About the author

Bruno Hannemann was born in rural Romania (now Ukraine), in a tiny village that counted only souls, albeit *live* ones. He has lived mainly in the United States, but also in Romania and Germany. Having served two years in the U.S. Army, he delved into the study of Russian and German literature and language at UC Los Angeles, the Free University of Berlin and at his Alma Mater, the University of California, Berkeley, concluding with a Ph.D. in German literature. Subsequently he accepted a position at the University of New Mexico, where he taught German and Russian literature, language and culture. At present, he lives with his wife of many years in Konstanz, Germany.

DON'T FENCE ME IN
A QUEST FOR FREEDOM

Bruno Hannemann

DON''T FENCE ME IN
A QUEST FOR FREEDOM

Vanguard Press

VANGUARD PAPERBACK

A CIP catalogue record for this title is
available from the British Library.

ISBN 978 1 78465 975 2

*Vanguard Press is an imprint of
Pegasus Elliot MacKenzie Publishers Ltd.*
www.pegasuspublishers.com

First Published in 2021

**Vanguard Press
Sheraton House Castle Park
Cambridge England**

Printed & Bound in Great Britain

Dedication

To Edel, my wife, my love, my friend and my companion. My special gratitude for her encouragement, her invaluable insights and suggestions, as well as her emotional support. Thank you for being in my life, for caring and nourishing me during the long process of writing this novel.

Acknowledgements

My heartfelt thanks to all my friends, colleagues and acquaintances who have stimulated, inspired, challenged and supported me during my long journey while writing this work. My special gratitude goes to Kenji Barrett for his patience, dedication and unflinching diligence during the reading of the first version. I am equally grateful to professor Rainer Rumold for his emotional support, his unabated encouragement, as well as his insights and subtle criticism. Furthermore, let me convey my deep appreciation to doctor Dirk Petermeise, my staunch friend and helper, who has always been at my side, when the need arose.

Historical Fact

In July and August of 1945, fourteen Nazi POWs were hanged in Fort Levenworth, Kansas, after being convicted of murdering their fellow inmates; others faced similar charges, but were lucky to be acquitted.

WHERE IS PRIVATE FELCHEN?

"Isn't it wonderful?" my friend, Hans, cracked, as he let his eyes sweep the endless expanse of the surrounding prairie. "The end of the world is welcoming us with open arms."

"Yes, nasty arms wrapped with barbed wire," I remember adding, wrenching a hard-won chuckle out of myself.

We had just stepped off the train at the rail yard of Murphy, a flyspeck of a town on the southern edge of Colorado. It was June 4th, 1943. A scorching sun ruled the sky like an absolute monarch, making the light breeze that tingled our faces feel oven-like.

"By the way," I went on, scratching my head. "Did you hear anything about the turmoil that happened last night in the car ahead of us? I've heard rumors that a corporal was pushed out of the moving train by Lt. Spaeth for having said that we might lose the war."

"Well, that's not what I've heard," Hans shot back, flexing his beefy arms and heavy shoulders. "According to Lt. Spaeth, the corporal you are talking about was a very unstable fellow, a Viennese, with suicidal tendencies. He was deranged and lost his mind. Apparently, he blabbered out a lot of nonsense that insulted many of his comrades, then opened the door and jumped off the moving train. That's what crazies tend to do."

"Are you sure?"

"Well, no. I was not there. But I'd put my faith in Lt. Spaeth who is a very dedicated and highly decorated soldier."

"That Spaeth may be a dedicated and highly decorated officer," Peter Keller, lanky as ever, elbowed in, "but he's also a cross-eyed Nazi and a murderer. I just talked to a friend of mine — I won't mention his name — who witnessed what happened. And he told me that Lt. Spaeth got into a heated argument with Manfred Felchen, an Austrian, about the war. Felchen claimed we'd lose it. The lieutenant called him a traitor and started punching him. Well, they got into a vicious scuffle. That burley Spaeth got the upper hand; he grabbed Felchen, dragged him to the door and kicked him out of the moving train."

"This is a barefaced lie!" Hans shouted, lips trembling and struggling to compose himself. "You better watch out spreading lies like that. Spaeth is an honorable man and a good comrade who deserves well of Germany.

And that Felchen was known to be an Austrian backstabber, a coward and a pathological lier."

"That's not what I've heard," Peter rebutted, standing his ground. "I sure hope there will be an investigation… by the Americans, and soon! Yesterday!"

"Screw you!" Hans snapped, puffed up his enormous chest, raised his fist and with a pronounced flare of anger toward Peter he inadvertently lapsed into a spell of candor, snarling, "You seem to be in cahoots with the traitors as well. Too bad some dedicated patriot didn't take…"

Swarms of scathing sibilants and fricatives jammed the air.

"Come on, you guys," I cut in. "What difference does it make. We're all in the same boat, POWs of a beaten army heading for a lockup behind barbed wire."

"What do you mean by 'beaten army'?" Hans shot back at me. "We, Rommel's Africa Korps, are only a small part of it. Just because we lost Stalingrad and chased out of North Africa doesn't mean we're going to lose the war. What did Nietzsche say? 'That which does not kill us, makes us stronger.' We'll bounce back, mark my word. We still have our Fuehrer! Never underestimate our Fuehrer! And our German scientists who're working on the Wunderwaffe."

Hans turned away, grumbling and cursing, while Peter, Dieter and I rolled our eyes and shook our heads.

"Too bad," I breathed. "We were such close buddies; we fought in the trenches together."

Though stirred, we were able to shove the quarrel to the back burner, devoting ourselves to more urgent issues that were bugging us. After all, we hadn't only been beaten in battle, we were also thoroughly sapped, worn to a mere shadow of our former selves. It started with enduring thirteen days spitting and retching in the bowels of an American troop bucket on the rough seas of the North Atlantic, shaking in our boots that our own U-boats would target us and send us to kingdom come. And upon arrival in New York, we were squeezed like sardines into the seats of Pullman cars for four miserable days and nights, mere castaways, deprived of sleep, drubbed by headaches, constipation, swollen feet and ankles and bucketfuls of anger.

After lining up in formation and filling our canteens with water, we started marching. That was easier said than done. Weighed down with our packs and hampered by exhaustion most of us were barely able to move — much less march in a lockstep, the way we were supposed to. The searing sun, as well as the relatively thin air added to the challenge we were faced with. Mercifully, nobody dared rush us.

Yet watched we were. Distrustful as ever, the Amis couldn't resist drumming into us, that we were nothing but a mob of Nazi brutes. Why else would they've set up those manned machine gun nests along the road? Lowering our heads, we plodded along, some stumbling over our own feet and sweating like horses. Every once in a while, we ground to a halt to take a breath, slake our thirst or strip ourselves of jackets, even shirts, until most of us were bare-chested like a wild horde of galley slaves.

After almost an hour of crippling strain, several watchtowers edged into our view, linked by two rows of barbed wire fences. Beyond it, small, single-story barracks began to emerge from the haze.

"Must be our camp," Peter Keller added, as we drew closer. "Out in nowhere, surrounded by grasses and brush for miles upon miles. The Amis sure know how to clip our wings."

"You bet. Hopefully we'll still have our feet," I jested. "That is, if we get them back!"

"To me, it looks more like a penal colony," Dieter Krumm sneered, "girded by barbed wire fences and flighty guards with loaded guns. Even in my wildest dreams I never thought I'd end up in a godforsaken place like this. I don't know about you, but I feel like a felon: beaten down, homeless, our pride in the shit hole, a bunch of convicts, that's what we are."

"You know, I feel very much the same," Peter added. "At the same time, it doesn't help us to be grouchy. Things could still be worse. We'll have to see how it'll all turn out."

"And what *we'll* make out of it," I said. "We just don't know what'll come at us."

I shuddered at the thought of ill-prepared guards manning the towers, gripping loaded rifles. With the mere flick of a finger, they could send a hail of deadly slugs at us. Branding us all Nazi thugs didn't help. The climate, being poisoned as it was, made me brace for the worst.

Clenching our teeth, we finally reached the camp itself, which occupied an area of hundreds of acres, six hundred and forty we were told later. No sooner had we come to a standstill, than a few of us slumped and fell, calling into action American medical personnel with stretchers. Nine of our soldiers were rushed to the hospital to be treated for heat stroke and circulatory collapse.

Subsequently we were divided up and assigned to various housing facilities, the officers to officer quarters and we enlisted men to company barracks. From afar the barracks had the appearance of large garden sheds

13

that had been hastily hammered and nailed together. In fact, as the various construction sites indicated, some of them had yet to be completed. Like most slipshod edifices, they sat on blocks of concrete, offering a hollow crawlspace underneath, where — so I found out later — a tangle of pipes and wires squeezed in to live in a precarious balance with roaches, black widows, presumably even rattlesnakes.

Designed for bare-boned, no-nonsense functionality, these quarters happened to be equipped with sleeping rooms, commonly shared lavatories that could dispense hot and cold water on demand, shower rooms and toilets. No question, in terms of hygiene the Americans were definitely ahead of us. Their toilet bowls, for one, were unrivaled in their ready-for-battle efficiency. Deep-throated and spotlessly clean, they'd burst forth with ferocious gushes und gurgles that would within seconds smash and suck down the most stubborn of stools. I should know! What baffled me, though, was the fact that they lacked even the smallest of dividers, much less stalls separating them. What did the builders think? I, for one, shuddered at the thought of knocking knees with somebody and pinching my nose, while heeding an urgent call of nature.

Yet the accommodations, mercifully, seemed to embrace ideas that were almost the opposite. Instead of large dormitories, we were given rooms that would put up no more than four enlisted men. Moreover, measuring eighteen by twenty feet they were partitioned by two walls. A cast iron stove that was supposed to provide warmth during the winter quaintly sat in the middle of each room. Unfortunately, little thought had been given to furnishing these quarters, to making them livable. Chairs, tables, night stands and wall lockers were conspicuous by their absence.

Aside from that, there were also some pleasant surprises — our bunks. Not only did they come with clean straw mattresses, white sheets, blankets and soft pillows, but each bed also displayed two white socks and a neatly ordered assortment of toilet articles: a bar of soap, a hand towel, a toothbrush, toothpaste, a razor and a comb.

"An inkling of civilization," Peter bellowed, stroking his chin.

The room, Hans, Peter, Dieter and I were assigned to happened to be uncomfortably hot, stuffy and infested with thousands of moths, many of them dead. They covered the floor, the beds, the footlockers and every other horizontal surface, while those still alive buzzed frantically at the window panes. Our first task was to sweep the floor, wipe the footlockers, the beds and chase the live moths out. Next, we stripped and jammed into the shower. Most of us preferred showering cold. Being the first shower since New York, it was a great pleasure to cleanse ourselves of the sweat and grime, or simply let the cool water ripple down our hot and weary bodies. I relished it so much that I must have spent twenty minutes in there.

Less than an hour later, we were rounded up at the parade grounds, where we were welcomed by Col. Henry C. Hutchins, Capt. Shepherd and Lt. Conroy. Standing on a pedestal, handsome, tall and taut, Col. Hutchins began by commiserating with us about our arduous journey all the way from New York to Murphy. "I feel for you," he claimed, placing his hand on his heart and lowering his head. He went out of his way to mention the loss of Cpl. Manfred Felchen whom he officially declared as missing. Though he admitted that the circumstances were murky, even that 'foul play' may have been involved, he refused to go into details. He said that the War Department in Washington had been informed about it and that a search team was already underway to find the body. He promised to immediately start an investigation to find out what exactly happened.

Since Capt. Shepherd was designated to be in charge, the colonel momentarily handed the reins over to the captain. He was a stocky fellow with a broad, round head whose top was as bald and shiny like a seasoned saddle, save for two strands of comb-over. He was quick to lay out his plans. Speaking in a soft, southern drawl, he ordered everybody who had been present in car four last night to appear before him to be questioned. He was confident that he'd get to the bottom of this case, assuring us that justice would prevail.

In the end, Col. Hutchins also addressed the lack of furniture in our quarters, claiming he was fully aware of the problem and pledged to find remedies soon. Stressing repeatedly that he was interested in a smooth running of the camp, he believed in the principles of self-government according to the Geneva Convention. He would rely on our own chain of command to discipline ourselves and see to it that order would be maintained.

Once Col. Hutchins and Capt. Shepherd had exited from the scene, Lt. Conroy filled us in on the setup and running of the camp itself. He was a lanky, loose-limbed fellow with a bullet head and the face of a short-order cook. Nervously twitching his shoulder, he ordered us to strip, toss our soiled and smelly uniforms and underwear onto several big tarps and then drop back into line again. Standing there naked in the heat of the searing sun, we were puzzled as to what the guards were up to. Thankfully comic relief soon steered us into a more mirthful mood. It so happened that right at that moment three women in uniform, presumably visitors from the Women Army Corps, came walking past. Having lacked any contact with the other sex, we instantly inundated them with a hailstorm of wolf-whistles, as well as horny and goatish hoots. The women, meanwhile, watching us standing there in the full glory of our birthday suits couldn't help but holding their mouths and snicker. One of them, a short, thick-set redhead, stopped and, clicking her heels, even chose to honor us with a snappy salute. At that point we lost all restraint. Like a horde of pickled teenagers we whistled, hooted, stomped and clapped. Some blew kisses and made lewd, orgiastic movements, their hands venturing to places where the sun never shines.

It was a brouhaha that showed no sign of dying down. Worried that things might spiral out of hand, Lt. Conroy eventually grabbed the loudspeaker. "You stop that right now, or else. Attention! *Ach-tung!*" he barked. To no avail. If anything, we ratcheted up the frenzy. It was as if we'd just been waiting for the occasion to give our full vent to all the anger and frustrations of the past few weeks.

Eventually things *did* calm down, just before a group of doctors and their helpers, all clad in white coats, made their appearance.

"First, we'll give you a quick medical check," the lieutenant announced, his face still tense. He shoved a flat wedge of gum tween the flaps of his lips and began chewing it, crushing the Wrigley wrapper as if he were strangling a lizard. "Later your clothes will be searched for contraband," he bayed.

Accompanied by the lieutenant, the doctors then started to go down the rows to check out each one of us. The white-coat examining us was a middle-aged, bespectacled man who even happened to speak German, albeit with a Viennese accent.

"I bet he's an Austrian Jew, " Hans lampooned. "I can see it on his nose and forehead."

"Yeah," Helmut added, smirking. "That fucker can't wait to cut off our foreskins."

Despite taking this as a joke, we still were a bit nervous. Newspaper images of sly, hook-nosed Jews armed with knives, and breathing unbridled vengeance still crowded our minds. Luckily the doctor didn't feed into our prejudices; he turned out to be surprisingly benign. After inspecting our skin, he bent down and told us to pull back our foreskin and squeeze our glans. Most of us submitted, although unwillingly. Not so Anton Breuner, one of our comrades, a medic no less. When the doctor approached him, he just stood there, as if deaf and dumb.

"Hoeren Sie nicht?" (Can't you hear?), the doctor admonished him. "Ziehen Sie Ihre Vorhaut zurueck und quetschen Sie ihre Eichel!"

When Anton still showed no sign of budging, the doctor, now visibly irritated, moved to carry out himself what he'd ordered Anton to do. At that point Anton, hissing "Hauen Sie ab, Sie Judenschwein!" (Get lost, you Jewish pig!) forcefully slapped the doctor's hands.

His hackles raised, the doctor whispered something to the lieutenant, who in turn made a note of it.

Once the medical inspection had been completed, the lieutenant grabbed his bullhorn, declaring, "As to the search of your clothes, I want to remind you that some items will have to be confiscated because they present a great security risk to every one of us, you included."

Peeved, we braced for the worst. And when, twenty minutes later, we were handed our clothes again, we noticed that the word 'contraband', had been considerably expanded to include private items such as nail scissors, pocket knives, watches, shoulder patches, ribbons, medals and other military paraphernalia, items which had slipped through previous searches.

"Once again these bastards are ripping us off," I whispered to Hans, not knowing I would be eclipsed by Otto Kirst, another of my comrades, who shouted out aloud, "You mean to say that my ribbons are a security risk?"

"Are you accusing us of stealing?" the lieutenant snarled, seeking nods from the guards.

"Yes, I am," Otto burst out, fuming.

"You better be careful what you're saying, soldier," the lieutenant bellowed, turning red in his face. And addressing the first guard, he added, "This, smacks of insubordination. OK, Dick, why don't you see to it that this soldier's taught some manners. And," pointing his finger at Anton, "this one, too."

Both Otto and Anton, who had barely finished dressing, were shackled and led away. It was an injustice that cried to heaven. Needless to say, we all rooted for them. Hans, me and others even tried to talk to the lieutenant, hoping to impress on him that both were right, Otto on speaking the truth and Anton on sound American values of hygiene. But the officer brusquely brushed me aside.

"Both are clear cases of insubordination," he insisted, bristling affectedly. "I will not tolerate enlisted men ignoring the orders of an officer. You guys better rip off those chips on your shoulders," he bellowed at us, his face flushed with anger. "You are p-r-i-s-o-n-e-r-s of war now and you are in America. Yes, in A-m-e-r-i-c-a! You better get that in your gourds. Let's be clear, we beat the shit out of you. You and your Thousand-Year Reich. It'll soon be nothing but a fucking heap of rubble and ashes."

We booed. Hans and many true believers even dared waving their fists, which in turn angered the lieutenant even more. He was beside himself. His head wobbling with military swagger, he reached down and fondled with his handgun, even taking the safety catch off.

That muzzled us to silence. All we did was shake our heads. Later we heard that both Otto and Anton had been put in solitary confinement on bread and water for two weeks. Now we knew the way the wind was blowing. What hypocrisy! I felt like strangling that ass in its lion's skin.

OUR TOP DOGS

Embittered, we braced for surprises and pain, wondering what we could do to foil our honcho. While passing a trash barrel, I got hold of a day-old copy of the Denver Post, my first American newspaper. My curiosity rose on tiptoe and once back in the barracks, I lost no time delving into it, eager to find out what was happening in the war in Europe. Unfortunately, the news coverage was very limited, dominated by a hodgepodge of local issues and ads. As if by accident I stumbled on a small column on the bottom of page two, headlined 'NAZIS REBUFFED IN RUSSIA'. It claimed that the German Army faced stiff Russian resistance at the battle of Kursk, bringing the German offensive to a grinding halt. The confrontation was dubbed as the biggest tank battle in history.

I was at a loss, shaking my head. I couldn't wait also showing this scoop to Hans. As expected, he turned his thumb down. Adopting a weary, petulant, droop of mouth, he called it, "Typical American propaganda not worth the ink it's printed with. Their T-34s are no match for our Tigers."

"I'm not so sure," I countered. I cited the first battle near Kiev, where we won but also suffered heavy losses where Ernst and Peter, two very close buddies I originally enlisted with were torn to shreds by a Stalin Organ.

"Sure, but sacrifices are to be expected," he said, "if we want to gain *Lebensraum* and build a German empire. The overriding thing is that in the end we came out on top."

"*Lebensraum,* victory, German empire!" I shot back. "I can't hear that any more. How about the masses of people who were slaughtered?"

I was shocked that Hans appeared to be so utterly devoid of any human feelings, viewing our comrades as expendable cogs in a big tank that rumbled across the steppes of Russia. What I hushed up in our exchange about my experience at the battle of Kiev was a festering doubt about our mission. It kept following me, clawing its way into my brain and finally settling with a thud. It was a wake-up call that would raise the uncomfortable question why we were in Russia in the first place, why in the hell we had even started this war. The answer was anything but flattering. It wasn't until I received orders to join Rommel's elite Africa Korps, with a promise of entering officers' school, that my belief in our mission began to wax again, only to plummet to another low on our trip across the Atlantic all the way to Murphy.

My train of thought still deeply mired in Russia — curious how memory clings to events that pack an emotional wallop! — I happened to find myself in the mess hall where we were fed dinner, hungry stomachs at long tables. Let me add, we were pleasantly surprised at the great variety and abundance of choices, from sausages, pork chops and fish, not to mention eggs, noodles, potatoes and three different vegetables. In addition, our palates were treated with coffee, cake, even ice cream. Save for the ice cream, which most of us were unfamiliar with, it felt as if we were attending a rich farmer's wedding in prewar Germany.

At the end of our feast, we all kept wondering why the Amis were treating us so well. Was it because of an assumed mutual understanding that their soldiers in German POW camps would be treated likewise? as Peter, Dieter and I argued. But, as always, Hans chose to differ. "It's all part of a pacifying gesture," he claimed. "The Amis want to worm themselves into our good graces. Deep down they're scared shitless of us. I bet they can already hear the rumbling of our Tiger tanks and the stomping of our boots. Stop laughing! I heard our diplomats in Berlin are also trying to win over the Mexicans who've been forced into an alliance with the Americans. Many of them are very resentful toward the gringos, as they call them. Now wouldn't that be something if they'd spill across the border from the south and try to take back what once belonged to them? And they're not the only ones that could cause trouble for Uncle Sam and make his knees wobble. Back in the hinterland, in Pennsylvania, Illinois, Ohio and Iowa, our German Bund is ratcheting things up to a boil. And many Indian tribes are disgruntled as well. All they may need is a shove to rise up against Roosevelt and his clique of Jewish capitalists. Our agents are busy working with the chiefs of the various tribes to foment riots."

"Yes, and all the knights from the castles in the air come parachuting down and start fighting for the German cause," Peter responded, shaking his head. "Forgive me, Hans, but have you ever thought of getting your head examined?"

Hans was fuming, clenching his teeth. "You're damned traitors, snakes in the grass," he barked, his voice a ragged tear in the muted fabric of the mess hall. "One day we'll make you eat your words! You can bet on it." He puffed up his enormous chest like a rooster among a gaggle of hens.

Come bedtime, we stripped to test our mattresses. I slept like a baby. No, better. Miraculously my bladder held until six a.m., when we were rattled out of bed by a shrill bell. We all rushed into the washroom at once,

20

elbowing each other for a washbowl. I chose a hot shower instead, later shutting down my pores with a cold one.

Our first roll call came at seven a.m. It was governed by outright confusion. Actually, it started with simple basics. We were ordered to line up in rows of five and the guards, edgy nitwits most of them, were told to count heads. Yet each time they came up with a different number, none that matched the number in the book. It was highly embarrassing for them, the more so since we ridiculed each false count with vigorous salvoes of laughter. Finally, Lt. Conroy, flustered, stepped in. And, lo and behold, he came out with the right count. Some of us clapped. Hans and I didn't. Our grudge against the man ran too deep. Besides, we suspected he had fudged it to put the kibosh on the embarrassment.

Regardless, we finally made it to the mess hall, where once again we were treated like guests of honor. It must have been before the war, on our headmistress's fiftieth birthday, when I had last sniffed and sipped a cup of genuine 'bean' coffee, to be followed by such goodies as milk, butter, peanut butter, various jams, several kinds of soft breads, oatmeal, corn flakes, scrambled eggs, bacon, ham, processed cheese, you name it. U-mm! Did we stuff ourselves! The only weak link: the mushy white bread. But that was no more than a speck of dust on a Rembrandt.

As an afterthought, we POWs were actually treated more generously at the chow line than the average Joe at his breakfast table, who happened to be on rations. At least that's what Dieter told us, adding that such a preferential treatment was bound to stir up a lot of resentment against us outside the camps. And having lived in Pennsylvania for more than a year, Dieter knew America better than any of us.

Our first big challenge came a day later, when the administration issued an order that each one of us had to be fingerprinted and photographed. "To complete the records," Lt. Conroy stated. We felt that they treated us like criminals and we weren't going to take this without a fight. Since we had no choice, we tried to sabotage it by smudging the fingerprints or stiffening our fingers. As to the mugshots, many of us took the ink and smeared our faces, disfiguring them by painting mustaches, thick brows and grotesque beards on them. Some of our comrades even managed to have their pictures taken twice, first for themselves, the second time for others who planned to escape, and later did indeed escape. There was no end to harassing the guards and the service personnel. Lt. Conroy in particular was up in arms. Rumbling on the shoestrings of ability but buckets of bile, he made sure that those troublemakers who openly resisted were apprehended and brought before disciplinary boards. Most of them ended up in the stockade on bread and water.

All that created a climate of tensions between us and the Amis that was further compounded by the clash over the building of furniture and our raids of the construction sites. Since the administration failed to respond to our needs to furnish our quarters, a group of fourteen officers and soldiers, I among them, resolved to take matters into our own hands. Luckily, there were several construction sites which stored large quantities of lumber, some stacked up to six feet high. They offered an opportunity we simply couldn't let pass. And once darkness had settled, we'd sneak through the fences and raid the sites, grabbing whatever we needed — scraps of wood, whole boards, two-by-fours, nails, screws, even some hammers and handsaws. This was strictly *verboten,* lest we take the tools and 'stage a general uprising'.

I might add, there were even signs specifically warning us not to trespass. But we paid only scant attention and, at the beginning at least, nobody seemed to mind. Until one day, when a guard caught Gerold Fischer and Georg Enslin carrying a stack of boards to their quarters. All of a sudden, things came to a head, rising all the way up to the camp commander, Col. Hutchins. Although our colonel had a good stage presence, he proved to be short in every other respect. He was soaked in the sour brine of pious malice, always seeking ways of blaming others for his own shortcomings. Accused of losing control, he immediately issued a bulletin, threatening anybody caught with a piece of lumber with severe punishment of four weeks in the stockade. As to the shortage of furniture, the actual reason for the theft, he once again promised to do the utmost to rectify it. Yet he failed to act on it. He'd simply claim that he had solved the problem, that the number of raids on the lumber had dropped precipitously. When the builders complained that they hadn't, that they still continued, although more stealthily, in the wee hours of the morning, he ordered armed guards to protect the sites. This turned out to be an unjustifiably harsh measure considering our unmet need for furniture.

Equally harsh were the off-hand decisions that Lt. Conroy issued. And when we asked Col. Hutchins to review them and, where wanting, cancel them, he first gave in to our wishes. But once again, he failed to follow through. Nor was there any measurable progress on the investigation into the death of Corp. Manfred Felchen. Although most of the questioning by Capt. Shepherd had been completed, he claimed that it wouldn't amount to much. Any closure would hinge on an autopsy. But the body still hadn't been found. There was no trace of it, leading to the assumption that coyotes or other wild animals might well have dragged it off. Regardless, the search would continue.

Another sore point was our governance. Our oily charmer decided to lean toward a do-nothing, hands-off approach, using the Geneva Convention as a fig leaf. That might have been justified if our commando structure had widespread support. However, that was no longer the case, since our former tight cohesion had hopelessly frayed. For the first time we were free, even encouraged by our captors, to voice our opinions on anything that touched us. This created a healthy ferment but also a political vacuum, which in turn was filled by none other than our dyed-in-the-wool Nazis. Unified and well-organized, they were known to be most rabidly anti-American and believers in the myth of a final victory. That included Col. von Wiese, Hans, Lt. Spaeth, Lt. Borchart and others. Although they despised the colonel, they were also pleased by him, particularly by his lax style of governing. To them he was simply a 'useful idiot'.

Diametrically opposed to our Nazis was the swelling number of those who had deep-seated doubts about Hitler and his movement. Some, particularly the communists, Austrians, Alsatians and other nationalities such as Czechs, Poles and Ukrainians who had also embraced the swastika thought that holding on to the belief in the Fuehrer and what he stood for was the greatest of self-delusions. In the eyes of the Nazi diehards, these skeptics were promptly branded as traitors who deserved special treatment — good thrashings, deadly beatings or the gallows. Already on day two they had solidly entrenched themselves, setting up a Gestapo-like organization and kangaroo courts that quickly identified apparent turncoats and traitors who should be persecuted and punished. Almost every night gangs of these true believers would drag them out of their beds and beat them up or, worse, giving the 'Holy Ghost' (*Himmelfahrtskommando)* treatment, killing them under the guise of suicides. Even those of us who raised the slightest doubts about Germany prevailing were warned to toe the line, or else. That created a far-reaching chilling effect, a reign of terror that engulfed the whole camp. Case in point, when on the first Sunday after arrival our chaplain, Anton Gruber, called on his congregation "to pray for our poor and ravaged Fatherland" and voiced his hope that peace may soon be in the offing, he was instantly booed by our true-believers. And once he'd left the pulpit, he was heckled, pushed against the wall and threatened to be beaten up.

Barely two days later, Lt. Tankred Buchner who had voiced some muted criticism of the Fuehrer was rudely awakened one night by a mob of nine officers and enlisted men, dragged outside and beaten unconscious. He was found four hours later by accident, barely hanging on to his life. He was rushed to the hospital where he was treated for a concussion, a broken jaw, nose, arm and ribs. According to a subsequent investigation by Capt. Shepherd, he had been selected by a pack of Nazi bloodhounds who claimed that he was a traitor. Self-righteous to the point of arrogance, they considered it their duty under the Geneva Convention to discipline all those who voiced defeatist ideas. Two officers, Col. von Wiese and Lt. Borchert, even had the gumption to demand that Buchner be turned over to them as soon as he'd be ready to leave the hospital to be declared guilty of high treason and publicly hanged.

Sadly, almost every day our Nazi zealots continued to bait the field with signals as nuanced as a swelling number of bloody, thrashed bodies and forced suicides. Indeed, the situation got so tense that a number of soldiers, fearful of their safety, specifically pleaded to be protected by American guards, who in turn secretly admired the strict discipline of the German camp, run mainly by Nazis. Most of us, however, chose to safeguard ourselves by keeping our thoughts close to our chests and our hands in front of our mouths. Although I was never personally threatened, there were many occasions when I, too, held my tongue, especially when dyed-in-the-wool Nazis, my friend Hans included, happened to be around. That made us outsiders feel as though we were fenced in twice, once by the barbed wire of Americans and, far worse, by the thought-police of our Nazis.

Incidentally, among the various duties that Hans's new position in the Nazi hierarchy required was posting bulletins of German victories every morning in the barracks. It was part of the 'psychological warfare' that could have been issued by Josef Goebbels personally.

All that happened in bright daylight. And what did Col. Hutchins do? Nothing, naught. At first, he claimed that it was Hans's right under the Geneva Convention to do what he did. Later he came with the excuse that it was too early to intervene, since we were just few in numbers. New POWs would arrive every day. He'd hold back from setting up a permanent structure and a semblance of order based on justice until the camp would be filled up. Sadly, there was much hold on his word as a wet eel on its tail.

OUR DAILY ROUTINE

Despite these dreadful developments, most of us still managed to settle into a certain routine that consisted of reveille, showering, roll calls, eating (usually far too much!) and sleeping. Since we were exempt from working the first two weeks, boredom and apathy gradually began to settle in. I saw many dawdling away their time. The more active among us, however, soon sought and found a fair number of diversions such as participating in sports activities — soccer, handball, volley ball, ping pong, track and field, or delving into various handicrafts. Those drawn to more intellectual pursuits were encouraged to enroll in seminars teaching Latin, Classical Greek, algebra and philosophy. And if you had a more artistic bent you could occupy yourself with painting, play-acting, singing or learning to play musical instruments. We even formed a choir that dared perform on stage. The repertoire consisted mainly of German *Volkslieder*. But it also included several American songs, some of which were bound to ruffle the feathers of our diehard Nazis. Incidentally, our favorite tune happened to be Cole Porter's cowboy hit *Don't Fence Me In*, the same song that had already cocked our ears at our arrival in New York. Eventually it would gain such a widespread popularity that most of us — me in the lead — learned it by heart.

Although I got a charge out of letting my bass-baritone fill a room or hall, my favorite pastimes were learning English and play-acting. Already at the orphanage I had also starred in some classical plays and when Wolfgang Riem offered a course in theater, I was among the first to enroll. An experienced actor himself, Wolf would occasionally also write plays, mostly comedies, and he couldn't wait to stage them at our theater that, unfortunately, was still in its construction stage.

My other flirtation, the English class, happened to be taught by my roommate Dieter who, had it not been for his German accent, would have been called fluent in English. Open-minded and affable, Dieter was very unconventional in his approach. His primary goal was to teach us how to communicate better with our captors, the Americans, to talk and engage with them. "I want to build bridges," was his slogan. All that was poison to our dyed-in-the-wool Nazis, who had long targeted him.

The teaching material consisted primarily of American comics and funny, witty dialogues some of which he wrote himself. They depicted typical everyday encounters between Americans, more often than not with an absurd twist, including typical behavioral patterns Americans frequently use.

Changes that would raise the dust was the periodic arrival of hundreds upon hundreds of newcomers, almost all of them ex-soldiers of Rommel's Afrika Korps. At the end of June, the camp was rim-full, roughly holding fourteen hundred enlisted men and two hundred and forty-five officers. Deprived of an excuse, Col. Hutchins, finally called on all POWs to attend meetings within the various companies and compounds, for the purpose of electing spokesmen who would represent our interests vis-a-vis the administration and to voice our grievances and needs.

Responding to the demand, our company quickly formed a committee to take charge of the election process. Its chairman asked everybody to nominate a candidate. Altogether thirty-one candidates, many of them officers, were designated, Hans, Dieter and I among them. Dieter was nominated not least because of his good command of English and his knowledge of the American way of life.

It turned out that Col. Horst von Wiese won the crown of being our primary spokesman, not only because he was one of the highest ranking officers but also because he was forceful and, besides being a true-believer, for his command of English. Hans, Lt. Ludwig Spaeth, Lt. Ernst Borchart and Lt. Wolfgang Riem garnered many votes as well, and Col. von Wiese instantly offered them various other leadership positions. I may add that our theater director, Wolfgang Riem, was the only one who didn't belong to the inner clique of the Nazi zealots.

ESCAPE IS LAWFUL

To be fair, not all of the dealings and machinations our zealots tried to push through proved to be harmful or detrimental to us. High on their agenda was also their laudable demand that we POWs be treated respectfully, in accordance with the Geneva Convention. It was a cudgel they swung well, reminding the Amis again and again that we were endowed with certain rights, that even though they were in charge, they couldn't push us around as they damn well pleased.

Indeed, these true-believers were the first to bring up the apparent injustices done to both Otto and Anton who were still held in the stockade. Better yet, right after our election they stormed into Col. Hutchins's office and demanded an immediate release of both. Although the commander first stalled, but when von Wiese and his supporters relentlessly kept up their pressure, even threatening to appeal the cases to the Swiss Legation and the Red Cross, Hutchins buckled. It was our first triumph, which tickled us pink. Never mind that both would have been released four days later anyhow.

Equally important, it was also our firebrand Nazis who saw to it that we all had access to the Geneva Convention, which had been denied to us before. In fact, Hans lost no time handing me a copy in English and I, Peter and Dieter began reading and discussing it. Having never seen this important document before, we were astonished at its forthrightness, especially in reference to the rights of POWs. The particular section we right away pounced on was the one that dealt with the question of escape. What appeared most riveting, were the articles 47 to 51. Although they did not state specifically that escape was a 'right', the leniency in punishing such an offense, suggested that it was at least tolerated. That's what Dieter claimed after carefully reading these articles. "Frankly, I was surprised myself," he said.

"That's interesting," I chuckled, shaking my head. "Actually I've been thinking about escaping for quite some time. I felt I had been breathing the air of freedom ever since I stepped off the boat in New York."

"But who hasn't?" Peter snapped. "Hell, the Amis shoved it down our throats by the shiploads. It created a real glut. Every second word they used was 'freedom' or 'liberty'."

"Yea, directed at us who were all fenced in," I went on. "And nobody can blame us for not listening. Needless to say, what they drummed into us gradually began to whet our appetites, at least mine."

"You sound like you're seriously thinking about skipping the fence?" Dieter pressed.

"Haven't you? I know it would be very tough. You'd need to plan it meticulously to the last detail. That might take months. The other night I saw myself hiding in the laundry truck, or digging a tunnel that burrowed underneath the fences and come up on the other side."

"The first option might be suffocating, but could be done," Peter noted. "The second may be much tougher. I've heard that ground is unusually hard. Herbert Volkner, who's trying to plant some trees, told me it's almost like soft rock. And where would you get the tools? You won't get very far using your fingernails."

"Well, we would have to be inventive," I chipped in. "We might be able to get a hold of some shovels at the construction sites."

"It's not impossible," Dieter observed. "You might make it and escape in grand style. But a bigger problem than getting out may well be *staying* out, I mean evading the police or the FBI. Unfortunately, the odds are not good. In fact, it's damn near hopeless. Think about it, the flat terrain surrounding the camp, coupled with the lack of vegetation to hide makes it almost impossible to get away. And, let's face it, we're out in nowhere. Where would you go? America is a very big country. Its coasts are thousands of miles away. Unlike in Europe, there's no big city around for hundreds of miles where you could immerse. I wish I could be more optimistic. I heard Capt. Shepherd recently joking that the odds of you succeeding are as good as two-hundred fiddlers' farts turning into a symphony. Although Shepherd may be a bit self-serving, but still."

"It probably depends a lot on your preparation," I emphasized. "How about slipping across the border to Mexico? I've heard that the Mexicans are very friendly toward us Germans."

"I've heard that, too," Dieter said. "But you shouldn't forget, just getting to the border is more than five hundred miles. Besides, the Mexicans are allied with the Americans. I've heard they even have an extradition treaty with the United States. I'd try to milk Capt. Fahrenbach who's setting up an Escape Committee. He'd know more about it."

"Good idea," I said. "- I'm not saying it would be easy. But it would still be worth a try. Leaving that barbed wire behind you would at least regain your self-respect and dignity. It would be adventurous, too. By the way, what would they do if they caught you, anyway?"

28

"They'd probably bring you back and put you in solitary confinement for three to four weeks," Dieter explained. "It's a toss-up. But they certainly wouldn't make you face a firing squad 'cause you've done nothing illegal. The stickler is, not all of the American officers have read the Geneva Convention, much less regard it as a law the United States has signed."

FLOWER POWER

At the end of June, four weeks after our arrival, all enlisted men were requested to fulfill a certain amount of work, inside or outside the camp. Inside we could do such tasks as collecting laundry, garbage, be useful in shops and kitchens or tend the camp's lawns, the shrubbery and trees and maintain the landscape. Outside we could help farmers working in their fields, picking fruit, harvesting crops, chopping weeds, or lend ranchers a hand, tending cattle and sheep, or cutting wood and cleaning up. We were even promised some pay, 80 cents a day, albeit in coupons. Owning any real American dollars was *verboten* for fear that this might help us escape.

I was the first to volunteer for farm or ranch work, eager to seize any opportunity to get away from our Nazi zealots. But just as important was the wish to leave the dreariness and cheerlessness of the prison camp. Facing the barbed wire every day had turned into a haunting experience for me. It had literally etched itself on the inside of my eyelids, forcing me to stare at it every morning and evening when my eyes were shut. So leaving the camp behind and entering the wide open spaces was nothing short of an hosanna for me. It invariably gave me the illusion of freedom, despite the fact that we were always guarded by an armed American soldier.

Aside from that, I longed to get in touch with ordinary Americans, civilians, farmers and other farm workers. And quite unlike Hans, my wish was to talk to and engage with Americans, to find out how they think, act and carry on was very much alive as well. Moreover, I also was eager to polish my English, which was still mediocre, so flawed that any country bumpkin would immediately identify me as a German. And, unlike my Nazi brethren, I hoped to get a feel for America, to figure out what makes this huge country tick.

While most of us were told to pick water melons, peaches, and apricots or harvest beans, squash, celery and tomatoes, a dozen of us were taken to Earl Perkins's run-down cattle ranch, where we were given the task to clean up and repair things. Located fifteen miles south-east of the camp, it encompassed a huge spread, stretching from the west-side of a dry creek all the way into the wild mountain range toward New Mexico's border. The owner, Mr. Perkins, appeared to be an unyielding, headstrong man in his early sixties. Tall and lanky, he was heeled with a wry face, whose skin was

30

shriveled like an old apple. So deep were the neck wattles and the folds in his jowls they could easily have served as hideouts for a number of insects. Like a common cowboy, he was wrapped in dusty, down-home denim duds, worn cowboy boots and a big, sweat-rimmed felt hat. And he wouldn't want to be seen without a big colt.

What struck me most was his aloofness. He was always dreamy and withdrawn, a loner weighed down by oodles of prejudices. Although he had requested us, he refused to meet with us, much less shake hands. When we accidentally ran into him later on, he'd still dodge us. Nerved and puzzled, I tried to open him up by pitching a question at him, about the size of his ranch or how many heads of cattle grazed on it. But all he did was shrug his shoulders.

All the negative impressions notwithstanding, the experiences at the ranch left an indelible impression on me. Callow that I was, the sheer expanse, the giant dome of a blue sky and the wild, untouched nature simply overwhelmed me, not without a tinge of apprehension, I might add. It gave me an inkling of the freedom Cole Porter's song *Don't Fence Me In*, celebrated: "*Oh, give me land, lots of land under starry sky above…*" For the first time I was able to fill the idea of freedom our ears were stuffed with daily with palpable images of a life filled with unconstrained movement and individual rights, none of which I'd been familiar with. Worse, such a vision hadn't even nibbled at the edges of my rigid German brain, awash as it was with the churning brew of the Nazi myth, including all its confining boundaries.

Our job was to fix fences, bury carcasses, bones and skeletons, pull weeds, cut down unwanted vegetation including brushwork and trees, get rid of the rusted wrecks of cars, trucks and machinery that had been sitting there for decades, tidy things up around the ranch house, kill rodents and rattlers, repair the ranch house, cars and trucks. I suspected that Perkins, growing old and shaky, wanted to spruce up the ranch in order to put it on the market.

More than a week had passed but the climate still remained as hostile as it was on day one. Frustrated and disappointed, I asked our guard, Marvin, what was rubbing the old man.

"Good question. I just know, his head is crammed with deep-seated suspicion. Time and again he keeps badgering me for assurances that 'them krauts' or 'Nazis' were 'good boys,' that they carried no firearms, machetes or knives."

"Why would he even hire us?"

"Beats me."

Mr. Perkins's suspicion, for all I know, may well have been fueled by his wife, Eleanore, who was literally frightened by our presence. Whenever she could, she avoided us, as if we were afflicted by some sort of moral leprosy. A pear-shaped dumpling with doughy cheeks and a button of a nose, she'd barricade herself inside the ranch house, where she could stealthily watch us from behind the curtains. Although she'd always prepare a lunch, it was her Mexican helper, a young girl of about sixteen, who had to dish it out to us.

Forget our good works that were visible daily. We simply couldn't gain the couple's trust. Until one day, when their daughter Mildred, a strikingly attractive businesswoman, pulled into the cleaned-up driveway with a shiny new Oldsmobile that may have been bigger and more luxurious than our Fuehrer's Mercedes. She was accompanied by Janice, her alluring, seventeen-year-old daughter. We were told that Mildred hailed from Denver and, when she bounced out of her Olds, she right away showered us with warm praise.

"I'm delighted how things have improved," she impressed on her dad, letting her eyes sweep the area around the ranch house. And pointing at us, she added, "Aren't they terrific German boys? Who'd have thought they could do such a good job, getting rid of the clutter and whipping everything into shape. I'm glad I hired them."

Earl remained tight-lipped but smiled at us like a half-wit. The next day, though, both he and Eleanore seemed to have made a complete turnabout. For the first time they smiled at us and treated us with some courtesy, if not respect. Not only did Eleanore prepare an exceptionally tasty lunch, consisting of smoked turkey, a green salad, toasted bread, sour pickles and mustard, all to be washed down with a good brew from Milwaukee, but she also bid us to join them in their dining room we'd never even seen before. At first, our guard, Marvin, stuttered some objections, pointing out that this violated strict military rules, that we had to be served outside at the camping tables. But Mildred quickly muzzled him, accusing him of having no heart.

Since Mildred and her daughter, Janice, were also present at the table, we readily engaged them in a conversation. In fact, I sat next to Janice who, encased in an appealing olfactory bubble, was a very self-assured young woman with a pair of captivating hazel eyes, a straight, small wedge of a nose and shiny chestnut-colored hair which was tightly bound in a long ponytail. She must not have had time to look into the mirror because smudges of chocolate donut-icing covered the area to the left of her crimson lips, which added an odd, childlike twist to her appearance. Let me emphasize that Janice was my first contact with an American girl, with any girl for over a year. Suspecting that she liked me, I often sidled up to her. And, by golly, she seemed to tolerate, dare I say? even welcome my advances. Several times she praised me on my 'noble table manners', of using both my hands and eating with knife and fork. Moreover, she also complimented me on the use of my English, often giggling when I mispronounced a word. She was so sweet, I felt tempted to lick the chocolate donut-icing off the gooseberry fuzz of her cheeks.

In addition, this daisy-fresh girl was exceptionally curious about life within the POW camp, even about me personally. Using a winsome toss of a voice, she inquired about my age, how long I had been in America and what I wanted to do with my life after the war. She expressed hope that the fighting would soon be over, so we could go home to our families. We also talked about her future. She told me that she planned to study medicine at the University of Colorado in Boulder and become a doctor. I encouraged her, emphasizing that there were few professions that could do more to help mankind.

Dare I say it? I was smitten by this girl, spending the evening and part of the night musing and blissfully digesting my experience. And the next day I thought of picking a bouquet of wild flowers for her. Since it wasn't easy to find any close by the ranch house, I asked Marvin if I could venture up to higher elevations that looked more promising. He reluctantly gave his OK, after he'd wrest a promise out of me not to escape. Curiously enough he even made me place my hand on Earl's Bible, swear an oath of loyalty, while looking him in the eyes. Me, a German!

As I keep rummaging through the leafage of my memory, I'm finding that my little hike paid off handsomely. Not only did I find the prettiest flowers, bursting with a great variety of shapes and colors — yellow, red, white, blue, even purple. As if by sheer luck, I also stumbled on an old, worn horseshoe. Granted, it was covered with dirt and rust, but after rubbing it against the bark of a tree, it would regain its original bright shine. I'm at a loss of words to express how thrilled I was for holding a good luck charm in my hands again.

As I wound my way down, I began to have doubts about giving the bouquet to Janice. I feared that it might be too direct, too daring a message. What would she think, not to mention her mother? Flowers from a German POW? In the end I decided to hand them to Mildred, her mother, who was more than thrilled.

"Wow!" she rhapsodized. And turning to Janice, she added, "Aren't they gorgeous?"

"They sure are," Janice fluted in a barely suppressed yelp of excitement. "They look a little wild with those grasses you added. Actually, they're more beautiful than anything you find at the florist in Denver."

"You're a real gentleman!" Mildred purred. And, pursing her lips, she actually planted a kiss on my cheek. "What's your name again?"

"Friedrich Graf, but most call me Fritz."

"I'm curious, Fritz, where did you find all those wonderful flowers?"

"Well, it wasn't easy. As you might know, there are hardly any around here. I had to hike up to higher elevations."

Mildred found a vase, filled it with water and placed the bouquet right in the middle of the dining room table. It was so picturesque, it begged on its knees to be painted. The flowers further ingratiated me and my comrades with the Perkins, to the dread of our guard who was caught speechless. In the following days the Perkins treated us as an integral part of the family. It was so uplifting to all of us that we momentarily forgot that we were POWs cooped up in a prison camp, surrounded by two high barbed wire fences and trigger-happy guards manning the watchtowers. Which is why I can say without reservations that the final days spent at the ranch belonged to some of the fondest memories of my time as a POW.

BULLETS ARE HISSING

The contrast between life on the ranch as opposed to that behind barbed wire couldn't have been starker. For one, inside the camp we hardly ever encountered any women, much less established contact with them. The very lack of feminine decorum made our daily course of events not only less savory, it added a harsher, infinitely more confrontational atmosphere to it. Case in point: It must have been two days after the 'flower' episode. It was searing with the mercury rising well above the century mark, enough to wrench drops of sweat from a shriveled cactus. We did what routine had prescribed for us. We showered, ate supper and devoted ourselves to our favorite pastimes. Some of us played a musical instrument, learned how to paint, attended courses in English, mathematics, American history or play-acting. Others, the more physical among us, played soccer or handball. As for myself, I spent my time practicing conversational English and rehearsing Wolfgang Riem's play *Our Victorious Hosts*, where I played the part of an American lieutenant. It was a satire whose aim was to skewer the American Army, its lackadaisical attitude toward any kind of authority, its lack of discipline and a slew of other glaring deficiencies, especially when compared to the German Army, let alone the unforgiving practices of Rommel's elite Afrika Korps. Let me say, I was thrilled playing the lead role, impersonating a fumbling American officer. It also spurned me to closely watch the live specimen of American officers, their way of talking, but particularly their body language.

Unfortunately, our relatively playful atmosphere was about to change drastically as soon as dusk settled. I happened to sit on our little porch glued to my English lessons, pronouncing phrases and learning dialogues by heart. Thankfully there was a light that allowed me to continue once it got dark. As I leaned back comfortably in a chair and read a witty exchange, I was ruffled by hoarse shouts coming from a tower nearby, followed by a couple of shrill whistle trills. Seconds later, several shots rang out in short succession. I heard a whizz and then a thwack, close to my feet, in fact. Baffled, I yanked my head down and what I saw scared me stiff. A bullet had hit the very leg of the chair I sat on, a mere two inches from my right foot.

Farther away, a rough and tumble turmoil followed. I heard screams and shouts, as if something ominous was happening. The center of the scuffle appeared to be several hundred yards away, at a construction site. The ruckus went on for about half an hour, when it abruptly died down, swallowed by the night.

I was bewildered.

Next morning the rumor mill started grinding away. Over breakfast I heard that two of our comrades, officers no less, had been shot dead for no apparent reason by a guard in Tower 7. But nobody knew for sure, not even Hans. Since I soon left for the ranch, it was not until supper that I found out what had happened.

"From what I know," Hans told me, anger gripping his face, "there was also a casualty, Capt. Eduard Markwart. He was shot dead by Pvt. Chaplin who manned Tower 7. He claimed he'd received orders from his lieutenant all the way up to Lt. Col. Hutchins to fire at anyone caught taking lumber from the construction site."

"You must be kidding, everybody has taken lumber from the site, you, me, officers, enlisted men."

"I know, and from the beginning, since our arrival. Otherwise, we wouldn't have any furniture. Those bastards!" He shook his head in disgust.

"That private must have been drunk," I ventured. "He just fired bullets haphazardly into the night. One of them almost hit my toes."

I told everybody what had happened.

"Well, at least you're still alive. Capt. Markwart wasn't so lucky. He was just entering the construction site when a bullet hit him. He was taken to the hospital, but they couldn't save him. An hour later he was pronounced dead."

"Damn!" I shook my head. "Shot dead, for a few lousy pieces of lumber. This cries to heaven."

"You're right." Livid, Hans clenched his fist. "The whole incident is in clear violation of the Geneva Convention. This time they won't get away with it. I already talked to von Wiese, and we'll report it to the Swiss Delegation and the Red Cross. We will not rest until those responsible have to answer a few questions. That includes the whole chain of command, from the guard who fired the gun all the way up to Hutchins, that mealy-mouthed ass of a commander."

A couple of days later we were called upon to attend a memorial, held by Chaplain Anton Gruber. Lined up on the parade grounds around the swastika-draped coffin of our comrade, we all stood there with doleful faces, hanging on to every word of the chaplain's somber and moving funeral speech. Once Gruber had ended, Col. von Wiese manned the podium and delivered a fiery speech, stressing that Capt. Eduard Markwart did not die in vain; he gave his life for our Fuehrer, Adolf Hitler, and the German fatherland, adding that one day his death would have to be atoned for. "In the name of our Fuehrer there will have to be reprisals," he shouted. "Let's all salute our comrade in the hope that this hour will come soon."

We all stood at attention and raised our arms for a stiff *Heil Hitler*. It was followed by the *Horst Wessel Song*, the Nazi battle hymn. We formed columns and followed the eight comrades who carried the coffin to the camp's cemetery to lay him to rest. While the coffin was lowered into the grave, Bernd Breitner, a Viennese, played the somber soldier song *"Ich hatt' einen Kameraden"* (I once had a buddy) on his mouth harp, and many hummed right along. It was all very solemn and festive.

Actually, I was anything but joyful when von Wiese and his zealots praised the Fuehrer and intoned the Nazi battle hymn. Caught in a dilemma, I wrenched a painful compromise out of myself, simply because I knew of no other way to render homage to our comrade who had died in vain due to American negligence.

Like no other incident, this deadly shooting shattered not only the relative peace within the camp, it caused a profound upheaval. Most of us, whether enlisted men like me or officers, were angered at the Amis, more specifically at the camp's administrators. Our spokesman, von Wiese, lodged a strong-worded complaint to Col. Hutchins, as well as to several other officers who were in charge of the guards, accusing them of negligence at best and incompetence at worst. Copies of the report were also sent to the American representatives of the Swiss Legation, which represented German interests. That sparked an investigation, hearings were held and testimony was taken from as many as twenty-three witnesses, Hans and me among them. Mid-July a representative of the Swiss Legation visited the camp to discuss the shooting with the camp commander and officers in charge of the guards, and to check on our living conditions. Although he didn't voice any open criticism, it was quite clear that he disapproved of the way the camp was run. A full, detailed report of his findings was later completed and sent to the State Department.

The consequences of all these investigative actions were not long in coming. By the middle of August, a little more than four weeks after the incident, Col. Hutchins and von Wiese received the final report. It turned out to be anything but flattering for the camp commander and the officers in charge of the guards, Capt. Commager and Lt. Barber. The first ones to bite the bullet were the officers at the helm of the guards, who were relieved of their duties at once. Shortly after it was Col. Hutchins's turn. Having been accused of being irresolute and incapable of issuing clear and binding orders, he was dismissed from his command, demoted and sent to another POW camp in Illinois. At last, there was Pvt. Chaplin, whose loose trigger finger had caused all the turmoil. An appointed Judge Advocate, Lt. John Pincer, who investigated his actions, recommended that he be court-martialed. Unfortunately, the military court, citing confusing, even contradictory instructions by the officers in charge, claimed there wasn't enough evidence to let him stand trial.

Incidentally, Wolf Riem who happened to be present when Col. Hutchins received the report, told us that the colonel looked bewildered, at sea. "Like a senescent octopus, he sputtered nothing but an inky cloud of syllables under whose cover he hoped to get away with murder."

We were generally pleased by the outcome, even though we would have liked to see Pvt. Chaplin convicted of negligence and incompetence as well. Looking forward, we wondered how the new camp commander, Col. Peter Sullivan and his executive officer, Major Robert Binford, would turn out. Sullivan was a fireplug of a man in his forties, so blond and blue-eyed he could have been a German. It was rumored that he'd had combat experience in Europe, that he was not only a strict disciplinarian with an iron fist, but also a staunch opponent of the Nazi movement — a man of no nonsense who reportedly spit fire when our Fuehrer's name was mentioned.

Well, it didn't take us long to find out. Set on tightening the reins from his first day in office, he called von Wiese, Hans and several other sergeants and officers to his office and admonished them in no uncertain terms that from now on law-breaking would no longer be tolerated. Anybody caught violating the rules would be severely punished. This would even apply to minor offenses such as stealing lumber and swiping food from the kitchen. In addition, he also prohibited the display of Nazi symbols, such as swastika flags or other Nazi paraphernalia. This included the use of the Hitler salute, singing Nazi songs such as the *Horst Wessel* battle hymn and displaying the picture of Adolf Hitler at our bunks, lockers or bulletin boards — widespread habits among our diehards.

THE SWASTIKA RULES THE ROOST

As expected, such sweeping prohibitions were quickly challenged by our spokesmen who cited our rights under the Geneva Convention. Being stiff-necked supporters of the national socialist movement, they were particularly stung by Col. Sullivan's hostile actions against those who believed in Hitler and the Nazi ideology. Besides complaining to the Swiss Delegation, they chose the path of confrontation, even provocation, regardless the cost.

Hans, forever at the forefront of provoking the Amis, also coaxed us, Dieter, Peter and me, to join him in acts of sabotage against Sullivan and his ilk. "We want to squeeze their balls until they're nothing but mush," he said, turning his hand into a tight fist.

We'd just come back from supper and were sitting around the raw coffee table of our quarters.

"You know that I'm on your side, Hans," I offered, "but I don't see the point of using such a strategy of head-on provocation. I'm also for resisting, but in a smart, crafty and cunning way."

Peter agreed. "A public showdown is not in our interest. I'd give the Amis a chance to save face."

Dieter nodded as well. "More brains and fewer fists is the way to go."

Hans was taken aback. "As you know, Sullivan hates all Germans who don't bow to him and his flunkies. Somebody has to show him that we can't be pushed around. What makes you such damn pussyfoots?"

"I think your and von Wiese's strategy will only aggravate the situation," I told him. "It may lead to a complete clampdown."

"Let him clamp down on us. But we have to prove to him that we're a tough bunch who can stand up to him. The harder he keeps pushing, the harder we'll push back. But we have to be united."

"That sounds heroic but they would still be in charge. If the Swiss won't come through and tame them, then we're in for an un-winnable fight. Remember, they've got the guns. Granted, we would gain a little more respect, or hatred, but it's not worth the price we'd have to pay. There could be bloodshed."

"Whatever the cost, we'll fight for our honor, our Fuehrer and the German fatherland. Any compromise, no matter how small, is defeatist, licking the boots of the Amis."

"You know I'm not for licking the boots of the Amis," I shot back. "But I'm not in favor of provoking them just for the sake of feeling good. That's childish."

Hans gave me a quizzical stare. "You, Peter and Dieter!" he burst out, red-faced, his voice a ragged rupture in the texture of the room. "You've let yourself be ensnared by the Americans to the point of dancing according to their tunes. What happened to your tough German spines? You're violating the oath you have given to our Fuehrer and our German fatherland. You're bowing to the Amis, to their superficial way of life. Your brains are already mired in that gooey American peanut butter you've been cramming down your throats every day. Pretty soon you'll get into the habit of getting rubber-soled boots and chewing gum, too, looking like bovines chewing the cud. Aren't you ashamed of yourselves?" He shook his head, turned around and headed back to his bunk, growling.

Unfortunately, the true believers once again got the upper hand, strong-arming everybody. So most of us continued to use the Hitler salute and display the swastika whenever the occasion presented itself. Worse, four days after the first meeting, Hans and several hardcore officers, including von Wiese, sneaked out of their barracks at night and, using ladders from the construction site, painted red swastikas smack on the windows of the commandant's building.

When Sullivan entered the office in the morning, all he saw was crawling, bristling swarms of swastikas. Even the small piece of lawn displayed a large swastika that had been dug into the sod. Livid with rage, he promptly ordered Capt. Shepherd to start an investigation in the hope of apprehending the perpetrators. Within days, five of our men, Col. von Wiese, Lt. Spaeth, Lt. Borchart, as well as Hans, were identified as prime suspects. It was whispered that a stool pigeon had been given the names to the Amis. In any event, the suspects were forced to face a disciplinary board. Goaded by Col. Sullivan it was swift in dealing with the cases and meting out unusual and severe punishments. Each one received sentences of twenty-one days in the stockade on bread and water.

When the news of their convictions was publicized, the camp turned into a hornet's nest. Most of us couldn't help but feel unconditional solidarity with our comrades, even those who were straddling the fence. Von Wiese, Hans and all the true-believers triumphed.

"Nobody could have united us more than Sullivan," Hans told everybody. And glaring at me, he probed, "Does that finally convince you?"

I nodded, dealing him a wry smile. Actually, I was still straddling the fence. While I opposed the provocation, I also had my quarrels with Sullivan who in my estimation overreacted, raising the confrontation to yet another level. Since the sticking point was the display of swastikas and Nazi emblems, the protest came in the form of even more of the same. Our jagged fire-wheel suddenly popped up on most outlandish surfaces. It was scratched into the silver ware, onto doors, walkways and parade grounds, even showing up on the roofs of the barracks. Many bitter-enders painted little swastikas on their foreheads, cheeks and, yes, teeth. And some of them who worked for local farmers even used their thumbnails to slice swastikas into peaches and plums. The swastika became as ubiquitous as carrion flies on a rotten carcass.

Enraged, Col. Sullivan didn't sit on his hands either. Within the first week alone, he made sure that altogether sixty-four of our men ended up in the stockade for breaking rules. In fact, the stockade was overflowing and other buildings had to be found to incarcerate all the culprits, most of whom had committed only minor pranks.

The whole camp was walking on a tightrope.

Barely twelve days later the Swiss Delegation stepped in and after a thorough investigation it declared that the rules and the punishments Col. Sullivan had set up were arbitrary, disproportionate and in violation of the Geneva Convention. Rumors made the rounds that Sullivan reacted in disbelief when he read the report. But a few days later he agreed to significant concessions such as allowing the Nazi salute and the display of swastikas and pictures of Hitler on bunks. Most of us, especially the Nazi bullheads, viewed these concessions as a clear defeat and an encouragement to keep up the pressure.

Von Wiese, Hans and the other instigators, now freed, carried the day. "Now we are fingering Sullivan's balls, one by one," Hans commented when he came back to our barracks. "All we have to do is to tighten our grip and squeeze until he rescinds the rest of his nonsensical rules."

Von Wiese, expressing an unwavering confidence, likewise declared that the fight would continue, suggesting again that we, being top dogs, might well be planning ahead to forming the advance guard of a German invasion. Rumor had it, he was already looking into establishing contact with other German POWs at camps in Illinois, New Mexico, Arkansas and Texas, as well as members of the German Bund in Pennsylvania, Ohio,

Illinois in the hope of joining forces, with the goal of eventually marching into Washington D.C. and taking over the government.

Swell-headed and swaggering, our Nazis also exploited this partial victory to tighten their grip on the German camp even more, with truth being its first casualty. Daily, by way of their bulletins, they beat the drum for a German victory on all fronts, despite the fact that things looked more hopeless every day. Never did the German Army retreat, much less face defeat. Worse, these fanatics jumped on everybody who got used to reading American newspapers. And those who dared to utter even the slightest doubt about our winning the war, were declared back-stabbers and told in no uncertain terms to shut up or else.

Tightfisted Gestapo units would roam through the camp hunting down and beating up all those they deemed 'suspicious'. To give you a glimpse, walking back to the barracks during the night of the Fourth of July, I encountered a group of ten Nazi thugs who had surrounded Pvt. Manfred Froehlich and Cpl. Heinz Schumann. I had met both of them before and found them to be fair, level-headed fellows you would want to rub elbows and guzzle a beer with. In fact, I used to play soccer with Schumann on the same team, while Froehlich was an outstanding student in one of my English classes. Stepping closer, I instantly noticed that the air was bristling with tension. Veins puffed up, saliva splattered and mouths blustered with rage. "Deserters! Traitors! Back-stabbers!" the leader of the mob, Lt. Spaeth, barked at the two men, pushing and shoving them. Accused of having thrown Pvt. Manfred Felchen out of the train, Spaeth was infamous for being one of the most rabid Nazi thugs in the whole camp. Blustering, he and his men, all burly toughs, were ready to strike, just waiting for a counter-thrust from the two.

"Leave us alone," Froelich shot back. "We haven't done anything to you."

"Not to us, but to our German cause!" Lt Spaeth hissed, forcing out a laugh. "You've been caught spreading enemy propaganda, that our Fuehrer is a madman and the war is lost."

Feeling empathy for Schumann and Froehlich, I elbowed my way into the circle and pleaded to Spaeth and his lot, "Come on, you guys, what difference does it make? We're all Germans. We stuck together in the fight for our country, even risking our lives. We should all be thankful that we're still alive. Why don't you leave them alone."

"Sounds like you're one of them, too," Spaeth bawled at me. "Maybe we should take you to task as well."

"I think he's on our list," another in the back shouted.

At that point, one of the Nazis must have punched Schumann. But, being a muscular fellow, Schumann punched back, and seconds later it was a free-for-all. Insults criss-crossed, fists started flying and groans rang out into the night as Spaeth and his gang soon piled on Schumann, Froehlich and me. Although we three tried to stand our ground, trading punches and kicking, we soon realized that we were woefully outnumbered. All we could do was taking to our heels. I was lucky. Since Schumann and Froehlich took off in the other direction, I couldn't tell what happened to them. All I heard was a frightful muddle of yelling and shouting, even gun shots. I feared for the worst.

Upon entering our barracks, I ran into Dieter and Peter. Seeing my bloody face and hands, they right away offered their help in stopping the bleeding and applying plasters.

"What in the hell happened?" Peter wanted to know.

When I told them about the confrontation, they just shook their heads and cursed the Nazis.

Next morning, during breakfast, Hans let me know that both Froehlich and Schumann had been hospitalized, in critical condition. "I heard there was a big scuffle among ten comrades last night just outside of this mess hall," he explained, his eyes riveted on my cuts and lesions. "They must have been dead-drunk on beer and some home brew. Anyway, there were those two or three troublemakers who got very quarrelsome. Apparently, they mocked and derided others for being Nazi pigs and warmongers. Well, a brawl started. When the American guards belatedly got wind of it and started to arrive at the scene, those who could quickly dispersed, except for the two instigators. What can I say, they got what they deserved. They should count themselves lucky that they're still alive."

When Hans had ended, I almost had to throw up. This was the pinnacle of cynicism — blaming the victims. Was that my good friend, Hans? I wondered who'd be next.

When, early in the morning, the camp commander, Col. Sullivan, heard about this horrible incident, he was furious, once again. He was supposed to have cursed like a trooper. "Fucking Nazi thugs. If I catch them, I'll castrate them, even if it costs me my stripes!" He promised to conduct a thorough investigation and bring the perpetrators to justice. To find them he instantly issued a bulletin, in which he called on all those who'd witnessed or heard of the incident to contact him personally, or Capt. Shepherd who was put in charge of the investigation. Their identity would of course be kept secret.

When I came back from a day's work on the farm and read Sullivan's bulletin, I wobbled. Should I? On the one hand, I, too, was enraged at the brutality of Lt. Spaeth and his thugs and the glaring injustice of their actions. But then again, I felt not quite ready to betray my comrades. I was unable to admit that these past years as a fighting man, the tight bonds of comradeship in situations of life and death, of triumph and defeat, were based on nothing more than a deception. Or was it just cowardliness that prevented me from being resolute? The fear of being found out by these fanatics, of being marked as a traitor like Peter, Dieter and others or, worse, facing the same fate as Schumann and Froehlich? I strongly suspected that Hans and others of his fellow believers were watching me closely for signs of coziness toward our captors. And if, God forbid, they were to find out that I was a stool pigeon, I knew that my days would be numbered. So I dawdled, waiting to see how Capt. Shepherd's investigation would proceed.

But then two incidents soon made my flesh creep. On the morning of August 13th, barely four days after the beating, I was stunned that Peter and Dieter were not lying in the bunks. There was not even the slightest sign that they had slept in them.

"What's going on?" I pumped Hans who was still in bed. "D'you have any idea what happened to them?"

"Beats me. Maybe they skipped the fence."

"I doubt it. They'd have told us."

"Why do you ask me?" he snapped. "Who knows where they are. They may have crawled up Sullivan's asshole, enjoy the warmth and pray he doesn't take a shit. All I know is that both of them are nothing but damn traitors." He turned and pulled the blanket over his head.

As I shuffled to the washroom, I ran into Helmut who happened to be quartered next door. We got into a chat. I told him about the absence of Peter and Dieter and asked if he knew anything about them escaping.

"I've never heard anything about that. I only know that there was another brawl last night. The usual thing. Apparently, some people got badly hurt and had to be committed to the hospital."

"Oh brother!"

While Helmut was drawn to the wash-basin, I made my way to the john. I always made sure to be the first to empty my bowels, so I wouldn't have to knock knees with somebody else. As I picked a bowl, I somehow sensed that something looked unusual, suspicious. The center of the floor appeared as if somebody had wiped it with a mop. It was a crude job that left dirty, reddish-brown streaks on the concrete. At the fringes I even detected stains and drops of blood. Startled, I followed the streaks into the shower room. A sharp, acrid stench assailed my nostrils. As I raised my head, I was struck dumb. There was a body dangling from the rafter, its head in a tight noose. It was badly beaten up, with blood crusting the blueish face and urine mixed with feces dripping from his trouser legs and onto his boots. It reeked like hell. A written cardboard sign suspended from his right foot read: 'I'm a traitor to my country'. Staggering even closer, I recognized that it was none other than my friend and roommate, Peter Keller. Yes, Peter!

I was shocked out of my mind, breathless. Flashbacks of deserters strung up on tree branches by General Schoerner's bloodhounds along forlorn roads in Russia caught up with me. Worse, the whole trauma of the Russian assault, to the tone of a Stalin organ, unfolding before my eyes. I was so dazed, so benumbed, I couldn't even remember what I did. I only know that hours later, I found myself in the infirmary, stretched out on a cot. Having just emerged from the daze, a medic informed me that guards had picked me up half-naked, wandering around the camp aimlessly and disoriented. Dr. Moor, who treated me, claimed that I'd had a mental breakdown. He made me swallow a handful of antidepressants and suggested that I spent a day in the hospital for observation.

Toward the evening, as I shuffled past the other beds on my way to the john, I suddenly heard somebody calling my name. The voice was very weak, barely audible. I turned my head. It came from a patient who was so heavily bandaged I couldn't even recognize him.

"I'm Dieter, Dieter Krumm," he whimpered as I approached him.

"Dieter! Oh my God, what happened to you?"

He was close to tears. "The Nazis beat us up last night. Peter, Arno Eggert, Johann Klett and me, after we walked out of our English lesson. They accused us of being traitors. They almost broke my jaw and I lost many of my teeth. Eggert and Klett didn't fare much better. They are in the other ward. I don't know what happened to Peter."

"You mean... I can't believe it!" I was ready to throw up. "These were our comrades we fought with in the same trenches elbow to elbow. Bastards, gangsters, that's what they are."

I shook my head in disgust. Thank God I'd failed to attend the English lesson. Needless to say, I couldn't bring myself to tell him about Peter. It might have done more than break his heart.

MY MEXICAN CONNECTION

Peter's murder as well as the clubbing of Dieter and the other comrades came as a profound shock to me, comparable to the loss of my friends Ernst and Peter in Russia. I'd become very amicable to both of them of late. During our English lessons, we often digressed and freely shared our views about Hitler and the war.

On a more personal level, the whole onslaught by the Nazi thugs once again hit home, making me wonder about my own fate. I knew I could no longer count on the protective hand of anybody, including Hans. Quite the contrary, I played with the thought that Hans, a grudger that he was, may well have played a part in Peter's murder and the beatings of Dieter and the rest.

Indeed, when I ran into my former pal on the way back from the bathroom two days later, he acted decidedly unsure, I dare say, even devious. Though he barked, "Good morning," he wouldn't look me in the eye. He seemed to be in a great hurry, twisting and squirming, as if he was about to slip out of his skin. I had never seen him acting in such a way before and I wondered, *Would I be next? Had I not overdrawn my portion of luck already?* These and other questions hung over me like a dark cloud. I wondered how I'd be able to share a room with a thug who wouldn't think twice about breaking your jaw or forcing a noose around your neck.

The fuse was hustling, jostling. Never before had I felt as disheartened and hopeless about the run of things in the camp. *But life will go on,* I tried to drum into myself. Eager to prove it, I made sure to slip beyond the barbed wire whenever I could, to dip into a world where people intermingled and treated each other in a civilized way. Still, I couldn't quite shake off the negative effects of the turmoil, the most bothersome of which appeared to be the lack of sleep. More often than not I felt so weary that picking watermelons and squash turned into a real chore. The heat did the rest. Jay Jennings, our guard, who had sworn to Mr. Muncie that he wouldn't have to worry about our productivity, repeatedly warned me that I'd barely done three quarters of my quota. And even that would have been impossible without help from Pancho, my Mexican friend.

Pancho happened to be one of a handful of young Mexican laborers who'd been hired to buckle down with us. Being about my age, he was much smaller than me, yet stocky and muscular. Broad-faced, gap-toothed and slightly slit-eyed, he sported high cheekbones, a curved, bony nose and dark-brown eyes that sparkled like a pair of polished gems. His low forehead, hemmed in by a full thatch of black hair, might have led our Nazis to put him on the lower rungs of the evolutionary ladder, just above the chimpanzees. Thank God I'd dropped such racist nonsense long ago, at the latest after our capture in North Africa.

From the first day there was a natural affinity between Pancho and me, and we immediately struck up a friendship. Our common status as underdogs may have helped, but there was something else at play I couldn't quite fathom. What I admired in him was his stoic resilience in the face of adversity, matched by a boundless curiosity. Though bare of any formal education, Pancho was one of the most curious fellows I'd ever met. He never tired prying me about my hometown, Berlin, about Alemania, Europe, Russia, North Africa and my life as a POW.

Come to think of, there was another attribute I treasured — his cheerful mood. Never did I see him downcast or gloomy. Like the rest of his compatriots, he always whistled or hummed some Mexican song or other, even during work. "Time pass faster," he claimed. Yet I had a hunch that there was an inner wellspring at work, an equanimity whose roots may well reach way back into a hard-won Indian frame of mind.

We clicked as though we were brothers. The only downside in our relationship was our lack in adequate communication tools. Both of us were weak in English. And Spanish was as Greek to me, as German to Pancho. Though my English was marginally better than Pancho's, we often had to fish for words or use our hands, fingers and facial expressions to chat, converse or to exchange our views, about our work, about Germany and, most often, about America.

Although Pancho was thankful that America provided him with a job and a livelihood, he didn't hold back in his criticism of his host. He reminded me of the black waiters we talked to on the train from New York. They compared their lot to dingle berries in the anal fold of a huge white rear end. Although not quite as graphic, Pancho didn't hold back his mind either, especially when white Americans weren't around. "Gringos talk much about freedom, but only talk," he told me and my comrades during a lunch break. "You free in America if you white. If skin is brown, you are like dirt kick with boot. They like *Mexicanos;* we are tough and work hard. They like our girls, too, but only for cleaning houses or for pick-ups, you know, take to bed. But we get no respect. For Gringos we are dirty Mexicans, good for hard or dirty work they are too lazy to do themselves.

"You go to bar or dancing hall," he went on, the air whistling through the gap in his teeth like the hiss of an overheated teapot. "Maybe you come out dead. They beat me only for *looking* at white girls. Yesterday I went to drugstore buying Aspirin. There was long line. When I wait and come to saleslady, she look to me and say: You wait, the others, Gringos, come first. Happen all the time. What a life, ha?" He shook his head in disgust. That's why he didn't want to stay in this country, he told me. Never! As soon as he had some money in his pocket, he'd be on his way back to Mexico, where he'd build a small adobe house. "You come visit," he added. He mumbled something I couldn't understand, got up and took off. A minute later he came back with a large piece of brown wrapping paper and a pen. He tore off a small piece and scribbled the address of his parents in Chihuahua on it, assuring me that they would always welcome me, with smiles and tasty *antojitos.*

Mexicans are very friendly to Germans, he claimed. "They think you good people, honest and working very hard." He knew of a whole colony about a hundred miles west of Chihuahua, thousands of them. They are called *menonitos.* They have their own villages, with churches and schools. And they still speak German.

That pricked my ears. "Germans in Mexico? Not far from Chihuahua?"

"Yes. Sorry, me no *mapa.* But me draw one." He grabbed a piece of brown wrapping paper and a pen and began drawing. "OK, this here El Paso," he said, drawing a little circle and adding, "And this here Rio Grande, for us Rio Bravo." With one stroke he drew in the stretch of this long river from El Paso all the way to the Gulf of Mexico. "This here border, *frontera.* And here Chihuahua, *ciudad,* three hundred kilometers from El Paso." He drew another little circle, as well as the road between these two cities. "And here is Cuauhtemoc, very small town." He just made a little dot southwest of Chihuahua. "Here *menonitos* live." He made a large circle around Cuauhtemoc and then handed it to me.

That sparked my interest. "How far is it from here."

"Oh, very far. Maybe seven hundred miles."

"Wow, that far? I wonder, how many days would it take to get there?"

"Three, four days with bus, *mas o menos.*"

That was sobering, enough to put the idea of escaping on the back burner.

Sadly, I saw my friend Pancho one more time. According to my diary, it was Friday, the 27th of July. Come Monday, I was suddenly, without prior notice, trucked to another farm, owned and operated by Charles

48

'Chuck' Johnson and his sons. It was only three stone throws away from the Muncie farm. Yet we had no way of reaching out to each other, dropping our friendship into the arms of our memory.

BE CAREFUL WHAT YOU WISH FOR

But let me first tell you what came to pass at the camp. One Friday night I was busy playing my part in the dress rehearsal of Wolfgang Riem's satirical play, "Unsere siegreichen Gastgeber" (Our Victorious Hosts). It went quite well, thank you. I was at ease, in complete control of my part. Never did I have to fish for a line. Only one actor, Hermann Bischoff, who impersonated an American private, stumbled twice. It was later whispered that he had hours before received a heart-wrenching letter from his relatives in Hanover. His aunt, Bertha, had written that Hermann's whole family had perished in the last British air raid on Hamburg. Showing great empathy, Riem first thought of postponing the premiere, but Bischoff gritted his teeth, insisting that he would be ready for the premiere the next day. And he was, albeit with some hiccups.

The long-awaited performance, which was not only attended by the German camp, but also by a few American officers, was a resounding success, with four curtain calls. Its satire was biting, depicting in telltale individual scenes the disorder within the American Army, the lukewarm attitude of its enlisted men toward their officers, indeed, toward any authority, the inability or unwillingness to follow orders and march in lockstep, the way we in the Afrika Korps did, even in our defeated state. This dilemma would reach its comic climax in the last act. Frustrated at the incompetence of my men, I, as the American officer in charge, once raised my hands in despair and shouted, "How can you lead an army, if you have hundreds of different steps."

The contrast between the two armies couldn't have been sharper, nor the laughter greater. And yet I had the distinct feeling that the satire frequently backfired in a funny, quite unexpected way. While the Americans, with all their foibles and shortcomings, may have skittered across the stage as screwballs and nincompoops, they never lost their semblance of being human. Many of their zany acts were even likable — far more so than those of the Germans whose devotion to a culture of stiff discipline and order made them look like a bunch of narrow-minded, humorless blockheads. This applied particularly to the German Captain, Kurt Sommer, who acted as he was supposed to, as a stiff-necked robot.

This weird twist wasn't entirely lost on some of the German officers, who showed a pronounced dissatisfaction with the performance. According to them, the Americans were presented too affectionately, too likably, whereas the Germans came across far too rigid, stiff as ramrods. They blamed Riem, insinuating that he intended to spread anti-Nazi propaganda. But the actors, including me, were also pounced upon, some slack of poetic license notwithstanding.

"You acted quite well," Captain Olaf Kinkel told me after the show. "The way you stuttered when you gave an order to your enlisted men was superb. You showed quite clearly that you lacked the backbone to be a good officer who can bark commands and lead soldiers. But then you twisted that in a way that made us feel you were too much of a gentleman to boss people around. So your weakness in character got turned into a human strength, and you begged everybody to like and admire you for it. And they all did exactly as you wished. Of course you realize that you can't run an army in a climate like that, whether it's German or American."

I smiled. "Maybe that wouldn't be so bad," I heard myself saying. "It might make wars less palatable."

"You're a romantic dreamer. That will never happen. But if I were you, I'd be more careful with your words."

By the way, when I got back to our quarter, Hans lashed out at me, also claiming I portrayed the Americans far too favorably. "As an American lieutenant you were far too likable," he insisted. "You completely forgot the likes of him treated us like shit after our surrender, and still do, even now. That shows on which side you're on."

FLIRTING WITH OUR ALLIES

The sun hung overhead, fat as a giant pumpkin, splashing the fields of our new workplace with an overabundance of sparkles and luster. Called the Johnson Farm, it was only two miles east from the Muncie homestead, and sometimes I played with the thought of taking to my heels at our lunch hour to see my friend Pancho. Sadly, that wish never left the dream stage.

While picking fruits and vegetables, my comrades and I happened to get acquainted with three young and pretty Japanese-American women, Matsuko, Yuki and Sei. Actually, we had ogled them a day before already, albeit at a distance. We had even wolf-whistled them and shouted complimentary remarks. But this time, thanks to the change of mind of the owner, we were lumped together in an effort to harvest tomatoes in a huge field the size of a football stadium. This allowed us to come face to face with each other, often on opposite sides of the same stalks. Having never had a chance to meet Japanese girls or women before, we were curious, most eager to engage with them, not only because they were part of the opposite sex. We also considered them to be allies in arms, distant friends. And during our first lunch break, while we were all sitting around wooden camp tables and munching on our sandwiches, we immediately struck up a conversation. Unfortunately, they were so shy and constrained that it was well nigh impossible to squeeze anything out of them. All they did was to sit there, smile and giggle like a gaggle of schoolgirls. It wasn't until the end of our lunch break that they loosened up a little.

I was particularly fond of Matsuko and, from all I could tell, she of me. Marcy, as she preferred to be called, was a relatively tall, slender woman with finely chiseled features: a short, perfectly straight nasal ridge, shapely lips, prominent cheek-bones and a high forehead that was framed by a page-boy hairdo with bewitching, girlish bangs. Even though I introduced myself as Fritz Graf, she insisted on calling me 'Viking', because, being blond and blue-eyed, I reminded her of a character in a movie about those Germanic marauders she'd seen a couple of years ago. I laughed, pointing out that the Vikings were a free people, while I was anything but.

Having placed myself next to her, I besieged her with questions about herself and how they ended up in this godforsaken place. Gradually, step by step, she overcame her giggles and matter-of-factly told me about her fate. She insisted that she was an American who was born and raised in California, becoming increasingly more emotional, particularly when she touched on the forceful relocation she and her family had to face. While she conceded that most of her countrymen were very pleasant and friendly people if you met them individually, she also claimed that the American government couldn't be trusted.

"It's very suspicious, even paranoid," she insisted. "Look at us. We're loyal citizens who were forcefully uprooted from our homes and farms in California and moved to a Japanese Relocation Center in Amache, a few miles east of here, just because we were of Japanese descent. It's crazy. Two of my uncles are even fighting in the American Army. And we, who haven't lifted a finger against America, are put behind barbed wire. It's pure racism. Our constitutional rights don't mean a thing. I hate to say it but they're all hypocrites up there, the politicians, the judges, even our president."

The injustice Marcy told me about hit me particularly hard. My mind harked back to the complaints of Pancho, my Mexican friend, and the black soldiers and servants on our initial train ride from the East Coast had told us. So much for the claim that America, unlike Germany, was a democracy, more, the Mother of all Democracies, where the rule of law reigned supreme, where every citizen was treated equally and with respect. I was more than disappointed, I felt *disillusioned*, as if Uncle Sam had suddenly stumbled badly and fallen flat on his face.

"How about you?" Marcy asked. "You're being guarded, too. How did *you* get here?"

When I told her about my fate, she right away drew parallels. "How do *you* deal with being in chains?"

"Well, it's very hard on me. Frankly, if I couldn't get out of the camp, like working on the farm here, I'd probably go crazy," I remember saying. I also brushed on the tensions within the camp, the toxic civil war we were engaged in and about the killing of my friend, Peter Keller.

She shook her head in disgust. "Don't you have American guards who protect you?"

"Not really. We're more or less on our own."

"That's awful. How can you stand it? Have you ever thought about escaping?"

"Who hasn't? But it's not that easy."

"Have you?"

"Well, yes, many times. But frankly, I wouldn't know how to go about and where to."

That was about it. The return of the guard wouldn't let us go any farther. Yet our exchange, particularly Marcy's willingness to escape roused me to the point where it wouldn't let go of me. My fear of becoming another victim of the Nazis also played a role and, when I got back to the camp, the thought arose of teaming up with her, of escaping together. I envisioned us heading south, bolting to Mexico, where we could probably find shelter with Pancho's parents in Chihuahua. From there we could head to the Pacific coast to catch a freighter to the Philippines, China, or Japan. I had no illusions. It would be very risky. The FBI, everybody, would be on our tails. But we were both young, full of beans; excitement would trump any fear of the unknown.

Anyway, I couldn't wait to discuss my pipe dream with Marcy. Luckily, the tomato field we harvested was huge. I figured we would be at it for another two or even three days before we'd be finished. That might give us time, diminishing the chances of being torn apart. When, next day, we managed to get together again I was able to draw Marcy aside and approach her about my escape plans, half-baked as they were. Surprisingly, she was very receptive, even enthusiastic. But Mexico? No, thanks, that wasn't for her. She suggested Los Angeles instead, where she had some relatives who would help us go into hiding. Her greatest worry was that we might not be able to stay under the radar of the FBI and the local police. In any event, she asked me to give her some time to think it over.

Unfortunately, owing to a glitch, we were prevented from getting together for more than a week, and I was about to get cold feet. But, as if by a stroke of luck, we were able to touch elbows again, a whole lunch hour serving as our frame. Since the guard had left momentarily, we seized the opportunity to sneak away into a cornfield nearby, in the hope of having a little tete-a-tete. I'd gotten hold of an old poncho, which I spread on the ground between two-and-a-half feet high cornstalks. Clods beneath made it a rough lair. But we were young, and well — in love. Cheek to cheek, we delved into the subject of our escape. We pledged to each other to pull it through and promised to work on the details over the next few weeks.

Naturally, we couldn't resist necking, kissing and fondling each other. We didn't intend to go all the way, always mindful that the guard might return and catch us in the act. But then one thing led to another and before long we were about to do what young people starved for love are in the habit of doing. But just as my fingers were fumbling at Marcy's panties, echoed as it was by a muted squeak of passion on my lover's side, we were startled by some rustling.

We froze.

"I'll be damned, a fucking kraut and that slit-eyed Jap floozy!" suddenly came booming through the cornstalks. There was more rustling and seconds later he stood there in front of us, arms akimbo and grinning from ear to ear. "What in the hell d'you think you're doing? Celebrating that German-Japanese friendship of yours? Pull up your fucking pants, both of you! Double time. This ain't a pick-up joint! This is a wholesome American farm. You're here to pick tomatoes, not screwing. I want to see you back at your working area in five minutes. Do I make myself clear?"

It was none other than Pvt. Jay Jennings, our guard, an athletic fellow who was as tall as the surrounding cornstalks. Naturally, neither Marcy nor I were in the mood to ask questions, even though Marcy was deeply offended by Jennings's remarks. Clenching our teeth, we simply did what he'd ordered us to do. We dressed and joined the workforce. And as the afternoon dragged on, we picked our tomatoes, easily filling our quota.

Naturally, we were apprehensive. We had reason to fear that Jennings would turn us in and that we might receive some sort of punishment. Mercifully, he never did. He more or less acted as though our love encounter had never happened. God bless his soul, he didn't even mind me getting together with Marcy and talking, as long as we stayed out of the cornfield.

THE COOING OF THE STOOL PIGEON

Meanwhile, the drama inside the camp showed no signs of dying down. After a grace period of three weeks, there was yet another attack on so-called traitors. This time three enlisted men and one officer were so badly beaten that they had to be committed to the hospital. In the wake of this violence, Sullivan issued yet another urgent bulletin, in which he called the beatings of these honorable and peaceful soldiers cowardly acts by a gang of Nazi thugs. "We have to stop these Nazi gangsters," he wrote. "To accomplish that, I want everybody who has any information that could lead to the arrest and conviction of these blackguards to step forward and report them to Capt. Shepherd. Once again, I offer secrecy and extra protection to anybody courageous enough to follow their conscience and help us stop this menace in its tracks."

Enraged by the brutality and cowardice of the diehard Nazis and hoping to make the camp a little safer, not least for myself, I finally resolved to cut the umbilical cord that tied me to Hitler's army and make my way to Shepherd's office. Suspecting that the Nazi thugs might be on the lookout for me, I purposely chose a meandering detour to throw anybody who might spy on me off the scent.

Luckily, everything proceeded according to the plan. The secretary guarding the office, a curly-haired corporal in his late twenties, was all smiles when I entered. "I'm Dave," he said, stretching out his hand. "What can I do for you?"

I explained that I had some information Capt. Shepherd might be interested in.

"Oh, you want to blow a whistle on the Nazi marauders? Well, you're at the right address. Unfortunately, Capt. Shepherd's presently out at a meeting. But he should be back in less than fifteen minutes. You can wait right here in his office." He led me to the office and offered me a chair. "Would you like to have a sundowner and something to nibble?"

"Sure."

A minute later, Dave brought me a bowl of crunchy peanuts and a tumbler filled with ice and a brown liquid. "It's a smooth Bourbon from Kentucky," he added with a smile, setting it on a small coffee table to the right of me. "They tell me it's the best," he added, showing me the bottle.

The Bourbon was indeed special and, pleased by the treatment, I moved my elbows, guzzling the smooth Bourbon, munching on peanuts and letting my eyes sweep around the office, which struck me as a bit drab, colorless. On the wall, behind the desk, hung the mugshots of President Franklin Delano Roosevelt, the Generals Eisenhower and Patton, and some other military leader. I suspected it was Capt. Shepherd. The desk was cleaner than an airport runway, save for a smaller photograph of a chubby-cheeked, bespectacled woman with a Mamie Eisenhower hairdo hugging two cute tots.

Trying to fend off boredom, I lifted a newspaper out of the wastebasket. It was the Denver Post. Smack on the first page, under the headline RAF RAIDS HAMBURG, it reported that the Royal Air Force had for the third time bombed Germany's second largest city and most important harbor. 'Total losses may well exceed 40,000', it stated. I assumed that most of them were civilians, women, children, and old people.

I was more angry than shocked. *Where was Goering's Luftwaffe??* a voice in me screamed. *Why didn't our antiaircraft guns blast these Limeys out of the sky? We can't even protect our own air space. And yet Hans and his ilk still dream of bombing New York and invading America. How delusional can one get? These diehard Nazis are no longer soldiers; they're cases for a psychiatrist. They should be taken to a lunatic asylum, sooner rather than later. Or...*

As I revved up my anger, Capt. Shepherd burst into the room. I rose, saluted and introduced myself. After giving me a bone-crunching handshake, he slipped behind his desk and whipped his rear into the chair.

"Thanks for steppin' forward, soldier," he drawled in a heavy southern accent, leaning forward with both elbows. "I know it takes a lot of guts to do what you're doin'."

"It does," I remember confiding in him. "When you do that, you're renouncing everything to become a traitor in the eyes of your comrades, regardless of your justifications, because that's what you fought for, in many cases until death. Ever since my enlistment at the age of seventeen the German Army has been my home. So it takes conviction and a lot of guts to cut the cord."

"I follow your feelin's," he replied with a slightly condescending smile. "Le' me just say, I could never have joined a bunch that is led by such a croakin' hellhound like Hitler. Anyway, it must feel good to dump all that Nazi crap like you're doin'. Frankly, I don't know what's buggin' 'em fuckin' Nazis. What a thankless bunch they are. I've done a lot'a livin' in my days but I don't get 'em. Here we're treatin' 'em with respect, we're housin' 'em, we're feedin' 'em, we're givin' 'em medical care. Down in Bama we'd say we're wiping their asses with purple velvet. And yet these fuckers turn around and spit in our faces and keep harassin' us with their crawly swastikas." He paused for a few seconds, as if harnessing himself, and then, raising his voice, went on a harangue. "These bastards should all be hanged," he thundered. "You know what I'd love to do? I'd love to strip 'em, cut off their gonads, their pricks, their whole shebang and then string 'em up, one by one, with my own hands, all of 'em. That's what I'd do. I'd love to watch them twitchin' in the noose. And I want to thank you, soldier, fo' tryin' to help me gettin' started."

For a moment I thought my ears had haywired me. When I realized that they hadn't, I feigned a spell of dizziness.

"I'm sorry, Capt. Shepherd," I slurred, holding my head. "I'm feeling miserable. I think I have to throw up. I'm afraid I guzzled too much Bourbon on an empty stomach. You wouldn't mind, would you, if I came back tomorrow."

"Sure. Can I he'p you in any way?"

"No, thank you. I just want to go back to my quarters and lie down."

I got up, shook his hand and left.

FEELING HAUNTED

I was visibly relieved and when I stepped out of Capt. Shepherd's office. Unfortunately, that lasted no more than a few seconds. It so happened that through a slight inattentiveness I was forced to cross paths with a German lieutenant, whose name I couldn't remember, although his face looked familiar. I greeted him with polish, as I'm in the habit of doing. Only later, as I continued my walk, did it dawn on me that this lieutenant could very well be one of the Nazi ideologues who would immediately suspect that I, coming out of Shepherd's office, could very well be a stool pigeon. If so, he'd straitaway report me to the camp's Gestapo, in which case my goose was as good as cooked. The blood-curdling image of Peter Keller hanging from the rafter hovered in my mind's eye, scaring me out of my wits. I lashed out at myself for having been so flighty, so careless.

Ever since Peter's hanging and Dieter's thrashing, repeating bouts of angst, coupled with a deep-seated suspicion, held a tight, merciless grip on me. Whenever I crossed paths with Hans and his clique my stomach would turn into a virtual butterfly cage. *Will they soon be after me?* More often than not I caught myself swiveling my head or spinning around at the slightest sound. Several times I thought I heard steps behind me, yet a check bore out that the dread was just in my mind. When I took a walk at dawn or dusk, but especially during darkness, I became all eyes and ears. I braced for a gang of fanatics to pop up at any time, to give me the 'Holy Ghost' treatment. I only hoped I could prevent that by taking to my heels or fighting to the very end.

Both options, needless to say, required a strong, muscular body. So I began steeling myself, if only to give them a taste of what they could expect. Almost daily I submitted myself to a rigid Spartan workout, including running, sprinting, wrestling, weight-lifting and boxing, and that on top of working in the fields. I simply couldn't take any chances. Besides, going to the limits also improved my sleep.

But there was yet another reason why I became so obsessed with physical exercise. Just as much as I feared the Nazi ideologues, I loathed the sweet life of the camp, the cradle-to-grave care we received. I was afraid it would sooner rather than later lead to a state of satiated contentment. Daily I watched my compatriots gulping down far more pork chops, corned beef, potatoes, bread, cakes and ice cream than their bodies could possibly absorb. Their appetite knew no bounds. Some stuffed themselves like porkers in a pigsty. Just two weeks ago, I overheard that some of my comrades had already gained more than ten pounds since their arrival. More and more of them needed bigger pants because their potbellies couldn't be squeezed into their old ones. Even I, who spent so much energy working in the fields, had already gained more than three pounds. One doesn't need much wit to know that such a life can only breed sloths, degenerates and wretches. Quite frankly, I was worried that I could end up like that as well, although up to now I was able to keep my weight within a span of four belt holes.

GETTING READY TO BAIL OUT

Mercifully, the apprehension and angst that plagued me was limited to the confines of the camp. As soon as I left the barbed wire behind me, I breathed long sighs of relief. Because here I could drop the role of a mangy alley cat and slip into the skin of a human being. Only beyond the barbed wire I could ease up, relax, be spontaneous and funny, in short, be myself, not unlike some of the characters in the American comic strips. Or, better yet, the happy-go-lucky cowboy in Cole Porter's *Don't Fence Me In*.

Tasting that pinch of freedom only made me long for more. Unfortunately, the contact with Marcy had once again been broken. I had no way of communicating with her. While she and her sisters continued to pick tomatoes, we POWs had to break our backs in the damned pumpkin field. It wasn't until Monday, nine days later, that 'Chuck' Johnson changed his mind and made us go back to the tomato patch. I distinctly remember the day. It was scorching hot, making the quicksilver easily swell into the lower three digits and the air quiver. We were all drenched in sweat. The only relief was that, unlike picking pumpkins or squash, we were lucky enough to harvest most of this precious fruit standing up, or bending down halfway.

Physically resilient, I easily topped my quota. That pleased Pvt. Jennings, so much so that he left me alone. I was even able to choose my own row, allowing me to join the three Japanese sisters who'd started at the other end. As an extra bonus, I managed to pick the same stalks with Marcy who greeted me with a broad smile and a shy kiss. "My Viking!" she buzzed. "I was afraid I might never see you again." I found her unusually tense, frequently turning her head as though she felt watched by a guard. But I managed to calm her and with time she began to relax. We even began to joke and laugh together. Like children we teased each other; more, we even dared exchange a series of kisses. At one point I picked an overripe tomato, squeezed it into my mouth and then pulled Marcy over to share it with her.

Later, as we walked to our lunch break, we dropped our play and slipped into our adult roles again. Our guard was off and we took the opportunity to go over our escape plan again.

"Any progress?" I pressed.

"What a question! I've been lying awake night after night thinking about it, figuring out how we should go about it."

"Good."

"But I think I'd need another week or two to work out the details. We have to 'cause without good preparation we'd be caught in no time."

"I fully agree. But let's set a deadline. How about September 11th? That's a Saturday. It's more than four weeks from now."

"Good. You know, one of my uncles has an old Chevy that just sits there. He wouldn't mind loaning it to me."

"Great! So we wouldn't have to take the bus. Have you driven it?"

"Yes, but only short distances. It seems to run quite well. I still have a valid California driver's license. That shouldn't be a problem."

"I'd also ask your uncle for a good road map."

"Good that you remind me. But if he doesn't, I probably could get one someplace else."

"You could pick me up at a back-road not too far from the gate of the camp, and we could then head south, into New Mexico."

"Yes. You know, I found out from my mother that we have some distant relatives in Mesilla, near Las Cruces in southern New Mexico. It's a brother of my grandmother on my mother's side. I'm sure he wouldn't mind giving us shelter."

"Sounds great! I wonder if you could also get me some civilian clothing, like a pair of pants, a shirt and a sports coat?"

"Good idea. But it may not be easy 'cause we Japanese are a lot shorter than you."

What a rendezvous it was. I came away thrilled, bouncing with joy. A deadline was set. *Now things will get serious!* So when I got back to the camp, I sat down to make a list of what I would need for a successful escape. Fortunately, we had an Escape Committee, which could be of help. I had heard that they had access to a large pool of talents, cartographers, photographers, chemists, tinsmiths, tailors, and trained craftsmen who, with a scant supply of raw materials and great ingenuity, would be more than willing to forge documents, letters of identification, social security cards, driver's licenses and what have you. All they needed was an etched template carved on a scrap of linoleum, some ink, bits of cardboard and a cleverly devised stamp, painstakingly whittled and chiseled from a raw yam or potato. Unfortunately, this help also came with some drawbacks. The committee was dominated, so I was told, by diehards such as Capt. Fahrenbach and his clique. That pricked my ears. I was afraid that they might have heard something about my attitude toward the Fuehrer, or worse, my visit to Capt. Shepherd.

And, indeed, when I had my first opportunity to join them at the table in the officer's quarters, I couldn't help but feel veiled spikes of suspicion directed at me. To begin with, I received not the smallest gesture of welcome: no smiles and a few noncommittal handshakes. I knew right then that I had to be on my toes. Already Capt. Fahrenbach's first question was shot through with dubiousness. It centered on the purpose of my escape. Well, I put on a studied mien and told him that I intended to skip across the border to Mexico in the hope of making my way down to Veracruz. I'd heard that some Nazi yoke mates had settled there. Needless to say, I quashed any mention of just trying to get a taste of freedom.

"What, for God's sake, do you want to do in Veracruz?" Lt. Borchart, Fahrenbach's right hand, asked. "Find a nunnery to have a little fun?"

I grinned. "Actually, I wouldn't mind, but I heard that nobody gets out of those joints without a dripping dick. Hans Henkel told me that, with a little luck, I could sneak onto a freighter as a stowaway and make my way to Portugal or Spain. From there I could hitch a ride to Germany to rejoin the army. It's been my home since I was seventeen. I think our Vaterland desperately needs me."

That, brightened faces. Fahrenbach even smiled.

"Right on, our Fatherland needs fighting men more than ever. We must win this war, come hell or high water. Come to think of it, we can even give you some addresses where you can find help." He pulled out a manila folder, fetched a piece of paper and scribbled down two names and addresses.

"Thank you, that'll be of great help to me."

"Let me just add something that may come in handy when you cross the border. I'd stay away from El Paso. They've got as many agents from the FBI and the Border Patrol there as cockroaches in their sewers. It's better to pick a spot a little downriver, Presidio, for instance. It's almost empty. There are hardly any people down there. And it's only about two hundred kilometers from there to Chihuahua."

He also handed me a list of suggestions for avoiding capture, going over each item. A lot of it was common sense, such as carrying some cash to enable me to buy something to eat and rent a room to catch some sleep. But some were new, for instance the advice that I should do it alone. "Two fugitives," he claimed, "arouse much more attention than one." (I thought of Marcy, but made no mention of her.) His prodding that I should put my tongue on the shortest leash possible made good sense, because people

63

would quickly pick up your accent, regardless of how fluent you are in English. As did his tip that I should get away from the camp as far and as quickly as I possibly could and that it was best to slip into big cities because there you could submerge more easily. "There you are no more than a needle in a haystack," he added. "The bigger the haystack, the better your chances of being undetected. Of course, it goes without saying that we can forge almost any document that you'd like to take along with you. We suggest that you get a Social Security card, because that's what you need most if you apply for a job. And a driver's license for simple identification. What also comes in handy is a draft board certificate showing that you reported to enlist in the American military service, but was declared 4-F, that is unfit to do the job. We could also, if you so wish, counterfeit a certificate issued by the War Department that declares that you're a citizen of Switzerland, the Netherlands or Denmark, who's been in this country since 1939 and has a right to remain here. Our forgeries are so sophisticated, with all the stamps, seals and personal pictures, they can even fool the best FBI agents. You just have to tell us what you want, what kind of name and background you want us to put on there."

"I will, thanks."

"Remember we will do everything in our power for you to have a successful escape, so you can rejoin our fighting forces. We have to win — we will win this war. We owe it to our Fuehrer. Heil Hitler!"

In the end, Lt. Borchart also came up with a few suggestions on how to get out of the camp itself. There were several options. Leave in the back of the laundry or garbage truck, or just sneak away from the work detail at the farm.

I had something else in mind, but wasn't sure, not yet, anyway.

While the days wound past, I carefully weighed all my options, the pros and cons, until I finally settled on a plan of action. I'd simply put on an American uniform and walk out of the gate. I already had access to the specimen I wore in the play. It was a perfect fit.

No sooner said than done. I contacted Wolfgang Riem, begging him if he could loan the uniform to me. He was curious to know, why I wanted it. But, when I told him about my plan to escape, he began to waffle.

"I like you, Fritz, and I don't mind you taking the uniform," he said, with a pat on my shoulder. "But if they catch you, they'll put the blame on me. And I'd have to face a disciplinary board."

"I know what you mean, but there must be a way…"

"It just occurred to me. I could let you swipe the uniform. In that case you'd shoulder the responsibility. You just have to tell me when you need it so I can leave the door unlocked. How does that sound?"

"It's a deal. I'd need it by September 10th. There's another thing. Would you mind me taking a few of your contraptions, like fake beards, mustaches and eyebrows I could glue on to disguise my identity?"

"No, not at all. You can take whatever you want."

He led me to a sideboard and pulled a drawer that had a fair selection of masks and masquerading items. I picked a small, light-brown beard, a mustache and some eyebrows.

As we walked back to his desk, I chanced to see a rack of shoes of many sizes. "Whose shoes, are they?" I inquired.

"Oh, those? They belong to the theater. I picked them up at a Goodwill store in Murphy."

"I wonder, could you spare a pair?"

"Sure, feel free."

I took a sturdy pair of leather shoes, hardly worn, with clean stitches and tough soles. Unfortunately, they turned out to be a tiny bit too small. But without socks, they fitted me like a glove. Besides, they were the most striking footwear I ever owned, especially when polished.

"Thanks so much for your help, Wolf," I said, wrapping them up in newsprint.

We shook hands.

"I wish you all the luck in the world," he said. "Judging by the way you played Lt. Murray couple of weeks ago, you should have no difficulties. I'll cross my fingers. Who knows, I may soon want to follow you. Those damn true believers scare the hell out of me. I don't want to end up like Peter."

"You said it!"

GETTING MY HANDS ON GREENBACKS

I now pretty much had everything I needed for my escape, save for money. So far, my nest egg amounted to less than $6, which wasn't nearly enough, or so Fahrenbach warned me. Food and lodging would quickly diminish these savings, he added, figuring that I'd need at least triple or quadruple that amount to tide me over, until I could get hold of a job. These were hefty sums to scrape together, especially since we weren't paid in real dollars but in coupons.

It was no secret that GIs in general were hot for all kinds of Nazi paraphernalia, as well as souvenirs made by us prisoners. The most curious craving was for our insignias. And it occurred to me that I could somehow profit from satisfying this need. What if I made some of these things and sold them, the craftsman and businessman in me kept thinking? Although I had easy access to a workshop and also a limited number of tools, I needed certain raw materials, sheet metal or aluminum. Not unexpectedly, my request for these materials was immediately denied on the grounds that I could fashion weapons, knives or even guns. That left me no choice but to use my own wits. We all used toothpaste, which was contained in soft metal tubes. Better yet, they could easily be melted down and, poured in a mold, shaped into whatever you wished. Fortunately, as a kid I had dabbled in tin casting; I had even made my own tin soldiers. The soft metal I found in the tubes of toothpaste available in the PX for almost nothing. Well, I got myself four tubes, squeezed out the contents, cut them open and melted them down. Then I poured the liquid into various molds I fashioned out of shoe polish cans. Everything proceeded smoothly and within a few days I'd managed to turn out Iron Crosses, SS Death Heads, Eagles, shoulder clasps and other insignias. The most iconic was the Iron Cross, which also happened to be most in demand. This was the first insignia I cast, then painstakingly painted it black and white and scuffed it a little so as to feign some wear. Of course it was a fake, yet it looked so real that only an experienced craftsman could tell the difference. I doubted if any of the GIs could. Nevertheless, selling it, at least for cash, proved to be much harder than I'd expected.

The first person I practiced my talent as a salesman on was Jay Jennings, our guard at the farmstead. While I was busy picking tomatoes, he happened to show up as part of his patrol. It was shortly before the lunch break. "How you doin' with your quota?" he barked, tucking in his shirt.

"I think I'm slightly ahead."

"Good job, Fritz! That goddamn heat never stops." He wiped the sweat off his brows. "Say, where's Marcy today?" He feigned a knowing grin.

"Somebody told me she and her sisters have started picking at the other end," I replied. "Say, Jay, can I ask you a question?"

"Sure, shoot."

"Maybe you know already, on my time off I tend to keep busy buying and trading Nazi insignias," I said, pulling the Iron Cross out of my pocket. "You know, stuff like that."

I slowly unwrapped it, treating it as if it were a crown jewel, and showed it to him.

His eyes sparkled. He pursed his lips and nodded approval. "Not bad! Not bad at all! How much d'you want?"

"Well, it's not cheap," I said. "As you know, it's very valuable, highly prized stuff. There's a big market for things of that kind. But since you are my guard and you have been especially nice to me, I'd give it to you, let's say for $4."

"Hm! That's a lot of bucks for a tiny thing like that. But I kind'a like it."

"As you can see, this piece is old. It has witnessed a lot of combat, even on the Russian front, I've been assured. As you can see, the craftsman who made it paid a lot of attention to detail."

"It kind'a shows."

"It's really special. You could hang it up on the wall of your living room or around your neck, at a party. Your friends and relatives would be dazzled when they see it. Just imagine."

He smiled. "I tell you what, I'll go to the PX tomorrow morning and get you the coupons."

"That's very kind of you, Jay, but I'd really prefer if you paid me — well — in cash."

"Cash? Why would you want cash? You can't spend it anyway. Besides, it's against our regulations. I'm not allowed to give you any dollars, even if I wanted to. They'd bust my ass."

"Well, what I'm offering you is a really special kind of keepsake. Even our Fuehrer wears one on special occasions. I might add, the Iron Cross goes far back into Prussian history. The first one was issued in the early1800s. The same is true of your dollar bill. There is, as you know, a picture of George Washington on it, the founding father and the first president of your great country. That's something very special for me. One day, when the war has come to a close and I get back to Germany, I'd like to show such a dollar bill to my kids and grandkids as proof that I was in America and that I learned something about the history of your great country."

"Hm!" he hawked, then put his hands up to his chin and stood there for a while.

"Did you say four bucks?" he finally asked.

"Yes, four bucks. They all say it's a good deal."

"OK, I'll take it." He pulled out his wallet and counted the George Washingtons into the palm of my hand.

As I handed him the Iron Cross, he hemmed and then rejoined, "I must say, you're one of the shrewdest salesmen I've ever met. I'm just glad the farmer's daughter, Jeany, isn't around, or we could really hear some laughter and groaning in them cornfield over there." He then roared with a round of guffaws.

This was my first sale, and I jumped for joy. Once back in the camp, I must have looked at and kissed the portrait of George Washington, his forehead, eyes, locks, nose, chin, yes, even his overly tight lips more than ten times. Things were looking up. Other sales followed in quick succession, using the same sales pitch, with slight variations. I deliberately worked on perfecting my English, peppering my pitch wherever I could with witty colloquial expressions, even slang. Some I copied from the funnies. In the end my salesman act worked so well that I raked in compliments, even from American officers who had an excellent command of English. But most importantly, my efforts paid off handsomely. My fake medals sold like hotcakes, so much so that I soon hired a helper, Heinz Zwinger, who assisted me in my workshop. And when the demand for the simple Iron Cross slacked off, I began changing it carving a swastika into the center where both beams cross. Since there was more work involved, I charged a dollar more, a total of $5. That meant bidding farewell to George Washington's aristocratic, slightly perfumed image and accustom myself with Abraham Lincoln's down-to-earth portrait. It goes without saying that Lincoln was palpably closer to my heart. I reveled in his natural, unpolished appearance, his craggy features, scraggly beard, slovenly kempt hair, not to mention his gritty, unwavering look. I got a kick out of how his image reigns over the banknote, presenting a real leader who keeps pushing himself out of the fence-like frame the Federal Reserve tried to contain him in. Lincoln reminded me of us or Cole Porter's cowboy. He loathed to be fenced in.

The dollars, meanwhile, added up and before long I had almost a hundred and $40 in my billfold. I couldn't help it, I swooned for joy and frequently played with the thought of taking Marcy out to dinner, as soon as the opportunity came my way, to a fancy, candle-lit restaurant, where filet mignons and champagne were served, where waiters swirled around us as if we were a famous Hollywood couple. I imagined myself in an exquisite, pinstripe Brooks Brothers suit, while Marcy would be decked out in a silky evening gown, displaying a draped neckline.

Apropos Marcy, I ran into her two more times, picking tomatoes and pumpkins at the Johnson farm. These encounters gave us a chance to strengthen our commitment and refine the blueprint of our escape. Everything appeared to be rock-solid, from all I could tell. There was no doubt in our minds, I could depend on her as much as she could on me.

PLAYACTING IN REAL LIFE

Time flew, although not exactly in favor of our much-touted Thousand-Year Reich. Somehow, I saw it coming: On the eighth of September a wheel happened to spin off the Berlin-Rome axis as Italy officially surrendered to the allies. It was another blow to Hitler and his bootlickers, including our diehard Nazis. Yet they were far from admitting it. Quite the contrary, Hans, for instance, viewed it even as a favorable development. "Finally, we get rid of those wimpy spaghetti munchers," he said, when I showed him the headline of the Denver Post. "They were nothing but clumps of lead on our ankles; all they did was slowing us down and sucking us dry. I remember how happy Rommel was when he no longer had to deal with them, turning them over to the Limeys who had to feed them and treat their dripping dicks. All I can say is 'good riddance'! Now we have a free hand."

"A free hand to do what?" I grilled him. "The Russians are closing in on Smolensk."

"You will see a counter offensive very soon. We'll beat the shit out of the Russkies. Take my word for it."

I kept mum, thinking, *Dear fellow, you're beyond help.*

Actually, my mind was already focusing on something else — my escape. I had resolved to travel lightly, to take along only the barest of necessities, an extra pair of socks and underpants, an undershirt, a small roll of toilet paper, a bar of soap, a towel, a canteen of water, two sandwiches, my horseshoe and my precious diary, which consisted of a wild assortment of yellowed leaves of different sizes, interspersed with pieces of thin cardboard, and dried flowers. I made sure that the dollars and the various documents, my Social Security card, a Colorado driver's license and a draft board certificate, showing that I was declared 4-F, were safely tucked away in my wallet. Within an hour I had gathered all these belongings and stuffed them into a small American army bag I stacked in the crawl space beneath our barracks. Later, after the last roll call, I headed to the theater. The side door was unlocked, just as Wolf promised. Making sure that nobody was around, I sneaked in, rushed over to the rack, lifted the uniform including the cap from the coat hanger, wrapped them in a newspaper and slinked out the door. When I got back to the barracks, I waited until the air was clear, then crept into the crawl space and stowed the bundle away, next to my army bag.

To say that I was jittery would be an understatement; I was on pins and needles, like a parachutist who was about to be dropped into a patch of prickly pears. I kept wondering how everything would turn out tomorrow. After all, I was still a bungling stranger to this huge country whose horizons were crowded with a sheer endless forest of question marks. Would my command of the American vernacular be good enough to avoid detection? Could I pass as an American? Could I, as a German, avoid falling into the trap of pronouncing the 'th' like an 's'? How about our habit of mixing up the 'v' with the 'w', especially when under stress? Or counting with the thumb rather than the pinkie? The slightest misstep could instantly shatter the whole scaffolding of my precious illusions into a pile of dust.

Marcy and I planned to drive as far south as possible, hopefully reaching Albuquerque, New Mexico, or even the farm of her great uncle near Mesilla. How far would we get? Would there be cops on the road? When gassing up, would the attendant notice that there was something fishy about us? Where would we spend the first night? And how?

I went to bed early but couldn't sleep a wink. I felt like a ping pong ball in a mountain stream. Hans snored: harsh, raucous like an old percolator. Damn, did I long for dawn! But time dragged on and on, like molasses on a cold day. At last, I must have fallen asleep because I remembered dreaming of being free, of floating on a pink cloud the shape of a hippo. I looked down on the camp. I even saw the two barbed wire fences surrounding it, when the sound of the bugle brutally cut me off, chucking me into consciousness. It was chased by a shrill whistle, announcing a new day, a day that begged fervently to be seized. Five thirty. *My last reveille?* I leapt out of bed, grabbed my toilet bag and rushed to the latrine. It was still very dark outside. Thin rain-streaks crosshatched the windows. The bowls, thankfully, were still up for grabs. I snagged the last one near the wall. Having unburdened myself, I had a quick wash. "Bastards!" I snapped with an audible exclamation mark, as I glanced into the shower room, where Peter had been lynched by the Nazi thugs. I even showed them the filthy finger, with gritted teeth.

Back at the quarters. "Guten Morgen," I greeted Hans who, having just arisen, went through his stretching exercises. At one time he moved his arms in such a way that I thought I saw a swastika, with his head in the middle. Dieter was still deep in a slumber. Turning away, I fluffed my pillow and pulled the sheets and blankets tight. I was going to leave my area behind in an orderly fashion, as if facing an inspection. After all, I was a soldier of the Afrika Korps not for nothing! Following my daily routine grounded me, giving me my footing back.

A light, silent rain was falling when I trudged to the mess hall. I felt my appetite rising, as if my body somehow sensed that I could soon be starving. I tucked into a hearty breakfast consisting of two eggs, a big portion of hash browns, three slices of toast, and two cups of coffee. I also bagged three apples and fixed myself two double-decker sandwiches to take along.

On my way back to our quarters, the rain had dwindled to a light sprinkle. Dawn was about to break. After I'd shaved and cleaned my area, I fell in for the first and hopefully the last roll call of the day. My name was called, but it sounded as though it came from another planet. Nonetheless I responded with a full-blown "yes."

Back at the barracks, I bided my time. As soon as the coast was clear, I stepped outside, slid and wound myself into the crawl space. It was uncomfortably tight down there. I couldn't even kneel, much less stand up. Still, with a few deliberate movements I managed to take off my old German garb and slip into the American khaki uniform. I also glued on a mustache, shoved my horseshoe into my pocket, and minutes later stepped out as an American second lieutenant, with insignia, headgear and all.

I dusted myself off, took hold of my American army bag, squeezed some good luck out of my horseshoe and turned my step toward the main gate. I had already practiced my officer's gait during my theater performance, with the aim of striking a perfect balance between firmness and ease. I knew the guard saw me coming. As I approached the shack, I first waved flirtatiously at Marcy, who was parking outside the gate. Then I fixed my eyes on the guard and, casually raising my hand, blurted, "Hello," dropped a hint of a salute and, oops! slinked past. I still heard him hollering, "You have a nice weekend, sir."

"Thank you, I will," I remember mumbling. And, under my breath, *"You bet your ass I will."*

Anyway, I never looked back.

When I opened the car door, Marcy first stared, then, shaking her head, burst out laughing, big guffaws. I assumed it was the uniform, but it turned out to be the mustache, which she thought made me look like Groucho Marx, at least around the eyes and nose. Her good cheer rubbed off on me, although my outburst may have been more a mutated sigh of relief. The dew of sweat covered my forehead and temples.

We hugged and kissed. Indeed, our passion reached such a pitch that the mustache slid off, ending up in Marcy's mouth. She choked and spit it out. This triggered another round of hearty laughter, outbursts that put tears into our eyes. Looking back, it may well have been our first laughter of freedom rising from way down of our bellies.

ON THE SANTA FE TRAIL

"Sorry, but we really ought to get moving," Marcy urged.

"I agree. But shouldn't we first take a look at the map?"

"Don't worry, I know the road, at least until we get to the highway leading south to New Mexico."

Marcy started the Chevy, revved it up, and we took off, leaving behind billows of dust. Our first destination: Murphy. Since it was still early in the morning, the traffic was light, even in town. What impressed me was the general courtesy of the drivers, their laid-back attitude. They simply stopped when they saw a pedestrian who wished to cross the street, regardless of traffic lights. This was also true of people as a whole. Most smiled when they spotted us easing to a halt at the traffic lights. An older gentleman and two young boys even honored me with a military salute. And I, playing a real American lieutenant, paid homage with a snappy version of my own, drawing from my part on the stage.

Leaving Murphy behind, we headed south, up Raton Pass. A sign informed us that we were on the famous Santa Fe Trail, where once covered wagons, facing fierce attacks by marauding Indians, passed through. The engine clanked and coughed while the throat of the carburetor was practicing strange gurglings. What was most uplifting for me were the trees, conifers, and way up near the pass, green meadows with flowers. The landscape looked more and more like home, except for the space, the wide open, sheer endless space. It helped that shafts of sunlight flooded the scene. Thrilled by the green-yellowish sheen, I asked Marcy to turn off and take a short break. When we stepped out of the car, we first stretched. After we had taken a leak, we both changed clothes. I quickly defrocked the lieutenant, making a free civilian out of him. Granted, the clothes Marcy had brought along could have fit better, but I had long learned never to look a gift horse in its mouth. Yes, the pair of pants could have been a bit longer and tighter at the waist, but I had no wish of prancing at a fashion show. Nor did Marcy mind. In fact, we right away celebrated our change by hugging each other. I started singing *Don't Fence Me In*. Marcy followed me, even though she had trouble with the lyrics, and we fell into a little two-step dance. What I appreciated most was not only Marcy's litheness, the way she turned and responded to my guidance, but also her subtle feeling for rhythm.

As we turned, shuffled and shimmied, I sensed a space unfold inside of me, a huge spread that made me feel as if I had given birth to something auspicious, wrapped as it was in the aura of freedom. I felt like being in a meadow of four-leaf clover up to my jowls. Sitting down, we shared a sandwich and, yes, a large apple.

When Marcy went back to the car to groom herself, putting on some facial cream, combing and setting her girlish bangs, I strayed into the meadows to take a look at the flowers, bushes and trees. I eventually came back with a small bunch of wildflowers, handing it to Marcy.

"It's a freedom bouquet picked by Arne from the wild shores of a Norway fjord," I whispered, pecking her cheek.

"Thank you, this is so sweet of you, my Viking."

We kissed each other again.

"Sorry to cut this off," she said at one point, "but we should really get moving."

I wrapped the stems of the flowers in a wet handkerchief and stuck the bouquet into the ashtray on the dashboard. Marcy, meanwhile, tried to start the Chevy. Sadly, in vain. Like in a tedious cranking, the engine failed to catch.

"Stop and try again," I suggested. She did, but the motor still refused to turn over.

I checked the various gauges. The water temperature was way up, which I attributed to the fact that we'd pushed uphill. Nor had Marcy's lead foot spared the engine. Shaken by worries, I opened the hood and peeked at the water level. It was way down. Once I had filled it up, I told Marcy to turn the key again. And, hallelujah! this time it caught, albeit timidly, taking several attempts.

We made it back to the highway which, mercifully, soon wound down from the pass into New Mexico. All of a sudden, zooming around a curve, the land opened up, displaying a vast expanse, a veritable feast for our eyes. Save for a few volcanic mounds that cocked up like pimples and buttes of black lava, it was covered by fawn-colored grass, dark shrubbery and tiny dots, presumably cattle, reminding me of a handful of tossed cloves. Only far out to the west did I see an imposing mountain range, which, according to the map, carried the mysterious name of 'Sangre de Cristo', Blood of Christ. Some of the highest peaks even displayed specks of snow. Above them hovered a few lavender clouds that looked like forlorn vessels of a larger fleet beyond the horizon. The boundless stretches of plain, mesas and lofty mountains ahead were nothing less than breathtaking. As we stopped on the shoulder and let our eyes sweep from one horizon to the other, it was sheer impossible *not* to be uplifted and carried away into a sublime feeling of freedom, slumbering in the lap of eternity.

Alas, it would soon turn more sobering as we dipped down into Raton, a squat town that could have been used as a Western movie set. Spreading out at the foot of the pass, it embraced a sizable railroad hub and a number of historical buildings, among them, believe it or not, even a small opera house. Feeling rushed, we decided to make a short stop at a grocery store, where we picked up a loaf of bread, a chunk of yellow cheddar, six sticks of beef jerky, a can of pinto beans and a few apples. But as we approached the cash register, I had reason to perk up. No, not so much at the huge, bird's nest of a hairdo and pumpkin breasts that the lady who rang up our groceries happened to display, but at the way she looked at us.

"Did you notice?" I pressed Marcy on our way out.

"You bet, she leered at us as if we're strange birds of a dark feather. We better clear out of here fast."

"I know what you mean. On the other hand, she won't have time to blow the whistle. The store was busier than a honey jar full of ants. And she was the only one at the cash register."

Nevertheless, neither of us wanted to tempt fate. So we slipped into the car and, having cranked it up a couple of times, whisked out of town. While we zoomed down the highway, I took the horseshoe out of my pocket, squeezed and rubbed it and then placed it on the dashboard. This gesture had a visible calming effect on me. And, by way of radiation, presumably also on Marcy who, by the way, managed to cut a matchless figure behind the steering wheel.

Our goal was to get as far away from Murphy as possible in the shortest amount of time. Fahrenbach had it right; the closer to the camp, the greater the danger of being caught. With this goal in mind, I kept my eyes peeled for anything that might put a spoke in our wheels. Luckily, everything ran according to plan. Marcy turned on the radio and were soothed by the gentle murmuring of some crooners. Come nine a.m., we gobbled up to the news. There was a murder in Albuquerque, yet no mention of the war where thousands, indeed, millions lost their lives. It was as though the war didn't even exist out here. Nor did we hear anything about our escape, which soothed us.

We zipped past herds of cattle and sheep, but also pronghorn antelopes, hoofed quadrupeds I'd never seen before. Occasionally they grazed very close to the fences that were packed with scraggly skeletons of

76

tumbleweeds, or so Marcy called them. Thousands of feet above turkey vultures kept wheeling, on the lookout for a carcass or a sickly animal. Not unlike in North Africa, I also witnessed fierce whirlwinds tottering across the countryside, picking up and swirling around dust, tumbleweeds and God knows what. Actually, one of them happened to cross the highway less than a hundred feet ahead of us. Feeling the impact, I even reached over to help Marcy steady the steering wheel.

Yet, the scare that frightened us happened to come from another, quite unexpected source. As we breezed along at about sixty miles per hour, a fancy Packard happened to pass us on the left. At the same time, somebody on a motorbike, lights flashing, was closing in on us from the rear. "It looks like there's a cop who wants us to stop," Marcy hissed, wrinkling her forehead.

"No! Damn!"

I was shaking in my boots. I already saw myself in the stockade on bread and water, fenced in by barbed wire once again. I grabbed my horseshoe.

"I'm afraid we have no choice. I'm going to stop."

As she eased down on the shoulder, the cop drew closer and closer. We both braced for the inevitable. But then, by golly, he'd simply roar past.

"Praise the Lord!" I said, heaving a long sigh of relief.

"Aren't we lucky! By the way, are you superstitious?" Marcy quizzed as we gathered head again.

"Superstitious? Not that I know of."

"It's the horseshoe," she said pointing to it. "It's the second time I've seen you grabbing and rubbing it. You don't believe it'll bring you good luck, do you?"

"Well, it's funny. I've been told it brings you good luck, regardless whether you believe in its magic or not. I guess this last scare is an example. Having said that, I should add that just squeezing and rubbing it makes me feel better, you know, calmer. It's almost like being able to grab a crutch before you fall."

"That's *more* than funny!"

"Maybe you're right. — Actually, it all goes back to Emma, the headmistress at the orphanage in Rummelsburg near Berlin where I grew up."

"Oh, you were an orphan?"

"Yes, and Emma was an ersatz-mother of sorts. Anyway, she always had one of those luck charms she got from *her* dad who claimed that it saved his life during the First World War. So when I joined the army, I thought that it couldn't hurt to get one myself. I eventually got mine from an old blacksmith. He told me it came off an old Belgian draft horse that pulled a brewer's dray in pre-war Berlin. You should have seen it, it was worn shiny, having clip-clopped thousands of times over countless cobble stones. That was bound to add a lot of magic to it. And from all I could tell, it helped me save my life, too. My buddies all agreed with me. They called me the 'lucky boy'. As you might expect, this horseshoe became very precious to me. Sadly, when we had to surrender in North Africa, an American corporal snatched it away from me. That really hurt, literally 'cause when I resisted, that scoundrel started to punch me. He almost broke my jaw. Anyway, without my horseshoe I felt kind of exposed, vulnerable. Until about two months ago, when I stumbled on this one, while I was working on the Perkins' ranch." I held it up. "As you can see, it's worn as well. It's got character! It looks like it has many good and prickly yarns to tell as well, you know, range stories about fierce rattlers, spiny cactuses, wailing coyotes, sly cougars, stubborn cattle, lonely cowboys and charming girls in jodhpurs and fancy Western blouses."

Down the road we eased to a halt in Wagon Mound for gas. An odd, elderly attendant, who was as wrinkled as he was toothless, stepped out of a rickety service station. He was wearing a cowboy hat, a black pair of pants hitched up by a twain of suspenders, a white shirt, an open leather vest, all stained, yet embellished by the flair of a bolo tie with a stunning nugget of turquoise twice the size of Marcy's tongue. "Fill'er up?" he mumbled, squinting at Marcy.

"Yes."

"Dang hot!" he said poker-faced, swishing an hoary arm across his forehead. "Where you folks from?" He glared at me, as though I'd dropped down from the hidden side of the moon.

"Denver," Marcy snapped.

"Denver?" He shoved his lower lip up to his scraggly snot-catcher and nodded. "Nice, but too dang big. Too many hoity-toity people steppin' on each other."

Besides filling the tank, he also wiped our windshield with a sponge and shammy cloth, checked the oil and the tires.

Having refilled our canteens, we shuffled to the restroom. It was a place stamped into my mind owing not least to its biting stench, but even more so on account of a gruesome story that appeared on a small sign pinned to a dead tree nearby. It described the fate of twelve Santa Feans, including a well-known doctor and his family who, in 1850, were allegedly ambushed and taken hostage by Indian marauders. When a posse from Santa Fe was sent to free the family, it was horrified to find the body of the doctor's wife propped up against the trunk of the tree. Come worse, the posse later stumbled on ten more dead bodies, including the doctor himself.

Reading the story, a shiver raced down my spine. I imagined being caught in such a raid myself. It conjured up Karl May's stories I voraciously devoured during my childhood, wondering how it would square with May's romantic characterization of the American Indians.

After cutting through Las Vegas, the wide open plain soon ran its course and we were greeted by a greener, hilly landscape, mainly dotted by dark-green juniper bushes and small pine trees, especially as we turned west and pushed on toward Santa Fe. Originally our goal was to reach Albuquerque, this tongue twister of a town, stay there in a cheap hotel and then leave early in the morning, in the hope of reaching the farmstead of Marcy's great uncle by the end of the day. As it turned out, these aspirations were soon to be exposed as vagaries of our imagination. For as we tried to grind up Glorieta Pass, our old Chevy, believe it or not, ran out of breath. It stuttered and coughed a few times, then convulsed to turn comatose.

"Shit!" Marcy hurled against the windshield, shaking her head.

Fighting off a stupor, I checked the heat gauge. It was way up. There was also an unpleasant smell as though something in or around the engine, oil and rubber, was burning. I even noticed a wisp of smoke rising from the hood.

"Damn, I had the feeling that something wasn't right," Marcy blurted out. "The car just didn't respond when I stepped on the gas. It seemed weak, washed out."

I got out and lifted the hood. The water in the radiator was way down, even though we'd filled it up an hour ago. I'm no mechanic, but I suspected that the head gasket had already incurred some damage when the engine ran hot going up Raton Pass and that the impairment was now compounded.

"Damn, what can we do?" Marcy asked.

"I suggest that we wait for twenty or thirty minutes to let the engine cool down and then try again," I said, nearly as clueless as she.

We waited for twenty minutes and then tried again. The starter cranked fine, but the engine showed no sign of kicking in.

"Let me hitchhike back to that little town we just drove through," I volunteered. "Maybe I can find a mechanic who could help us. It shouldn't take too long. You could stay here in the car."

"But don't you stay too long. Remember that awful story at the gas station just an hour ago. This is New Mexico. They don't only shoot Westerns here; they practice them daily."

79

"Really? I promise."

I rushed over to the other side of the highway and stuck out my thumb. Luckily it took only about fifteen minutes before a beaten-up Ford pickup truck stuttered to a halt. The driver was a friendly, older Hispanic, whose face featured a pair of dark, deep-set eyes, a thick, prominent soup-strainer and two wooly brows. Smiling like a hungry beggar, he introduced himself as Francisco. When I explained our troubles to him, he said he might be able to help. "Let me take a look," he offered with a distinct Spanish accent.

So he turned around and pulled up behind our Chevrolet. Once I had introduced him to Marcy, he walked over to our car, lifted the hood and leaned into the engine compartment, checking the radiator, the oil level, the engine block and the various hoses and cables. Apparently not finding what he was looking for, he slid his head under the car and, touching and pulling a few things, looked up with a knowing smile. "I think your radiator is leaking. There's hardly any water in it. Your engine probably overheated and then conked out."

He checked the motor again and, knitting his brows, said, "It looks like you also blew the head gasket."

"Do you know anybody who could repair it?" I pressed.

"There's nobody in Pecos who could fix it. But I know a good mechanic down the road in Santa Fe who could. I could tow you to his shop. It isn't all that far."

There goes our money, it flitted through my head.

"How long would it take to repair it?"

"It's hard to say. It depends how fast Tony could get the parts."

I glanced at Marcy and nodded. She nodded back.

We shook hands.

"Say, what's your name again?" Francisco asked.

"Fred," I said, "and my girlfriend's Marcy."

Giving us an appraising look, he quizzed, "Where you from?"

"Denver," I said.

"I mean, where you *really* from?"

"Well, originally from Switzerland," I said.

"And I'm from California," Marcy added.

"From *Switzerland*?" He gave me a sidelong glance.

There was an awkward pause. *What in the hell is he up to?*

He must have noticed our uneasiness because he quickly diverted attention to the task at hand. "OK, Fred, lem'me get a rope, so we can hook up your car to my truck. And then we're set. But I want one of you to stay in the Chevy 'cause somebody'll have to hit the brake when we're goin' downhill. I don't want you to rear-end me. It's gonna come very soon."

"Listen, Fred, I wonder if you can take the steering wheel," Marcy begged. "I feel very uncomfortable driving under such conditions."

"Sure."

With a few flicks of the wrist, Francisco did as promised. And with the rope in place, he disappeared into his cab. We, meanwhile, jumped into the Chevy, me behind the steering wheel. Francisco waved with his hand, revved his truck and off we went, up and over Glorieta Pass, all the way to Santa Fe.

SANTA FE

We squeaked and rattled to a halt at Tony Romero's garage, a ramshackle corrugated iron shack that was squeezed in by a motley jumble of old rust buckets. It reeked of gasoline, oil and lubricants. Tony, a wiry, middle-aged fellow with a greasy handlebar mustache and a full shock of hair greeted Francisco with smiles and an *embrazo*. And once Francisco had introduced us, he walked Tony over to the Chevy, lifted the hood and, pointing to the radiator and the engine, showered him with a jumble of words, unfortunately in Spanish, but liberally sprinkled with English. Meanwhile, Tony himself stuck his head into the engine compartment and checked the various parts, particularly the head gasket and the radiator.

"Well, the way it looks to me," he said in heavily accented English as his head emerged, "your radiator has to be replaced. Probably a new head gasket'll have to be installed, too. All in all it would cost you about $110.00."

"How long would it take you to repair it?" Marcy wanted to know.

"Maybe four days, *mas o menos,*" Tony said, wiggling his hand. "It depends how long it'll take to get the parts."

"Four to five days?" Marcy looked up to me, hurling a bundle of question marks at me.

We stepped aside. "I'd let him do it," I whispered. "But we'll long be gone when it's ready. We might have to get rid of the car. Or you could come back later to pick it up."

"OK, I want you to go ahead," Marcy told Tony.

As we shook hands, we asked Tony if he knew of an inexpensive hotel or motel nearby.

"Yes, there are several within walking distance." He told us the names and addresses of three, even giving us directions.

Having given Francisco $5 for the towing, we took our bags out of the Chevy and started walking. "What did you mean when you said, 'We might have to get rid of the car'?" Marcy asked.

"Well, we have to move on. We've already lost four hours with that clunker. Pretty soon they'll be on our tails. Maybe we can come up again after we've settled at your great uncle's. We'll have to see how things develop."

"I'd want to pick it up again."

Our first stop was Sunrise Inn, a small motel south of the town's center. Having never seen a motel before, I was impressed not only by the pragmatic and expedient outlay, but also by the use of the mud-brick architecture, examples of which I'd already seen in North Africa. With its thick brown walls that were smoothly rounded off on top, it looked so comely, so down to earth and inviting that I was instantly taken by it. Yet it also seemed so out of place that I wondered if we were still in America.

There were a lot of cars parked in front of the units, showing that the rooms were very much in demand. They seemed clean as well, and the price of $3.25 per night was reasonable. The owner, an older, haggard gentleman with a shriveled face, a cowboy hat and a bolo tie ogled us in a funny way. He couldn't quite swallow that we had no car. Worse, he wanted to know how we got here.

"On foot," Marcy quipped, raising her leg.

Frankly, I was ready to walk away, but Marcy had already agreed to the terms. So she filled out and signed the registration form. As we walked to our apartment and turned the key, my heart pounded in anticipation of spending the night with a woman, whom I had grown very fond of. It was the first of such a rendezvous in more than a year, and I had a hell of a time bridling my primal urges. *"Bridling,"* what was that? We had barely dropped our bags, when I clasped Marcy from behind, trying to embrace, fondle and kiss her.

"Please, Fred, not now," she pleaded, pushing me off. "Control yourself. Please!"

But I wouldn't listen. Instead of holding back, I pulled her down onto the bed where I forced myself on her. Yet she stubbornly fought me with her hands, legs, her whole body.

"Stop it! Control yourself!" she hissed.

But she might as well have hissed at a wall. It was embarrassing, a raw scene, and looking back I'm deeply ashamed of myself. I was reminded of similar incidences in Russia, when I was still a blundering Nazi madcap. But I was older now, infinitely more experienced. And this was Santa Fe, America, and the woman in question was American. The rules of the game had radically changed. Sadly, I was unable to grasp that, at least not until Marcy's incisors got hold of my lips and chopped into them. I was so stunned that she managed to wrestle herself free, run out the door and shut it with a commanding bang.

Poked, I jumped up and hurried after her, pleading, "Marcy, Marcy, listen to me. I apologize; I'm very sorry. Please forgive me. Please!" With blood-smeared lips, no less.

Marcy finally came to a halt way down the street. As I caught up with her, I saw a changed woman. Her eyes were defiant, scornful. "You know what you are? A brute, a barbarian with a penile entitlement. You should be *ashamed* of yourself." The stitchless seam of her eyelids ajar, she let her lips curl forward beneath her whorled nostrils, a sign of unmistaken disdain.

"Please, Marcy, forgive me. I'm deeply sorry. I didn't know what I was doing. I promise, it'll never happen again."

She just shook her head. "That's what you all say. And I thought you were different."

With the sour apple of remorse in my throat, I eventually persuaded her to come back to the room. And after I had treated my bloody, swollen lips, I suggested that we shower, dress up and then take a stroll to the town's center. "And if we see a nice restaurant, I'll invite you to dinner," I added with a raspy warble.

"That sounds more like it."

I looked at my watch. "Not to change the subject, but you know what? Back at the camp, they're going to have the first roll call without me."

"Does that mean that they'll put out the first bulletin for your arrest?"

"I hope not. You see I asked Helmut to call 'here' when the guard shouts my name. He's a very reliable soul; he promised to do the same at the roll call tomorrow morning as well. That way we'd have more time to get away. Actually, if everything goes according to plan, the Americans won't know until tomorrow night."

"Let's hope you're right and Helmut doesn't have a weak spell."

Twenty minutes later, shortly before sunset, we were on our way to the Plaza of Santa Fe, a faint waft of soap and lilac perfume trailing us, blended as it were with the sweet fragrance of pinons and junipers. Marcy looked particularly captivating, wrapped as she was in a black polo dress, a stitched leather belt and a pair of red ballerina shoes, all of which brought out her lithe, shapely figure and the muscular calves of her legs. My attire was much more modest, owing to the fact that I was confined to wearing what Marcy had brought along — somewhat short, dark-brown gabardine pants, a simple leather belt, a white cotton shirt and my pride — the handsome dress shoes Wolf had given me.

Perhaps I should also mention that, by sticking on my false mustache and eyebrows, I had slightly altered my facial features. *Why give away your real face?* I reasoned, painfully aware of my role as a lamster.

I was again captivated by the mud-brick buildings — they call it 'adobe', Marcy corrected me — we came past along the way. Quite unlike their Victorian neighbors, they appeared as though they had heaved themselves out of the earth, displaying their dark brown or tawny walls as if they intended to make a statement of humility. At the same time, they also embodied a subtle sensuality, owing to their apparent massiveness, their rounded curves and softened edges that invited the viewer to stroke them. Squinting at them, we fancied them to be genuine sculptures as much as functional buildings where people live or businesses thrive. One of the most appealing among them appeared to be the La Fonda Hotel, a three-story complex located right on the Plaza. That was true outside as well as inside. Indeed, the coziness of its lobby, but particularly the ambiance of its adjacent restaurant, appealed to us so much that I dropped all pretensions and reserved a table. It helped that President Teddy Roosevelt had once been a guest here, or so a plaque in the lobby stated.

We eventually secured a cozy, candle-lit table close to the entrance. Our waiter appeared to be a Mexican by the name of Pedro whose English sounded as if he were snorkeling in a muddy waterhole. But he was very friendly, cloyingly so, going out of his way to please us.

Having grabbed the menu, I flipped through only to be shocked at the prices of the various dishes and drinks. They were way beyond our reach, although I strained to keep a stiff upper lip. What surprised me was that Marcy was shocked as well.

"Ouch!" she said, her forehead a ripple of worries. "I'm sure we can find a Mexican restaurant that's much cheaper. Remember we may have to pay for the car. All I have in my pocket is $150. We simply can't afford it."

"Come on, Marcy. Enjoy it; you are invited. We have to celebrate our freedom! When things get tight, I can always wash dishes or work on a farm."

Marcy reluctantly gave in, mellowed I suppose by the sentimental tunes of Broadway favorites played by a versatile and gifted pianist. Quaffing on a glass of champagne, we placed our orders. Marcy chose a dish of half a game hen, wild rice, cauliflower, green salad, accompanied by a glass of California chardonnay, while I was craving for a sirloin steak, garnished with potatoes, string beans and a fluffy green salad with anchovies, all to be washed down by an oaky California merlot. For dessert, we shared a chocolate tart and a cup of coffee. Both meals turned out to be worthy of the occasion — mouthwatering. My steak was especially savory, a most tender and juicy cut of beef. If there was a small wrinkle, it had to do with my table manners. Oblivious of my status, I started eating like a

German, with the fork in in my left hand and the knife in my right. Thank God, Marcy quickly reminded me of the blunder.

Other than that, the atmosphere was decidedly mellow and carefree. Like the rest of the guests, we tried to engage in softened, candle-light conversations. When Marcy accidentally brought up the question of the car and our tight budget again, I suggested that we ban all such talk. That helped raising the evening to a most memorable experience for both of us, and as we walked back to the motel, we felt so animated, we shimmied with both our hips attached to each other.

LAUGHTER AND TEARS

Blessed with luck, the joyous mood continued to hold us in thrall, lifting us over the threshold and right into our cozy adobe cubby. Marcy, mercifully, had forgiven me for my shabbiness. At the very least she held no grudge against me. Despite the irritating ichor which occasionally oozed from my lips — the tip of my tongue helped atone for my sins — we passionately shared our love for each other. For most of the night, we were head over heels into a variety of amorous acrobatics venetian blinds were invented to conceal. Let me just say, the jiggled bed never stopped grumbling, and when the morning knocked on our door, we were still entwined.

While we tucked in our own, modest breakfast, including the free coffee available at the reception, we also touched on our immediate plans again. I argued that we couldn't stay in Santa Fe, as inviting as this town had been, was simply too close to Murphy and far too small to provide a hiding space. In spite of the fact that it harbored a surprising number of people belonging to several different races and colors, Whites, Indians, Hispanics and Mexicans, it lacked a big anonymous crowd we could immerse in. For better or worse, we stuck out, not least because our racial differences. I doubted that there were many Santa Feans who, having watched us, would fail to remember our faces, most conspicuously when they'd appear on an arrest warrant.

Although Marcy yielded to my argument, she once again brought up the question what to do with the car. "I can't just abandon the Chevy," she yammered, close to tears.

"I thought we had settled that already. — Look, Marcy, if we're really serious about our escape, we ought to jump on a Greyhound today, on one that would take us at least to Albuquerque, hopefully even to Mesilla, where your great uncle lives. And once we've settled in you can still get the car."

She took a sip of coffee and, cutting a sour face, glared at me as if trying to bite my lip again. "You caught me unawares at Tony's. You know that won't happen."

"Why not? It's up to you. Look, Marcy, we have no choice. We've got to get moving. The FBI will soon be breathing down our necks. Tomorrow at the latest, they'll put out an arrest warrant, with our pictures and all. It will be displayed in every law enforcement office, government building and most newspapers."

"With our pictures?"

"With our pictures. And our names. And… who knows what. It's not hard to imagine what they'll write. I'm sure you remember what Jennings, our guard at the farm, said, when he caught us in the cornfield. You can be sure that they'll soon cast out their dragnet."

Marcy stared at the wall, looking cheerless, disheartened. It was very hard on me, exasperating. In my final effort to pull her over, I embraced her, tenderly kissed her cheeks as best I could and padded her on the back. "Look, Marcy, we haven't got much time. Please!"

I rose, grabbed my bag and stuffed my belongings into it. "I checked the bus schedule in the office. There's a Greyhound leaving for Albuquerque at 10:20. We could still catch it."

"Oh, Fritz, that's not how I pictured our trip." She glared at me as if she hovered on a different planet.

"Neither did I. I know, it's tough. All we can do is make the best of our situation. Just sitting there, moping and staring at the wall will only make things worse. Come on, Marcy, I beg you. Pull yourself together."

"I don't know," she said, heaving a sigh. "I'm so torn."

"Marcy, don't you chicken out!" I warned, losing my patience. "Remember, you and I pledged that we were in this together. We've got to hurry. I'm gonna rush over to the office, pay the bill and then we'll be on our way to the bus station."

"Sorry, Fritz, I can't. I simply don't feel good about it."

I shook my head. "I don't know what to say. This is very cowardly of you, Marcy. You should be ashamed of yourself."

"Regardless of what you say, I won't go," she said in an unwavering tone of voice. "You have to go by yourself. I'll stay here until I can pick up the car. And then I'll make my way back to the camp."

"Back to the camp?" I swiveled my head in disgust. "To the barbed wire! So everything we did and dreamed together was for naught? A life of free movement without the pricks of the barbs. Gone, dissipated like a wisp of vapor out of a bathroom vent."

Marcy only stared at me, tormented, as though gone through the wringer.

Neither one of us had any words. We both knew that we would in all likelihood never see each other again. Shaken, I rushed over to the office and paid the bill. Marcy was in the bathroom when I returned. When she came out, I asked her if she had changed her mind. "No," she said, resolutely turning her head. "Have you?"

"No. I'm heartbroken that it didn't work out. But I'm still thankful for having met you and sharing so many happy hours with you, I really am. I'll never forget you, Marcy. Whatever happens, I hope you have a most happy life and a safe return. Here is my share of Tony's bill," I added, handing he $60.

"Thanks so much," she said, dissolving into tears. "Meeting you was like a dream that has come to an end. You were my Viking. My imagination ran wild with you and me together. Good luck to you on your journey to freedom. I hope and pray, they won't catch you."

We hugged and kissed, choking with tears.

DOWN THE RIO GRANDE

Ichor oozing from my lips, I grabbed my bag and stumbled out of the room. The bus depot was farther than I'd expected, but my falling into a vigorous stride helped me muffle my disappointment and loss. On the way I stopped at a dumpster near a grocery store, pulled the uniform out of my bag and tossed it in. Having finally reached the depot, I rushed to the ticket office. As I approached the window, I felt butterflies fluttering all the way up my esophagus. I was overly self-conscious, almost as if my English and my body language were being tested and found wanting. So far Marcy had usually handled our contacts with people. Now I was thrown back onto my own. My mental motto: avoid verbal bloopers. Being still about twelve feet away, I fished the money out of my pocket and, simulating a yawn, asked for a one-way ticket to Albuquerque.

The man behind the window was chewing tobacco. "One twenty-four," he finally uttered in a scratchy rasp of a voice.

I gave him $2. "What time?"

"Ten twenty," he snapped, handing me the ticket and the change.

I breathed a sigh of relief for having passed my first test so smoothly. Still having about fifteen minutes to squander, I walked out of the building and around the whole bus depot. Passing a garbage can I picked a newspaper, The Albuquerque Journal, out of it. I checked the news and was relieved that it didn't carry a scoop about my escape. No mugshot, nothing.

Contemplating my recent past, I was able to log a flicker of insight into Marcy's conundrum. Gradually, very gradually, I began to understand why she was so torn. It hadn't even come up that, by providing me a means for transportation, she'd actually taken a huge risk. *She could be accused of aiding the enemy or, worse, of treason. Conviction on any of these charges might well carry a long jail sentence, even the death penalty. Marcy's dream of a liaison with a Viking could easily flip into a nightmare.* All that weighed on me like a ton of wet adobe bricks.

Minutes later I boarded the bus. I was able to secure a window seat. Making myself comfortable, I chanced on a well-preserved, if sweaty baseball cap, which stuck in the gap between the seat and the outside panel. Although blue, it had the white letters N.Y. sewn across its front. After a little adjustment it fit me perfectly. Now I looked like a real American, a Yankee. *If only it weren't for the accent!*

I happened to share a seat with Dick, an older, rosy-cheeked fellow who repeatedly tried to strike up a conversation. He kept smiling at me as if we had known each other for years. Back at the camp, Dieter had told me that, as a rule, Americans tend to be friendlier to strangers than we Germans. A basic goodwill toward others is ingrained in the national psyche, I remembered him saying, especially in the American West. That's also the reason why they tend to smile much more than we do — sometimes like idiots! — most notably when they see somebody, even a complete stranger, who arouses their curiosity. From all I could tell, I must have fit that mold. Chances are Dick suspected all along that I wasn't a native because he right away wanted to know where I was from.

"From Santa Fe," I told him abruptly, giving him a hint that the last thing I wanted to is talk. Although I felt like shit being so rude, I hoped he'd stop talking altogether. "Keep your tongue on the shortest leash you possibly can," I recalled Fahrenbach drumming into me. In addition, there was a second reason. Or was it the first? It so happened that Dick happened to suffer from a bad case of halitosis. Each syllable he uttered was accompanied by — I wish I could be more gracious! — a puff of bacterial stench that seemed to come straight from the dregs of his lower intestines.

Fearing that my answer might not dampen his curiosity, I deliberately turned away from him, pretending to be focusing my attention on the landscape that rushed past. Well, he finally got the message, letting me turn inward, to the events of the past evening and night. Abandoning myself to a wistful mood, I fondly conjured up the dinner down to its smallest details, the smell of the candle, the fragrance of Marcy's perfume, the bewitching hollow below her neck, her everted lips, her girlish bangs, her giggles, her cheeriness, her supple, youthful figure when she bounced to the bathroom, reminding me of a ballet dancer. I indulged in reveries of our sexual embrace, squeezing out the last drop of pleasure. *For God's sake, who could ask for more?* If only it hadn't come to that painful ending.

As we rolled down toward Albuquerque, the dwarfish pine trees and juniper bushes vanished in favor of even sparser vegetation such as grasses and scraggly shrubs, reminding me of some desert areas in Tunisia and Lybia. The intense preoccupation with Marcy was also rudely pushed aside by worries about my escape route. I wondered how the itinerary would proceed. I suspected that a warrant for my arrest with a mugshot would be publicized by nightfall at the latest. This meant that the danger of being caught would increase more than a hundredfold. Yet I trusted that my fake mustache and eyebrows, coupled with the Yankee baseball cap and the waning day would help me dodge the police and the FBI. My provisional goal was to reach the farm of Eisako Kobayashi, Marcy's great uncle, in Mesilla. I wondered how he'd react when he opened the door and saw me without Marcy. Frankly, I braced for the worst.

At 11:40 a.m. our grey behemoth pulled in at the Albuquerque bus depot. I stepped out into a muddle of people of different racial makeup — Hispanics, Indians, Mexicans, whites and even some blacks, standing or sitting on their luggage, bags or the curb, patiently waiting for their buses. I first headed to the ticket office, which was located in the main building. All of a sudden, just as I approached the building, two policemen armed with truncheons and handguns came striding toward me. *What if they're looking for me?* It was too late to change course. Any evasive movement would have been a giveaway. Indeed, even acting insecure, like shortening my steps, letting my eyelids flutter or raising my hand to greet them, could well have been taken as a hint that I was hiding something. Desperate, I instantly grabbed my horseshoe and conjured up the comedy 'Our Winning Hosts', wangling myself into believing that, "All the world's a stage and people merely players". So I squared my shoulders and kept walking straight toward my nemeses, holding my head high, as if nothing had happened. And when I came within range of the cops, I looked them in the eyes, simulated a wan smile and slipped past.

As I entered the building, I felt relieved, as light as a down feather. For all I know I even registered a smile when I stepped toward an open ticket window. The man behind it, a swarthy fellow with shiny black hair was busy cackling on the phone, gesticulating as if he were a cheap, Neapolitan comedian.

Once he'd put down the receiver, he glared at me. "What do you want?"

"Las Cruces, one way." I felt pleased for having reduced the words to an absolute minimum. Fahrenbach, I reckoned, would have given me a slap on the back.

"One sixty," he said.

"When and where does the bus depart?"

"One fifty, gate two."

The word thanks sat on the tip of my tongue, just waiting for the last punt.

Since I was hungry, I walked around in the hope of finding a diner or luncheonette. I soon came across one. Called Pablo's Kitchen, it was crammed with people. *A good sign*. I checked the menu. The variety of dishes available, Mexican as well as American, was truly astonishing. What I particularly appreciated were the low prices. So after finding a booth, I ordered a portion of *carne adovada*, marinated pork, cut into little cubes, rice, a large scoop of pinto beans and three corn tortillas. Being a Mexican dish, it was hot and tasty. Possibly a little too hot. Anyway, I eventually walked out gorged, chased by a sequence of hiccups that would stubbornly follow me for fifteen minutes or more.

I also stumbled into a secondhand store that was called Goodwill, and not for nothing. The prices were stunningly low. Many items were sold in cents rather than dollars. I often stood there amazed when I saw the great range of goods at such low prices. At any rate, I soon found a well-made Austrian rucksack, which was almost new, a blanket, a waterproof poncho, woolen trousers, a sturdy shirt, a pocket knife with a large blade and a can opener, a lined travel jacket with a myriad of pockets, as well as a pair of lightly tinted sunglasses.

Having barely walked out of Goodwill, I showed my own goodwill. I took all my personal belongings out of my bag and stashed them into the rucksack. The bag itself, a durable, but also bulky, unwieldy specimen, I handed over to an employee.

"Thank you, thank you for thinking of us," he beamed like someone who'd won a jackpot.

On my way back to the bus depot I passed a drugstore whose shop window displayed a wide array of hair dyes for ladies. *Why, I could dye my own blond hair brown, or even black. What better way is there to disguise your identity?* I didn't need a shove. So I walked in and, acting as though I was set to do Marcy a favor, bought myself a bottle of dark-brown dye.

Later I boarded the Greyhound to Las Cruces. It was packed. Most of the passengers were Hispanics or Mexicans. Once again, I secured a window seat at the rear. At first, as we weaved through the southern part of Alboocurkee, as the folks down here chose to pronounce it, I focused my attention on the urban landscape, the homes, gardens, businesses and streets. I was astonished how impoverished the area was, especially compared to those trim and tidy towns we passed through by train coming from New York. Granted, even there we had witnessed poor areas, slums dotted with shacks and inhospitable streets. But in that part of this huge country, they were the exception, whereas here they seemed to be the rule. Many houses were mere shacks, hovels, surrounded by trash and wrecked cars. I witnessed poorly clad children playing on dusty, inhospitable streets that were neither paved nor seamed with sidewalks. *Dirt poor. Scraping by. Chewing pork rinds. Hardly a pot to piss in.* In America!

93

Leaving this sprawling settlement behind we passed through more and more agricultural areas. Harvested fields and fruit orchards scurried past, as did small scraggly towns. They were almost all located along the valley floor of the Rio Grande. Water seemed to be the life blood of this valley, the Rio Grande being the Nile of New Mexico, on a much smaller scale, and without the temples, to be sure. Again and again I was reminded of the desert areas of North Africa. And yet, this was America. *But was it really America?* I kept asking myself. *This mighty land that was going to vanquish Germany? That built all those bombers, tanks and guns? That harbored all those great universities, scholars and scientists?* I racked my brains but failed to come up with an answer that could put things to rest.

Eventually, once we had left the small town of Hot Springs, the lack of sleep of last night finally caught up with me. I felt weary, and before long I'd dozed off. My head even appeared to have dropped onto my neighbor's right shoulder, urging me to apologize. But save for this tingling embarrassment, I didn't really wake up, until the coach barreled its way into Las Cruces.

It was scorching when I stepped out of the womb of the Greyhound, over a hundred degrees Fahrenheit, a scale I still lacked a good feeling for. It didn't take me long to orient myself. One look at my watch and the shadow of a telephone pole and I knew where I was, at least in terms of directions. Having found the street that led south to Mesilla, I positioned myself at a stop sign and stuck out my thumb. Within minutes a pickup stopped. The driver, an older gentleman with a craggy, sunburnt face, was gracious enough to crank down the window.

"Where d'ya wanna go, soldier?" shot out of the cab.

I was flabbergasted. *How did he know? And what does that entail? Would he also pump me about my service?* I felt ill-at-ease.

"To Socorro," I said.

"You're on the wrong side of the street," he snapped back. "You've got to stick out yer thumb over there." He pointed to the stop sign diagonally across the intersection.

"Thanks."

He revved up the engine, leaving me stuck in a cloud of blue smoke.

Of course, I never dreamed of going to Socorro. I just came from there. All I wanted was to protect myself from the hailstorm of questions this gentleman might have unleashed on me.

So with the well-meaning gentleman out of sight, I stuck out my thumb again. This time a young man stopped in a beat-up jalopy. He was so short, his chin — I kid you not! — may have touched the lower swing of the steering wheel.

"Where you go?" he asked, jerking back his head as if he intended to challenge me to a fight.

"Mesilla."

"Mesiya! Me go there, too." He smiled, opened the door and waved me in. He looked and acted like a chummy, affable fellow, reminding me of Pancho. He had his radio going full blast with Mexican music. Sonic gusts and waves from trumpets and fiddles crammed the cab, easily drowning out an average human voice. *Serves me well,* I assured myself.

"*Donde en Mesilla?* Who you want to see?" he out-shouted a flurry of trumpet sounds.

I scrambled for the address of Eisako Kobayashi's farm.

"Here," I said, handing him the slip.

"*Oh, japones?*" he nodded, giving me a big smile. "Calle del Oeste? Me know. Me know."

What a stroke of luck! He's chauffeuring me right to Eisako's doorsteps. "*Gracias!* I really appreciate your help." I offered him a handshake, introducing myself as Fred.

"*De nada,*" he said. "Me? Eusebio."

He stepped on the gas, giving the car, as well as us, a mild whiplash. Mercifully, he slowed down afterwards, as we headed down Main Street and Avenida de Mesilla, passing car lots with gaudy flags, gas stations and strings of small businesses, interspersed with cheap, weathered homes. Gradually the town frayed into dilapidated buildings, empty lots and small fields, some barren, others still very green and pleasing to the eyes. As we whisked along, silhouettes of houses loomed on the horizon again, shimmering in the hot haze of the afternoon.

"Mesiya," Eusebio said, pointing ahead.

Ten minutes later Eusebio scraped to a halt, enwrapping the car in a huge cloud of dust.

"Kobayashi live here," he said, pointing to a small, wooden homestead, surrounded by a low hedge, with an attractive, neatly kept garden unfolding behind it.

"*Muchas gracias,*" I said, giving him a firm handshake. "That was very nice of you."

As Eusebio drove off, I opened the gate, shuffled to the front door, and rang the bell. It took a few minutes before a small old man with a shriveled, weather-beaten face opened the door. "Can I help you?" he piped in a thin, weak voice.

95

"I'm Fred Luthi," I said, squeezing out a smile. "You must be Mr. Kobayashi."

"Yes," he nodded, returning my smile.

"Well, I'm Marcy's friend. She told me to pass on greetings to you."

"Where is she?"

I explained that she is in Santa Fe, that her car broke down, which is why she couldn't come. But that she is well.

"Oh, you are her German boyfriend? She wrote me a letter two weeks ago. She promised she'd come visit us with you. Is she still coming?"

"No, unfortunately not. It's a big repair that may take several days or even weeks."

"That's very bad," he said, wincing and wringing his hands. "What are we going to do? You are a German POW, right?"

"Well, yes."

"Please don't misunderstand me, Mr. Fred," he said, writhing as though under pain. "I would very much like to help you. But our government wouldn't look on this kindly, especially since we are Japanese. They'd accuse us of helping the enemy. We would be traitors to this country. My wife and I could really get into deep trouble. They give you the death penalty when they catch somebody doing that."

"I fully understand," I said, nodding. "I wouldn't want to be a risk to your life, either. But maybe you could tell me where I could find an inexpensive hostel or hotel."

"There are some in Las Cruces, or farther down the road in El Paso. But if you only look for a place to sleep, I know a barn with lots of hay just down the road. It's no more than half a mile from here. You might have to jump the fence. But you're tall; that would be easy. There are no dogs or people around that area. But there could be cows. As I recall, there is even a watering place, where you could wash yourself." He described in detail where the barn was located.

"Thanks for telling me," I said, adding, "By the way, is there a diner in town?"

"Yes, La Posta. It's a very inexpensive but good Mexican restaurant. It's easy to find. It's located right on the plaza."

"Do they also serve breakfast?"

"Yes, a very good breakfast, tasty *huevos rancheros*. They'll last you all day."

"Thank you. I appreciate your help. — Um, could I still ask you for a little favor? Could I refill my canteen?"

"Certainly, go right ahead. There's a faucet right to your left."

"Thanks."

We shook hands. I re-filled my canteen, shouldered my rucksack and started walking down the Calle del Oeste all the way to a narrow dirt road that veered off toward the west. I followed it and after a quarter of a mile the barn showed up, surrounded by a barbed-wire fence. I saw no cows, but I did pass by a watering place, a sizable cistern with a trough attached to it.

The barn happened to be full of fresh hay that must have been mowed very recently. The homey fragrance, the peace and the softness were so tempting that I immediately gathered some to cock a bunk. Stretching out, I conjured up idyllic scenes of my childhood and youth. It was in a barn out in the country where Lotte and I made love. She was experienced, while I fumbled as a tenderfoot. I felt so sheepish. I wondered how Marcy would have reacted if I'd told her that.

Somehow, I must have fallen asleep, because I woke up when it was already dark. Rising and stretching myself, my thoughts skipped back to the camp. *They must have had the last roll call.* Helmut had promised to shout "here" twice, when my name was called, first on Saturday night and then again on Sunday morning, but not Sunday night, meaning that my escape would be known to the camp's administration by now. *Tomorrow at the latest the hunt for my scalp will start.* A bitter pill, indeed. All I could do was to stiffen my spine and be wary.

Fully aware of the challenge ahead, I calmed down, ripped off my mustache and fake brows, stripped and, grabbing my toilet case and towel, made my way to the trough, where I gave myself a good scrub. I also washed my shirt, my T-shirt and underpants, all of which I hung out to dry on a rotary swather that sat inside the barn. I saw no need to advertise my stay at the 'hay-hostel' to a farmer or cowboy who might accidentally swagger past.

Pinched with hunger, I unwrapped the provisions I'd purchased in Raton. They were rather meager, a few sticks of beef jerky, a couple of slices of stale bread, an apple and a can of pinto beans. Yet I gobbled it all up like a starved dog at a dumpster, giving credence to the old saw that hunger is the best cook. Good old Emma came to mind. Since it was too early to go to sleep, I fetched the flashlight Marcy had given me, and began writing my diary. I now realized that I'd gathered a whole slew of new impressions and experiences during the past few days and putting them on paper took me more than two hours. I also studied the map I had taken out of Marcy's car, hoping to get a clue as to the area I'd try crossing the border into Mexico. Unfortunately, it lacked the gritty detail necessary to make a preliminary decision. I came back to what Fahrenbach had suggested, namely that the stretch along the Rio Grande south-east of El Paso would be the most promising, largely because of its remoteness, as well as the density of its vegetation, the trees and bushes I could use as cover.

But "Night is the mother of counsel," as one of my teachers at the orphanage used to say. And tomorrow the sun would rise again for another day. Tired, I added more hay to my bedding, fluffed it up and, covering myself with my new blanket, stretched out and dozed.

A FAMILIAR FACE

I woke to hoarse sounds, followed by a cacophony of mooing and throaty noises. It was five past seven. Dawn was about to break. Rising, I took a swig of water, grabbed my toilet case and a towel and shuffled out to the trough. The air was fresh, yet mellow. What a joy it was to splash cold water on my face and torso. I got so carried away, I didn't even notice that I actually had an audience — a healthy bevy of curious bovines, five of them. I wished them a good morning.

Once back in the barn, I lifted the clothes off the swather. Though still a bit clammy, I still slipped into them, trusting they would dry in no time. Having set up my little mirror on a wooden brace, I glued on my mustache and the eyebrows. Next, I grabbed the bottle of dye I'd picked up in Albuquerque, went back to the trough and began rubbing the stuff into my scalp. I also pinched a bit of grease from the running wheel of the swather and smeared it on my face, my neck and on my hands and arms.

The results truly amazed me. Although that swarthy fellow who peeked at me from the mirror may not have matched the cast of an average Mexican — too tall, too Nordic, Germanic! — he did come close. Certainly, nobody would have taken this fellow for a 'Viking', any more.

Now set, I grabbed my rucksack and, cocking my baseball cap over my left ear, turned and was on my way. I felt a light breeze at my back. The sun dimmed, as light clouds began moving into the area. Worse, out on the western horizon some heavy bedding with morbid ambitions pushed its way into my direction.

Surprisingly the plaza of Mesilla was already teeming with people, mostly Mexicans and Indians. They gathered around La Posta, the restaurant that Eisako recommended, and a Mexican grocery store called *La Tienda*. Mexican trumpet and fiddle music blared from a radio that sat at the entrance. The looks of the people, the music, the widespread use of Spanish, the whole atmosphere felt as though I was in Mexico already. Even the smell — roasted peppers and mesquite — was Mexican, or what I presumed to be Mexican. Thankfully, nobody seemed to pay any attention to me, which I found very comforting and reassuring to boot.

Feeling pangs of hunger in the pit of my stomach, I was drawn to La Posta, where I secured a seat at a secluded corner booth. Almost all of the dishes were Mexican. Taking the advice of Eisako, I ordered a plate of *huevos rancheros,* consisting of eggs sunny side up, smothered with green chile and jalapeno peppers, a large helping of pinto beans, rice, salad and three maize tortillas. All of this very tasty grub was served by a heavy, bosomy Mexican waitress, dressed in a wide skirt and artfully embroidered blouse, reminiscent of the kind Ukrainian peasant women were wearing on Sundays.

Unfortunately, as I leaned into my huevos rancheros, I couldn't avoid coming face-to-face with an incident that was bound to put me on guard. The prompters were two cops who happened to walk in and place themselves at a table close to mine. Dressed in full regalia, with spiffy uniforms, polished badges, even heavy colts dangling from their hips, they seemed to take a special interest in, well, me, Fritz Graf. Notably one of them, a tall, lanky fellow, whose piercing peepers and orbital ridge reminded me of a battle-hardened Neanderthal, simply couldn't take his eyes off me.

Come to think of, the nosiness of these cops didn't come exactly out of the blue. After all, it was Monday morning and, according to my figuring, the camp authorities in Murphy would likely know by now that I had broken loose. In that case, a mugshot of me should have appeared in today's paper, setting in motion the cops and FBI agents in Colorado, New Mexico and Texas to find me, none other than Cpl. Fritz Graf. True, my effort to change my appearance with the help of various makeups, greases and coloring agents may have given me a little cover, but being the tallest and most Germanic-looking fellow around made me conspicuous, enough to increase the risk of being cornered. The fact that I caught myself red-handed eating my breakfast with knife and fork, only aggravated my dilemma. In short, I braced for being questioned, arrested, handcuffed and sent back to Murphy. I was ready to skip the huevos, to rise, pay up and take to my heels. Actually, I had already raised my hand, but the waitress, being overburdened, was slow in coming.

Meanwhile, casting sidelong glances at my foes, I expected them to get up any time, strut over and, fondling their colts, ask for my identification. What would I tell them? Yes, what? That I was a young American who, due to an ailment, had been classified 4-F, i.e., exonerated from serving in the military and produce the evidence Fahrenbach had faked? Yes, a red-blooded American who just happened to have an appetite for Mexican dishes? In my heavy 'Cherman aktsennt' no less! I'd have burst out in laughter, had my situation not been so tense, the tunnel I found myself in so dark. *But, Fritz, every tunnel has a light at the end,* I heard myself whispering, only to be chased by the question: *Maybe, but would it come in time?*

Well, as nutty as it seems, it actually *did* come. It showed up in the shape of a cute Mexican filly, accompanied by a pearl string of high-end giggles. More to the point, she was as pretty as a kissing doll, endowed with a sweet button nose, dark, wide-set eyes, a large forehead, topped by a mop of curly, black fluff. Like the waitresses, she was dressed in sandals, a blueish ruffle-skirt and an embroidered, tightly fitting blouse that veiled a pair of shapely knockers. Better yet, this miss — Aida was her name! — happened to head straight to the table of my foes. Batting her eyelids and exposing her bronze legs, Aida began jesting and flirting with the cops, mercilessly baiting them with coquettish movements, glances and come-hither-looks. At one point, she even dared ask them what they would like to order, touching her thighs, belly, buttocks and breasts.

The cops, meanwhile, were going batty. Leaning back and roaring with laughter, they'd jest, jeer, banter and, flinging off sexual innuendos, lustfully slap their thighs. They were totally focused on her, to the point where I didn't even exist any more.

I couldn't but laugh in my sleeve. What a relief it was, to watch my sworn enemies getting their teeth pulled, and closer to my chest, not to be watched any more. I felt like blowing kisses to Aida. Had it not been for the coincidental appearance of this lascivious offspring of Lady Luck, I'd likely have lost my freedom and my dreams of a new beginning. And when I stepped out of La Posada, the inside of me smiled, soaking every nook and cranny of my brain with the balm of happiness. Clenching my fist, I looked forward to the future with a cheerfulness I hadn't experienced before. I couldn't wait to take on the challenge of crossing the border.

With La Posta at my back, I first paid the grocery store La Tienda a visit. As I stepped in, I right away felt drawn to the newspaper rack. It carried a small selection of American and Mexican publications. Grabbing the topmost copy, my heart instantly skipped into double time. It turned out to be today's issue of The Las Cruces Sun, a thin local daily. I stepped aside and unfolded it, holding my breath. And wouldn't you know it, there it was, a mugshot of yours truly smack on the front page, accompanied by two others, Lt. Christian Kurland and Sgt. Heinz Boehn. All three were part of a scoop captioned with: 'Dangerous Nazis Escaped. $250 REWARD FOR EACH OF THESE MEN'. According to the camp's administration they broke out of the POW camp in Murphy, Colorado, on Saturday at the latest. "One of them, Cpl.l Fritz Graf, has allegedly teamed up with a Jap woman who slipped out of the Relocation Center in Amache, Colorado. According to unconfirmed reports these allies in arms were last seen in Santa Fe, New Mexico. There is no trace of the other two men. But it is assumed that all three are heading to the Mexican border. Agents of the FBI, personnel of the border patrol, sheriff's deputies, police and other law enforcement personnel are taking part in the search. Officials are authorized to pay the reward to any person who is aiding us to capture these men. A warning: They may be armed and dangerous.

Even though I'd expected to see my mugshot in the newspaper, I was still shocked. I must have looked as if I'd stepped into a lion's den. *Now it's official. They just painted a bull's eye on my back and blew the horn for the hunt. Two hundred and fifty dollars for my head! Alive or dead!* That would notch up things. I knew it would be tough and challenging, that J.Edgar Hoover and his G-men would spare me nothing.

Since I was in dire need of provisions, I ventured deeper into the store. Luckily, I found everything I needed: bread, corn tortillas, cans of beans, carrots, apples, shoe polish and a large chunk of a semi-soft Mexican cheese called *queso menonita.* I faintly remembered that Pancho had already mentioned this *queso*, so named because it's made by Mennonites, a group of German settlers in Chihuahua.

Another whiff of Mexico, I concluded as I stashed the groceries into my rucksack walked out of the store, clenching my fist. Full of vim, piss and vinegar, I yearned to hand myself over to a Mexican adventure, to walk all the paths, alleys and and trails that had the word freedom stamped on their sleeves. Although I had heard about the ancient civilizations that once thrived there and had seen pictures of pyramids, I viewed it as an enigma, a place with an aura of mystery. I wondered how I would find my way in this colorful, multifaceted land, especially since I didn't know any Spanish, let alone Indian tongues. As I've mentioned before, Spanish was Greek to me. That is, almost. I did have a glimmer of some Spanish *words,* but only because they sounded Italian. And the tint and pitch of Italian was somewhat familiar to me since we chanced to fraternize with our Italian allies in North Africa.

The first and thorniest question that loomed in my mind was how to get to the border. After weighing my options, I decided that hitchhiking would be safest, provided it was done in a savvy way. Namely, if I carefully picked the driver. If the ride with Eusebio had taught me anything, it was the presumption that Mexicans who know hardly any English would be the best bet. To begin with, I wouldn't have to talk much. And whatever I did say wouldn't be listened to critically. A fellow like Eusebio couldn't care less, even if he were able to catch me mispronouncing a word. In addition, having a common bond of being underdogs should not be underestimated either. Nor would he be drawn to identify my face, simply because he wouldn't likely stick his nose into an English language newspaper

With all that tumbling around my mind, I trudged over to the main artery that sliced north and south, looked for a stop sign and raised my thumb. Being in a rural place, drivers of all stripes stopped and generously offered rides. Unfortunately, most of them turned out to be white Americans who were far too friendly, too affable to pass my test. It wasn't until the fourth try that I got what I wanted — another Eusebio. Diego was his name, a stocky, bow-legged young chap with a meaty face, chubby cheeks and a pair of bulging eyes. Steering an old small Ford pickup, he originally hailed from Ciudad Camargo, south of Chihuahua. Or so I managed to squeeze out of the Spanish monologue he sputtered out like a machine gun would bullets. As far as I could gather, he intended to whisk down to El Paso to pick up a kid brother of his.

Anyway, Diego kept shooting the breeze, mainly about his family — he had three *ninos* — his job, the backbreaking, poorly paid drudgery of picking chili peppers and, worse, cotton for white farmers. Me? I listened and nodded. Occasionally, especially as we drew closer to El Paso, I caught myself parroting some of his Spanish words or even phrases. (I was especially fond of the vowels because of their clean, straightforward articulation.) *What better way to learn a new language?* For Diego, however, my performance must have been no more than comical entertainment, making him break out in repeated bursts of laughter not least because of my frequent mispronunciations, often with an Italian or even German twist.

Needless to say, I couldn't possibly keep up. To put it squarely: I didn't have a tongue of my own. But being primarily a listener was a role that fitted me like an old glove. All Diego wanted to know was the disclosure of my *destinacion*, where I wanted to get off. Since I already knew that he'd only go as far as El Paso, I said, El Paso, adding that my real goal was Presidio, Texas. Yet I also tried to make clear to him that I intended to stay away from the border crossings because of the *policia y agente de policia.* Somehow it just slipped out of my mouth, and I immediately tried to suck it back in again, for fear that he might consider me a scofflaw. But Diego would turn around and smile a most charitable consent at me, emphasizing, *"Eso se comprende."* (That is understood.) *"No me gusto la policia ninguno."* (I don't like the police either.) I hope I mirror his words and actions correctly when I say that he unexpectedly snarled and added in a spitting tone of voice that "we Mexicans" are nothing but '*basura*' (trash) to them.

When we reached El Paso, more specifically the crossing of Paisano Street and Stanton, Diego squeaked to a halt, only to tell me in so many words that he now had to turn off toward the border, adding that if I get to Chihuahua, I should also visit his *padres* in Ciudad Camargo.

Thanking him for the invitation, I said that I might take him up on his offer one day.

Smiling at me, he pulled an old, badly worn map of Mexico out of his glove compartment and unfolded it.

"*Aqui* El Paso," he said, pointing to a red dot. He also showed me where Presidio, Ojinaga, Chihuahua and Ciudad Camargo were located, even retracing the roads between these towns and cities. I smiled, pointing to the map and then to me, while repeatedly nodding. He intuitively knew what I wanted, and in the end, handed me his map.

"*Muchas gracias!*"

"*De nada,*" he snapped with a broad, all-inclusive smile. "*Buena suerte!*" (Good luck!).

We hugged, wished each other well and parted with a robust "*Adios!*"

I was ready to jump for joy. Did I not have a destination and a map? Was I not already within a stone's throw of the border? And yet it was barely twenty past ten. Never mind, that dark clouds were roiling the sky and it started to drizzle. Getting cold, I wrapped the poncho round me and via various alleys headed to the bus depot in the hope of catching a Greyhound that would take me all the way to Presidio.

But the official behind the window, a crusty fellow, just laughed at me. "Presidio? That's way in the boonies. Only roughnecks wanting to shoot jackrabbits and rattlers would think of going there. No, there ain't nothing there for Greyhounds."

MEET A MUDSLINGER

Disappointed, I trudged back to Paisano Street and, always on the watch for cops, tried my luck with hitchhiking again. This time it was much harder to pick my choice of a driver. Try as I might, I was unable to flag down a Mexican driver. Losing patience, I shoved a piece of carrot into the left side of my mouth, in the hope of making it appear as if I were suffering from an infection of my molars. If anything, that provided me with a pretext to garble my words, or even stay mute, when somebody pitched questions at me.

This time I chanced to pick an old, bald-headed Mexican-American who drove a plush, luxurious Cadillac. Yes, a real Cadillac! "Where d'you wana go, young man?" he asked with a broad, affable smile.

"To Presidio," I mumbled, simulating pain in my jaw.

"You're at the right address. Jump in!"

Climbing in besides him, I introduced myself as Fred.

"I'm Enrique," he said, licking his chops. "But most people call me Hank. Got some problems with them choppers of yours, and spout, too?"

"Yeah, they hurt," I mumbled.

Unlike Diego and Eusebio, Hank spoke fluent English, albeit with a slight Spanish accent. I guessed his age as seventy, yet the looks of his face may have nudged that up a little. It was pasty and puffy, sporting a warty, alcoholic nose and pea-like eyes that were hardly visible. At the same time, Hank was impeccably dressed in a pinstripe suit, a classy white shirt and a flashy tie, as if he'd spruced himself up to attend a wedding. Aftershave mixed with vinyl permeated the cab.

"Say, where you from?"

"Switzerland."

"Switzerland? I've been told that you've got lots of mountains, cheese, chocolate and hardworkin' people. And you're neutral!"

"Yeah."

"I wish we were neutral, too. We should damn well mind our own business and not stick our fingers in this war. Let them Europeans handle their quarrels themselves. Don't get me wrong, I don't like that big-mouth Hitler either but we shouldn't support Churchill and his ilk. The damn Brits just want us to fight their war. That Roosevelt keeps listening too much to that old bulldog. FDR was good at the beginning, but lately he's turned into a warmonger. He should be held accountable for all them dead bodies bein' shipped back every day from the war."

Once again, I just nodded, acting as if I agreed with him.

My constant nods must have encouraged him because he rambled on and on about President Roosevelt, calling him a criminal and Congress his flunkies. He blasted them for legislating gasoline rationing and raising taxes. According to him, Uncle Sam quit being the aloof uncle and turned into a common thief who kept on rifling the pockets of all the hardworkin' people.

Hank's monologue, needless to say, got on my nerves. It was childish at best, full of whitewash, distortions and outright hatred. Here was a man who, judging by his car and his suit, had achieved a high level of well-being. By any measure, he had climbed the ladder of success and seemed to be cruising comfortably along the American way of life. Frankly, you'd expect that a fellow like him would voice some praise for those who'd made this possible, including the president, high-ranking politicians and the American system of government, as faulty as it may be. And yet he did the opposite. Grumpy, he dumped pitcher after pitcher of bile on them, green, slimy bile. He was nothing but a grouch who kept biting the hand that fed him.

That was my verdict. I couldn't help but scratch my head at the man's attitude. At the same time, I couldn't help being stunned how freely he carried on to say what was bugging him. Again and again, he called Uncle Sam a crook who is running a corrupt enterprise and the president a scoundrel, even a criminal, and thought nothing of it. Being a German, I repeatedly felt urged to compare Hank's America to Hitler's Germany. *What if a German were to voice such criticism about his government, not to mention the Fuehrer?* I asked myself. *Well, you know what would happen. He'd immediately be arrested by the Gestapo, denounced and thrown into a concentration camp, where he'd rot away without ever seeing the light of day again.*

Yet, while all of that kept rumbling in my craw, it wasn't until much later that the full significance of this ride I shared with Hank would dawn on me as my first meaningful civics lesson that would leave a lasting impression on my mind. It taught me in a negative way what free speech is all about, thus opening a window onto the American system of fair play I hadn't noticed before. More, it brought home to me that the desire to escape from the prison camp was part and parcel of the same ideal — the yearning for freedom. It was a shame that I had to turn my back on America, the very country I was beginning to grow fond of. Despite all the glaring imperfections, I might add, the many shapes of racism and other injustices I'd encountered along the way.

Well, it took us almost six hours of driving often on dirt roads through a parched, monotonous landscape until we reached the little frontier town of Presidio. It had rained, more on than off, for most of the way, but it was tapering off as we coasted down the hill from Marfa. Trying to avoid any contact with agents of the border patrol or FBI, I begged Hank to stop way on the outskirts, a wish he failed to grasp.

"Why on earth would you want to get out *here*? There's nothin' but rattlers that are goin' to lunge at you. Come on, I'll buy you a cold beer at that joint down there."

"Thanks, Hank, I really appreciate your offer," I mumbled around my carrot. "But you know, the dentist told me to stop drinking."

"OK. I get you," he growled, shaking his head. "Still…"

"Thank you so much for giving me a ride," I said, grabbing my rucksack.

A FATAL ENCOUNTER

Frankly, I was a little worried that my latest maneuver may have had the opposite effect of what I'd intended. Instead of concealing my identity, I may have inadvertently brought it into a glaring light. Anyway, crunching the piece of carrot, I instantly left the road, ducked under the fence and headed down to the Rio Grande, to an area a few miles upstream from the town. Across the river the blue mountains of Mexico remained my fixed points, drifting more in than out of the cloud cover. Unlike the higher-lying desert area, the valley floor appeared to be lush and green, dense with vegetation, mostly willows, cottonwoods and other riparian growth. Having crossed a dirt road, I finally reached the banks of the river. I was astonished that it was carrying so much water, and with a loamy, muddy hue. *It must have dumped a lot of rain upstream.* Following a narrow trail presumably used by anglers, I began searching for a spot along the shore where the water would be shallow. I originally intended to slosh across it, carrying the rucksack on my head. At the same time, the spot should also offer me good cover until nightfall. Incidentally, whenever the ground happened to turn wet and muddy, I always made sure that I turned around and walked backwards, just to confuse or mislead a nosy border guard.

It took a while until I found what I was looking for. The spot was above a little bend that the river had carved into the landscape. The water may have been a tad deeper than I'd wished for, especially along the northern shore where I planned to enter. But who was going to quibble? Farther out, about fifteen feet from the bank, there was a sizable willow tree. Having been uprooted somewhere upstream, it must have gotten stuck on a shoal. As I watched it tilting diagonally up from the water like a big broom, I wondered if I could somehow take advantage of it.

I eventually settled down under a large cottonwood, hoping it would provide me with some shelter. I pulled out Diego's map and tried to orient myself. Sadly, it was not detailed enough to give me the clues I needed. Feeling hunger pangs, I took out my poncho and spread out my provisions, a loaf of bread, a chunk of queso menonita, a can of beans, as well as some carrots and apples. As bad luck would have it, it started to drizzle, just as I was about to open a can of beans. So I quickly gathered all the goodies, placed them under a log, slipped on my travel jacket and poncho and slowly began to put down my supper. Just in time, as the outlook turned from bad to worse. The drops grew bigger and bigger, smacking the leaves with tiny thuds, and soon it poured cats and dogs. Everything turned dripping wet, not to mention cold.

After stashing away my supplies, I got out my mirror and smeared my face with shoe polish, until I began to look like a replica of Winnetou, a noble Apache in Karl May's novels. Now set, I pulled in my legs and snugly leaned against the trunk of the tree, preoccupied with stitching together my flight plan.

The rain, meanwhile, had slacked off a bit, falling with a steady sibilance that sounded like distant frying. As dusk settled, I got up and once more checked the spot where I hoped to wade in. I'd poke the water with a stick. It seemed to be deeper than I'd expected. And the current was quite swift and muscular as well. *Could I withstand it all the way to the willow?* Just to be on the safe side, I decided to pick an entry place farther up the river, to make up for a possible drift. As I made my way back to the cottonwood, I saw some lights flickering on the other, Mexican, side. It was about a kilometer upstream. As far as I could tell, they must have been flashlights, and every once in a while, I was able to detect a lot of commotion. People hustled to unload what seemed to be huge bundles from a truck, carried them to the water's edge and dumped them into barges. I assumed they ferried them across the river but it was already too dark for me to see. *Why at night?* I wondered, an unlicked cub that I was.

Minutes later I heard at least two vehicles speed up the dirt road on our side. I suspected it was the American Border Patrol. They must have had direct access to the river, because all of a sudden, powerful searchlights lit up the banks on the Mexican side, including the hustle and bustle. In fact, one barge loaded with bundles was just in the process of crossing. It had almost reached the halfway point, when shouts rang out and, seconds later, a barrage of gunshots. One of them must have hit the searchlight because it instantly shut off. Since it had started to rain again, it was sheer impossible for me to tell who fired at whom and when, and who was winning or losing the skirmish. I only noticed that the man who pushed the barge with his pole must have been hit, because the boat turned and drifted rudderless down river.

It was the last phase of the twilight, and the rain once again came down relentlessly, weaving a dripping-wet web of water threads. *Now or never!* So I slipped off my shoes and dropped my pants, but left the poncho on. Yet, while I was bending down to stash both items into my rucksack, I heard some rustling and crackling. *Must be some wild animals,* was my first thought. Looking up, I recognized the outline of a tall figure standing on the trail, with a flashlight pointing at me and shouting, *"Manos arriba!"* (Hands up!)

His words were Greek to me, but the message traveled more on the tone of voice than it did on words. Slowly straightening my knees and torso, I raised my hands to face him. He was a mere fifteen feet away.

Actually, I was more stunned than ruffled. As a battle-hardened soldier, I had stared death in the eyes several times. Moreover, I'd also been fortunate enough to experience close-combat training while fighting Russian partisans, some of our most feared nemeses. Wary, I let the man, who I suspected to be a Border Patrol agent, step closer. Now nine feet away, I shouted, "Stoy!" (halt in Russian, a natural reflex), slammed a branch at his legs and instantly ducked. He fired, but over my head. A split second later, I lunged full tilt at him, ramming my head into his chest. He groaned and slumped, enough to allow me wrest the gun out of his hand.

"Manos arriba!" I bellowed as he rolled sideways to rise.

He raised his hands, cringing with pain and trembling with fear.

Now I was the top dog, though not for long. Seconds later, there was another crackling and, riding on a beam of light, a man's voice, "Manos arriba!"

His buddy? I instantly dodged behind the first agent and, using him as a shield, fired a shot in the direction of the newcomer. It was not my intention to hurt him; I did it simply to prove to him that I was decidedly not in a playful mood. Unfortunately, he instantly fired back, not once but twice. The first shot barely whizzed past me, ripping my poncho. The second struck the first agent, his buddy, hitting him. Possibly in the head, but I'm far from sure. As I watched him collapse, I instantly aimed my gun at the newcomer but then saw him turn and bolt into darkness. His action, needless to say, left me puzzled, bewildered.

A WETBACK IN REVERSE

I had no time to waste. I feared that within minutes the second agent would be back, and with helpers equipped with the latest searchlights and armaments. I also knew, that I couldn't expect any mercy. Stashing the handgun into the rucksack, I lifted the pack onto my head and waded into the river, with the willow as my intermediate goal. Unfortunately, the depth was about to confirm my worst fears. With each step I sank in deeper and deeper and twelve feet in, the water was high enough to touch my shoulders. Moreover, I also had to brace myself against the current. It was a sheer impossible task, given that most of my body remained submerged, while hands and arms were tied up with balancing a forty-pound rucksack on my head. With each and every step I saw myself drifting down, well beyond the imaginary line I'd set for myself. In fact, I had already passed the willow, which loomed large in the middle of the river. Mercifully, my feet soon touched a shoal and, now leeward of the willow, I was able to recoup the drift. Shivering, I dropped my rucksack on the trunk and rested, clasping my torso in an effort to keep warm.

Darkness had settled, engulfing the river in a brooding mood. The rain still kept coming down relentlessly, in cold, wet snippets. My mind spooled back to the wounding or even death of the agent, when I suddenly saw the flashing of lights of what appeared to be two vehicles. I knew that they'd be coming for me. *Now I really carried a bull's eye on my back, and one that might dig into my flesh and begin to fester.* I also suspected that they'd be equipped with new searchlights, as well as top-notch sharpshooters and the best guns money could buy. Lucky for me, there was no vehicular access at the site of my crossing, as far as I could tell. Nor would flashlights be of much use. Even the most powerful beams would in all likelihood fail to penetrate this closely knit mesh of rain. Still, I wasn't in the mood to take any chances.

Once again, I lifted the rucksack on my head and took on the other half of the river. Thanks to a stroke of luck the water level rarely rose beyond my nipples. The only setback: I was getting weary, even drowsy, my concentration was dropping off sharply. A small lightbulb began flaring up inside my skull, prodding me to see the word 'hypothermia' written all over an imaginary wall. It was scarily familiar to various scenes I experienced

111

during the Russian winter of 1941. And when I finally scrambled up the banks on the Mexican side, I was shivering and shaking, almost like a soldier facing a firing squad.

Acutely aware that I couldn't slack up, I quickly pulled out my towel, cast off the poncho, stepped out of my underpants and rubbed myself dry. Next, I slipped into dry underpants, a pair of woolen trousers, a warm shirt and a precious travel jacket, all of which I covered with my 'wounded' poncho. Once I'd put on my dry socks and shoes and forced myself to jump up and down for about ten minutes or so, I gradually began to feel as if life was about to embrace me again.

During the last slog I had largely been oblivious to the threat I faced from the Border Patrol. Indeed, it wasn't until the river was at my back that I would once again pay renewed attention to the action unfolding on the other side. Luckily it had almost died down. All I saw were flashlights, reminding me of Tunisian fireflies, scurrying around the vegetation, presumably in search of somebody — me? A smidgen of amusement, followed by a feeling of triumph surged within me. I was tempted to shout at them that they are making fools of themselves. Instead, I quickly reined in my bubbly feeling. After all, it wasn't over yet, not by a long shot. Fahrenbach had warned me that simply crossing the border, didn't mean all that much, pointing out that FBI agents and military personnel were known to frequently cross into Mexico themselves in their effort to hunt down fugitives. Fully aware that I was still in danger, I went about wringing out my wet underpants and rolling it into my towel. And having shouldered my rucksack, I clenched my teeth, set my jaw and soldiered on.

It didn't take me long, to stumble onto a dirt road. Unfortunately, it was awfully muddy, furrowed by horse tracks as well as deep, water-filled ruts that seemed to have been carved only recently. The previous attempt of people ferrying questionable commodities across the river came to mind. Yet, I neither saw nor heard anything, save for raindrops striking leaves, gurgles and trickles. Staying on the high shoulder, I began trudging downriver in the hope of reaching the Mexican settlement by the name of Ojinaga, or so the map had promised. It was supposed to be located on the south side of the river, opposite of Presidio, close to where the Rio Conchos is swallowed up by the Rio Grande.

I must have covered some four to five kilometers when I came across another large river, which I assumed to be the Rio Conchos. Funny, it appeared to carry even more water than the swollen Rio Grande. Crossing the river on a wooden, ramshackle bridge, I happened to catch sight of a light. It twinkled from the sashless window of a small, brush-thatched adobe dwelling whose stucco had partially crumbled off the wall. There was a big pile of burned garbage next to the entrance. Soon other dwellings loomed, all loosely lashed together by a web of dirt roads, many of them as muddy and filthy as gullies. I first blamed it on the downpour, but it appeared as though most mud walls were naturally slumping, yearning to return to the clay they'd risen from. Seldom had I seen a town that lifeless. I encountered not one soul, a fact that suited me just fine. The only live creatures I came face to face with were stray dogs. Despite my effort to draw a big circle around them, they kept following me, barking and barking on end.

What struck me most about this clutter of primitive dwellings was its scruffy, hand-to-mouth poverty, which reminded me of some areas of Tunisia and Libya. The fact that some huts showed cars parked near their entrances didn't dim that view. What were they but outdated American models that may have been in disrepair? Indeed, a great number of them appeared to be flat-footed, rust-covered wrecks overgrown with weeds and accompanied by worn-out refrigerators and kitchen stoves. This made some neighborhoods look like small-scale junkyards. As I let these images sink in, I began to understand why so many young Mexicans were drawn to the United States.

Eventually I came across a broad artery, the Boulevard Libre Commercio that housed a number of run-down stores, a *tienda,* a liquor store, a taco restaurant, a gas station and, yes, even a motel. Most of them were shut down. I was dead on my feet, and when I saw the motel sign, I stopped. It carried the promising name of 'Casa de Eva' whose gaudy sign portrayed a half-clad bosomy girl with thick, bee-stung lips and a flowing blond mane. I felt very much tempted to rent a room with a comfortable bed in the hope of enjoying a good night's rest. Actually, I had already approached the office when a homunculus inside me taunted me. *You're risking your freedom, possibly your life, for a night of comfort.* Well, I did listen. More than listen. I turned around and trudged on, even raising the stakes by switching to a hidden alley that ran parallel to the boulevard.

At last, I reached the outskirts, where I was greeted by a welcome change. The stores with their garish signs and dilapidated mud shacks gradually scattered in favor of neat adobe farm houses, surrounded by irrigated pastures, harvested fields, large wooden barns and sheds for animals. I followed the arrow that pointed to Chihuahua, located some two hundred kilometers up the road, where Pancho's parents were supposed to live. I hoped and prayed that they'd offer me shelter for a few days at least. After that, things would likely fall into place, or so I trusted.

Yet, the chances of getting there quickly were practically nil, and worst of all, also fraught with danger. The road looked bare and forsaken, its potholes full of water. I didn't even see a single vehicle I could have flagged down. Getting close to exhaustion, I had to find some kind of shelter, ideally a dry, enclosed place where I could catch some sleep. The rain had pretty much wound down by now, and every once in a while, the clouds broke up, letting pale moonlight peek through. Finally, as I staggered past a cotton field, I spotted a small shed with a corrugated iron roof. Luckily, there were no farmsteads nearby, relieving me from being pestered by dogs. Taking the occasion by the forelock, I slipped under the fence and made my way to the shed. It was a muddy, suck-stepping slog, but helped by my flashlight I was able to avoid the worst of the slosh and puddles. Unfortunately, I soon noticed that the shed was already occupied, by no others than two bulls, both of which started to become agitated. They turned around and looked as if they were ready to charge. One of them even stomped, wagged its head and made some throaty noises, while the other actually came toward me. Knowing very little about bovines, I thought it wise to hold myself back and be patient. It worked. Before long both animals calmed down and sauntered off.

An archipelago of cow-pies, softened by the rain to the point of dissolution, crowded the entrance. It reeked, but not as badly as I'd expected. Sloshing through and approaching the shed, I splashed the inside with my beams in the hope of finding a niche where I could build a bunk. Well, I did, indeed, find one, way in the back, behind a trough and hay rack, adjacent to a narrow feed alley. Better yet, there was a gap way on the left that allowed me to squeeze through. Later I noticed that the feed alley even sported its own gate that opened to the outside. And, as the long streak of luck would have it, there was plenty of straw and hay stacked up back there. Within minutes, I had made a comfortable bunk for myself.

Stretching out, I scarfed down a can of beans, a chunk of queso menonita and an apple, basking in my fortune. When I finally stepped outside to take a leak, I noticed that it started to drizzle and, before I had closed my fly, it was coming down hard again, this time as slush, even hail. It was a real squall that sounded like a battering of bullets.

Once under the roof, I took a swig of water and hit the fluff of hay, for the second time in a row. Lying there and listening to the hail pellets hammering the roof, it was time to recapitulate the day. What a whirl it was! What struck me hardest was that horrible mishap, just hours ago. I felt terribly sorry for the guard whose life may have been snuffed out and wondered what I could have done to prevent it. Well, I didn't get very far. Soon fatigue overwhelmed me, robbing me of a possible answer.

A BUMPY ROAD

Once again, it was a hoarse 'Moo, moo, moo' that tore me out of my slumber. My watch reminded me that it was already past eight, meaning that I must have slept more than nine hours. I rose, rubbed my eyes, stretched and opened the gate. A herd of about fifteen cows and the two bulls stood there at a distance of a hundred feet, goggle-eyeing me. The rain and hail had waned and a single beam of sunlight stabbed through an oval window, bright as aluminum. The ground was still soggy and muddy, speckled with dissolving cow pies. While taking a long leak, the heartbreaking incident of last night, raised its fist, again. I had no answer. All I could do was shake my head, sigh and gingerly raise the flag of crass survival. Or was it simple egotism?

Letting my eyes roam the area, I detected a concrete stock tank filled with clean water. So I got my toilet bag and towel, tiptoed over and began scrubbing my face and my body. It felt fresh, like a recall to life.

As I tucked in some bread, a large piece of queso and an apple, I mulled over the itinerary, foremost keeping my safety in mind. Once again, I felt tempted to hitch a ride on the highway again, but then ditched the idea for being too risky, especially during the daytime. I was still too close to the border. Trusting that the worst was already behind me, I browned my face and neck with shoe polish again, glued on my mustache, took my rucksack and struck out toward the west. The clouds had dissipated, swished away by God's mighty hand, and the sun's rays bathed the land anew, adding a fresh, lemon-hued sheen to it.

As I trudged on, the landscape gradually began to change, turning dryer and dryer, more desert-like. Grasses, lanky bushes, dwarfish trees with small pods of agave and yucca plants replaced maize and cotton fields. Farms began to fade away in favor of large cattle ranches, and every once in a while, I saw neat ranch houses with accompanying barns, horse stables and corrals.

A few kilometers west of Ojinaga I encountered a river once again. The map was not detailed enough to show this intersection, but common sense told me that it was the same Rio Conchos I'd crossed before, going east. Having reached the western side, I stopped, pulled the pistol out of my pack and pitched it into the river. I felt relieved getting rid of the last vestige of my painful border crossing.

Since the river meandered pretty much parallel to the highway, I thought it could well be an alternative route for me — one that would not only be attractive but, most importantly, also safer, where I wouldn't have to worry about encountering police or, God forbid, FBI agents. I also assumed that there must be roads that flank the river. Cutting through slabs of up-thrusted layers of limestone and chaotic tumbles of rock, I soon spotted a dirt road that followed the river upstream, staying fairly close to the northern shore. A small sign at an intersection promised that it would lead me to Cuchillo, San Pedro and El Pueblito.

As luck would have it, I soon found myself in the middle of a cultivated, rural landscape that surpassed all my expectations. Fields, fruit orchards and pastures dotted by horses, donkeys, cows, goats and sheep flanked the roads, followed by well-tended adobe farmsteads. The unabashed sunshine helped give the valley a bucolic, pastoral sheen I hadn't seen since the train ride through the Midwest. Nowhere was there any indication that the bloodiest war in history was raging. I came across sturdy, hardworking people who were astride burros or labouring in the fields. Dark-skinned and small in stature, they reminded me of Mesitzos or Indians. They were exceptionally friendly towards me, smiling as if I was some messenger from the beyond, who bouht them good tidings. Since it felt awkward to pass them just with a smile, I usually hollered *"Buenos dias!"*

"Buenos dias," it echoed, usually twice as loud.

As a fugitive POW, I cannot emphasize enough that I found these gestures to be most uplifting, as though the Mexican people had laid out a personal welcome mat for me.

Cuchillo was the first pueblo I happened to enter — gingerly, so as not to arouse any attention. Toward the center of this tiny Santa Fe, near its well-tended adobe church, I came upon taco and fruit stands, as well as a sizable *tienda.* Since I was running low on provisions, I dropped in. The store carried almost everything I needed, including tortillas, queso, small sausages called *chorizos*, chili peppers, canned beans and corn, tomatoes, bananas and, last but not least, *aguacates,* a green, ovoid fruit I had never seen before, much less tasted. And, save for the canned food, everything was not only fresh but also dirt cheap. When the smiling, rotund saleslady had added it all up, my bill ran less than $2. I also looked for a newspaper in the hope of finding a description of what happened last night at the Rio

Grande. But all I saw was a thin, four-page weekly, which carried local news, yet not a word about the border incident.

Having stashed the provisions into my rucksack, I found an idyllic spot on the banks of the Rio Conchos, spread out my poncho, laid out the various edibles and, with lush vegetation and the rushing water of the river in the background, surrendered to my first Mexican feast. And talk about an appetite! I packed in so much that I later had no choice but to yield to a Mexican *siesta,* my first. The only disappointment came with the aguacates. I found them not only hard to chew, but also tasteless, as if eating raw potatoes. I pitched most of them into the river.

When I woke, it was already three o'clock. I still plodded another five kilometers upstream, until I passed an old shack located in a weed patch beyond a rusted barbed wire fence. It stood there all by itself, thirty feet from the banks of the river. Curious, I took a look. It was messy, full of garbage, dog-eared cartons, empty tequila bottles and a skeleton of an animal, presumably a dog. While trying to rid the shed of the trash, particularly the bones, I ran into a little scare. It came in the shape of a scorpion that was hiding under the pelvic bone of the animal. Zapping the critter, I cleaned out the rest of the garbage, picked some grass and heaped up a bunk again. Next, I took my clammy clothes out of my rucksack and hung them up on the willow branches nearby. And listening to my stomach, I treated myself to a light supper, consisting of cold beans, tortillas, tomatoes and green chilis.

Satiated, I gathered the experiences of the last two days in my diary, repeatedly shaking my head at the events that had gone so awry. The shooting of the Border Patrol agent again grieved me deeply. I wondered if he had a family, a wife and children. If so, what would they do in the face of this sudden loss. How could they feed themselves and keep their house warm.

Shortly before sunset, an old man wandered up the river with a self-made fishing rod in hand and a bucket full of fish, earth worms and insects. I tried to talk to him. Although he didn't understand any English, we still managed to communicate, I using my broken Italian, my hands and a repertoire of mimicry. He wanted to know where I came from (*De donde viene?*) and where I was heading to *(Adonde va?)*. But wary of divulging too much, I acted as though I couldn't understand him.

Weary — my legs felt like lead stumps — I was ready to call it a day. I shuffled back to my shack and, having relieved myself, stretched out. The fragrance of my grassy bed reminded me of Mesilla and, by extension, also of my years as a youngster in the Hitler Youth. It was as quiet as in a tomb, except for some dogs that barked far, far away into the night. At first, I slept like a marmot. It must have been around midnight when I was aroused by a high glissando of intertwined whines and howls that soon swelled to a chorus. I assumed it was a social gathering of a species of wolves. Straining my ears, I listened with abandon to their wild and feral message. It was a chorus of nature that reminded me of the howling of wolves in the steppes and woods of Russia. (Later I was told they were coyotes.)

As I tried to get back to sleep, I felt a weak rumbling in my stomach and my intestines. At first, I paid little attention, trusting that it would go away by itself. But it showed no sign of budging. Quite the contrary, it intensified, spiking in wild throbbings and heavings, followed by bouts of nausea. I quickly jumped off my bunk and rushed out, and not a second too soon. It burst out of both ends, with an explosive force that scared me out of my wits. For all I know, I must have crouched there for more than an hour until I'd shat and spat out all the tortillas, beans, cheese, tomatoes, chilis and whatever else I had downed the past day or two. In the end I was left with nothing but the bitter taste of bile in my mouth, accompanied by a blasting headache and a crippling weakness.

Full in the grip of misery and wretchedness, I crawled back into my shed and tried to rest and, if possible, go back to sleep. Instead, I ended up on a wild goose chase. Time dragged on and on. The night showed no sign of ending. At last, a thin crack of dawn inched over the eastern horizon. Yet the misery showed no sign of waning. Forget about ingesting anything; even nibbling on tortillas or bland cheese made me retch again. All I could do was to drink water, and more water. Unfortunately, by noon I was running out of it. So squeezing the last ounce of strength out of my body, I got on my feet, shouldered my rucksack and step by step dragged myself to San Pedro, the next village. It was more than five kilometers up the road, too far for a body wrung with agony. Fierce headwinds further aggravated the slog. Yet I made it, albeit with long pauses along the way, when I was close to fainting. Mercifully, the village also had a small *tienda* that sold water out of a large dispenser, where I could fill my canteens and pay by the liter.

MY FIRST MEXICAN MENACE

Wary of my physical limits, I staggered my way back to the shack, where I stretched out again. Mercifully, I was able to doze off for a few hours. In the late afternoon two ten-to-twelve-year-old boys dropped by, peeking into my shack. I talked to them using my Italian, English and my mimicry. They wanted to know where I'm from. I was very wary, afraid of revealing too much. I was all the more dumbfounded, when less than three hours later a local cop shows up. He caught me slouching, covered with my blanket up to my neck.

"Oh brother!" I sighed to myself. *"That's all I need!"*

Here he stood with the swagger of a bantam cock confronting a rival, a stout, five-foot *mestizo*, whose face was marred by a long scar that raced from his mouth all the way to his left eye. He was decked out with a big sombrero and a uniform that glittered with an exuberance of badges and insignias. He also sported a broad bandolier around his chest stuffed with bullets and a silver-plated, quick-draw holster that cushioned a heavy colt with a pair of shackles dangling from it.

With my hands under the blanket, I fumbled to find my horseshoe.

He instantly pulled his colt, shouting, "Manos arriba!"

I jerked up and raised my hands.

"Hablo espagnol?" he barked at me, a frown on his face, as he stepped forward.

"No!"

"Where you from?"

"Switzerland."

"Switzerland?"

I explained to him in English that I was a Swiss naturalist who was studying the fauna and flora of the Chihuahuan desert, but that I fell ill because I'd ingested some spoiled food.

"B-b-bacteria! G-g-gastro!" I stuttered, fishing for words and pointing to my stomach. I hoped he'd be indulgent toward me. I also identified myself, showing him the papers Fahrenbach had faked.

But instead of looking at them, he ordered me to stand up and raise my hands, then with a raised finger he jumped down my throat in a hot crackbrained drumroll of a lecture, crammed with the sound of Rs that

120

reminded me of a mad crow in defense of a juicy morsel. Once done, he pulled out a warrant jam-packed with mug-shots. Next, he began scrutinizing my face, my eyes, my hair, only to go back to his mugshots. He repeated this process several times, his mimicry covering the whole gamut from wrinkle-browed seriousness to breaking out in smiles — sleazy smiles, his lips had forgotten before they reach the eyes. Worse, with his hand fumbling his holster, he often displayed a sense of pleasure, even smugness, like a cat pawing a frightened canary.

All this was unmitigated torture. I was scared out of my wits. *Now he's got me!* I kept thinking. Yet, all of a sudden — had my horseshoe smiled at a miracle? — he folded the warrant, stuck it into his jacket and started checking my papers.

"Oh, suizo!" he suddenly fluted with a broad smile.

Somehow, they must have impressed him because he pushed up his lower lip and nodded repeatedly. *"No gringo?"* he asked, wiggling his head.

"No, suizo!"

"You come from *Estados Unidos?"*

I nodded.

"Sus documentos, pasaporte, por favor."

I once again showed him the faked papers, adding "That's all I have. *Todos!"*

"No forma migratoria?"

"Lo siento. But they told me at the border in Ojinaga that I don't need this as long as I stay close to the border."

"Who say that?"

"A Mexican custom official," I feigned.

He shook his head. *"Estar incorrecto!* 'Rrong! You khave guns?" He spit out the words like a mouthful of curdled cream.

"No."

He told me to turn around and put my hands up, so he could search me. He also checked my rucksack and the hay of my bedding. Not finding a weapon, he bounced back to the *pasaporte* and the *forma migratoria.* "You break law. I arrest you."

"Arrest me? For a piece of paper?"

"Yes, you break law!"

Acting as though he loosened the shackles from his holster, he suddenly paused and then put his fist under his chin, as if he were racking his brains.

121

"But me *sympatico con usted.* You Swiss *sientifico.* Me help you. You khave — dollars?"

I nodded, then slowly pulled my wallet out of my pocket and handed him three dollars.

He shook his head. *"No basta! Mas!"* (Not enough! More!)

I added another two dollars.

He smiled broadly. *"Bienvenidos en Mexico. Buena salud! Feliz viaje!"* he yelped and, adopting his cocky swagger again, made his way back to the road.

Oh, my Lord, was I relieved. *Praise to the sinister practice of bribery.* I meant it. After all, it saved me; it offered me nothing less than another shot at freedom. Yet, while I was still savoring the momentary mental lift, I saw the cop turning around and strutting back. I braced for more trouble. *What in the hell is he up to now?* I wondered. But when I noticed a broad smile on his face, I felt somewhat eased.

"Se me olvido." (I forgot.) "You sick?" he said, touching his belly. *"Necesito un medico?"*

"Si."

"Me know Yolanda. *Ella es una maravillosa curandera.* She khelp you, *problemas gastricas?"*

"Si."

"She come, OK?"

"Si, muchas gracias."

The police, your friend and helper? Could there be a shred of truth in that German saying? In the meantime, I was still stuck in my misery. Since any attempt to eat something, and may it simply be a plain tortilla, would have caused me to retch and vomit, the only measure I could take was to drink water, and more water. I knew from our experiences in North Africa that my intestinal havoc was in all likelihood caused by some sinister bug and if I'd stay hydrated it would eventually be flushed out.

MY CURANDERA

Dead-tired, I stretched out again and dozed off. Half an hour later I was torn out of my slumber by a knock. Raising my head, I was able to make out the face of an old, shriveled woman peeking in at the entrance. The reddish-brown color of her skin, high cheekbones and the folds of her eyes made me guess that she was of Indian extraction. She wore a hand-woven vestment of burlap and linen that made her look simple, but dignified.

"Buenos dias, yo soy Yolanda, una curandera," she introduced herself, a bit stingy with her smile. *"Tienes un dolor de estomago y intestinos? Me puede ayudar."* (I can help you.)

"No hablo espanol," I replied, smiling and raising my hands, palms upward.

"No hablo ingles," she retorted, giving me a measured smile.

I threw off my blanket and rose.

She grabbed her large leather bag, stepped up to me and drew a line down her belly, then palpated it and mimicked an explosion, even pursing her lips and imitating the sound of a wet whistle. *"Tienes diarrea?"*

"Diarrea? Si, si!" I flashed back, overjoyed that I was able to catch that pivotal word. Or was it her mimicry?

She nodded, then stepped outside again to gather some rocks, twigs and branches. And within minutes she had built a small fireplace and lit a fire. Having rolled up her sleeves, she cracked open her bag, grabbed something and tossed it into the fire. Seconds later a balmy scent of incense hit my nostrils, uplifting me. Next, she rummaged up a copper bowl, a large glass, a canteen, a bottle filled with a liquid and several bags. With a flourishing sleight of hand, she poured water into the bowl and, having set it on the fire and stirring it, sprinkled it with herbs, roots from the bags and liquid out of the bottle. Once the concoction had come to a boil, she let it cool down, poured it into the glass and urged me to drink it. Aside from the encroaching darkness, the smoke of the fire and the fragrant vapor rising from the bowl, the whole ceremony was embedded in a spiritual soundscape of murmurs and chants of cryptic sequences *(Indian?)* that left me spellbound, *me,* a former Nazi who'd never even shaken hands with a protestant pastor.

Following the ceremony, she told me to lie down on my grass bedding, unbuckle my belt and lower my pants and underpants, short of exposing my genitals. Having warmed her hands, she dripped some fragrant oil into her palms and began massaging my belly, chanting intermittently. It felt most comforting and soothing.

That was the end of her spell. She wished me a good night's rest. *"Buena salud!"* she fluted and, promising she'd be back tomorrow morning, shuffled away.

Still befuddled from the ritual, especially its spiritual spin of it all, I took a leak and then stretched out and cuddled myself on my grass bedding. With Lady Luck hovering over me, I dozed off instantly and slept through until the crack of dawn lit up the shack.

Emerging from my sleep, I didn't know where I was. There was something unreal, chimerical about me and my place on this earth, as if I were doped. Only gradually, step by step, did I regain my footing. I tried to recall the events of last night, the image of Yolanda murmuring her chants as she stirred a concoction. I conjured up scenes of witchcraft I'd read about as a kid, losing myself in the labyrinthine world of Grimm's fairy tales. Worried, I called myself to order, switching back to the episode of Yolanda massaging my belly, which still had an oily sheen. I touched it. Amazingly it felt sound, almost normal. Even a hint of hunger began to stir. It wasn't until I got up and tried to walk to the river that some lingering remnants of yesterday's misery made themselves felt. Not only did I feel drained but my body ached as though it had gone through the wringer.

Having washed myself, all in slow motion, I fetched two tortillas and a slice of queso and began to eat, very deliberately, with extended pauses of chewing. After all, I hadn't eaten anything for more than thirty-six hours. Yet the food stayed in, miraculously so! With yesterday's exhausting slog to the village still in my bones, I had no illusions concerning my physical condition. So I hunkered down, hoping I could perhaps continue my trek tomorrow, or the day after, depending on how fast I could bounce back. Thankfully I didn't feel pressed for time. Nobody was expecting me. Nor was there any other reason that nagged me to leave. I considered myself to be relatively safe, safer than any time since I'd left the camp. While I continued to think that the border was still too close for comfort, I felt heartened by the way yesterday's encounter with the cop had ended. It had been the first real test in Mexico. And had I not passed it? So what if I lost a few dollars? It was still a bargain. I bagged a valuable stock — knowledge. That there was such a thing as a Mexican magic wand, a key that would unlock the toughest door — *mordida.*

Shortly past nine, Yolanda came tip-toeing toward my shack again. I was leaning against a willow close to the banks of the river, working on my diary, and yes, woolgathering.

"*Buenos dias, Yolanda,*" I cheered. "*Mi curandera milagrosa.*"

I hugged her and pecked both of her cheeks.

She smiled.

"*Com'esta usted?*" she beckoned softly, as if a starving mouse had piped an apology.

"*Bien!*"

Overjoyed that I was doing well, she handed me a bag, telling me (and mimicking) that I should make ample use of these *hierbas* whenever I'd encounter gastro-intestinal problems. That at least seemed to be her drift. In addition, she volunteered to give me some advice on how to avoid an intestinal *infeccion*. Unfortunately, most of what she said was well beyond my ability to grasp. Baffled, she pointed to my rucksack and pulled down her lower eyelid. Finally, it dawned on me, she wanted to see my provisions. And when I showed her the green chili peppers and the tomatoes, she warned me that I should wash them well before eating and that I should be careful with hot peppers.

Needless to say, I felt greatly indebted to my gentle healer and at the end, I offered her a gift of $5 for her services. But she wouldn't take more than a single George Washington. Before we parted, she insisted on giving me a solemn blessing.

I stayed at the shack for another day, the seventh day since I'd left the camp. It was hard to believe that it had only been a week since my journey began. Somehow it felt as if I'd been on the road for several months already. Thanks to Yolanda's help, the recuperation was right on track and by evening of the 17th of September I had pretty much regained my old strength. I was ready to push on, come tomorrow.

The light was seeping out of the day. After catching up on my diary using my flashlight. I still boiled some water from the river to fill my canteens and to wash the tomatoes and chili peppers. At peace with myself and the world, I hit the hay, pulled the blanket up to my chin and fell into a slumber, so deep I didn't even hear any coyotes howling, if howling they did.

J. EDGAR HOOVER'S CLAWS

After a long trek, stained as it was by a nasty run-in with a bunch of *zorillos* skunks, I finally wound my way into Chihuahua, a colonial city and the capital of Mexico's biggest state. My diary recorded the 27th of November, shortly before the sun disappeared behind the Sierra Madre Occidental. Everything had proceeded according to plan, rousing another batch of gratitude in me. And having reached a city so far away from the border — it was almost four hundred kilometers to El Paso! — made me feel so much freer and more secure. Actually, I got so carried away by the thought of melting into the anonymous crowd that I even saw myself dropping my false identity.

Stopping at the first big intersection, I pulled out the slip with the names and address of Pancho's parents and showed it to an older, tottering gentleman with a stooping gait and a cane.

"Con permiso, senor, donde esta — Calle numero diez?" I asked.

"Calle diez?" he said. *"Esta...* You speeka *ingles, no?"*

"Yes."

"Lo siento, Calle diez, esta on other side, *oest."* He pointed toward the west. *"Aqui,* kheer, *este. Comprendo?"*

"On the other side of the city."

"Esta lejos de aqui. You teike bus *Numero seis.* OK?"

I nodded. *"Muchas gracias, senor!"*

It was already too late to pay Pancho's parents a visit. Nor was I in the mood. My appearance, let's be honest, was not likely to evoke trust, much less liking. Sadly, I looked like a tramp — grimy, scruffy and grungy. My unshaved face reminded me of a hedgehog that had just emerged from a dense thicket. Nor had that foul smell completely left me. I was sure, my friend's parents would have been taken aback had they seen me in my present state. Keeping all that in mind, I resolved to spruce myself up first. So I decided to check into 'El Torbellino', one of the first little hotels at the northwestern outskirts. It was a nondescript place, other than being painted in a stunningly bright blue, as if it hoped to pull the sky down to earth. A promise?

"You look for room?" the middle-aged lady who stirred behind the reception desk asked me with a gruff tone of voice. She had a torso like a whiskey barrel and cheeks like small pumpkins that quivered as she spoke. Looking daggers, she'd measure me from top to toe, while maudlin *ranchera* tunes kept bleeding from a background radio.

My looks, no doubt! I figured. And her nose may likely have picked up the unpleasant remnant from the smell oozing from my rucksack and possibly from my clothes, too. In any event, her mien signaled to me that she had already shoved me into the lowest of her drawers. The *senora's* unsavory reaction aside, I was pleased that she spoke some English.

"How much is a room?" I pressed.

"One night, one dollar, ten centavos. You pay now, OK?"

"OK," I nodded and handed her the money.

"*Numero cinco,* five," she snapped, swiping a key from a pegboard and waving me to follow her.

It was a very small room with a narrow bed and nightstand and an adjacent bathroom that was so tiny I could hardly turn. As I entered, a stale, slightly fetid smell rose up my nostrils. Yet, from all I could tell, everything I needed seemed to be in place. No blue heaven, but for one dollar, who'd want to quibble? Anyway, I thanked the lady and made myself comfortable.

I first took a shower. The water was tepid, the plumbing wretched, pitiful. I tried to turn the lever for *caliente* (warm) and it fell right off. I also shaved, cut my hair and washed my clothes, although in tepid water. Now fresh and fragrant, I turned toward my basic bodily needs. Taking a knife, I tackled my first mango, then munched on canned beans, a chunk of queso, corn tortillas and green chilis, all of which I downed with a bottle of Mexican beer. Finally, having caught up with my diary, I hit the sack and drifted off. The Cantina resembled a beehive that had just been stirred up by an unlicked beekeeper. It was so crammed with customers that I hardly found a seat. Little wonder. The hearty breakfast of *huevos rancheros*, eggs and scoops of pintos all smothered with a zesty salsa couldn't have flattered the palate more. While tackling the beans, I began wondering how the Mexicans, who downed beans like we Germans do potatoes, avoided making themselves unpleasantly conspicuous in public. *Are they perhaps anatomically different? Do they have different bowels, longer intestines, handed down to them by their Indian ancestors? Or do they have some hidden magic I was not privy to?*

Once back at the Torbellino, I gathered my things, heaved my rucksack onto my shoulders and began striding in the direction of downtown. I made my way through the streets, plazas and parks, past precocious mansions, all the way to the historic heart. I was struck by the color and glitter. People, even the beggars, were dressed in bright-hued, often showy clothes, decked out with glittering junk-silver jewelry. I saw many women wearing flowing polka-dotted skirts, ruffled, flowery blouses and headscarves. Mexicans obviously treasure bold colors, I concluded, flamboyant pageantry and theatrical presentations.

Being in dire need of pesos, I walked into the next bank, where I exchanged $20 into pesos. I got a wad of bank notes and coins. *What a flimsy currency, especially when compared to the dollar!* Having noticed in the cantina that some people had turned up their noses at me, I first sought out a drugstore where I intended to buy a bottle of perfume. Unfortunately, all I could find was a lavender fragrance for *senoras*. Regardless, I grabbed it and liberally sprinkled myself, hoping to drown that godawful smell. Only later did it dawn on me that I must have smelled like an *hombre,* a regular customer of whorehouses.

Curious to find out if there was any news about the border, as well as the war, I also picked up the local newspaper, the *Diario de Chihuahua* and a de rigueur — a Spanish-English dictionary. In search of a quiet place, I decided to head to the central park, *El Palomar,* where a bench promptly invited me. I had barely taken a seat and unfolded my paper when I was besieged by swarms of urchins and beggars. *"Senor, dame dineros, por favor,"* they'd keep on pestering me. Having finally fended them off, I was badgered by a bevy of women who kept pushing trinkets, home-made dolls, attractively painted pottery and little baskets. Most of them were poor folks, Indians or mestizos who didn't even have the means to afford leather shoes; they came either barefoot or in *huaraches,* cowhide sandals, although some were made out of sisal or used car tires.

One of them, a stocky young wench, who was hawking cute little hand-made baskets all strung up with a rope, was particularly persistent. Wearing a richly embroidered white blouse and a blue flower cup skirt, she was endowed with shiny reddish-brown skin, fiery eyes, rows of white teeth, all framed by raven-black hair that hung down in tight plaits. *"Cestas hermosas, cestas hermosas!"* she'd keep purring. Noticing me glancing at one of her baskets with an oblique randing that dangled way at the bottom, she dealt me an alluring smile while pointing to the object of my interest. Yet, as she shifted her hips and bent down to reach for the basket, her right breast unwittingly bobbed out of her blouse, almost brushing my face. Saluting its owner, it was a most shapely specimen, whose dark-brown areola with its uneven seam and its light nipple left me spellbound.

The wench met my reaction with a grin. Unfazed, she straightened up, waited a few seconds and, using her free hand, casually shoved her gem back into the blouse again. Then she pushed the basket into my face and

128

cracked a smile. *"Diez pesos — te lo vento barato, senor!"* (Ten pesos — you can't buy cheaper, sir) she piped holding out her palm.

Mesmerized, I pulled out my wallet and handed her a limp bill of pesos. It wasn't until much later that I began to fancy that she might well have been a hooker and that the baskets a mere pretext she used to lure me. But I quickly took it back, with a hint of shame, no less.

Presumably encouraged by the sale, more vendors and beggars showed up. Pretty soon I was so besieged that I felt strangled. I couldn't even read a line, much less a paragraph. Indeed, I had no choice but to get up and buzz off. Eventually I found a small cafe where I could find some peace. I ordered a cup of coffee and some *dulces* (sweets).

Since the place wasn't very busy, the waitress didn't mind me taking my time leafing through the paper. Hell, I even tried to read some news clips aided by the dictionary. It was an arduous, wearisome task that tested my patience like no other. I might mention, there was one news item in particular that struck me. It dealt with the war, more specifically the Russian front. It stated that the Red Army had liberated Smolensk. *Which meant of course another blow to our once so glorious German Army!* That touched a soft spot. Newsreel images of us taking Smolensk in the fall of 1942 came to mind. There was only one solace: the defeat could only shorten the bloodshed.

Heading for the bathroom, I went past a counter with a whole stack of *Diarios*. Among them were older copies, more than a week old. On the way back, I picked up a few and hopscotched through them. Once again, the issues were too local to arouse my attention, save for the one of September 16th. It happened to contain a longer report about Mexico's northern border, dealing with the smuggling of marijuana across the Rio Bravo near Ojinaga. Way at the end it also touched on the mysterious killing of a border guard — yes, he died! — that took place on the night of the 13th of September. While the investigation of the incident by the FBI had apparently not yet been concluded, preliminary reports leaked to the press hinted that the likely murderer was Fritz Graf, a German POW who had escaped from the prison camp near Murphy, Colorado, on September 11th. According to eyewitnesses, Fritz Graf had later crossed the Rio Bravo into Mexico. There was a warrant out for his arrest on both sides of the border. Anybody who had any information about his whereabouts should immediately contact the Federal Police. The reward for his capture had been increased from $250 to $5,000. Attached was a warning: He's armed and highly dangerous.

I was struck dumb. The article confirmed the worst of my fears — standing accused of murder by the FBI and facing arrest. *What a blow! The worst of all possible outcomes.* The most dreadful and unexpected aspect was J. Edgar Hoover's reach across the border, at least into Chihuahua. It dashed my hope of finding a safe haven in this northern Mexican city. But there was little I could do, except be very watchful and keep doing what I had done since my escape. And that included changing my appearance to remain incognito and avoiding the cops.

Set, I instantly seized the bull by the horns: I grabbed my rucksack and headed back to the lavatory. Just to be sure, I locked the door, then dug up my shoe polish and began smearing it generously on my face, neck and hands. Next, I opened the dye bottle and began washing more pigment into my locks. To complete the job, I also glued on the mustache and the eyebrows. A final check in the mirror: not perfect, by a long shot, but pretty good, the best I could do. While I was far from looking like a real, dyed-in-the-wool Mexican, I came closer than ever. Most importantly, I had tweaked my appearance to the point, where the POW mugshot J. Edgar Hoover had of me could only partially identify me. Incidentally, the Mexican straw hat I picked up minutes later to shade my head with was no more than icing on the cake.

PANCHO'S PARENTS

In the early afternoon I caught the bus to the home of Pancho's parents. It sat far out on the western outskirts, a little south of the *Cerro Grande*, where the expanding city had chopped its way into the surrounding desert. It was a very modest, pitch-roofed adobe dwelling that was surrounded by a few fruit trees and large clay pots from which a riot of geraniums and petunias spilled almost to the ground. Spiny ocotillo sticks tightly knit together with wire girded the whole plot.

As I approached the wooden gate, dogs started barking furiously. I rang a small bell that hung down from a gallow-like contraption. An older, grey-haired gentleman with beady eyes, pushed down by a pair of bristly, grayish-black brows, stepped out of the door, shouting something at the dogs, which instantly stopped barking.

"Con quien hablo?" (Who are you?) he inquired, as he approached the gate. He eyed me with a skeptical mien.

"Con Fritz, senor. Yo soy un amigo con Pancho en Colorado." (I'm a Pancho's friend from Colorado.) I should stress that at that time I still used my real name.

"Oh, me conto acerca de usted," he said, smiling. *"Aleman?"*

"Si."

"Me llamo Francisco, Francisco Gutierrez."

"Mucho gusto."

He squeezed open a squeaky gate. We shook hands. He had the grip of a blacksmith, even though the small finger was missing. *"Bienvenido en Chihuahua.* Welcome."

Watching the flanges of his nose, I noticed that he'd picked up my lavender scent. But he didn't mention it. Instead, he motioned me to follow him, up the steps into his home. We entered a small living room that was jammed with dark, wooden furniture of a heavy and massive feel, among them a bulky sofa, two sturdy armchairs and an imposing sideboard that displayed a good number of photographs, presumably of the family. Above the sofa hung a picture of a smoking volcano, and in the right-hand corner, elevated on a pedestal, stood a large, four foot high statue of the Virgin of Guadalupe, the Mexican Holy Mary.

Having offered me a seat in one of the bulky armchairs, Francisco hollered something at Erlinda, his wife, who must have been busy in the kitchen. She instantly rushed in to join us. She was a small, stocky woman without any noticeable hips, all stem from the shoulders down. Her high cheek bones and slightly slit eyes pointed to an Indian or mestizo extraction.

Francisco introduced me, stressing that I was a friend of Pancho's, an *Aleman*. She acted shyly, almost subserviently, even dropping a halfhearted curtsy when she shook my hand.

"You like coffee, *cafe Mexicano?*" he asked me.

I nodded vigorously.

While Erlinda left for the kitchen, he insisted on giving me a tour of their tiny home, whose floor plan barely covered seven hundred square feet. They had built it just three years ago, partially with the money Pancho had sent them from *los Estados Unidos.* Although the home was connected to the electric grid, there was no running water. However, just last year they had installed a manual pump behind the house that supplied them with the needed water for their personal hygiene, cooking and for watering the garden, although it wasn't quite enough for a flushing toilet.

He also showed me both the front and back ward emphasizing that he and Erlinda were very fond of gardening. It was a tough task because of the dry desert climate and the poor, alkaline soil. Besides the roses, some of which were still in bloom, he and Erlinda cultivated various flowers, not to mention an array of vegetables, beans, squash, potatoes and tomatoes. He claimed that during the past few years their harvests had been so bountiful that, during the spring and summer seasons, they could sell most of their vegetables for good money at the local market. Although now, being the end of fall, most beds lay fallow.

Flattered by my praise, Francisco chatted non-stop. He spoke a very broken English, which he picked up during a one-year stint in the fields of California's Central Valley near Fresno. That was in the early thirties. But, having not practiced it for more than ten years, it was very strenuous for him and he invariably kept on sliding into Spanish, or a funny mix. Still, I understood most of what he said. Watching his body language helped.

Yet, there was more to come. Making his way beyond the vegetable beds, Francisco also wanted me to take a look at their chicken coop which sheltered about fifteen chickens. They lay eggs every day, he claimed, enough to sell some of them to their neighbors. Next to the chicken coop, there was a small stable where they raised three goats.

When we got back to the house, Erlinda had already set the coffee table in the living room. She had brewed a robust, dark-roasted coffee with beans that grew in the highlands of Chiapas near the Guatemalan border. As for the cream, she offered goat milk, which gave the coffee a curious, slightly feral flavor. She also served some home-made cookies. Though buttery, they tasted cloyingly sweet, like most of the Mexican 'dulces'.

Both Francisco and Erlinda were eager to hear how Pancho was doing, if he was healthy and in a good mood, how he liked his work, if he had a girlfriend and when he would come back to visit them. After I had given them my impressions in a sputtering hotchpotch of Spanglish, livened up with plenty of gestures and mimicry, Francisco repeatedly itched to draw me into a discussion about the United States.

"Como gusto los Estados Unidos?" (How do you like the United States?) he wanted to know. But no sooner had I made an effort to say something cheerful about the American way of life than he furrowed his whiskered eyebrows, crumpled his chin and, cutting me off, tried to answer the question himself. Initially I thought he simply might be impatient while listening to my stuttering. But as he went on and on, I became ever more convinced that he was set to get something off his chest that touched him very deeply. He became so impassioned and high-pitched that Erlinda, feeling embarrassed, repeatedly reminded him to calm down, a gesture that seemed to whip him up even more.

Incidentally, since he began to slide more and more into Spanish, I failed to understand a large part of what he said. But I got the gist of it. In any event, Francisco made it quite clear that he was anything but fond of the big neighbor to the north, which to him was a soulless giant who valued only money. He had an unpleasant penchant for blaming the troubles of the world on it. According to him the United States was one of the most arrogant, imperial countries the world had ever witnessed. All the gringos want is to dominate the world, and Mexico in particular. To him they were nothing but scoundrels and thieves, claiming that they had already stolen two thirds of the Mexican land mass, a territory in the western United States reaching all the way from Texas to the Canadian border. Curious as it may seem, he sided with none other than Hitler and us Germans, blasting Mexico for becoming allies of the United States. He called President Camacho who helped to negotiate this alliance a *faldero* of Roosevelt, a lapdog. Acting on the premise that the enemy of my enemy is my friend, he claimed that most Mexicans feel the same way, and that Hitler was a courageous leader, and challenging the United States was the right thing to do. He badly wanted him to win, although at the moment it didn't look as if he could. But if ever Hitler's going to be defeated, it is because of the prowess of the Russians, not the Americans. To make things short, Francisco praised us Germans as

133

if they were the most trustworthy, smartest and heroic people the world had ever seen.

I sat there, agape, out of my wits. Never had I heard any foreigner uttering such accolades about Germany. It appeared as if Hans was batting the breeze. Actually, it was none other than Fahrenbach who had already alluded to the widespread sympathies many Mexicans were showing for our cause. And Francisco squarely echoed what the diehard Nazis in Berlin, as well as those at the camp claimed all along. What he said seemed so incredulous that there were moments when I thought that he wanted to demonstrate to me that he was on my side, or at least against my former captors, the Americans. I couldn't help it, in the end I came away with the conviction that his fondness for anything German might well have served as a stalking horse for his anti-Americanism.

Having finally shed what was rubbing him, he asked me if I was hungry. When I nodded, he nudged Erlinda to prepare some supper. While she was busy in the kitchen, he offered me some *pulque*, an agave drink. It was so different from anything I ever had tasted before and it took a few swigs to get a feel for it. Sipping his pulque, Francisco was curious to know what led me to come to Mexico. I skimmed over my escape from the POW camp. Instead, I tried to convince him that I came here to get to know the country and its people, to study their customs and culture, including the Indians. He was impressed and honored, claiming that Mexico was a fertile ground for doing studies of that sort.

"We have a rich culture here," he emphasized. "It's much richer than the gringo culture up north. You will find more than you expect, much more."

He added that in case I needed shelter, I could always stay with them. He regretted that he couldn't offer me a bedroom, but I could sleep either right here on the sofa in the living room, or on a narrow bed in the toolshed that was attached to the house.

Since I showed interest in the toolshed, he was quick to show it to me. It was a primitive shack, crowded with all kinds of garden tools, pots, lumber, as well as bundles of fragrant herbs that were suspended from the ceiling. Still, I found it preferable to the living room. More importantly, it would give me some privacy. The lack of a bathroom or toilet was quickly solved: Francisco handed me two buckets, one for clean water, the other for waste.

For supper, Erlinda served tasty enchiladas and beans, apparently leftovers from their lunch. Francisco once again came back to his pet peeve — *los Estados Unidos*. Knowing what he would say, I feigned fatigue and

134

left for the tool shed, where I worked on my diary for more than an hour, until I hit the sack. At first, I slept soundly for an hour, until I was torn out of my slumber by rustlings. *Must be rodents, mice perhaps.* When I turned on the light, the rustling stopped. But as soon as I turned it off again, it started all over again. It was very annoying. I knew of no way to stop them. It looked as though it was a nuisance I had to live with.

When, in the morning, I mentioned it to Francisco, he apologized and suggested that we bait some mouse traps. He promptly brought three of them, cut up some bacon and, after baiting them, set them up in the shed. In the meantime, Erlinda had prepared a sumptuous breakfast, consisting of eggs, beans with green chilis, tortillas, goat cheese and coffee. I relished all of it. Seldom had I tasted food that was so garden fresh and hearty, and I told them so.

THE UNEXPECTED

After breakfast, Francisco suggested that he'd like to show me the town, which he praised as one of the cleanest, most prosperous, culturally progressive municipalities in all of Mexico. "It's not only the capital of Mexico's largest state," he stressed, "but it also has a fascinating history." He emphasized that Chihuahua was the capital of *Nuevo Espana's Provincia Internas,* which stretched from California to Texas and south to Sinaloa and Coahuila.

Half an hour later, we sauntered about the Plaza de Armas, Chihuahua's historic heart. It happened to be dominated by such architectural show pieces as the huge, baroque Metropolitan Cathedral and a neoclassical City Hall. Both seemed to be erected to impress, even intimidate the populace. As I stood there squinting at them, I felt a deep urge to commiserate with the average Mexican citizen who surely must feel humbled, even crushed, by these overbearing heavyweights.

Thankfully, the plaza itself paid little attention to them. It was in the grip of pulsating vitality, of color, the din and the hustle and bustle of life. The warm and beaming Sunday undoubtedly helped drawing out the people. We walked past rows of vendors, shoe-shiners, beggars, ranchers and cowboys in large Western hats and floppy sombreros, all surrounded by flocks of pigeons. At one point we stopped to watch Mariachi musicians who, wrapped in dashing, black, silver-buttoned suits, were abuzz, playing saccharine trumpets and weeping violins in tunes about forlorn love.

Drawing closer to the huge cathedral we couldn't avert our eyes from four faithfuls who, down on their knees, their skin torn to the bones, pushed their way to the portal. One of them, wearing a crown made of cacti, mercilessly flayed himself with a scourge spiked with spines. He was outdone by a cripple who, clad in blood-stained sackcloth, carried a huge, three-meter-long cross, made of branches of thorny cacti strapped to his back.

"Penitentes!" Francisco sniffed, shaking his head with contempt. *"Loco, loco."*

In the same breath my host praised the cathedral as one of the outstanding examples of colonial architecture in Mexico, comparable to the finest in Europe and far more artistic than any church north of the Rio

Bravo. Since out on the plaza, it had turned more than toasty, we were drawn to the cool, cavernous inside. Here the air was heavy with incense and the somber sounds of an organ composition, as well as the breaths and sweat of more than four hundred and fifty believers who crammed the benches. Many of them murmured prayers, an anathema to Francisco who claimed to be a staunch atheist. We took seats as well, if only to cool down and rest our legs. While we sat there, way in the back, Francisco couldn't help making disparaging remarks about Catholicism, as well as the statue of the Virgen de Guadalupe in his own living room, quickly emphasizing that he tolerated it for the simple reason that it kept the peace in the home.

Upon Francisco's suggestion we walked up Avenida Juarez, the most representative boulevard of the town. Its sidewalks teemed with vendors belting out their offerings to passersby, couples, ladies and girls strolling arm in arm, older gentlemen bent over their canes, mothers with strollers, toddlers and kids, beggars holding out tin cans or open palms, you name it. The boulevard was jammed with *paisanos* on rattling carts cracking whips at their burros, perennially honking American cars, and huge buses and trucks that spewed out billows of smoke into the air. The traffic was hopelessly congested, and every once in a while, it came to a complete standstill. Sweating, we stopped at a pulque stand, where I treated Francisco to a glass of that curious, habit-forming drink. It was a quiet eddy in the runnel of life.

Beyond the curb, a two-horse landau, carrying two elegantly dressed couples, came to a squeaking halt. *"Hacendados ricos,"* (Rich landowners) Francisco snapped, pulling back his mouth. "The revolution should have done away with them. But they're always coming back."

Their spruced-up, handsome horses, taking advantage of the pause, unplugged the pucker of their anuses and began dropping a whole chain of steaming globoids onto the pavement — an act that caused the ladies to turn up their noses, while the men lightheartedly chortled it away.

"As a boy I couldn't wait to gather these steamy balls and spread them over our garden," Francisco commented, laughing heartily.

"So did we back in Germany," I added. "We would never sneer at a shovel of free fertilizer. It does wonders for the vegetables and flowers."

"I know what you're talking about. We have a neighbor who has four horses, and every other week Erlinda and I grab our wheelbarrow and head over there to load up on manure. I've worked tons of it into our soil."

Just as the traffic began moving again, Francisco grabbed me by the arm. "Look, Fred," he said, pointing to a Jeep and a green limousine that followed the carriage. "That's what I was talking about yesterday."

137

I stood there dumbstruck, overwhelmed by a gush of panic. Both vehicles were not only American, they actually belonged to the United States Army and were crammed with American officers.

"What in the hell is the American Army doing here?" Francisco hissed. "Are we not a sovereign country? See, that's what I don't like about our political leaders. These damn gringos treat us as if this was their own backyard."

He hawked up a thick lump of slobber and, resorting to a curious twist of his tongue, hurled it so it spiraled to the ground.

By the way, I wholeheartedly agreed with Francisco, if for no other than my selfish reasons. The Mexicans were far too cowering, indeed, toadying toward the United States. I, for one, wouldn't mind at all if they took a much tougher stance and told them to mind their own business.

If anything, this last incident was yet another rude wake-up call, reminding me once again that it was foolish to lull myself with a false sense of security. It would behoove me to stay and move in the shadows, even deep within Mexico, peeking over my shoulder and keeping my eyes peeled at all times.

After being on our feet for more than three hours, Francisco and I decided to stop at *La Casa de Milagro* for lunch. Francisco had praised the cafe as something special. "It's stylish, historical. It used to be a hangout for Pancho Villa."

"Let me invite you," I insisted, as we entered.

"But you need your money."

"Don't worry. I still have a few dollars."

I was struck by its ambience and the decor that had the air of the turn of the century. The walls were slathered with starkly yellowed photographs, showing Pancho Villa as a cattle rustler, fighter, politician, *generalissimo* and, last but not least, a ladies' man. Thanks to Francisco's doggedness, we secured a table in the imposing courtyard, where, surrounded by live music that weaved through lush tropical plants and flowers, dined on savory *antojitos* (appetizers), which we downed with Mexican beer. We had barely taken our seats when Francisco took the liberty of plunging into the life of Villa and his military exploits, including his raid on Columbus, New Mexico, he sacked in 1916. That, in turn, led to a pursuit by the American Army deep into Mexico. But all in vain. He was able to dodge every move by the gringos, accomplishing a feat that boosted his legendary status. Francisco, for one, was full of praise for his fearless attitude that restored the honor of Mexico, as well as for his political accomplishments during his short stint as governor of Chihuahua. He characterized him as a leader with a social conscience who seized the property of the rich hacendados to use the money to build schools for children and to help the poor by driving down the prices of the basic staples, *frijoles, maiz, carne,* and *huevos* (beans, corn, meat and eggs).

At one point, my host palpated his belly and politely excused himself. As he got up to head for the sanitario, two tall, well-dressed gentlemen, led by a waiter, came ambling past our table. Both wore grey fedoras; both spoke English, that is, American. They were deeply engaged in a discussion of some sort. I caught only snippets of it, but from all I could gather they grumbled about the Mexicans who were 'dragging their feet' in following what they had agreed upon. They also made ample use of the words 'corrupt', 'deceitful' and 'bribes'.

Government officials, possibly even Hoover's men? A cold shiver ran down my spine. Worse, it got stuck and refused to settle.

While I was in the middle of gnawing at, what had become a phobia of mine, Francisco returned to the table. "Is there anything?" he asked, staring at me. "You seem to be on edge."

"Well, I am." Taking a swig of beer, I told him about the episode with the Americans.

"Oh, you're making too much out of it. It's not you; it's part of the American swagger. You better get used to it, they're all over the city. They're here because they want to take over."

Even though I couldn't care less about Francisco's pet peeve, the presence of the 'American swagger' in Chihuahua did ring an alarm bell. It led me to the conclusion that I should get out of this town as soon as possible.

On the way to the bus that would take us back to Francisco's home, we walked past the gigantic prison, surrounded by countless guards with loaded guns. In awe of the sheer size of the complex, gobbling up several blocks, I was curious to know why Mexico would be in need of such a big prison.

Francisco squirmed. "Yes, we have a lot of big prisons," he finally mumbled, heaving a big sigh. "I know it may not look like, but we are a very violent country. We've always been. Everybody owns guns. And people use them, too. Every day, especially when their honor is questioned."

"Oh?"

"Yes, you may have noticed that there are many beggars on our streets and plazas. That's no accident. We have a lot of poor people, often Indians, who just scrape by."

When we got back to the Guitierrez's home, Erlinda served a light supper. Unfortunately, I had to abstain; I felt a slight rumbling in my stomach again. It reminded me of the one near San Pedro. I feared for the worst. But after I slugged down some herbal tea, with a sprinkle of Yolanda's blend, I began to feel better. Still, I chose to excuse myself and withdrew to my shed. It was a full day, and I carried countless impressions in my head that begged to be recorded.

Shortly past ten, I undressed, stretched out and drowsed off. The three mouse traps Francisco had baited must have done their job, because I heard not the slightest rustlings. But, cursed that I was, that didn't help me much. Early in the night I was ambushed by several harrowing dreams that shook me to the marrow of my bones. Though I couldn't remember any details, I faintly recalled that they dealt with my arrest and being led to the gallows, in Texas, of all places, somewhere near El Paso.

Still quivering when I got up, I sneaked into the garden, stuck my head under the pump, and pushed down the handle. The fierce gushes of cold water sobered me up and rung in the new day as well. As I, spruced up, entered the kitchen, the table was already set, meticulously so, as if a gaggle of fairies had been at work. It was of course Erlinda, who also bent over backwards to serve me. I tucked away a twin of sunny-side eggs, goat cheese, pinto beans and tortillas. Thanking her, I made my way back to the shed, where I grabbed a spade, headed out to the backyard and started digging up the soil to prepare it for spring planting. It was sheer joy, the relish and smack of the soil, to thrust the spade into the earth, lift it up and turn it over, making it tumble in raggle-taggle chunks. Thanks to the horse manure it was loose, almost fluffy and, yes, full of earth worms, ideal for plants to weave their network of roots into. Inevitably and regrettably a fair number of these poor crawlers were cut to pieces, wriggling in agony.

This task, needless to say, reaped me salvos of praise and gratitude from Erlinda, not to mention Francisco. *"Muchas gracias, Fritz,"* Francisco cracked, bouncing with joy. "You are so helpful, we wouldn't know what to do without you. You will have to stay here with us." Erlinda even eulogized me as being a godsend, explaining that my digging came just at the right time, like a good rain during a severe draught. She claimed she had badgered Francisco for weeks to get the garden ready for spring planting. But he, suffering from a bad back, had always dawdled.

Needless to say, the widespread American presence in Chihuahua continued to weigh on my shoulders and when we sat down for lunch, I politely revealed to my hosts that I'd want to leave tomorrow for a smaller town. I mentioned Cuauhtemoc, simply because Pancho had praised it as being a stronghold of the Mennonites, a group of German settlers. I hoped I could somehow blend in and become inconspicuous, perhaps even get a job in their community.

"I'm running out of money. I have only a few dollars left."

What I didn't mention was my need to get out of Chihuahua to feel safer. I wouldn't dare bring this up for fear of raising a red flag.

"I'm afraid we can't help you much with money," Francisco said. "And the Mennonites wouldn't be of much help either, as far as a job is concerned. I've heard they only hire their own people. You have to be part of their community and religion. They're very pious, you know."

"Oh really?"

That was a big disappointment to me.

"Yes, unfortunately. But maybe there may be a chance of getting a job someplace else. What kind do you have in mind?"

"Well, I'm pretty good as a carpenter, making furniture from scratch. But I could also do ranch work, anything. I'm quick to adapt."

"Can you ride a horse and take care of cattle? Could you do the work of a *vaquero* (cowboy)?"

"You bet! I'd be delighted. My first job in the U.S. before I met Pancho was on a big ranch, where I also worked as a cowboy."

"Good. You see, I have a nephew, Guillermo Padilla, who is a *caporal* at a big *hacienda* about nine kilometers northwest of Cuauhtemoc. He has around a thousand head of cattle under his wings that have to be taken care of. There is always something to do, like branding them, driving them up and down the meadows in the mountains or to the slaughterhouse, castrating young bulls, building and mending fences and keeping the wolves, mountain lions and those damned cattle rustlers at bay. There's a lot of physical, often challenging work involved."

"I don't mind that at all. Quite the contrary, I'd love to do work of that kind."

"Most of the ranch is located in the higher, remote part of the country that's quite unlike other parts of Mexico. They get much more rain and even snow, so it's much greener there, more beautiful. There are trees up there, meadows with flowers and creeks. It's wild, beautiful hiking country. And good for hunting, too. The hacendado, Don Leonardo, is a proud but generous man. Here's what I'll do. I'll write Guillermo a letter, explaining why he should give you a chance. And tomorrow you will deliver it to him. He, his wife, and his two sons are hardworking, honest and goodhearted people."

Cole Porter's *Don't Fence Me In* came to mind. *Could I actually live to see and breathe the freedom trotted out in this song?* It's as if I was in a dream. When I noticed that I wasn't, I still hung on to the belief that Lady Luck was about to embrace and cuddle me.

"I don't know how to thank you for your kindness," I gushed, giving Francisco a spontaneous hug. "But could I ask you another small favor?"

"Sure."

"I'd prefer if you'd mention in the letter that I'm Fred, a Swiss, instead of Fritz, a German. With the war still raging and all the Americans around us, it's simply too dangerous to be called a German."

He gave me a funny look but then caught himself. "I understand," he said, smiling knowingly. "Incidentally, you might want to know how to get to the hacienda. First you'll take the bus or the train to Cuauhtemoc. It's a very small town of a few thousand people. It's known as the commercial center of the Mennonite colony."

"Yes, Pancho already told me."

"Anyway, I'd take the bus. It's cheaper than the train and just as fast."

Both Francisco and Erlinda volunteered to accompany me to the bus depot. It was a chilly morning, making me seek the sun's rays that squeezed in sheafs through a gap between the *Palacio de Gobierno* and another high building. The bus, a huge silvery cocoon, was warming up its engines, swirling billows of blue-grey exhaust into the clear morning air. Most of the passengers who crowded around the door were Mestizos and Indians, although way in the back there were three tall, bearded men in outdated black suits, white shirts and funny leather boots that looked almost medieval. Each one carried a big briefcase, as if they were into white-color work.

"*Menonitos,*" Francisco informed me, watching me follow them with inquisitive eyes.

When the driver, a burly, middle-aged man with a swarthy face, balding, comb-over, head and a waxed handlebar mustache finally opened the door, I gave Francisco and Erlinda an *abrazo*. "Thank you so much for your hospitality," I gushed. "You're very generous people. You treated me like your own son. Like Pancho."

"*De nada, de nada,*" Francisco spouted, chuckling. "It was our pleasure. We hope to see you again. Actually, the hacienda is not all that far. Erlinda and I may even come visit you one of these days. Don't forget

142

to hand the letter I gave you to Guillermo and give him a warm *embrazo* from us."

"I sure will," I said, getting in line.

FOOT-LOOSE AND FANCY-FREE

"Would you know the road that leads to the hacienda Buena Vista?" I asked a young blond Mennonite, in High German to boot.

"Oh, Sie sprechen Deutsch?" he snapped back. "Ja selbstverstaendlich." (Naturally.)

Smiling at me, he gave me detailed instructions, adding a warning that the road may be very rough, dusty and steep at times.

"Danke schoen," I said and, wishing him a pleasant day, shouldered my rucksack and started walking. Thanks to the smallness of the town I had no difficulty finding the road. Indeed, the young man wasn't kidding. Ruthlessly gouged out of a starkly beautiful landscape, it was studded with potholes, rocks and pockets of fine dust, milled by trucks. But I didn't mind. After sitting on my rear end for almost two hours, I looked forward to stirring my limbs.

Trudging along for about twenty minutes, I heard a large truck droning and squeaking uphill. I positioned myself and stuck out my thumb. It tottered to a halt amid a large billow of dust.

"Para donde vas?" (Where do you want to go?) the driver shouted.

"A la Hacienda Buena Vista, senor."

He leaned over, pushed the door open. "Subete que te llevo! "(That's where I'm heading.)

I lifted my rucksack into the cab, climbed up and shoved my buns next to him. A stench of tobacco smoke, of the crude, homegrown kind, hit my nose, blended as it was with garlic and some other smell I couldn't make out.

"Hablo espanol?" the driver, a grey-haired man in his fifties, pressed. He was a small fellow with a broad, shriveled face, deep-seated brown eyes and a three-day beard, whose pepper seemed to be losing the battle against a stubborn wave of salt.

"Poquito."

"Me llamo Pedro," (My name is Pedro.) he said, extending his hand. "Y como te llamas?" (What's yours?)

"Fred."

"Aleman, menonito?"

"No, Suizo."

"Suizo?"

He mumbled badly, and I had to listen carefully to grasp even half of what he said. If I understood him correctly, he was working for a rancho to the north of the hacienda. But he promised to let me off at a certain fork. From there it was less than one kilometer to the hacienda.

The ride turned out to be much rougher and bumpier than I had expected. They must have had rough weather because large parts of the road were badly washed out. We also had to ford two very swift-flowing arroyos, but thanks to Pedro's driving skills, he managed to pull through without much ado. Gradually the vegetation changed from grasses and shrubs to small trees, oaks and junipers. Closer to the arroyos we encountered taller ponderosa pines with their long, bushy needles glistening in the sun.

When we reached the fork, Pedro screeched to a halt. *"Mucha suerte!"* he said, as I opened the door.

I thanked him for the ride, shook hands, threw up my rucksack and started walking. The road curved upwards, but soon dropped into a hollow with a creek flowing through it. On the other side of the creek the road took a sharp bend and followed the creek upwards. Trudging up the road, I soon heard dogs barking. But I kept going. All of a sudden, they came charging at me, four of them, barking on end. *Canine windbags?* I froze. One of them, the biggest and most hostile, edged very close to my left leg. "Oh, c'mon," I said in a calm baritone, in German, no less, "you should know better." Seconds later, I slowly reached down with my hand and, gently, very gently, touched his head, petting him. And surprise, surprise, he dropped all pretensions, sat down and looked up at me with an amiable face. I continued to pet him and gently reproached him for having been so mean. And somehow, he appeared to understand me. Or was it the tone of voice? In any event, he lowered his head as if he was ashamed of himself.

The others, meanwhile, just stood there, watching us interact. I kept stroking and reproaching the dog for about ten minutes. When, at the end, he began licking my hand, I slowly started moving again. And the dogs started walking with me, peacefully, like lambs.

As I entered the courtyard through a flamboyant gate, guarded by two muscular stone lions, with oversized, boastful manes, a small, shriveled woman gingerly approached me. *"A quien buscar, senor?"* (Whom are you looking for?) she asked, smiling meekly.

"Senor Caporal Guillermo Padilla," I said, pulling out the letter and showing it to her.

"Oh, Guillermo? You'll find him at the bunkhouse over there." She pointed to a long white adobe building with a red tile roof. *"Donde esta su caballo?"* (Where is your horse?)

"No tengo caballo." (I have no horse.)

She looked at me in disbelief, as if the tip of my nose had winged away.

Having walked over to the bunkhouse, I knocked on the door. A young boy, aged about twelve, opened it. "Are you looking for somebody?" He impressed me as a bright kid with an inquisitive look radiating from his sparkling eyes. I said that I'd like to speak to Caporal Guillermo Padilla, that I had a letter for him.

"Oh, to my dad," he said in Spanish. "But he's up there at the horse corral." He pointed to an area behind the bunkhouse and offered to show me the way.

The corral was up the creek, about three hundred meters from the bunkhouse. It held about fifteen horses that jammed the upper corner of the pen, away from the stream. In the open area, down below, I saw three men busily selecting and feeding said animals.

When we arrived at the fence, the boy hollered to his dad, "Hey, Dad, there's a man who wants to talk to you."

"I'll be right over," it echoed.

It took a few minutes before he could free himself and exit the corral. He was a small wiry man in his middle thirties with a dark, shining face, shortly cropped black hair, dark-brown eyes, plus a sizable wart on his left nostril that reminded me of a blackcurrant.

We shook hands.

"I'm Fred," I said in Spanish. "Your uncle, Francisco Gutierrez, told me to talk to you about a possible job here at the hacienda." I pulled out the letter and handed it to him.

"From Francisco and Erlinda?" He looked at it, smiled, tore it open and started reading it. "So how are they?" he wanted to know, once he was through.

"Quite well, as far as I could tell," I said. "They are such a hospitable, generous couple."

I also conveyed him additional greetings from them, adding that they had praised him as a trustworthy and goodhearted man.

He smiled, licking his lips. "Francisco says you're Swiss and you worked on a ranch in Colorado?" he said after a while. "What kind of job was it? What did you do?"

"Well, I took care of cattle, erected fences and did whatever needed to be done on a ranch. I can also work with wood, do carpentry, furniture."

"Hm. Well, Fred, if it were up to me, I'd give you the nod. But I'll have to consult with the manager and the patron first, because they have the final say. They're the ones who have to pay you. Unfortunately, the budget is tight right now and the pay is not all that good. But you get free room and board. And life is good up here. You'd be living in one of the most beautiful parts of Mexico."

"I believe you. Let me just say, I didn't come here to become rich. I need a job, that's all."

"Anyway, both the *gerente* and the *patron* will want to talk to you. Let me find out if they're around right now."

He turned to his son. "Antonio, why don't you show this gentleman around so he can get an impression of the hacienda."

While his father headed for a small cottage that was surrounded by a well-tended flower garden, Antonio took me on a tour of the various buildings, the bunkhouse, or living quarters of the vaqueros, the two little cottages, one where his family lived and that of the gerente, the manager. Last but not least, he showed me the manor house, the stately residence of the hacendado, Don Leonardo Gomez y Izaguirre. Built out of sandstone in a colonial-baroque style, it had the appearance of a small castle, with a tower and all. This two-story colossus sat on a hillock, overlooking not only a pond and the hacienda itself but also offering a breathtaking view, a 'buena vista' of the surrounding landscape. On a very clear day one might even get a glimpse of Chihuahua, so I was assured. To the north side there was a fruit orchard studded with apple, plum, and pear trees, a vegetable garden and large fields, where, according to Antonio, they planted corn, alfalfa, oats and occasionally also wheat.

Having made the rounds, Antonio led me back to the cottage where he and his family lived. I met his mother, Teresa, and his cute little sisters, Maria and Rita. And while I waited for the return of Guillermo, Teresa offered me a cup of coffee and some dulces.

Fifteen minutes later, Guillermo was back, filling me in that the gerente, Luis Avila, would be ready to speak with me. I slugged down the rest of my coffee and then followed the caporal to the gerente's cottage. Guillermo introduced me to a small, wiry man with sunken-in cheeks, a high forehead and thin, dark-brown hair. After we had shaken hands, the caporal started praising me as an experienced vaquero who'd earned his spurs on 'model' ranch in Colorado. The gerente put on a poker face.

In the meantime, we had taken seats at the kitchen table, I directly opposite the gerente who lit a cigar and leaned back in his chair. Using a tricky, self-effacing demeanor, he began to question me about the work on the ranch and also to pry into my past. With my butt on the hot seat, I knew that I had to be agile, not to mention imaginative. Still, several times I couldn't avoid getting into a bind. But whenever that happened, Guillermo would quickly jump in, blaming my short and incomplete answers on my deficiency in Spanish. More, in two cases he even answered for me, presumably saying what Luis wanted to hear.

In any event, the gerente seemed satisfied. Still, he insisted that we see the hacendado before he could offer me the job.

"It's up to Don Leonardo to give his blessings," he said somewhat pompously, as if he were referring to an audience with the deputy of the pope. "We're very lucky he is here today."

Squeezing a booklet under his arm, he led us up to the mansion. He knocked on the door. A young mestizo woman opened it. She was dressed in a loose, flowery skirt, covered by a blue, checkered apron and an embroidered blouse.

"Buenos dias, Demesia," the gerente said. "I'm sorry to disturb Senor Don Leonardo, but could you ask him if he might possibly have half an hour at his disposal?"

"Uno momento." She left.

Three minutes later she was back. "You're lucky, Senor Gomez is awaiting you in his office."

"Muchas gracias."

DON LEONARDO AND CAROLINA

The hacendado's office happened to be located on the second floor, partially in the tower that stuck out, hugging the northeastern corner of the mansion. The door was a crack open. The gerente, with pearls of sweat running down his forehead, gingerly knocked.

"Entra!" a full-throated voice bellowed.

We gingerly entered, into a room whose floor was laid out with expensive oriental rugs, while the walls were covered with paintings, antique oil portraits with dark patinas, etchings of horses, as well as sundry hunting trophies: antlers and horns of various forms and sizes, heads of bears, mountain lions and even sharks. My eyes were also drawn to the huge ornamented fireplace, in front of which lay a big bear skin with a lifelike stuffed head, jaws wide open as though ready to charge. The hacendado, Senor Don Leonardo, sat in a leather swivel chair, behind a huge hardwood desk that was stacked with papers, folders, framed photographs, as well as a tablet that displayed some symbol I couldn't quite make out. Prominently standing on both sides were bronze sculptures of horses in motion, one in the middle of a vertical leap with a backward kick, the other in a prancing jump with the hind legs raised.

A handsome, broad-skulled man in his late fifties, he busied himself with some paperwork, barely looking up when we entered. It took him several minutes before he raised his head and faced us. "Why don't you sit down," he said, stroking his tightly cropped, grey beard.

We placed ourselves on the chairs, forming a semicircle around the desk.

He cleared his throat, pulled out a cigarillo and lit it. "Well, what is it, Luis?"

Thanking Senor Gomez for receiving us, the gerente began his plea by mentioning the shortage of vaqueros in view of the breaking of wild horses and driving the cattle down from the mountains. Then he went on to argue that he'd found the man who could more than do the job. "It's Fred," he announced, introducing me. "He is a Suizo."

I rose, strode to the desk and shook Don Leonardo's hand. It was slack, noncommittal.

"You are a Suizo?" he asked, as if in disbelief. "So what brought you to Mexico?"

"My scientific studies, but also adventure and curiosity. Mexico is such a fascinating country."

"Isn't it!" He dealt me a brazen grin.

"Let me mention that Fred has a lot of experience as a vaquero," Guillermo interjected. "He worked for a long time on a ranch in Colorado."

"Oh?" Senor Don Gomez took a puff at his cigarillo, drummed with his fingers on the desk and shifted in his chair. "Listen, Luis," he finally said, with an unassailable aristocratic equanimity, "as I told you before, you can hire all the help you want, as long as you stay within your budget. You know that we all have to tighten our belts, don't you?"

"I'm fully aware of that," Luis said. "You can always count on me." He still mentioned something about the horses that I failed to understand. Having concluded it, he added, "That's pretty much it. I want to thank you so kindly, for approving the hiring, Senor Don Leonardo."

The hacendado took another puff. "Well, is there anything else?"

"Not that I know of," Luis said.

We all got up, paid our respects and left the office.

Walking down the broad, winding stairway, Luis, Guillermo and I happened to bump into a young, most eye-catching woman. She was blessed with an oval, symmetrical face, enhanced by stunning, dark-brown eyes, a small, tip-tilted nose with alluringly sculpted nostrils. All that was domed by a healthy stock of shiny jet-black hair she'd pulled back and bundled in a ponytail. Coming back from a horseback ride, she was wearing fine English riding boots, black jodhpurs and a white, embroidered blouse she filled to the point of bursting. As I recall, she also held a fiery-red jacket in the crook of her arm, while a classy flat black felt hat dangled down her back.

"Buenos dias, Senorita Carolina," Luis and Guillermo exclaimed, dealing her a broad, almost subservient smile.

"We hope you had a good ride," Guillermo added.

"I did, thanks to you. You're always giving me the best horses."

"It's our pleasure," Luis said, bowing deeply.

Smiling, the woman suddenly shifted her eyes toward me, lifting her brows and pouting her lips. Guillermo immediately picked up on it. "I want you to meet Fred," he said, waving his hand toward me. "He's our newest *compadre*. We just hired him today."

150

"Encantado de conocerla, mucho gusto," I said, bowing as if I intended to kiss her hand. Nor did she fail to notice my gesture, or so the string of sprightly giggles seemed to suggest.

"Do I detect an accent?" she inquired in English, slowly withdrawing her hand. "Where are you from?"

"Switzerland."

"Oh, you are a Suizo?" she said with a rhapsodic tone of voice.

"Yes, but I'm very glad to be here at this beautiful hacienda. I also find Mexico to be a very fascinating, most mysterious country."

"That it is fascinating and mysterious, sometimes too much so. But you have to tell me about Switzerland. I've read somewhere that it's the most beautiful country on the face of the earth."

"That may be an exaggeration."

The gerente, meanwhile, was getting skittish. "I'm afraid we've got to get going," he said. "It is always a joy seeing you, Senorita Carolina."

"Asimismo." And, addressing me, she added, "I really mean what I said about Switzerland. I can't wait to hear about it. Let's keep in touch. It shouldn't be that hard, now that you're working here at the hacienda."

"I agree."

Both Guillermo and Luis gave me a smile of consent. Not that I needed it. For I was already smitten, brimming with expectations. Carolina's image was about to drift through my mind like a florid hot-air balloon wafting in a gentle breeze.

A HUMBLE VAQUERO

Once back at the cottage, the gerente told us to take a seat, then ceremoniously opened his book and, asking me to spell my name, recorded it with a flourish that might lure a Jesuit scribe to break into a chuckle. Guillermo and I soon rose, shook hands, showed our gratitude and left. While heading back to the bunkhouse, I thanked the caporal for his support, conceding that without his help I wouldn't have gotten the job. Yet, all he did was wave his hand and smile knowingly.

Having entered the bunkhouse, he assigned a wooden bedstead to me. He also showed me the kitchen, the wash room with its small soapstone sinks and cold showers and — beggars can't be choosers! — a smelly latrine that seemed to rely on nothing more or less than the force of gravity and lest I forget, on the ability to hold one's breath. Later, once I had taken my first cold shower, I joined the rest of the vaqueros, fourteen of them, in the kitchen for supper. I helped myself to a bowl of hardy goat(?) stew, pinto beans and maize tortillas, all very garlicky and tasty, prepared by Teresa, Guillermo's wife. We'd gather at a long wooden table, sitting elbow to elbow on hard, knotty benches that made me lean forward and shift my weight onto my elbows. The word had somehow gotten out that I'd worked on an American ranch. That sparked scads of questions about the breaking of horses, the handling of cattle and sheep and quality of life in the rich Estados Unidos. Some had friends and relatives working in California, Texas, Arizona and they shared their impressions and experiences with the others, many of them relating to narrow-mindedness and racism of some sort or other.

Yes, I'd listen to the conversation, but only politely, with one ear. My mind was someplace else — in blue heaven on the wings of angels. Who could have been more gratified than me? Not only did I get a job and a safe place to stay, out in the beautiful country to boot. To top it all, I felt immeasurably blessed by getting acquainted with Carolina, a most captivating woman, who seemed to be curious about Switzerland. Ca-ro-li-na — what a mouthful of thoroughbred vowels! They bounced off my tongue like hot chestnuts on a roast.

Once in bed, the images of walking through heavily meadows finally lulled me to sleep. Unfortunately, it didn't help me *staying* asleep. The snoring of my neighbors and the intermittent mooing of some cows in the corrals would often arouse me. As did the repeated hee-hawing of a burro and the call of a rooster very early in the morning, when the crack of dawn was about to brighten the eastern horizon.

At six sharp, Guillermo stumped into the dormitory and hand-clapped us out of bed. We all rushed to the bathroom, yet nobody dared to shower. Now reasonably clean, we all jammed into the kitchen, where we served ourselves with a hardy breakfast that included fried eggs, beans, queso menonita and tortillas.

Later, I joined Guillermo who graciously offered to take me under his wings. Together with two other vaqueros, I was handed long maguey ropes. Having slung them over my shoulder, I made my way to the horse corral. The task was to rope a drove of wild horses, three-year-old colts, Guillermo and a file of five vaqueros had rounded up way on the outer reaches, the northeastern mesas of the hacienda only two days ago. According to Guillermo there was a stunning number of about five hundred horses roaming out there.

Lassoing and roping these captivating animals were tough and challenging jobs. Having never seen a human being before, these wild *caballos* were scared pee-and-shitless, so much so that they'd all jam themselves at the farthest corner of the corral, away from the gate. Watching us entering, some were so spooked they rose on their hind legs and tried to scale the fence that consisted of rugged, four inches thick poles tightly wired together.

The first thing Guillermo did when he entered the gate was to stride up to the horses and pick a few of the healthiest and most appealing specimens. Unfortunately, when the colts saw us coming, they all bolted to the other corner, away from us. It happened to be piled up with fresh horse dung, drenched with pee. And it reeked. Yet, being a seasoned horseman, Guillermo didn't mind. Quite to the contrary, he'd pick a spot on the fringes of this equine outhouse, go down and actually start rolling in the horse manure. Rising, he suggested we do the same, arguing that if we smelled like horses, it would make our job easier, smoother.

"Instead of taking you as a complete stranger, they may look upon you as an uncle, or distant relative," he claimed without his tongue in cheek. "That's what horse sense is all about." Since he happened to be our caporal, most of us followed his advice. In the end, each of us exuded the stamp of an unmistakable equine whiff.

Let me add, I'd never done that kind of job before. Seldom had I been so out of the loop. Short of following orders, I was condemned to carefully watch and try to imitate what my fellow vaqueros were doing. But I adapted. And what I lacked in skills, I tried to make up in strength and agility. Since I was considerably taller and also stronger than the other vaqueros, I could better wrestle the horses down, forcing them to surrender. As expected, they never did this willingly; they jumped, kicked and bit so forcefully that none of us walked away unscathed. It was raw nature pitted against human prowess and craftiness. But in the end, we had the upper hand, hobbling and shackling these proud and stunning creatures that only days ago roamed the mesa in unbridled freedom.

Although we initiated the breaking of these creatures, the heavy lifting was done by none other than Guillermo. He was the ultimate tamer, the *amansador,* as he was called, a role that was the most challenging by far. Among the first horses we set up for him was a ravishing colt, whose front legs we had looped so tightly that once released, it immediately hit the dust, a crushing humiliation that left the animal stunned. At that point Guillermo quickly seized the opportunity. In a split second, before the colt could bounce back, he'd kneel on its neck, then grab its head. Holding it tightly against his chest and sliding his hand over its eyes, he began caressing it, all the while uttering soothing words. Nor was this the end. With the colt's front legs immobilized, Guillermo also had us hitch the hind legs to the neck. Next, he slipped the hackamore over the muzzle and ears and tied it up with the hind legs. Now that the colt was all trussed up, our tamer took a breath and stepped back.

Meanwhile a motley flock of spectators had gradually trickled in to watch the spectacle. Some of whom I was able to recognize, such as Teresa and her three children, the wife of Luis Avila with her four children, Demesia, Don Leonardo's domestic servant, and her five children. But there were also other spectators, among them, last but not least, Senorita Carolina. Inspired by the children, they all actively participated, clapping, cheering, rooting, laughing, stomping, booting, hissing, hooting, whistling and cheering. Within minutes the corral had turned into a small circus and we, as well as the horses, into dramatic actors. That inevitably heightened the pressure on us to perform. I, in particular, felt that most acutely, not least because Senorita Carolina was one of the spectators.

I might add that she had long wormed herself deeply into every fiber of my mind. Although the encounter on the staircase had lasted only a few minutes, her words, her gestures, indeed, her whole appearance, had set ablaze fantasies that preoccupied me day and night. I was overwhelmed by an intense desire craving for fulfillment. Yet, I didn't know how to set things in motion. Luckily a small window would soon open. It so happened

154

that at one point the action would shift fairly close to the fence, where my heartthrob was standing. I quickly seized the opportunity, tipping my hat at her. And she responded by tipping her's to me. Our eyes locked; we exchanged two flashes of warm smiles.

Not immune to a little chivalry, I, the valiant knight, would try my utmost to impress my lady in terms of boldness, agility and strength. Never mind that most of my action happened to take place on the colt's blind side which she could only partially see. I gave my best, aided by a drama of the colt that showed no sign of abating. Although its fate was sealed, it still refused to buckle. Snorting, frothing, gnashing teeth and whinnying, it whirled, kicked, thrashed hoofs and reared up, all for a miserly half-turn, followed by yet another humbling spill. Having found its legs once again, it would fare not a whit better: It spun, twisted, strained to cut a circle but instantly lost its balance and thumped back into the dust again, badly whacking its cheek and shoulder. These sequences repeated itself no less than four times, albeit with slight variations, and each time the colt took longer and longer to get on its hoofs and complete its kicks, twists and turns. Little by little the brawn, pluck and grit began seeping out of it. In the end, with its snort and swagger quelled, it would just stand there, motionless, staring empty-eyed at us.

At that point, everyone broke into applause. As Guillermo led the tamed animal out of the corral to the nearby *potrero* (field) I instantly followed him, but decided to stay closer to the fence with the intention of slinking past my heartthrob. Indeed, I came so close that I was able to brush her hands. It was a fortuitous move because as we touched, she slipped a small note into my hand. I was so thrilled I could have turned a somersault. But unable to read it at this point, I shoved it into my pocket and followed the caporal and the colt.

Having come to a standstill near a pole, Guillermo handed me the rein. Let me just say, I sympathized with the animal. And to express my feelings, I started stroking its head and neck, while at the same time whispering to it in a steady, soothing voice as if it were a prayer, which instantly had a calming effect.

Minutes later Guillermo came back with a blanket, a saddle and a long piece of burlap and, folding the burlap, he began rubbing the colt's muzzle, its head, its belly, its legs, even its genitals and butt. When, in the end, he placed the cloth back onto the muzzle, the colt gave a hint of neighing, but showed no sign of moving. The rest, the placement of a blanket and a saddle, Guillermo did with a professional touch. Having tightened the cinch, he took off the hackamore and replaced it with the headstall. Next, he gathered the reins, slid his foot into the stirrup and mounted the colt. Thankfully, the animal took it without much discomfort, save for folding back his ears for a few seconds. But as soon as Guillermo pulled the reins, it calmed down, assuring me that he had finally embraced our caporal as his 'uncle'.

Not taking anything for granted, Guillermo still had a little dry run up his sleeve. He reined the colt again, this time to the right, and the colt effortlessly drew a semicircle. Still strained, he decided to try a short, four-hundred-meter walk, then turned around and headed back. All of it unwound smoothly, without the slightest incident. Now high on the horse, our amansador relaxed, smiling away his tension. There was no longer any doubt that the colt had finally been broken to harness, and Guillermo's mission had ended with a panache. We all gathered and congratulated him for accomplishing such a feat. Unfortunately, Senorita Carolina had already left by then.

Incidentally, while my celebrated mentor was on his final test-walk, I had nervously pulled the note out of my pocket. It smelled of perfume, more precisely, lilac. I unfolded it. Written in flamboyant, self-assured letters, it read as follows:

Dear Fred,

Let us get together. Tomorrow is Sunday and you are off work.
I will saddle two horses and wait for you at ten a.m. near a tall
ponderosa about six hundred meters up the creek. I want to hear
about Switzerland. Hope to see you,
Carolina

I was about to jump for joy, and turn two cartwheels to boot.

Come afternoon, my compadres and I kept busy hobbling and preparing two other colts, which, so rumor would have it, Senor Don Leonardo was putting on the market for sale, some in Texas. The whole procedure took more than four hours and when it ended, darkness began to settle. We were all tired and hungry, not to mention grey with dust and soggy with sweat. And, boy, did we reek! Our hands were raw from the handling and pulling of ropes. When we finally got back to the bunkhouse, we dropped our dirty clothes, scrubbed ourselves or took showers and then went into the kitchen, where we served ourselves a tasty meal of tacos stuffed with a medley of seasoned kid, queso and lettuce. The chef? Teresa. After supper some of us still hung around the *hogar* (bunkhouse), watching the flames and talking about wild and tamed horses. One of the vaqueros, Luis, brought a guitar, another pulled out a mouth harp, and together they

156

played songs, while the rest of us kept singing along. Most of these tunes were very touching and sentimental, romantic laments, dealing with unrequited or forlorn love, betrayal of the heart and loneliness — feelings I hoped would only happen to others, not me.

I sneaked away early, into the kitchen, where I began to corral the day for my diary. And, once again, what a day it was. Some parts even took on a dreamlike quality. I'm referring to the portentous note Carolina had slipped me. Yet not all the events that came to pass proved to be edifying. To be sure, the hustle and bustle in the corral was most adventuresome, not to mention, stirring, and the gusto with which I hurled myself into the fray could be seen as a testimony to my commitment. However, when, at the very end, the rumor reached my ears that these broken horses were corralled to be sold on the market, doubts began to creep into my mind, pinching a very sensitive nerve. I couldn't help it, I began to feel a deep empathy for these creatures and their fate. *Who gave me the right to take away their freedom and crush their wild spirit? To force them to spend their lives in human bondage? In the stable and under the crotch of some rich man who could afford to buy them, for no other reason than to serve his vanity.* Still closer to home: The thought of my own fate began to crowd my mind. The intoxicating feeling of freedom in the days following my escape, but most notably in the aftermath of my arrival at the hacienda was still fresh and palpable, as was the perennial fear of losing it through some foolhardiness or bad luck. That mental whiplash in the shape of the ghastly dream of my arrest and the foreboding execution only three nights ago still sat deep in my bones. What was life without freedom? Liberty! What a treasure. Or was it a drug? Cole Porter's hit *Don't Fence Me In* thrust itself onto the forefront of my mind again.

MY FIRST DATE

Sunday, my first on the hacienda, proved to be most worthy of its name. It turned out to be unabashedly sunny, a fall day out of a picture book. Although it started chilly, cold, close to freezing at sunrise, gradually the sparkling shower of photons would take away the bite, while nourishing the illusion of warmth and friendliness. Adding to that was the weather within my mind, whose barometer not only matched the 'Sunday' outside, it surpassed it. Anticipation churned up a wondrous pleasure, letting me revel in the fore-gleam of an erotic encounter.

After getting up, I rushed to the shower. I wanted to make damn sure that I didn't reek of horse manure or, worse, stud piss. When I turned on the faucet, I thought I was back at the Russian front. The water was so cold I involuntarily jumped up and down, twisting and dodging just to bear its stings, stitches and stabs. Goose-pimpled from head to toe, I carefully shaved my cheeks and the upper part of my neck, but let my beard stand. Since I'd stopped dyeing it, it was about to take on a distinct 'Viking' sheen the past few days, neatly matching my thatch. Adding a little spiff, I put on the best pair of pants, made of dark-brown cotton cloth I'd bought in Chihuahua. It provided a cutting contrast to my white cotton shirt. And, with the horseshoe snugly in my pocket, I was ready.

Making sure that nobody was watching me, I made my way over to the creek and then, following it, ventured upstream. Occasionally the riparian vegetation, most of it leafless by now, was so dense that I had to veer off occasionally. But I easily managed to find my way back, and within twenty minutes I had reached the ponderosa, a weather-beaten giant that must have stood guard for hundreds of years. Unfortunately, to my great disappointment, Carolina, my heartthrob, was nowhere to be seen. Then again, a glance at my watch reminded me that I was early, by more than ten minutes. *Would she think I was overanxious?*

I waited, anxiously biting my lips and clutching my horseshoe. Time dragged its feet, jamming its toes. *Had she forgotten?* Well, at last, full ten minutes later, I heard the snorting of horses. And, all of a sudden, there she was, high on the horse, her face bathed in a full-blown smile.

"Perdon por llegar tarde," she said, her lips curling into a smile and dimpling her cheeks.

She was dressed in the same garb as yesterday, only now she *wore* her red jacket and her flat, wide-brimmed black felt hat. Unlike yesterday, two black curls, one right, the other left, dangled down all the way past her cheeks, adding a frame to her alluring face. She lowered her eyelashes until they almost caressed her cheeks, then lifted them again like a theater curtain.

"Well, yes, I waited more than an hour."

"You are a *diablo*!" she flashed back with a grin.

I offered to help her get off the horse, but she put me off politely, then elegantly lifted her glutes out of the saddle and dismounted. With my hand on her waist, I gently pulled her toward me and buzzed her cheek. The sweet scent of lilac struck my nose, lifting my spirits.

"Que dia magnifico!" she rhapsodized

"Heavenly!" I burst out in English. "Not a cloud in the sky."

"Oh, you prefer to speak English?"

"Yes, if you don't mind. Somehow, I feel more comfortable. My Spanish is beyond awful. I always feel as if my tongue were in a harness and somebody else kept pulling the reins. It's less than a month since I entered Mexico."

"I wouldn't know how you feel but let me say you're doing exceptionally well for somebody who's been in this country for such a short time. So you've also been in the United States?"

"Yes, but only a little more than six months."

She began to flesh out her impressions of the United States, which were quite favorable for a change. She particularly praised the high standard of living, as well as — yes — the freedom. She also defended waging a war against the Nazis, whom she denounced as brutes.

"Where were you in the United States?"

"In southern Colorado. I worked on farms, as well as on a big ranch. But yours is so much more beautiful."

"I think it is quite beautiful. That's why I'm here and not in Mexico City, where my brother lives. Although at times it gets a little lonely out here. It's at the end of the world, you know."

"I do know. That's why I'm here."

"Well, I wonder, would you be interested to see a little more of our hacienda?"

"Sure would."

"I thought we could ride up a little way into the mountains. I know a place near a lake, where we could spend the afternoon."

"Sounds very alluring."

159

We mounted the horses and started to ascend, she leading the way. Yet whenever the vegetation allowed it, she fell back and we rode side by side. We veered off the creek and trotted, cross-country, in a northwesterly direction. The terrain gradually began to change. The vegetation became denser and denser. More species of trees made their appearance, madrones and ash, and they were taller, the trunks heftier. We encountered rabbits, frightened away quail and even wild turkeys, birds I'd never seen before. Thankfully, we came across a trail that ran along another creek. We followed it. At last, after about an hour and a half, we reached a *cienega* (bog, swamp) that was overgrown with willows and *carrizos* (tall reeds) and, shortly thereafter, we stood in front of a small lake.

"This is Beaver Lake, one of my favorite places on the hacienda. I have been visiting it since I was a kid. I have many fond memories, including an encounter with a she-bear and its three cubs. It kept bothering us, until Jorge, my brother, chased it away with hand clapping and rock throwing."

"How beautiful but also scary," I said. "It feels as if we're in central or northern Europe."

"Yes, it's very unique. You know, there are even *truchas* (trout) in there. My dad always keeps it stocked. We have seen eagles swoop down and catch them with their claws."

She selected a sunny spot on the northern slope, where we could overlook the whole lake, dismounted and tied up the horses. Carolina unfolded a large, colorful Indian blanket and, pulling all kinds of provisions out of her saddlebags, neatly stacked them up at the upper end.

"Thank you, that was very thoughtful of you," I commented.

"Well, what's a day in the country without a picnic?"

"Sure. I thought of bringing something along too but I couldn't find anything. Teresa must have hidden all the cheeses and tortillas."

She unwrapped a stack of tortillas, goat cheese, *carne asada*, smoked turkey, roasted red and green peppers, avocados, apples and pears. And, having opened two bottles of beer, she clinked hers with mine.

The hard, brawny work during the past few days had given me a good appetite, magnified as it was by the taste and quality of the provisions Carolina had brought along. Nor was this lost on her. "You're eating like a galley slave," she said. "And so zestfully!"

"Well, I'm always grateful when I'm served good food. The joy of eating comes naturally, once you experience hunger."

"Oh, you did?"

"Yes, many times."

Once we had finished, I excused myself. Upon returning, I checked the water. "It's not bad," I said. "I think I'll take a swim. Let's both jump in."

"It's much too cold. It's already late October. Besides, I didn't bring a bathing suit."

"Who cares? What's wrong with skinny-dipping?"

I pictured both of us naked, frolicking in the water. And later, warming each other on the blanket. The bare images of our bodies inundated my mind with an intoxicating concupiscence.

"But Fred, we've just met. I'm not that kind of a girl."

Well, I made it to the shore, showed her my back, dropped my clothes and in I was. As bad luck would have it, it turned out to be much colder than I'd expected. I had to swim full throttle just to keep my body away from hypothermia. Getting weary, I eventually switched from breaststroke and crawl onto my back, kicking and waving my arms.

"It's very refreshing," I shouted. "If you survive that you'll probably live to be a hundred."

"Who wants to live that long?"

"I do."

Maybe I did, but what I didn't want was to stay in much longer. It wasn't so much the cold, it was the fear that my pendant down under might shrivel to nothing, to a tiny knob. Indeed, it may have done so already. *What,* I shuddered, *would Carolina think, when she sees a withered dwarf?*

I was in a quandary. But as I drew closer to the shore, I was struck by a flash of inspiration. Instead of swimming ashore with a breaststroke and facing my heartthrob head on, as I had in mind, I could use a backstroke and, once in the shallows, I could rise to show my back and glutes. And, ashore, I'd instantly slip into my underpants. Thought and done! And it worked. I was spared any embarrassment, and Carolina possible sighs. All she did was laugh.

Since we didn't bring a towel, I had to dry myself off by lying in the sun. Actually, I tried to draw closer to Carolina, to cuddle up with her, but she kept pushing me off.

"Don't be so impatient," she'd say. "We hardly know each other. Why don't you tell me about your home country, Switzerland. I'm very curious to hear about you, too, and your family."

Having never been to Switzerland, that presented a challenge. Luckily, I had heard about this jewel of a country from people who had traveled there. Moreover, I had also read about it in papers and books. The rest of it was left to my imagination. And, judging by Carolina's reactions, her many

"Ohs", "Ahs" and other blurts of surprise, I must have done a fairly decent job. Anyway, she was fascinated.

What Carolina failed to understand was how a country not even half as big as the State of Chihuahua could stay neutral and independent, especially in the face of the brute force of the Nazis. Nor could she grasp, why I left such a peaceful, neutral country. My prayer-wheeling answer, that I found life in Switzerland stifling, even suffocating and that I, being young and curious, longed for adventure, exploring other countries and cultures, failed to satisfy her. I could always see the slightest internal dissonance by the way she flared the flanges of her nostrils and spared her smiles.

"How long have you been away traveling?" she wondered. "I mean..."

"Since the fall of 1939."

"That's four years," she said, shaking her head. "How about your family, your mother, father, your brothers and sisters — don't you have any desire to see them?"

"I neither knew my mother, nor my father. An old granny found me near a garbage can. I was a tiny baby, who had just been born, or so I was told. Since I had no parents or relatives, I was placed into an orphanage. That's where I grew up. When I was seventeen, I escaped and began fending for myself. I worked in many different jobs not only in Switzerland, but also in Germany, Russia, Italy, North Africa, the United States and now Mexico."

"You mean, you have lived and traveled in all of those countries?"

I nodded. *How easy it was to flimflam. Or was it simply playacting?*

She shook her head in disbelief. And rightfully so! "It must have been terrible growing up as an orphan," she harped on, as if in thought. "No mother, no parents, no family, no relatives. I can't even imagine living like that."

"Well, I had no choice and no way of comparing. All I can say, it was tough. I had to fight to survive. It was a dog-eat-dog struggle. I never knew life in any other way."

"I've never met anybody like you. You remind me a little bit of those *golfillos* (urchins) who live on the streets in Mexico City."

She leaned over toward me, pouted her lips, as if she intended to give me a kiss, but then shrugged back.

"We've been sitting here for more than three hours," she suddenly said, getting up and stretching. "I feel like moving my legs. Let's walk around the lake."

"Good idea."

Carolina stashed away whatever was left of the provisions. I dressed, and we started walking. To begin with, she was a bit awkward on her feet, given that she wore stiff English riding boots, on uneven ground to boot. At times, when we encountered obstacles, such as the inflowing brook, rocks or branches, I offered her a hand, but she turned me down. "Thanks so much, but I think I can handle it," she let me know. She pretty much stuck to my heels, and everything seemed to go well, until we entered the last stretch near the lake's outlet. Confronted with a large bog, that was dotted with ponds made by beaver dams and overgrown with willows, we had to draw a big circle to get around it. At one point we were forced to cross a gushing creek. I suggested hopping from one rock to the next. Unfortunately, some of them were quite slippery. I once again extended a helping hand, but she insisted on taking up the challenge herself. But luck tends to be very capricious. Jumping to a small rock, Carolina slipped, lost her balance and tumbled head over heels into a clump of willow reeds. I rushed to the rescue. Luckily, nothing appeared to be broken, although she didn't get off unscathed. Besides hurting her left wrist, she twisted and sprained the ankle of her right foot in such a hapless way that, writhing with pain, she couldn't move at all. I actually had to pick her up and carry her over to the other side, where I made her sit down. Next, I pulled off her boot and her sock. The ankle showed the first signs of swelling and discoloration.

"We have to cool it down immediately," I suggested, "or else it may keep on swelling."

She whined; her face took on a pleading air. I intuitively bent down and kissed her ankle. That visibly soothed and calmed her to the point where she even uttered a joyful gurgle. Encouraged, I also hugged her and caressed her leg, back and head. Yet, balmy as my effort might have been, it did little to curb the swelling. Since we didn't have any ice, I took her foot and gently began dunking it into the cold water that gurgled down from the lake. "Wow, that's cold!" she burst out, repeatedly moaning like a kid.

"No pain, no gain!" I countered.

Having dried her foot and ankle with my shirt, I slowly piggybacked her back to the original picnic area.

Owing mainly to the accident, the hike had taken us more than two hours. The horses neighed and whickered when they saw us approaching. I rolled up the blanket, fastened it to the saddle of Carolina's horse and helped my patient to mount, so we could head back to the hacienda. Carolina once again insisted that we return to our original meeting place, the tall ponderosa.

"I think, it would be better if we parted right there," she said. "People talk."

"I understand," I said. "But you need help. How will you be able to get off the horse and go into the house?"

"Don't worry, Demesia will call for some help. — I'm sorry, but I must go back alone, without you. You see, people shouldn't know that we've been riding together all by ourselves. They wouldn't think it was proper for a young woman. I'd risk losing my reputation. And all a woman has is her reputation. These are our customs. You have to remember, we're in Mexico."

"Oh, I had no idea you were that strict."

"Well, actually I'm... But that doesn't count all that much." She unconsciously tugged at a loose strand of hair and let her voice drop reflectively. "Besides, there's also my dad. I don't know how he'd respond if he found out that we're seeing each other. He might not like it. In fact, I'm afraid he wouldn't like it at all. It's about the hacienda and who will inherit it. He's very conservative, set in his ways like an old mule hobbling to his water hole. For him it's family, family, family. He thinks he has to uphold a family tradition that goes back all the way to the seventeen hundreds, way back to the Spanish crown, when Mexico was barely on the map. Because that's how long this hacienda has been in our family's possession."

"That's crazy. These customs remind me of those European aristocrats held on to. But in Europe they're pretty much a thing of the past."

"Well, not here. Anyway, I've gotta get going. My ankle's really hurting."

Having reached the ponderosa, I dismounted and handed the reins of my horse to her. "You know you have to put ice on it as soon as you get home, again and again."

"I know. And I will. Let me just say thanks to you, especially for helping me after the accident. You are a wonderful man, so helpful."

"Thank you, the pleasure is all mine." I clutched her hands. "Thank you for inviting *me*. Sharing this day with you was an unforgettable experience for me. Just being around you makes me feel so cheerful and merry that I would want... Maybe we can get together again soon. I thought of a bar or dancing hall somewhere in the vicinity where we could shake a leg. But, I'm afraid it would have to wait until your ankle's been cured. And that could take weeks."

"Well, I hope I can speed it up. I promise, I'll try as hard as I can. But as soon as my ankle's healed, we'll do it."

164

"That would be fun."

Using my hands, I cradled her right leg and kissed her ankle again. She giggled like a toddler. Then, calming down, she unlatched her heart, sighing, "Oh, Fred, I wish I could have you around me more often."

There was a long, deep pause. We locked eyes. My Adam's apple bobbed nervously.

"As to your question about a dance hall," Carolina said, breaking the silence, "I know of one in Cuauhtemoc. It's called El Flamenco. That's where a small band plays dancing music every Saturday night. It's kind of earthy, real Mexican, a gathering place for a lot of young, crazy people to go wild."

"Let's go! I can't wait. This time, I'll invite you. Who knows, I may go wild, too. But say, how can we get down to Cuauhtemoc?"

"We could ride down on horseback. Actually, Dad also has a car, a fancy Packard. I could get it, but he'd want to know what for. And, frankly, I'm not quite ready to tell him about us."

"Well, what's wrong with horses anyway? I'd prefer them to those 'horseless' carriages."

"I would too. Anyway, I'll let you know as soon as my ankle gets better. I'll once again give you a written message. But since I want to avoid creating a big stir that will make people's tongues wag, I won't come to the corral. Instead, I'll give the message to Juana, Demesia's daughter, who will hand it to you."

"Fair enough."

I still stroked her ankle and shook her hand before we parted.

What can I say, Carolina had pulled my heartstrings to the point of ripping. I was smitten, in love. I panted for her, the more so since she warned me of the hurdles that stood in the path to her heart. I couldn't think straight any more. Everything swirled around her in gusts of exaltations. I worshipped her, I ennobled her, elevating her to the status of the perfect woman. I imagined her sitting high on the horse, the reins in her hands, laughing, slightly raising her delicate nostrils, dropping her jaw and opening her oral cavity to the point where, aside from her perfect rows of teeth, her salmon-hued tongue and gums, my eyes could pierce as far back as her soft palate and alluring uvula guarding the isthmus of fauces.

What was I, a poor fugitive, in comparison? A young barbarian reaching for an unknown treasure that could be the subject of painters and sculptors. What would her father, not to mention his ancestors, who peeked at me from the portraits in his office, say, if they saw me embracing their offspring? "No way! Be gone! Get yourself a wench of your own standing."

165

To be blunt, I was beyond being in love. I was sick, shaken with fever, stripped of an appetite and the need to sleep. Although I tried to keep the affair secret — I wouldn't want to hurt Carolina — I failed miserably. It became known Monday morning at the latest, when I reported to Guillermo for work. He noticed right away that I had changed, and not for the better.

"You look so absentminded," he said, staring me in the eyes. "Are you sure you can still rope these wild horses? You know, they'll notice right away when somebody is daydreaming. If they sense that your resolve is weak, they won't buckle under. They'll jump, kick and bite if you try to rope them."

"Oh, I think I can handle them."

Well, reality was not in the mood to match my words. I'm afraid Guillermo was right. The first horse immediately picked up that my head was someplace else. In any event, as I came around the back to rope its front legs, I was struck by such a kick into my rear that I was sure my pelvic bone had shattered, worse, crumbled. For a moment I thought that *I* would be the one who couldn't make it to the dance floor on Saturday night. But thanks to my sturdy physique I managed to shake it off. Still, it was a wake-up call that had to be taken seriously. And it was embarrassing. Luckily, I had Jorge, a competent partner, who could take over the most dangerous work.

THE BUDDING OF DREAMS

I got through the week reasonably well, despite my daydreaming. Thanks to Jorge's steady hand, we managed to break eight wild horses. What flustered me during all those days was the fact that I never got a glimpse of Carolina. Nor did I receive a message. It wasn't until Saturday afternoon, while we were trying to rope the ninth horse that Demesia's daughter showed up at the gate of the corral. She smiled at me, and when she waved her hand, I knew it was Juana who carried a message. I tipped my hat and walked over to her, and she handed me that precious pink note from Carolina. My nose instantly picked it up. Trying to avoid being seen, I breathed in the lilac scent and shoved it into my pocket, where it began to stir and blaze.

Half an hour later, shortly past four, Guillermo called it a day. Leaving the corral, I pulled out the note and, bracing myself, began reading it.

Dear Fred,
Please forgive me for being so tardy. It looks as if I have to postpone our dancing date. I apologize. I did everything I could but my ankle, although improving, is still very tender. I can hardly walk, much less dance. May I suggest next Saturday?
I miss you. So does the ankle, especially your warm…
From the bottom of my heart,
your Carolina

Naturally, I was disappointed. I had yearned feverishly for this rendezvous. I even thought of presenting a little gift to my sweetheart. Unable to find fresh flowers, I had written a little love poem on a sheet of paper, wreathed with a depiction of colorful flowers and singed the fringes to make it appear old and yellowed. This, the first token of my love I intended to hand to my heartthrob right after I'd hugged her. *And now, was it not all for nothing?* Or so my first impulse proffered. But after reading the note again, I had a change of heart, not least because of Carolina's last few lines. *Did they not implicitly match my own feelings?*

I reminded myself to be more patient, to wait until next Saturday. I had long noticed that nothing poked the fire of passion more than the anticipation of love. In the meantime, I went about breathing, doing my job and enjoying life, unlike many of my comrades who were either stuck in the prison camps or, worse, still dying in a mindless war. That is, I *hoped* I could. Actually, it turned out to be not that simple. For one, regardless of how hard I tried to be my old, reliant self, my emotions continued to be tethered to Carolina. She pulled the strings, at least I assumed she did. I wondered how I could please her, make her less resistant to my advances.

Come Sunday, Guillermo's son Antonio and I packed a lunch, saddled two horses, and together explored the hacienda's land holdings toward the northeast, where they bordered on the Mennonite colony. They were characterized by expansive, grass-covered mesas, dotted by creosote bushes and cacti in the lower-lying areas and junipers, live oak and gnarled red *madrono* in the higher elevations. Carved up by creeks and arroyos, these grasslands were much more arid than the area around the hacienda, reminding me of the eastern part of Colorado and northern New Mexico.

Born on the hacienda, Antonio turned out to be a fine-tuned horseman and bright kid who knew the area like his own pocket. Most of the time we let the horses walk but occasionally, when the terrain allowed it, we'd fall into a trot, even a gallop. I immensely enjoyed riding through a wide-open country, unhindered by fences or walls, so much so that I inadvertently broke into Cole Porter's tune.

"Oh give me land, lots of land, and the starry skies above
Don't fence me in
Let me ride through the wide open country that I love
Don't fence me in…"

I recalled when we warbled our cowboy tune at the camp, we all assumed that the content was no more than a dream, a wild illusion. But now it felt as if the dream had come true, for me at least. Had escape not metamorphosed into arrival, flight into sanctuary, war into peace? Again, and again, I shook my head in amazement how generous Lady Luck had been to me. (Or did my horseshoe push her?) Not only had she protected me when I needed it most, she also kept pouring her fortune over me, a cornucopia crammed with such precious goodies as freedom, happiness and — lest I forget! — love.

But let me leave those lofty heights and return to the ground, the flat mesa. Led by Antonio, I got introduced to many distinct features of this land, determined to a large extent by the availability of water. Unlike the table lands, the stream beds, gulches, and arroyos were populated by willows, cottonwoods and other riparian vegetation. We encountered swarms of birds, two rattlesnakes, rabbits, coyotes, as well as herds of pronghorn antelopes and wild horses. Sadly, both the antelopes and horses immediately took to flight when they saw us approaching.

Back at the hacienda, we happened to cross paths with Demesia who was in tow of another, quite attractive woman I'd never seen before, much less met. Clad in a blue blouse, bolero jacket, and fine gabardine slacks, she appeared to be in her late forties or early fifties.

"It's Imelda, the hacendada," Antonio whispered worshipfully to me as we approached them.

Determined not to let the opportunity pass, I walked up and introduced myself.

"Oh, you are Fred, our new Swiss vaquero? I'm Imelda, Carolina's mother. Glad to meet you. I have already heard about you."

"I hope good things," I said, smiling. I studied her face, trying to detect features she may have passed on to Carolina. Indeed, the shape of her eyes, her nose and her mouth reminded me of my heartthrob's, although her skin was a bit darker and not nearly as smooth.

"Yes, indeed," she said. "Well, how do you like it here on our hacienda?"

"I'm ecstatic. Antonio and I are just coming back from a horseback ride to the wild, northeastern grasslands. It was a breathtaking experience. There was no other place I'd rather be."

"Yes, it can be very beautiful out here. But it's especially flattering to hear these compliments from somebody like you, from a Swiss. I have heard so many bad things about Europe. Maybe you can explain to us one day what is happening there. I'm sure we'll be seeing each other more often. Anyway, I'm pleased to have met you."

OUR DEBUT DANCE

The new week started out with the same, roping the rest of the wild horses, six in all, for Guillermo to break, so they could be sold. Midweek we got ready to start the stock drive. First, we were kept busy working on the large holding pens extending to the north of the estate, repairing the fences, gates, water tanks, fodder racks and whatever else needed to be whipped in shape. That stretched well into the weekend — a weekend that was brimming with anticipation.

On Saturday morning, as I was in the middle of driving new cedar poles into the ground, Juana, Demesia's daughter would show up again. She greeted me with Senor Fred and, beaming, handed me another note. Once again, I had to be patient. Later, when we all broke for lunch, I pulled it out and unfolded it.

Dear Fred,
I hope you didn't lose your patience. Let me just tell you that my ankle is fully healed. In any event, I've asked Jose to saddle two horses. They'll be waiting for us at six by the large cottonwood three hundred meters down the creek. We could take a shortcut to Cuauhtemoc. This should take us less than an hour. I suggest that we first have a bite to eat. I know a cozy restaurant in town. I'm looking forward to seeing you. It's been too long!
Warm greetings,
Carolina.

At last! I sighed, my heart beating out of range, so much so that it even cramped my appetite. At one o'clock we were back at the fence. Luckily, we were able to pretty much finish the job. At four, Guillermo raised his hands and clapped. I rushed back to the bunkhouse, stripped and braved a cold shower, which sobered me up and gave me a ruddy patina. Clean as a whistle, I slipped into my white shirt, a dark-brown pair of pants, grey socks and brown dress shoes. A few tucks and pulls here and there made me inch toward my humble crest. I grabbed my poem, slipped it under my shirt, and off I went.

Carolina was already there, standing near her horse, the reins in her hand. She looked captivating, sporting a black bolero with red cuffs, tight white blouse with blue stitching, a red gathered skirt that opened toward the bottom like a budding poppy and, last but not least, black ballerina shoes. She wore her hair loose, letting it fall in curls. Better: lovelocks. I watched her earrings dangling against the swell of her jaws and the cute parentheses framing her mouth. I let myself be dizzied by her cute dimples sitting symmetrically in those little whirlpools of her cheeks.

A bubble of lilac engulfed her.

"Finally!" I said, giving her a hug and a kiss on the cheek. "It's been so long."

"How true. I'm very sorry, Fred. I feel the same way. But it was a wise decision to wait. Now my ankle is back to where it should be, and tonight I'm ready to prove it."

"I want to first give you a poem I wrote," I said, pulling the sheet of paper out of my shirt and handing it to her. "It's dedicated to you."

"Thank you so much." Her eyes widened when she unfolded and read it aloud.

> *T'was love at first sight, I confess.*
> *You'd just blown in from a rousing ride,*
> *Wrapped in jodhpurs and boots, no less,*
> *Enclosed in a bubble of lilac, sloe-eyed.*
> *Your hand would reach out,*
> *Leaving me smitten, in awe of your clout.*
> *Your image at once cast a spell on me.*
> *I knew right then, I'd have no choice,*
> *But to share my days with you, in glee,*
> *And nights to boot, in counterpoise.*
> *Let's make it more than just a gleam*
> *Of a phenomenon we call a dream.*

"Wow! I've never known anybody who wrote a poem about me," she said, catching her breath. It was as though she intended to give me a kiss on my lips, but at the very last moment caught herself and deflected it onto my cheek. I was overcome by a feeling of inadequacy. The image of her dad sitting behind that huge oak desk, surrounded by all the somber portraits of his ancestors, flashed across my mind. What was I but a simple vaquero and one with a dubious past to boot? I couldn't tell if she'd noticed my awkwardness. But there was a pause.

171

"Thanks again," she said hastily. "I suggest, we take the shortcut I told you about. It's a horse and cattle trail, you know, kind of rough. We should get going. I'd like to get there before it gets dark."

She stepped into the stirrup, swung her leg over the horse's loin, whipped her bottom into the saddle and got going. I did likewise, following her. It was uphill and down dale, but we made good headway, thanks not least to our husky horses. And forty-five minutes later the first dwellings of Cuauhtemoc edged in our range of vision.

We dismounted in front of Casa Vieja, tied up our horses and entered. It was an unassuming but bubbly eatery, crammed with a clamorous crowd of people, some of whom, curiously enough, were Mennonites. Housed in a building whose fortress-like walls were made out of adobe bricks, it offered traditional Mexican fare at reasonable prices, which I greatly welcomed because I hardly had any money. My dollars were long gone, seeped through my hand. Thankfully, Luis Avila, the gerente, had been so kind to offer me an advance of 600 pesos, but I knew next to nothing how much a dinner for two would cost. And, let's face it, I didn't want to give my date the impression that I was a cheapskate.

Owing to the fact that Carolina knew the owner, we were quickly seated at a table for two, located in the liveliest of rooms near a window. It was set with a white tablecloth, blue cloth napkins and two lit candles. The ambiance couldn't have been more romantic. To begin with, we picked a bottle of red Rioja. More precisely it was Carolina who thought the occasion demanded it. For dinner, she selected carne adovada with *arroz, frijoles, pico de gallo* and a green salad, while I picked *enchiladas de pollo, arroz, frijoles,* as well as a green salad.

As soon as the waiter had served the wine, I toasted to 'the future of our budding relationship'. We clinked glasses. I thought that the occasion should be sealed with a kiss. Yet, once again, Carolina turned away, offering me no more than her cheek. In our subsequent conversation, she revealed to me that she'd had a long talk with her dad. They talked about Jorge, her brother, who lives as a bon vivant in Mexico City, where he mingles with the film crowd, with actresses and actors, as well as artists of every stripe. She informed me that her father despised him because he led, what he dubbed, such a debauched life, but most of all because he showed no interest in the running of the hacienda.

She also touched on her dad's financial woes. Apparently, the contract with the government to buy five hundred cattle per year from the hacienda was running out and had to be renegotiated. According to her dad, this sale was crucial for the financial stability of the hacienda. As usual, the government official in charge demanded an outrageously high bribe her dad refused to pay. Yet without it the contract had no chance of getting renewed.

"If Dad can't get the contract, we may well have to sell large chunks of land," Carolina said, knitting her brow. "Too bad, it's a buyer's market right now. There are swaths of land for sale. The price per hectare has plunged to the point where the land wouldn't bring all that much. Besides, such a sale would further shrink the profitability of the hacienda."

"You don't mean the hacienda could go broke?" I asked, shaking my head in disbelief.

"Yes, that's precisely what we're all worried about. I only hope we can weather the turmoil. Let's see how things shake out. Dad always has a tendency to exaggerate our troubles. But selling land is about the only ray of hope I can see at the moment."

"I'm shocked to hear that. I always thought you live on a rock-solid ranch."

"That's what *I* thought. But you know all things have a beginning and an end."

She was on the verge of tears. I reached over, took hold of her hands and squeezed them. There was a hint of a smile, followed by a long pause.

"Here's to us," I finally said, raising my glass, "and to the evening ahead of us."

"I agree. We've got to seize the day." We chinked glasses.

"I don't want to belittle the problems you discussed with your dad, but did you mention anything about our relationship?"

"No, I didn't. It's still a little early. We've only met twice. Things have to settle first. I'll bring it up one of these days."

"Are you afraid he might not approve of it?"

"Well, yes, knowing Dad. He's a small despot who never gives in without a big fight. My mother is much less rigid. She's usually on my side. But I'm old enough to make my own decisions. And if he wants to fight, so be it."

I found that very refreshing and raised the glass to her grit.

Buoyed by the romantic, candle-lit atmosphere and the tippling of the Rioja, Carolina was able to brighten her mood, becoming much more chipper, even amiable. I, too, unshackled, getting bolder, so bold in fact I even managed to steal a real kiss from my sweetheart. It was nothing more than a superficial meeting of our lips. Actually, I tried to penetrate, but failed. Still, it had a lot of hope riding on its back.

Once again, my heartthrob was unusually curious about my past, about my early years in Switzerland, as if she suspected there was something fishy about my previous account. Well, I managed to swing far back, holding her to a colorful yarn about the Alps, the life in the country, working, yodeling and all. I faked, invented and cooked up stories about Swiss vaqueros, dairy cows, driving them out to green pastures, milking them and, in the end, rolling fat wheels of Emmentaler through the narrow streets of mountain villages. While I felt increasingly embarrassed about my gift of the gab, Carolina seemed to savor my stories. She repeatedly referred to the Mennonites, claiming that many of them originally hailed from the Switzerland I'd depicted.

At the end, while we were munching on wedges of chocolate cake and talked about Europe, we also touched on the war. "I'm glad the Nazis are now getting a dose of their own medicine," she opined. "I just heard on the radio this morning that the Russians have finally figured out a way to clobber the German Army. I just hope the tide has turned for good and the bloodshed will soon come to an end. The world can't stand by and watch the slaughter of so many innocent people, especially Jews."

Although I applauded her remarks, I also felt a deep empathy with my comrades who were in danger of being blown to pieces. And for what? The glory of our great leader, Adolf Hitler. I wondered how she'd have reacted had she known that her Swiss charmer had actually received a medal of bravery from the German Army.

The dance hall stood on the other, southern, side of the town, but a ten-minute ride and we stood right in front of it. It was an old mud-brick building whose high, lime-washed walls were propped up by several buttresses, some of which were so crooked the walls actually leaned into the building. I also noticed cracks, especially on the other side of the entrance, where the walls seemed to have sagged. Although the dancing hall may originally have been a granary or a horse stable, it was now the navel of Cuauhtemoc's youth.

We dismounted, tied down our horses, handed a youngster 5 pesos to watch them and threaded our way through the crowd to the entrance. There was a long line, but it moved quickly. I paid 10 pesos for both of us. It was my guess that more than three hundred young people jammed into its interior, which was decked out with strings of lights — bulbs dangling from cables fastened to a wooden roof frame. Mantled in colorful paper bags, they served as magnets for a motley assortment of insects swirling around them. They, in turn, must have lured various birds, even two small falcons in search of a late-night supper. How they were able to sneak into a dancing hall was a mystery to me.

The dance floor itself was nothing more than a shiny surface of concrete. It looked as though it sagged toward the other side, away from the entrance, where a five-man band played mostly Mexican tunes. As we entered, it wrestled with the American popular song *Moonlight and Roses*, familiar to me from the camp.

Although most of the tables, the ones close to the dance floor, had already been taken, we were able to secure one farther back, surrounded by a noisy, tumultuous crowd. The air was thick with a curious mixture of cologne, sweat, leather and a faint reminder of horse dung, soaked in you-can-imagine-what. Most of the guests chose to guzzle beer, as did I. My *carina*, however, preferred a fancy cocktail, as well as a portion of guacamole.

No sooner did the waiter set the orders on our table, than we took to the dance floor. The band, made up of an accordion player, two fiddlers, a trumpeter and a drummer, chose to play Jacinto, a fast and fiery Mexican evergreen, I'd never heard before. But Carolina had, and fondly so; she was virtually carried away by it, going into raptures, as if she were possessed by a demon. Endowed with a natural feeling for rhythm, she had quickly unshackled herself and, tossing back her open mane, rocked, stomped, swirled, swayed, sashayed and shimmied her way through the crowd. The range and execution of her movements left me awestruck.

What happened to the sprained ankle?

With insects swarming around the Mexican lanterns, the accordion warped, chirping and chittering, the trumpet rapping and blaring, and the violins whining, whimpering and gusting, Carolina and I kept dancing one round after another, never ever missing one, until we were both out of breath and drenched in sweat.

"Fred, I think we deserve a pause," my *novia* sighed, pearls of perspiration running down her forehead and cheeks. "Let's go outside for a while and cool down."

"Good idea."

I put my arm around her and we stepped outside. It was a cool night with barely a stirring in the air. According to the radio Carolina listened to, those residing in higher elevations might be pinched by the first frost of the season. The moon was just a little short of full, coating Carolina's flushed face with a soft, pale sheen.

"Wasn't that fun?" I commented after we had placed our bottoms on a stone wall. I praised her on her dancing skills and her fiery temperament. "When you raised your arms over your head and stomped your feet, you reminded me of an Andalusian Gypsy. I mean it as a compliment."

"Don't worry, I bagged it as one. Actually, you're not that far off. My ancestors did, indeed, come from Andalusia. Of course, it goes without saying that I'm not a Gypsy. But I actually admire the Andalusian Gypsies, at least when they're dancing Flamenco. I watched some of them performing in Mexico City. Yes, I really enjoyed myself."

"It showed, except for the last two dances maybe."

"Oh, you noticed? Yeah, unfortunately it was my ankle. I must have overdone it. Anyway, I felt it. I may have to slow down, if you don't mind."

"Of course not. But maybe we should first take a look."

"Sure." She raised her right leg onto the wall, pulled up her skirt and pushed her sock down.

"Oh, it's even swollen," I reminded her. "Meaning, it's inflamed. You've got to get the swelling down, otherwise it can't fully heal."

I kissed and stroked it. I also gave her a light massage.

"Oh! Fred! It feels so good!" she blurted out. "I wish, you were around more often."

"Well, my *carina,* the choice is yours."

"I know, I know. If only…"

"If only… what?"

"Well, we'll have to see."

We stepped into the hall again. This time we agreed to pick only the slower dances. Shortly after we'd taken our seats, the band played the old favorite La Paloma, whose German version I had heard way back in Berlin. I couldn't let that pass. So when I got the nod from my sweetheart, I gently put my hand around her waist and led her out onto the floor. Unlike before, I pressed her close to me, to the point where I felt her bosom and her thighs. With her head snuggled up against my shoulder, I repeatedly kissed her forehead and brushed my nose over her hair, getting drunk on the fragrance of her sebaceous oil, blended as it was with the lilac of her perfume. When the violins waxed especially sentimental, I remember bending down and offering her a soul kiss. To my great surprise, she actively responded to my move, after hesitating at first. I was greatly relieved. Finally, we were entwined. At the same time, her willingness also stirred my loins, kicking my Cowper's gland into full throttle. Soon a wet blotch began to appear around the fly of my pants. Since it was noticed not only by Carolina, but also by the other dancers, it turned out to be a great embarrassment to me.

We finally decided to leave the dance hall shortly past eleven, owing not least to the increasing pain in Carolina's ankle. This time we decided to ride the regular road. We were both worn, yet thoroughly content about the outing. We talked, joked and laughed most of the way, about the flimsiness of the dance hall the good-natured spirit among the Mexican youth, mentioning also their lack of decorum, their clumsiness, shabby clothes and their awkwardness of bumping into others or stepping on their toes, without apologizing. Carolina commented on their drift of bunching up in front of the band owing to the downgrading of the dance floor.

We got back to the hacienda a few minutes shy of midnight. We saw no light burning anywhere. Everybody seemed to be asleep, at least we hoped so. At any rate, Carolina didn't mind us riding our horses all the way to the stable. With them whinnying to each other, I instantly heaved myself out of the saddle and then helped my *novia* out of hers, but not until I had kissed her ankle again, accompanied by some ancient *Zauberspruch* (magic chant) I'd heard murmured to me by a matron at the orphanage. My *novia* was ravished, giggling like a five-year-old who had just won a tickling contest. Waxing confident, I reached up, slid my arm under my heartthrob's right bun and lifted her out of her saddle. All I heard was a squeak of surprise, followed by laughter.

"*Hijole!* Are you strong!"

"That shouldn't surprise you," I said, holding her tight. "I can't let you go now 'cause you're an invalid. I have to take care of your ankle. It needs my attention. I'm a Samaritan. Duty is calling me."

"But I…"

I sealed her lips with a kiss, *a la francaise*. Our tongues, after initially playing ring-around-a-rosy, eventually settled into a semi-classic dance: they first moved together in unison, then crossed and intertwined each other, until finally loosening the tie to become undone.

My hands, meanwhile, had minds of their own. While the left held on to her waist, the right went for my *novia's* buttocks, stroking them. However, at that point Carolina became stubborn. "You're a *cabron* (billy goat)!" she spit, staunchly pushing me off. "Be a man; tame yourself."

I turned a deaf ear, goatish as I was. It wasn't until she slapped my face that I got the message. I yielded, offering her an apology.

That soothed her. Not only would she calm down, she even managed to squeeze out a cackle.

"Since you're going to be busy during the week," she said matter-of-factly, "how about getting together Sunday in two weeks? We could take our horses to the canyon lands down south. It's very beautiful there. The vegetation and the rock formations are truly spectacular. We could take a hike in one of the canyons. I'll bring along the provisions and backpacks."

"Sounds wonderful. I realize that you may still have some trouble with your ankle but couldn't we do it a week earlier? I'm off, you know."

"Sorry, I already promised to accompany my dad to church. He doesn't go regularly, yet every once in a while he feels he should. It's important for him to be seen, especially with me."

"Too bad. It's going to be a long wait for me."

"How about me? In your case, time will go very fast. You're going to be very busy up there in the mountains. By the way, I want to thank you for the invitation. It was a wonderful evening. I enjoyed myself so much."

"So did I. It was special. I'll never forget spending this evening with you, regardless of what happens, the dinner, the dances and, yes, also the kisses. What a privilege. It seems unreal. Think about it, there's a savage war going on. People are getting killed by the thousands while we were dining, dancing and having fun."

"I know. *Innocent* people. Women, children and old people. And Jews, just because they're Jews." She shook her head.

There was a minute of silence.

"I have a feeling we don't count our blessings enough," I said.

"How true. Our worries are tiny compared to the worries of the world. Our hacienda still is almost a Shangri-la."

"I don't know what a Shangri-la is, but I've never had it so good. Incidentally, how is your ankle?"

"It's swollen. I feel some pain, especially when I'm standing up."

"Be sure to put ice on it."

"I will. I'm glad you reminded me. — But I have to go now. See you Sunday in two weeks at nine, at the tall ponderosa again."

"I'll be there."

"Goodnight, my *guero*. And sweet dreams."

"Goodnight my *novia.* I'll miss you."

We kissed one more time.

I should note that instead of reveling in sweet dreams, I suffered through one of the worst nights in recent memory. My *cojones*, for some reason or other, throbbed and ached all night, to the point where I began to seriously worry about losing my potency.

SUN, SWEAT AND DUST

We were hand-clapped out of bed at five. It felt as if I were back in the army again. A quick wash. After breakfast, we, altogether eight *vaqueros,* saddled eight horses, gathered a few shotguns, an axe and a saw, two tents, bedrolls, and an assortment of pots, pans, plates, utensils, as well as all kinds of provisions. Having loaded them on our two pack horses, we climbed our trotters and began trekking up the mountain in an effort to drive the cattle down from the high mountain meadows and funnel them into large holding pens. As I was told by Guillermo that some of them, the heftiest and burliest, would then be driven to the trailhead in Cuauhtemoc and sold to the slaughterhouses. The others would stay in the pens until next spring, fed and sheltered from the inclemency of the weather.

Mercifully, the pain in my gonads had faded away by Sunday morning. That untangled me from my worries, making me receptive to new experiences, of which the cattle drive was one. There was a whiff of adventure in the air

With a few exceptions close to the hacienda, the ride turned out to be a long and arduous slog, across a most challenging terrain such as arroyos, creeks, gulches, ravines and canyons, as well as along abysses and chasms that might spook our horses shitless. It was one of the wildest, most forbidding landscapes I'd ever come across. From God's abode, it must have resembled a huge wad of crumpled packing paper, sprinkled with green confetti, specifying higher regions.

Yet we were a tough bunch, as sinewy as the deer and pronghorn jerky we chewed to curb our appetites. I recalled the ride up the mountains on the ranch near Murphy, and how drastically the vegetation kept changing, as we gained in elevation. Not unlike at the ranch, we, too, moved up the ladder from grasses and shrubs to dwarfish oak, juniper, pinyon, albeit at higher elevations. As our train of horses snaked and zig-zagged its way up even higher, small ponderosas began to appear, standing far apart in stiff competitions with pinons and madrones. They in turn were soon kept in check by tall and imposing conifer forests, dominated by tall ponderosas and majestic Douglas firs. The latter ruled the mountains — save for the areas with easy access. There, dogged Mexican lumberjacks had chopped down large swaths of those huge trees and hauled them off for timber, while at the same time making room for lush mountain meadows, where many of our cattle spent the warm season.

Guillermo had his eye on one of those meadows, located close to the Continental Divide. We happened to arrive there shortly before sunset. The temperature was dropping precipitously. On the fringes of the meadow, in the shadow of a tall ponderosa, there stood a small wooden shack. It was occupied by Sabine, an old hermit, whose main task was to protect the cattle from rustlers. Only five feet tall, he had a shriveled face, highlighted by two glittering ogles that were bursting with curiosity. With his white beard and his broad-brimmed hat, he looked like a figure from another, bygone age.

Although he projected the gentle appearance of a Benedictine monk, I soon began to have doubts when I saw a rifle hanging from one of his walls. According to Guillermo, he was a sort of poet-philosopher, who had written several volumes of poetry published in Mexico City and even in Madrid. In his previous life he'd been a Jesuit priest who allegedly left the order in disgust because it had no room for his ideas. Curious as to how he survived up here, I was told that, every once in a while, Tarahumara Indians supplied him with grub. Occasionally he also ventured out with his rifle to bag a rabbit or even deer. His water needs were met by the run-off of rain water from his roof, which he collected in a barrel.

Sabine warned us right off the bat that we should be bracing for a clear and frosty night and that, of late, there were marauding bears in the area. "If I were you, I'd hide my provisions in tree branches they can't reach," he said. "The bears are now extremely hungry before hibernation. The other night, they even brought down a calf. That's very unusual. It was in the dead of night, and I couldn't possibly have saved it."

"Thanks for the advice," Guillermo said. "Fred, you're in charge."

Having unsaddled the horses and letting them trot off into the meadow, we all joined in unloading the pack horses. While four of us pitched the tents and three busied themselves with finding and chopping firewood and building a fire, I tried to locate some tree branches where we could safely suspend our provisions. Luckily, I did indeed find one nearby, but unsure whether it would prevent the bears from reaching the grub, I milked Sabine for advice.

"You've made a good choice," he assured me.

We fell into a chat. He asked me where I was from, and I offered my usual response. He said he admired Switzerland for staying neutral, but wondered how long it could. The pressure must be enormous. Like Carolina, he, too, condemned Hitler, calling him a *maton* and *belicista,* a thug and warmonger.

I was curious about his poetry. He felt flattered, but then put me off politely, saying that, being a foreigner, I'd have enormous difficulty understanding it. Besides, poetry was an art in its death throes. "Ours is a prosaic age," he claimed. "I'm living at a time that has long passed. Somebody once called me a Don Quixote among the Mexican writers."

Less than an hour and a half later, we all, including Sabine, sat around the campfire and gobbling up beans, steaks and tortillas. The warmth of the fire made us feel snug. The temperature had already dropped and crept toward zero. Thankfully we were prepared. According to Guillermo the tents and our thick bedrolls would shelter us and keep us warm.

It was a long and grueling day, and my eyelids became heavier and droopier. Worse, I had yet to string up several bags of provisions. Having woefully underestimated their heft, I was forced to climb the tree and venture out onto the limbs before I could safely tie them down.

Tired, drained, we hit the sack at nine p.m. Several hours later, close to midnight, we were roused by growling and groaning bears. Lured by the scent of our grub, they tried to pull down the bags. It sounded as though one may have climbed the ponderosa, but then, trying to reach the outer end of the branches, lost its grip and thumped to the ground. The racket also startled the horses. Frightened, they snorted and stomped. We were all rattled. Peace was not restored until Guillermo jumped up, grabbed a rifle, rushed out and fired a few shots in their direction.

We perked up at five again. It was still dark and shivering cold. Hoarfrost coated the meadow, reminding me of Germany. Our cook, Jose, gathered some kindling, tossed it onto the charcoal, stoked it and soon the flames lit up the area around the shack and tents. I climbed the ponderosa, untied the bags and dropped them into the arms of Jose. Warmed by the fire, we wolfed down our breakfast and sipped our coffee. Once we had satisfied our stomachs, Guillermo told us to mount our horses, spread out and round up the cattle and drive them to another, very large meadow lying a little below. Since they'd gathered in clusters, it was easier than I'd anticipated. Within hours we had rounded up close to nine hundred head, and before noon had accomplished the first phase of the drive.

Five of us rode back to the upper meadow, folded the tents, gathered the bedrolls, all the kitchen ware, the rest of the provisions, the shotguns, and loaded everything onto the pack horses. Sabine, who had picked up his few belongings, did likewise. We mounted our horses, our poet climbed onto a pack horse, and off we went, heading down to the lower meadow, hoping to join the rest of the crew. Far above us, four *zopilotes* wheeled in a postcard-blue sky, scouring the landscape for carrion. And farther to the south, I saw two even bigger birds with huge wing spans riding the thermals. "They're condors," Sabine explained to me, smiling. "Aren't they majestic? They're the biggest birds in the Americas. Sadly, they're in big trouble. We've cut down their range and shot at them. Their days may be numbered. I really feel for them."

Now that we'd all gathered, the real drive could begin. Up in our saddles, we hastened to draw a narrow horseshoe around the herd, the open end pointing toward the drift of the drive. Cracking our rawhide whips, we whistled, squeezed and then goaded the animals into moving, generally in a northeasterly direction. There was a lot of mooing, pushing, shoving and jostling but once the throng got going, things smoothed out. It helped that the route we chose was much more gradual and less dangerous than the horse trail on the way up, though quite a bit longer. After a few hours, we changed course and started heading east. Unfortunately, as we descended into more arid areas, the cattle kicked up huge billows of fine dust. Besides making us look like blanched miners, the dust got into our mouths, settled on our teeth, clogged our ears, noses and eyes. Worst of all, it made normal breathing wishful thinking. I don't know what we would have done, had it not been for the bandanas we could wrap around our mouths. Adding to the discomfort was the fact that, as it warmed up, we were dripping with sweat. That came on top of the stale sweat of yesterday which, due to the lack of water, we'd been unable to scrub off. All that marked us as a most smelly lot. What may have blunted the edge a little was the fact that, apart from clogged noses, we were among equals and that *all* of us stank to high heaven.

Since most of the terrain sloped in the direction of our drive, we made good time and shortly past five we had already reached our goal for the day — the bottom of a small canyon. Thanks to a clear stream that flowed through it, there was plenty of water, as well as green fodder for our cattle. And the herd took advantage of it right away, drinking, foraging and resting in the shade of large cottonwoods. Once we had unsaddled our horses, pitched our tents and had a bite to eat, I, too, was drawn to the stream, where I threw off my garb and scrubbed off the dust and the sweat. That's all it took to feel human again. Adding a little kick to my joy, I even caught a couple of trout (by hand, no less), which I later skewered, fried over the camp fire and put away.

With the approaching night, we all gathered around the camp fire again, sharing stories about past cattle drives, even assaults by cattle rustlers. Given my poor command of Spanish and my lack of experience, I could only listen. Like at the meadow above, we sacked out relatively early, shortly past nine, mindful that the sleep would be short. Each one of us was called upon to do two hours of guard duty to prevent rustlers from swiping our cattle. My beat happened to be from twelve to two.

Thankfully, the night held no surprises in store. Unlike at the meadow, we sighted neither bears nor rustlers. Only once in a while did we hear cattle mooing and coyotes yowling and wailing. The latter again reminded me of my first winter in Russia, when I heard the wolves howling into a starry, merciless sky. Back then, I was as green as a bowl of salad, marinated to the core in Hitler's Nazi ideology. That was barely two years ago. How far I had traveled, how much I had changed. Or was it the world that had changed *me*? Be that as it may, I couldn't but shake my head in wonder.

The rest of the drive turned out to be much more burdensome and enervating. Since it got warmer and drier, the dust kicked up by the cattle became even worse than on the previous day. The long slog and the lack of water had drained the cattle as well. They were weary, tired and cranky. Often small bunches of mooing and groaning cows and calves would trot off into the bushes in search of shade. To get them into line, we had to crack our rawhides, yell and whistle at them. Sometimes they simply refused to move, and to force them back to the herd we had to use sticks and strike their ribs or hipbones.

The most weary and vulnerable were the calves. Having grown up in a half-wild state, they'd never seen a human before, much less one sitting high on a horse. They were literally scared shitless, with plenty of green goo running down their hind legs. Watching them stumble along the last few kilometers, especially on that last rocky stretch down the arroyo, I felt sorry for them. But all that whistling, shouting and shoving eventually paid off. I fully shared Guillermo's joy when he announced that we had managed to save the whole herd without a single loss.

I may note that the drive — we covered more than fifty-five kilometers — was quite challenging for us too, worsened by the billows of dust, the physical strain of sitting erect for so many hours and, worst of all, the lack of sleep. Nobody was happier than we and, after having funneled these worn-out critters into large holding pens and providing them with water and feed, we were finally released. Before we stepped into the bunkhouse, we knocked off the dust. And once inside, we scrubbed off the pancake makeup and went about cleaning ourselves. Never had I seen so many of my compadres taking cold showers.

Come Wednesday, we gathered around the various stock pens. First, we separated the yearling steers, more than three hundred of them, from the other cattle. Four of us, including me, were selected to drive some of them to the railhead in Cuauhtemoc. From there they would be shipped, so we were told, to slaughterhouses in Chihuahua and Mexico City, where they'd face the hammer when they entered and eventually come out as raw sides on a hook. Somehow these critters must have had an inkling of their fate. The closer they came to the railhead, the more stubborn they became, as well as frightened, even scared to death, or so their frequent bowel movements indicated. They dropped everything they had, coating their hind legs with thin green muck. They mooed, bawled and groaned and, whenever they had a chance, they'd run off into the bushes. Occasionally they'd even take a stand when we, trying to make them join the herd, cracked the whip or whistled to them. Two of my fellow vaqueros lost their temper, whipping them with their rawhides or lashing out at them with their thick ropes, accompanied by wild screams and curses.

I for one couldn't help but feel very sorry for those animals. *What a shock they must go through. After living peacefully in a semi-wild state high up on the lush, almost Alpine meadows, those two-legged brutes with sweat-stained sombreros, leathery, crumpled faces and calloused hands would all of a sudden appear and, cracking their whips, drive them into inhuman, crowded stockpens, or to more misery and eventual death in a filthy, smelly slaughterhouse.* More often than not, I was tempted to raise my voice, mentioning precisely these objections. But in the end, I always held my tongue. I couldn't, I wouldn't want to risk my job, much less be separated from Carolina.

It was tough on me. I heaved deep sighs of relief once we had delivered these animals to the stock pens near the railroad station. While all three of my compadres rode back, I took advantage of the occasion and stayed in town for a few hours. I left my horse at the cattle pen and sauntered through the streets. I went into shops and bought some clothes, a pair of attractively ornamented cowboy boots and, last but not least, a classically elegant silver bracelet for my heartthrob.

Eager to find out what had happened at the front, I also picked up a copy of the Chihuahuan *Diario*, went into a coffee shop and, sipping on a heady cup of Mexican coffee, tried to peruse it. As usual, there was hardly any international news in it. All I found was a small report on page five that disclosed Russian troops were pushing back the Germans near Kiev. Kiev, the city, where in the fall of 1941 Ernst and Peter, my two best friends, were mowed down by a Stalin Organ. According to General Zhukov, the city would likely be recaptured in the next few days. On the western front there was reportedly little movement.

The rest of the week I spent feeding cattle and inspecting them for possible injuries or diseases. The bull calves also had to be branded and castrated, two unpleasant tasks I had never witnessed before, much less done. I watched both, the practice of heating up a branding iron and burning a certain mark of ownership into the hide of a live animal, as well as slicing open the scrotum and tearing out the testicles. The first appeared to be cruel and barbarous, the second nothing less than pitiless savagery that brought me to the cusp of throwing up. Yet I seemed to be the only one who reacted with such loathing. My Mexican compadres went at it with a nonchalance, a happy-go-lucky attitude, as if they were cutting down a dead tree.

At first, I shirked doing either. But I did help rope the animals and prepare them for these procedures. It wasn't until Guillermo politely called me to account that I, too, began to face the music, at least partially. With great reluctance, I roped, grounded, restrained and branded, as well as ear-tagged a full sixteen of these bull calves. It was nauseating, for the eyes no less than the nose. The stench of burning hide got so stamped into my mind that any similar smell would invariably conjure up images of my most loathed stint as a vaquero.

As though this weren't enough already, on Friday, one day after we had started castrating, we were served *cojones de monteses* for lunch. Teresa, our cook, would even praise them as *verdadero manjar,* a real delicacy, better than prime *bistec*. She even offered me a piece to taste, not knowing that I was close to retching. I swore never to touch them. My disdain surged so far that I seriously considered becoming a vegetarian. Sadly, I didn't quite make it. But I did go halfway: from that time on I'd never touch beef again.

'THE MURMUR OF THE COTTONWOOD'

"You're early," I cracked as I approached her.

She was sitting in the sun near the ponderosa. The horses rested close by. She was dressed in a blue blouse, a pair of khaki pants, hiking boots and a broad-brimmed, beige felt hat.

"Oh, am I?" she said, getting up and greeting me with a wide smile.

I took off my rucksack. We dropped our hats, hugged and kissed.

"Tempestuous as ever," she said, catching her breath.

"Passionate, I hope! Anyway, I'm so happy to see you. It's been so long."

"For me too."

"I almost forgot. I have something for you, a little gift you might appreciate."

I pulled the silver bracelet out of my rucksack and handed it to her. "This is a small token of my love for you."

She opened the case and took it out. "How beautiful. It perfectly fits my taste. Classical! Less is more. Thank you so much. You're such a gentleman."

She kissed me and then slipped it over her wrist. "Wow!" she burst out.

I squeezed her head with my hands and kissed her forehead. "So how has my *novia* been? Has she recuperated? How's her ankle?"

"Quite well, thank you. And the ankle's much better, too. All I can say is I followed my doctor's advice. I put a lot of ice on it. I think it's fine now, ready for a hike."

"Touche! Oh, what a day."

"Typical fall weather. Dry, sunny, cool nights. But warm days."

"So tell me, where are we going? You are my guide now."

"As I told you, to the canyon lands. They're about twenty-five kilometers to the south. It'll take us about an hour and a half to get there. I've been there many times, as a kid. It's stunningly beautiful. There are colorful rocks, sparkling creeks and a lot of vegetation. The trees and bushes are probably in their fall colors now. But getting there isn't going to be easy."

"Like everything else that's worthwhile, including..." I looked at her and nodded.

186

"Me?" She broke out in laughter and then, pulling in her lips, smiled.

I picked up my rucksack. We put on our hats, mounted the horses and, with Carolina in the lead, started trotting in a southerly direction. Leading us was a narrow horse trail that seemed to slice through the landscape against its natural grain. From the beginning, big boulders or large colonies of prickly pear cacti blocked the way, forcing us to zig-zag to the right and left. Rocky and sand-filled arroyos fringed by dense vegetation had to be crossed. The worst obstacles we encountered were those tight ravines that made us dip down on one end and climb out on the other, occasionally through narrow gaps, in the hope of reaching a new plateau. At times our horses got so frightened that we had to dismount and lead them by the rein past dangerous precipices, escarpments, or narrow switchbacks.

In the end, it was all worth it. Or so Carolina claimed, as she drew the reins and came to a halt. "That's what I'm talking about," she said, sweeping her hand through the air.

"Wow! Spectacular! What a confusing tangle of canyons back there, and to the left, too. By the way, is this still part of your hacienda?"

"Don't we wish. No, it belongs to another spread. But my dad knows the owner and is on good terms with him."

We stood at the rim of a medium-sized canyon. Down below, a stream meandered through the valley floor, glistening like a ribbon of silver. Stands of deciduous bushes and trees, now all in their fall colors, lined it.

We trotted down the escarpment through talus and detritus, past oaks, pinons and junipers, all dwarfed by several tall pinnacles and spires, until we finally reached the valley floor. Carolina right away aimed for the stream, for a large cottonwood right by the banks, whose leaves blazed with gold. Having found a sandy spot, we dismounted and took off the blanket, as well as the provisions. While the horses strayed into the stream, we spread the blanket and made ourselves comfortable.

"Are you hungry?" Carolina asked as she opened a bag of victuals.

"For what?"

"For food, you scoundrel." She dealt me a knowing smile. "Or should we first take a hike?"

"Let's eat something first. The hike won't run away."

She pulled out tortillas, enchiladas, avocados, chorizos, a chunk of queso menonita, even a bottle of Mexican Tomas and two stemmed glasses.

I grabbed the bottle, pulled the cork, poured some wine into the glasses, and handed one to Carolina. "Here's to us!" I said, lifting my glass, "and to a bright future — together!"

"Yes, and to Lady Luck, who has brought us together in such a curious way."

We drank, locking eyes.

I bent down, pushed up the cuff of her right pant leg, shoved down the sock and kissed her ankle and then, rising, also her lips. She giggled.

"I don't know about you," she said, smiling suggestively.

With all the morsels begging us, we jumped at the opportunity and ate to our hearts' content, chasing our mash with hearty gulps of wine. At least *I* did. The weather, the delicacies, the whole ambiance — it felt as though we were in the land of milk and honey. Wallowing in idleness, we slipped into the roles of children, occasionally even babies: we snuggled up and caressed each other; we whispered endearments and sweet nothings into each other's ears. And — boy! — did we hug and kiss one another. We knew no fences or hedges; no part of our body was off-limits to our hands, lips and tongues. One thing led to another, and before we became fully aware, we were engaged in the one crucial act we all owe our lives to — making love.

Yet, my heartthrob, after giggling, chuckling and baby-whispering, began to sound as though she were at the opposite end in the throes of death. "Oh, my God, I'm dying!" she gasped repeatedly, with an audible exclamation mark no less. At the same time, judging by her facial movements, how sensuously she opened her lips, flared her nostrils, deepened her dimples and closed her eyes! — she seemed to be on the very pinnacle of life, or even frolicking in the seventh heaven of delight. That's where I found *myself*. In any event, we both savored our quasi-religious moment to the fullest, with a majestic, gold-leafed cottonwood guarding our carnal adventure. The line, 'And listen to the murmur of the cottonwood trees' from *Don't Fence Me In* bubbled up within me.

Once our afterglow had waned, we ventured on our hike, sauntering arm in arm and, playfully, in shimmying motions, bumping into each other's hips in a triumphant sashay of love. Nor did we miss a chance to kiss each other. I may mention that Carolina's ankle, thankfully, held up surprisingly well. Having left the horses behind, we managed to trek a big loop, all the way to the western end of the canyon, where it culminated in a natural amphitheater, with sheer stone walls and a waterfall bursting into the viewers' section.

On the ride back from our outing we once again stopped at the ponderosa. Carolina insisted again that we separate, that I walk back to the hacienda all by myself, as though nothing had changed. "But Carolina, why all this secrecy?" I countered. "Why can't we admit to everybody that we're in love with each other?"

"As I told you before, I don't want people talking. You don't understand, I'm a woman, and my reputation is at stake here. If I lose it, I'm done. Besides, there's my dad. He'd have a fit."

"Let him. He'll calm down again. The same goes for everyone else. Sooner or later it'll be out in the open anyway. Or are you afraid to be seen arm in arm with a smelly vaquero?"

"Fred! How dare you even think that way. You know I love you, but I do need a little more time. I beg you to be patient. Please! What we could do is see each other more often, like during the week, when you get off from work. We could meet up here. Let's say Wednesday at seven?"

I nodded, reluctantly. We kissed and said goodbye.

Needless to say, I was disheartened. Yet there was nothing I could do, short of being patient, of meeting and embracing Carolina in secrecy and keeping up the pressure on her to lift that cloak.

Come Monday morning, I found myself back doing my ranch work, branding and ear-tagging more bull calves. But my head was somewhere else, lashed to my novia. Thoroughly gaga, smitten, I could think of nothing but her, her brown almond eyes and their perfect distance to each other, the angle between her nose and her upper lip, her delicate nostrils, her trow-like philtrum, the triangular facial shape and the angle of her chin, not to mention the bewitching dimples in her cheeks when she smiled. I was spellbound by images of her taut, silky-smooth bosom, scented with lilac and tipped by pullulating brown buds, her well-deep belly button, embedded as it was in a light swell of abdominal fat and, last but not least, her lush, jungly *mons pubis*, whose black hue was so rich and intense, it almost looked dark blue.

I saw my *enamorada* again, in the flesh, on Wednesday night, at the ponderosa. Dusk had already settled. She came high on her horse, and as soon as I lifted her off, we embraced and passionately kissed each other. We communicated only in gestures. We didn't even take the time to speak to each other. Except once, when, slightly raising her red gather skirt, she baited me. "You wouldn't be hungry, would you?"

We both laughed.

"Of course, or I wouldn't be a scoundrel," I said, lolling out my tongue.

"I like scoundrels; I like them served hot so I can eat them up. Especially when it's a blond Viking." She ran her fingers through my hair.

"Bon appetit!"

She had brought her dazzling Mayan blanket, which had been fully in the know about our secret. Not wasting any time, we soon found a spot near the creek, spread the blanket, cuddled, fondled, and kissed one another. We exchanged sweet nothings and somethings by the bushel basket, while the creek gently gurgled in the background. Unfortunately, unlike under the cottonwood, it was a bit chilly and we couldn't simply slide into the roles of Adam and Eve. With our skin mostly covered, we were unfairly hampered. But we knew how to help ourselves. While my novia was more measured, I, forever hungry, carpeted her face, her ears, her neck, her arms, and after tossing her panties aside, every fleshscape below the navel, with ardent kisses. A hopeless victim of my own libido, I surrendered myself to my senses, sucking in her lilac perfume and the fragrance of her skin and hair. Curiously, what captivated me most, and embarrassingly so, was the very odor that tended to repel most people — that musty, yeasty scent that keeps on rising from the very depth of a woman's pelvis. *What other quirks do I have in common with canines?* I wondered. All I can say: it was pure joy, with a sprinkling of privilege, to serve my Andalusian *condesa*. And she paid me, her *guero,* in the currencies of giggles, moans and groans, the whole aural repertory of lovemaking. If those sounds of pleasure revealed anything to me, it was the inkling that the way to Carolina's heart started somewhere on and under her skin.

Once again, my novia, after some initial baby-whispers, whimpered herself into her 'Calling of the Lord'. It was a shudder so intense that I momentarily feared that she'd had some sort of stroke or fit. Yet it was probably nothing more than her gesture of unconditional surrender.

During our long afterglow, as we lay there rolled up in the Mayan blanket, we chatted about our lives and what the future would bring. She tossed out hints of us staying together for good, indeed, of getting married.

"You know, I'm watching my days very closely, but what if I get pregnant?" she suddenly burst out, tightening her grip on my torso. "It could still happen. Have you ever thought about that?"

"Well — not rea-lly," I stuttered. "But you can always count on me. I would take full responsibility for my actions."

She also wanted to know if I would be willing to stay at the hacienda, possibly even take it over if something happened to her father. "I have heard much praise of your work from several sources," she said. "You already understand how a hacienda works. I personally think you would make a grande hacendado, I mean it."

"If the hacienda still has a pulse. You told me just a few weeks ago that it could well shuffle off."

"Yes, but things have improved a little. Two days ago, Dad let me know that the government official had lowered the bribe and he's now weighing the option of simply paying it and signing the contract. But he hasn't made a final decision. Mom and I pushed him to do it."

"That sounds encouraging. And your thought that I would make a great hacendado is very flattering. But have you asked your dad what *his* plans are? I'm sure he has thought about it. And he may well have his own ideas as to what should happen in case of his death. Just trying to read his mind, I'd say he's looking for someone other than a poor vaquero to take over his hacienda."

"You're probably right. I don't think you'd pass the sniff test right *now*. But he might well change his mind if we get married. Just think about it."

"I will."

So far, I hadn't given much thought to most of these questions, weighty as they were. Frankly, I was also a little surprised, not only about Carolina's proposals, but also about myself, my own lightheartedness. I'd looked at the relationship more from the lens of a mutual, sexual attraction, of an adventure that might eventually run its course, not without tears at the end, and possibly worse. Never had I plumbed the gravity of it. As to the question of my eventually becoming an hacendado, I'd never in my wildest dreams mulled over such a possibility. Having been brought up in a very traditional, highly stratified society, I had only seen the large gap between the rich and the poor, the burgher or aristocrat being the upper crust and a peasant or worker the lower. I'd always assumed that this was the natural order of things. And as an orphan and, later, a common soldier, I was convinced that I, Fritz Graf, was scraping an area close to the bottom. As far back as I could remember, I unwittingly accepted the notion of being caught in the threads of my background like a fly in a spiderweb.

Yet, while I was 'caught', I also wriggled. Secretly I cherished the illusion that I could free myself, possibly find a ladder and, who knows, even climb a rung or two. That was also one of the reasons I joined the German Army. I'd heard that you could rise in rank if you proved yourself, even become a big shot if you tried hard enough. It was for the very reason that I liked our *Fuehrer:* Because having been an upstart himself, he'd always tried to give those at the bottom a lift, while dealing the old stuffy order of monocles the shaft.

CONTEMPLATING THE FUTURE

Though this illusion of climbing up the ladder and becoming an officer dissolved in the thin air of the American prison camp in North Africa, it was nourished again during my stay at the camp, especially during my stints on the farms and ranch, when I first saw Americans of all walks interacting. It didn't take me long to notice that in America you could find ladders at almost every corner. Better yet, you could get them at a very reasonable price, well-crafted and unusually sturdy specimens to boot. Unlike their German counterparts, their rungs carried such promising messages like, 'Try me, if you want to smile', or, 'If your soles touch this, you'll be handsomely rewarded', or, 'Don't be shy, you won't regret it'. Some displayed pictures of new, elegant cars, of alluring women, of homes and mansions. One of the most memorable rungs in the upper half showed a stately building named 'University of California' whose doors were thrown wide open. I was so struck by raptures of enthusiasm when I first saw them that I raised my leg in an effort to try them out. But low-rung guards forcefully held me back, shouting, "This ain't for you. Get back behind the barbed wire, you fucking kraut!"

This was the end of my American dream about ladders, rungs and ranks. Welcome to the Mexican apparition.

Well, here in Mexico, I saw myself as I was: a poorly paid vaquero who worked in the good graces of Carolina's father. *What was I but a servant to the family of the hacendado?* I always reminded myself. *A servant also to Carolina, who was a quasi condesa to me.* It had never occurred to me that she'd look upon me as being on the same footing, 'worthy' of her, her sexual fling with me notwithstanding. Yet, all of a sudden, I was promoted from a poor vaquero who rolled in the horse manure soaked with urine, who had to scrape bovine excrements off his work clothes every night, to an hacendado, a conde of sorts. Now if that didn't open up new vistas, nothing would. It was as if all my experiences here on the hacienda had struck roots.

On a more practical note, my sweetheart and unflagging promoter also asked me at the end of our rendezvous if I could help her pick up a new hardwood bedstead and a vanity at the railway station in Cuauhtemoc. "It's a birthday gift my dad ordered for me. It'll be on Friday afternoon, day after tomorrow. Enrique will come along also. Later I would invite you both to dinner at the Casa Vieja."

Who was I to turn her down? "Of course, I would be most pleased to serve you, my lady," I said affectedly, bowing and waving my arm. "May I ask madam condesa when her birthday might be?"

"Certainly. It's not until the beginning of December, on the sixth."

"Are you going to be celebrating, madam condesa? And would I, your faithful servant, be invited as well?"

"There will be a party, and servants, as you well know, always have their place at such events."

"I am very much obliged, madam condesa. As to your furniture: Of course, I, as your loyal servant, would be most happy to carry it to your boudoir and set it up, notably your bedstead. As your humble servant, I might even be obliged to sacrifice myself inaugurating the lair, but only if madam condesa so expressly wishes."

"What an impertinence! Don't you have any manners? You are a vaquero, period, while I was born to be a blue-blooded Andalusian condesa. I want you to be mindful of your social standing. What makes you think you can have a liaison with your lady? You're not a conde yet, by a long shot. I hereby discharge you of your duties as of today. You are fired!"

"Please, forgive me, madam condesa. I humbly apologize."

We laughed and laughed until our bellies hurt.

A NIGHTMARE IN BRIGHT DAYLIGHT

The ride on that old Ford truck was a bumpy, jolting affair, and dusty to boot. Enrique, the driver, tried his best but couldn't do much about the old, washed-out road snaking its way down to Cuauhtemoc. I sat near the right door and Carolina, my *amante,* got sandwiched in the middle. The mood was jovial, decidedly upbeat. Just to be together with Carolina was always uplifting, especially for me. Nor would this Tom Thumb of a town, budge much when it came to feelings of joy and laughter. Our evening at the restaurant, not to mention the romp at the dancing hall were still vivid in my mind. Isolated that I was up at the hacienda, I always welcomed little changes, even if it meant no more than visiting a restaurant or watching the hustle and bustle of people on the plazas and streets.

Yet, on this very day, all these good vibes were destined to be turned upside down. We had barely approached the northern outskirts of the town, when we unexpectedly ran into a barricade. It was manned by five uniformed men with black combat fatigues. Heavily armed with pistols and rifles, they kept pointing their firearms at our truck. Stupefied, I first suspected that they might be banditos who were out to rob us. But Carolina, as well as Enrique insisted, they were Federales, as the federal police force was called.

Coming to a crawl, one of them bellowed at us to pull over. It turned out to be a stout, beefy lieutenant who nervously waved us onto the shoulder.

We all wondered what had happened. I in particular grew very jittery. But Carolina quickly tried to calm me down. "They probably want to *catch* some banditos who'd pulled something off in the area."

Enrique, meanwhile, followed suit and quickly pulled over to the shoulder.

"Get out, arriba las manos!" the lieutenant bellowed, still pointing the rifle at us.

I was the first to step out. For some reason or other I seemed to attract unusual attention. All of a sudden, I was surrounded by three cops who looked me over.

"*Donde estan sus armas?*" (Where is your gun?) the lieutenant shouted, as he patted me down.

"No tengo armas," I said.

"Americano?"

"No Suizo."

"Suizo?" He looked at me in disbelief. *"Como se llama?"*

"Fred Luthi."

"You khave pasaporte?" he bawled in Spanglish.

"No, but I have other identification papers."

"I want to see."

"Unfortunately, I don't have them with me." I gave Carolina, who was standing just four meters away, an imploring glance. But she was busy answering similar questions.

"Hm! You khave *carta migratoria.*"

"Sorry, I don't."

"No pasaporte, no carta magratoria, no documentos. Es caso muy interesante!" He grinned. "Let's shackle him and take him to the police station," he told the other three policemen in a throaty Spanish.

"No, you can't take him!" Carolina shouted, dashing over and embracing me. "He hasn't done anything. He's no criminal. I can vouch for that. He is a very reliable vaquero who has been working at our hacienda for years. My father, Don Leonardo Gomez, will be very upset if he hears you're arresting him. He knows a lot of people in the highest circles, even the governor. You will have to answer some tough questions if anything happens to him. What in the hell is the charge anyway?"

"He khave no papers," the lieutenant said. *"Immigrante ilegal, transgresor de la ley."*

While they shackled me, I saw the lieutenant buttonholing Carolina. According to snippets I pieced together there had been a deadly prison riot at the State Penitentiary in Chihuahua. Apparently, some felons had set fire in their cells, killed their guards and managed to break out.

"Regardless of what you say," I heard Carolina shouting, "this is a case of mistaken identity. Fred is not the criminal you're looking for. He is a peace-loving man. I won't let you take him." She clasped both arms around me.

The lieutenant claimed that he is a professional man who follows the law and he had to take me to the station, where I would be investigated. If I'd turn out to be an honorable man, not the felon they're looking for, I would be released right away.

But Carolina wouldn't be subdued. She fought for me like a hellcat. Flying into a rage, she showered the lieutenant with insults and threats. But all that was in vain.

"Don't worry, Fred, I'll fight for you, come what may," she shouted, as they separated us. "I'll get you out!"

While two policemen held her back, the lieutenant jabbed me with his rifle toward a car. I was rudely pushed into it and spirited away to the police station.

Located on the other end of town, it was housed in a whitewashed, large adobe building. Upon entering, I was unshackled and taken to a primitive jail cell that was attached to the back of the building. Windowless, it had a cement floor and a corrugated tin roof held up by raw, wooden beams. The only light, aside from the iron-barred entrance, came from a naked light bulb dangling from the middle of the ceiling. The cell happened to be chock-full with about twenty-five other suspects. Besides being oppressively hot, it reeked of disinfectants and human feces. The latter came from a latrine, actually a hole in the ground, located way at the other end, opposite the entrance. Luckily there was also a faucet nearby, where we could get water.

At best, the facility was woefully inadequate for taking in and processing so many people. It looked as though we were simply dumped there, with no plans to register, much less interview or investigate us. I saw only one policeman and two guards, who were all armed with pistols. The suspects, all of them Mexicans, were very unruly. Frustrated that nothing was moving, they constantly rattled the iron bars, shouting obscenities at the guards. But the guards simply ignored them, sitting there at a small table, smoking cigarillos, playing cards, burping and breaking wind. Occasionally one would get up and, grinning, arouse the suspects' anger by shouting obscenities at them, making them livid. That was his way of having fun, for all I know. When some suspects spat at him, he cleared his throat and simply spat back. One time, he got upset, untangled a hose and sprayed all of us with water. Actually, he did us a favor since we were all suffering from the heat.

At one point I heard Carolina's voice again, arguing with and shouting at the police officer. I suspected that she'd demanded to talk to me, but they refused to let her near me.

Every once in a while, new suspects arrived, and they were all crammed into our cell, until we were about fifty. It was close to unbearable. We must have waited for more than three hours, when at last a higher-ranking police officer showed up and announced we would all be transferred to the State Penitentiary in Chihuahua, the same prison where the riot had taken place. Two buses were waiting outside to haul us there. So, one by one, we were shackled and led to the buses — battered American school buses from San Antonio, Texas — and ordered at gun point to take our seats.

An hour and a half later, our buses tottered to a halt at the massive gates of the Chihuahua State Penitentiary, close to the train station I'd walked past with Francisco. It was short of the fifth hour. We were ordered, at gunpoint again, to disembark, form a line and march into a black-topped courtyard. The guards, presumably still in shock over last night's riot, were extremely jittery, and each one of us was thoroughly frisked for weapons or explosives again. I and some other suspects even had to drop our pants, so the guards could poke into our rectums in search of knives and whatever else they might be looking for.

Gradually other buses from other towns in northern Mexico kept pulling in and more and more suspects came pouring into the courtyard. In the end there were around two hundred fifty men milling around, while guards got busy setting up long tables. Subsequently they ordered us to fall into one of five lines, with an upper limit of roughly fifty suspects each. With pen in hand, they began registering each one of us. We were asked to give our names and to show them any documents we carried with us to prove our identity. Unfortunately, I had none, a fact which my guard countered with a smirk and a thumbs-down gesture. To him I was an Americano with three question marks, or so he put me down. In the end, we also had to pose for a mugshot.

Once the registration had been taken care of, we were led three flights up, ending up on an iron catwalk, which allowed us to peek into a prison yard below, now deserted. A stench of disinfectants, mixed with the smell of burned wood and fabric enveloped us. One story below, way to the right, my eyes were drawn to a whole row of smoke-stained dungeons, whose floors and doors were smeared with a dark substance that looked like dried blood. We also passed several prison cells that still seemed to be occupied. The vacant ones were reserved for us, two to a cell. The guards randomly picked a pair. I hoped and prayed I wouldn't have to share my cubby hole with some cutthroat.

Well, after some shoving, grating and banging of steel doors, I found myself in a raw, naked prison cell shaking hands with a fellow named Emilio who hailed from Juarez, just across the Rio Bravo from El Paso, Texas. He was a young, sturdy man with a friendly complexion. His button eyes, buried in a broad, fleshy face with a broad stump of a nose and prominent orbital ridges, seemed to signal a certain mellowness, possibly even a willingness to compromise, or so I hoped. Though he was considerably shorter than me, he was blessed with broad shoulders, a barrel of a torso and unusually muscular arms.

Barely bigger than a large closet, our cell had a small iron-barred window on the opposite side of the door. But since the night was about to catch up with us, the only source of light came from a small, fly-specked, 40-watt bulb dangling from the ceiling. Right below the window was the latrine, a mere hole in the cement floor, with a slimy bucket sitting beside it. As I stepped closer, an acrid stench of urine and feces surged up my nose. Attached to the wall was a leaking faucet, whose water dripped into a cracked and filthy porcelain sink. Each of us was provided with an iron bunk which, bolted to the wall, was covered by thin, soiled pads. Conspicuously absent were the bare necessities such as toilet paper, towels, bedsheets and blankets. According to Emilio, these articles were considered to be luxuries that were expected to be furnished by relatives and friends.

I wondered if Carolina knew about that too.

Since I would have to share the cell with Emilio, my first concern was to get to know him a little better. I was eager to engage with him about setting up rules to make our life here more bearable. He was a bit shy, looking up to me. Luckily, he spoke some English, which was of invaluable help. Having heard through hearsay about the violent nature of Mexican jails, I tried to win him over to forming an *alianza* whose purpose would be to counter aggressive behavior toward us and defend one another in case of threats to our well-being or lives. He was very much in favor, thanking me for bringing it up.

We'd also discuss our arrests and what we could do to get out of here. Emilio's answer was simple: mordida, paying bribes. Touching on the absurdity of our experiences, he claimed that he was arrested for doing nothing more than being in the wrong place at the wrong time. There was a shooting and he happened to be in the vicinity. If I understood him correctly, the crime was in search of a perpetrator, and since he was nearby it promptly found him. This is Mexico, he went on, going on a tirade about the chaotic conditions and the outrageous injustices in his home country.

As he worked himself up into a rage, there was a rattling at the door, followed by the opening of the Judas hole. Seconds later, a small tray stacked with six tortillas and a bowl of beans was pushed in. Hungry, we both pounced on it, squarely divided everything and then tucked it away. Thereafter we rolled out our pads, turned off the light and stretched out.

Although fagged, I couldn't for the life of me go to sleep. The arrest and the aftermath were a nightmare come true. I wondered how, if at all, I could counter such a haphazard turn of events. The future looked bleak, bleaker than a winter day in the vast steppes of Russia. *What in the hell can I do to get out of here, and fast?* I kept asking myself again and again. Yet I failed to come up with a plausible answer. The only effective weapon to cut the chains seemed to be a hefty wad of money, a mordida. Unfortunately, all I had was a few pesos, filthy, worthless lappets you could at best wipe your butt with. There was, of course, Carolina. She'd promised to get me out. Unfortunately, she didn't even have an idea where I was. Nor did she have any money. And her dad… If only I could meet with her, talk to her, plead with her. She was my anchor, my sole and only hope.

The rest of the night was eaten up by barking dogs far, far away, rattling snores and occasional shrieks of despair by inmates suffering from some anxiety attacks or communicating with the various bats in their belfry. Every hour, on the hour, I heard the clanging of church bells. Yet I failed to detect the slightest hope in it. Quite the contrary.

The morning came with the sound of a horn, reminiscent of the sirens during air raids in Berlin, when I was on furlough. I got up with a throbbing headache, wished Emilio *Buenos Dias* — which struck me as an irony — and shuffled to the latrine, where I squatted over the hole. Since there was no toilet paper, no paper at all, I knew no other way than to clean my anal crevasse with nothing but water, helped by my hand. *Was I back in Tunisia or Libya?* I also washed my armpits and dried them with my handkerchief. At seven, we made our way down — via rickety, creaky steel ladders — to the prison yard for roll call. The procedure took more than an hour, but in Mexico time was as abundant as the grains of sand in the desert.

Breakfast came in the form of a thin maize mush and tortillas. Sadly, it was neither enough to live on, nor sufficient to die. Subsequently all the inmates, more than four hundred of us, were turned loose into the prison yard. I felt as though I'd entered a boiling cauldron jammed with the scum of the earth. What I saw after weaving through at the fringes made my blood run cold. Never in my experience as a civilian had I witnessed so many battered, swollen eyes, mouths and chins, not to mention broken noses, bowed-out chops, bloody and bandaged hands and arms. At times, when I stood there squinting at it, I momentarily thought I was at a convalescent home for soldiers who had just returned from battle.

On edge, Emilio begged me to stick together. "You never know," was the phrase he used. And we did, and for good reason, it turned out. As he stood there to orient himself, he was instantly heckled by three filthy thugs, who squeezed him for money or goods, such as radios, blankets, clothes and other usable things. When he told them that he was poor and all he had were the clothes and shoes he was wearing, they barked at him to hustle his relatives or friends and make them deliver the money or goods to him.

"I'm a poor and lonely guy," he shot back. "I have no relatives and friends who have money or goods."

"You're a lying bastard, that's what you are," I heard one, the leader, barking at him.

Within seconds they'd cornered him and began pushing and shoving him. One pulled a homemade knife, a *trucha,* and threatened to cut his *garganta* (throat). At that point I couldn't be quiet any longer. Using a thick German accent, I politely urged the thugs to stop harassing him. That seemed to have a calming effect, initially at least. It didn't escape me, that two of them respectfully looked up at me, all the more because of my size and stature. A footnote: I was by far the tallest and brawniest of anybody around, possibly of the whole yard. Lucky for me, I stuck out! Indeed, two of these ruffians were smart enough to bow and scrape. But the third, the stocky, bowlegged fellow who wielded the trucha, seemed less impressed. Raising his knife, he pranced and strutted like a rooster among a flock of hens. More cocky than deft, he even showed me how he'd cut my throat. I bristled, clenched my fist and, resorting to a swift uppercut, struck his chin with such force that the blow may well have dislocated his jaw. Anyway, it hung there, grotesquely out of joint, like a useless part, that didn't belong to his face.

My intention was to set an example. Unfortunately, I couldn't prevent him dealing me a cut on my left arm. Though shallow, the wound was annoyingly messy, begging my handkerchief and shirt to stop the bleeding.

Emilio suffered a cut as well.

Meanwhile, the other two cutthroats had rushed to help their buddy and together they buzzed off. But after a few shuffles, one of them stopped, turned toward us and shouted defiantly, "Watch out! We're gonna get you yet!"

At least that's what the tone of voice and the horizontal thrust of his hand suggested.

Stuck with bleeding wounds, Emilio and I made our way to the *enfermeria.* And whom do we meet there? None other than the snotty swaggerer. Being taken care of by another medic, I was unable to tell exactly what the condition of his jaw was. But Emilio claimed he overheard a nurse saying that his jaw had suffered a serious fracture. "That means, he'll be out of commission for a while," he commented. "That can only help our cause."

"Maybe, but I assume he'll be replaced in no time," I said. "Somehow I have a feeling that it may just be the beginning. I'm afraid, we've done no more than stab into a hornet's nest."

A nurse quickly cleaned and sealed our cuts with bandages.

As we left the medical facility, we both looked at our wounds as part of our initiation rite, thankful that these thugs aimed for our arms and not our guts. Stripped of any illusions, we instinctively knew that we had to watch out, be on the tip of our toes, constantly look over our shoulders and, if challenged, act quickly and decisively. Or else we might soon be carried out horizontally, with our throats cut and tags dangling from our toes.

STUCK IN THE CAULDRON

Although I may have gained the respect of these thugs, I also reckoned that Emilio and I couldn't rely solely on ourselves. Two men, even the strongest and quickest, were not enough of a threat to desperate cutthroats, of whom there were too many.

"What we need are more comrades in arms," I drummed into him, as soon as we got up, "or they'll make mincemeat out of us."

My roommate wholeheartedly agreed.

So, both of us got busy recruiting allies. Watching some confrontations, we'd try to engage with the victims, offering our help and inviting them to join our coalition. And, lo and behold, everyone showed interest; three of them even burst out with enthusiasm, as if it was a question of life and death, which it was. That was reassuring. Calling our partnership 'Los Lobos' (The Wolves) we shook hands and promised we would watch out for each other, and instantly intervene whenever one of us was attacked. One of the newcomers proposed that we actively recruit still other inmates who felt threatened as well. And Emilio came with the idea of putting some money into a common fund we could use to buy truchas and other weapons. Although we all knew that all these moves could never guarantee absolute safety, they made us feel a little more secure in an environment characterized by random violence.

Our group of six Lobos happened to gather again during lunchtime, where we occupied the end of a long table. United by a common cause, we began chewing the fat, hoping to get better acquainted with one another and discuss srategy. Over a bowl of pinto beans, tortillas and vapid enchiladas, we tried to hammer out some details we had touched on previously.

Well, we happened to be in the middle of things when a guard approached to tell me to step aside. He grinned and told me a very *hermosa chiquita* was asking for Fred — me. My pulse spiked, my hands trembled. I jumped up and followed the guard to the Visitors' Room, which was jam-packed with about fifty people. My novia immediately caught my eyes. Although she was still attractive, there was a tinge of sadness about her, livid rings around her eyes. I was beside myself. "Carolina!" I shouted as though I yearned for an echo. We fell into each other's arms. Tears welled up in both of our eyes. Sobbing, we held on to each other for a minute or longer. I drank in her lilac perfume, and for a moment I felt as though we were hugging each other under the ponderosa pine near the hacienda.

"Forgive me for smelling like a skunk," I apologized.

"Forget about it. What counts is that you're alive. It must be awful in here."

She stared at my bandaged arm.

"Worse, it's hell on earth. One of those thugs already attacked me. Thank God I was able to prevent the worst. I'll tell you later."

"How awful! There were several articles in the 'Diario' about it, the riot, the chaos, the gangs in particular, how they terrorize all the other inmates. Now I know why the Federales targeted you specifically. 'Cause you reminded them of Bruce Wozniak, a tall, blond inmate who allegedly started a prison riot right here at the State Penitentiary. According to the report, he and ten other felons, allegedly killed seven guards, took their guns and broke out. As of now they are still on the lam. Wozniak, their leader, reportedly is an American from Brooklyn. And the Federales are feverishly looking for him and the other felons, combing the whole state and beyond."

"You must be kidding. No wonder they are interested in me. But I'm not Bruce Wozniak. Sadly, I can't prove, I'm *not* him. It may be too late anyway. They got me on another charge: of being an illegal immigrant."

"This must be a joke. Regardless, we'll have to get you out, and soon, or they'll carry you out flat as a bread loaf. That's what I've read in those articles. I had no idea. Many of these inmates belong to ruthless gangs that practice extortion. They prey on other inmates who become their victims. They in turn have to beg their relatives to give them money and goodies which will end up in the hands of the gangsters. If the victims resist, they're beaten to pulp or killed. They mentioned some cases where the inmates' relatives had to sell their homes to save the lives of loved ones in jail."

"Yes, they already tried to shake us down and get some money out of us, me and my roommate. And when we resisted, they tried to stab us and threatened to cut our throats. But I hit back hard. Unfortunately, I couldn't prevent the guy from hurting me too." I showed her the cut. "Knowing those thugs, I'm sure they'll try to avenge the blow I dealt them. I expect them to gang up on me. But I'll be ready."

"You're crazy. They have knives. They may kill you." She shook her head in disgust. "Fred, we have to get you out of here, and fast. You shouldn't even be here. Your arrest is an absurdity. Have you been able to talk to anybody about your case at all?"

"No. I tried to, but I couldn't get through. It's Saturday, you know. They told me at the registration last night that it'll take several days before they'll take a look at it."

"Rest assured, I'll do whatever it takes to get you out."

"It may take some money, a lot of it."

"I'm afraid it will. We'll see. I've heard from one of the guards that they have a *papazote*, an attorney, somewhere around here. He helps certain clients to buy themselves out."

"You mean a shyster who squeezes you for mordidas?"

"Yes, I'm eager to talk to him. He'll be back tomorrow. By the way, have you talked with Guillermo about me?"

"Yes, I told him you had some problem with your immigration papers, but you'll probably be back by the end of next week."

"How about your dad? Did you tell him about us?"

"No, but I will in the next few days. He wanted to know why I needed the car this morning, but I just made something up. He'd be horrified if he found out that I'm visiting you in jail."

We still talked about the prison conditions, the lack of guards and the poor sanitary conditions in particular. I also begged her to go to my locker and select a set of clothes, plus socks and underwear, as well as fetch some bedsheets, a towel, a bar of soap and — most urgently! — some toilet paper.

"Yes, there is another thing. On the top shelf of my locker, you'll find an envelope that contains a few documents, particularly one stating that I'm a Swiss citizen. There's also an old horseshoe. It's inside a little burlap bag. It's a talisman of mine, and I would really appreciate it if you could somehow hide it in your pocket and then hand it to me during your next visit. The guards might think it's contraband. So you'll have to be careful."

"Gosh, you don't believe in stuff like that, do you?"

"Well, no, but it really helps me, you know, emotionally. Just bear with me, I'll explain it to you another time. There is another thing. You mentioned a while ago that you've been reading the paper, the 'Diario'. Do you still have it?"

"Sure." She pulled it out of her bag and handed it to me, then promised to be back Monday at the latest.

"Be alert, my *guero*," she said after we hugged and kissed one more time. "Stay away from those cutthroats. And try not to worry. We'll get you out of here one way or another. I miss you so much."

HELL ON EARTH

I felt so much better after Carolina's visit. There were even a few tiny crumbs of hope I'd gathered from it. Still, I harbored few illusions. I expected more dark clouds ahead, churned by the capriciousness of Mexican life and the frightening lack of transparency of its judicial system. Nor did I find the proverbial silver linings. But who knows, life is known for its capriciousness, especially in Mexico. Perhaps with a little rigging, barrels full of luck and, last but not least, *sumas de dinero* for a hefty mordida, I might just be able to wriggle myself free.

Luckily, our alliance seemed to bear fruit already. By staying together in one corner of the prison yard, Emilio and I, as well as our four buddies, managed to avoid any other dangerous encounters. We got together again at supper to refine our strategies.

Once back at our cubby hole, I unfolded the *Diario* and stuck my nose into it. As expected, the news was almost exclusively local and frothy like the head atop a glass of beer. True, the article on the conditions in the jail was enlightening. I also found a small item on the second page that got my attention. It dealt with the Russian liberation of Kiev on the seventh of November. The sacrifices on the German side were staggering, so the report claimed. Young lives were snuffed out by the thousands. The news still felt like a knife in my guts. I could easily have been among them. It may have been Emma who had told me once that we all live on borrowed time. God knows what will happen in the courtyard the next few days.

On Sunday, the day of the Lord, things were a little quieter. For one, the prison yard wasn't nearly as crowded. Many inmates were flocking to the Visitors' Room to greet their relatives, who brought them pesos, provisions and necessities that would make their lives here a little more bearable. Emilio's girlfriend, both of his parents and one of his sisters showed up as well. He insisted that I meet them. From all I could tell, they seemed to be very decent, upright citizens who wouldn't want to get involved in any crime, much less the murder Emilio was accused of. They were dressed in their Sunday attire, having made their way down from Juarez by bus. Though poor as church mice, they still provided Emilio with a few pesos, enchiladas, *carne asada,* avocados and oranges, all of which my roommate freely shared with me. It was a real family gathering, and I as Emilio's compadre was part of it. Everyone was cheerful; sometimes they laughed so heartily as if they attended a country wedding. I was amazed at the knack of Mexicans to resolutely push aside the many bitter pills they had to swallow and squeeze the last drop of joy out of the moment.

Before I left the Visitors' Room, I also had a chance to talk to Jorge, one of the friendly guards, about the *papazote* who could possibly help me. I was told that his name was Feliciano Villareal who supposedly occupied an office on the first floor, way on the southern end of the prison complex. Although Jorge didn't know him personally, he knew Pedro, one of his *ayudantes* (assistants). Better yet, in exchange for a few pesos Jorge even declared himself willing to pump Pedro for an appointment with Senor Villareal.

The new week started on some auspicious notes. First of all, Jorge informed me that Pedro had assured him of the feasibility of seeing Senor Villareal at three o'clock in the afternoon. That buoyed me: I felt like a feather in a breeze. An hour later, Carolina came to visit me again. After we had hugged, she opened her bag and handed me a few necessities, a set of clean clothes, two towels, bedsheets, toilet paper, my documents and — not to forget — my horseshoe. But most importantly, she informed me that she had talked to her dad about her involvement with me.

"Really! How did he react?"

"He threw a tantrum. He thought that it was a big mistake on my part to rush into such a relationship. I should have talked to him before. He also mentioned that I, as his only daughter, as the apple in his eye, had a sacred obligation to the family, that there was a certain tradition that should be observed."

"That probably means you should have picked somebody who is more worthy than me."

"You may be right. He always comes with tradition, family and obligation whenever he has a chance. But I wouldn't take all that as set; it's not hewn in granite, or even sandstone."

"Let's hope so, or else… By the way, did you mention anything about helping me to get out of here? Like money for a mordida?"

"Yes, I did, at the very end. He flared up again, claiming that you fully deserve being thrown into jail, that he'd sensed from the beginning that you had a criminal streak down your back. He made a big deal out of your illegal entry. To him it shows that you would be ready to disregard the law, any law, to suit your own purpose. As to our plan to buy you out, he steadfastly maintained he didn't have any money, that the hacienda was in a financial crisis and he was fighting for its survival. All that should be taken as a red flag."

"Damn! That sounds awful. Did he mention anything good about me, like my work at the hacienda?"

"Sadly, no. I think it all boils down to the fact that you're not the son of an hacendado. If you were, he'd praise you to heaven. But don't lose heart. I'll keep pushing, I promise. Knowing him, I think he'll eventually come around. We'll have to get you out of here. Any new incidents or developments?"

"No, we were able to keep the thugs at bay." I told her about our alliance.

"How about the papazote? Have you found out anything about him?"

"As a matter of fact, I have. Just this morning. His name is Feliciano Villareal, and he has an office on this very floor. Better yet, I've already set up an appointment with him. It's going to be today at three. I'm looking forward. I've a feeling that things are beginning to move a little."

"Good! Do you think you need my help?"

"I don't think it's necessary. Maybe it wouldn't even be a good idea. Because if he sees you, he might think there was some wealth backing me. He would in all likelihood jack up the mordida."

"Maybe you're right. At any rate, I told Dad that I'd be back by three o'clock. What can I say, I wish you a lot of luck. You'll have to tell me how things went. I'll be coming in on Wednesday again."

We hugged and kissed each other, and then my *carina* was off, gone. And I was condemned to join the cutthroats again.

Back at the cauldron, things had turned from bad to worse. Our *alianza* was very much under stress, indeed, close to crumbling. The thugs, feeling their oats in my absence, dared going on the offensive. I had barely left, when Emilio and the other members were accosted for money again. When they resisted the gang began to batter, worse, stab them with their truchas. They put up a good fight but, surrounded by a dozen cutthroats, they stood no chance. In the end they looked like they had come back from a battlefield. Emilio was hit very hard. His blood-drenched face was swollen to the point where he couldn't even look out of his eyes, any more. His arms and torso were covered with stab wounds. The three others fared even worse. All of them had to be treated in the intensive care unit of the enfermeria.

Encouraged by their success, the thugs dropped all fear and began attacking me as well. Luckily, I, together with two of my buddies, was able to fend them off. I fought like a madman, knocking down and out at least three of them. But the price was high. Short of any garrotes or truchas, I couldn't avoid taking two other stab-wounds, one on my torso, the other on my right arm, as well as a cut on my chin, all of which had to be treated. My face, my fist, my whole shirt was splattered with blood. Carolina would have fainted, had she seen me.

VISITING THE PAPAZOTE

Two hours later, I wound my way to the papazote, Feliciano Villareal. Even though I suffered from the cuts and wounds, I felt a little more upbeat. When I got to the office, Pedro, the ayudante, made me wait for ten minutes, claiming that Senor Villareal was busy with an important matter. At last, the abogado defensor cracked the door open and, without glancing at me, made a curious two-finger gesture to his ayudante. Pedro bowed and then informed me that his boss was now ready to receive me and I should follow him.

The office was surprisingly spacious, at the center of which stood a hardwood desk, with a comfortable swivel chair, as well as three chairs for visitors. Behind the desk, a large window, framed by bookcases, let in a feeble shaft of sunlight. Close to the right wall there stood a chaise longue, a round coffee table and three more chairs. Above it hung a large painting, depicting a wingspread eagle, whose claws grabbed a huge snake.

The head honcho, Senor Villareal, was a corpulent man of about forty-five with a gleaming pate, a puffed-up face that was cratered by previous acne, a fleshy nose, small eyes and very large ears whose tips bent away from his skull as if they tried to catch a breeze. I introduced myself, extending my hand. His handshake was surprisingly tight and resolute, a characteristic I'd learned to appreciate.

Remaining seated, he waved his hand at Pedro. The ayudante bowed and left the room.

"Sit down, please," he said in English. "What gives me the pleasure?"

He dealt me an enigmatic smile that had at least two gold teeth in it, then pulled a cigarette out of a case, lit it and blew several perfect smoke rings toward me.

I offered him the usual scoop, that I was a Swiss citizen who was working as a vaquero at an hacienda and that I was arrested in Cuauhtemoc on Friday for being in Mexico illegally.

"I wonder if you could help me getting released, so I can go back to work," I added. "I hear you're a seasoned lawyer who can assist people in legal trouble."

He smiled. "Yes, that's my job. So, you say you have no papers, no passport, no immigration card, nothing?"

"No *Mexican* papers. Unfortunately, my Swiss passport was stolen on the train when I traveled from New York to Chicago. But I have an official American document verifying that I'm a Swiss citizen."

I pulled it out of the envelope and showed it to him. He looked at it and then handed it back to me. "Well, I think I can look into your case. But it'll cost some money. I have to make a living, too."

"How much would it be?"

"Five thousand pesos, if it's only a violation of immigration policy."

"Five thousand pesos?"

My response seemed to irritate him. He drew in the cigarette smoke and blew his rings again. "How much is your life worth to you?" he snarled. "I can see you've already had some fights. Well, if you stay here long enough, you'll face certain death because you're going to be sucked into a vicious circle that keeps grinding on mercilessly. The more you fight to survive, the more enemies you make. And the more enemies you have, the higher your risk of being stabbed or killed. Chances are, you'll join a gang. That'll require you to adapt to certain rites of passage and a violent code of behavior. In that case the gang will become your family. You'll gradually lose your previous identity, your relationship to your family, your parents, your girlfriend, your wife and your children. It may give you a few months more but life will be pure hell."

He leaned forward, putting both elbows on the desk. "And without my help," he went on, "you may never get out of here. Remember, you're in Mexico! In less than a month, papers will disappear. Records get lost. I know from experience. Parents, mothers and fathers, come here all the time looking for their sons. All in vain. Nobody can find them. Why? They're probably dead. But there's no record of them dying either. Officials can't even tell the parents what happened, why their sons are gone, how they departed and where to, because they don't know. Only God knows, but in Mexico He's always light-years away.

"Even if they'd find their son, they'd no longer recognize him. He'd be somebody else, a thug, a cutthroat, a murderer. Sometimes I have the notion that the whole penitentiary is under the thumb of Huizilopochtli, that bloody Aztec guardian god who was lord over life and death. His thirst for the blood of warriors was unquenchable, so history tells us. Slurping it by the copper kettles kept him alive."

I was startled, so benumbed I couldn't even dare ask a question, much less find any fault or crack in his argument. But when he depicted my hopeless condition as a 'vicious circle', I preferred to tilt more toward the image of a 'death spiral'. Overcome by a sudden sense of foreboding, I felt

210

a quick jolt of fear and the icy breath of death in my face. Dread and despair took hold of me, shaking me to the marrow of my bones.

There was a pause.

"I wish I had a more upbeat story to tell you," Senor Villareal went on, tearing me out of my emotional dungeon. "I'm thinking of a peaceful prison yard, of hovering angels who blow their trumpets and sing hymns of joy and goodwill. But back to your case. If you agree with the conditions I've laid out, I'll study your case, and then we'll see from there. I'd want you to come back, let's say, on Wednesday. Why don't we do it at the same time, at three o'clock. Is that suitable?"

"Yes," I said, "I'll also try to get the money."

"Good! I promise to do whatever I can to get you out of here. But I must warn you, my influence is not infinite. There are many quirks in this business. Remember, I have to deal with many other people, officials, who have their own agendas that might not agree with ours."

He rose, came around the desk, shook my hand and hollered, "Pedro!"

Pedro came rushing in and bowed. "Yessir?"

"I want you to take this gentleman back to the yard, and don't forget to tell Jorge and the other guards, that he's under my protection. Have I made myself understood?"

"Yessir!"

I followed Pedro and, arriving back at the yard, he instructed Jorge and three other guards to keep an eye on me. Let me comment: I found Pedro's instructions not only reassuring, but I also knew how to appreciate their practical consequences. Case in point, it didn't even take ten minutes before I was heckled by a gang again. But unlike in the past, the guards immediately elbowed their way in and, wielding their truncheons, warned the gang to disperse, or else. And it did, miraculously so. It was a welcome change, the more so since the guards' protective shield not only covered me, but also Emilio and the other compatriots who hung on to my coattails.

All that helped us recover some of our self-possession. The truce held.

Tuesday was ushered in with two surprises. First of all, it rained. Actually, it was more like a drizzle, but still. I relished breathing the moist air that came with a quasi-herbal fragrance of creosote and other desert vegetation reminding me of the hacienda. In the early afternoon Jorge called me, urging me to head to the Visitors' Room. Some people from Chihuahua wanted to see me. I rushed there. And whom do I see there sitting on a bench? Francisco and Erlinda. Having heard from Guillermo about my troubles, they couldn't comprehend what had happened to me, shaking their heads in disbelief when I told them my version. In any event, they wanted to tell me they were on my side. Erlinda even promised to pray for me, invoking the Almighty to intervene on my behalf. They also brought me some enchiladas and a cheesecake Erlinda had baked especially for me. I thanked and hugged them, promising I'd soon come to visit them, dig up the soil in their backyard and haul in the horse manure. They gave me a hearty laugh. In the end they wished me a lot of luck and when we said farewell, I saw tears in their eyes.

ON THE RAZOR'S EDGE

Wednesday packed even more glad tidings for me. In the early afternoon, Carolina showed up again. She was shocked out of her mind, when she saw all those bandages. "Oh, my God, what happened?" she pressed, shaking her head.

I told her about the trouble we had in our bund because of my absence. But most importantly, I informed her in detail about the meeting with the papazote, particularly about his services and his conditions.

"Wow, 5,000 pesos!" she burst out, shaking her head. "That's a big chunk of money for such puny legal help."

"No question, it is a huge mordida, especially if you don't have it, like me. But in all fairness, included in it is also a protective shield. Without it I might not be alive any more. Besides, what choice do I have? What's the alternative?" I told her about the 'death spiral'.

"Oh, *guero mio!* How awful!" She grabbed my hands. Tears welled up in her eyes. She started to sob.

"I do apologize for creating so many problems for you," I remember telling her.

"You do, but it's too late for blaming anybody," she commented, sobering up. "We've got to get these 5,000 pesos. And the only source I know of is Dad. So, as soon as I get back tonight, I'll grab a gun, put it on his chest and demand he loan it to me."

"I don't know how to thank you," I said. "It takes a lot of courage. To soothe your dad a little, you could tell him I'd promise to work for him without pay to make up the 5,000 pesos, regardless of how long it may take. I'm serious."

"That may help. By the way, there is another thing that might be of interest you. I was supposed to have my days starting Monday, but they didn't come. All I'm saying is I might, well, be *embarazada,* pregnant. Now that's not hundred percent sure, but I just thought I should let you know."

I was thunderstruck. "Are you serious? You mean I'm going to be the father of your child?"

"Yes, Fred. That's what it looks like."

I hugged her, I kissed her, until the guard tapped my shoulder and told me to curb myself, or else.

"Did you tell your mom and dad? I mean…"

"No, not yet, because it could still be a fluke. But I will certainly tell them in the next few weeks."

"Oh, Carolina, I still can't believe it. This changes a lot of things. Anyway, did I tell you that I've scheduled another meeting with the papazote in an hour?"

"No. But when you see him you could tell him he'll get his 5,000 pesos as soon as the end of this week. Actually, it just occurred to me, I think it would be a good idea if I came along, now that we know the fee. He is a man, a Mexican man. Maybe I could charm him a little. Who knows, he might even lower it to 4,000."

"It couldn't hurt."

Carolina left for an hour and then came back.

I was in the yard, when Pedro came to remind me of my appointment. We made a little detour to the Visitors' Room where we picked up Carolina and together, we headed to the office of the papazote. Unlike before, there was no waiting.

When we stepped in, Senor Villareal's eyes were only on Carolina. He was all smiles as well, the outer edges of his up-turned lips straining for his long, pendulous earlobes. I introduced her as my fiancée and the daughter of Don Leonardo Gomez y Izaguirre, and him as a renowned abogado. They shook hands. He even bowed a little to mimic a hand kiss and then offered us a seat, hastily moving a chair in Carolina's direction. His eyes still riveted on her, he was curious to know where the hacienda was located, how big it was and how many cattle roamed the land. It took him several minutes before he'd settled down to business.

"As I promised you, I delved into your record," he started off, finally switching his eyes toward me. Then he quickly debunked my arrest by the Federales as an idiocy that typically happens during a dragnet search. He also belittled the charge of entering Mexico illegally. All that was grist to my mill and I couldn't help but rejoice. At the fringes of my brain, I already saw myself paying a fee and then stepping outside as a free man with an overjoyed Carolina in my arms, patting her belly.

Pausing for a moment, the papazote lit a cigarette, blew a few perfectly round smoke rings, cleared his throat and put on sober mien.

I braced.

"What complicates your case is something completely unrelated to the arrest or your illegal entry," he said, wrinkling his forehead. "And that's your record of the time *before* you entered Mexico. What you did or didn't do in *los Estados Unidos* is what drags you down. I don't know if you're aware, but for the American FBI you are nothing less than a fugitive from justice. According to them you were originally Corporal Friedrich Graf, a German POW at the camp in Murphy, Colorado. Then you fled the camp, assumed a false identity, taking the name Fred Luethi, shot at and killed an American guard at the border and made your way to Cuauhtemoc."

"What?" Carolina cried out, her hair standing on end. "I can't believe it!" She stared at me as if I were the spawn of Satan.

"But that's a lie," I burst out. "I didn't kill anybody. It was his buddy who killed him, accidentally."

"Maybe. We don't know. Only a trial could bring the truth to light. But that's for the Americans to resolve. Anyway, the FBI issued a warrant for your arrest a few days after you skipped the barbed wire fence. And since we have an extradition treaty with our northern neighbor, we're required by law to send you back to the United States. That would close the book. By the way, the FBI has promised a reward of $10,000 for your arrest. We'd probably get the money if we'd turn you in."

I was shaken, out of my mind. "You can't send me back," I recall pleading. "Granted, I was a German POW who fled from the prison camp. But I swear to God that I didn't kill the guard."

"You may be right. Remember, it's only an accusation. Actually, I may be able to…"

"You're nothing but a damn liar!" Carolina interjected, finger-stabbing me. "You lied to me again and again. You lied to everybody. You're nothing but a fraud! How can anybody believe what you say. I've had it with you!"

She jumped up, took her purse and was about to rush out of the room. But I clutched her arm and pushed her down. She tried to wrest herself free. In vain.

"Please, Carolina, I want you to sit down and listen to me," I pleaded with her, glaring at her. "So far you've only heard one side. But there is another side as well. You've got to hear my story. Granted, I lied to you. But I *had* to lie. I had no choice. I was a young soldier of a defeated army, stuck behind barbed wire, in a prison camp, where I was about to be killed by diehard Nazis, as one of my friends actually was. I had to flee in order to stay alive. At the same time, I also yearned to live as a free man. And once I skipped the fence and was on the run, I had to take on a false identity in an effort to stay free. My lies were nothing more than a tool I used in defense of my freedom. They didn't harm anybody, anywhere.

"And when I slipped across the border into Mexico, I had to keep on lying. If I'd told people, you and everybody else, the truth, the Federales

215

would sooner or later have arrested me and cart me back to the United States, where I would have had to face a trial by court martial. I, a German soldier, in a country that is entangled in a deadly war with my country. It doesn't take much imagination to guess what would happen. I already had nightmares in which I saw my body dangling from the gallows. And now that my lies have been exposed, I've come full circle. If, God forbid, I were to be deported, I would have to face the very outcome I tried so desperately to avoid, a biased court-martial reaching a verdict of guilty and a final shove to the gallows."

I was in a high flutter, close to tears. Some may even have trickled down my cheeks, for all I know. I remember dropping down on my knees and clutching Carolina's thighs. "I apologize from the bottom of my heart for lying to you, Carolina," I pleaded. "At the same time, I won't spare asking you, what would *you* have done in a situation like mine? Would you not have used lies, forgeries and other subterfuges to cover your tracks just to stay alive?"

There was a tense pause. The papazote drummed with his fingers on the desk. I cast piercing looks at Carolina, trying to pick up subtle facial cues. I could see she was moved. And so was I, watching her, arresting her with my eyes.

The first who broke that deafening silence was curiously enough the papazote. "I understand you, I really do," he said, eyeing me with a whit of sympathy. "I wouldn't want to face an American court-martial either, not as a Mexican, and least of all as a German soldier. Let me just say your case is very tricky because of the international law that's involved. But it's not as bleak as it appears on the surface. As I look for solutions, I can even see a crack of light at the end of the tunnel. The Americans, as far as I know, have no clue that we have you in our custody. For them you're still on the lam, a fugitive from justice. And I may be able to come up with a strategy to keep it that way, regardless of our cross-border agreements with the Americans. Screw the gringos!"

He puffed up his chest ever so lightly.

"You see, I happen to be acquainted with the official who is in charge of the office dealing with our obligation under the international treaty and the extradition procedures. I could talk to him. Now I can't promise anything, but there is a chance he'd simply ignore your case when he comes across it. Of course, there's a lot of risk and maneuvering involved and that's costly, very costly. And time-consuming. We are in Mexico, after all."

216

"What are we talking about?" Carolina asked. It was her first comment after her hysterical outburst.

I took heart and breathed a sigh of relief. Yet I also braced for the shock.

"Well, let me see." The papazote scribbled some numbers on his pad, added them up and then said, "It's in the vicinity of 50,000 pesos, give or take a few."

"Fifty thousand?" I countered, swiveling my head. "That's oodles of money."

"Sure, but remember your case is very intricate. It involves a lot of risk-taking. Think about it, if something goes wrong, it would amount to an international scandal that could turn very ugly. The Americans would never forgive us. They'd not only scrap our 'favored nation' status, but even use it as a pretext for invading our country and deposing a number of officials, perhaps even our president. Remember, they've done so in the past."

"Fifty thousand! I don't know how we can pay such an amount," I sighed, glancing at Carolina who looked as though she was on tenterhooks. "We're too young and poor to have that kind of money."

"Couldn't you come down a little?" Carolina begged, her forehead a ripple of worries. "I implore you, Senor Villareal. I just told Fred an hour ago that I'm pregnant. We want to get married and raise a family."

The papazote paused, then looked at his numbers, cleared his throat and said, "All right, how about 45,000?"

We agreed, reluctantly. Anyway, we promised to bring him the money by Friday, shook hands and left.

Pedro led us back to the Visiting Room. The first thing Carolina did was to apologize for giving me the cold shoulder. "I'm deeply sorry," she said, batting her eyes. "I overreacted when the truth about you was revealed. I got completely overwhelmed by hatred and contempt. I felt so offended by your lies that I was ready to ditch you. It was something very personal that tore into my pride. But after hearing your heart-wrenching pleading and also the papazote's argument, I began to have second thoughts. What you and the papazote said made perfect sense. I concede I'd probably have done the same thing. I really would."

"I understand. How do you think I felt when I lied to you? Miserable! I felt so bad that I even thought of making an exception and telling you the truth. But then I changed my mind again. I feared that it would create a terrible mess, simply because everybody else already accepted my lie as fact. I was Fred, the *guero suizo*. And that was that."

"By the way, what is your real name again? I forgot."

217

"Friedrich Graf, but everybody called me Fritz."

"Does Graf mean anything?"

"Actually, it means 'count' in German, a title of nobility, as crazy as it may sound."

"Gee, isn't it funny! Deep down I had an inkling that you were of the nobility. Wait until I tell Dad. He'll flip out."

"I doubt it."

"Now that we all know the truth, the hard part will be to convince Dad to give me the money for the mordida. It won't be easy. Besides despising you and being very tight with his pesos, he's indeed facing a serious financial crisis. But I'll find a way to get the money, you can rest assured. I have two potent trump cards up my sleeve."

"That you're pregnant, with me as the father?"

"That's one. The other is that you're a 'Graf', a conde."

"Knowing him, I can imagine how he'll react. He'll say that the second is a lie, too. And in some way, it is. Graf is just my name, not a title. To begin with, I didn't even have a name. I was a nobody, when they found me as a baby. They christened me Graf at the orphanage."

"So what? He doesn't know that."

"But he could easily find out. He could call his Mennonite business partner. Anyway, I expect you back on Friday. And don't you forget the pesos!"

Willy-nilly, I made my way back to the yard. Although the infighting for status, position, and money continued unabated, the tender truce between our *alianza* and the gangs generally held up. Only on very rare occasions, were we challenged to duels, at which point the guards quickly intervened. As if by a miracle, not one of us was beaten up or injured. Emilio in particular was pleased, as well as surprised. And he needed it most because his past injuries were far worse than mine. Assuming that I was behind these changes, he repeatedly showed his gratitude, generously offering me gifts he received from his parents. When, at one point, he asked why we were so unexpectedly spared the fighting, I only shrugged, suggesting that he should enjoy the peace to the fullest because it might not last.

MY SAVING ANGEL

Come Friday, Carolina appeared as expected. She looked pale, worn, with dark rings around her eyes. At the same time, she was in an upbeat mood, smiling. We found a corner in the Visitors' Room, way on the other side of the entrance.

"I have it!" she hissed even before we'd hugged. She pulled out a thick, brown envelope with sheafs of thousand-peso notes. "You can't imagine what a fight it was," she sighed. "Dad just wouldn't give in. We haggled for two days and nights in a row. Stubborn as he is, he did not capitulate, until early this morning. Actually, it's a bank loan he had to co-sign. It has to be paid back within a year. So the pressure will be on us. It will be tough. But the most important thing is to get you out of here."

"I don't know how to thank you, Carolina. You've saved my life!" I hugged her and held her for a while until the guard warned me. "I'm curious, what did your dad say about me?"

"Well, in his eyes you're not worth one 'stinking peso'. These are his words. You simply fall short in every respect."

"What else is new?"

"Precisely! Of course, I described you the way you really are, things that I picked up being with you, what the papazote said, and what you revealed about yourself, including your real name. But he brushed it all aside, calling you a common scoundrel. Once a liar, always a liar, was his motto. The fact that you were afraid of facing a trial in America indicated to him that you actually are a murderer. When I mentioned the praising comments about you by Guillermo and the gerente, he just sneered at them. He was especially upset that I'd become pregnant by *you*. He even wanted me to abort the baby, offering even to pay for it. He insinuated that your intent was to marry into our family to eventually take over the hacienda."

"There we go. A leech, a legacy hunter, who blew in from nowhere to mine a rich seam."

"Kind of. Another thing that really irked him was the fact that you're a German. He especially targeted your military service in Hitler's army. I might add, he'd always been very leery about Germans, actually our whole family is. Partially it is derived from the fact that we're, you know, Jews."

"Really? You mean… I always thought you were Mexicans who originally hailed from Spain. Catholics. Didn't your father attend a Catholic service in Cuauhtemoc a few Sundays ago?"

"Yes, he did, but that's just for show. He wants to fit in. Deep down at his core he's a real Jew who actually loathes the Catholic church. You see, our ancestors were Sephardic Jews, bankers and merchants in Andalusia, where they had to face a lot of religious and racial discrimination, fanned mainly by the Catholic church and by Torquemada, the leader of the inquisition. In 1492 King Ferdinand of Spain gave them an ultimatum to either convert to Christianity, suffer persecution, or get the hell out and leave Spain for good. Well, they decided to ditch Spain and settle in Mexico. Needless to say, they never looked back. Dad has kept their diaries; he's very proud of them. Many are even written in Hebrew. He used to read parts of them to us children. They are very gripping, full of heartbreaking stories about the foul play, barbarity and savagery committed by the Spanish administration and the Catholic church. So, naturally, we as a family are very sensitive to any kind of discrimination. And the wanton persecution and even killings of Jews in Germany has incited our anger and wrath anew. We find these actions against an innocent minority atrocious and despicable. I must tell you, I myself can't help feeling a certain antipathy toward anything German as well. And when the papazote brought to light that you weren't Swiss, but German, and a soldier in Hitler's army to boot, I felt like throwing up."

"I can follow you. I might have felt the same way."

"Of course, these kinds of feelings shouldn't be applied to individuals. I'm convinced that there are bad Germans, but also many good Germans."

"I'd hope so."

"That's common sense. Because it would be very unfair to declare every German guilty of atrocities against our people. It would in essence be reverse discrimination. Having said that, I hope you didn't commit any brutalities against Jews, while you were a soldier in Russia."

"No, I didn't. I was a soldier in the regular army. It was the SS that committed the brutalities."

"Oh? I'd still like to hear something about your service in the German Army. But here we are talking about the past. What we should do, now that we have an envelope stuffed with money, is to move on and look into the future. In fact, I'm ready to plan for a big Mexican wedding, that is if you still feel like walking down the aisle with me, my *guero aleman.*"

"You can't deceive me, *mi idola andalucia.* I saw your tongue poking your cheek, turning your cute dimple into a knoll. You have to forgive me

220

if I try holding the horses. Sure, things look a lot better. But the feeling that I'm still sitting on a shaky roller coaster hasn't quite left me. I can't help but brace for the next curve or downward slide, with the wheels spinning off. Remember, I'm not out of this god-awful place yet. There are still many things that can go awry."

"That's understandable, especially from your perspective. But I can't help looking ahead. Maybe the fact that I'm already in the family way has something to do with it."

"Oh, so it's certain?"

"Pretty much. I can already feel it in my body. Anyway, we'll find out for sure in less than an hour from now."

"So you're gonna see the doctor? Well, I wish you good luck. I'll cross my fingers and rub my horseshoe that the exam will proceed smoothly, with no hiccup and you'll know for sure if you're pregnant, or not."

"Thanks. I must say, I feel much more hopeful right now. Although I wouldn't mind catching up on some sleep."

Carolina took her leave to see her medico whom she'd known since childhood. And when we met again two hours later in the Visitors' Room, she radiated a confidence and self-possession I'd not seen in her lately.

"Do I look as if I've got a tiny creature in my belly?" she asked, touching her abdomen and smiling.

"You sure do." I couldn't help but touch her abdomen as well, at the peril of getting a warning from the guard who suspected some hanky-panky.

"Well, that's what the doctor said. And he should know. It looks as if I'm on my way of becoming a mother."

"Of a love child."

"Of a love child," she repeated, nodding her head and giving me a kiss. "I like that. A German-Jewish-Mexican love child!"

"Touché! By the way, are you aware that we're in the process of building bridges, when the whole world is busy tearing them down? Who'd have thought this was possible? I'm sure Hitler would cough up all the saliva from way down his throat and spit it at me if he heard about my blood ties with a Jewish woman."

"You're probably right. I never viewed us from such an angle. That's what I like about you. You are not only a real sweetheart, but also a *pensador* (thinker). And a good lover!"

"Thank you, I appreciate such compliments, especially now. I gobble them up."

"You deserve them," she said, adding with a tinge of pride that Dr. Garcia, her doctor, gave her a certificate of excellent health, besides telling her to come back in four weeks.

While we were bantering about our relationship, Pedro showed up to remind us of our appointment. We followed him wending through the labyrinthine hallways to the papazote's office.

Thankfully, Senor Villareal was in cheerful spirits as well, welcoming us with a big smile. He even bussed Carolina's hand. And once we had taken our seats, he lit a cigarette. "Let's start with the bad news: for the Americans you're still a fugitive from justice," he said after blowing his rings. "That I won't change, and you'll have to deal with that burden on a strictly personal level. If I were you, I'd try to stay away from the United States. I'd also get a Mexican immigration permit. That way you wouldn't face arrest here. I could give you the name of an official who would issue one for a relatively small fee. If a police officer gives you any trouble, you'll just have to hand him a small mordida. He'll know how to appreciate that because he's so poorly paid."

He scribbled a name and address on a piece of paper and handed it to me.

"Carlos could help you get the permit, Herr Graf."

"Thank you. I appreciate that."

"Well, that pretty much wraps up the bad news," he went on. "The good news is that the Mexican government won't turn in your name to the FBI for now. I was assured that by a high government official after hours of tough negotiations. For Mexico, you simply don't exist, momentarily at least. Since you're a nobody, there can't be any record of you and you can be released immediately. The record we have of your recent arrest will simply vanish."

"You mean you can just make it disappear?" I asked incredulously. I always knew that money could talk, but that it could actually conjure up miracles of that kind was news to me.

"Yes, I've been authorized to do that by the Mexican Government. That was part of our agreement."

"So he can be released right now?" Carolina pressed, still skeptical.

"I don't see why not," he said. "Pedro and Jorge will personally see to it that the door to the Avenida Terrazas will be opened for both of you."

"Well, thank you so much for your services," Carolina said, handing him the brown envelope. "Here is your fee."

He quickly opened it, grabbed the pesos, counted them, and, smiling, stuffed them back in. He took a puff from his cigarette and blew his rings. "Is there anything else I can help you with?"

"No, that's pretty much it," I said. "Thanks for getting me out of here, and so quickly."

"My pleasure, Herr Graf."

We shook hands. He called Pedro and gave him the proper instructions. While the ayudante led Carolina back to the Visitors' Room, I rushed up to my cell to gather my belongings. On the way down, I decided to peek into that seething cauldron one more time to give Emilio and my other comrades a farewell. As expected, it turned out to be a very somber occasion for them to see my parting. Several feared for their lives. It was heartrending for all of us. But what could I do? I knew of no way to fix the Mexican system of *in*justice.

When I entered the Visitors' Room, Pedro, Jorge and Carolina had gathered already. Minutes later the door at the penitentiary's portal opened magically and we stepped out unhindered into the bright sunshine of the Avenida Terrazas. It was an indescribable feeling for me. I was ecstatic, intoxicated, bouncing with joy. I hugged Carolina, I kissed her, I rubbed her belly. "I don't know how to thank you, Carolina," I burst out. "First, for sticking with me and fighting so bravely with your dad to get the mordida. I'm deeply indebted to you. I promise to try as hard as I can to pay back the bank loan you and your dad signed. If it hadn't been for you, I'd in all likelihood have perished in there, never to be seen or heard of again."

"Or extradited to the United States and put on trial. Anyway, I'm gratified everything worked out well. Seldom have I felt as good fighting for somebody as I did for you."

My head stuffed with four-leaf clovers, I picked her up and swirled her around. Passersby stopped and turned their heads, probably musing this fellow is out of his mind. And, indeed, I was. Even Carolina suggested that I curb myself, if for different reasons. She worried that my wounds might ooze.

A LEGITIMATE FAKE

After we walked over to the Packard to drop my belongings, my heartthrob invited me to a small nondescript cafe for a cup of coffee and a slice of cheesecake. Later, after strolling through downtown, she suggested that we celebrate my miraculous release with a dinner at the famous La Casa de los Milagros. This was the stylish, historic restaurant Francisco and I had dined at. Although I was very fond of its flair, I felt a little uneasy entering, fearing once again I might bump into American government officials. But Carolina was so fired up about that swank restaurant that I reluctantly gave in.

We took a table at the far corner of the airy courtyard dotted with an array of gorgeous tropical plants. I tried to breathe in the exotic atmosphere, which was heightened by a live marimba band. No matter, I was unable to relax. Even the glass of wine I guzzled down failed to ease me up. Spooked that I was, I simply couldn't banish the images of those American agents that came past our table the first time around. Although the odds of their being present now were relatively low, I repeatedly caught myself looking over my shoulder or allowing my eyes to comb through the courtyard in search of clues pointing toward the presence of Hoover's sleuths.

Carolina quickly picked up on it. "What's the matter with you? You look as if somebody is following you. You're not getting paranoid?"

"I hope not," I said, bent over my spicy *carne a la tampiquena*. "But my experiences the past few months, particularly the arrest in Cuauhtemoc and what I just went through in that hell hole, has been more traumatic than I originally thought. I feel I have aged at least ten years in the past few weeks alone. It's no fun worrying you could get arrested anytime again, like right here at the Milagro, or when we step out onto the street."

"That's why it's so important for you to get the immigration card as soon as possible."

"You're right on the dot. It would make me feel a little more secure. Every bit helps. How about tomorrow morning? I wouldn't mind spending the night with you, the lady of my choice, in a small hotel right here in town."

"Sounds good."

"But can we pay for it? Remember, aside from the dinner tonight and the hotel, we'll also have to pay a mordida for the immigration card. I have no more than 5 pesos in my pocket."

"Let me check." She pulled the purse out of her handbag and started counting her pesos. "Luckily, I still have almost 4,000 pesos with me. What do you think? Would it be enough?"

"It should be. They can't take an arm and a leg for such a little wisp as an immigration card. If they do, I'll bargain with them."

I pulled the slip of paper with the name and address of the government official out of my pocket.

"I'd say, let's do it," she said.

I gave her a kiss. *"Oh, mia judia mexicana!* You know, you are truly a godsend to me. What would I do without you?"

"You could rub your horseshoe harder," she chuckled, "so the sparks would fly and horses neigh."

"Dios mio, you're very unfair. You have nothing better to do than making fun of me."

Following Carolina's suggestion, we got a room at the Hotel Jardin del Centro, a comfortable inn located not far from the main cathedral I had visited with Francisco. Like the 'Milagro', it contained a lush courtyard filled with tropical plants, even caged birds and a quaint restaurant to boot. Our room, looking out onto the courtyard, was unusually quiet, save for the thundering bells of the cathedral, which rang when we stepped in.

While I made myself comfortable, Carolina decided to rush back down to the reception in order to call her dad, just to inform him that she wouldn't be back until noon tomorrow. When she returned, I was already in the shower. She joined me. We jumped for joy; we burst out laughing and shook like jelly. Later we cuddled, kissed and made love. It was the first for us on a regular bedstead, and we took full advantage of it. It wasn't until Carolina froze, raised her hand and hissed, "Sorry, Fred, you are bleeding!" that we untangled. I was shocked. Three of my wounds had burst, oozing ichor and blood. All the sheets, as well as the bedding were smeared with it. It was an unholy mess that eventually would cost us a bundle of pesos.

After a hearty breakfast of eggs and beans, we made our way down Avenida Juarez to the Federal Palace, a massive building in the city's center. We soon found the office of Epitacio Quintana, the federal official the papazote had recommended. We first had to talk to his *secretario*, Porfirio Santillanes. After we'd given him the reason for our visit, he led us into an anteroom. After waiting for about ten minutes, we were led into a large room, whose walls were cluttered with pictures, photographs as well as paintings, of various presidents of Mexico. In the middle of the room stood a massive hardwood desk decked with the Mexican flag and a bronze sculpture of a jaguar, whose front paws held down a huge, writhing snake.

I chose to mention Mr. Quintana last for a simple reason — he was hardly visible. Being a midget of a man, he drowned in his huge armchair. However, what he lacked in size, he compensated with his lively demeanor and his distinctive appearance. Although he may have been close to fifty, he had a very youthful appearance, marked by a pair of sparkling eyes, a small but cutting aquiline nose, bony cheeks, a classic handlebar mustache and a full thatch of black hair with a light tint of grey at the temples.

We introduced ourselves, emphasizing that Senor Feliciano Villareal had recommended we see him regarding an immigration card. We shook hands. He offered us a seat and, using a high-pitched voice, asked in broken English if I had a passport or some identification card. I showed him the document that the Escape Committee at the camp had faked for me. He looked at it, held it against the light and then put it down. "Khave no more?" he asked, stroking his mustache.

"No, regrettably not. I had a Swiss passport, but it was stolen from me on the train when I left New York."

He scribbled something on a piece of paper. And, pointing at me, he said, "So you want immigration card. You come to our country — when?"

"Let me think. On the 12th of September, in El Paso, Texas."

He made a note of it. "*Por que* no immigration card *entonces*?"

"He means why didn't you get an immigration card right then?" Carolina jumped in.

"Well, nobody mentioned that I needed one."

"Always, *siempre, invariablemente.* You no Mexicano, you *estranjero, comprende?*"

"*Lo siento*. I should've known."

He also asked me if I was working, and where, if I'm a criminal, possessed weapons and how long I intended to stay. After I had answered all those questions, he said that I could get such card but that there was an official fee for people like me who broke the law.

"How much is it?" I asked.

"*Tres mil pesos.*"

"*Lo siento,*" I said, shaking my head. "I'm just a simple vaquero. I have a pregnant wife. I can pay no more than 2,500."

"*Tres mil! Esta regla.*"

"Two thousand five hundred," I repeated, driving the words in like stakes into the ground and acting as if I was ready to get up and leave.

He threw up his hands. *"Como quieras, 2,500. Estoy de acuerdo."*

"Bien!" I said, giving Carolina the nod.

She opened her purse and put the sum of 2,500 pesos on his desk.

He counted it and promised he would tell his secretario to write out the card and then he would sign it.

"Es legal en Mexico para uno ano. Bien, other things you wish?"

"No, gracias. Eso es todo."

He called the secretario and gave him some instructions. We shook hands, I thanked him, and we left for the anteroom. Ten minutes later, the secretario came back and handed us the immigration card, as well as my faked document. We checked it, thanked him and were on our way.

"Thank you again for the 2,500 pesos," I sighed to Carolina as we stepped out of the Federal Palace. "It's really adding up. I feel so indebted to you and your dad. — But look at the immigration card. Now that I have another faked document, I may soon be able to prove that I'm a real, *legitimate* fake. I pray it'll help me to avoid another stay in a Mexican jail."

BACK IN THE FOLD AGAIN

After a comfortable ride in Don Leonardo's luxurious Packard, we pulled into the courtyard of the hacienda. Carolina let me out near the bunkhouse, but not until we agreed to a new rendezvous on Wednesday night at six at the ponderosa. She said she'd like to have a talk with me about the wedding and exchange ideas about our budding family. While she pulled up to the mansion, I headed for the bunkhouse, enjoying anew the peace and quiet of the place. Somehow everything looked much friendlier to me, not to mention clean, as if it had been scrubbed. The ground was wet, suggesting that rain had fallen, enough to drive up earthworms.

Incidentally, I was warmly welcomed by everybody, Guillermo, Teresa and four fellow vaqueros who were present. Besides telling me how much they had missed me, they showered me with a hailstorm of questions, particularly about my stay at the penitentiary. Let me say, they treated me as if I were a decorated veteran who'd just come back from a successful war on the other side of the globe. Eager to satisfy their curiosity, I suggested we all sit down in the dining section of the bunkhouse. Over a cup of coffee and some sweets I gave them a rough sketch of my recent misfortune. They just shook their heads and gaped their maws when they heard about the randomness of justice, particularly the violence at the penitentiary, the gangs and their sinister practice of extortions. To them, all that must have appeared like a crime thriller. As if my yarn wasn't enough, Guillermo even goaded me to show my wounds, bandaged as they were. I could also sense they knew about my involvement with Carolina, although nobody raised it.

Having satisfied their craving for sinister stories, I grabbed some grub, shouldered my rucksack and took off on a long hike, going almost as far as the cienega, where Carolina had sprained her ankle. Pushing myself out in nature helped clear my head and cleanse my body, and when I came back four hours later, I felt like I'd been reborn. A full moon rising on the eastern horizon would cast a magic spell over the landscape. Armed with my immigration card tucked away in my billfold, a new life was about to begin, a life in peace, free of worries and turmoil, at my sweetheart's side. But first I was preoccupied with putting my things in order, washing my underwear, socks, shirts and cotton pants, polishing my shoes and boots and, not to forget, catching up on my diary, which I had neglected so flagrantly the past few days.

The new week found me in the holding pens again, working with our cattle. I helped feed them, inspect them for ticks and diseases and brand more calves. Nor did I mind, especially since my head was someplace else — with Carolina. I wondered what I could do to show my gratitude toward her. What bothered me was the lopsidedness of the relationship: she, the giver and I, the taker. I had the uneasy feeling that such an unbalanced linkage would inevitably lead to a loss of respect for me.

Wednesday didn't come soon enough. Once I was off work, I took a cold shower, put on clean clothes and made my way up to the ponderosa. I happened to arrive a little early. But she soon came too, high up on the horse, equipped with a broad smile and her usual cheerful disposition. I helped her get out of the saddle by lifting her off in such a way that she couldn't but fall into my arms. It drew a chuckle out of her. We kissed.

"I had such a yearning for you, Carolina," I sighed. "How *are* you, my novia?"

"I'm very well, thank you. I can feel it growing." She patted her belly, pulled off the blankets and spread one out. Having shed our jackets, we lay down and pulled the other blanket over us. We hugged and kissed, pausing only to catch our breath and to exchange sweet nothings and flatteries. The baring came naturally, piece by piece, until we were Adam and Eve — stark naked.

The afterglow came much too quick. Resting there arm in arm, I wanted to know how her pregnancy made itself felt.

"Thanks for asking. Actually so far quite benign. My breasts feel a little larger and more tender. But there's something else you might like to hear, namely, that my desire has actually risen. I often wake up at night thinking wouldn't it be nice if you were with me and we could… you know what."

"I already noticed, you were unusually voluptuous tonight."

"I was. I could hardly wait."

"Well, I would suggest we get together much more often. Couldn't you leave your window open so I could sneak in every once in a while?"

"But Demesia would soon notice. And so would Mom and Dad."

"So what?"

"You don't understand. How many times do I have to tell you that we're in Mexico. Anyway, I don't want to be called a slut."

"That doesn't make any sense. They probably know already that we're sleeping with each other."

"How do you know that?"

"Well I've heard insinuations."

"Bull! Even if they knew, I'd still feel very uncomfortable letting them know."

She was very flinty about her position, and I soon dropped the subject. Instead, we broached the topic of our marriage. She came very close to rebuking me for failing to tell her in simple language that I wanted to marry her. "In Mexico, it's the duty of the man to ask the woman if she'll marry him."

"Forgive me for not having done so, but let me make clear I am fully committed to ask for your hand. You can take my word for it."

"You know, according to our Mexican traditions, you will even have to go to my dad and make an official wedding proposal. He would then approve me to be given in marriage to you."

"But what if he says no? From what you've told me, I'm not so sure he'll give his nod."

"Well, I'd make sure beforehand that he'd give you thumbs up. I'm quite sure he would."

"Why don't you do that, and then we can set up a date when I can present my marriage proposal. It just occurred to me, would he ask me questions about my family and background?"

"He might, knowing him. But I'd tell him the truth, if I were you. I've told him quite a bit about you already."

"Well, yes, but you've made it very clear to me that he doesn't like me, that I'm not on the level he expects of a groom."

"Oh, I'd take that with a grain of salt. He'll come around, I know he will."

"Well, if that's the case, why don't you set up a date with him?"

"I will."

We also touched on the question of my future occupation, once we were married with me being the head of a family. I told her right away that I couldn't possibly continue to work as a vaquero, nor would I want to, even if her dad would pay me more.

She nodded.

"Nor would I want to consider an offer from your dad to learn the job of running the hacienda in the hope of eventually taking it over after his death. I simply can't see myself in the role of an hacendado. That may well surprise him, since he's dubbed me a legacy hunter who'll use his wile to heist his one-and-all from his family."

Actually, it was a moot point since she doubted her dad would ever propose something like that. At the same time, she didn't shy away from asking how I'd support myself, her and a child.

OFF TO THE FUTURE

"I'm particularly worried about paying back the bank loan for the big mordida to the papazote and how we'd make a living as a family," Carolina goaded me. "We need some money. I'm expecting my dad to give me the rest of my inheritance, but that would eventually run out as well. We can probably stay here on the hacienda for a while but what would *you* do? There is no job for you, no future."

"I fully share your concern, Carolina. But I simply haven't had the time to seriously think about these questions."

I tried to explain to her — a bit too defensively, I fear — that after my escape I'd been totally preoccupied with wiggling away from the dragnet of the FBI. And then came the challenge of arriving at the hacienda, working as a vaquero, my falling in love with her, the shock of my arrest and jailing, the buyout, the release and finally that big bolt out of the blue — her pregnancy.

"The events were so jam packed, they came hurtling at me with such a speed that I didn't have time to catch up with them, much less find answers," I heard myself telling her. "Think about it, this is the first time I've received the hint of a foothold in Mexico, tenuous as it may be. Which leads me to another question, namely that of acquiring Mexican citizenship. There must be laws specifically targeting foreigners who marry Mexican citizens."

"I'm quite sure there are. But to get the government officials to move on such a request, you may have to pay another hefty mordida. Regardless, I'll find out. I've already told you about Jorge, my brother, who lives in Mexico City. He'd know, or know somebody who would. By the way, while you were in the dungeon, I called him and we talked about the financial crisis Dad's confronted with. I also told him about our relationship, and about you, too, your arrest, jailing and the mordida the papazote demanded. I don't know if I've told you but he's a playboy of sorts and a great charmer, very bright and well educated. After completing his secondary education, Dad sent him to the University of Chicago to study economics and finance. Sadly he never finished. Though occasionally he still works as financial advisor for a few rich families in el D.F.

"Actually, he could really make big bucks if only he weren't so lazy, maybe undisciplined would be a better word. I think I mentioned already that he likes to mingle with the film crowd, actresses, actors, filmmakers and artists of all stripes. You know, cinematography is a thriving industry in el D.F. right now. In fact, he himself has played several minor roles in movies. He mentioned that the movie director he worked for is in the planning stages of a new movie. If I remember correctly, it's about Jewish refugees who flee Europe in a freighter that is later torpedoed by a German U-boat in the Gulf of Mexico. The way he described it, there's also a part for a German sailor who's drifting in the shark-infested waters and struggling to get aboard the life raft. But there's a lot of resistance from the refugees. It's a real moral dilemma."

"I can well imagine."

"You may wonder why I'm telling you all this. It so happens the director is still looking for an actor to play this part of the sailor. And that's where you may be coming into the picture. Jorge wondered if you might be interested in auditioning for it. He thinks you might be well-suited for such a role and there's a fair chance you might even get it, especially since you served in the German military and have an intimate knowledge of it. And you're good looking! I'd do it in a flash, if I were you. You've got nothing to lose."

"That sounds very tempting. Why have you waited so long to tell me about it?"

"Well, there were more important things on my mind, like finding the money to buy you out of jail. It just occurred to me, acting in movies is very well paid and if you'd get this role we could probably pay off the bank loan and still have some money in the bank. And, who knows, if you do a good job, you might eventually get another part in another movie."

"That's the best news I've heard in a long time."

"Didn't you tell me once that you're very fond of playacting, that you played in the theater while you were in the prison camp, that you even made an elegant escape from the camp in the uniform of an American lieutenant. And your playacting since then is not to be sniffed at either. You filled out the role of a Swiss citizen so well that everybody fell for it, including me."

"I admit, it's always fun to leave yourself behind and slip into the skin of another person. Of course I'd love to play a role like that. But, come to think of it, there's also a snag. I'm afraid that the FBI might recognize me and send a bunch of Hoover's bloodhounds after me."

"Here we go again," she said, shaking her head and rolling her eyes. "Fred, please do me a favor — drop your paranoia. Frankly, I wouldn't

233

worry. These film people have excellent makeup artists who could change your facial appearance so much that nobody would recognize you. You could even insist on it. Besides, by then you'd in all likelihood already be a Mexican citizen. And I doubt that our government would extradite you to the U.S. if you are a Mexican actor. If, God forbid, you should get in hot water, you could simply pay a mordida to one of our officials. It might cost you a little more, but as an actor you could easily afford it."

"Wow, you sound like a slick abogado mexicano, a Mexican shyster. Come to think of it, you may be right."

"I know I am."

"I was just thinking, in case I'd get a part, I'd probably have to work in Mexico City, wouldn't I?"

"Yes, unfortunately. But you would only be busy when the movie is being shot."

"Sure, but I'd have to leave you."

"Not necessarily. I could go with you and we could stay with Jorge or in a hotel. I get along with Jorge very well. We are on very friendly terms. He's the most generous person I know. He's always inviting me to visit him. Of course, I can't promise anything, but it's worth trying. I'll call him tomorrow."

"Please do. Carolina, you are an angel. Still, I'm worried."

We met again two days later, on Friday. It had suddenly turned much colder. Out west, winter barreled through the canyons on the breath of fierce winds. Guillermo predicted frost for tonight. As I walked up to the ponderosa in my warm jacket with a hood, I braced for the day when these rendezvous might end. What then? There was still a small barn that was located more to the north, but it was twice as far away from the bunkhouse.

When I arrived at the ponderosa, Carolina was already waiting for me, sensual as never before. We had hardly spread our Mayan blankets properly, when she was already grabbing me, making lewd moves, indeed, almost offering herself. Never before had I encountered a woman who was so assertive, so desirous. It was a change I found rather amusing. Holding myself back and letting her initiate things was a real joy for me.

Once we were able to catch our breaths, Carolina brought up her plans for the future again. Her head resting on my chest, she couldn't wait to tell me that she'd talked to her brother, Jorge, twice already, on Thursday and today, only an hour ago. "He told me he'd had a good chat with Senor Alarcon, the director in charge of the movie," she said, getting very animated, "and he reaffirmed the odds for getting the sailor role were pretty good. But you'd have to appear in person, present your credentials and then undergo an audition. Jorge stressed you should make up your mind quickly, because the parts were filling fast. By the way, he wanted to know more about you. Well, I told him about your childhood as an orphan and about your service in the German military. That stirred him quite a bit, and he's eager to meet you. He offered us his apartment. We could stay there all by ourselves."

I was thrilled, almost euphoric. "Why don't you call Jorge tomorrow, and tell him that I'm looking forward to meeting him and urge him to set up an appointment with the director sometime next week. What would be best, going by bus or train?"

"Neither," Carolina whispered. "I'll ask Dad if I could take the Packard."

"Oh, we would go together? That would be great. I'm really looking forward to breathing the air of a big city."

"But not literally; it's filthy, poisonous. Still it would be fun nonetheless, like a short vacation. Quite frankly, I wouldn't mind getting out of here for a week or two, as beautiful as it is. Mexico City is a very exciting, cosmopolitan place. Granted, parts of it are very dirty and inhospitable, but there's a lot of beauty also, like tree-lined boulevards, parks, street cafes and restaurants, not to mention all the art galleries, museums and the ancient Aztec ruins of Tenochtitlan. And there is a lot to see of Mexico just getting there."

"Sounds like going on a honeymoon. Unfortunately, it all depends on the whims of your dad."

"Well, yes, that could be a stumbling block. But I think if I push hard enough, he'll give in. The car just sits there in the garage, looking pretty. The mechanics in Cuauhtemoc have told him time and again that it should be driven more, especially on long trips. And going to Mexico City is quite a stretch. If everything goes according to plan, we may be able to do it in three days. I know my way; I've done it several times. And we could switch. You know how to drive a car, don't you?"

"I think I do. I've driven all kinds of military vehicles, but never passenger cars, and certainly not in Mexico."

Carolina also told me her dad wanted me to present my wedding proposal tomorrow afternoon, at three, in his office. She thought it was a formality because he'd already approved it.

"But you know Dad. He pays great attention to protocol. If I were you I'd shave, look clean and dress up, put on the best shirt, pants and shoes."

"You're going to be present, aren't you?"

"No, I'm afraid not. He insisted on seeing only you. He said he knows my thinking on marriage already but not yours. Don't worry; it won't be a big deal. My guess is he'd want to know how you feel about bonding for life and about raising and caring for a family. Stuff like that."

At the end, I brought up the question of our rendezvous, more specifically where we should meet, now that the winter was approaching. I suggested again that I could visit her at the mansion. But she would have none of it, citing her reputation, as if she were a nun watched by a mother superior.

"How about that cute little barn toward the north?" I threw out. "It's a little far. But for you and your horse it wouldn't make that much of a difference."

"Good idea. *Vamos!* How about Sunday night."

"But don't you forget the Mayan love-blankets."

"You're telling me!" she said, laughing. "Anyway, by Sunday night I'll know a little more about our D.F. trip. As I said, I'll call Jorge tomorrow. Hopefully he has set up an interview with the film director already. By the way, when Dad, Jorge and I talked about you, questions popped up I simply couldn't answer. One of them was your service in the German Army. How was it? Were you drafted and where did you go? Were you a Nazi?"

"Well, that's a disturbing story that's hard to stomach for somebody who wasn't part of it. And frankly, I'm reluctant to go into it, unless you promise never to hold it against me."

"OK, I won't."

"It was in spring of 1941. I was a dumb, lanky and awkward kid. I had just turned seventeen. I was still at the orphanage in Rummelsburg, outside of Berlin. The atmosphere was stuffy and confining. I was in a bind; I longed to get out into the real world but didn't know what to do with myself. One day, I heard the army was looking for recruits. It needed soldiers for the Barbarossa campaign, the invasion of Russia. I might add that two of my buddies, Ernst and Peter, soon followed me, and we three thought that joining the army would be more or less a continuation of the paramilitary games we enjoyed at the Hitler Youth. It promised adventure, comradeship and also advancement — a life that matched most of our wishes. So we signed up. First there was this awful bootcamp. But later, once routine had put a stamp on our lives, it got more and more gratifying. And eventually the army became our family, our home. We were all forged into a tightly knit group where we did everything together to the point of melting into a brainless jumble of Aryans. We ate together, slept side by side, cleaned the camp, marched together, roared nationalistic marching songs, fired our rifles, cracked stale and filthy jokes and let farts ricochet off the walls. You could say we floated in a bubble of juvenile, intoxicating swagger."

"I believe you."

"Those were heady days. Even when we marched into Russia and things turned ugly, we still stuck together. There were cases where one of us would sacrifice his own life to save a comrade. We were daring, ruthless barbarians, all part of an efficient, merciless fighting machine that scared the shit out of the Russians. We were the Blitzkrieg, the lightning war in the flesh, especially when we swallowed our Pervitin pills. Our captain praised them as energy pills. And they were, sort of. They made us alert, fearless and invincible; hell they even curbed our need for food and drink. It was only later, much later, at the camp, when I found out that Pervitin was a dangerous, mind-altering pep pill, a methamphetamine that also contained cocaine."

"You mean to tell me that you were drugged-up when you fought?"

"Yes, some of us even got addicted. Thank God they often ran out of pills. But when we had them, nothing could stop us. Or so we thought, fools that we were. The first big test came on the outskirts of Kiev, and although we eventually beat the Russians, we also suffered a lot of casualties, including Ernst and Peter, my best buddies. That was a real shock to me, and for the first time I began to doubt our invasion of Russia and the war. Of course by then it was already too late. I no longer had any choice but to keep on doing my duties as a soldier. Anyway, I must have done it so well that I even received a medal for exceptional bravery. Our captain even urged me to attend officers' school. Well, when the North African campaign started, many of us were assigned to Rommel's army. And it was there that everything ended with the surrender to the British and Americans."

"It sounds like you were a staunch believer in the Nazi myth."

"Yes, I'm ashamed to say, although I never was a member of the party."

"When did you really wake up and change your mind?"

"It was a gradual process. The first doubts sneaked up on me already in Russia, when Ernst and Peter were killed. Other big jolts hit me when we were taken prisoners in North Africa and during the train ride from New York to Murphy, when we watched trains with all the military equipment passing us. But the real wakeup call happened at the camp, where I became a bitter opponent of the Nazi regime, especially after Peter, my buddy, was murdered by Nazi thugs, just because he refused to toe the line. In fact, I was only a whisker away of turning into a traitor."

RUBBING ME THE WRONG WAY

Early on Saturday morning, I took another hike way up to the pond. It was cool, even frosty, but clear and sunny. Along the way, I glimpsed a few rabbits, a flock of turkeys and a herd of deer. The pond was lightly frozen over, glistening in the morning sun. Coming around to the outflow of the pond, close to where Carolina sprained her ankle, I watched beavers chopping at branches and twigs and dragging them down and up into their burrows. Always ready to challenge myself, I tried my hand at catching some trout. Although the water was so cold my hands quickly stiffened, I still managed to get hold of four *truchas,* two large ones weighing almost two pounds each, and smaller fry. I quickly gutted them and strung them up, pulling a barbed willow twig through their mouths and gills.

When I later handed them to Teresa, our cook, she was full of praise, not to mention curiosity, wondering how I'd caught them. When I told her she just shook her head in disbelief. She fried them and served them for *comida.* I relished them, though most of my compadres, not knowing how to carve them up, cursed them for their vicious bones, comparing them to cactus spines.

After lunch I took a cold shower, shaved and slipped into my my best white cotton shirt, my seasoned dark-brown pants and my pair of dress shoes. The hike had flushed my face, giving my skin a ruddy glow. Complimenting myself, I wended my way to the mansion and rapped on the door. Demesia opened it a crack and stuck out her head.

"*Buenos dias, Senor Fred.* Senor Don Gomez is awaiting you in his office."

She led me up the stairs and gingerly knocked at the door. *"Entra!"* a voice resounded.

I stepped in. Don Leonardo sat in his swivel chair behind his desk, bent over, his eyes riveted on some document. To my great surprise, he wore a *yarmulke,* a skullcap. Nor was this all: near his right hand, stood a tiled tablet displaying a blue Star of David. Sniffish as he was, he wouldn't even deign to give me a glance, much less a greeting.

I bristled. *"Buenas tardes!* Senor Gomez," I belted out.

He twitched, looked up and, having cleared his throat, said,"*Buenas tardes!* Senor, uh, Luthi."

"Since you are the head of the family, I came to ask you to approve the marriage of your daughter, Carolina, to me, Fred Luthi. The *boda* (wedding) will in all likelihood take place sometime in early December, at which point your daughter will officially be my wife and I her husband." I'd rehearsed these lines and they came out snappy, which made me feel as if I were on stage.

"I have taken note of your request, Senor Luthi," he said, straightening up and glowering at me with a toad-like stare. "Or maybe it would be better to call you by your real, your German name, Fridrik Graf."

"Friedrich Graf, I beg you!" I pointedly ruffled him with the German guttural 'ch'.

He was taken aback, harrumphing. "Thank you, Senor Graf. Please sit down. So you are asking me for the hand of my daughter. Well, before we can proceed, I would like to ask you a few *preguntas* (questions), if you don't mind. You are still a very young man. Are you aware what it means to enter the bond of marriage with my only daughter, Carolina?" He leaned back and rocked in his chair.

"No, not really. I have never been married before. But I love Carolina and I'm committed to make the best of it. I cannot promise more."

"You shouldn't. I have heard you are an *aleman* by birth and nationality and that you grew up as a poor *huerfano* (orphan). At seventeen you left the orphanage and enlisted in Hitler's army. You were eventually taken *prisionero de guerra* by the Americans and brought to Murphy, Colorado, in *los Estados Unidos*. You escaped from that prison camp and came to Mexico as a *fugitivo*. The American FBI has accused you of having brutally murdered a border guard as you crossed the Rio Bravo. That's very troubling to me, to all of us, as it should be."

"I understand. But I didn't do it. And there is no evidence that I did. I have never killed a human being outside a military engagement, much less brutally."

"*Seguro?*"

"*Muy seguro!*"

"Carolina has told me that you fought as a German soldier on the Russian front. Did you ever encounter any Jewish people in the towns and villages you came through."

"Yes, I did."

"Tell me, did you shoot at them? Did you kill them?"

"Of course not. I'd never kill defenseless people. Unfortunately some of our SS troops who infiltrated the territory after we had conquered it may well have. Or they may have rounded them up and taken them away to concentration camps. At least that's what we've heard. I admit, it was a very sad and brutal chapter in our history, which I feel deeply ashamed of. That's all I can say."

"You should be. You may know by now that we are a Mexican-Jewish family, whose roots go back deep into Spanish history. There are obviously great social and cultural differences between you and Carolina, some would say unbridgeable canyons. How would you reach across, especially in the case of conflicts or crises that may erupt at any time?"

"Frankly, I don't know. It depends on the case in question. All I can say is I'm always ready to talk with Carolina when something comes up that is disturbing or hurtful to either one of us. Thankfully, we're both rational people. I'd listen to her arguments, and I expect her to listen to mine. And if we can't solve our conflicts verbally, we can always, well, go to bed and make love."

He glared at me as if I'd stepped out of a bughouse. "What do you mean, make love?"

"Hacer el amor con algun, coito," I said, smiling. "Follow our biological urges."

He acted as though he were nibbling on a spoiled oyster, but then called himself to attention, harnessed himself and threw up his hands in a gesture of helplessness. "Although I still have many *reservaciones* about you, Senor Luthi, especially as related to your past, I trust Carolina made the right *decision* to enter the bond of *matrimonio* with you. It's her choice. She will have to live with it. That's why I have decided to bow and give you her hand. I hope and pray that you will lead a happy and harmonious life together."

We shook hands.

Carolina was already there when I wound my way up the cattle trail. At least her horse was, whose rein was fastened to a hardy juniper that stood to the right of the barn. The barn was a ramshackle structure, which, at one end, leaned into an abandoned holding pen. Raw and weather-beaten, it must once have served as a depository of hay.

The gate was ajar. I stepped in, catching her as she fetched some hay to provide a cushion for the blankets she had brought with her.

"Fred, there you are! I've been looking for you," she said, as she, flashlight in hand, saw me. "I may have come a little early. I misjudged the distance. I thought it was farther."

"Come on, be honest, you couldn't wait to see me. And neither could I, seeing you, my *novia*. I wouldn't want to have it any other way. As

240

always, I'm overjoyed being near you. Maybe it's the pregnancy, but you are more beautiful than ever. I really love you, Carolina. For me, you are a dream come true."

I raised my hand and brushed over her eyebrows and down her tip-tilted nose. We hugged and kissed. I inhaled her lilac, but even more so the intoxicating smell of her hair and her skin.

"So how did it go yesterday?" she was curious to know, as I helped her spreading the blankets. "Did he give you my hand?" She raised her right hand.

"Well, he gave me your right hand all right, but unfortunately not your left. Or the rest of you, for that matter. That's what I felt, anyway. What can I say, things got a little testy at times. Of course I expected that. My lance was tilted. He just doesn't seem to like me. Still, the way he carried himself was unbecoming, bad-mannered, even rude. He's nothing more than a puffed-up, pompous ass, a Don Quixote who still lives back in the sixteenth century. I told myself not to mention his name any more, lest he fail to sink into darkness which he so richly deserves. Sorry about that."

"That's Dad. No apologies needed. At the same time, you should never forget that same pompous ass is the very person who signed the bank loan that paid for getting you out of jail and saving your life. More than that, he's also given us the Packard to go to el D.F."

"Glad you reminded me of his better side. In all fairness, that's all very generous of him. But he did it unwillingly. You practically had to force him."

"Well, I've long learned that you can't please everybody. He's still very much stuck in his ways, tilting his spear at windmills. The most important thing is that he didn't say no. You can always bargain with him, at least I can. You just have to know how. The last time I talked with him I hinted that we would both leave the hacienda and tie the knot someplace else, in case he'd deny us getting married here."

"Oh, so you did put a zip gun to his head. Smart! You're a jewel. But say, what did you hear from Jorge?"

"Glad you asked. He did come through, as expected. But let's leave the details for later."

"Wonderful! — But why are we still on our feet?" I hugged her, lifted her up and swirled her around, then dropped to my knees, kissed her tummy and put my ear to it. "Did I hear some gurgling?" I said, grinning.

"It's probably my supper being digested."

241

"Oh, Carolina, couldn't you be a little more poetic? You could've said that it was the first effort of our unlicked love child to imitate a famous tenor or soprano."

"Fred, you're crazy. But that's what I like about you, embellishing things with an artistic flourish."

I placed myself on the blanket and pulled her down toward me. She came more than willingly; indeed, my *novia* was as sensual, as lustful as ever. Rising again, we stripped, she not without a wily tease, the first I had seen since my stint in North Africa. Not only did it kick my Cowper's gland into overdrive, but it also aroused me to the point where I was ready to pull her down, pounce on her and… Yet Carolina managed to calm me down, to delay action, guiding me instead into a rich offering of petting, stroking and kissing. At last, we couldn't but move on, abandoning ourselves to the carnal pleasures God had given us. Or was it perhaps his fallen angel?

Reaching the angle of repose, we let go, listening to the hum of silence. After a while, Carolina came to life again. Her head resting on my chest, she murmured that Jorge had managed to secure an appointment with Senor Manuel Alarcon, the director of the war flick, *They Came From Afar*.

"It will be on the 20th of November, eight days from now. That would give us plenty of time to get to el D.F., possibly even settle in for a few days. My suggestion is, we should leave on Wednesday or Thursday at the latest."

"Good. I'll be ready. By the way, did he tell you anything more specific about the movie?"

"No, not that I recall. I doubt that he's read the screenplay."

"Well, thanks again for doing that for me. I'm just thinking, if I could get my foot in the door, anything might follow. God knows, with a little luck it may even develop into a career. In any event, I'm really looking forward to the challenge. The only thing still worrying me is that the FBI and its hounds might recognize me when I appear on the silver screen."

"I thought we'd solved that already."

"Well, not completely. I'm still tense. I know good makeup artists can do a lot. But in the long run it may be advantageous to find a plastic surgeon who could give me a few tucks here and there. I understand there's a good number of them in el D.F. To tell you the truth, I wouldn't mind if my nose were a little smaller. And, frankly, my ears could also benefit from a little surgery so they wouldn't stick out so far."

"You're nuts. Let me tell you, you're not only looking *good*, but unusual, distinct. And when you put on a suit you strike me as being absolutely distinguished. I'm not alone who thinks that way. You may not have noticed, but when we walked around Chihuahua I saw scores of girls and women turn their heads when you walked past. Blond, blue-eyed, as well as tall, with broad shoulders and the torso of Atlas. And that in Mexico, of all places! No wonder the Nazis liked you. I dare say, you're the best advertisement for the master race I've seen. Hitler, Goebbels and Goering are lame, degenerate cripples compared to you."

"You're exaggerating."

"Exaggerating? They would have cringed from jealousy if you stood next to them. But if you had enlisted in the Mexican army, our president would have promoted you to the rank of general, on looks alone. That's why I think you'll get a part in the film. You've got the looks, *novio mio,* believe me. I just hope it doesn't go to your head what I've just told you."

"I think I'm well beyond that. I've been humbled too many times, especially lately. I'm very thankful that I've gotten this far. What more could I expect than to be loved by such a captivating woman like you?"

"You're flattering me!"

"I mean it. Actually, under ordinary circumstances I would long be dead. It may still happen. Who knows, the FBI may catch up with me one of these days. They'd probably see less your handsome fellow in me than the typical specimen of the 'blond beast' the Nazis celebrated."

"Fred, stop it! Please!"

ON THE ROAD

When I got back to the bunkhouse that night, I was so high-strung I couldn't sleep a wink. Things Carolina said whirled through my head like scraps of paper in a twister. I already saw myself on the film stage, playing a German sailor, a bit stiff and correct maybe, but unflappable, always true and dedicated to his mission. I had watched them for years, knew them inside and out, their demeanor, their gestures and their way of speaking. I knew what stirred them and what not. Granted, their language would necessarily have to be Spanish. Yet it would have to be a broken Spanish with a heavy German accent and intonation. Who but me could master that best? I could simply go back to my own stuttering efforts in the Spanish tongue.

Back to ground zero: I spent two days in the holding pen, working on cattle, feeding them and checking them for diseases. In the meantime, I gathered my clothes, shoes, toilet articles, my papers, my horseshoe and other items I would need on the trip, and stashed them in the suitcase Carolina had loaned me. Very early on Wednesday — it was still pitch-dark — I waited at the gate for Carolina who soon came wobbling down the hill in her big white Packard. She hobbled to a halt and stepped out of the cab. Her hair was tangled, unruly, the way I liked it best. We hugged; I brushed her cheeks and her lips, but she hardly responded. Having put the luggage into the trunk, we slid into the cab, closed the doors with a soft thump and off we went, wending our way down to Cuauhtemoc. The headlights punched into the dark, flipping up and down with each bump, letting the leafless shrubs and trees appear in an eery, unearthly light. Like skeletons on an x-ray, I thought. At the first Pemex station we filled the tank, then took the road to Chihuahua. After about fifty miles we turned a sharp south toward Parral and Durango.

Designed for a smooth ride, the Packard sat on a very soft, ladylike American suspension. Although it may have increased the comfort, it was not without pitfalls. This huge eight-cylinder, being heavy like a boat, had the tendency to become an easy victim of the centrifugal force. It could lean dangerously into curves to the point of tipping over or ending up in a ditch.

I offered to drive, but Carolina insisted on keeping the steering wheel to herself. I wondered if her dad had warned her not to turn it over to me. Whatever, she hoped we could get as far as Durango, possibly Fresnillo, on the first day although that would depend on the traffic, the road conditions and the weather. Luckily, it was dry. Nor was there much traffic, especially on the long and lonely stretch to Parral. We whisked comfortably through vast expanses of parched, steppe-like grassland, dotted with occasional creosote bushes. Toward the southeast the sun peeked through a rose-colored layer of clouds, flooding the land with a beige sheen. To the west the rugged foothills of the Sierra Madre kept us company. We encountered herds of cattle, pronghorn antelopes and swarms of birds, though hardly any cars. They were so rare that the oncoming driver would greet us with a broad smile and the friendly gesture of an open palm. The only drama that broke the monotony was an occasional whirlwind bumping across the landscape, picking up dust and debris.

Responding to my question, Carolina delved into her stay in el D.F., which lasted almost four years. She attended a boarding school for gifted children catering to the cream of Mexican society. Taught by Jesuits, the curriculum was very demanding and to pass she had to hold her nose to the grindstone. During her stint, she happened to fall in love with a certain Carlos, the son of the president of Pemex, the nationalized oil company. But the relationship was doomed from the beginning by the narcissism and self-absorption of Carlos. Carolina eventually dropped him, although they kept up a loose friendship. In fact, Carlos still keeps calling her every once in a while, inviting her to visit him in his mansion in Acapulco. But she hasn't seen him in years, at least that's what she claimed.

We made good time and by eleven thirty we had already reached Parral, a small, scruffy town with a rich history in silver, copper and lead mining. The narrow and winding one-way streets were not easy to navigate. Since high noon was only a few ticks away, we decided to stop for lunch. Over a tasty meal of tacos at *El Gavilan Poliero,* Carolina informed me that as far back as the seventeenth century enslaved *indigenas* (natives) were busy digging up these various metals from its rich veins. The latest boom ended in the late nineteenth century, when most of the stone villas and mansions still adorning the streets were built. Nowadays, the town is mainly famous for the murder of Pancho Villa, the flamboyant bandit and colorful revolutionary hero.

"Admirers, droves of *campesinos,* but also to many Mexican patriots still flock to his grave," Carolina informed me with a sneer. "Thirty thousand admirers attended his funeral that had a most macabre sequel: shortly after his burial, his corpse was beheaded by political opponents who would have liked to do the very same when he was still alive."

I shook my head in wonder. "What do you think of him?"

245

"Well, if you ask me, he doesn't deserve his heroic stature because he carried out his raids and his revolutionary crusades mainly for personal aggrandizement. For better or worse, we Mexicans are incurable romantics. What counts in our country is the high-minded, revolutionary gesture, not the result. And such a gesture Pancho Villa sure had in superabundance, just like the rest of our revolutionary heroes you see statues of on every street corner. One of my teachers compared them to operatic heroes. Unfortunately, we Mexicans have a curious tendency to live down to a hostile caricature the Americans have of us."

"How many did you have, heroes I mean?"

"At least a handful. They did virtually nothing to help the poor. People are as poverty-stricken as before. Many have to go to America to find work and make a living."

South of Parral it got a little greener, which pleased my eyes. Unfortunately traffic thickened, especially as we drew closer to Durango. Worse, the pavement and bridges also narrowed dangerously, forcing us to slow down and stay fully alert. At times only centimeters separated our mirrors from those of the oncoming cars and trucks, testing the nerves of Carolina and also mine. I saw her repeatedly cross herself and murmur prayers.

"There are too many head-on collisions on Mexican highways," she said matter-of-factly during one of our stops, "and a good number of them are deadly. That's why you see crosses by the bushel along roads, *descansos,* as we call them. They signal that somebody lost his or her life at this spot and is resting now."

"Yes, I saw them already in New Mexico and Texas."

Battle-hardened, I again offered to relieve my novia and take over the steering wheel. But she resisted, mumbling something about her father's insurance, that it might not pay if I were to drive and get into an accident.

Come Friday, we whisked past the bull breeding and wine producing area between Aguascalientes and Lagos de Moreno. As we drew closer to el D.F., the traffic became heavier and ever more dense and chaotic. Straying animals, people astride donkeys, horse, or donkey-drawn carts, bicycles, motorcycles, buses and other decrepit rust-buckets thronged the road. Wary, Carolina gripped the steering wheel and slowed down to a walking pace. Still, she barely missed hitting a dog. Gone was the blue horizon in favor of a blurring haze, just as Carolina had predicted. Instead of entering a gleaming metropolis, we encountered the encroaching horrors of a wasteland with its shanty towns, mange of detritus, its heaps of smoking garbage tended by a host of scavengers, men, women, children, babies and gray heads included. A stinging blend of smoke and dust, car exhaust from belching buses and trucks, feces and carrion, ravaged our noses. Did I not also notice some metalliferous taste on my tongue?

At the first big traffic light, vendors leaned into our windows, hawking flowers, fruit, *chicles* (chewing gum), crucifixes, and live chickens. A scruffy Indian boy even stuck a live iguana right in my face, making me shrug back and turn up the window. *This is supposed to be the Mexican capital?* I asked myself. My mood dropped to the dregs. *What an urban monstrosity!*

At one point, we had to stop at a Pemex station to fill up. We stepped out into an air that was so filthy that we both choked. Carolina was particularly hard hit presumably because of her pregnancy. Besides complaining of a dizzy feeling, she started to wheeze and cough, gasp and gag. I tried to be helpful and again offered to take over the steering wheel. At first, she turned me down, but minutes later came around: "But you have to promise to drive very, very carefully. I don't want to get in trouble with Dad."

Having been warned of the dangers inherent in its soft suspension, I started out very slowly, weaving into the flow of the traffic. Gradually I began to feel more confident and figured I would drive the car all the way to Jorge's apartment. It was stop and go. Thankfully, I'd long learned to be patient. But then, we had barely entered el D.F. and a stretch where the traffic began to move more briskly, we were suddenly motioned over to the shoulder by a police officer, a *tamarindo*. Clad in a dark-brown uniform, he stood there at a filthy turnout, beside a rusty, dented police car.

"Mierda!" I hissed, shaking my head. To say that I was nervous, would be an understatement. I was on tenterhooks.

Watching me, Carolina put her hand on my shoulder and said, "Don't worry, we'll get out of this mess one way or other."

That soothed me a little. And having come to a stop and turning down the window, I asked matter-of-factly, *"Que pasa?"*

"Senor, limite de velocidad esta forty kilometer," the cop said in a polite tone of voice. "But you drive seventy."

"No puede ser, senor! It can't be true, sir! I drove less than forty. I watched my speed very closely."

"He's right," Carolina elbowed in. "He drove about thirty-five and certainly no more than forty."

"You stay out of this, senorita," the cop barked, jutting his jaw. And turning to me again, he insisted, "I watched you driving seventy. You fast, speeding. Your *licencia, por favor?"*

"Lo siento, no tengo una licencia?"

"What? You don't khave license."

"My friend just took over the steering wheel at the Pemex station up the road because I felt dizzy. You see, I'm pregnant." She bloated her stomach. "I did it to avoid an accident."

"Bien! El coche es tuya?"

"No, mio padre," Carolina said.

"Tienes algunos documentos?"

"Si." She fished them out of her handbag and handed them to him. He looked at them, checked the license plate and returned it.

"Americano?" he wanted to know, facing me again.

"No, suizo."

"Suizo? You khave *pasaporte*?"

"Sorry, I don't. But I have an immigration card." I pulled it out of my rucksack and showed it to him.

He looked at it. *"Esto valido, pero no tienes pasaporte?"* he said, shaking his head. *"Es imprescindible tener un pasaporte.* (You've got to have a passport.) You come to *comisaria."*

No, not again! Stark images of the jail in Chihuahua pulsed through my mind. I gave Carolina a glare of desperation.

"Lo siento, senor," she said. *"Pero tenemos no tiempo. Esta una infraccion de trafico, como no? Solo por curiosidad, quanto costa la boleta?"* (It's a traffic violation, isn't it? I'm just curious, how much is the ticket?)

"Doscientos pesos, senorita. Two khundred pesos."

"Two hundred pesos? How dare you? That's *exorbitante!"* She pulled out a scratch pad and began writing down the license plate number of the cop's car. "By the way, what's your name, sir?"

"You want name? *Por que?"*

"To report you to the Secretary Teofilo Diaz-Arrelano at the *Secretaria de Turismo.* He is a relative of mine."

The officer appeared flustered, then bowed and said, *"Oh, lo siento. Es no importa.* Me sorry. You OK. *Buen viaje! Buen viaje!"* He waved us on.

We switched seats again and drove off.

"Damned, that was a close shave," I sighed out. "He had me by the cojones. Congratulations! You pulled no punches. You really startled him."

"I got so upset with that bastard when he tried to blackmail you."

"For me, the whole incident was a wake-up call. I'll have to apply for citizenship, get a passport and a driver's license as soon as possible. I'm a sitting duck for those cops."

"I agree."

Leaving the shock and the shanty towns behind, we gradually pushed and shoved our way into this ghoul of a city. Fortunately, things improved somewhat as we drew closer to the center. Although the poorest of the poor, most of them indigenas, still crowded most traffic stops, things did look up. Often the contrast couldn't have been starker and more stunning. We drove past well-tended parks with monumental statues, huge baroque palaces along tree-lined boulevards, where well-dressed couples in horse-drawn carriages or American convertibles, even luxury cars like Cadillacs cruised along.

"They look like they own the future," Carolina commented as a young couple in a sleek Lincoln passed us.

We purposely skirted the old center, heading south instead of east. We finally purred to a halt in front of a mansion on the poplar-lined Avenida Venustiana Carranza in the southern park-like district of Coyoacan, within a stone's throw of the Plaza Hidalgo. According to Carolina, Coyoacan was once an independent *pueblo* outside of the city and, originally, after the fall of the Aztec empire, the haunt of the conquistador Hernan Cortes and his Indian mistress La Malinche.

"Now, as the city bursts at its seams, Coyoacan is gradually being swallowed up by it, and in a few years it will have turned into another suburb."

NIBBLING AT ACTING

Compared to the filth and extreme poverty of the shanty towns, Coyoacan, this cobblestoned enclave with its captivatingly stuccoed colonial houses and villas, many of them tastefully painted in bright purple, russet, blue, green and yellow, turned out to be a feast for the eyes. My jaw dropped at the burst of color, the sprightliness of the street cafes, restaurants, bookstores and small shops. It didn't surprise me that this district, in Carolina's words, rose to become *the* artist colony of Mexico. "This is the place where the painter Frida Kahlo, the muralist Diego Rivera, and many other famous painters, sculptors, singers and actors are living and working. It's here where the Mexican films are made. And where the Russian revolutionary leader Leon Trotsky chose to live and, sadly, also die. He was murdered by agents of Stalin's KGB only two years ago."

"Oh, Trotsky was here in Mexico?" I wondered.

"Yeah, but as a political leader he was no longer influential. I guess sensuous Mexico pulled him down to a more biological level. That is at least what Jorge thinks. He even met him once at a party Frida Kahlo staged in her home. He claims that Trotsky's brains kept sliding down into his pants and were consumed by his cojones. According to the grapevine he also engaged in a liaison with Frida Kahlo."

We hopped out of the car and rang the bell. It took several minutes before the door opened and a young, handsome man appeared. Wrapped in a pair of white pants and a navy-blue, double-breasted cotton blazer, he looked and also acted like a full-fledged dandy. "Carolina, my little sister!" he shouted, smiling and opening his arms. "I've been waiting for you."

"I hope so," Carolina snapped. *"Ay, muy guapo!"*

They hugged and kissed.

"Allow me to introduce Fred Luthi, my fiancé."

"Mucho gusto," I said, as we shook hands.

"It's my pleasure," he retorted in fluent English, although with the rolling 'r' of a crow on mind-altering mushrooms. "Carolina has told me a lot of good things about you, but also about your terrible experiences at the penitentiary in Chihuahua."

"She did?" I said, smiling and giving her a kiss. "Thanks to your sister, all that is behind me."

"Let's hope so," Carolina burst in, shaking her head.

"Well, what are we waiting for? Let's get your luggage. As I told you, you're welcome to live in my apartment during your stay. It will be all yours. I'll leave as soon as you're settled."

We carried our luggage up the stairs.

A head shorter than me, Jorge had a definite Near-Eastern, Semitic appearance. His face was narrow, hatchet-like, as if it had been designed in the wind tunnel, dominated as it was by a bony beak of a nose that shadowed his piercing coffee-brown eyes and a thin black mustache. His shiny black hair, heavily pomaded, was ruthlessly slicked back.

Jorge's first-floor apartment was not only spacious but also very luxurious. It had all the modern conveniences I could think of, a large carpeted living room with a huge sofa, several comfortable armchairs, a coffee table, a tastefully tiled kitchen with a gas range and a refrigerator, and a bedroom with a huge queen-size bed. The walls were dotted with modern abstract paintings. Several large sculptures of shapely girls and women dotted the floor. The whole flat was unusually bright, with its large windows looking out toward the east, as well as the south.

"If it's clear, I can see the two snow-covered volcanos, Popocatepetl and Iztaccihuatl," Jorge commented, as I tried to orient myself. "Although nowadays it doesn't happen very often any more. The air is too dirty. By the way, can I offer you a drink? I can mix a good margarita. But I also have a fair selection of wines and an excellent tequila reposado that tastes heavenly."

Carolina opted for a margarita, while I thirsted after the tequila, which turned out to be an aged, amber-colored Mescal *con gusano*. Its bottle contained a plump, whitish caterpillar to prove it had a high enough percentage to kill and to preserve it, or so Jorge informed me. We clinked glasses. I took the occasion to thank Jorge for his generosity in letting us stay here in his abode, but most notably for arranging the interview with the film director, Senor Manuel Alarcon, tomorrow morning. I asked him if he had any tips helping me make a favorable impression.

"I'm glad you asked," he spouted, revealing to me that in order to get a foot in the door he had deemed it wise to add a few 'minor things' to my biography. He claimed he had told Senor Alarcon that I had been a top student at the Drama School in Zurich and, being a full-fledged actor, I'd played important roles in several German plays, tragedies as well as comedies, on various stages in Zurich and other Swiss towns. "So don't be surprised if he'll ask you about it," he added, biting off a titter.

I was stunned that Jorge would take it upon himself to fictionalize my biography. Yet I also bought his argument for fibbing on my behalf, only to help me.

"The biggest hurdle will not come tomorrow but on Monday, when you will have to return for an audition," he went on. "Senor Alarcon will most likely hand you a script with a dramatic dialogue in Spanish you'll have to act out during the audition. There will be Senor Alarcon and several experienced actors watching your presentation. They will later decide whether or not you'll get the part."

"How long's the script?"

"It varies. I would say about ten pages for an audition that may take half an hour or so."

"That'll keep me busy tomorrow and on Sunday," I said glancing at Carolina. "You'll have to help me with the pronunciation and the meaning of the words."

"Sure, I'd be happy to."

Before he left, he promised he'd pick me up at about nine thirty in the morning and take me to the film studio. Carolina could come along as well. In fact, Jorge thought it would be to my advantage if she did.

Weary and hungry, we found a small restaurant just around the corner where we got a bite to eat. The waiter brought a candle and lit it, setting Carolina's olive skin aglow. How attractive she still was, despite the pregnancy and the long and strenuous drive. I also picked up a newspaper, *Reforma,* and began reading it. According to a report hugging the front page, the Russians continued to make progress pushing the German Army out of Odessa. I cringed as usual. The only consolation I could come up with was my conviction that the more negative the report, the sooner the war might end.

"And wouldn't it be nice if the FBI's manhunt for the murderer of the border guard were a thing of the past as well?" I hinted to Carolina.

"That would be a godsend."

Once back at the apartment, we crowded into Jorge's shower, splashing on end, only to be drawn to a comfortable bed.

In the morning, we rolled out of bed late. A pale, tired sun edged into our bedroom, even stroking our faces. Both volcanos, Popocatepetl as well as Iztaccihuatl, showed themselves only in blurry outlines.

Carolina first brewed a strong cup of coffee, while I raided Jorge's fridge for provisions needed for a wholesome breakfast. Luckily everything was there: eggs, tortillas, beans and a hot salsa. I let my elbows fly, finding a pan and some oil, cracking eggs and, within minutes a spate of huevos rancheros begged to be served. Carolina was astonished at my sleight of hand. And when I asked her how my huevos tasted, she burst out in roaring laughter. "What's the matter?" I poked.

"Well, as a man, you'd never ask anybody how 'my huevos' taste, especially a lady," she warned me. "Because in Mexican Spanish huevos is also slang for 'balls'. Nor would you want to approach a man with *Tiene huevos?* or he might deal you a blow to your chin. If you want some eggs, you simply say *Hay huevos?*"

"Thanks for saving me some trouble. Actually, in German it is somewhat similar. Although, as a rule, German men are not nearly as prickly about their manhood."

"I hope they don't have reason to be," she kidded me.

Shortly past nine thirty Jorge arrived and after a few polite exchanges we headed down to the car. Ten minutes later we came to a halt in the back of a movie studio, La Via Lactea. It was housed in a modern, austere, off-white Bauhaus building, whose wall was embellished with a colorful mural by Diego Rivera showing scenes of Mexican history. We followed Jorge inside. Unfortunately, Senor Alarcon was not in his office, but his secretary, Liliosa Flores, a heavy, round-faced woman, told us that he would be back shortly. In the meantime, we could wait in Senor Alarcon's office, a sizable, square room with two large windows facing the street, a small desk and a huge, round coffee table surrounded by a large leather sofa and tubular steel furniture. Several heavy, abstract stone sculptures dotted the floor, while the walls were covered with posters of movies, movie stars and a large painting of a pained Frida Kahlo sitting in a wheelchair. We took seats on the sofa and the chairs. Liliosa brought some coffee, a hefty, no-nonsense brew, and some pan dulce.

As we slurped our coffee and let our eyes feast on the art, a high-pitched voice cut in, "Forgive me for being tardy."

Our heads turned. Through the door came a short, rather corpulent man in his early fifties. He looked like a streetcar conductor, sporting a pair of chubby cheeks, large dark eyes, and a hard, bony nose that protruded like a ship's prow. Below his distinct neb, a vigorous salt-and-pepper mustache fanned out to shade most of his upper lip, while a tousled mane, interlaced with silvery strains, framed his forehead. Unlike most Mexicans, he refused to flash an inviting smile. All he did was chew on a fat cigar.

We rose, although he insisted that we remain seated, hissing, "*Sientese, sientese!*"

Jorge introduced us. Shaking my hand, Senor Alarcon offered a "Willkommen in Mexico" and quickly joined me and Carolina on the sofa, sidling up to her. Turning toward me, he let me know in fluent American English that he'd traveled around in Switzerland. But that was before the war, six years ago. He praised the beauty of the country, the lakes, the rivers, the mountains, the small towns and the cities, but then added somewhat apologetically that he found the people rather stodgy and stiff. He admitted it might have something to do with the fact that he had been in Italy before and, his being Mexican, enjoyed the Italian lifestyle.

"Forgive me but I found them lifeless," he said, giving his cigar a vigorous puff.

"Well, why do you think I left for Mexico?" I couldn't resist snapping with a smile.

"Touche!" And switching the subject, he said, "I understand you would like to get a part in one of our movies. What do you think qualifies you? Aside from your appearance, that is."

"Well, I don't know what Jorge told you about me, but I have studied acting at the Schauspielschule in Zurich, and I have had quite a bit of stage experience in Switzerland, particularly playing soldiers. That's a weakness of mine. You see, I come from a military family. My grandfather was a captain and my father is a colonel in the Swiss Army. I've also been in Germany before the war, where I frequently watched German soldiers marching in military parades. That helped me pick up their demeanor, their gestures and their way of playing their roles." My boasting came so naturally, as if I believed it myself.

Seeing Senor Alarcon's eyes lit up, I instantly rose, clicked my heels and proffered a snappy salute, shouting, "Leutnant Luethi, Herr General, ich stehe zu Ihrer Verfügung!" (I'm at your disposal!)

Everyone, including Senor Alarcon, burst out in laughter, rich, round globes of it that would drift in the air like soap bubbles.

This sleight, unexpected as it was, must have impressed the *zorro viejo* (old fox), as Jorge chose to call him. Rising, he gave his cigar a good puff and then returned my salute, shouting, "Bravo, lieutenant. At ease!" adding, "We have to apologize when it comes to a military salute. We Mexicans are not quite as snappy as you. Thankfully, I venture to say."

Having asked a few more questions about my acting qualifications, Senor Alarcon shuffled over to his desk and picked up some sheets of paper. "This is a scene from the film's screenplay *They Came From Afar*, he said, handing them to me. "It's the part of a German sailor who is the lone survivor of a sunk U-boat. He's desperately trying to get on a life raft crammed with Jewish refugees who have just survived the German torpedo attack. I want you to learn it by heart, so you can present it at the audition. Let's see, would Monday morning at ten fit your schedule?"

"It would be perfect."

"Well, let's go ahead then. I and some other movie people, actors and actresses, will likely be present. Obviously, I cannot guarantee you'll get the part. Good luck!" He puffed again.

I rose and thanked him for offering me the opportunity. We shook hands and left.

"Congratulations, you played the role of a petitioner with panache worthy of a seasoned actor," Carolina gushed, as we walked back to the car. "I dare say, with your performance you're almost halfway of getting the part."

"I agree," Jorge chipped in. "You've made a very good impression on Senor Alarcon. I could see it in his face. That's quite a coup. I know him a little — he is not easily impressed."

"Let's tread carefully," I dampened both of their enthusiasm. "I'm not there yet. I still have to earn my stripes. Maybe you can both help me learn my part. It's all in Spanish, and my Spanish is worse than that of a five-year-old indigeno. "

Both promised to help.

We rattled to a halt on the cobblestones in front of Jorge's haunt. Up at the apartment we all settled down. Jorge and Carolina made themselves comfortable on the sofa and began reading the *Reforma,* while I turned my attention to the screenplay. It started out by giving me a quick rundown of the plot, at the center of which is a Jewish mother with her two tots who, like fifteen other refugees fleeing the Nazis in Europe, find themselves on the freighter CONFIANZA from Lisbon.

The first destination happens to be Miami, Florida, where the refugees hope to find compassionate officials who will grant them asylum. Yet, after dropping anchor and mooring in the harbor for two days, the captain is informed that the freighter must leave within twenty-four hours. Short of other options, he leaves the harbor and begins steering the CONFIANZA toward Veracruz in the hope that Mexico will show more heart. About three-hundred-fifty miles northeast of Veracruz a German U-boat sights and targets the CONFIANZA. The torpedo is a direct hit. Nine passengers, women, children and old people, including the captain and the crew, perish in the shark-infested waters. Eight lucky ones scramble onto a life raft, among them a mother with her two tots.

As the survivors move away from the giant oil slick, dead bodies and flotsam, they're soon pestered by a German sailor, Kurt, who begs to join them. Traumatized, he is floating in the water nearby. He is the sole survivor of the U-boat that was hit and sunk with the help of American airpower. At first the refugees steadfastly refuse to let the sailor grapple aboard. But eventually they soften their stance and take him in. As the days pass and the provisions diminish, as the fierce sun and heat beats down and muscular winds batter the raft, the nerves of the rafters are fraying, and before long, a thin majority decides to toss the German overboard. Still, the sailor, fighting for his life, keeps clinging to the boat — the more so since sharks are mercilessly closing in on it. He again makes heartbreaking pleas to come aboard. Eventually they pull him back in, just in time, it turns out. Meanwhile the raft, catching a favorable current, washes ashore at a remote beach about twenty kilometers south of Veracruz. Exhausted and dazed by the trauma, the refugees are found and taken in by families of Mexican *pescadores* (fishermen) and paisanos, and cared for.

Attached was the dialogue depicting the interaction between the refugees and the sailor. My task for the audition was to learn and embody the role of the sailor. Since he was a perpetrator before he became a victim, it required the utmost emotional sensibility.

Stirred by the plot, I was more than eager to take up the challenge and immediately went to work. To get a better grip, I translated the pivotal Spanish words into German and made them my own. Later, after a light comida at a small restaurant around the corner, I delved into the script. Carolina and Jorge not only helped me with the pronunciation and the meaning of certain words and phrases but also gave me valuable insight into their emotional content and the proper use of facial expressions and gestures. It helped that both slipped into the roles of the other passengers, taking up their dialogue. We practiced and drilled until late at night, at the end of which I was ready to make my first presentation, albeit with the text in my hand.

Next day, on Sunday, we rehearsed the same dialogue several times again, refining the diction, enunciation and articulation, as well as the body language. For most of the day we kept going at the preparation hammer and tongs, until my head started spinning.

At last, the day of reckoning had finally arrived, accompanied by a light, welcome drizzle. Though it may not have turned the valley green, it did cleanse the air. After a hot-cold shower and a hearty breakfast, I once again delved into the dialogue, licking it into shape. I felt very comfortable with it. Shortly past nine thirty, Jorge arrived and we whisked back to the studio. Senor Alarcon was already expecting us. He introduced us to Senores Gallegos and Battista, two experienced, middle-aged screen actors he had picked to evaluate my performance. In the wake of some chit-chatting all six of us headed to a small movie theater, equipped with a little stage.

"Well, are you ready?" Senor Alarcon approached me. "Today the stage is yours. By the way, you can peek into your screenplay if you get stuck."

Having rubbed my horseshoe, I grabbed the manuscript and walked up onto the stage. And once up there I was no longer Fred. I was Kurt, the ragged, disheveled sailor who found himself at death's door. Acting as though I clutched a rope, I began pleading with the refugees to let me board the life raft. I begged them, I implored them, I beseeched them. In heartbreaking outbursts, I appealed to their empathy and their conscience. I argued that I was anything but the Nazi monster some had dubbed me; that I was only a common sailor who had been drafted into the military; that I had no choice; that I would have faced the firing squad had I resisted; that I, doing my duty in the submarine, had been staunchly opposed to firing a torpedo into the steamer, but was overruled; that I was above all a human being who, just like they themselves, had a father, a mother, sisters and brothers; that I had a fiancee, whom I fervently loved; that we planned to marry once the war was over and have a family; that I hoped to see all of them again; that I wanted to live; that they shouldn't abandon me to the sharks. I was so wrapped up in my role I occasionally even uttered gushing and gurgling sounds to enact Kurt's peril of drowning. And when the call for help reached its most desperate pitch, I wailed and whimpered not only in Spanish, but also in German, giving Kurt's despair a more immediate, authentic ring. Even though this rendition deviated from the screenplay, Senor Alarcon burst out in a volley of spontaneous applause.

When I came to the end of my performance, I thanked Senores Alarcon, Gallegos and Battista for the opportunity to audition for the part, as well as for listening to my presentation. I also gave special thanks to both Carolina and Jorge for coaching and encouraging me all weekend long, emphasizing that without their help I could never have taken on such a part. Winding up, I bowed to a warm shower of applause.

Having left the stage, I was surrounded by everybody. They all tried to shake my hand and cheer me on. Carolina embraced me and placed a smacking *beso* (kiss) on my cheek.

"You were *magnifico*!" she spouted. "I'm really proud of you."

"Good performance, Fred," Senor Alarcon added, patting me on the shoulder. "I'll call you in the afternoon."

I handed him Jorge's telephone number and, following Carolina and Jorge, left the building.

Outside, the drizzle had thronged into a full-fledged downpour. That boosted my good cheer, and for the first time made breathing a joy. Instead of driving back to the apartment, Jorge made a small detour, stopping at El Fuego restaurant.

"I invite both of you to a *comida fuerte del dia*," he announced. "It's one of the best-kept secrets in town."

The eatery was jam-packed. Luckily Jorge knew the owner and, having slipped him a 10 peso bill, he promptly found us a table. Over a hot and savory *comida,* the lunch of the day, we talked about the audition and the movie project. For both Carolina and Jorge it was virtually certain that Senor Alarcon would pick me for the role. Jorge even suggested that I should plan ahead and prepare myself for the shooting, which could begin within months. According to him, the scenes centering on the steamer and the life raft would probably be shot in and around Veracruz. He claimed he'd met some of the cast's actors and actresses. The role of the mother, for instance, would be played by Elvira Mendez, a young, ravishing Mexican actress. In fact, he jokingly issued a warning about her charms, insinuating she was known as a siren and an eye-candy to the male gaze. I countered he wouldn't have to worry, I was deeply in love with Carolina. That seemed to calm Carolina, but lured a wry-mouthed smile out of Jorge.

We leaned into our food, guzzled beer, and chatted for more than two hours, leaping from one topic to the next, the war included. They were of the opinion that Germany, exhausted by the daily onslaught from the east as well as from the west, would surrender within the next six months. I wasn't so sure any more, but expressed hope that they were right. Eventually we ran out of topics that aroused our attention, and when Jorge and Carolina turned to Mexican politics, I grew restless. Anxious about missing Senor Alarcon's call, I begged Jorge to take me back to the apartment.

The rain had retreated, when he let me out in front his apartment. Bountiful shafts of sunlight, reminiscent of sheaves of wheat, stroked the city, dotting it with a fresh sheen. I rushed up to the apartment, while Jorge and Carolina zoomed off to meet with friends in a cafe downtown. Entering, I instantly tore open the windows to let the clean air drift in. Toward the south-east, Popocatepetl and Iztaccihuatl, both capped with new snow, proudly displayed their regal grandeur, standing sentinel over the valley. It was a breathtaking and awe-inspiring sight, one that Hernan Cortes may have enjoyed in 1521, after he'd conquered the Aztec empire. Or so Jorge had reminded me when we first arrived. To watch those two giants, I placed myself in a comfortable armchair in such a way that I could just look up from Jorge's broadsheet.

Minutes later, the telephone rang. *That must be him,* I reckoned, twitching nervously as I lifted the receiver. But it was a high-pitched, feminine voice asking for Jorge. *"Lo siento, hoy no esta,"* I said going back to the newspaper, which also carried some news from the war. Unfortunately, I was too tense and expectant to concentrate. According to my diary, I'd skipped through a piece about the bombing of the hydro-electric plant in Vemork, Norway, by the American Air Force. That's where our scientists were producing heavy water that was needed to build an atomic bomb. The article claimed that the destruction of this plant made it virtually impossible for Hitler to build such a weapon. It was supposed to be one of the *Wunderwaffen* that, according to the Fuehrer, would eventually change the outcome of the war in Germany's favor. I still recall that I spontaneously applauded the American action. Jorge and Carolina might be right after all that the Thousand-Year Reich would collapse much sooner than I'd expected, leaving nothing but rubble and a trail of dust. *Could it be a Christmas gift?*

Shortly past two, the phone rang again. This time it was Senor Alarcon. "Am I speaking with Senor Luthi?" he asked.

"Yes, that's me."

"Senor Luthi, I just want to inform you that we have agreed to offer you the part of Kurt, the German sailor. Your performance…"

"Thank you so much, Senor Alarcon," I burst in. "I really appreciate that."

"Let me just say, your performance during the audition was very good, except for your Spanish pronunciation. That'll have to improve considerably before we start shooting. Fortunately some of that deficiency can be remedied. We have access to several excellent language instructors who can work with you on your Spanish diction." He gave me two names, Pedro Saltillo and Dolores Reyes, including their telephone numbers. "I suggest that you contact them right away. The shooting of the first scenes will start no later than the middle of February in the area around Veracruz. But the scenes where you will appear will be shot a month or even two months later. I hope we can complete all the footage I need in about three months. I just want to let you know, so you can plan ahead. I also have a copy of the whole screenplay for you. You can pick it up any time. If you have any questions, call me. Please give my greetings to Jorge and don't forget to embrace your lovely fiancée Carolina for me."

259

I was thunderstruck, floating on a pink cloud with the feel of a foam mattress. It was nothing short of a dream. It wasn't until two hours later when Jorge and Carolina appeared that I grew more certain and was able to share my joy with somebody.

It goes without saying that they were enraptured when they heard the favorable news and the warm greetings from Senor Alarcon. "See, what did I tell you?" Jorge shouted, patting me on the back. Carolina embraced and kissed me. All three of us danced a ring-a-ring-o'-roses. Always ready to celebrate, Jorge pulled out all the stops, offering margaritas and other drinks. Later we walked to the Cafe de Durango, another of Jorge's hangouts, where we continued our revelry. Besides enjoying our dinners, we slugged away almost three bottles of Chilean bubbly. It wasn't until two o'clock in the morning that we trudged our way back to the apartment, so soused that we could hardly climb the stairs.

Next morning, we slept almost until noon. After a hearty breakfast, Carolina whisked me to the studio to pick up the screenplay. I couldn't see Senor Alarcon; he was reportedly busy jawing with a high government official about subsidies for his project. But Liliana, his secretary, had several copies, and she willingly handed me one. It was a thick, typewritten tome. And when I got back to the apartment, I couldn't wait to delve into it. Besides being curious about the nitty-gritty of the scenes, I was eager to get acquainted with the dialogue between the other players of the cast. A surprise came right at the beginning, when I read that one of the authors were Raimondo Alarcon and Fernando Ulibarri. I was completely oblivious that, besides being a movie director and businessman, Senor Alarcon was also a writer. The fact that he was all three made his stature rise to unknown, monumental heights.

As to the cast itself, initially the whole huddle of the seventeen refugees, as well as the captain, first catches the eye of the camera when the freighter is miles east of the Florida coast, near the Bahamas. When I read about these vulnerable people, many of them seasick and scared stiff, bracing for an attack by a U-boat that would suddenly pop up out of nowhere and then fire a lethal torpedo into the hull of their vessel, I reminisced about my own journey only six months ago. But the comparison was lame, self-indulgent. I was a battle-hardened soldier who'd to expect the dread of dying, while they were civilians, old people, women and children, who'd been beaten down by the fear of ending up in a concentration camp.

According to the script, I, that is, the German sailor Kurt, wouldn't make my appearance until much later, when the German U-boat is first sighted. At that point, the camera catches me inside the sub, showing my scruples about the decision to torpedo the freighter, but also executing the command, even though it was in conflict with my conscience.

A NEEDLE IN A HAYSTACK

Being part of this huge cauldron called el D.F. was bound to arouse strange, dissonant feelings. While I found the stench, squalor and human misery nauseating, I was also lured by opportunity and, last but not least, the feeling of safety. Unlike in Chihuahua I didn't feel threatened. Quite the contrary, I felt safer here than in any other place in Mexico or the United States. The reason was simple: Here I was the proverbial needle in the haystack — undefined, anonymous, invisible. Nobody, save for a few people of goodwill, knew that I was a fugitive of justice; nobody even knew who I was. Nor would anybody care.

All that instilled me with a feeling of ease and lightheartedness I hadn't experienced lately, a frame of mind Carolina had not only noticed but also praised. And so had Jorge who complimented me for having grown wings. Although I fully savored my feelings, I was also aware that I could only hold on to it, if I'd get my foot in the door and become a full-fledged Mexican citizen with a passport at all. With that goal in mind, I, together with Jorge, headed to the Secretario de Relaciones Exteriores, located on the Plaza Juarez in the historic district.

As expected, there were long lines, but Jorge, foxy as ever, found a way to get around them. In any event, we were soon able to speak to an official who promptly provided me with the information and forms I needed. He urged me to apply for naturalization as soon as I got an *Acta de Matrimonio*. And once I'd received my citizenship papers, I could petition for a passport. He handed me the necessary forms. Unfortunately, the process could take months, although there were ways to hasten it — with the help of a mordida, of course. He wouldn't commit himself, saying in effect that the cost would have to be negotiated.

That soothed me somewhat, although I was still vexed with the question of how to pay for the bribe. My pockets were drained. Yet Jorge assured me, that by then I may already have received the first paycheck from Senor Alarcon.

"I don't know about you, but I need a cup of coffee," Jorge announced as we stepped out of the office. "Let's go to the El Popular. It's emblematic of the city. And it's close, just around the corner."

I followed him, jostling through a beehive of people, mainly indegenas. We passed more beggars, two organ grinders and, shortly before the entrance to the cafe, I almost bumped into an *escritorio,* where a ragged clerk was sitting behind an old Smith Corona. Using two fingers, he kept tapping out letters to relatives and lovers, deeds and wills, all for people who couldn't write, so Jorge informed me. "That's the problem in Mexico," he added with a grin. "We've got too many illiterates."

The cafe itself was a loud and bustling place, albeit somewhat shabby. A rotund waitress in a spotted, off-white apron led us to a table. Next to us sat three scrubby, off-duty cops, sipping tequilas and chattering with two, what seemed to be, *calientes,* with flaming red hair and shaved eyebrows, stuffed in blue and pink dresses to the point of bursting. On the other side, a little farther away, five older gentlemen in threadbare jackets but with bow ties kept hugging a round table. Some puffed unfiltered drags, others slurped *cafes con leche,* while heatedly discussing local politics, especially Mexico's relationship with America.

We ordered a cup of coffee each with milk from a separate jar, plus a platter of pan dulce. Leaning back in our chairs, we chit-chatted about Mexico City, its culture, its bloody history and the Spanish conquest. Since this was Jorge's pet peeve, he soon took hold of the reins, although his disapproving, even faultfinding attitude puzzled me.

"You have given me so many grim and disenchanting impressions of this beehive of a city," I finally threw in. "I've heard so much about the gory Aztecs, their bloodthirsty god Huitzilopochtli, the choking air, shanty towns, the indegenas, the mud and temblores, I'm just curious as to what if anything keeps you here?"

"Good question," he said, taking a long sip and grinning. "I concede, life can be pretty wretched and ugly here in this teeming cauldron. But you know what? I wouldn't want to live anywhere else. First of all, I'm very fond of my flat in Coyoacan. It's convenient, beautiful, close to ideal. I have a circle of friends in the world of art and the cinema I couldn't have in any other place. And even in this chaotic city, hidden underneath all the poverty, there's a ferment, a creative vitality and an anarchic freedom that's unique. You always feel as if you're living on the edge, near the abyss. It's an air of nihilistic poetry you breathe every day in the streets, shanty towns and cafes you wouldn't find anywhere else. Just look around this place and you get some inkling of what I'm talking about. It may be a little bit what Berlin in the twenties and early thirties must've been, full of gloom and despair, grins, grimaces and cackles. Georg Grosz comes to mind."

"That's where I'm coming from," I said. "From Berlin. Unfortunately, I wasn't part of the upper crust or of artist circles. Being young and green, I caught sight of the turmoil from a different perspective, from the very bottom of things, the dregs. When you're confined to an orphanage, you don't have the luxury of seeing the art in the despair surrounding you."

Recapitulating what I had been told about my early childhood, I wondered if one of the ladies at the next table could've been my mother who, shying away from the responsibilities of taking care of me, simply dumped me in a place next to a garbage can.

"I see what you mean," Jorge conceded. "Things do look different from worm's-eye view."

"It's one of the reasons why the Nazis had so much support. They came in with sharp elbows, fists and big brooms to sweep the place clean and put everybody to work. And people seemed to like it. I, too, was impressed. But these bullies also started the war and… Well, you know what happened, is still happening, I'm afraid."

When we got back to the apartment, Carolina was sitting on the couch, sipping a mixed drink and reading a novel. Besides mentioning to her that we just came from the Cafe Popular, I also informed her about the obstacles I'm facing to get Mexican citizenship, reminding her that I'd have to be married first.

"I wondered," she said stroking her belly. "We should get going right after our arrival at the hacienda."

"Good idea," I said, giving her a kiss.

Since we were already approaching suppertime, she invited us all to dinner at the Cafe de Tacuba, a quaint, historic gem of a restaurant in the heart of the city. Having been a frequent visitor when she was still in a liaison with her former boyfriend, she found no ceiling in her praise.

"I want it to be festive," she said with a slight swipe at Jorge. "Mexico is more than the Cafe Popular and the zocalo."

To get ready, we all showered, scrubbing off the grime and soot of the city. Shuffling out clean, Carolina spruced herself up, donning black slacks, a tasteful blue poncho and attractive silver earrings and touching up her face with light makeup and lipstick. While I slipped into a white shirt, pinstriped suit and oxford dress shoes, Jorge insisted on showing up in tan golf slacks, a black shirt, light-brown loafers and a boater. We all looked like we stepped out of a Hollywood movie, eliciting the crack, *"Muy guapo!"* out of Carolina.

We piled into the Packard with Jorge at the wheel. Being a fast and ruthless driver, he hardly ever showed any consideration for pedestrians, especially jaywalkers. In fact, in one instance I saw him purposely speeding up as if he intended to scare the person.

Carolina hadn't overstated. The Cafe de Tacuba was one of the most beautiful restaurants I'd ever seen. What it lacked in size, it more than made up in sensuous charm, coziness, not to mention ambience. With its colorful tiles, its brass lamps, beamed ceilings and, last but not least, its eighteenth century paintings, most notably the one of nuns preparing food in the kitchen, it gave us a feeling of a peaceful historic atmosphere long gone. The quality of the cuisine, including offerings from many regions of Mexico, was hard to surpass as well. The flavor of the *carne asada* with a smothering of *mole poblano,* a spicy sauce made with chilis and chocolate — yes, hot chocolate! — was as unusual as addictive. So were the tamales, made with chicken, tomatoes and jalapenos, rolled in corn tortillas. The exquisite dishes, swilled down with Chilean wines and garnished with Jorge's juicy anecdotes about movie actresses and actors, made the whole evening at this unique cafe a most memorable culinary event, adding a harmonious ending to our short stay in el D.F.

Leaving behind this beehive of a city, I'll never forget how carefree, how lighthearted I felt being there. At the same time, it was also a great relief to turn my back on the poverty, the shanty towns, the beggars, harlots, the grime and crime. And what a joy to finally breathe clean air again. Carolina was especially affected by the foul haze that suffocated the capital. "I don't know how Jorge can stand it," she said.

TYING THE KNOT

Back in the fold of the hacienda, we were welcomed like a couple who'd traveled around the world. They all badgered us to tell how it was in el D.F. and what we experienced — if the traffic was still as congested as they had heard and if the police had to deal with more than ten grisly murders a day, or if we felt any temblores that made the most beautiful palaces crumble.

"And what about the air?" Guillermo was curious to know. "Is it true people actually choke to death? And why don't they do anything about it?"

We told them and they listened with wide eyes and open mouths.

Once we'd settled, Carolina and I gathered our personal documents and headed down to *Registro Civil* at the *Municipio* of Cuauhtemoc one morning with nothing but marriage on our minds. Everyone had told me it would be easy to find a civil magistrate and in a few hours we would walk out of the wedding chamber with the *Acta de Matrimonio* in our hands. Giddy as I was, I'd forgotten we were in Mexico, where it's always a good policy to lower one's expectations and brace for the unexpected.

That appeared to be truer than ever. The whole process turned out to be most cumbersome, worse, frustrating experience. Besides filling out a Marriage Application and paying a fee, we were told that we had to prove we were both healthy adults. That part still proceeded smoothly. We rushed to the local health clinic just ten minutes away, where we submitted to a chest x-ray, as well as blood test. When we handed the results to the magistrate, the obstacles multiplied like bluebottles on a smelly piece of meat. I was told that, being a foreign national, I would first have to apply for a permit to marry a Mexican citizen. It would be issued by the federal *Secretaria de Gobiernacion — Officina de Migracion* in Chihuahua. Unfortunately, it would take some time, perhaps two months to get a response. Worse, I'd also need to show a passport and a birth certificate. My immigration card alone would simply not do it.

When I explained that I was assured by an official at the *Secretaria de Relaciones Exteriores* in el D.F. that I'd have to get married first in order to apply for a passport, the official simply shrugged his shoulder. *"Esta es regla,"* he mumbled. Besides, I would also need a passport and a birth certificate to get our Marriage Application approved.

Here we were, stuck in the vicious circle of the Mexican bureaucracy. Though it had the odor of the German obedience to fixed rules, we were still in Mexico, where the 'regla' could be circumvented with the help of that magic wand called mordida. Indeed, the official in charge was willing to turn a blind eye on both requirements if the bribe was hefty enough — 600 pesos. Once again, we drove a hard bargain. But having a weak basis for negotiations, we finally settled for 400. Since I didn't have a penny in my pocket, Carolina pulled out her purse. Notwithstanding, we were warned it might take months before the permission from the official in Chihuahua would arrive.

In the meantime, I went back to playing the role of cowboy again, taking care of the cattle in the holding pens. I also read through the whole movie script and started to learn my part by heart. It was a major challenge, mainly because of my weakness in Spanish. Again and again, I encountered words I'd never heard before, much less used. Still vividly recalling Senor Alarcon's critique, I frequently consulted Carolina about the pronunciation. And what a demanding taskmaster she was! I often had to pronounce a word or phrase five times before we could proceed to the next. Never had I strained my tongue and other oral muscles more than during the sessions with her. Thankfully, Spanish is a phonetic language; its pronunciation is much more predictable than the English tongue's. And its rules are more binding, showing fewer exceptions. That helped. Yet, as in any major language with a long and rich literary history, there were many unknown subtleties and devilries lurking below the surface, especially for a foreigner like me.

Like before our trip, we continued to meet at the barn, often three times a week. Since it was usually dark when we got there, I had to rely on my flashlight to read the words and phrases. Sitting on a blanket for more than an hour may have been bearable as a provisional solution, but it wasn't very comfortable or conducive to learning. Besides, we also had to face a cold spell, which forced the mercury below freezing, giving us stiff hands, cold noses and goosepimples.

"Can't you find a room in your mansion that has chairs, a table, a bright lamp and, while we're at it, a sofa or a bed?" I baited Carolina. "I don't know why we have to hide our relationship. It doesn't make any sense. Everyone knows that we're a couple. The sparrows keep twittering from the rooftops in bright daylight that you are *embarazada* and I was the one who sowed the seed. Our trip to el D.F. only confirmed what they'd known for weeks already."

"Come on, Fred, knock it off," she snapped at me again. "As I told you before, it won't happen before we officially get married. That's all there is to it."

We also discussed the big wedding celebration here at the hacienda. She thought that, since this was going to be an outdoor event and the cold months were approaching, we should postpone it until spring. "I was thinking about March or April. We can't set a date anyway. Who knows how long it will take to get permission from the government. That'll give us a little slack."

I couldn't but agree. Knowing how slowly the wheels of the Mexican bureaucracy turned, I urged her to call the magistrate and pester him. Well, she did, and eight days later a city official in Cuauhtemoc called her back, informing her that the *permiso* from the *Oficina de Migracion* in Chihuahua had finally arrived. We were urged to dress up, come down with two witnesses, recite the marriage vows and get our *Acta de Matrimonia*. We jumped for joy. Carolina immediately asked her mom and dad to act as witnesses. While her mom felt honored to attend the ceremony, her dad issued his usual threadbare rebuff, growling something about finding somebody else. But a day later, he reluctantly bowed.

The day of our wedding, a Friday, greeted us with plenty of sunshine and a bit of hoarfrost that enwrapped the grasses and shrubs with a fresh, sparkling coat. After my daily routine, I slipped into my suit, shirt and shoes, girded a Windsor-knotted tie around my collar and, feeling chipper, if slightly nervous, headed up to the mansion. The Packard in its full luster waited at the entrance. I rapped at the door. Carolina opened it. She was dressed — I had to rub my eyes! — in a traditional white wedding gown.

"I must be at the right address," I said, giving her an abrazo and a beso. "Muy guapa!"

She giggled. "Yeah, isn't it nice? You wouldn't guess it, it's my mom's. She wore it at her wedding forty-six years ago. Doesn't it fit me?" She spun around like a primadonna.

"Beautiful! You look like an angel floating on a silvery cloud."

"Yeah, the white is deceptive, *embarazada* so." She chuckled, touching her belly. "Anyway, we'll be ready in a minute."

She disappeared. Two minutes later she came back with both parents in tow. Imelda, her mother donned a bell-shaped, purple skirt, a white blouse and a black jacket, while her dad appeared in a grey flannel suit with a white shirt and a flamboyant, red-striped tie. "*Buenos dias!*" I greeted them, embracing her mother and shaking her father's hand which felt as spongy as a decaying carp.

All four of us ducked into the Packard. Having taken over the steering wheel, Don Leonardo started the car and, revving it up twice, we began wobbling down the rock-strewn road to Cuauhtemoc, and straight to the *Municipio*. The secretary who sat behind a rickety typewriter received us with a smile and, having pulled our papers out of the drawer, promptly informed the magistrate of our arrival. He turned out to be an unusually tall, dignified man with a full shock of grey hair, bushy, black eyebrows, a nicely trimmed mustache and soft, glistening eyes. More, he welcomed us with a big smile, shook our hands and, apologizing for the long delay, led us into a small court chamber. A large bouquet of fresh flowers embellished a table near the entrance, suggesting that the chamber found use for nobler purposes as well.

Presumably a judge by profession, Senor Fidel Archibeque asked us to be seated in the front row and without pausing issued a call to order. Talking slowly and deliberately in his baritone voice as if he was an emissary of the Lord personally, he then introduced the ceremony by stating that marriage must be one of life's greatest moments, stressing that it wasn't only a personal matter but, being the root of the family, it laid the foundation for any civilized society. After he had elaborated on his statement, which I only caught snippets of, he moved to the exchange of vows, urging both the bride and the groom to step forward and hand him the rings.

"Fred Luthi, are you ready to take Carolina Gomez y Izaguirre as your wife?" he asked, addressing me.

"I am, yes, very much so," I announced, stumbling slightly, which drew a chuckle out of Imelda and a sneer from Don Leonardo.

"And you, Carolina, are you prepared to take Fred as your husband?"

"Yes, I am," she said self-assuredly.

Bathing his face with a gratifying smile, Senor Archibeque then proceeded to ask both of us if we could promise to love, honor and cherish each other, to the exclusion of all others. He dealt me a knowing twinkle.

Having concluded the exchange of vows, he turned to the swapping of rings, asking both of us again if we were prepared to take each other as wife and husband and spend our lives together, to have and to hold, in sickness and in health, for richer or for poorer and promise to love each other.

"Fred Luthi, with this ring I thee wed," he pronounced, wiggling the ring onto my finger and later also on Carolina's. He concluded by comparing our marriage bond to a couple of different threads woven in opposite directions that can form a lasting tapestry. It will take love, amor. Otherwise, it won't work. Indeed, amor should form the core of your marriage. In addition, it will also take trust and goodwill, to know in your hearts that you want the best for each other, to stay open to one another, to learn and grow together, even and especially during hard times. It will take faith to walk into the future with your partner, not knowing what the future may bring. It will take commitment to hold true to the journey you both now pledge to share together.

"Fred and Carolina, in so much as the two of you have agreed to live together in matrimony and have promised to love each other by these vows, I now declare you to be husband and wife.

"Congratulations, you may now seal your love and marriage with a kiss."

Having embraced and kissed each other, we followed Senor Archibeque to the secretary's office, where we all signed the *Acta de Matrimonio*. He then handed us the document, congratulating us again. We shook hands and minutes later we were on our way.

Instead of driving back, Carolina suggested that we invite her parents to a comida at the Casa Vieja. It was the first time I had a more intimate encounter with both of them. Over a bottle of Spanish cava and a tasty meal, we talked about the future, the baby, the financial problems that plagued the hacienda, our excursion to el D.F. and my acting engagement. They both praised me for my quick acquisition of Spanish and my determination to succeed in my new acting career. Even now, her father continued to act niggardly. But I was not going to hold any grudges. For me, it was nothing less than a breakthrough and, letting bygones be bygones, I bowed by expressing my appreciation for all the help they'd given me, especially while I was stuck in jail. That helped clear the air, lower tensions and possibly even build a tenuous rope bridge across the huge gap that separated us. And when we walked out of the restaurant, we were all very relieved.

Taking advantage of the light thaw having descended on us, I brought up the question, very gingerly at first, of my moving to the mansion. For the first time ever, Carolina was receptive, now that we were married, and she promised to discuss my wish with her parents at the next opportunity. Well, the next day she informed me that both her mother and her father were in favor of letting me move in, although on a trial basis at first.

"That's what my dad insisted on," she said, rolling her eyes. "I wouldn't take it too seriously."

Again, I was not going to argue and quietly bagged the offer. So I gathered my belongings in the bunkhouse and carried them over to the mansion, where I was told to place them on Carolina's bed for the time being. For the first time I had a chance to enter her room, which was located on the ground floor. I must say, I was impressed. It was a spacious and tastefully decorated chamber with an attached bathroom, carrying a distinctly personal flavor. Most of its hardwood floor was covered with Persian area rugs, one more beautiful than the other. Two large windows, one looking south, the other east, let in plenty of light. The walls were covered with two large hardwood wardrobes, several bookcases and paintings, most of them representational, with a few abstract examples in between. Besides a large hardwood bed and two night stands, both flaunting tiffany lamps and one a radio, there was a small coffee table surrounded by a sofa and two armchairs. A fancy tropical-hardwood writing desk commanded the space below the southern window. Close by, hemmed in by bookcases, a cozy reading corner with an art nouveau lamp and a comfortable leather armchair invited the inquisitive mind to spend time in mental pursuits.

Once I'd dropped my belongings, Carolina offered that I could later tuck them away in her wardrobes. But come tomorrow, I'd be able to move all of them into a room located next to hers. It had to be scrubbed down first. Actually, she let me peek into it. A gurgle of joy escaped me. Brightened by a big window, it was furnished with a small bed, a tiny coffee table and two chairs. It was the first room I could call my own, and I looked forward to taking charge of it.

Next day I kept busy moving into my room, finding additional furniture that suited me, but also shaping and decorating it according to my own taste. Luckily, the mansion's attic contained a treasure trove of old furniture, as well as lamps, paintings, books and what have you. And I was free to pick whatever suited my taste. My eyes were fixed on a writing desk, two comfortable chairs, several lamps, a wardrobe, a large table and three paintings of landscapes that spoke to me, like a stunning depiction of a snow-covered Popocatepetl. Most pieces were easily carried down by myself; for the writing desk, the wardrobe and the table I called for help.

I was especially fond of my writing desk. Though small, it was a sturdy hardwood specimen with large drawers on each side. I placed it right under the window to take advantage of the daylight.

Being settled, my next goal was to apply for Mexican citizenship and a passport. I knew it would be an arduous, time-consuming and possibly expensive effort. Yet what choice did I have? I still felt very vulnerable. The process of applying for marriage had shown me once again that I wasn't out of the woods just yet. I couldn't quite shake off the uneasy feeling that Hoover's bloodhounds were still on my scent, would continue to be, at least until the end of the war, possibly even beyond. If only that carnage would wind down soon! Although the odds of that happening were long. Stalemates were the rule, except perhaps on the Russian front.

In the first session at my desk, I began to fill out both applications. Unfortunately, once again I was asked to provide an *Acta de Nacimiento,* a birth certificate, as well as a passport of my home country. Like on previous occasions, I explained that both my passport and my birth certificate had been stolen, but that I was born on March 17th, 1924, in Kreuzlingen, Switzerland. I promised to take an oath, if necessary.

Well, I stuck the applications into a large envelope and, adding four passport pictures, a copy of the *Acta de Matrimonio,* the *Permiso* for marrying a Mexican citizen and a check for more than 1,000 pesos, rode down to the post office in Cuauhtemoc, registered it, and sent it off to the *Secretaria de Relaciones Exteriores* in Mexico City. I was hopeful that I'd have a good chance of obtaining these valuable documentos so that with friendly nods from Lady Luck and a few rubs of my horseshoe, I could drop my stateless status and put my troubles behind me. But living in the land of manana, the first damper wasn't long in coming. I didn't even get a notice acknowledging the receipt of my application, much less the documents themselves.

I also began listening to the radio, particularly the newscasts beaming from several stations in Texas and Arizona. With time I became hopelessly glued to them. Later, Carolina, who for the first time was suffering from morning sickness, joined me. We heard about the heavy bombardment of Berlin by the Royal Air Force, wondering what was so 'royal' when thousands of civilians, mothers, children and grandparents were choked to death by the subsequent firestorm. The news that our highly decorated Field Marshal Rommel, the former commander of the Afrika Korps, had been appointed to be commander in chief of the Fortress Europe, suggested the war would probably drag on longer than most of the commentators thought. The greatest threat to the *Reich,* some suggested, would probably come from the east, where the Red Army continued to make steady gains.

Christmas rolled around with all the festivities and celebrations a Catholic country like Mexico could conjure up. It goes without saying that the hacienda was too isolated to come up with any ritual worth mentioning. But what we were lacking, the town of Cuauhtemoc more than made up. It hurled itself into the fray as if it wanted to prove its status as a regional go-getter. Very early, in mid-December, Las Posadas, colorful candle-light parades and parties, were held, leading up to Christmas. Thanks to a very active Jesuit priest, Monsignor Bertoni, it also staged Las Pastorales, shepherd plays. Performed mainly by amateurs, they depicted the story of the shepherds' passage to Bethlehem and the devil's attempt to bewilder them through a series of mishaps. Carolina and I couldn't resist watching one such show. I liked it so much that, when an actor fell ill, I volunteered twice to play the devil.

Christmas Eve, we celebrated by going to a Mass in Cuauhtemoc. That is, Carolina's dad placed the Packard and the big truck at everybody's disposal to catch a free ride. While Carolina, I, her parents and a visibly pregnant wife of a vaquero crammed into the Packard, most of the families piled onto the truck's flatbed and, frolicking and singing, we all rocked down the rough road to church. Watching the children swept up by cheer and mirth, I couldn't help being reminded of the last Christmas we celebrated during a lull in the fighting during the Russian campaign.

Later, upon our return, everybody was invited to the dining hall of the mansion for a traditional Christmas dinner, which included such morsels as antojitos, chiles rellenos, tamales, carna asada, *guajolote* (turkey), and *jamon* (ham), along with fruit juice, beer and wine. For dessert, we were served delicious pastry. Although most of us may remember the gathering as a culinary treat, it also had a very festive ring to it. We exchanged small gifts, sang Christmas carols and listened to speeches by Don Leonardo, Imelda, as well as the gerente. At the end, Carolina spontaneously rose and burst into a speech as well, announcing she had recently married me, at the same time apologizing that the big wedding celebration would have to wait until March. She also called on everyone to count their blessings and pray for those people who were suffering from persecution, disease and hunger.

All in all, it was a most joyous and touching Christmas, one that would long linger in my memory. Seldom had I seen a gathering of people so swallowed up by light-hearted cheer, mirth and merriment. What I appreciated most: All social differences had — puff! — mysteriously vanished, making it appear as if we'd always been one big, happy family.

The New Year was swept in with a big snowstorm coating the hacienda with a bridal white fluff. Measuring thirty centimeters, the snow bent grasses, bushes and tree branches and made walking very cumbersome. Rousing, I wrapped myself in warm clothes, grabbed a snow shovel and began clearing the main walkways between the various buildings. I also checked the cattle in the holding pens. Thankfully, they didn't seem to suffer any jitters. They just stood there, stoically glaring at me. By next day, most of the snow had melted, leaving only a smattering in shady areas, and mud, *montones* (piles) of mud.

Carolina, meanwhile, kept hitting one hard patch after another. Despite girding herself in her eating habits to smaller meals several times a day, the nausea and vomiting showed no sign of abating. Nor was her skin, having always been immaculate, spared. Her forehead and cheeks, down to her neck and nipples, mysteriously turned blotchy, blemishing these areas with a brownish pigment, that looked like a frost-burned plant. Come worse, she also suffered from heartburn in the center of her chest, accompanied by belching and a yucky taste in her mouth.

Having been spoiled by good health, her physical maladies visibly weighed on her, preoccupying her for hours. They even forced her to give up riding her horse, one of her favorite pastimes, as well as reading and listening to the radio. All I could do was sympathize with her and give her all the support I could. I made sure she was served certain dishes and drinks that reduced her nausea. I caressed her and bedded down with her, which she continued to enjoy. Thank God she also had Imelda, her mother, who never tired of comforting her and dripping soothing words into her ears. She knew how it felt, having been through the same maladies decades ago.

Mid-February, during a violent rainstorm, Jorge came to visit us in a fancy Bugatti that belonged to one of his female admirers. He was as jovial as ever, witty and piquant. Apparently Don Leonardo had threatened to cut his allowance because of the financial difficulties. Yet Jorge wasn't willing to submit without a good fight, insisting that his dad had violated the contract they'd signed more than nine years ago. Forever at odds, both used the family's get-togethers during meals to throw brickbats at one another.

Lacking a bone of contention, Carolina and I spent a good number of animated, candle-lit hours with Jorge, sitting snuggly in Carolina's cubby, with Jorge and I guzzling countless bottles of wine and snacking on antojitos and other morsels. At one time — it was on Saturday, the last day before his departure — Jorge insisted on tackling Mexico's role in the war, Roosevelt and Camacho and the American meddling in Mexican affairs. Being on the side of Mexico, he claimed that the gringos were once again disgruntled with Camacho. They accused him of promising to cooperate only to drag his feet when it came to the question of delivering, especially on the international agreements he had signed with Washington. Jorge portrayed it as a war of words with the cannon shots coming mainly from the gringo stronghold. He was particularly incensed by the American diplomat who was reportedly caught off-guard saying the time was ripe to once again send a bunch of marines to the 'Halls of Montezuma' for an extended camping trip. "For us this is no laughing matter," he concluded. He tactfully paused, inserting tiny coughs during the gush of sound.

When Carolina insinuated that Mexico may indeed fall short of following the spirit of the agreements, he admitted more could be done but blamed most of these deficiencies on a slow, poorly paid and utterly corrupt bureaucracy.

I nodded, mentioning my own disappointment with respect to my applications for naturalization and a passport. "It's been three months and I haven't heard a word," I told him.

"That's a good example but awful nonetheless," he said. "I sympathize with you. You want me to check what's holding up the process? But you'll have to wait a few days until I get back and settled."

"We can never satisfy the Americans, regardless of how hard we try," Carolina sighed. "Actually, I'm more interested in hearing something about the cultural life in el D.F. Do you have any sizzling stories about Frida Kahlo, Diego Rivera, Siqueiros, Orozco and Rufino Tamayo? And how about the film directors, actors and actresses?"

"Yeah, how is Senor Alarcon doing?" I pumped. "Shouldn't we start filming soon?"

"Oh, he hasn't informed you?" Jorge perked, taking a big sip again.

The candle, having given its best for several hours, was edging toward its rigor mortis, leaving a churrigueresque mess on the table.

"No," I said. "Why, is there something?"

"Yes. I've heard from a reliable source the old zorro couldn't get the government subsidy for your film project. And he absolutely needs it to move forward."

"You must be kidding!" My mouth went dry. And so did Carolina's. Did I not even hear a muffled snarl, *"mierda?"* I recall grabbing my glass and gulping down more than a mouthful, one that almost made me choke.

"No, from what I've heard, the project is in deadlock, at least for now."

"How awful," I said, shaking my head and taking another swig. "Carolina and I put so much hard work into it, and hope, and now it's all for naught. And I'm not even talking about my plans for the future."

"Sorry! I just wanted to let you know. I guess I shouldn't have told you." He gave me a friendly pat on the back. "But if I were you, I'd hang in there. Knowing Alarcon, I wouldn't be surprised if he still has a few other irons in the fire, or rabbits in his hat."

"I'd call him tomorrow," Carolina suggested.

"I wouldn't," Jorge replied. "The whole debacle is extremely embarrassing to him. Besides, it wouldn't bring much. He couldn't tell you anyway which way the project's going."

Jorge's news was a big blow pulling away the ground from under my feet. All of a sudden my whole plan for the future and everything hinging on it was cast in doubt. I wondered what I was going to do with myself, how I would pay back the debt I owed. And what about supporting a family? What would I do if, God forbid, the bureaucrats in their whimsies rejected my applications for citizenship and a passport? I'd be totally stuck in limbo, without any legitimacy. And being illegitimate had always been a trauma of mine with very deep roots, reaching way back to my beginnings, being born out of wedlock and raised as an orphan. All that weighed on me like a ton of bricks. I already saw myself, pride in the gutter, standing near the Cafe Popular, with a tin in one hand and a help sign in the other, begging for mercy.

That same night I bought up my misgivings and fears in a pillow talk with Carolina. She, too, was worried about me — us. At the same time, she wasn't nearly as pessimistic.

"Listen, Fred, you're taking everything too seriously. Let's wait and see. Things are still very unsettled, I admit; but they're not as bad as they look. As Jorge said, Alarcon is a go-getter; he could still pull the cart out of the mud just yet. And those bureaucrats who process your applications may just be plain lazy. Too bad you can't talk to them. A little mordida would give them a spur. But, trust me, it will work out. I'll bet in a few months you'll be a Mexican citizen with a passport and all. And even if they don't come through, it won't be the end either. As Jorge likes to say: 'Sin esperanza pero tambien sin desesperacion' (without hope, but no reason to despair). We'll adapt, trust me. Besides, worrying won't help you anyway. 'Ojala,' God willing, my grandma used to say, when her plans were stymied by something or other."

"That sounds like the 'inshallah' the Muslims use when a sandstorm is burying their village."

"You may be right, ojala might well be derived from the Moors. They were long a dominant force in southern Spain. But what I'm trying to say is we Mexicans are always guided by something larger, more random, than our own tiny will. You can call it fate stepping in and overriding everything we humans do. I think it's healthy if you can shrug things off every once in a while."

"That sounds too nebulous for me. Forgive me, all that has a whiff of old wives' tales, of superstition. We already have too much of it. Superstitions are as common as dandruffs."

"Says who? Fred! An enlightened fellow who rubs his horseshoe whenever a dark cloud appears on the horizon. Do you believe it helps you?"

"Frankly, I don't. But I can't deny I feel a little better when I do, more confident, more buoyant."

"Sounds like that's your way of chickening out. Why not admit that it influences you in a positive way? It's our Mexican ojala sneaking in through the backdoor, if you want my humble opinion."

"By God, the Jesuits sure taught you something. I never really thought about it. Maybe we're all superstitious, some more, some less. Maybe that's the reason so many of us believe in some sort of a god. But there are still some major differences. If it's a temblor or sandstorm hitting us, I can be very stoic. They're natural disasters over which we humans have no say. But lazy, incompetent and corrupt bureaucrats are in an entirely different category. They have nothing in common with some nebulous, supernatural power. They're supposed to be public servants. Yet here in Mexico they mainly serve themselves. Their behavior could be changed. I'm puzzled why the Mexican people, who've stirred up so many revolutions, don't get upset and start demonstrating for an end of incompetence and corruption. Why they don't hit the streets and plazas."

"I agree, we should. But if we headed to the zocalo and demonstrated doesn't necessarily mean things would change. Some sixth sense tells me they wouldn't. These patterns are too deeply ingrained in our culture."

"I'm afraid you're right. As a whole, Mexicans tend to shrug off responsibility for their actions. And nobody seems to care. It's the reason why everything goes to seed or crumbles. That's what you see all too often in this country, where things simply break or fall apart, and nothing is being done about it. Nobody takes responsibility, nobody is accountable, because some nebulous power has done it. Human actions are shoved into manana, into an indefinite time in the future. The Mexican deadline is manana. It's the emblem of Mexico, together with the squatting *campesino* who's idling away his time under a huge sombrero."

"I admit, that's largely true. But don't forget, it's this infamous practice of corruption that saved your life. You said yourself that if they'd caught you in your often praised *los Estados Unidos,* they would have hanged you," Carolina lashed back, visibly stirred. "And take a look at your own country, Germany. You celebrate the 'Triumph of the Will', the human will. And to what end? War and destruction, racism, mass killings, bloodshed and suffering! Granted we had our bloodthirsty Aztecs, but we'd never start a world war."

"Because you're too weak, too incompetent, worse even than the Italians," I couldn't help but snipe.

"Just imagine, a Mexican Hitler told us to marshal our will to attack our pet peeve, the gringos up north, our people would burst out laughing.

They'd think, he's nuts. Granted we're imperfect, weak and disorganized, but we don't kill people randomly, we're not criminals."

Her last words went straight to the marrow of my bones, the more so since the 'Triumph of the Will' had also been at the core of my catechism, my recent rejection notwithstanding. And Carolina — there comes the sting! — was well aware of it.

A NEW NEMESIS

I don't believe in fate, yet life on the hacienda was too good to be true. Something had to give.

"Could you please pass me the queso?" I asked Carolina.

"Claro."

The foursome of us, Carolina, Don Leonardo, Imelda and I, were sitting leisurely at the end of our large dining table, enjoying a lush breakfast. While I, still numb from a bad dream, was busy cutting off a piece of queso, the doorbell chimed. I still heard Demesia opening the door and having an exchange with some men. Unfortunately I couldn't understand what they were saying. I only noticed that the tone of their voices was unusually harsh. Seconds later, Demesia, all wrought up, came rushing back to the table, drew up to me and whispered into my ear, "Senor Luthi, there are three *tira* (cops) at the door who claim they are from the *Policia Judicial Federal*. They want to talk to you."

"Policia Judicial Federal? Seguro?" I might add that the *'judiciales',* as they were called, had a most sinister reputation.

"Si senor!"

Shocked, I instantly dropped my utensils, jumped up and grabbed both of Demesia's arms. "Tell them I'm not here."

All eyes were riveted on me. Carolina was aghast, covering her face with her hands, while Don Leonardo puckered his lips mockingly and shook his head.

"Sorry, but I have to get out," I hissed, rushing to my room, grabbing a jacket and the horseshoe, and making a run for the back door. As I stepped out, I noticed a dubious figure lurking on the right side, about four meters from the door. Spotting me, he quickly pulled a pistol and shouted *"Alto o disparo!"* I ducked and lunged at him, aiming at the hand with the gun. Although I succeeded in knocking it out of his hand, I was unable to get a hold of it, embroiled as I was in a *mano a mano* fight. He struggled for hammerlocks and choke holds, whereas I preferred punching him with my fists. Luckily, I was soon on top of him. Since he continued to strike back, I grabbed him by the throat and dealt him a potent blow to his chin. He snapped back and groaned. Having knocked him out, I instantly took to my heels. Just in time. I could still see another cop slinking around the left corner of the mansion, shouting, *"Alto o disparo!"* I ignored him. Shots rang out but, anticipating them, I had already hit the ground. I heard bullets whizzing past me. When the last shot popped off, I was already crawling behind the juniper poles of the uppermost corral. Hearing the cop coming after me, I rose and hustled up the slope, past some junipers into a dense thicket near the creek. I knew I had to get away as quickly and as far as possible, assuming that these vigilantes would soon comb the area. It helped being acquainted with the terrain. So I kept forging ahead, frequently looking over my shoulder or stopping and listening, just in case. Thankfully I neither saw nor heard anybody.

I must have covered some five or six kilometers before I, out of breath, allowed myself to take the first break. It was chilly, yet dry and sunny. The grasses and shrubs were still covered with hoarfrost. Sitting beneath a large madrone, I took a deep breath and squeezed a wry chuckle out of my mouth. My head was brimming as I tried to get a grip on the turn of events and why the judiciales were on my heels. I couldn't help but blame it on my applications for citizenship and a passport. Assuming they may have tracked me down as a fugitive from justice in the United States, I wondered what I could do to avoid being caught in their dragnet. One thing was certain, to stay free I would have to be on the run, at least for the foreseeable future. Sadly, the hacienda, my present hiding place and home, could no longer serve as my haunt. I certainly couldn't live there any more. At best I could set foot on it only stealthily, if at all. What a blow! The mere thought of forsaking Carolina, my one and all, made me eat my heart out. I couldn't conceive of spending my life without her. Nor she without me, I was sure. Since we were a couple, I was worried the judiciales might try to interrogate her in my stead. How would it affect her, notably her pregnancy? I had noticed she'd become much more touchy lately, more vulnerable.

Once again, the painful realization that my foothold in Mexico was tenuous and that my identity would remain elusive, was thrust upon me with a brutal and humbling clarity. I was a foreigner and would continue to be a foreigner, as well as an orphan, regardless of the roots I struck and ties I forged. Once again I was condemned to be on the run. Wondering where I could hide, I came to the conclusion it would have to be a big city like el D.F. Only this huge cauldron could provide me with the ray of hope I needed. Like the proverbial needle in a haystack, I could mingle with the crowd of people. To get there, I could take a bus. Just to cover myself, I pulled out my wallet. I counted several thousand pesos. I was sure that Jorge would help me find a place. Maybe, just maybe, Carolina could eventually join me there, too. And once the war was over, things might relax, or so I hoped.

At least things stayed momentarily quiet, which soothed me a little, although my stomach was still rumbling. Once again I felt drawn to hike down to the hacienda again, but then resisted. I feared that the judiciales might well hang around all day. *Don't take any chances,* I told myself. My thoughts went back to Emma Burgdorf who, pursing her lips and raising her finger, would always stress that "Patience is the best remedy for every trouble."

I waited and waited until, finally, dusk began to creep over the land and silently settle through levels of lavender. Starving, I got going. Luckily, since most of the walk was downhill, I made good headway. Still, it took me more than an hour to reach the outskirts of the hacienda, just beyond the upper-most corral. I tried to stay away from the mansion and approach the complex from the south, the bunkhouse. By then it was getting dark already. I made short moves, sought cover, lay low and waited, as though I was at the head of an expeditionary force. It was eerily quiet. I didn't even hear a horse snort or a cow moan, much less a human voice.

As I reached the southern edge of the bunkhouse, I faintly heard somebody whistling a tune. It sounded like the popular song "La Paloma". It must have come from the other side, where the main entrance was located. Encouraged, I kept skulking toward the last corner. A shadow suggested that there was a light burning near the entrance. Peeking around the corner, I saw none other than Luis, the vaquero and guitarist, sweeping the *soportales* (porch) and whistling some other song.

"*Eh, Luis, ven aqui!* (come here)," I whispered, curling my finger.

Startled, he turned. "*Ah, eres tu, Fred!*" He leaned his broom against the wall and came shuffling toward me. "*Anda, que sorpresa!* (What a surprise!)*"

"*Dime, judiciales pasarse?*"

"*Si,* all gone!"

"*Seguro?*"

"*Si, seguro, muy seguro, senor.*"

Relieved, I stepped onto the porch. We shook hands. Luis couldn't wait to tell me that those nasty judiciales, three of them, had been busy all day to fine-comb the whole area, leaving no stone unturned and that everybody prayed they wouldn't find me. Well, they finally left in the late afternoon.

"*Con las manos vacias!* (empty-handed!)*" he emphasized, riveting my eyes and laughing.

After jabbering for a minute or so, I made my way past the manager's house all the way to the mansion, wary, always on the lookout. I rang the bell. Demesia carefully opened the door a crack. *"Senor Luthi, aqui tiene!"* (Mister Luthi, you are here!) she said, staring at me as if I'd come back from hell. *"Nos todos preocuparse por usted. Como estas?"* (We were worried about you. How are you?)

"Tengo frio y hambre, mucho hambre." (I'm cold and hungry, very hungry.)

I stepped in and rushed over to Carolina's room. I rapped on the door. I heard a weak *adelante!* I pushed the handle and entered. Carolina was in bed, but jumped up when she saw me. "Fred! Oh, my God!" She heaved a deep sigh. "You made it! Where have you been?"

I rushed over, hugged and kissed her. "On a hike. Where else?"

"Hike? I was so worried about you. When I heard the shots, I thought those bastards had killed you. One even claimed he hit you."

"They tried to, those jerks, but I was able to dodge them."

"I was out of my mind. But shortly later, while the cops were combing the area, Demesia told me Antonio had actually seen you getting away. I assumed they just wanted to scare me to death. You can't find a nastier bunch than those judiciales. They've really got a chip on their shoulder! They kept interrogating me for a whole hour, me, a pregnant woman. It was scandalous. They wanted to know everything about you, what you do for a living, who your friends are, if you have guns and where you keep hiding them, even what foods you're eating and if you're talking at night in your dreams. They claimed you were a murderer, that they had the evidence. They also threatened Dad and me for being complicit in the crimes you committed because we harbored a fugitive. That would cost us dearly. We'd have to face time in jail."

"I'm sure it's those sly Americans who are behind it. The Mexicans are only their lackeys. The whole incident has the whiff of Hoover's bloodhounds. Say, what did you tell them?"

"I kept telling them they were barking up the wrong tree; that you're the most loving and peaceful man I ever met. But they ridiculed me as being gullible. Their mantra: You were simply a liar who knows all the dodges. So they came back with the same questions again and again, hoping to grind me down. It was pure torture. Still, I held my ground, but at a price. 'Cause when they left I felt so sick I had to throw up. I was worried stiff about our baby. I couldn't have pulled myself out of it alone. Thank God Mom came to my aid. She constantly stood by my side."

"Those bastards!"

"Once they had left, I had a big clash with Dad, for lashing out at you. He had the gall to defend the judiciales for trying to arrest a thug. He also turned against me for having married you, pushing me to cut all ties with you at once, to divorce you and turn you in. Imagine, turn you in! If *I* wouldn't do it, *he* would."

"You mean...?"

"I don't think so. What he said angered me so much I actually challenged him to make good on his threats. And if he did, I'd leave the hacienda for good and he'd never see me again. And Jorge would feel the same way. That must've hit home 'cause he never mentioned it again."

"What a *gusano*! The good thing is there's nothing devious about him. You can always count on him being a full-blown asshole."

I hugged and kissed her again. "Are you feeling a little better?"

"Of course, who wouldn't feel better if somebody you like flatters you with a kiss, especially in times like these?"

"I know it's tough for you. The nagging question is what to do. I'm afraid from now on these judiciales are going to be on my heels. They know where I am, and I expect them to be back, probably soon. I'm condemned to carry this menace around like the thug his ball and chain. What I'm saying is, I can't live here any longer. I have to leave the hacienda. I have no choice."

"No! You can't leave me, especially in the state I'm in."

"I know, it's awful. But I know of no other option. The only place I can think of is a big city, el D.F. Only this vast and sprawling city offers the anonymity where I could immerse. Everywhere else, I'm afraid, I'd have to face arrest, jail, extradition and possible death. What I thought of is getting an apartment in Mexico City, perhaps in Coyoacan or San Angel. Jorge would probably help me. And once I'm settled, you could join me. Eventually I'd try to get a fake passport, so I could sneak out of the country, to Guatemala, Costa Rica, Chile or Argentina, just in case they'd track me down. But the odds of that happening would in all likelihood be low."

"Maybe. But that'd be very costly. How are you going to pay for all of that?"

"Well, that's a problem. But I'll find a way. I have to, I have no choice. Maybe Senor Alarcon will still come through with his movie. Who knows, he might even give me an advance."

"Maybe, but you can't count on it."

"I also thought of Jorge. He's always been a very generous fellow. Actually I wouldn't mind calling him. He'd understand my predicament. But first I'll have to get something to eat."

I headed for the kitchen where I found tortillas, cold cuts and beans. I gobbled them down greedily. Later we called Jorge. He couldn't have been more forthcoming and supporting, promising to help me find an apartment. The odds were pretty good. There were ads in the papers every day. In case it wouldn't work, I could always contact an *agente immobilario*. One of his girlfriends was acquainted with a sharp one. In the meantime I could stay at his place. When I asked if he had heard anything about the funding of the movie, he said things looked a little better and Senor Alarcon appeared to be slightly more optimistic. Yet a final deal hadn't been struck, not yet, anyway, although he hadn't had a chance to talk to the old fox lately.

"I think you're right, it probably would be best if you headed to el D.F. all by yourself," Carolina said after we had put down the receiver. "I could join you later, once you've found an apartment. It won't be easy, but with Mom's and Demesia's help I may be able to make it."

FAREWELL TO SHANGRI-LA

It was a harrowing, wretched night for both of us. We were wide awake, tossing and turning until the morning seeped through the south-eastern sky. While Carolina was intermittently plagued by cramps, I was in the grip of angst, with cold sweat running down my spine. Every little creak or grate made me shudder, dreading that the judiciales were already in the mansion and, gestapo-like, would shackle me and take me away. I was so wrought up, so tense, that my member, ordinarily chirpy, couldn't even rise to the occasion. It was the first for me. I was mortified. But Carolina calmed me down. "Don't worry," she said. "It happens to the best of us."

I was dead-tired when I rolled out of bed and shuffled to the bathroom. After a quick shower, I went about dying my hair and my eyebrows black. Using Carolina's makeup and dark shoe polish, as well as my old mustache, I tweaked my facial appearance further, to the point where I could hardly recognize myself. Once I had devoured a quick but hearty breakfast, I grabbed my hat, a suitcase and my rucksack and piled them into the Packard, and together we hit the road, heading to the bus depot in Chihuahua.

When we arrived there we ran into a tamarindo who hung around the ticket office. I was not going to take any chances. After all, this was Chihuahua, the town where I'd experienced the baptism of hell not too long ago. So I stayed back and, keeping an eye on the cop, let Carolina purchase the ticket. Within minutes, we had located the bus to Torreon that was besieged by a motley cluster of travelers. We joined them. Carolina and I still had almost half an hour to talk about our separation that weighed heavily on both of us. While she brought up the question of my safety, I voiced my worries about her health. I kept wondering if her stomach cramps might be more than a short-lived intestinal irregularity — a symptom of big trouble ahead, perhaps? I urged her to ask her doctor about it during her appointment an hour from now.

The final parting proved to be most heartbreaking for both of us, amid well-wishing, hugs, kisses and also tears.

Luckily, the bus ride went smoothly, without incident. Whenever I encountered any cops, I made sure to sneak around them in a big semicircle. They didn't even pay any attention to me, which was reassuring. In any

285

event, after spending a night in a cheap hotel in Torreon, I was able to continue my journey next day, stopping in Zacatecas and San Luis Potosi. From the first day on I frequently caught myself falling asleep in my seat. It wasn't until the third day that our bus finally rumbled into this snarled megalopolis. Dead tired and stiff, I was relieved this drudgery was finally coming to an end.

"I hardly recognized you at first," Jorge said, as he opened the door. "Quite wicked that mustache of yours! It fits you quite well."

We threw our arms around each other in a tight abrazo. "I'd be damned if those judiciales would ever make you out," he added as he grabbed my suitcase. "I'd place a bet on it they won't. You're too smart for them."

"Thanks, but pray that you won't lose any money."

"I don't think so. Anyway, welcome to the heart of Mexico. I concede, the air could be a little better, but it was far worse last week. We also had a light temblor about two weeks ago. You see, things are quite lively around here."

He was dressed like a playboy with black silk shirt, a yellow tie, a brown v-neck vest, tan golf slacks and punch-hole Blucher Oxfords.

"Can I offer you something to drink?" he asked, after I'd seated myself on his sofa.

"Just a glass of water. -You have to excuse me, Jorge, but I'm pretty tired. It's been a long journey."

He poured me some sparkling water and himself a glass of red-inked Malbec. Toasting me, he pumped me about Carolina. "How's she doing?"

"I wish I knew." I told him she was seeing her doctor in Chihuahua the day I left. "I hope she has recuperated and found out that her stomach cramps are not pointing to something more sinister. I think it was the emotional turmoil of the raid, as well as her dad's hostile stance toward me. The good thing is that Imelda and Demesia are always at her side and that she can consult with a good doctor."

"That's sort of what she said, when I called her last night. But she has a tendency... Well, let's call her later."

He also showed me a stack of ads from newspapers, offering apartment rentals. "Thank you so much. I really appreciate your help."

"Come on, Fred, you're like a brother. By the way, I've also had a talk with Vicente Ulibarri, a real estate agent, today, and there are quite a few rentals on the market, including the southern suburbs of Coyoacan, Churubusco and San Angel. If you want me to, I can make an appointment."

"Let's first try the ads. It's cheaper. I'm strapped for money you know."

"I can help you a little. Dad's been more generous, now that he paid the mordida and signed the contract with the flunkies in the government. I also made a little money in financial consulting."

"Thanks, that's very kind of you."

"By the way, on Friday I've made an appointment with Senor Alarcon. As I told you over the phone, he's still in the process of negotiating with the government about the funding of his project."

"Good! I was going to call him. But that's no longer necessary. I don't know how to thank you for all these favors."

"Who knows, one day I may need your help. In any event, I want you to feel right at home here. The provisions in the refrigerator are for you. Meanwhile, I have an errand to make. I'll be back in about three hours."

I stripped, showered, shaved, unpacked my suitcase and treated myself to a light but savory supper. As usual, Jorge's refrigerator was filled to the brim with all kinds of goodies. Filled and scrubbed, I took to the couch, where I stuck my nose into the 'Reforma'. Outside of the national news, it reported that Eisenhower had been appointed to be the Supreme Commander of the western allied forces and that the Red Army was about to crack the German stranglehold on Leningrad. Another Russian unit was advancing into eastern Poland. Especially the latter once again raised hopes that the war might not last much longer.

I also searched some ads regarding apartments for rent. One was in the North Roma district, the other in San Angel. I cut both of them out.

When Jorge came back, he called Carolina. We chatted for more than half an hour. She said she was pleased my journey had proceeded without incident and I was safe and in good hands, adding that the judiciales had not come back, as yet. When I broached the question of her state of health, she was a bit hesitant, but then claimed she was feeling a little better. According to her doctor the cramps were caused by an intestinal inflammation that could be cured with the help of medications. She had taken the pills and they seemed to be effective. She stressed that her mother and Demesia helped her a great deal to get past the worst.

"Frankly I feel worried," Jorge commented later. "Though she claimed she's feeling better, I didn't hear that in the tone of her voice. It contained virtually nothing of her usual *joie de vivre*. On the contrary. I know my sister. She can never admit she's ill."

"Now that you mention it, I think you may be right. The tone of her voice seemed to contradict her words. I don't think she's well at all. Like you, I'm worried, so worried in fact that I would hop on the bus and go back tomorrow, if I didn't have to dread the judiciales. Hell, I wouldn't even have left her. The thin silver lining is that she's cared for by Imelda and Demesia."

"Let's hope for the best. I'll call her tomorrow again. By the way, I'll leave you to yourself. I'll be back tomorrow at about ten. I can accompany you on your search for an apartment, if you like. Four eyes always pick up more than two."

"Yes, by all means."

Carolina's condition weighed on me, the more so since I felt so utterly helpless, hobbled.

SETTLING IN THE CAULDRON

I was torn out of my sleep by the howls of sirens that weaved its spaghetti-like sounds through the neighborhood. It was six o'clock and still dark. Two fire engines raced past. There must be a house aflame nearby, I assumed. Minutes later I smelled a stench. I bailed out of bed, feeling like a zombie, staggered into the bathroom, hunkered down on the toilet seat and squeezed my bladder. Given my erection, it took some effort, not to mention time.

It had been a horrible night again. I was visited by frightful dreams revolving around a pregnant woman who sat next to me on the last bus from Quereraro to el D.F. She suffered from a massive hemorrhage. We all tried to help but didn't know how. Before the bus came to a halt she, shrieking *Socorro! Socorro!* died in agony. Her baby struggled to survive.

Trying to blot out my dream, I brewed a robust coffee and prepared a lavish breakfast with huevos, frijoles, queso menonita, chiles and tortillas. That breathed new life into me. A new day was about to break. Toward the south-east, a thin-lipped crack of light had just climbed over the giant shadow Popocatepetl had cast. I walked down to the mailbox and retrieved the *Reforma*. With the fragrance of freshly brewed coffee still saturating the apartment, I grabbed myself a city map and, having made myself comfortable on the sofa, perused the ads Jorge had given me. As I studied the map, I noticed my deep bias in favor of the southerly suburbs, Coyoacan, San Angel and Churubusco. What particularly caught my attention were two offers on quiet streets in Coyoacan. I quickly located them on the map, rentals I'd want to take a look at first. One was only a stone's throw away from Jorge's apartment, not far from Frida Kahlo's domicile. Next came the promising offer in San Angel, another attractive suburb, as well as an apartamento in Churubusco, a district to the east.

Pleased with my finds, I turned to the newspaper. Farther into it I stumbled on a news clip about the liberation of Novgorod by the Russian army, coupled with a spearhead deep into eastern Poland. It also mentioned that there was fierce fighting on the beaches of Anzio and Nettuno, south of Rome, where the American Fifth Army prepared a landing in the hope of bypassing the defenses of the Gustav Line. The German Army, using Panzer units and railway guns, obliterated the beachheads. Badly exposed, countless American GIs lost their lives.

Shortly before ten Jorge arrived and, with ads in hand, we headed out to take a look at the various apartments. We examined six of them but unfortunately none suited my taste. It was a chore, and as the afternoon waned we finally called it quits.

Back at the apartment, we called Carolina. Mercifully, the medicine had been working and she was doing much better, or so she claimed. When Jorge and I raised some doubts, she got flustered, insisting that our attitude did little to boost her recuperation. Quite the contrary.

"If you're facing an ailment, you have to think positively," she insisted, also quoting her doctor. "Only an upbeat attitude helps the patient. If everything goes well, I'll see him again on Monday. By then I'll know more."

As to our search for an apartment, she urged me to pick a beautiful, roomy one with lots of light and a view. It should also be in a safe, leafy neighborhood, somewhere in Coyoacan or the surrounding area.

"I'll keep that in mind, but I also have to watch the cost," I reminded her.

"Naturally. And please call me. I always like to hear your voice. You don't know how much I miss your laughter and good cheer. Life without you is kind of drab and boring."

Friday morning Jorge and I went to see Senor Alarcon at the film studio. My mood was tinged with a feeling of guarded optimism, swayed in large part by Jorge.

The reception was as before, friendly and relaxed. The old fox was his usual self, crafty, witty and more loquacious than anybody I'd met before. "You came to find out if our project will get funded," he sputtered, wrinkling his forehead. "Unfortunately, I can't tell you because I don't know it myself. The good news is we are still negotiating. The government officials haven't given up on me, nor I on them. So there is a crack of hope. I pray it will widen to let the sun peek through. That's all I can tell you."

"Too bad," I said. "By the way, I would like to tell you that I'm going to move to el D.F. But I haven't found an apartment yet. I'm presently staying with Jorge. That's where you can reach me. I'd really appreciate if you let me know as soon as a decision is made."

"You can count on it. Maybe I shouldn't tell you but my gut feeling tells me it will go through. We just have to be patient, very patient. I know it's hard on you, being a foreigner, especially a Swiss. For us Mexicans it is much easier. We get it at birth. Patience is a gratuity that comes with our mother's milk. I even dare say that the word itself and the whole gaggle of synonyms that swirl around it was invented in Mexico."

Next morning, Jorge and I once again ventured out on our search. We took a gander at various offers located in North Roma, near the green lung of Chapultepec Park, as well as Churubusco. But every one of them had certain shortfalls or flaws. It wasn't until we stepped into a tenement on Madero, a tree-lined street near the Plaza San Jacinto in San Angel that our spirits received a pleasant lift. It perched on the second floor of a two-story house that was just a few years old. It was bright, spacious and in excellent condition. We were thrilled, and we assumed that Carolina would be, too. We also took a fancy to the owner, Senor Fidel Aznar, a small, fidgety man with a shiny bald head, beady eyes and a drooping mustache faintly reminiscent of Pancho Villa's.

Everything seemed to click, the only drawback was the price: the rent was more than a hundred pesos higher than equivalent apartments we had looked at. I politely mentioned it to Senor Aznar at the very moment when a white-haired, pear-shaped woman came to join us. He introduced her as Julia, his wife and soul mate. She must have been busy in the kitchen because she trailed a whiff of enchiladas after her. Shorter than him, she was a jovial, cheerful mama with a dark, shriveled face and lively blinkers that glistened like two highly polished gems of amber.

At first, Senor Aznar wouldn't budge. He repeatedly came back to the argument that his rental was simply better, hence the higher price was fully justified. Although I didn't dispute that, I humbly mentioned that I just didn't have the money to pay for it. I kept pointing out to him, but also to his wife — especially to his wife! — that I'd just married and that Carolina, my wife, who'd soon join me, was highly pregnant, adding that life in this big city was prohibitively expensive for a newly married couple. I pleaded with them that such factors should also be taken into account. I said all that, albeit somewhat clumsily, given that my Spanish was still far from up to snuff. Mercifully Jorge helped me, always pitching in words, when my tongue failed me.

Anyway, Julia couldn't but stop nodding; she even inquired when the baby was due. She gave her husband a questioning look, as if to say, "Can't you be a little more generous toward this poor man and his family?" From all I could tell, he was annoyed by her gestures. But while he pursed his lips and shook his head, she kept on smiling and nodding. It was a classic marital seesaw.

"Bueno!" he said after a while. *"Esta quatrocientos pesos. No lo haria por menos."* (It's 400 pesos.)

"Trato hecho! (It's a deal.)"

We shook hands. Julia uttered a stream of subdued giggles and clucking noises.

Once back at Jorge's place, I couldn't wait to call Carolina. She sounded much better, insisting the stomach cramps were gone. Whether it was indeed the case, or simply her will to think positively, was hard to tell. I wasn't going to test her. Instead, I congratulated her and told her about the apartment. "You'll like it. It's located on a tree-lined street in San Angel. It's so clean, it feels and smells like new. The owners, an old couple that lives downstairs, are very pleasant. Of course it's completely empty. I still have to furnish it, although it shouldn't take long. I expect it to be ready in a week or so. When are you coming?"

"I'd come tomorrow but I don't know how to get there. Taking the bus would probably be too strenuous, considering the condition I'm in. I don't want to take any risks, especially after those cramps. The doctor has warned me not to overdo it."

"I agree. You shouldn't. There must be another way. I tell you what, Jorge and I will talk it over. We'll call you back. I truly miss you. Give my regards to Imelda and Demesia."

The next few days I was in over my head furnishing the place. The Aznars, generous as they were, gave me free rein to sort through their storage shack in the backyard, where I came across an old bed, a sideboard, a table and two chairs. Both the table and the chairs were a bit rickety, but I sat down and, with the help of Fidel's tools, repaired them.

In another burst of generosity, Jorge ushered me into a big department store downtown, where he bought me a new mattress, sheets, blankets, comforters, towels and bedspreads. Later he lured me into a huge thrift store run by the Salvation Army. There we were able to scrounge up a used writing desk, dishes, silverware and kitchen utensils for a bargain-basement price. Laura, one of Jorge's women friends, chipped in an old leather couch, a coffee table, two night stands, three Diego Rivera and Siqueiros posters and several Indian rugs, two of which I suspended from the walls of the living room. Within four days, I could boast of a fully furnished apartment. True, the various pieces could have been prettier and matched better — no, simply matched! — but beggars can't be choosers. Besides, a jumble of styles can also unfold some charms.

Virtually everything I needed was there, except a good radio, perhaps, and come Thursday, the seventh of February, I staged my first housewarming party. Aside from Jorge, I invited the Aznars, Fidel and Julia, as well as Laura Lopez, one of Jorge's generous girlfriends. The latter turned out to be a most intriguing, eccentric woman, who refused to fit the regular bourgeois mold. To begin with, her face had a peculiar triangular shape, with a broad forehead, framed by blond shingled hair, tapering off toward her chin. Her eyes were of an iridescent, emerald green. Clad in beige culottes, a beret, and a rust-colored blouse with a sweetheart neckline, she expressed a free, unbound spirit. Her hourglass figure, her broad shoulders and her taut and very pointed bosom, suggested that she might well cling to some pretensions beyond herself.

I had catered carne asada, pico de gallo, guacamole and tortillas from Jorge's hangout. Savory as they were, these dishes, helped by various beverages such as Mexican beer, Chilean Sauvignon Blanc, Mexican Tomas and a choice tequila were bound to lift the spirits. They all enjoyed themselves. And it got quite lively, especially as the evening progressed. Some guests dipped their beaks and the topics switched to politics and religion. Unfortunately, Laura, who happened to be on the outer left fringe, soon got into a fierce spat with the Aznars who, being devout Christians, defended conservative values and lifestyles. Whenever she mentioned Marx, Engels, or Stalin — yes Stalin! — they steadfastly invoked the Virgen de Guadalupe, Jesus and the Almighty. All that was an odium to Laura. Soused, she became shriller and shriller, dropping one clanger after another. She finger-stabbed and scolded them as *tarados, tontos, idiotas,* morons, fools, idiots. It was awful, unbecoming. Highly embarrassed, Jorge repeatedly apologized to the Aznars and beseeched his girlfriend to tame herself. In vain. On the contrary, she began to tongue-lash him as well, even giving him the finger. At that point Jorge lost his cool. He yanked her from the sofa, dragged her down to his car and sped her home.

The whole scene was also embarrassing to me. Besides apologizing to the Aznars, I pleaded with them not to hold her behavior against me. "Laura gave me several pieces of furniture," I told them. "That's why I invited her. Other than that she is a complete stranger to me."

Thankfully they accepted my apology. *"Mas vale valo conocido que bueno conocer,"* (It's better the devil you know than the one you don't.) Fidel said prophetically. "I hope I don't have to lock eyes with her any more. I'm sure one day our good Lord in all his graciousness will forgive the poor soul."

A WELCOME VISITOR

Now settled, I felt very pleased about the choice I'd made. It was the first time in my life I had so much space of my own. Attached to it was a feeling of independence, indeed, freedom, which I savored beyond anything. I could come and go whenever I pleased. As an additional benefit, I was able to draw closer to the Aznars, even befriend them. Both turned out to be shakier than I'd assumed. I took that as a call, and I couldn't wait to make myself useful to them, stay at their side when they needed help. And being generous people, they more than returned my favors. Almost every other day Julia, a whizz in the kitchen, brought me leftovers, at times complete dishes, zesty meals which were as becoming as they were tasty. Occasionally I'd so much food that I had Jorge over. He was more than flattered, always relishing Julia's culinary morsels.

Since I didn't have a telephone, they let me use theirs. To get my own, I had to wait until the end of February. At last I was able to chat with Carolina and Jorge. Actually, the first ring came from Jorge who invited me to dinner at El Fuego, his hangout. I should drop by his place. He had something he was eager to show me.

Well, I hopped on the bus and half an hour later I rang the bell. He bid me in and, as usual, suggested that I take a seat on his sofa. "What would you like to drink?" He smiled slyly, as if he had something up his sleeve.

"How about a glass of full-bodied Argentinian Malbec that bursts at its seams?"

"Don't you want something sparkling, something with a fizz?"

"Hm, what's the occasion?"

"I can't tell you."

"Did Senor Alarcon call you? Stop playing the secret-monger. Stop tormenting me!"

"Be patient. You're too slow to adapt to our Mexican ways, my friend. Don't you remember any more what the old fox told you?"

He fetched a bottle of Chilean champagne, carefully wiggled the cork out of the neck and filled three glasses, one of which he handed to me.

"Why don't you take a big swig and then close your eyes, until I tell you to open them," he said with a big smile.

Well, I did just as told. For twenty seconds or so I saw nothing, but I did hear some rustling I couldn't identify, followed by a ripple of snickering. "Now you may open your eyes," he said.

I did. I was thunderstruck. In front of me stood — *were my eyes bluffing me?* — none other than Carolina, smiling as though she'd stepped into seventh heaven.

"I'll be a monkey's uncle! Carolina!" I shouted, lunging forward, throwing my arms around her and giving her a long kiss, until we were both out of breath. "You are here. What a surprise!"

"It's been far too long," she said.

"You're telling me? But, say, how *are* you? And how's our *bebe?"* I stroked her belly.

"We're both doing quite well. Thank you. The baby's growing, as you can see." She rubbed her bulging abdomen.

"No more cramps?"

"None, thank God."

"It scared me."

"This joyful tangle begs for the blessing of Bacchus," Jorge butted in, handing Carolina a glass and holding up his own. "Let's raise our glasses."

"Viva!" I joined in. "Here is to life, love and happiness! Let's also add freedom." Flutes were clinking and elbows bending in a bubble of cheerfulness.

"Say, how did you get here?" I prodded Carolina, once we had settled down on the sofa. "You didn't drive, did you?"

"No, I rode a bicycle, you know those lean Italian wire ponies. No, seriously, I came with Dad. He had some urgent business to take care of. You know, with high government officials, about the supply and delivery of beef. Stuff like that."

"Oh, I hope he won't get the idea of squealing on me, when he's up there mixing with the big shots. From what you told me…"

"I don't think he'd do that. I know he wouldn't. I'd vouch for him. Besides, the way you look now, with your dyed hair and mustache, I doubt that the judiciales would recognize you."

"I hope you're right, 'cause I can't take any chances. By the way, why isn't he here, your dad, I mean?"

"He always likes to stay at the Monte Carlo downtown."

"You're not going to ride back with him, I hope?"

"Not if I can help it. No, I'm going to stay here. With you, provided you're willing to take in a bloated *moza* (wench) like me."

"Well, she might still come in handy if she can swing a broom and a dust rag. And make use of pots and pans."

"*Oh, una criada* (a serving wench)?"

"Why not? If I can afford it. No kidding, knowing you, I'd guess you might like the place, as well as its location. I selected it with you in mind. And wait until you meet my landlord Fidel and his wife Julia. They are the sweetest people I've come across in a long time, a rare breed of Christians in the true sense of the word."

"Like black swans," Jorge quipped. "That reminds me of Laura who feels so guilty about the way she behaved at the housewarming party that she didn't have the nerve to call you or the Aznars to apologize. But she wants to make up by inviting you all to a cocktail party at her place. Are you doing anything this Saturday evening?"

"No," I said.

"We would be delighted to come," Carolina nodded.

"OK, I'll pick you up at seven. You can also invite the Aznars, although I doubt they'd want to risk another encounter with Laura."

We still spent more than three hours at El Fuego. The dishes were cheap and yet very tasty. That made up for the air we bowed to breathe. It was so thick with cigarette smoke, stale breath, cheap perfume and earthy sweat, it could have been sliced with a dull machete.

"How charming," Carolina burst out when she stepped into the apartment. "How cozy and comfortable. You must have pilfered some ideas from interior decorators."

"Wait until you see it in bright daylight! Anyway, I'm glad you like it. I did what I could in such a short time. Let me stress, everything you see is unfinished, a work in progress. You can add and change whatever you like."

"Really?"

"Provided I agree," I added with a crack of smile. "But knowing you, I will."

"That's reassuring."

As soon as Carolina had unpacked her suitcase, we treated ourselves to hot showers, barely making it before the water turned cold. Once in bed, I felt like a sailor who had been two months at sea without a bromide. Thankfully Carolina relished my passion; I dare say, she couldn't get enough of it.

We woke early, at the crack of dawn. A rooster somewhere in the neighborhood relentlessly cock-a-doodle-dooed. Other than that it was quiet. We crammed into our small bathroom, then dressed and got busy preparing a breakfast, a rustic huevos motulenos, tortillas smothered with fried eggs, ham and a sauce made with tomatoes, peas and a smattering of cheese.

Now the day could begin. I first wanted Carolina to meet the Aznars. So we went downstairs and knocked on the door. Julia answered. *"Buenos dias, Julia,"* I singsonged, hugging her.

She had barely replied to my greeting when Fidel inched up at her back and blinked over her shoulders. Both were smiling as if the Virgen de Guadalupe personally were paying them a visit.

"Permitame que te presento Carolina, mi esposa." I said.

"Encantado de conocerlo, mucho gusto," they both replied, as if completely attuned to one another.

"Entra, por favor," Fidel mumbled, offering us a seat on their big sofa.

A warm, cozy fragrance, a blend of coffee and pastries surged up our nostrils. *"Quieres una taza de cafe o te?"* Julia followed. And some dulces to nibble on. She also had a few delicious *bunuelos,* crispy pancakes, left.

We politely declined, pointing out that we'd just eaten a big breakfast. But we would gladly take a raincheck.

Riveting her eyes on Carolina's belly, Julia was curious to know how the pregnancy was going, in which month she was and if she could be of any help. We are one family here, she said. Their door would always be open and Carolina could come any time, even at night if need be.

Carolina had never experienced such a friendly reception from strangers before, and she thanked both Julia and Fidel for their warmhearted congeniality. *"Mil gracias! Mil gracias!"* she gushed, as we rose. *"Que Dios te bendiga.* (God bless you.)*"*

Stepping out into the street, I suggested that we take a stroll around our charming, cobble-stoned neighborhood, which, not unlike Coyoacan, prided itself on being the home of many artists, writers and diplomats. I tried to show Carolina the beautiful Plaza San Jacinto, the very center of San Angel, with its many shops and outdoor stalls selling Indian handicrafts. Passing swarms of vendors and an accordion player, we were soon drawn to the medieval Iglesia de San Jacinto with its stately dome and rich interior, its onyx font and carved wooden screen. We also visited the Casa del Risco, a well-preserved colonial mansion, which was wrapped around two eye-catching courtyards, one decorated with a flamboyant fountain.

Although the sun seemed to give its best, it was powerless against the bad air that had settled over this huge valley. Mindful of Carolina's condition, we soon ended up at the famous flower market with its wealth of flowers, some of which I had never seen before, as well as its profuse arrangements. Stopping at one of the stalls, I bought Carolina a fiery red rose.

PARTY WITH FRIDA

Laura's dinner party on Saturday night turned out to be rather entertaining, to say the least. She had invited more than thirty guests, mostly artists and actors, to her haunt, a very modern, spacious and bright Bauhaus spread on the eastern edge of Churubusco. It was sparsely furnished in a minimalist fashion with tubular steel furniture, glass tables, cabinets and cupboards and decorated like an art gallery, with abstract paintings, sculptures and ceramic pieces of many different shapes and sizes. Laura received us with an unctuous politeness, thanking us again and again for coming and apologizing for her former misconduct. She also introduced us to the other guests, praising me lavishly as an incipient actor of whom they will hear more the next few years.

We had barely mingled and chit-chatted with another couple when the bell rang again and in came a big and fleshy hunk of a man. He was pushing a wheelchair. All of a sudden all eyes were on him and, even more so, on the person in the wheelchair.

"That's Diego and Frida," Jorge whispered to us. "They're together again, wouldn't you know it? It won't be for long. It's a love-hate thing; they simply can't let go of each other."

Well, Frida lost no time taking center stage, staying in her wheelchair no less. Clad in her traditional indigenous Tehuana dress with a long fluffy cotton skirt and a colorfully embroidered blouse, she looked crassly out of place in Laura's modern surroundings, a bit like an Aztec princess boarding a sleek jetliner. Somehow she looked drained, as though in agony, with her prominent, seagull eyebrows that weighed heavily on her dark-rimmed eyes, winging away from her deep naso-labial folds and her incipient mustache. Yet, all that was only the surface. Once surrounded by an iridescent halo of friends, admirers and well-wishers, she'd suddenly burst into blossom, laughing and gesticulating away whatever was bothering her.

"What are you waiting for?" she shouted to a waiter. "I'm thirsty and hungry. Why don't you get me a bottle of tequila and the antojitos? What kind of service is this here?"

As soon as the waiter had served the order, Frida began munching on the antojitos and guzzling tequila, out of the bottle, as if it were beer. It didn't take long before she was lit to the gills, bantering and telling one dirty joke after another. Lighting up a cigarillo, she minced no words, blaring out that most men were lousy lovers, smug, self-centered quick-squirters, who had not the slightest idea what women need. They'd never heard of feelings, intimacy and affection. She even named names, including Trotsky, Diego and other men she'd allegedly slept with, which is why she'd turned to women.

"I had to," she claimed. "Only women know how to make love."

"Isn't she a riot?" Jorge commented. "I wonder where all that vitality is coming from. I've never met a more tenacious character than Frida."

Meanwhile we also met and chit-chatted with the other guests, including Diego Rivera, who at first looked as though he was fighting down a belch or hold breaking wind. Later he kept on talking about several big projects in New York, San Francisco and other cities in the United States. For him these cities in their present state were all capitalistic monstrosities Field Marshal Joseph Stalin would eventually erase and then rebuild as proud, shining citadels of socialism.

Once the crowd around Frida had thinned, Jorge introduced us, me and Carolina, to her. Noticing an accent, she wanted to know where I'm from. "From Switzerland," I told her.

"Aus der Schweiz?" she asked. "Then we can speak German. My father was German. And proud, too. He even sent me to German school here in Mexico to learn good German. But the teachers were far too rigid, like military officers, and I soon left.

"You must feel relieved that the Germans are being clobbered by the Russian Army," she commented, "that Hitler will no longer pose a threat to invade your country. It's all because of the great leader Joseph Stalin."

While Frida kept on praising Comrade Stalin as an outstanding military genius, a revolutionary leader and a true visionary, a quake suddenly shook the ground. Vases tumbled off ledges, glasses and cups toppled and crashed. It was as if hell had broken loose.

"Es un temblor!" somebody shouted. Everybody, us included, hustled toward the door, jamming it. Some stumbled and fell.

Minutes later, everything had settled down again. Frida still sat in her wheelchair, shaking her head.

A BIG FAMILY

"Somos como de la familia aqui," Julia pressed home, sounding as though she was reciting a profession of faith. It didn't only *sound* as though. It actually *was*! Julia, but also Fidel, made sure their mouths found a place in their hearts. We *were* a family. Never had I felt more at home than with the Aznars here in San Angel, where we enjoyed a frugal yet comfortable domesticity. Although the apartment itself may have been a bit cramped, we couldn't have had it better. Almost every day Julia shared her delicious dishes with us. And when we needed something, we simply knocked on their door. From the third week on, we'd even enter when they were gone.

It goes without saying that we also returned their favors whenever we could. I helped them repair things around the house, inside and outside, carry heavy objects and tend their garden. We also did errands for them, buying groceries, medications and other essentials.

I had no reason to complain. I had a roof over my head, a loving wife and an extended family. But life in this big city was, well, rather expensive. It helped that Carolina could count on some money from her dad, but it wasn't much. (I suspected that he was purposely keeping her on a short leash because he loathed to give me any slack.) Yet, even though we were very tightfisted and avoided any entertainment, cafes or expensive restaurants, we soon noticed that we didn't have the means to cover our expenses. Granted, I could have asked Jorge to help us out. He had done so before and he'd surely have lend a helping hand, had we asked. But we didn't want to approach him on our knees like beggars. It was as simple as that: We were in dire need of some income. I needed a job.

One day, on the way back from the market, I walked past a house where workmen were installing a new and fancy front door. Hearing them chanting a popular song, I stopped, greeted them and, praising their work, fell into a chit-chat with them. Upon my asking, they told me they were employed at a local *carpinteria*. They also claimed they had plenty of work, so much so that they could hardly keep up with the demand. That pricked up my ears and, being curious, I pumped them for the name and address of the owner.

An hour later, I paid the carpinteria a visit. It was housed in a well-kept adobe building, not more than twenty minutes away from our apartment.

Up on the roof there was a huge sign that read: CARPINTERIA, Propietario Alfredo Rodriguez. Below it, in smaller letters, was the claim: *'Si es de madera, ven a vernos!'* (If it's made of wood, come see us!). Entering, I asked the lady at the counter if I could speak to Senor Rodriguez. Within minutes he stood in front of me, a stocky, square-jawed man of about fifty, with a broad, low-profiled nose and thick black eyebrows, reminding me of two caterpillars locked in a sweet love encounter. I introduced myself, mentioning I'd once worked as a *carpintero,* a joiner, in Switzerland, and asked him if he had a job for me. A man of few words, he propped his chin up with his gnarly hand for a few seconds and then waved me back into his workshop. Having led me to a work bench, he handed me a few raw pine boards, showed me where I could find an extensive array of woodworking tools, hand saws, mallets, try squares, wood chisels, files, gouges, hand screws, planes, sandpaper and a glue pot, and then told me in so many words to fashion a small cabinet door, identical to the face of a sample hanging on the wall.

Actually, that suited me quite well. I may have mentioned before that I had been an apprentice joiner way back at the orphanage. I also built some furniture at the camp, and I knew how to handle most of these tools. So I rolled up my sleeves and got going. Taking a good look at the sample, I carefully measured the various parts, cut the pieces with a saw and, applying the glue where necessary, assembled them. I was pleased how effortlessly my buried skills rebounded, and within half an hour the door was done. Though nothing fancy, it was a clean, solid piece of craftsmanship. It even exuded a light shine, thanks to the linseed oil I found in one of the cabinets.

I called Senor Rodriguez. He inspected the door, nodded his approval and grumbled, *"Yo te pago 550 pesos por mes. Te puedes empezar por la manana a las ocho."* (I'll pay you 550 pesos per month. You can start tomorrow morning at eight.)

"Trato hecho!" (It's a deal!)

So, as unlikely as it may seem, I'd slipped into the role of a carpintero. It was a good job, and from Monday to Saturday I cheerfully went to work every day, especially since my coworkers were such an easygoing, happy-go-lucky bunch. Even more so than my friend Pancho in Colorado, they'd whistle, trill, warble, sing, tell jokes, laugh and act crackbrained as if they were enjoying themselves at a fiesta. Nor did it seem to hinder their performance. Quite the contrary, I'd wager their batty attitude actually increased it.

Our job revolved around fabricating and installing doors, cabinets, as well as making furniture, beds, tables, chairs, sideboards, wardrobes, you name it. Although the pay could have been better, it helped us immensely to make ends meet. There was another aspect that deserves mention: the work filled my day. This was of great importance to a restless idler like me.

A PASSPORT AT LAST

Fidel's truck growled and squeaked, while the pendant of a blue Virgen de Guadalupe, suspended from the mirror, swayed and shuddered with every pothole, and in Mexico that meant nearly always. It was Saturday morning. The air had an unpleasant bite, as though it drifted out of some sort of a smelter nearby. Toward the southeast, Popocatepetl spewed a huge cloud of ash and vapor into the sky, towering like a frazzled whirligig. We, Fidel, Carolina and I, were heading to the flea market. With the pesos of my paycheck in my pocket, I hoped to find a radio and some tools. Carolina would be looking for some lamps and kitchen utensils. And Fidel came mainly to watch people carrying on in the clamor and ferment of a big marketplace.

After parking the truck, we sauntered toward the stalls, full of expectations. And what a cornucopia of sensuous impressions it offered. I felt as if I were a kid again. Right at the beginning, a little aside, almost blocking the first aisle, a crippled juggler tried to keep a number of balls, hoops and ninepins in the air, but rarely succeeded. Entering the aisle, we let our eyes feast on people haggling over the price of an alluring Mayan rug or a shapely copper kettle. There was a profusion of goods, among them many that struck our fancy. Too many! Oddly enough, quite a few glistened and smelled as though they were brand new. To which Fidel proffered an answer: They were most likely pilfered, stolen. That dampened our mood a little. But after a while we managed to shake it off as the poor people's version of a grass-roots, soak-the-rich socialism. Little wonder then that we came across so many gloating indigenas.

Already halfway down the first aisle, Carolina stumbled on a handsome tiffany lamp that she adored but — ouch! — the price was steep, outside our reach. She dealt me a begging look. So I gathered my wits and began haggling, using methods I'd learned from one of Mussolini's soldiers in Tunisia, and in the end got that jewel for a little more than half the price. Down another isle, I chanced upon a high-quality American radio, a Zenith that could receive long and shortwave programs. I had seen and heard an identical one in the office of a Capt. Shepherd at the camp in Murphy. Gripped, I chaffered the vendor — a young Mayan? — down to less than half. But only to invite some eye-opening second thoughts from Fidel: "What if it doesn't work?" He had a point. I walked away, smarting.

Twenty meters down I shuffled to another halt again, at a stall that tastefully displayed several typewriters, all kinds of stationery, sheaves of writing paper, various inks, envelopes and a fair number of fountain pens that begged to embellish a desk. One of them, lying next to a wooden box close to the edge, had the looks of a Pelikan, a pricy German brand. I immediately recognized it being the same or a similar model Emma Burgdorf used when she signed an important document. My! Was I captivated.

Having watched me, the vendor heaved his enormous belly forward, grabbed the pen and handed it to me. "Two hundred peos," he said, with a smile full of crooked teeth. "It's a good buy."

I tried it out, scribbling something on a piece of paper. It felt so snug in my hand and wrote heavenly. Its stub-like tip easily lent itself to broadening the stem, bend or loop of a letter, indeed, even to drawing fanciful Arabic letters. Delighted, I haggled. But the vendor refused to come down. He just kept smiling, as though he had me by the balls.

"Es demasiado caro," I said. As I tried to give the pen back to him, he bent forward and accidentally pushed a small wooden box over the edge. Having dropped onto the hardpan, little booklets tumbled out, spilling over the dusty ground. From my angle I wasn't able to see them. But Carolina did.

"Whoa! Fred, look, they're passports," she whispered, nudging me.

"Yes, real passports. I bet he's hawking them."

Are you sure?"

"Yes, I bet he's hawking them."

The vendor, meanwhile, was down on his knees picking up these colorful booklets and putting them back into the box. As he rose, I pointed to them and asked him if they were authentic.

"Si, muy autentico," he said. *"Quieres comprar un ejemplo?"* (Would you like to buy one?)

"Tal vez. Let me take a look at them."

He handed me the box. I grabbed the first one, an American specimen, and opened it. It looked damn real, official. With pictures, personal entries, signatures, stamps, government seals and all.

"This is amazing," I said to Carolina, shaking my head.

I flipped through the various other passports. Most of them had once belonged to men, except for one. Most were Mexican, but I also came across a Brazilian, an Argentinian, and, not surprisingly, five American

305

versions. Aside from the Mexican booklets, I also scrutinized the American exemplars. I particularly zeroed in on the pictures. Well, most of the men had dark hair, from black to dark brown. Five were partially or totally bald. More than half of the Mexican men wore mustaches of various shapes.

However, the picture I found myself most drawn to was the one that used to belong to a fellow with the name of Lars Stenson. The reason for my appeal was simple: His facial features were similar to mine, the way I used to look without my outlandish makeup. Stunned, I showed the picture to Carolina. She looked, rubbed her eyes and looked again. "You almost look like twins, bi-zygotic perhaps, but still." She said 'almost'. As always, there were indeed some differences, small as they may have been. For one, Mr. Stenson's lips were thinner, his nostrils flared less than mine, his eyes were a little more drawn in, and his ears fanned out more, besides being smaller. He was older as well, by more than seven or eight years perhaps. And although he was an American, he claimed Goeteborg, Sweden, as his place of birth.

Always looking forward, I habitually focused on the similarities, which galvanized me to the point where I could hardly contain myself. No question, I had to get a hold of this passport one way or another. At the same time I thought it wise to keep the acquisition secret. Under no circumstances would I want Fidel to witness it. Although I liked and respected the man, I was afraid that he might talk, as was his wont. Worse, that he could tell the neighborhood that Fred, his subtenant, was in the market for passports. So I put my object of desire down, stepped aside and urged Carolina to take Fidel and head to the next stalls down the aisle. "Entertain him," I whispered to her. "I'll catch up with you in less than ten minutes."

As soon as both were out of sight, I turned to the vendor again. I picked up the passport and, praising his overall selection, tried to milk him. *"Quanto costa, senor?"* I let my voice trail off a trifle to downplay my eagerness.

"Quinientos, senor. Esta muy valioso."

"Quinientos? Es demasiado caro. Que parece trescientos?"

"Lo siento, senor, quinientos."

"Es demasiado caro," I repeated, dropped the passport and started shuffling away.

"Senor! Senor!" I heard him shouting after me. *"Quatroscientos cincuenta."*

I stopped, shook my head and proceeded again, hoping to force him into another, still lower bid. But he was stubborn. Torn, I eventually bowed, turned, walked back, handed him 450 pesos and bagged the passport. At the time that was a huge amount of money for me, almost a month's wages.

I soon caught up with Carolina and Fidel and, having bought what we needed, soon headed back to the truck. The ride over the dried and furrowed mud was very jolting, forcing Fidel's virgen into uncommonly wild swings, as though aiming for a Charlston — a performance that drew some worried glances from her worshipper.

Heading home, the passport never stopped sizzling in my pocket. Every once in a while I let my hand slide into it to check if it was still there and to get a feel for it. No sooner did we arrive at home than I pulled it out, handling it like a hallowed keepsake. I began admiring the golden eagle clawing an olive branch and a bunch of arrows. Wondering what it all meant, I gingerly opened it and began riveting my eyes on Mr. Stenson's somber mug. I also checked out the entries, then pensively shoved it away into my pocket again. I felt euphoric, as if I'd hit the million dollar jackpot.

"From now on I'm going to be Lars Stenson," I gushed to Carolina who had just come back from the kitchen. "At least to the Mexican police and the FBI. That'll be my snook at J. Edgar Hoover."

"You must be crazy!" she huffed at me. "That Lars Stenson's probably still alive. Some pickpocket may have simply swiped this passport from him. In that case there would be two Lars Stensons walking the streets of Mexico City. Hell, you might even run into him one day when you go shopping for groceries."

"Sure, I might, but the chances of that happening are very slim in a big city like ours. And even if our eyes met, he still wouldn't notice I had assumed his identity. The same goes for any Mexican cop who'd stop me on a street. He'd have no way of knowing that either. If he sees the passport, he'll assume that I'm the real Lars Stenson, simply because I *look* like him. I don't even think it would be a problem at the U.S. border. Although that would have to be tested."

"I hope you're not fooling yourself. This is the second time you've changed your name. That may call for a psychiatrist's couch. You definitely have a paranoid tilt, like somebody who's scared of his own shadow."

"Maybe so. But what do you want me to do? Capitulate? Let's face it, officially I'm a fugitive from justice. I may never be able to completely shake off that curse. All I *can* do is playing it safe, especially after that bone-chilling assault by the judiciales. I'd do anything that'll help me stay free, and I have a hunch that this passport will assist me in doing just that. At best, it's a sort of freedom charter. At the very least, it'll act as a bromide that'll soothe my mind when I see a cop approaching. And it may also help me sleep better. I hate to wake up in a panic at every creak and grate, expecting armed cops to crash through the door. Nightmares of that kind have struck me five times the past three weeks. That's why I'm so euphoric about that passport. It's nothing short of a godsend. Yes, my official name will change, but for you, our friends and our acquaintances, I'm still Fred."

"Well, Fred, what can I say? I just hope and pray it'll work."

When I lay in bed that night I kept wondering where, in America, this Mr. Stenson chose to live and why he was here in Mexico. I was curious what he did for a living, if he had a family, a wife and children. The thought that he may no longer be alive also crossed my mind. *Perhaps he was murdered during a robbery? After all, the papers were full of such crimes.* Wherever my thoughts may have strayed, it pained me that I knew virtually nothing about the man whose identity I was about to steal. Had done so already.

Next day, on Sunday, we invited Jorge for lunch. Over antojitos and a Bohemia, I couldn't resist letting him in on my new acquisition. I also offered to show it to him, but only on the promise that he'd keep it to himself and tell no one, including his female friends and his dad, particularly his dad. And when I handed the reddish-brown booklet to him, he was flabbergasted, as well as curious. I also told him where I'd picked it up.

"At the flea market?" he chortled. "Where else? We're in Mexico after all!"

He congratulated me, telling me that it was an exceptional buy. He fully shared my view. It would give me a certain measure of protection from the police in the next few years.

"The cops?" he said, waving his hand palm down. "They only look at your mugshot. If that's identical or close to the face they see in front of them, you're safe."

He opened it and compared Stenson's photo to my face. "I don't think you have to worry," he said matter-of-factly. "At least here in Mexico. But if I were you, I'd stay away from the northern border. You never know what the gringos have up their sleeves. And they're organized. They may even have a record of stolen passports, yours among them."

"Oh, I have no desire to test Hoover's bootlickers, at the moment at least. But, say, wouldn't some cops — I'm thinking of those nasty judiciales — pick up on those little facial differences?"

"They might. But you could probably do something about them. I mean tone them down, cosmetically, making slight changes to your face. You know Laura knows a good plastic…"

"Fred, I wouldn't," Carolina butted in. "Don't listen to him. We've discussed that already. I like you the way the good Lord made you."

Jorge took a big swig of wine. "Well, he'd only have to do very small tucks and pulls," he went on, showing it on his face. "You'd hardly see the difference. You'd be surprised what a good surgeon's nimble hands can do."

I nodded. "Frankly, I wouldn't mind getting an opinion from him."

"I would, if I were you. Darn, I forgot his name and address. I'll dig it up when I get back home. I'll call you."

Carolina sneered at her brother and, turning to me, said, "I think you could sail along without any surgery. It just occurred to me, there may be a way to actually tuck and pull Stenson's *picture* a little. I could well imagine that a good forger or counterfeiter with a lot of experience could doctor it in such a way that sober Mr. Stenson would look more like *you* than the other way around."

"Hats off to you," Jorge said, nodding approvingly. "Good thinking! You deserve a toast. Here is to my smart li'l sister."

We raised our glasses.

"Coming back to your suggestion," Jorge added, glancing at Carolina. "I'd bet that there are more than a few of those forgers and counterfeiters around. They could be right under our noses. Frankly, I wouldn't mind tracking some of them down."

"I would appreciate that," I said. "A good forger could be very helpful. I should know. We had an excellent one in the POW camp. I probably wouldn't be here if one of those crackerjacks hadn't faked my first identity card. At the same time I could imagine profiting from a surgeon as well. Why choose either side? One doesn't exclude the other. We could tuck and pull on both ends and meet somewhere in the middle. What's wrong with a good compromise?"

"Regardless, something is bound to work," Jorge said. "For the next few years at least. The only problem that might arise is when the passport expires and you have to renew it."

"Sure, but that's not until 1948," I added with a sigh of relief.

"Oh, that's a long way off," Jorge mused. "We could have ten temblors by then and our proud Metropolitan Cathedral might have turned into a giant rotten molar or sunk into the mud. But kidding aside, what I'd do soon is getting a tourist card, an FMT, under your new name. You can get it at the National Immigration Institute. Just tell them you lost your old one. Or that it was stolen from you. Hah, hah! It may cost you some 50 pesos or so. You couldn't buy a cheaper sleeping pill! But I'd watch out, there are a lot of scruffy pickpockets hanging around that area. Keep your passport close to your chest. It wouldn't be fun if you had to buy it back at the flea market again."

He couldn't bite back his laughter. Nor could we.

MORITZ, MY FORGER

The run-down, haunting mansion sat on a weed-choked plot on the fringes of the southern suburb of Churubusco. All windows were shuttered, except the ones along the basement. When I rang the bell, an old mechanical device, I heard some rumbling. But it took a while until somebody finally opened the door, although just a tiny crack of it.

"Quienes es?" (Who are you?) he barked at me. *"Que quieres?"* (What do you want?)

I introduced myself, telling him that Carlos Montoya had recommended him, and that I needed some help with my passport.

"Sind Sie Deutscher?" (Are you German?) he asked in high German, softened by very peculiar Yiddish and Viennese inflections and intonations.

"Nein, Schweizer." (No, Swiss.)

"Schweizer?" He looked at me as if he didn't believe me.

Bracing for a bang, I quickly wedged my shoe into the crack, only to watch the door open magically.

"Kommen Sie herein!" he snapped, striking me like the lash of a whip.

As I stepped in, I extended my hand. But he acted as though he didn't see it. I felt snubbed, and not by anyone, but by a fellow who'd actually *profit* from being friendly. *Didn't he look like a beggar who'd be shaking a tin near the Zocalo?* Besides being disheveled and wearing a scraggly beard, he was small, frail and walked bent over. His face had the color of a moldy peach, dominated by a sharp, beak-like nose, hollowed cheeks and a high, wrinkled bulb of a forehead. He was wrapped loosely in rag-like clothes that seemed to match his slurring speech.

While I stood there near the door, a teapot started whistling somewhere in the back. "I've to get that first," he said gruffly, rushing over to what seemed to be a small kitchen.

I let my eyes sweep the place, but the dimmed light severely limited the range of my sight. What I could see was a lab, but an old-fashioned version that appeared to be frozen in time. It was equipped with a large kitchen sink, a microscope, various lamps, a wild array of bottles, tubes, jars, brushes and pens all crowded into a tiny space. A smell of biting chemicals mixed with glue, burnt tortillas, cumin and some other unknown substance saturated the air.

"What is it you want from me?" he barked at me, when he came back.

I showed him the passport, explaining that I had recently acquired it and asked him to make slight changes on the photograph, so as to look more like me.

"That's odd," he said. "You claim to be a Swiss who wants to become a Swede? And all that in Mexico?" He stared at me.

"I *am* Swiss!"

"You are as Swiss as the moon is blue and full of butterflies. You can't fool me. You're a fucking German! I detected that right away in your accent. I even know the city you're coming from — Berlin."

"You've got the ears of a Rottweiler."

"I do. I've come across many Germans here in Mexico and, I regret to say, most of them are Nazis. Well, I refuse to work for people who're gassing *my* people. For a long time I didn't even speak German any more 'cause it's the language of our henchmen."

He gave me a blank stare.

"You said 'most' Germans. How about the rest? If you lump everybody together, you're not much better than the Nazis themselves."

He paused, lowered his head and let his Adam's apple bop several times. "OK, why don't you take a seat," he finally went on, waving me unto the sofa, while he carefully lowered himself into one of his armchairs.

"You want to hear what the Germans did to me and my family?" Then he started to tell me the story of his tortured life, starting in a Jewish shtetl in the Bukovina, moving to Vienna, where he attended the university and later worked, all the way to his and his wife's flight to New York. Several times, especially when he depicted experiences that were extremely stressful, he turned very emotional. The worst happened in New York, where his entry into the United States was rejected on the grounds of a skin rash he was plagued with.

"They simply separated us, Elsie and me," he told me in a highly strained pitch, breaking down in tears. "The doctors and the immigration officials literally had to tear us apart. They kept telling me that I had to go back where I came from. Can you imagine? Back to where? The gas chambers?" He shook his head. "I was lucky to get on a freighter as a stowaway to Veracruz."

His tale, which faintly reminded me of the boat people in Senor Alarcon's movie script, cut me to the quick. Little did this man know that I once passed through the Bukovina, albeit trigger-happy, in a German uniform, helmet and stomping boots.

I should stress that it was the first time I was confronted face to face with a living human being who had suffered because of an action I might have been part of. I was deeply ashamed, and Moritz's depiction only added to it. What he went through was so gripping, his tone of voice so heartbreaking that I couldn't help but commiserate with him, to the point of getting up, walking over and hugging this frail man. *What did we Germans do to those innocent people? Was not I, infused to the tips of my hair by the delusion of being part of the master race, personally guilty of having caused all this suffering?* The answer was such a clear and resounding 'Yes' that I was about to drop on my knees and beg for forgiveness.

But Moritz, making sure to stay ahead of me, abruptly tore himself out of his own emotional embrace and matter-of-factly delved into the business at hand.

"OK. So you want me to touch up the photograph, make little changes. That's no problem. In order to do that, I'll have to take some close-up pictures of you. We can do that right now. Why don't we step over there, to that booth."

He got up and shuffled to the other side of the room, close to his perfunctory lab. I followed him.

"Why don't you go into the booth and sit down."

He fetched a camera, a Leica, mounted it on a tripod, told me to sit still and look into the lens and then snapped several pictures. Subsequently he focused the lens on my profile.

"That's it," he finally said. "I'll do what I can. Your passport will be ready next week."

I arose, hugged him, wished him a pleasant weekend and left, deeply lost in thought.

Five days later, I headed back to Moritz. This time he received me with the best welcome mat I could think of — a genuine smile. After hugging him, I handed him a little gift. He nervously unwrapped it and, turning it in his hand, started laughing. It was a blue crescent of a moon, studded with four butterflies made out of glass. Actually it was brown and blank when I first bought it, until I painted it and glued on the butterflies.

"You got me. You know, you're a crafty young man."

"Well thank you."

"Could I bring you anything to drink?" he asked, once he'd offered me a seat on his sofa. "How about a good tequila?"

"Sure, why not."

He placed a bottle of Tequila reposado and two liquor glasses, filled them and proposed a toast.

"To life!" he said, raising his glass. "How lucky we are that we're still among the living. We should celebrate that every day."

"I agree. It's a miracle we're still breathing."

"By the way, the passport picture came out very well."

He shuffled over to his workbench, picked up my passport and joined me on the couch.

"Take a look," he said. "You be the judge. Don't tell me your name is *not* Lars Stenson."

He was right on the dot. I could hardly see a difference between me and the mug of my Doppelgänger. We looked like veritable twins.

"Thank you so much! This will hopefully make my life a little easier."

To be truthful, I felt a little uneasy about the picture for the simple reason that it looked too much like the mugshot showing up on the arrest warrant the FBI and the judiciales had. Frankly, if I'd had a choice I'd have picked a picture that deviated a little more, so I wouldn't have been so easily recognizable. But these were some of the shortcomings I could live with. I trusted that being part of an official American passport, it would pass scrutiny, at least in Mexico. And for the time being I had no desire to travel to America anyway, where things might be riskier.

All Moritz wanted was 400 pesos. Since we got along so well, I chose to keep him company a little longer. Over the Tequila reposado, we chatted about our private lives, he about Elsie and I about Carolina. Elsie has promised to visit him soon. It's the second time. She may join him here for good. The winters in New York are hardly bearable. But she still feels she has to take care of one of her aunts who, unfortunately, is in ill health.

Upon leaving I promised to keep in touch with him.

TESTING THE BREAKING POINT

Meanwhile, I kept busy learning and playing the part of Lars Stenson, at least for public consumption and aside from my regular job as a carpintero. My first goal was imitating his signature over and over again, so it would come naturally. I also visited the Swedish embassy, asking for information on Sweden. I frequented various libraries in search of books depicting this Nordic country I knew next to nothing about but had always admired. I still remember our headmistress claiming that Sweden was actually far more Germanic than Germany, that Germany was a hopeless racial hotchpotch compared to most of Scandinavia. From what I heard, she got into deep trouble for saying that and later a Nazi true believer actually made her scarf down several big wedges of humble pie to the point where she almost choked.

The first test of my playacting my new identity came with the application for the Tourist Card, the FMT, at the National Immigration Institute, located on Chapultepec Avenue. Apprehensive, I had taken half the day off from work. But I must have picked the wrong time because it was filled to the brim with people. After filling out and submitting the application, I was asked by a grumpy, holier-than-thou official, where my old Tourist Card was. When I told him that I had lost it, he said there was a price for being sloppy. I — he always called me Senor Stenson — could pay it right now, otherwise it would take more than a month. I handed him 10 pesos. It greased the wheels: he turned around, checked my passport, compared the picture with my face, and determined everything was as it should be, that I was Mr. Lars Stenson and that was that. Never did he suspect the passport might belong to anybody else but me. And when he put the last stamp on my Tourist Card, I felt as if a big weight had dropped off my shoulders.

According to my diary, there was yet another incident requiring me to show my passport. It happened about three weeks after I'd received my Tourist Card. Carolina and I were passengers in Jorge's car. We were on our way to a special exhibition of Diego Rivera's paintings at the Bellas Artes Palace. Being late, Jorge was even more lead-footed than usual. Well, one suck-cheeked *tamarindo* picked up on it and flagged him down. Aiming for a hefty mordida, or so we suspected, he acted as though Jorge's speeding should be a mountain rather than a molehill. Be that as it may, he instantly ordered all of us to get out of the car, nosed Jorge's breath for booze and requested we all prove our identity. Luckily, I had my Tourist Card as well as my passport with me. He looked at the photo in the passport and immediately recognized me as none other than Mr. Stenson. Everything else proceeded smoothly as well, including Jorge's act of shoving the bribe into the tamarindo's open hands behind his back.

These two incidents, most notably their smooth sailing, added fuel to my hope that my new passport had enough heft to pass an even more stringent scrutiny, such as I might encounter at the U.S. border, for instance. It also strengthened my belief that I was on the right track. But just as I was about to regain the poise I'd nurtured before the raid at the hacienda, I had to face yet another incident that made me think twice.

In the late afternoon of June 21st — I was still at work — Carolina received a call from her dad. He was all up in arms. The reason: the judiciales had once again raided his mansion. Armed to the teeth, they had barged in at seven in the morning, flashed an arrest warrant with my picture on it, then combed through every room, turned everything upside down, sniffed out every corner, all in the search for that armed and dangerous *asesino, criminal, homicida,* Fred Luthi, the former me. They interrogated him, Imelda and Demesia for more than two hours to reveal where I was hiding. It was unbearable. Scared that it would happen again, he pleaded with Carolina to once again cut the cord with me, turn me in, divorce me and come back to the hacienda.

"Of course I flat-out rejected his dribble," Carolina claimed.

"Good! But how about him squealing? Did you lure him out if he had by any chance revealed our hideout here in San Angel?"

"Now that you say it, I did, again and again. But he stubbornly refused to commit himself. He always came back to the mantra that you were a murderer who ought to face justice."

"What a bastard! He's playing deaf and dumb 'cause he wants nothing less sinister than letting me dangle, twisting in limbo. That's his way of putting the thumbscrews on me. Oh brother!"

"Stop it! You're acting out your paranoia again. I don't think he's doing it consciously. Knowing him, I personally don't believe he'd ever squeal on us."

"You *believe!* I think you're naive, my dear. You've always underestimated him. If you want my opinion, this guy is molded by a wide mean streak that starts in his head and keeps running down his body, passing through his anal crack, all the way to his toes."

"Stop it, Fred!"

"Yeah, stop it. Who's the perpetrator here? And what am I but a victim? Actually, I was naive, too. Dumb me! I thought I could loaf in fairyland for a while, that I could rest on the laurels of my new passport. Welcome to the real world! I better pack my bags and move to a place where I can feel reasonably safe. Where I can finally get a night's sleep."

"Fred, be sensible," Carolina pleaded, hugging me. "You're safe here with me. I know you are. Think about it, Dad had months to turn you in. Guess what? He didn't. So calm down. Get off your paranoia treadmill!"

Well, I bowed to Carolina and stayed. At a heavy price it turned out. I couldn't sleep a wink. Every little noise, the creaking of wood in the windows, stairs and ceiling, the droning of cars, their squeaking to a halt, the cackling of people's voices, the slamming of doors, all of it put me on pins and needles. Worse, two times I was gripped by panic attacks making me shake like a full-fledged epileptic during a seizure. It was not until Carolina hugged me and whispered soothing, reassuring words and phrases into my ears, making me calm down a little.

I got up at the crack of dawn, tired and grouchy. After breakfast, I dragged myself to work. When I saw Senor Rodriguez, I told him I'd had a horrible night, that I was as tired as an old dog. I blamed it on the relentless barking of dogs in the neighborhood, but also on car traffic. Suggesting that this had been going on for a week already, I mentioned I might have to find a new apartment. In the meantime, I was looking for a simple shelter with a bed to get a night's rest. I knew he had a small shack behind the workshop. It was furnished with a bed and equipped with a water tap and sink, and I had seen him occasionally taking a nap there during siesta. To cut things short, I asked him if I could possibly make use of this shack for a week or so, until I'd found an apartment.

"Claro, no problema!" he snapped.

When I got home, I informed Carolina about the shelter. She got very upset, almost hysterical, accusing me again of you-know-what. "You're getting deranged. You should see a psychiatrist."

I debunked her diagnosis and, arguing that there were sound reasons for feeling threatened, I accused her again of being blind to her dad's mean streak. I regret to say, my words only made things turn from bad to worse. She simply could not be persuaded. Nor could she sway me, not even with her tears. Toward evening I packed a few pieces of clothing, a towel, soap, toothbrush and toothpaste into a bag and, bidding her goodbye, left.

Let me say, Carolina simply could not forgive me. Never mind that during the daytime I continued to visit her, sometimes staying with her for hours. We even ate supper together. Sadly, these visits continued to be marred with great tensions. It was unbearable. But unable to come up with a better alternative, I continued this arrangement for about three weeks, until our relationship turned so nasty, I feared it might break apart.

One evening over supper her patience reached an absolute ebb tide. "I cannot and will not continue to live this way," she sighed. "It's been three weeks you've been away at night. I've not heard judiciales knocking at our door. They had plenty of time to plan an arrest if they intended to. None came, *nadie*. I'm highly pregnant and married to a man who doesn't want to live with me. This is absurd. I'm not going to tolerate this any longer. So, if you refuse to stay here with me tonight, as is your duty as husband, I will start divorce proceedings as soon as I can."

"Is that an ultimatum? Are you sure you want to celebrate your dad's victory? That's why he didn't commit himself when you asked him about squealing on me. He always wanted to drive a wedge between us. Now he has succeeded, thanks to you."

"Look, Fred, I love you. But I'm also concerned about my own needs, and those of our baby. Don't bring Dad into the mix. He has his own agenda. I have mine. That's all I have to say."

These were harsh but clear words. There was a long pause. I was in a tight spot, stuck under the thumb of a dilemma. The angst of being in the crosshairs of the judiciales had settled deep into my bones. It felt like dancing a turkey trot with a saguaro. At the same time, I loved Carolina. I couldn't imagine letting her go and living without her. In the end I chose the most sensible option raising the white flag. I stayed, once again. But it was anything but easy. As before, I woke up at every little noise, trembling with fear that my nemesis might be plodding up the stairs at any moment to drag me out of bed, throw me in the slammer and hand me over to Hoover's bloodhounds.

Luckily, with time the angst gradually began to ebb, albeit at a glacial speed. It dawned on me that Carolina may have been right after all, that the judiciales had had plenty of time to nab me. But they hadn't. Which in turn made me wonder: *was Carolina right? Was I, indeed, suffering from bouts of paranoia?* It was a charge I couldn't quite shake off, as much as I tried to.

As the summer limped along, bringing much needed moisture by way of hefty, occasionally violent thunderstorms, Carolina was ambushed by cramps and bursts of pain in the abdomen. At first she blamed them on a sensitive stomach. But Dr. Salazar whom she consulted insisted that they were the first signs of normal labor. Indeed, these pains, accompanied by twinges of backache, not only increased in strength but also in frequency. They came at more and more regular intervals, indicating her doctor may have been right.

Anticipation couldn't have strained our nerves more. And all of a sudden a milagro rattled on our door. One Tuesday morning at the end of June, as I was ready to go to work she complained of a series of very painful contractions. "I feel it coming," she groaned.

"You do?" I said, feeling helpless. I wondered what I would do if — God forbid! — the head of the baby would unexpectedly emerge from between her thighs. Befuddled, I called on Julia to ask her for advice. She quickly came rushing up and began palpating Carolina's abdomen. After asking some pointed questions, she turned to me, smiled and rhapsodized, "Rejoice, Fred, an angel is paying her a visit."

Well, I got the message and quickly called the ambulance. I also informed Senor Rodriguez of our circumstances. And when the ambulance arrived, we all piled in and headed to the birth clinic of the University Hospital. We made it just in time. No less than an hour later a healthy boy would see the light of the day. Thanks not least to an experienced female doctor and two caring nurses, the last stretch turned out to be smooth, though much bloodier than I had expected. But Carolina took it in good stride. Once the umbilical cord was severed and the placenta had been expelled, the exhausted mom was given the bebe to hold. With the boy resting on her breast, I kissed and congratulated her on her bravery and toughness. "You did it! It's over!" I whispered, luring a wan smile out of her.

Three hours later, once Carolina had recuperated a little from her hour-long strain, we were allowed to take the baby and head back home. Although both mother and the newborn, whom we chose to christen Enrique Gomez-Stenson, were healthy and vigorous, it took some patience to cope with the demanding newcomer who readily let us know with piercing shrieks and screams when he was in need of something. Or thought he was. It was especially tough for Carolina and she frequently found herself stuck in the doldrums. She simply couldn't handle the perpetual demands the little suckler put on her. Unfulfilled with the role of mother, she perennially complained of being tired. What was most worrisome, she lost any sense of pride in her appearance and became increasingly unkempt, dowdy, like a petunia after a hailstorm.

Commiserating, Julia and I took up the slack and helped wherever we could. We changed and washed the diapers; we bathed and cleaned the baby; we bought groceries, we cooked and prepared the meals. Yet, regardless how much we tried to cater to Carolina's wishes, it was impossible to please her. To the contrary, our efforts were ridiculed, worse, answered with bursts of aggression, with me as the principal target. She even had the gall to accuse me of laziness and lack of responsibility. My plea that I also had to attend to my job was put off with a gesture of scorn. Never before, save perhaps for that pivotal scene at the penitentiary in Chihuahua, was our relationship under so much strain. The fact that it lasted more than a month made it especially nerve-wracking. It wasn't until the end of July that I started to notice some improvements. The trigger seems to have been Enrique, who for the first time broke out in smiles, repeatedly so, especially during bathing. I celebrated this event as a landmark, confirming that we had mastered the first stage in our effort to rear a child and were well on the way to a more normal way of life.

A BRAND NEW CHAPTER

Yet, what really turned the corner was an unforeseen, joyful incident that happened to burst into our lives. On Saturday morning, August 14th, the telephone rang. I was busy helping Fidel build a wooden tool shack in his backyard, when I heard Carolina's voice shouting from the kitchen window. "Fred, Senor Alarcon is on the line. He wants to talk to you."

I was startled. I had long deflated the hope the film project would ever get off the ground. Indeed, I had already played with the thought of opening my own carpinteria sometime in the future, as soon as I'd saved a little money.

"Forgive me, Fidel, but this is very important," I heard myself saying, dropping my hammer and rushing up the stairs. When I grabbed the receiver, I was so nervous it felt as if the good Lord himself was on the other end.

"Hier spricht Fritz... ah... sorry, Fred speaking." I stumbled but quickly caught myself, halfway, it turned out. My new alias, Lars, flatly fell by the wayside, embarrassingly so.

There were a few clicks and crackles. "Alarcon. Can you hear me? Am I talking to Fred?"

"Yes."

"Well, Fred, I just want to tell you that, as of this morning, the money for our film project has finally come through. That should make us all rejoice. I'm sorry it took so long. In any event, I plan to start rehearsing and shooting the first scenes beginning in November, most likely in and around Veracruz. Depending on the weather, of course. I want you to work on your script to get it down pat. How's your Spanish coming?"

"It's much better, but it still needs improvement."

"You said it! Take it to heart. Did I ever give you the names of the Spanish teachers?"

"Yes, but I haven't contacted them. I thought..."

"Please do. I'll give you the details later. Good luck with getting a grip on your part."

I was beside myself. I threw my hands around Carolina and whirled through the room with her, shouting "Wow! I can't believe it! Who would have thought? That's how haphazard things are."

321

"Estupendo! Que maravilla! Enhorbuena!"

Enrique started mewling and bawling. But this time it felt like music to our ears.

"Que milagro!" I hollered. "We have to celebrate that. We still have a bottle of champagne, don't we? Let's call Jorge and tell him to rush over. This calls for a toast."

Enrique started on another round.

"How about Fidel and Julia?"

"Yes, they have to join us too."

Carolina called her brother, while I headed down to the basement to fetch a bottle of champagne. On the way back I invited the Aznars. They were tickled to come, even though they failed to fully grasp the reason for this celebration.

It took Julia and Fidel less than fifteen minutes to show up, with Julia parading a big plate of antojitos, various snacks, in front of her ample bosom. Shortly later, Jorge knocked on the door, bringing along two more bottles of the bubbly. Cheery-eyed as if he'd hit the jackpot, he congratulated me most lavishly, kissing me on the cheek and claiming that he never had any doubts the project would eventually come to fruition. "You'll be a stellar actor!" he promised.

Once settled, he lifted one glass after another. Nor would I take the backseat, despite Carolina's repeated admonition to bridle myself. Well, it didn't take long to finish all three bottles, and soon both Jorge and I were lit to the gills. Had we not taken in Julia's morsels, we might well have staggered and stumbled down the stairs, even broken our necks.

Next day — thank heaven it was a Sunday! — I was saddled with a stubborn headache for most of the day. Still I goaded myself to dig up the film script and start reading my end of the dialogue again, aloud, with Carolina listening and correcting my pronunciation. I was surprised how much had slipped my mind. It was as if my Spanish had gone on a long vacation. Yet the words, once pronounced with an emotional edge, quickly came surging back, like the faces of people I had interacted with in the past. I also managed to call the two Spanish teachers, whose names and telephone numbers Senor Alarcon had given me. Both sounded very helpful, and I made arrangements for lessons. Since I was employed during the daytime, they would have to be in the evening.

Time winged its way, and swiftly at that. Putting in more than eight hours of work taking Spanish lessons, learning the script and helping Carolina care for Enrique more than filled my days. Every once in a while, when I had an hour or so, I scampered though the *Reforma* Jorge handed

322

me, usually a whole pack of them. I noted not without a certain satisfaction that on June sixth an overwhelming number of American and British forces made a successful landing on the coast of Normandy, opening up a new front to wrest France out of the German occupation. I couldn't help but side with the allies. However, my feelings radically shifted to the other side when I came upon an article that depicted how a fleet of no less than one thousand American bombers razed Berlin to the ground. I felt for the many victims, women, children and older people, who had nothing to do with the war. I wondered if Rummelsburg, the orphanage, was hit as well.

Nor was it quiet on the eastern front. There the Russian army advanced as well, crossing the Prut River and spearheading into Poland. Yet, what aroused me most was the event that took place on the 20th of July at the Wolfsschanze, Hitler's eastern headquarters. There high-ranking German officers reportedly tried to assassinate the Fuehrer but, as bad luck would have it, failed.

"Damned!" I pounded the word like a stake into the ground.

LEARNING THE ROPES

August, September, October soared past, thankfully smoothly, without incident. I savored the peace precisely because experience had taught me never to take it for granted. And while I cannot say I braced for another surprise raid, I made sure to stay vigilant with my ears pricked, eyes peeled and keeping my nose to the grindstone.

Yet the good news kept coming almost like the platters of antojitos from Julia. On the first Saturday in November — I was busy changing Enrique's diapers — Senor Alarcon came through with a call from Veracruz, informing me the rehearsals and shooting were about to begin. "Sorry I'm a few weeks late. The weather was very stormy. Do you have your part down pat?"

"I do. I'm already dreaming about it. You can count on me."

"Good! I want you to appear at the Mocambo Hotel in Veracruz no later than the 21st of November. It's right on the beach, about seven kilometers south of the city center. To get to Veracruz you can take the bus. The trip is about seven hours from el D.F. You should prepare yourself for a stay of two or three months. Starting on the 22nd, the first three to four weeks will be taken up with rehearsals. Then we'll start shooting the scenes, depending on the weather, of course. We'll follow pretty much in sequence according to the screenplay. The first scene involving the life raft won't be shot until the end of December, possibly even at the beginning of January. The whole crew will stop working from the 24th of December till January 2nd. I just want to warn you, it's not going to be the Seven Heavens. The sea can get very choppy. At the beginning there'll be a lot of crude oil, flotsam, even a few dead bodies floating around, so you'll get very dirty and grimy. And the water can get chilly too. So be prepared."

I was giddy with joy to delve into an altogether new chapter in my life. I couldn't wait to get ready, quit my job, pack my things, hop on the bus and take off to unknown shores. Sadly, Carolina was much less enthusiastic, and for obvious reasons. Although she applauded my becoming an actor, she was also wary of certain drawbacks. For one, I'd be sorely missed as an emotional support, as well as a practical hand. She'd be left alone to handle the many chores centering on the caring for Enrique. Sure, Julia would help. At the same time, she was getting old and increasingly more forgetful.

324

In addition, Carolina also expressed fear that I could fall in love with one of the actresses. "I don't know if you've read the articles appearing in the *Reforma* recently about the loose sexual mores running rampant among the film crowd," she reminded me of. "It's like 'little Hollywood', they kept warning."

"No, I haven't, but I can swear that I take our marriage very seriously. Besides, I don't think any of those actresses can hold a candle to you."

"Thank you for saying that but I'm not so sure. The pregnancy has definitely taken a toll. I'm not what I used to be."

"You will be; you'll bounce back in no time. You already have. I can see it in the way men glance at you. It just occurred to me, you may also be able to join me in Veracruz. I don't see why anybody would mind."

On the 19th of November I quit my job a decision that stunned Senor Rodriguez. Assuming the culprit was the pay, he offered me a ten percent raise. I thanked him and wished him and all my colleagues well. When I got home, I still did a few repairs around the house, gathered the things I'd need — the screenplay, clothes, underwear, socks and shoes — and packed them into a large suitcase. The next day, early in the morning I said goodbye. The parting was more painful than I'd expected. While we embraced, I had to kiss away Carolina's tears.

Seven hours later, I caught myself standing in front of the sprawling Mocambo Hotel. *What a place!* I was impressed by its antiquated charm, its breezy arches and terraced gardens. Better yet, I got a room on the second floor with a panoramic view of the beach and the sea. The weather was sunny, warm and so humid that it right away curled my hair. Unlike in el D.F. the air was stunningly clean, with a light breeze ruffling the sea.

Veracruz! It sounded like a chimera to me. No, it *was. Funny, I involuntarily ended up in the very place, I pretended heading to in front of our camp's Escape Committee. Yet, instead of catching a freighter to Europe to swell the ranks of our once glorious army, I more than ever rooted for its defeat.*

My first move was a call to Carolina, informing her of my arrival. I also described the hotel and my room and, praising the clean air, invited her to join me. After showering, I dressed and made my way down to the restaurant. A crew of fifteen people, among them Senor Alarcon, sat at a long table engaged in a lively discussion. Judging by the empty plates, I assumed that they had just eaten supper. I shook hands with Senor Alarcon who, after welcoming me, introduced me as Fred Luthi from Switzerland, the name I had long jilted. As I took a seat at the end of the table, he called a waiter. I ordered a plate of tacos al carbon and a beer. In the meantime more and more people arrived and Senor Alarcon introduced each one of them. We talked about the screenplay and the general guidelines involved in acting. Since it was all conducted in high-level Spanish, I had a tough time participating, although I understood most of what was being said. The Russian name of Stanislavsky, a name I'd never heard before, was bandied about like a wet ball at a soccer match. Everybody tried to get a hold of it but, slippery as it was, nobody really managed to.

Shortly after eleven, Senor Alarcon called on everyone to appear at ten in the morning in the Monterrey conference room for an orientation meeting. After that he called it quits and, although some stayed, most withdrew to their rooms. I still took a stroll down to the beach, where I breathed in the salty air and listened to the waves lapping up the beach.

After a good sleep and a hearty breakfast, we all, a motley crew of eighty-eight people, actors, actresses, cinematographers, camera operators, costume designers, makeup artists, sound specialists, set designers and carpinteros, gathered in the Monterrey room. Senor Alarcon welcomed all of us and then called the meeting to order. He first asked us to introduce ourselves and then proceeded to set the agenda and the timetable. He hoped once the rehearsal were wrapped up, we could start shooting the initial scenes, first on a freighter he had leased and later on the life raft. His latest plan was to finish the shooting by the end of February, weather permitting.

He then delved into his own ideas about filmmaking, what he had in mind with his project. The scenes he hoped to shoot should present the plight of these refugees in a starkly realistic setting, capturing real life situations visually as well as in sound effects — language, dialogue, storms, explosions, chaos. The goal was to achieve utmost credibility, authenticity and verisimilitude. He stressed the importance of dramatic action, a vivid depiction of human emotions — love, hope, joy, awe, disappointment, failure, dread, fear, terror, panic — so that the audience could experience the thrills and terrifying ordeals of these people vicariously, without being in harm's way and facing the dangers. Ideally he would have liked the involvement of all the human senses, lamenting again and again our inability to bring across such important sensory experiences as touch, taste and smell.

At twelve, Senor Alarcon granted us a breather, and we all withdrew to the restaurant, where a comida was served. The afternoon was specifically tailored to the actors and actresses, while the technical staff was granted a reprieve. As hinted before, Senor Alarcon championed the Stanislavskian credo or system of acting: He expected us to actually live the part we were assigned to play. If we failed, we wouldn't be doing our job as actors. "We must find the inner spirit of the character," he repeatedly emphasized, "so we can fuse it with our own emotions drawn from our past." We could achieve this by recalling feelings similar or analogous to those of the characters. Such acting would require tapping into our subconscious, demanding we engage in deliberate exercises, sitting down and concentrating on emotions we have experienced and writing them down so they could be acted out when needed. Responding to questions, Senor Alarcon even went so far as to encourage actors to improvise on their roles to catch sight of resonances not specifically spelled out in his text. Again, authenticity should trump everything, on occasion even the screenplay itself: to capture the character's inner turmoil, actors could distort their lines, mumble them, or choke on them. Even foreign words or phrases were welcome. Being a seasoned actor himself, he offered many graphic descriptions, which he illustrated with the help of practical examples, never failing to underline them with appropriate gestures. He himself had an exceptional talent for amusing an audience with comical exaggerations tending to the paradoxical, even absurd.

When we left at five, our heads were spinning. Yet his comments made good sense. In fact, I myself had followed them, unwittingly, largely unaware of them.

In the weeks to come, Senor Alarcon made each one of us perform our part, watched by his sharp eyes and ears. He was quite heavy on the tiller and when he didn't like a sequence, he jumped off his perch on the step ladder, rushed to the actors or actresses and explained what could be done better, including a detailed demonstration of the way he envisioned it. Being an unforgiving taskmaster and a stickler for detail, he picked up on the slightest imperfections. He'd mop his brow, frown, mutter and shake his head, even halting already remedied scenes, forcing the actors to go over them again and again, until he was satisfied. He was particularly harsh with Elvira Mendez, a stunningly beautiful actress who was supposed to play Bluma Rubin, a mother with two children. Her drawback: She repeatedly failed to act out her lines without stuttering.

"Can't you learn your lines?" the old fox scorned at one time, his eyebrows shooting up into his hairline. "What do you want me to do? Recruit a small army of stagehands holding up boards with your lines?"

Frustrated, Senorita Mendez, burst out, flailing away at him, "You sound like you don't want me to act at all."

"Dear lady, you may, indeed, be getting it."

He had a mordant wit and could be scathingly critical. Yet in all fairness he'd also praise certain performances, usually by clapping vigorously. He was particularly keen on fine nuances in pronunciation, gestures and body language. By the way, he also intervened in the dialogue I had with the life rafters, faulting me for my Spanish pronunciation. That came way toward the end of the rehearsals. And once he had released us, I walked up to him. "With all due respect, Senor Alarcon," I said to him. "As you know, I'm supposed to play a German sailor who is trying to speak Spanish. Wouldn't it be more authentic for me to speak with a German accent? Isn't that what Stanislavsky would prefer? And wouldn't the audience even *expect* me doing exactly that?"

"You know, you may be right. In any event, you shouldn't take my bickering too seriously. It's a gut reaction when I hear something that's a little off-key. You're doing an excellent job, Fred. Just keep on going."

KURT MUENZER AND BLUMA

"Enrique and I miss you so much," Carolina mumbled into the receiver. "It feels like you've been away for several months already. Are you coming home for Christmas?"

"Most likely, Senor Alarcon has mentioned something about giving us time off, but he didn't say when. I'll ask him and call you back tomorrow."

Well, next day I caught up with Senor Alarcon and he informed me that the rehearsals would wind down on the 23rd of December, so I could be back in el D.F. by Christmas Eve.

Since we were very busy, time broke into a vigorous trot and the 24th came in a twinkling. Luckily, I was able to catch a ride with Elvira Mendez. Driving a fancy Mercedes, she cut the trip down to a little more than five hours.

When she dropped me off at Fidel's house, Carolina was sweeping the sidewalk. "Wow!" she said, when I ducked out of the Mercedes. And, glancing at Miss Mendez, she pursed her lips, as if she intended to say something, but then kept mum, although her eyes spoke volumes.

That dampened our spirit, and it took a while before Carolina managed to recuperate. She'd put up a small Christmas tree, decorated with colorful ornaments and tinsel. The air was saturated with the fragrance of freshly baked cookies and the scent of burnt pine needles.

"I did it especially for you," she warbled, "to remind you of the Christmas you celebrated at the orphanage."

"Thank you so much. I really appreciate that."

On Christmas Day we exchanged Christmas presents. Carolina had wrapped up a new wristwatch for me, while I gave her a silver bracelet from Taxco. She had roasted a turkey and, besides Julia and Fidel, we had Jorge and Laura Lopez, his girlfriend, over for dinner. To heighten the Christmas spirit we also attended church services, which turned out to be very festive. Never mind that Enrique, who had learned to sit up all by himself, acquitted it with screams and piercing shrieks.

The time flew far too fast, and shortly after the New Year's festivities I was on my way back to Veracruz. This time I was able to hitch a ride with Benito Levya, an actor who also played a pivotal part among the people rescued in the life raft.

After welcoming us back on the evening of the second of January, Senor Alarcon reminded us that the shooting would start the next day and he expected us to come prepared. All the actors, actresses and the technical crew would be bussed up to the harbor in Veracruz, where we'd board the freighter CONFIANZA, the first film location. We'd be handed the clothing for our parts and receive the proper makeup, including hair style. Subsequently we'd have to be ready for their final rehearsal of the first scene, to be followed by the actual shooting. Since my first appearance before the camera was scheduled to start much later, I was the only actor to be excused. Still, Senor Alarcon urged me to attend the last rehearsals, so I would pick up valuable acting experience and the fundamentals of filmmaking as a whole.

It was a wise move, and I never regretted having witnessed the future in the making — the creation of make-believe. Though I was no stranger to playing feigned roles in real life, even as a tool of survival, it was nevertheless a novel world for me watching all the trickery in the service of conjuring up an illusory world that *could* have been real. I watched with amazement how the back-lot set of the Miami harbor and skyline, only constructed a few days before, was lit up. Its concept reminded me of the infamous Potemkin village in southern Russia, which was supposed to have been built as a showpiece to impress Katherine the Great. Curious, I fell into chats with the carpinteros and pintores who built and painted the backlot set. I was so itching to get involved I'd even give them a hand here and there.

While walking around and keeping my eyes and ears open, I learned a great deal about the practical side of outdoor filming on location and the logistics of cobbling together the various artistic skills of acting, designing costumes, using makeup, producing sound effects, building stage sets, not to mention choreography and photography to make everything click like a Swiss watch. What a production it was!

At first an electrically charged atmosphere filled the air, when an assistant clapper-boarded the first 'take' and Senor Alarcon bellowed "Lights! Action!" From then on things proceeded rather smoothly, and our 'head honcho' was pleased with the progress, although he didn't always show it, afraid as he was in spoiling us. In all, there were only three scenes he found wanting, two of them — surprise, surprise! — starring Elvira Mendez, he ordered to be retaken. That infuriated Senorita Mendez, and their relationship was bound to descend into testy shouting matches again. Rumor had it that, having never been his choice, she had been forced upon him by a 'string puller' high up in the government.

My first scene to be rehearsed and shot was staged in the bowels of the freighter, which had superficially been converted by our carpenters and painters to look like those of a submarine. Senor Alarcon had purposely included this controversial sequence in his script to show, despite the brutal decision to torpedo the freighter, not all Germans were evil Nazis. That there was even such a specimen like a 'good German', albeit with qualifications. Caught in a heartbreaking moral dilemma, the sailor Kurt Muenzer, was forced to quash the pangs of conscience to raise the lever releasing the torpedo. Had he resisted, he'd have faced death.

As I received the makeup for the role of Kurt Muenzer, I insisted my facial appearance be modified, to be made as unrecognizable as possible. Although puzzled by my request, the makeup artists did follow through. In fact, they did such an excellent job that my colleagues hardly recognized me any more.

Playing such a dubious character whose good intentions were crushed by unscrupulous actions presented quite a challenge. But good old Stanislavsky helped me get on the right track. I began searching my past, conjuring up many similar situations I'd weathered during the war. I imagined my nerves to be visibly on edge. And when I finally raised the lever, I started to tremble like a poor fellow hit with the death penalty. All in all, I must have done quite well, during the rehearsal Senor Alarcon applauded me twice.

Yet the greatest challenge came later, when I clung to the life raft and begged to be saved from drowning. Senor Alarcon hadn't warned me for nothing. What made playing the part of the sailor particularly testing was the hazardous nature of the physical environment: The water was unusually chilly, especially for me who had to stay in almost an hour. Worse, it was covered with a thick film of crude oil and tons of flotsam — a soiled doll, a backgammon board, shreds of clothes, a simulation of dead bodies, a tattered swastika and big chunks of lumber. It was a harrowing experience. I didn't only get cold but soiled and grimy as well. My uniform looked like a bunch of oily rags. Crude oil mixed with salt water sloshed into my mouth, eyes, ears and hair.

Senor Alarcon further compounded things by frequently changing the camera setups. Although it added more spice and perspective to the scenes, it also dragged out the shooting. Luckily, once the life raft drifted away from the oil slick and the debris, things improved a bit, at least for me. As I was allowed to climb up the raft and join the survivors, I was able to breathe a sigh of relief and warm up, although only temporarily. Minutes later I was pushed overboard again.

At that point a dose of stark reality happened to elbow its way into our world of make-believe. While I was out there playacting of being harassed by fictional sharks, and desperately pleading for my life, a voice suddenly bellowed, "Live sharks! Live sharks!" It was Benito Levya who, playing the sailor's nemesis, was shouting and pointing out to sea.

Struck dumb, I — we all — quickly spotted, a mere twenty meters away, at least five iconic triangles of three razor-edged caudal fins slicing through the water. They scared me and everybody else out of our wits. Luckily all hands immediately reached out to pull me back into the raft. By then, Senor Alarcon had caught on as well, barking into the loudspeaker, "Watch out! Live sharks! Everybody give Fred a hand!"

Incidentally, next day we faced a similar predicament, as several sharks threateningly circled the raft. Worse, one was spotted only six meters away. Once again Senor Alarcon stopped the action, making us face another long delay. Sadly, we didn't get into the next scene until three fishermen showed up in a trawler and, dropping explosives, chased these man-eaters away.

Later on, in a twist of supreme irony, a school of *fictitious* sharks would finally get the better of me, tearing and ripping at my legs and body in a bloodcurdling feeding frenzy. A primeval (unscripted) scream rang out from my mouth, encapsulating the agony but also shaking the life rafters to the very marrow of their bones. Dripping with blood — buckets of tomato sauce and juice — and being in the throes of death, I was pulled into the raft again, where I was entrusted to Bluma Rubin's maternal solicitude. Miss Rubin began to hover over me as if I were her own son, smothering me with a zeal easily outshining what Senor Alarcon had in mind. She stanched the bleeding; she bandaged me with her own clothes; she made me drink and eat; she massaged my body. Yet it wasn't so much *what* she did, but *how* she went about, her bearing, her tender strokes and loving words. All of it had the whiff of a deeper, more personal involvement. Lest I be misunderstood, *fictitiously* her affection for the sailor made good sense after all, she would later marry him. But as things played out on the life raft, fiction had already mutated into reality. Miss Rubin had been usurped by Elvira Mendez, a most beguiling woman, and the sailor — by me. Yet, it looked somewhat odd when the mortally-ill patient I played would feel aroused by Miss Mendez's seductive charms, not least when she brushed her hand over my fly, as she'd repeatedly do. Let me just say, I was pleased Carolina wasn't present to witness these scenes.

Out on the water the shooting entered its final dramatic stage. As the raft drifted aimlessly in the shark-infested waters and a searing sun mercilessly scorched everything in sight, tensions rose to their highest

332

pitch, especially after Simon, the smallest of Bluma Rubin's boys died of exhaustion. Ben Levy, the most vocal of my nemeses, called again for tossing "that Nazi thug" overboard. But Miss Rubin zealously argued for my stay on humanitarian grounds and in the end was able to sway most of the others. Two days later, the survivors were miraculously rescued by a trawler manned by wholesome Mexican fishermen. They took everyone aboard — some, like me (Muenzer), had to be carried — giving us first aid, as well as feeding us. Eight hours later the trawler with the life raft in tow pulled into the harbor of Antoh Lizardo, a small fishing village some twenty-two kilometers south of Veracruz, where the families of the fishermen received us with open arms, treating us like relatives.

That pretty much ended the shooting at Veracruz, as well as my memorable stay at the unique Mocambo Hotel. The rest of the scenes were rehearsed and shot at various studios in el D.F. They mainly centered on the exemplary care the refugees, and also Muenzer, received from the doctors and nurses of the Mexican healthcare system. Thanks to them and to Bluma Rubin's passionate advocacy, Kurt Muenzer fully recuperated, albeit with the loss of his left leg.

As time went on, they would fall in love and marry half a year later. Playing the love scenes between Bluma Rubin and the sailor, Elvira Mendez kept forgetting herself, going overboard. She insisted on playing passionate love scenes under a close-up camera lens, going full throttle, lying there arm in arm, eyes closed, mouth to mouth, captivated by our ardor. Being her designated lover, I tried to curb her, following Senor Alarcon's directive that the entanglement should be more *suggestive* than acted out. But it was all in vain at least until Senor Alarcon began to intervene. "Please, Senorita Mendez, you have to restrain yourself. I want the audience…"

"Bunk! That's old-fashioned. Trust me, I've got some experience in things like that."

"I know you played some harlots, and very convincingly at that."

"Shame on you!" she snarled, giving him the finger. "You owe me an apology."

"You may whistle for it. That is if you actually can whistle."

"What a mean bastard you are," she hissed. She was so enraged that she grabbed the clapperboard and threw it at him. Luckily it fell short.

He just stood there, poised like a monk. "Can't whistle, can't throw. Can you do anything, Senorita Mendez? Let me stress again, your love scenes are far too explicit. I want passion in the way of hints. My goal is to fire up the imagination. I want the audience to yearn for more and never get enough. Is that understood?"

"You and your method stinks," Miss Mendez screeched. "You're a damn despot. You'd even forbid a nightingale to sing."

"Damn, I must have ruffled the feathers of a wounded peahen," he mumbled. Snickering, he picked up the clapperboard and handed it to the camera assistant. "We'll have to take these two love scenes over again. No backchat. I'm the boss!"

As shown in the last scenes, the plight of the refugees, their suffering, and miraculous rescue received widespread media coverage in Mexico, Latin America, as well as in the United States. That wasn't entirely lost on the Mexican politicians, particularly the president who, scenting the political usefulness, promptly invited all these refugees to a state dinner at the *Palacio National*. In a seminal speech honoring their tenacity, determination and resolve, the president particularly stressed Mexico's professed values, "its openness toward the world, its boundless generosity and its widely admired humanitarianism as second to none on the face of this earth. We are a beacon to all nations. A world in search of answers is coming to Mexico," he claimed, looking straight-faced into the camera.

Incidentally, once the shooting was completed, it was whispered that Senor Alarcon disliked, even loathed the last scenes that paid the homage to the Mexican government, and its president. He thought it would cheapen the message. Indeed, his first script didn't even include any of them. Apparently he was forced to add them after some nasty quid pro quo negotiations for the government's financial support. As Elvira Mendez confided in me, Joaquin Sandoval, a high government official, had Alarcon by the cojones.

MY RUN-IN WITH A CACTUS

I swear, it wasn't me who made the first move. It was none other than Elvira. Of course, I had been warned. Aside from her salacious moves during the raft scenes, she had consistently flattered me as being the "best looking and the most highly gifted actor" she'd ever met. To be brief, there was no doubt in my mind that she aimed for some sort of a courtship with me. Yet I always resisted. There was something about her that told me to be wary.

On the eve of the last shooting day in Santa Cruz, Senor Alarcon invited all the actors and staff to a final party. Antojitos were served. Cava flowed freely. Miss Mendez who had managed to take a seat right next to me, began showering me again with praise that made my head spin. We filled the evening mainly with drinking, eating and talking shop, rehashing the pivotal scenes. It was getting late. Saying she'd want to go to bed, she buzzed my cheek, then raised both her hands and drew an airy outline of a female figure. Accompanied by a wicked smile, she neatly pushed the lower half apart, ending her aerial painting with a reversed V. She accomplished it with such an aplomb, finesse and sleight of hand, we all broke out in applause.

Who could deny it, there was something sexy about her presentation but, frankly, I didn't know what to make of it. Well, I should soon find out.

Shortly past one a.m., I called it quits and made my way up to my room. When I entered, I noticed a waft of perfume coming at me. Turning on the light, I was startled. There was something stirring in my bed, under the sheets. Well, that something soon turned out to be none other than Elvira Mendez. "Finally, where have you been?" she cooed, accented by a throaty, arrhythmic scratch of sensuality. "I've been waiting for you. You know I adore you, Fred. I really do."

She grabbed the sheet and shouting, "Tada!" flung it off. There she sat, stripped to the buff, thighs wide open like a barn door, hands reaching out for me.

I just stood there, speechless, glaring at her. Her lips were slathered with a glowing red lipstick, simulating an unmistakable echo of her vagina.

335

"What's the matter?" she cajoled, jumping up and rushing toward me. "Come, join me. You are my lover now. Remember, we're newly-weds. Let's do it. This will be our wedding night."

She fiddled on my belt and tried to pull down my pants. I pushed her back. "How dare you getting into my room!" I remember shouting. "What has gotten into you! You must be crazy."

"Crazy?" She let out a scream as if Lucifer himself had raped her. "Come on, Fred, why don't you drop your bashfulness," she added, settling down on the bed again. "You're a passionate man. I want you to make love to me, now." She stroked her pelt.

"Get the fuck out of here!" I barked, leaping onto the bed in the hope of grabbing her. Yet she always managed to wriggle away, giggling in fits of infantile spasms. At last I was able to corner her in the bathroom.

"Come on, Elvira," I pleaded. "Let's be sensible. I want you to go back to your room."

"What do you mean?" she hissed. "I'm not leaving until you've made love to me."

"Sorry, Elvira, I can't. I can't get it up. Maybe another time. Let's go back to your room."

Shaking her head, she instantly switched her mood and started sobbing. "Listen, Fred, you must tell me that you love me."

"I *must*? What is this, Elvira?"

We just glared at each other. I felt very awkward. Chastened by pity, I finally hugged her, held her in my arms and kissed her cheeks and forehead. "Now I'll take you to bed," I whispered. "Promise that you'll be a good girl."

She whimpered and then burst into tears, whining, "Nobody loves me. I feel so lonely."

I wiped off her tears, put my arm around her shoulder and put her to bed. It was close to two in the morning. Elvira was still sobbing.

To celebrate the end of the shootings, Senor Alarcon invited all of us actors and the crews of designers and technicians, as well as some high government officials, to a final party at the fancy Hotel Majestic, located in the Historic District near the Zocalo. With spouses and partners we numbered more than a hundred sixty-nine people.

The party was a real Mexican *fiesta,* a gala affair. Choice five-course dinners with drinks were served by elegantly dressed male waiters. A band of traditionally clad mariachi musicians, equipped with violins, trumpets and guitars, played popular tunes, as a cheerful feast for the ears, as well as for dancing. Sitting not far from Senor Alarcon and his wife Artemisa, Carolina and I enjoyed ourselves immensely. We hardly missed a dance, unless we were invited by others, for instance Carolina by Senor Alarcon and I by none other than Elvira Mendez. She came in fine feather, sparkling in a daring, flesh-colored sequined gown with a see-through sections on her bosom, her thighs and her buttocks.

Actually she had tried to flirt with me from the start to the embarrassment of Joaquin Sandoval, a high government official, who courted her. From the first move she tried to ensnare me, snuggling up close, placing her head squarely on my chest right below my chin, wedging her thighs into my crotch and whispering flatteries about my looks and my dancing into my ears. She also reminded me of my promise I'd allegedly made to her during that memorable nocturnal encounter at the Mocambo.

Feeling watched, especially by Carolina, I tried to counter her moves, short of pushing her off and creating a scandal. It was embarrassing. I bitterly rued having bowed to her invitation. But to Carolina the whole scene was an unqualified provocation — the more so since she had long suspected us of having had a liaison.

"You are betraying me, I know," she hissed at me, when I came back to our table.

My plea that I was a victim of the starlet's sexual advances fell on deaf ears. "I don't have any feelings for her," I insisted. "I really don't." I was even tempted to tell her about my tete-a-tete with her on that ominous night, but then buckled, fearing she wouldn't believe me anyway.

"Oh, yes! Do you think I'm blind?" Carolina mocked. "You're nothing but a scoundrel. Dad was right, once a liar, always a liar. All I can say, you won't get away with that."

When we got back home, she pounced on me again, giving her wrath full rein. Calling me a pathological liar, she told me that she'd refuse to defile her bed with me. Arguing heatedly for more than two hours, I finally bowed, grabbed some bedding and scrambled to my study.

Starting a new day, I had hopes that my yielding would eventually bear fruit and make her calm down. But once again I had misjudged the depth of her anger and resentment. She avoided even looking at me, much less engaging some sort of dialogue. She left early, clapping spurs to her horse, and came back late, while I spent most of the day working in Aznar's garden, repairing water faucets and playing with Enrique. It was late in the day and, having taken a shower, I shuffled out of the bathroom. Still musing about Enrique, I was startled by some movement behind the curtain. Next thing I knew, Carolina, fire tongs in hands, came charging at me. Shouting,

"These are the pricks you dealt me!" she tried to ram a three-inch barrel cactus into my crotch. Luckily, I managed to intercept her halfway, avoiding the worst. Still, she got me where it hurt the most. Needless to say, it took me all night to pull the stings out of my penis, my scrotum and my thighs and stop the bleeding.

Even though the party marked the end of the film project, I still kept in touch with Senor Alarcon, whom I considered to be a mentor of sorts. I remember chatting with him two and a half weeks after the party. Sitting in the studio cafe over a glass of Rioja, I asked him when the cutting would be done and the movie hit the theaters.

"Oh, there's still a lot of work ahead of us," he said, sighing and taking a swig. "It takes a long time to edit the material, cutting it to make it flow and then adding the various sound effects. It'll take months before it's ready for a private showing and another two weeks before it's released for distribution to the cinemas."

"You know I have a family to feed," I said. "And I'm presently unemployed. I just wonder if there are any chances of auditioning for another role. Besides, I'm also a skillful carpenter. I was an apprentice in Switzerland. I could help build movie sets."

"Oh, I didn't know. I wish I could hire you, but my hands are tied. What we're doing is very technical work that requires a lot of experience. But I know several other film directors and producers and I could ask them if they could employ somebody like you. I mean short term as a carpenter, to tide you over. But for the longer haul, I would stay with acting. It pays much better and may also be more satisfying. You've got the talent. I have no doubt that as soon as they see you playing that sailor, you'll get some other offers. You just have to be patient. Actually there's a great demand for actors who can play German soldiers and officers right now. Maybe we'll even lose you to Hollywood."

He snickered.

"Thanks for the compliment but I'd rather stay here. Hollywood is not for me."

"Don't say that. You could become famous in no time. Their films are distributed all over the world. Besides, they can pay you much more than we can even dream of."

338

BUILDING TEMPLO MAYOR

A few days later, Senor Alarcon called me back. I was busy repairing a window for the Aznars. "Fred, I've got a job for you," he told me. "Unfortunately it's not in acting but working as a carpenter and possibly also helping as set designer. It's not at our studio either but at another on Avenida Hidalgo, not far from the Palacio de Bellas Artes."

He gave me the name of the director, the precise address of the studio and wished me good luck.

Less than an hour later I sat in a comfortable armchair and faced Senor Francisco Benavidez in his opulent office, which was almost as big as a ballroom. The senor was a corpulent, round-faced man in his sixties who gave the impression of a buttered undertaker hawking top of the line coffins. He sat there in his big armchair content and self-assured with cheeks so chubby I could hardly see his eyes, especially when he smiled, which he often did. When I mentioned my skill as a carpenter, he asked for references. I gave him Senor Rodriguez's phone number.

He added a rough sketch of the film project he was working on and promised to call me back. Well, by late afternoon I had a job. I rejoiced. It turned out to be very interesting and, besides being plentiful, it paid quite well — almost three times more than I made at Senor Rodriguez's carpinteria. My task was helping design and build a set of the Aztec capital Tenochtitlan for the production of *El Pacer de la Venganza (*Revenge Is Sweet), a historical film about the Aztec uprising appropriately called 'Noche Triste' in June 1520, when hundreds of Cortes's soldiers and thousands of his indigenous allies were ambushed and annihilated by the Aztec Army. Those still alive experienced the horror of being sacrificed to the god Huizilopochtli in a most gruesome fashion, ending up at the 'Hueyi Tzompantli', the great skull rack that the Aztecs erected to taunt their enemies and demonstrate to everyone the ruthless power of their empire.

Our task was to design and build a mockup of the *Templo Mayor,* the center of this expansive city, and its surrounding canals, bulwarks of reeds, willows and mud bricks, as well as their Golgotha, a massive platform with an intimidating scaffolding where thousands of skulls were impaled on horizontal crossbeams. They were delivered in big crates, loaned to Senor Benavidez by several museums and archeological sites. Struck by curiosity,

I grabbed a long-headed, slightly yellowed specimen. My assumption was that it originally sat on the torso of an unlucky Spanish POW who was caught by the Aztecs to be sacrificed. Holding it in my hands, I instantly felt an affinity with this poor soul, christening him Rodrigo who may have hailed from a small town in Andalucia. While I turned it and looked inside through the holes, I conjured up the terror he must have experienced while facing his executioners. Wrong place, wrong time, I concluded. *How lucky am I to be born so late! And having been captured by Americans instead of the Aztecs. Yet, even that turned out to be more dangerous than I could swallow.*

Knowing next to nothing about this strange tribe, I made my way to various libraries where I delved into books and articles describing the Aztecs. Most enlightening was the account of Bernal Diaz de Castillo, Cortes's chronicler, who'd seen their capital Tenochtitlan with his own eyes. In addition I also read some more modern, scholarly studies and depictions by historians and archeologists. I came away impressed by the ingenuity of their architecture, their temples and pyramids and the splendor of their city and civilization. Not only were they known for cultivating and irrigating the land, but they also invented a hieroglyphic writing and a complex calendar. At the same time, it was hard for me to stomach their bloodthirsty barbarism. I reluctantly agreed with Jorge who never grew tired of denouncing them as bloodthirsty savages, even cannibals who nonchalantly scarfed down the flesh and the thickened blood of their enemies.

VICTORY CELEBRATION

Closely watched by the scull of Rodrigo who sat on a book shelf nearby, I tried to catch up with perusing a whole stack of newspapers Jorge had brought over. As usual, I was particularly curious about the European theater of war and pretty soon I'd sifted out plenty of articles. To begin with, things couldn't have been much bleaker for Germany. The ill will we Germans had unleashed on the world was finally coming home, and with a vengeance. American, English and Canadian forces had already smashed their way across the Rhine and kept on moving east toward Berlin, while the Russians had taken Danzig and Vienna and were spearheading the push to the German capital from the east. The proud German Army, my former home, was beaten to pulp, disintegrating. The promise of the *Wunderwaffe* had dissipated in thin air. As swastikas were hastily buried or burned, the only flags people waved were those of surrender — white. Germany experienced a veritable whiteout, sparking a shortage of pillow cases and bed sheets, not to mention coffins, crosses and tombstones.

"Let's have a victory party," Jorge bellowed into the phone. "Germany has surrendered. I just heard it on the radio."

It was Wednesday, the 9th of May. I had just come back from a day's work at the set and, having cleaned myself, helped Carolina in the kitchen prepare supper.

"Are you sure?" I asked, benumbed.

Even though I had heard about the advances of the Russian and allied forces the past few days, I somehow couldn't conceive that the German Reich would cease to exist. Had not Hitler hammered into us that it would last a thousand years?

"Yes, dead sure! The agony has finally ended. It's *Goetterdaemmerung* in Berlin. Hitler is finally dead!"

"Is there proof?" I wanted to know, as if I didn't trust him. I even toyed with a possible resurrection, just in case.

"No, but I'm sure the Russians wouldn't take any chances, if that coward down in his bunker hadn't taken the poison."

An hour later, having handed Enrique over to Julia, we found ourselves in Jorge's kitchen waiting for the pop of the bubbly. But before we all lifted the glasses, Jorge pulled a photo of a swastika out of his desk, asked me to hold it up over the countertop, then struck a match and set it afire. Once the ashes had tumbled onto the countertop, he raised his glass and announced, "Let us all drink to the Judgment Day of the most heinous criminal enterprise the world has ever seen. This is a victory for all of humanity. I think it'll change the course of history. I'd say, dictators of Hitler's type will probably be a thing of the past."

"I toast to a new world order that'll be more just and peaceful," Carolina added, lending weight to her brother's words.

While I also clinked the glass and toasted to the defeat of our murderous regime and those noble ideals Jorge and Carolina had uttered, I tended to be more skeptical. Maybe the atrocious killings the Aztecs practiced were still too fresh in my mind. Nor did I trust the Russians, Stalin in particular, who had slaughtered millions of innocent people as well. *"Was he a figure of the past?"* I wondered.

Moreover, I worried about the future, particularly of Germany. I feared the conditions the Russians, the Brits and the Americans might impose on the Germans would be overly harsh, vengeful and lead to a lot of suffering. This had happened after the First World War causing great resentment, rancor and hatred that sowed the seeds for another war sometime in the future.

On a more personal level, however, I felt a little more cheerful. I nurtured the hope that now, with the end of hostilities, I might be able to relax a little more, that the Americans may also turn more lackadaisical in their effort to catch me.

Many of these worries and hopes came unbidden to my lips as we sat there bending elbows and talking our ears off. It was well into midnight, when Carolina got up and declared that she was pooped out and wanted to go home. Half an hour later we lay in bed.

While Carolina immediately dozed off, I had a hell of a time easing up. For me the day had been too tumultuous, too earth-shaking to be wrapped into pajamas and put to sleep. It simply wouldn't let go of me. As I meandered, thoughts about my own past during the Nazi years would bubble up and inundate my mind with countless memories, one more troubling than the other. It was a canker sore my memory's tongue kept touching. Looking back at myself I could only shake my head in wonder. Little did I know that everything in life had a price tag and that some things, including blitheness and happiness, may not be worth the price you pay for. Obviously for me it was the idea of freedom, choice, personal expression, with all its ramifications. I had none, at least until I came to America. Far worse, I didn't even *know* that I had none.

The Spaniards came to America in search of gold and riches. I was involuntarily shipped to this continent to find myself, the freedom to follow my own inclinations, to deviate from a dictated path, then make decisions according to my own wishes and desires and to take responsibility for them. True, it was awkward at first, and demanding. I had to adapt to a completely new outlook on life. Before it had been so easy; I simply woke up, dressed, ate and followed orders. All of a sudden I was offered a rich serving of options from which I had to choose, and also weigh my decisions. It took me a while to grasp the rules of the game. But once I'd made them my own, I never regretted it. Quite the contrary, I became a grateful convert, grabbing every opportunity I could.

MY DOPPELGÄNGER

Work made the rest of May slip past at a fast pace. At the beginning of June Senor Alarcon called to inform me that the editing had come along well and that the film, *They Came From Afar*, would be released no later than mid-July. He felt very good about it. The life raft scenes had come out especially well. He promised to inform me as soon as he knew the specifics.

Saturday, at the end of June, summer came sneaking in hot and dusty. Gobs of baroque clouds roiled the sky over Popo and the mountainous southeast for the second day in a row, although down here scarcely a drop had spotted the ground. But tomorrow it probably would, or so Fidel predicted, and he was known to have a sixth sense when it came to the weather. That sparked worries that our roof, a flat contraption, might not fulfill its promise and protect us from the rain, much less a downpour.

Carolina, together with Enrique and Julia, had gone to the market to buy fruits and vegetables. The house was simmering quiet. Only once in a while did I hear some grackles making wild whistle sounds, interspersed with strange clacks and abrupt *shrieks*. I was trying to concentrate on an article about the 'Hill of the Serpents', a sacred place in the mythology of the Aztecs, when the bell started ringing. It turned out to be Jorge. He waved a copy of the *Reforma* in his hand as he hustled up the stairs. After a short embrazo, he placed the paper on the breakfast table and, turning over the first page, pointed to a specific news story, captioned with 'American Scientist Unearths Striking Evidence'. "You have to read it," he said.

Attached was a photograph of the scientist. And, oddly enough, the face looked like — me. Little wonder. Below the picture appeared the name: Lars Stenson.

"Mierda!" I lashed out. "I can't believe it. I thought he was dead."

I was too shocked to read the whole scoop. But skipping over it, I quickly gathered that it was about the excavations in the back of the colonial building that covered the area where the famous Aztec Templo Mayor was located. It stated that Lars Stenson, a professor of archeology at the University of California, Los Angeles, working with a team of eight other archeologists reportedly found a pivotal block of volcanic rock where the victims were tied up by four Aztec warriors to be sacrificed to the god Huizilopochtli. Two obsidian knives which supposedly served as instruments to cut open the live bodies to tear out the hearts were also unearthed nearby.

"So he's very much alive, that Mr. Stenson," I said, grinding my teeth. "I had gotten so used to this name, I considered it my own. I thought I could keep it at least until 1948. But all that was little more than a pipe dream. *Dammit!* Regardless of the effort to gain some footing, it feels as if I'm always being pushed back to square one, to being illegitimate, a baseborn bastard."

"I'm sorry for giving you this article."

"Oh, no, I have to thank you for it. It may actually save my life."

When I later showed this scoop to Carolina, she reacted with sadness but did not linger there. "It's damn unfortunate," she said. "But you can't change it. Here is what I'd do. I'd take a deep breath or two and start thinking what my options are. Of course, you could just hold on to the Stenson passport. So what if there are two identical Stenson twins in el D.F.?"

"No way. It scares the shit out of me. It serves as an invitation to the Americans to get involved. They probably did already. I'm seriously thinking of getting another, a new identity."

"In that case, I'd go right away to Moritz Finkelstein and talk it over with him. He may be able to help. You've got to find a way out."

The bus ride to Churubusco would have been short and forgettable, had it not reminded me of my dilemma again. Indeed, it even had a face. It belonged to a cop who happened to be aboard, barely two rows behind me. I got spooked, frankly scared. *One careless step, one unlucky coincidence and you're in deep shit.*

Although nothing happened, the incident made me wonder how many — if any — rabbits I'd left in the hat that might save me if things really would turn sour. It wasn't until two stops later, as I watched the cop getting off the bus, when I was shocked to notice that the very incarnation of my angst wasn't even a cop, that he was none other than some uniformed official of the merchant marine. I had fooled myself, embarrassingly so. Far worse, I was afraid that the dark-colored glasses of my anxiety had already shaped my view of reality. *Welcome to a new world!*

The mansion lay dreamily in the haze like a bewitched castle somewhere in Spain. The path past the gate was hot and dusty. There was not the lightest breath in the air. I knocked on the door and, putting my ear to it, listened. Hearing footsteps, I stepped back. The door opened a tiny crack. *"Quien es ese?"* (Who is it?) a voice piped.

"Lars Stenson."

"Oh, Herr *Sten*son!" it chirped, as if pleasantly surprised. Opening the door, Moritz dealt me an unusually hearty handshake and bid me in. "Please sit down," he said in German with his peculiarly soft inflection, waving me over to the sofa. "Can I offer you something to drink?" he asked, while I made myself comfortable.

"How about that tasty Tequila reposado you served me last time."

"Oh, you know what's good."

Taking a seat in a threadbare armchair opposite me, he offered me the familiar form of address, the "Du." Over glasses of tequila we began to schmooze about us, our families, our work, about Europe and, last but not least, about the collapse of the Third Reich and, yes, the liberation of the concentration camps. Several times his voice, pummeled by emotions, wavered and broke, and he started to sob, at which time I tried to console him with hugs. Incidentally, I also mentioned my stint in acting, an activity he registered with great interest. One thing led to another, as though everything had become fluid. Floating on the wings of tequila reposado, we must have chatted for at least an hour before he had the courage to ask, almost apologetically, why I had come by to visit him in the first place. And if he could do anything for me.

So I began telling him about the unexpected appearance of the *real* Lars Stenson and, as a consequence, my vulnerabilities and the challenge lying ahead of me. "I wonder if you could help me."

"Well, I can, but I'm afraid it may not be enough for you." He took a sip of tequila, accompanied by sucking in his lips with great relish. "You see, it's very difficult to forge American passports. Don't get me wrong, it can be done, but chances are you might get caught, especially at larger border crossings where they can afford to hire wizards who know what to look for. I've been told some of them have once been forgers themselves, so they know the tricks and dodges of the trade."

"Well, how about a Mexican passport?"

"Now that's another chapter. They are much easier to forge, no question. It's still a lot of painstaking work, but, yes, I could forge one for you. I'd usually take 5,000 pesos but in your case 4,000 would do it."

"Sounds good. How long would it take?"

"Oh, I could do it in a week and a half, mas o menos. If you want me to, I could take some pictures right now."

"Yes, but I first have to decide how I want to look. Come to think of it, I'd feel more comfortable if the new passport picture deviated more from my present Lars Stenson look."

"Why would you want to do that? I'd be more than satisfied if I had a face like Stenson's and yours. You're a good-looking fellow. I don't want to insult you, but with your clear facial features, your straight nose, your chin, mouth, your eyebrows and the shock of blond hair, you look like an epitome of racial purity, a real Germanic hero. You could have posed for that sell-out Arno Breker."

"Racial purity? You're embarrassing me. But I know what I'm doing, believe me."

You Jews have always had a weakness for the blond and blue-eyed Germanic hero, I was about to pitch at him, but then held back.

Although I knew that Moritz was on my side, I still didn't feel like revealing to him that the files of the FBI and the Mexican judiciales had a warrant for my arrest showing the mugshot of that same 'Germanic hero' he was talking about.

"Well, you have to make up your mind. But whatever look you choose, I just want to let you know I'm at your service. By the way, you'll also have to come up with a new name, a place, a date of birth and your present height."

Two days later, I was back. I came as a heavily mustachioed gentleman whose darkened eyebrows and facial skin all but matched the tint of his chestnut-brown hair.

Moritz was flabbergasted. "You look dreadful, like a floozy Latin lover who hangs around with the harlots at that cafe near the Zocalo. Tell me, why did you do this to yourself?"

"Stop asking questions, Moritz. I have my reasons. Anyway, that's how I want my face to look like, period."

"I don't mind the mustache, but your hair looks like — excuse my words — the dried and fluffed-up dung of a Mexican burro whose choppers are grinding away on an old broom."

"You've a knack of being funny. OK, Moritz, that's enough. Let's get down to business. Why don't you grab your Leica and we'll get going."

Besides all the other disguises, I also came up with a new name for myself. For convenience's sake I kept my Christian name, Fred. Yet the Swedish Stenson I jettisoned for the Flemish 'de Keyser' whom, 208 centimeters tall and blue-eyed, I specified to be born on the 28th of September, 1924, in Ghent, Belgium. Incidentally, the signature I added showed the swing and flourish of several hours of intense practice.

Eight days later Moritz had completed the job. I invited him to come over to our apartment and he gladly accepted. I right away noticed he was not his usual self. His Yiddish spritz and wit were conspicuous by their absence. I suspected that he'd gotten some bad news from Elsie. Once I had introduced him to Carolina, we placed ourselves on our sofa. And over a savory meal of antojitos and beer, we took a look at my new passport. From all Carolina and I could tell, it was a well-crafted forgery with an authentic flair. The photograph, the various entries, the stamps and the signature, everything was in place, striking us like a well-edged copperplate. I was particularly pleased with the mugshot, which made me look much darker, swarthier, more Latin in appearance. Of course, that would also require me to resort to cosmetics, to pencil the arches of my brows, to dye my hair and my budding mustache. But so what? That was peanuts compared to the price of freedom, indeed, life itself.

Anyway, Moritz, Carolina and I lost no time clinking glasses to my new identity, the third to be exact, in the hope of fulfilling its promise to protect me. Merely holding the passport in my hands had a soothing effect on me. And Carolina chimed right in. Comparing it to her own, she claimed that it was looking just as authentic as hers. "I just wonder how long it'll work," she added. "I hope you won't need a new identity in a year or so."

"So do I. I know it's far from a being permanent solution."

"Well, it should last a few years," Moritz countered, "if you stay away from our northern border."

"While it's not perfect," I offered, "it beats any alternative I know of."

"True," Carolina joined in. "Still, it's only a part of making a clean slate. You also have to change the name on the various bills and the bank account."

"That's a good idea," Moritz said, twitching with his left eye. "Of course, you can do as you please, but I think it would be most sensible if you'd put all that under Carolina's name, as long as you trust each other."

"That's no problem. All I'd need is an access to the bank account."

"It just occurred to me," Carolina chipped in. "It might be a good idea to also inform Senor Alarcon about your name change 'cause they're about to print the posters and send out the press kits and advertising material for the movie."

"Thanks, I'll do that right away."

We still talked about Europe, the collapse of the Nazi empire and the concentration camps, until Moritz got up and said, "Forgive me but I can't hear it any more."

THE PREMIERE

It was an event we'd all awaited with great anticipation — the red-carpet premiere and the official release of the film to the public. True, we, the actors, actresses and technical support staff had already watched a sneak preview of it at the studio theater. Although that turned out to be a jaw-dropping experience, it was easily dwarfed by the first public showing. It was nothing less than the litmus test of the production itself, accompanied by press releases, invitations to film critics, journalists, art aficionados and prominent politicians.

Aware of the ramifications, we were unusually nervous when the day arrived. As we approached the theater, we actors and actresses were spotlighted at once. Photographers pounced on us from all sides. Everywhere flashbulbs popped, robbing us of our sight. I almost stumbled. Incidentally, Elvira Mendez was present as well but, mercifully, she wouldn't even deign to glance at, much less approach me.

Finally, Carolina and I were ushered into the fifth row. Being familiar with the sequences, I decided to pay less attention to the action on the screen than to the *re*action within the audience. So I mainly kept watching the people surrounding us, their faces and body language, in the hope of finding clues as to how they were affected by the action on the screen. Actually, I'd learned that from the old fox who'd always reminded us of the emotional impact of our performance, how it would come across to the audience.

Luckily, from the raising of the curtains, I was able to notice that the viewers were being gripped, emotionally drawn in by what they saw and heard. They empathized with the characters, identified with them. I fancied that their emotions ran through the whole gamut from the fear of death to the bliss of being in love. Starting with such scenes as the denial of entry into the United States, the suicide of a desperate passenger and the attack of the U-boat, I saw them suffering, wrinkling their foreheads, dropping their jaws, being aghast, gnashing their teeth or clawing them with their fingers. Then again, they also felt uplifted. I even registered smiles and chuckles, when the bevy in the life raft was rescued by the fishing trawler or when Kurt Muenzer and Bluma Rubin uttered their vows. The scenes of the wailing mother hugging and kissing her dying son and of the blood-soaked sailor who was pulled into the life raft, really hit home. When a great number of women kept rummaging their handkerchiefs out of their purses and dabbing their eyes, I knew we had done something right.

After the show, Senor Alarcon and all actors, actresses and members of the technical crew gathered in a reception room adjacent to the stage to mingle with a select crowd of movie critics, journalists, film buffs and government officials. It was part of a promotion to meet with them and answer question about the film, our roles and future careers. As expected, they also beleaguered me. I was shocked, however, that they all called me Senor Stenson. Somehow — horror of horrors! — my name change hadn't gotten through. That instantly soured my mood, the more so since the name Lars Stenson also glared at me from all posters and advertising fliers, as I was more than apt to notice on the way out. Bracing for trouble, I cursed Liliosa Flores, Senor Alarcon's secretary, for having failed to do her job.

Carolina was anxious as well. "It's your own fault," she scolded me. "You should have gone to the studio personally to insist that your new name be used on all the publications regarding the film. You should've demonstrated that more forcefully."

"Sure, but that's all hindsight."

Early next morning I immediately called Senor Alarcon's office. Another feminine voice, belonging to Ida Gallegos, was on the other end. "Could I talk to Liliosa Flores, please?" I asked.

"Sorry, she's in the hospital. She's very ill."

"Mierda!" it bounced off my tongue. Offering an apology, I tried to explain what had happened, that I had told Senora Flores in no uncertain terms to use only my *nome de plume* on all matters pertaining to the film. But Senorita Gallegos steadfastly claimed she didn't know a lick about it.

Pissed off, I hung up. Unfortunately that didn't make things easier. Heavyhearted, I dressed, put on my boots and made my way to the plaza, where I picked up a *Reforma,* a *La Cronica* and an *Excelsior* from a street vendor. I then placed myself on a bench and tried to leaf through them. I soon found what I'd been looking for — the film reviews. Luckily, it turned out that the papers were full of praise for the film, calling it a gripping emotional journey, an epic adventure across the ocean and the Gulf of Mexico, full of action but also heartbreaking moral questions. It represented in a nutshell the war itself: a profound human drama with all the brutality, the suffering, the injustices and the ethical dilemmas it conjures up. Furthermore, the papers likewise acclaimed the acting, especially that of the actors and actresses on the life raft and the struggle they had to endure during the shooting on water covered with crude oil, threatened by sharks. My own performance — I was called Fred Stenson! — was applauded as

350

having been the most difficult, yet also the most convincing. One paper, the *Reforma,* however, dared question the ending, insinuating that it was too rosy, indeed, kitschy. Besides being a slap in the face of the Americans, it catered too much to the Hollywood myth of the 'Happy End' and the glorification of the Mexican government as sole guarantor of universal values such as compassion, tolerance, brotherhood, love and the milk of human kindness.

I concede, I felt flattered. Yet the praise could not blow away the dark cloud that hovered over my head. I strongly suspected that Professor Stenson would somehow get wind of the fact that his name and identity had been usurpt by me. *Would he try to contact me personally and ask about my name, identity and my passport? Or would he, God forbid, go to the American embassy and let it investigate the matter? Had done so already?*

I leaned toward the latter. I had to, I couldn't afford to fail. As in the past, when a danger of that sort was about to threaten me, I talked things over with Carolina. She opted for keeping the Stenson passport for the foreseeable future.

"As I've said before," she added, "there are countless names that are shared with two or more people. The bigger the city, the more there are. That's common knowledge. Even a simple telephone book will bear that out. There are probably more than fifty Francisco Gomezes in el D.F. I'm sure Professor Stenson knows that too. That's why he'd never walk up to you and accuse you of having stolen his name. Doing so would be absurd."

"Yes, but you forget, he also lost his passport, that is, his identity."

"That may be so, but he doesn't know *you* have acquired it. And neither would the cops."

"That would be true if I were an average Joe with no record. Unfortunately, I don't have the luxury of such a standing. I'm no needle in the haystack any more. The judiciales have long had me in their crosshairs. They'd be all too happy if they could catch me on whatever grounds."

"Don't tell me you're about to be on the move again." Judging by the tone of her voice she oozed bile.

"Look, staying here is far too risky. The name Stenson would inevitably blow the whistle on me. You remember what happened when they raided the hacienda? They did it twice. That's how eager they were to catch me. They're out to milk the gringos of $10,000, for all I know. There's no reason to believe things are any different now."

"But what about me and Enrique?"

"Well, I'd continue to see you, but maybe not here and not as often. You could come to visit me, wherever I am."

"This is awful! It's the end of our family. I should really have listened to Dad," she said, breaking out into a sob. "He warned me of you. I might as well get a divorce."

"Carolina, please don't use that word so flippantly. We'll eventually find a solution we can both live with. But as for now it'd be unwise to stay here. It pains me to say that. I'm very sorry."

"How about Julia and Fidel. What…"

"You can tell them I was in need of a little space. No, better yet, that I'm on a new film project. Look, Carolina, I know you're upset. But put yourself in my boots. I'm scared. I wish things were otherwise, peaceful, normal. But they aren't. I can't sit here like a barnacle on a rock and wait for those jack-booted scoundrels to rumble up the stairs, put me in chains and haul me to Texas. Let's face it, you and Enrique would be hit hardest if they arrested and extradited me."

She turned away and spitefully shook her head. "I'll do what I have to do, but it may surprise you."

"Good gracious, Carolina, what do you want me to do? Jump off a cliff? Put a noose around my neck?"

I first had in mind moving out of el D.F. altogether, to Cuernavaca, San Miguel, or Puerto Vallarta perhaps. But it would have broken my heart to be so far removed from Carolina and Enrique. Nor would I have wanted to quit the well-paying job building the 'Templo Mayor' for Senor Benavidez's movie set. So having settled on staying here, I began perusing offers in the various papers in the hope of finding a furnished room or, better yet, a small apartment I could rent. For safety's sake, I had in mind moving a little away from San Angel, to get beyond the claws of the judiciales. I thought of the area of Condesa, Roma Sur or Roma Norte, located on the southeastern end of the Chapultepec Park. Since Senor Alarcon had paid me handsomely, the price wasn't much of an issue.

As luck would have it, I soon found several ads that appeared promising. I checked them out and eventually settled on a small two-room apartment on Avenida Acapulco in the Roma Norte district. Another incentive: It was no more than half an hour away from San Angel. Wary of leaving traces, I made sure to gather all my possessions, my clothes, shoes, my diaries, my horseshoe, my books, the skull and my toiletry and stash them in several suitcases. Once again, the parting was most heartbreaking, even though I'd be moving only few kilometers away.

Carolina started to sob, when I gave her my address, as well as the name and phone number of my landlady. "Rosa, Rosa Rodriguez, is a very sweet, considerate woman," I tried to soothe her. "You can call her any time. She doesn't mind. Quite the contrary, telephone calls fill her days. Besides gossip, that is. Now, when the cops are coming, you can tell them you've been estranged from me for some time and you don't know where I am. You could mention that I had at one time talked about a film project in Acapulco, just to throw them off the scent. It may yet take a few days but I'd bet they'll show up. Anyway, let's keep in touch."

As early as Monday evening, I had just come back from work, Rosa called on me to come down. My wife wanted to speak to me. Startled, I lost no time. "Carolina, what's the matter? Did they harass you *already?*"

"Yes, but not the cops. It was journalists from various papers and magazines. They wanted to take some pictures of Senor Stenson and talk to him about his performance in the movie. They also mentioned Elvira Mendez and asked me if you had an affair with her."

"How rude. How insulting. What did you tell them?"

"Well, I told them I didn't know. But they didn't believe me. They were very aggressive, obnoxious. When I told them you are not here, they acted as though I wasn't telling the truth. It was very frustrating. They behaved like pit bulls, I simply couldn't shake them off. They didn't leave until I threatened to call the cops."

"The cops! Of all people! Are you out of your mind?"

"Well, who else?"

"Tell me, when are you coming over to visit me? I miss you, Enrique, and also Jorge."

"Well how about Saturday afternoon or evening? Would six o'clock be a good time?"

"Perfect! Just bring yourself and a good mood. But please do me a favor: keep looking back to make sure nobody's following you. They are a sneaky lot."

SACKCLOTH AND ASHES

Curious about the various comments about our movie but also about the developments in Europe, I had gradually turned into an avid reader of newspapers and weekly magazines. Every day after my eight hour schedule I would stop at an indigenous vendor who sat on packets and pick up several of them, and when I got back to my apartment I'd start leafing through and reading those articles that sparked my interest. Among them were of course comments about our movie. Although the warm showers of praise published right after the premiere had ebbed somewhat, they continued particularly in the letters to the editor and in the magazines. Some viewers wrote that they had never seen a more heartbreaking presentation of the suffering of the European refugees. My part, most notably the last stretch in the life raft, also received measured applause as well, much more than I had ever dreamed of. They found it gripping and captivating beyond words: that's why the unscripted 'scream' I spontaneously belted out appeared so timely and effective. It invited comparisons to the paintings of Edvard Munch I'd never seen.

All that was music to my ears, and I began cutting out many of those favorable articles. I collected them in a pile, and every once in a while, I grabbed one and bathed myself in the bubble bath of praise, especially when I felt down, which happened more often than I was ready to admit.

Naturally, I also came across articles that were anything but uplifting. They dealt with my home country, most pointedly with the concentration camps the allied soldiers had recently liberated. Many came with stark, gruesome pictures, showing detailed photographs of the gassing of Jews, men, women and children, whose numbers were staggering. According to reliable sources thousands, even millions were killed in cold blood, using modern, mechanical means. They brought to mind the true horror of the Nazi regime. The barbarism and brutality was beyond description. The fate of Moritz Finkelstein's relatives came to mind, as well as Senor Alarcon's fictional account of the refugees in our movie, which was based on facts as well.

While reading an article on the atrocities in Auschwitz, particularly the diabolic practice of turning human bones into soap, I was so touched that I got terribly nauseated. My bowels began to burn with the acid of guilt.

Unable to continue, I headed to Chapultepec Park for a long walk. That helped a little. Unfortunately, as I made my way back the nausea returned, this time stoked by a feeling of personal guilt, with disgrace and shame hobbling in its wake. It would haunt me that very night, robbing me of my sleep. Long buried images of Ukrainian Jews herded together by SS troops sprung back to life tormenting me. One angst-ridden Jewish woman with her tot, reaching out her hand and pleading for help as she tottered past struck my mind's eye, followed by other gruesome images in which hundreds of them were just shot in cold blood, defenseless, innocent people. We just stood there and watched the dreadful massacre, devoid of any feelings, as though this was part of the war. I'm deeply ashamed to say that a good number of us, including me, didn't even look upon them as humans. For us they were just vermin, roaches that deserved their lot.

Although this butchery was years away, its images haunted me; they screamed at me, especially at night. I simply couldn't shake them off. Like a thick-coiled whiplash they'd always come back from the pool of memory, sometimes washed-out, like shadowy apparitions. Nor could I comprehend my lack of feelings, my sociopathic bent, short of blaming them on the flawless brainwashing techniques of the Nazis that succeeded in molding an uncivilized mob of hellbent fanatics out of the clay of ordinary youngsters.

I was as chained to my guilt as a watchdog to his farmstead. And when Carolina and Jorge came on their first visit, they noticed right away that something was awry.

"You look sickly," Carolina observed after we had embraced. "Your face is pale, ashen."

"Are you sure you don't bleed grey when you nick yourself with the razor?" Jorge commented.

"Not yet, but who knows, it may still come to that."

I told them what I'd read, referring to the atrocities in the German concentration camps without concealing my own culpability. While they did not absolve me, they hastened to point out that the leaders of Nazi Germany, indeed, Germany and the German people as a whole, were accountable for the horror they had created.

"I've read somewhere that the allies will stage a big trial very soon," Jorge added, taking a swig of red Tomas. "And, judging by the general climate, I'm almost certain they'll handle those Nazi bigwigs with sturdy, old hemp ropes rather than kid gloves. By the way, how old were you when you volunteered for the German Army? I just wondered."

"Seventeen."

"Only seventeen? You were still a teenager. At that age your brain isn't even fully developed. I know I did all kinds of stupid things when I was seventeen. We all do. I remember getting damn close to shooting a friend who ran off with my girlfriend."

Carolina agreed. "It pains me to say it, but as hellish and abominable as these killings in the concentration camps and the war were, they are now past, a part of history that cannot be changed. We cannot bring back one single victim. All we can do is to keep remembering and fighting for a more humane and civilized world."

"That's right," Jorge chimed in. "While I understand your guilt feelings, I'd say you're a bit too harsh on yourself. As one of the commentators said, all we can do is to honor those innocent people who perished as martyrs for a better, more just and peaceful world in the future. It is upon us to show the world in words, pictures and monuments the face of these unspeakable atrocities the Nazis committed, all with the determination that they'll never happen again."

Hearing all that made me feel a little more levelheaded, calmer. The gulps of red Tomas may have helped as well, as did the subsequent conversation about the movie, particularly Jorge's praise of my performance.

I had decked out my dining table with savory antojitos I had picked up at a small restaurant nearby. We all snacked and guzzled wine or beer.

"By the way, I almost forgot," Jorge added after a while. "I found a short article in the *Reforma* which is very much related to your own experiences." He pulled a clip out of his briefcase that was titled, "Execution of German POWs in the United States."

I couldn't believe my eyes, when I read it. It stated that according to The New York Times altogether fourteen German POWs had been hanged by the American Army for murders they had committed in 1943 and 1944. The executions had been carried out on temporary gallows in Fort Leavenworth, Kansas, after a court-marshal found these Nazi zealots guilty of having murdered their own German inmates. These legal actions had been delayed because of possible retaliations by Germany. Among the names I also found four from the camp in Murphy: Sgt. Hans Henkel, Col. Horst von Wiese, Lt. Ludwig Spaeth and Lt. Ernst Borchart.

"Wow!" I commented. "Justice at last. The Americans are not shilly-shallying."

Capt. Shepherd had done his job, I concluded. Although a bit drastic, it was gratifying to hear that Peter was avenged at last. I felt as if a painful chapter had finally been closed.

In the aftermath, we continued to chew the fat and delighted in watching Enrique who repeatedly got up all by himself, stood there near the table for two or three seconds, and then tipped over and fell down again. He must have done that at least eight times. As far as I could tell it was his first major lesson in life — losing his balance and falling but also getting up again. What encouraged me was his pluck to always scramble up, yet even more the *way* he did it. As soon as he got on his feet again he'd spread his arms, look around and smile, as though telling the world, "Look what I can do!" Incidentally, Carolina let me know later that she used to act the same way when she was a baby. At least, that's what her mother told her. I thought about my own past. *Where was Emma Burgdorf?* I had so many questions.

THE HUNT IS ON

Early afternoon, shortly past two, dark clouds, reminding me of braids of steel wool, began to roil into the valley from the west. Together with two helpers, I was busy building a retaining wall between a canal and a pathway running along the 'Templo Mayor' when our secretary informed me of a phone call. "It's Carolina, your wife. She says, it's something urgent."

I rushed to the office.

"Fred, I had to call you," I heard Carolina in a high-pitched voice. "They've just left. The judiciales. Two of them. It was something!" She was flustered, in a tizzy, her words clawing for air as if they were choking.

"Damn! Listen, Carolina, I can't talk. I'm in the office here. Could you come to my place at, let's say, five thirty? Oh, sorry, I take it back. It may be too risky. They might follow you."

"I never thought about it."

"Why don't we meet at El Popular, close to the Zocalo? But don't forget to look over your shoulder every once in a while. I don't trust them; they might well be following you."

I was struck dumb. *They've got me in the crosshairs again,* a homunculus inside me hissed, as I walked back to the work site. Site, yes. But work? Only for the looks of it. I was out of it, body and soul. Stark images of my stint in the Chihuahua jail began haunting me. I don't even remember how I made my way to El Popular. I only recall it had in the meantime come down in buckets, that there were huge puddles all over and Carolina was already waiting in the doorway. She appeared tense, worried. I looked over my shoulder. I strained but detected nothing suspicious. We hugged, kissed and shuffled in. The air was thick with tobacco smoke and human ferment. We took a table in the left hand corner. There was a small window which was cracked open to let some air in. This was direly needed because at the next table three older gentlemen puffed unfiltered *Delicados* with abandon. The chairs, quite frankly, could have been more comfortable as well, but the atmosphere calmed me. I particularly treasured the stark anonymity of the place. People came and went, like passengers at a bus station.

"So tell me, what happened?" I pressed. "You said there were two. Were they armed?"

The waiter, thin as a rake, wrapped in a soiled white jacket, asked in English what we wanted. We ordered two cafes con leche.

"The judiciales, were they armed?" I heard myself coming back.

"Not that I could see."

"Of course, they usually turn up in plain clothes and conceal their weapons."

"Anyway, they asked to speak to my husband, Lars Stenson. They were gruff, and Enrique, whom I'd picked up, started shrieking as if poked with a knife. That tamed them a little."

"Smart of you. Kudos for Enrique! So what did you tell them?"

"Stop being so pushy! Anyway, I told them you're a movie actor and Lars Stenson is just a professional *seudonimo* you're using and that you're working in Acapulco on a new movie."

"Good girl."

"Woman, please! That seemed to confuse them. 'On a new movie?' they asked in disbelief. They wanted to know what your real name was and where exactly and in what kind of film you were playing. Well, I gave them your real name, Fred de Keyser, and pleaded ignorance to the rest of the questions. Before I forget, they also asked me if you had a passport under that name. I told them that I didn't know, but you had talked about going to Cuba and asked if one needed a passport to enter that country.

"They looked frustrated, insisting that you must be in possession of a stolen passport that belonged to Lars Stenson, an American professor. While one of them started searching the place, turning everything upside down, the other stayed with me. As he questioned me about your name, he hinted that officials at the American embassy are demanding to clear up the matter. He also mentioned that they had a couple of other important questions. They referred to your status of a POW, your escape from the camp and the killing of an agent of the Border Patrol, calling you a fugitive of justice in the United States."

"So they are informed about my past. Funny, I had an inkling of that. If anything, this shows it's the Americans, the embassy and Hoover's lackeys, who are pushing the judiciales. Regardless, they're going to be on my tail. And I was so naive to believe the war had laid all that to rest. So much for calling me paranoid."

Carolina just pursed her lips and sat there benumbed.

"Was there anything else they said or did?" I was curious to know.

"Well, yes. When the other fellow came back from his search, he insisted that you appear at their office to answer all these questions, or else they'll have to come after you with the full force available."

"So they invited me to hang myself. Well, I'm not quite ready yet. They'll have to get me. Actually, what saved me so far in their inexhaustible incompetence, the lackadaisical attitude toward their job. In any other country they'd have long nabbed me. Still, it would be foolish to rely on it. Which raises another question: How safe am I in my present apartment here on Avenida Acapulco? They may not have figured out as yet where I'm hiding. But one day they'll stumble on this place too. The anonymity I originally hoped to find here had vanished. There is no safety any more. To tell you the truth, I've been thinking of moving out of el D.F. altogether. How would you feel about that? We could perhaps rent a house in Puerto Vallarta or San Miguel. Money shouldn't be a problem. I just read an article that referred to some seismologists who claim a devastating temblor is long overdue and may hit el D.F. any time."

"Oh, they always say that. But move again? I'm so tired of hopping from one place to the next. I've gotten so used to being here in San Angel with Julia and Fidel. They're like parents to me, and also to Enrique, especially Enrique. I'm part of two reading circles. Jorge is close. And the city offers us a rich cultural menu, music, art, dance, museums. There are so many things going on you wouldn't have the time to take all of them in."

"Yes, that's all true. But what if the judiciales were to catch up with me? I still have nightmares going back to that Chihuahua hellhole."

Carolina shook her head and sighed. "Well, I'd hate to leave. But I also see your point. If we can't find a different solution, San Miguel would be the place. I've been there twice, maybe five or six years ago, and I must say I kind of liked it. It's a very picturesque colonial town on the hillside. There are lots of beautiful historical buildings, churches, quaint cobbled streets, and lively plazas. It's small, a bit confining, but it has a stimulating, almost international atmosphere. Many artists and writers from all over have settled there. The climate is very pleasant, cool nights, warm and sunny days with low humidity. It's about the best in all of Mexico."

"And it's got clean air. We have a guy at work who calls it his home. He praises it to heaven. Almost every weekend he heads back. He says it takes him a little more than three hours by car. And it's supposed to be a very delightful drive, once you get out of the city. He has invited me several times to come along. Unfortunately his parents have only a small house but he could recommend a nice hotel where we could stay."

"I believe all he says. Of course, compared to el D.F. San Miguel's still very small and, frankly, a little provincial."

"But that could have its charms, too. I wonder if we should give it a try one of these weekends."

"I wouldn't mind. We could ask Julia to look after Enrique. She'd be delighted."

MY CAREER TAKES OFF

"I'm glad I caught up with you," he said. "You're so hard to get hold of. Anyway, I have some good news for you. I wanted to ask you, would you be interested in playing a part in a new film project I'm about to get funded. This time it would be a Jewish immigrant by the name of Ignatz. It's a big role which would require a total commitment on your part."

"Very much so, Senor Alarcon. Of course I'd like to know more about it. Could I drop by your office? How about Saturday morning?"

"Sorry I can't. Could I perhaps invite you to dinner at the Bar La Opera on Friday night at seven? Your lovely wife could join us, too. I'd bring along the rough script and we could discuss the plot and Boris's part."

"Sure, I'd be delighted. And I'm almost certain Carolina can join us as well. If she can't, I'll call you."

Although I had heard of the Bar La Opera, I had never visited it. Located in the Historic Center, it was supposed to be one of the most lavish, opulent restaurants in all of Mexico, even more so than the Cafe Tacuba. Carolina had been there a couple of times, way back when she was a student.

Senor Alarcon arrived ten minutes late, but with a credible apology. He was in good spirits and, as always, intuitive, perceptive and unsentimentally witty. A master of grasping an incident, he cherished the habit of tossing each word up into the air, then adding spins, twirls, and velocity to hit a target. When he was in an upbeat mood, his syllables were puffy and muffled as though coated with tufts of felt.

"By the way, 'They Came From Afar' is doing exceptionally well at the box office," he started off. "It's beating all expectations, here and internationally. The American, French and even German adaptations will come out in the next few months. We should soon get some prizes too." And, turning to me, he added, "I thank you again for doing such a good job. I don't think we would have had such a success without your contribution."

"Well, thank you. It's your coaching that did it. I'm not kidding."

"You're flattering me. Sure, I may have helped you a little here and there. Actually you don't need much coaching 'cause you're a natural actor. I noticed that right at the beginning when you auditioned."

Even before the drinks came, the old fox had delved into his new film project whose provisional title was *Dulces y Aji rojo,*(Sweets and Red Chili). "I'm still in the process of writing the script," he said. "All the characters are in place and so is the plot."

Giving me an outline, he invited me to play the part of a Jewish psychology professor who'd fled Austria before the German takeover. While vacationing in Veracruz, Ignatz Cornfield meets Carlos who comes from a well-to-do Mexican family. Both are in different vessels out on the bay, when they're ambushed by rough weather. Carlos and his woman friend capsize and go overboard in shark-infested waters. Watching a tragedy in the making, Ignatz jumps in and manages to save Carlos's life. Later they toast to everlasting friendship.

Once back home in Mexico City they eventually become more and more aware of their unbridgeable philosophical and political differences. Having been fired from his job at a bank, Carlos is losing his mooring. He falls under the wings of Alfonso Herrera, a famous sculptor and communist zealot, and becomes radicalized. He joins a revolutionary movement whose final goal is to topple the Mexican government and replace it with a Stalinist dictatorship, ready to blaze a path to a just, utopian society.

Ignatz's efforts, meanwhile, center on drawing Carlos away from his ideological addiction by involving him in the pleasures of life. He introduces him to rousing women, to the arts, to boating trips and various sports activities. And at times Ignatz comes close to loosening the stranglehold the communist dogma has on his friend. But in the end Carlos falls back again. Together with other zealots, he is caught up in an assault on the presidential palace where he is fatally wounded in a shootout with police. Ignatz visits him on his deathbed in a touching, heartrending scene where he comes close to admitting that he had thrown away his life.

"It's a very contemporary theme," I commented. "Especially for Mexico."

"That's exactly the point," he replied. "It's a mirror of the madness that happens right under our noses. I'm thinking of the leftwing circles of artists surrounding Diego Rivera and Frida Kahlo, or, worse, other Stalinist ideologues such as Siqueiros, the famous sculptor, who attempted to assassinate Trotsky. They're all looking upon reality as a baroque opera conducted by none other than Joseph Stalin. That's Mexico in the 40s. Never mind the bloodshed and the dead bodies. In the end it's always the grand gesture that counts. In any event, I'll try my best to shed some light on those true believers. But I concede it's damned hard to keep pace with reality because it may well have turned into romantic fiction already."

"You have a point," Carolina cut in. "But wouldn't we need a revolution to lift workers, poor people, most of them indigenas, out of poverty? Our present government is anything but democratic. It's in the hands of oligarchs and their supporters who uses it for corrupt and selfish purposes."

"Of course, you're right, Carolina. But let me ask you: How are we going to change that? Would a revolution help set things right? I haven't seen the slightest evidence of that. We've had so many of them right here in our own backyard and look what we've got. The gap between rich and poor is wider than ever. The word revolution has been degraded to a cheap slogan. It sounds hopeful and brings virtually nothing. Remember we are in Mexico. We've always been good at romantic visions, yet utterly incapable of realizing them. Unlike the gringos, our northern neighbors. They've had only one revolution and yet they have the highest standard of living in the world. Every American breezes around in his own car. How did that come about? Well, they did it by rolling up their sleeves and doing the unromantic, nitty-gritty work of governing. That's how they have accomplished already what others can only dream of. Imagine Pancho Villa, one of our greatest and most admired heroes, chucking away his pistols and women and sitting down at a desk to write a good law or crunch numbers to figure out a fair government budget!"

He took a swig of wine and then barreled on. "And compare the *Estados Unidos* to Stalin's Russia, the model of our rabble-rousers. Even though they've won the war, they're still stuck in the mud. The deeper they sink in, the more they dream of a communist utopia, the classless society that's supposed to hover somewhere on the horizon. Of course, the horizon, being what it is, recedes with each step we take toward it.

"If you want my opinion, it's nothing but a brain child of depravity. Who'd want to live in such a utopia anyway? The suicide rate would skyrocket. Or we'd all die of boredom. And yet our artists and intellectuals keep propagating it as our great model. It's Absurdistan, that's what Ignatz calls it! And he should know. Quite frankly, if I didn't like some of their art, especially Rivera's, and have such deep empathy for Frida Kahlo, I'd be tempted to call them a bunch of spoiled brats who wear the communist garb because they want to show the world they are 'engaged' and have a heart for the poor. Doesn't that sound wonderful? Yet, while espousing stuff like that, these armchair communists keep on living high on the hog, showing off their mansions, munching on lobsters and steaks, partying and living like there is no tomorrow."

Senor Alarcon was in full swing. He almost forgot to tend to his fish a la veracruzana. "Forgive me, but I had to get it out. Anyway, let's get back to our project. He pulled out a provisional script and handed it to me. "OK, Fred, I expect you to play the role of charmer and tempter for a life full of adventure, of sensuality, intellectual curiosity, play and gregariousness, with all the ups and downs that come with it. After all, isn't it true that the sweetest, most aromatic honey is the one you're licking off the spines of a cactus?"

"Thanks," I said, glancing at the script. "I'm curious, when do you think you'll start with the rehearsals and the shooting?"

"Fair question. As you'll see, the actions require us to move around in many different locations. That's always cumbersome and takes time. I would say November, December and January. But don't hold me to it."

OFF TO SAN MIGUEL

"I want to thank you for hiring me when I needed it most," I told Senor Benavidez, "but Senor Alarcon has just offered me an acting engagement that'll keep me very busy. I have to move on."

He was very poised.

"I'm sorry to hear that," he said, puffing away at his cigar. "You've been a valued employee. We all appreciated your dedication and your craftsmanship. We'll miss you. I wish you good luck. Give my regards to Senor Alarcon."

It was a brazenly sunny and clear afternoon when we headed to San Miguel with Emiliano at the steering wheel. He was alert and twitchy like a young chipmunk, which was an asset on the streets of the city. But once we had left the shanty towns behind us and hit the highway, it turned into a handicap. Suffice it to say, the ride would have been considerably more enjoyable had Emiliano in his youthful lightheartedness not insisted on proving he could cover the distance in record time. It wasn't so much that I felt unsafe, I was afraid the tamarindos, the traffic police, might stop and search us. Although I had my new passport with me, it had become a habit of mine to stay away from cops as much as possible.

Thanks to the monsoon rains, the landscape had shed its tawny color and displayed a lush green which zipped past us like a ribbon suspended by a stiff breeze. Occasionally, when Emiliano had to slow down, hills brightened with wildflowers flashing their color. Before we knew it we zigzagged through Queretaro, a veritable jewel of a town, and wended our way to San Miguel de Allende, whose outskirts — it hurt me to say — looked cheerless at best. We encountered nothing but gas stations and scruffy clusters of dwellings, mere cement or adobe cubes with tin roofs, surrounded by dusty yards filled with car wrecks and other junk. Fortunately, that soon changed for the better. As we twisted and turned toward the center, the town began to fully unfold its colonial charm.

Emiliano had recommended the Hotel Ambos Mundos, which originally was an old hacienda, located within easy walking distance from the *Jardin,* the main plaza. Having signed up for a room and dropped our luggage, we ate a light supper at the cavernous dinette prepared by an indigena. Next we sauntered through the heart of the town which reminded me of hill towns in Italy I'd seen in picture books. Its peculiar charm came from its smallness. While Carolina found it a bit stuffy, it instilled in me a feeling of protection, security and worn, faded beauty. Aged, often colorful walls of handsome buildings rose from narrow sidewalks that were barely wide enough for one person. Everywhere we stumbled upon open doorways offering glimpses of dulces, accompanied by the fragrance of baking goods, or a profusion of colorful clothing and Indian crafts, woven baskets, rugs, ceramic figurines. Some open doors let us peer into courtyard gardens filled with luxurious tropical plants. The plazas were crowded with tourists and mothers tending their children, as well as elderly gentlemen who whiled away their afternoons. We were astonished seeing such a density of churches, which made us wonder if the residents were more pious than elsewhere.

Trying to find a scenic outlook, we ventured up small dirt roads that dissolved into the hillside. "This is the prettiest town in Mexico I've been to," I told Carolina as we paused to get a bird's eye view of the town and the surrounding area. "I could well imagine living here."

"Quite frankly, it's a little too small for me, too hemmed in. And there are too many tourists, especially Americans. Still, I think I could get used to it. I like the fact that everything is so accessible. You wouldn't have to hop on those dirty buses. You could do all your errands on foot."

"And isn't the air heavenly?"

Yet it was more than the air that made me sleep like a marmot. I chalked it up to feeling safer — almost as safe as during my first few months at the hacienda.

Next morning, after breakfast in the cozy dining room, I persuaded Carolina to pay a visit to a real estate office. We were received with free coffee and dulces by an unctuous young man with the name of Alfredo. "It's an excellent time to buy," he beguiled us, smiling like a saphead. "There's a huge economic boom just around the corner, now that the war has ended. Peace'll make everything bloom."

Listening to our preferences, he showed us pictures of several homes that had, "Hit the market only yesterday." Among them were two *gemas* (gems) he urged us to take a look at. "They'll sell like hotcakes," he claimed. Both came at a hefty price tag, rousing my frugal bent which had always served me so well. One 'hotcake' happened to be located on the northwestern side beyond the Arroyo de la Fabrica, while the other sat way up on the hill to the south, where the town grinds its way into raw nature.

Having nodded interest, we squeezed into Alfredo's truck cab and first rattled up the cobbles toward the southeastern hill where the road from Queretaro snakes in. Turning in toward the west, we finally crunched to a halt in front of a brown-stuccoed, one-story house nestling on a steep hillside. It faced southwest, looking down on the rooftops of the town and well beyond. Although we found the layout attractive and the location nothing short of spectacular, the structure itself made us raise a few tricky questions. What if a vicious rain storm or, God forbid, a temblor were to strike? Would such a fancy swallow's nest not simply lose its footing and slide down the hill? These were legitimate concerns, and we didn't hold ourselves back.

Alfredo chuckled. "You don't have to worry. That's all taken care of. The home sits on solid cement pylons that are deeply embedded in the hillside. Trust me, it's as safe as the pyramids in Tenochtitlan."

When we questioned the safety of the pyramids, Alfredo got our message. So we turned around and headed downhill again, this time toward the northwest, the opposite direction. Going west on Calzada de la Luz, the town gradually turned fluffier and more rural, particularly as we crossed the arroyo. After taking some sharp turns, we clattered up a gravel road.

"This is the one," Alfredo suddenly announced, pointing to a ranch house looming in the background, partially disguised by trees and brushwork. We grated to a halt just in front of the gate, amid billows of dust. Alfredo opened the gate and we followed him along a broad path that curved to the house. As we approached the big withered mesquite door, he fished out his keys and we entered. A musty smell strafed our nostrils. We stood in a hallway which, as Alfredo explained, led straight south to a patio door. To the left there was a sizable kitchen with an island in the middle. To the right a large dining room opened up. Adjacent to the south, close to the kitchen, a large living room aroused our attention. Following that were three bedrooms, the spacious one for the master and the two much smaller ones for kids and guests. They were accommodated in a pair of wings that jutted out into the large backyard, making room for a spacious, partially roofed patio in between. All rooms, save for the kitchen, were equipped with wide-board pinewood floors.

Everything seemed to be in good shape, including the lush patio which was dominated by a luxurious bougainvillea scaling the left, eastern flank way up to the roof and by other tropical plants, including a papaya and jacaranda tree, some of which drooped, apparently thirsting for water. Sauntering through the patio past the two bedroom wings, we let our eyes sweep across the lawn-covered backyard reigned by a huge, disheveled avocado tree.

"Carolina, look at that," I said, pointing to the horse stable, which stood close to the neighbor's fence.

"It's big enough for two horses," Alfredo remarked. We walked over and checked it out.

As we shuffled back, Alfredo stopped at a door not far from the kitchen entrance. "I almost forgot to mention that the home also comes with a small wine cellar. This allows you to store your wines, beers, tequilas, but also many perishable items such as fruits and vegetables at cool temperatures. Would you like to see it?"

"Of course!" I remembered saying.

He opened the door and turned on the light. We looked down a steep cement staircase twisting sharply to the right. "Watch your step," he warned us.

We slowly stepped down. A moldy, fungoid air, filled with swirling motes of dust enveloped us. We came to a spacious vestibule with three doors ajar. We stepped into one. Straight ahead an empty wooden storage bin covered the wall. On the right a small window filtered in a trifling of light.

"Un poco frio," Alfredo commented. "That's where the Villareals kept their wines and liqueurs. I heard they were quite some connoisseurs."

"Good for them," I said.

"There are several mansions in town equipped with tunnels that are running hundreds of meters to known safe zones," he went on. "That's how the rich families escaped with their money and jewelry during the revolution. Maybe with something even more precious — their own lives."

That pricked my ears!

When we descended into our Moloch on Sunday night, smelled the foul air again, saw the filth and decay and encountered the hoards of beggars, we were more than ready to drop the endless ifs and buts and cut the cord. We resolved to return to San Miguel, buy a home, pack our belongings and permanently move and settle there. To that end, we also decided to buy a car, an eight-cylinder 1941 Chrysler Town and Country Station Wagon one of Jorge's acquaintances wanted to dispose of. Although used, it was in excellent shape, almost new, and its bulging grille, its dark-brown color and attractive woodgrain paneling along its sides and tailgate added a rural ranch-like quality to it. Carolina instantly fell for it, praising its overall looks, its quiet but potent eight-cylinder engine and its spacious and sumptuous interior, awash in leather and wood.

"I hope I can show it to my dad one of these days," she said. "It's much more practical than his Dodge, which I think he once picked simply because Pancho Villa owned one like it."

"I could have guessed it," I quickly added.

Our new acquisition called on me to get a driver's license. But visiting a public office of that kind always made me feel uneasy even though I had my ways of hiding it. So I grabbed my passport, several pictures Moritz Finkelstein had made of me and headed to the Department of Motor Vehicles. Like all public offices in this land, this one was jam-packed with people. To get to the front desk alone took me almost an hour. Luckily, from then on things went rather smoothly, although not entirely without the hiccup calling for our ubiquitous Mexican grease.

Our first long ride, you might have guessed, guided us to San Miguel. We decided to take along a lavish picnic, turning it into a pleasure trip. Leaving Highway 57 after Queretaro we stopped near a meadow that was awash in greenery and motley flowers. We spread out a blanket, emptied our picnic basket, and feasted on the morsels that Julia had prepared for us. In the aftermath, I ventured on a little hike, where I picked a bunch of wild flowers and grasses, all of which I fashioned into a wreath that I later placed on Carolina's head. She looked so pretty, I felt urged to take a picture of her with my new Kodak.

Having dropped down into San Miguel, we once again chose the quaint and comfortable Ambos Mundos. Since we had more time on our hands, we made it a point to take another look at the home we'd checked out before, with the intent of buying it. Once again we were swayed by its space, its generous layout, its rural location and its fine condition. Yet our eyes also detected several streaks and stains on the walls of the kitchen and one of the bathroom where water had seeped in. The damage was negligible and we probably would have overlooked it, had it not reminded us that there might well be other defects we could have missed. Carolina in particular was worried that, bumbling neophytes that we were, we'd be inveigled into buying a pig in a poke. Having read a story about the collapse of a house infested by termites, she insisted we hire an independent inspector to sniff things out. Said and done. Although he demanded the hefty wad of 400 pesos, it was a good investment. Jose Bustamante must've had a very refined nozzle because he came up with a long list of various defects and rough spots. Luckily, he didn't find any termites.

Well, we handed the list to Alfredo who acted as though Senor Bustamante was way over the top. But he did pass it on to the Villareals, an old, rickety couple who'd moved on to an old-age home. Since they didn't question the defects, Alfredo immediately called on various craftsmen to go ahead with the repairs. In the meantime, we put down some earnest money and promised to come back as soon as the repairs were completed.

Five weeks later, by the end of September, we signed the contract. That is, it was Carolina who put down her John Hancock. Mulling over it, we both agreed she should be the sole owner. The reason? Safety! My motto: leave as few footprints as possible. Carolina didn't mind. She felt even flattered by my trust in her.

When we got back to el D.F., we began packing our belongings and cramming them into our station wagon to be hauled up to San Miguel. The wagon not only came in handy but also proved its mettle. The bigger pieces, the furniture, we transported with Fidel's truck. What amazed both of us most was the relative wealth of personal possessions we had accumulated in the past year.

I might add, this was the first time I'd ventured back from my hangout on Avenida Acapulco to San Angel. As always, it made me feel very uneasy, forever on the lookout for a possible appearance of the judiciales who were known for luring people into a trap. At one point, having seen a police car coming down the street, I spooked and immediately withdrew to the backyard, ready to leap over the fence if necessary. Luckily, it was only a traffic cop who zipped past.

As expected, the Aznars, Julia and Fidel, and Jorge, but also Rosa Rodriguez, were very saddened to see us leave. And no less puzzled. Every one of them, save for Jorge, kept pressing us to tell them why we were moving. And where to? Instead of answering, we continued to play tone deaf. That caused more awkwardness, even embarrassment. We couldn't possibly tell them that the deciding factor was safety, or the lack thereof. And neither could Jorge who knew all too well what was bugging me. At one time — I was just carrying parts of the bedstead down the stairs — Carolina inadvertently blurted out in Julia's presence that I had difficulty sleeping, of getting a night's rest here in the city. Unfortunately, that seemed to raise more questions than it answered, not to mention suspicion of illegal activities. After all, the Aznars were not only present when the judiciales made their appearance, they even faced questions as to my whereabouts. Moreover, it was common knowledge that these cops worked for the Federal Chief Prosecutor who in turn was responsible only for serious offenses such as murder and extortion.

Could they have suspected that I was an extortionist or, worse, a murderer? Perhaps not. At the same time, our relationship had cooled considerably the past few weeks. I couldn't quite shake off the feeling that they tried to avoid me. The most painful moment came with the final act of parting, particularly for Carolina. Both Julia and Fidel were in tears when we hugged.

"Please come and visit us any time," Julia begged Carolina. "You can stay here with us. But don't forget to bring Enrique along."

I was conspicuously absent from her invitation.

SETTLING DOWN

Life in San Miguel started with a hustle and bustle of activities, not all of them pleasant. Though we had brought along some furniture, the house still had a cavernous look to it as if it were a pendant of some government office. Our first task was to purchase kitchen appliances, a stove and refrigerator, so we could cook up some meals. As to the furnishing of the home, I pretty much left these tasks to Carolina. Thankfully, our tastes largely overlapped. Throwing herself into the fray like a newlywed, she picked such pieces I found appealing as well. That would also apply to the interior decoration. And when the first tables, chairs, wardrobes, lamps and bookcases came trundling in I'd generously complemented her. I particularly treasured her talent for creating an atmosphere of *Gemütlichkeit*, a particularly warm feeling of coziness.

To lessen her daily burden, my novia straight out hired a young indigena, Juanita, to do the housework and take care of Enrique who had been unusually irritated by the move. He'd usually show his annoyance in bursts of piercing shrieks, we knew of no way to curb.

Hoping to secure a room of my own, I immediately laid hold of a bedroom, with the intention of turning it into a study. I bought a large hardwood desk, a lamp, and a comfortable swivel chair. Since our stay in el D.F. I had already assembled a considerable library which now found their home in the bookcases covering the walls. No sooner had we settled down, than I found myself drawn to the basement. Inspired by Alfredo's remark about escape tunnels. I convinced myself of digging one of my own. The reason was obvious, the task formidable. To begin with, the cellar was encased in thick, almost impenetrable walls of concrete. Since I only envisioned a small opening, I first tried to crack the concrete with a brick chisel. But that yielded nothing, save for sweat and sore wrists. So I headed to a construction company where I was able to hire a sturdy young man who could handle pneumatic drills and hammers. Four days later, he appeared with a pneumatic hammer, a monstrous version of a chisel. I showed him the basement with the outline of a door drawn onto the concrete. He rolled up his sleeves and began assaulting it with the zest of a gold digger who suspected a big nugget hidden behind it. Unfortunately, he made such a nerve-rattling racket that the cups in the cupboard above fell into a fretful kissing mood. But he proved to be most deft, and in less than two hours he'd battered and hammered a perfectly rectangular hole through ten centimeters of concrete.

Luckily Carolina was out riding her horse or she would have skinned me. It was bad enough when I later started digging. She must have heard me swinging the pickax for the perfect blow because all of a sudden she stood there, arms akimbo, like a seasoned schoolmarm. "What on earth are you up to?" she hissed, shaking her head.

I gave her a rundown of my plans, including the reasons.

"Safety? I thought this was the reason you wanted us to move out here — to feel safer."

"Well, sure, I do feel safer," wiping the sweat from my forehead. "But that doesn't mean I can't improve on it. Think about it, wouldn't it have been helpful if we'd had an escape tunnel at the hacienda, when the judiciales came to nab me? On that day I got out because of my own agility and ruthlessness, plus a little luck from my horseshoe. If you don't look out for yourself, nobody will. 'Everyone carves his own destiny', I was told by Emma, my headmistress. I deeply believe that. That's why I worry. Sooner or later the judiciales will find out about my present hideout, too. I can't prevent that. All I can do is gird myself and play the hand I'm dealt with, and play it smartly and with cold-blooded determination. Had I not followed this conviction I would have long been dead, several times over. And when you look at it from that angle, this tunnel might well turn out to be the best investment we'll ever make. As with all tunnels there is light at the end, even sunshine. And that's where I want to be. And you should want me to be there as well."

"Investment? What you're doing is nothing less than an investment in your own madness." She shook her head in disgust. "You're endangering our whole house. Soon cracks will appear in the walls. What if the foundation collapses? Or your tunnel starts to fill up and flood when the monsoon rains come back? Or roaches, spiders, scorpions, rats and other rodents get in there and then into the kitchen?"

"I'll make sure the first won't happen. As to the second and third, I'll deal with them when I see the first roach."

"I'll give you three weeks. If you don't complete it by then, I'll be out of here."

"It's a deal."

Feeling the pressure, I hired two sturdy helpers, Alberto and Pedro, both indigenas. Even with their help, the digging was no Sunday school picnic. It was back-breaking work demanding brawn, stamina and gallons of sweat, not least because the ground was so unforgiving. For the most part, it consisted of hard caliche, decomposed granite with the firmness of soft stone. The crowbar I'd scrounged up helped loosen it and break it down. Still the progress only came at a snail's pace. The most I could do was a meter and a half a day, especially when rocks showed up. Losing my patience, I tried sprinkling the caliche with water. That helped soften it a little but at a stiff price — it created a muddy mess.

Nor were these the only headaches I was saddled with. These chunks of dirt and the rocks also had to be removed. We agreed that, being at the head, I'd shovel them into buckets, while Alberto and Pedro carried them up the stairs and, passing the kitchen, dumped them into the backyard. Not only did that take a lot of muscle but it also dragged dirt into house which annoyed Carolina further. She claimed, the hallway and kitchen had turned into a pigsty and that she was living at a construction site.

"I'm sorry," I told her. "I beg you to be patient. It'll be done in less than three weeks. I promise. Remember it will help us all."

My aim was to burrow under the backyard, past the horse stable where I hoped to exit. That would give me cover from the cops, helped by the profusion of shrubbery. If need be, I could skip our neighbor's fence and take to my heels. As we tunneled under and past the foundation of the left wing we found it very cumbersome to get rid of the dirt and the rocks, a deep vein of it. Worse, we were also hampered by a lack of air to the point where breathing became more and more difficult. With the obstacles mounting, I decided to poke through to the surface and then keep digging a deep trench, which I'd later cover, converting it into a tunnel. Despite encountering an irksome network of roots, we found the digging much easier. It wasn't until we reached the horse stable that we burrowed again to re-surface for the final exit.

It took us more than two and a half weeks to complete the raw job and another three days to build a scaffold, including the installation of two ventilation pipes, so we could fill the upper part and flush the trench. To make the tunnel more functional, I also installed a string of lights, including a switch at the entrance.

It goes without saying that my subterranean passage still had many rough edges begging to be smoothed. But that would take time. More urgent was the need to camouflage the entrance, which I accomplished by closing the back of the rack with plywood and adding wheels to its bottom. That way the tunnel's entrance would not only be invisible but could also be opened and closed quickly and without much effort.

To test the feasibility of my project, I pulled off a dry run, simulating a raid by the judiciales. One morning, while Carolina was astride her horse somewhere near the hills, I let Alberto and Pedro ring the bell at the gate, while instructing Juanita, our maid, to rush out there and, upon returning and reentering the door, shout "Fire." At that point I hustled down into the basement, moved the rack and, ducking into the tunnel's entrance, drew the rack back to the wall. I was pleased to say, things proceeded like a Swiss clockwork. The escape itself, if I may smugly say so, took less than five minutes.

All in all, I was most pleased with my mole dig. I looked upon it as a pledge to my freedom that would ideally provide me with that additional edge of security I'd always dreamed of, but so far had never been able to pull off.

As to the debris, the tons of dirt and rocks blemishing the backyard we, Pedro, Alberto and I, eventually heaped it up into an attractive berm we covered with flowers and shrubbery. It couldn't have been lusher. Even Carolina could barely conceal a compliment, pulling it off by pursing her lips while still smiling. But she refused to buckle and compromise herself verbally. Time and again she reminded me of Emma who was known to be unusually stingy in uttering a word of praise.

Finally I was able to settle down, play with Enrique, read the paper, as well as the movie script. The latter seemed way over my head. Luckily, I had almost two months to work on it. Occasionally I also put on an apron and cooked up a meal.

In late September, Jorge came to visit us with Laura, his woman friend, in tow. Playing tourist guides, we showed them the town, the most picturesque nooks around the Jardin and soulful streets of this four-hundred-year-old settlement, but also the Taboada, a *balneario* (hot spring), where we spent a whole day soaking in pools of hot mineral water. Actually, Jorge had seen it all before but that was more than five years ago.

They also had the pleasure to meet our neighbors, Carlos and Inez Sanchez and Felipe and Dolores Murillo, at a dinner party we hosted. We'd already had them over for a glass of wine shortly after we'd moved in. They had been unusually kind and helpful, lending us tools and giving us valuable advice. The Murillos even brought us a welcome cake Dolores had baked specifically for us. And Carolina had often chatted with Inez and Dolores, before she headed out on her morning ride, which was almost daily.

Both couples were much older than we. The Murillos, from all I could tell, may have been in their sixties and the Sanchezes possibly even in their early seventies. Still they were surprisingly hale and hardy. After greeting and introducing them to Jorge and Laura, we all withdrew to the patio, where we gathered around a candle-lit table, letting our eyes feast on the shock of our reddish-purple bougainvillea, the papaya and jacaranda trees, the fan palms, as well as the lush, tropical greenery in the center. The evening was mild and hushed. The breath of some fragrant essence filled the air. Occasionally a light fall breeze sighed in the branches of the avocado tree, while church bells chimed in the background. It felt like being in the anteroom of paradise, or so Carolina once whispered into my ears.

After some small talk, Juanita, began to serve the dinner, composed of enchiladas suizas, maize tortillas stuffed with chicken and covered with a sauce of melted cheese and cream, augmented by tostadas, crisp-fried tortillas smothered in refried beans, salad and guacamole. For drinks we offered beer, wine and tequila. Basking in the relaxed atmosphere, we engaged in animated conversations with a jovial bent. A hidden comedian, Carlos was especially gifted at telling jokes and spicy anecdotes about townspeople he knew.

We just broke out in laughter at one of Carlos's jokes when a sudden gust plucked thousands of petals from our bougainvillea and showered them on us, our heads, clothes and plates. They looked and fluttered like petite butterflies. It took us awhile before we were able to shake and pick them off.

I was still at it, when Felipe, curious as much as he was tipsy, began asking me about my past, where I came from and how I'd made my living. Damn, was I put on the spot! Obviously, answering him straightforwardly was out of the question. "Look, Felipe," I sighed, whispering in a voice choking with emotion. "I've had so many bitter and painful experiences in my past life, I'd rather not talk about them. Forgive me but I wouldn't want to tear open old wounds and poke around in them. Thank God it's all past. Frankly, I'd rather look into the future."

These words rolled off my tongue very effortlessly with an authentic ring because I myself believed in them. Needless to say, such a question never came up again.

We were all drawn into a joyous mood full of chatter and chirpiness that lasted until the very end. Once our guests had departed, Carolina and I chose to linger on the porch, soaking in the waning of the day. While Carolina's eyes were set on the starry sky. I let myself be lulled into the warm wrap of homeyness and domestic safety, to the point of even questioning the necessity of relying on a tunnel.

MY SECOND PART

Having heard from Senor Alarcon that the rehearsals would start no later than the 18th of November (1945), I began to seriously delve into the script. What I had long feared became true: compared to the sailor's role, this new part proved to be considerably longer and incomparably more demanding, verbally as well as in its body language. Although my Spanish had improved considerably, I still had a long way to go to achieve mastery, much less refinement. Daily I crawled through the gravelly shoals of Spanish words and phrases, wrestling with their meaning and pronunciation. Indeed, there were times when, coming across intricate scenes, I began to wobble frighteningly. More than once I came to the conclusion that the part was far too demanding for me, that I bit off more than I could chew. Hell, I encountered expressions I'd never heard before, some of which I couldn't even find in the dictionary. Yes, I faced the music, if only it hadn't come across as a cacophony. My plight was so disheartening I often caught myself feeling depressed and helpless, staring empty-eyed at the fan palms and the papaya tree. Seldom had I felt so out of place, a limp squid on a treadmill. Indeed, I was ready to call Senor Alarcon to tell him in so many words to drop me and find somebody else.

Fortunately, Carolina would have none of my gloom. "You cannot do that," she bristled, clenching her teeth. "Pushing the part away from you would be a terrible blow to Senor Alarcon who is counting on you. Think about it, that could well be the end of your acting career. And then what? What would you do? I'm not even talking about me and Enrique. No, Fred, you've got to get this defeatism out of your mind. I know you can. Besides, there is no other way. You just have to take the bull by the horns. You can count on me; I'll coach you."

These were clear and encouraging words helping me immensely in stiffening my spine. So I buckled down and under Carolina's tutelage delved into the script, working at it from early morning until late at night, polishing my pronunciation, the accent (a Spanish with a slight Viennese timbre), and refining the intonation and the gestures. I may add, my better half was a prodigiously strict taskmaster, making me repeat words, phrases and gestures until I'd reached perfection. Tirelessly, step by step she whipped me into shape, until I set foot on a fairly high plateau, where I began to feel more and more comfortable, at times even confident.

At the beginning of November, on *El Dia de los Muertos,* the Murillos invited us to a party in honor of Dolores's brother, Miguel, who had recently lost his life in a freak accident, when a terracotta tile fell off the La Parroquia parish church and smashed his head as he walked past, killing him. That happened two and a half months ago. Dolores and Felipe had set up an altar in memory of him, adorned with photographs showing him in various stages of his life, including the last one of him resting in his coffin. At the center sat a large sugar skull with his name inscribed on the forehead. The whole display was surrounded by candles, incense and flowers, gladioli, carnations and marigolds, with a towering pink and red Virgen de Guadalupe standing guard. Dolores, Felipe and a great number of relatives thronged around the shrine, praying and sharing memories and stories. Some were hiding their faces behind skull masks and black clothing, displaying freakish skeletal paintings. Others snacked on candy skulls and chewed bread in the shape of human bones. A shriveled old man frantically pulled on a large skeletal jumping jack. As the party progressed, things became more and more relaxed, even frothy. People laughed, bantered and joked about the Grim Reaper, calling him impotent, worse, laughable. I found all these theatrics most fascinating, so bizarrely contrary to anything I'd been used to.

They also invited us to partake in a picnic inside the cemetery. When we arrived, throngs of people jammed the entrance. We had to get in line to enter. It took us almost half an hour to elbow our way to Miguel's gravesite, where we encountered another of Miguel's sons who had stayed there all night chatting with his dad. Besides placing *zempoalxochitl* (marigolds), or flowers of the dead, on the grave, Dolores had brought along oven-warm, sweet loaves of *pan de muerto,* bread of the dead, various choice cheeses, chorizos and a bottle of aged tequila. She dusted off the tombstone, kneeled down and prayed to Miguel, briefing him on the kinds of morsels we were about to nosh and coaxing him into rising and joining us. To make the return more palatable, she related to him in flowery language all the wonderful experiences she'd had in the past two and a half months since his death.

Anything but idle, Felipe got busy setting off firecrackers, in the hope of summoning the spirits of his brother-in-law and other souls nearby. Four graves over, somebody played the guitar and everybody from young to old danced around the gravesite, calling on their dead loved ones to rise up and wiggle his or her hips with them. At another site a shriveled old man hugged a huge imaginary papier mache woman and danced a fiery tango around his wife's grave.

Although I didn't notice any corpse follow the lure and rise out of its grave, I can say with a some degree of certainty that everybody had a hell of a good time. For me it was an unforgettable event. Never had I seen death presented in such a farcical manner and when I came home I picked a bunch of marigolds and withdrew into my study. Having wreathed Rodrigo's skull with these flowers, I lit a candle and began engaging in a mental dialogue with him, calling him my compadre. We talked about life and death, light and darkness. In the end he repeatedly urged me to be mindful of my own mortality, to seize the day and savor life to the fullest. I promised to take his advice to heart and live accordingly. The only question was: would I be able to, weighed down by my precarious circumstances.

Our eight-cylinder station wagon purred along the highway, but then yielded to a deep ursine growl as soon as we gained in elevation. It was stuffed to the rafter with us — Carolina, Enrique, Juanita and me, as well as six suitcases, a picnic basket and a box filled with toys. We were heading to Veracruz. But, since we had to pass through that fetid Moloch el D.F. anyway, we decided to make a short stop to drop in on the Aznars and Jorge. Actually, it was one of Carolina's pipe dreams. I, for one, felt very uneasy, especially visiting the Aznars. I feared their home might still be under surveillance. Had not Julia told Carolina over the phone that two sinister fellows had been back two weeks after our move, questioning her and Fidel about me again?

Wary, I was not going to take any chances. So after letting her, Enrique and Juanita, out in front of the house, I quickly took off again, winding my way to Galvez, a side street less than five minutes away. Parking the car, I began checking the area for any signs of undercover agents. Luckily, I didn't detect anyone or anything suspicious. Yet a somber voice from within told me to be leery.

I might add, I felt a little more relaxed when we visited Jorge. I said a 'little'. That included keeping my eyes peeled and looking over my shoulder for anybody who might be spying on me. But that had long become a habit of mine anyway, as worrisome as it was necessary. Let me just add, I was greatly relieved when we finally left and approached the outskirts of this monstrosity of a city. Though the subsequent drive across the eastern plateau was relaxing, a piece of cake, up to the summit of the Cumbres de Maltrata at least. However, from then on, the next thirty kilometers down, up and down the Cumbres de Acultzingo proved to be hellishly dangerous, a nightmare in the making. Luckily, we got through unscathed, thanks not least to my defensive driving and quick reaction.

It was shortly past midnight when we, tired and worn to a frazzle, pulled into the parking lot of the charming Mocambo Hotel. As we stepped out, an unusually warm and extremely humid breath of air enwrapped us, making us feel as if we'd stepped into an unventilated laundry. Enrique, for one, instantly gave vent to his displeasure by responding with a piercing shriek.

Thankfully, Carolina and I were assigned an eye-filling room with a balcony and a view of the beach and the sea, whereas Juanita and Enrique were put up in a smaller chamber looking out onto the lush courtyard. We had deliberately arrived a day early in order to settle down and get a taste of the hotel, the town and the surrounding area. And it paid off. Roused by the morning sun beaming into our room, we put on bathrobes and shuffled out onto the balcony. The beach was still empty, save for two fishermen who were working on their boats and nets. The sea was as calm as a bathtub. We showered, spooned and then treated ourselves, including Juanita and Enrique, to a sumptuous breakfast in the restaurant. Returning to our rooms, we grabbed some towels, our trunks, bathing suits, a few provisions and headed down to the beach, where we made ourselves comfortable under a shady *palapa* and let our eyes wander. A movie camera for hire would catch a lazy, playful line of white frothed surf curled up the beach, which was crowded with little birds scurrying back and forth, while seagulls wailed at a distance. The water was warm enough to invite us for a dip. Having cooled off, we breathed in the peaceful atmosphere, strolling up and down the seashore, watching bathers, vendors and also fishermen, busy mending their nets and repairing their boats.

Later in the afternoon, we instructed Juanita to take Enrique to the children's playground, while we explored the town's center around the zocalo, the cathedral and the Palacio Municipal. From all we could tell, it was one of the most swinging, frolicking towns in all of Mexico. Senor Alarcon had already mentioned that the *Veracruzanos* were even more relaxed and easygoing than most Mexicans. They were known to celebrate their carnivals with a flair second only to Rio and New Orleans. Anyway, we were amazed watching them thronging the streets, cafes and arcades, where Mariachi bands and string trios played every day, all day long and well into the night. In addition to music the locals also displayed a special affinity for dancing. Everywhere we went we came across dance halls, where seasoned dancers performed the crazy, wild *zapateo,* as well as the calm and composed *danzon.* Lured by the crowd, we, too, entered one and,

381

after we had a bite to eat, we danced until we were breathless, drenched in sweat and rousing happiness.

"If that isn't carpe diem, then the saying isn't worth its ink," I cracked. "It faintly reminds me of Cuauhtemoc but three levels higher. Do you still remember?"

"How could I forget, I with my sprained ankle? And your magic kisses. You know, it feels as if we're on a honeymoon. I always missed going on one, but most of all celebrating a real wedding. You may not remember, I had planned everything, especially the big wedding party. And then..."

"...those nasty cops barged in."

It was close to midnight when we had our last swirl. Once back to the hotel we grabbed two towels and headed down to the beach. It was dotted with gaggles of young people. A gentle breeze, wafting in from the southeast, ruffled the leaves of the nearby palm trees that lined the promenade. Up, toward the north, the glittering lights of Veracruz illuminated the sky, as well as the shore, creating intermittent sparkles. Sitting there, loosely embracing each other, we watched the tide, the coming and going of the surf, some tongues lashing all the way up the beach, almost reaching our feet. It set the stage for a contemplative mood that had a profoundly soothing effect on me, mellowing me to the point of dissolving my ego and instilling in me a curious lightness of being I hadn't felt for a long time. I felt as if life had fallen out of time. Gone were the worries about being hounded, vanished the burden of being a husband as well as a father, ebbed away the funk of taking on the role of Ignatz. If only I could have held on to that moment, make it lasting!

Next morning, we were served a late breakfast on our balcony. Shaded by a big umbrella our eyes were drawn to the *Playa Mocambo* and the tamed sea beyond that lay tranquil in the morning mist. Little by little our film crew trickled in — actors, actresses, technicians and other support staff. All I recognized was the cameraman and a few assistants. But as I headed down to pick up a newspaper, I chanced to bump into Senor Alarcon who trudged up the stairs with three bellboys in tow. We shook hands and exchanged some comments about the fog on that treacherous highway and the unusually warm and humid weather down here on the coastal plain.

"Forgive me, Fred, I have to rush," he excused himself shortly after. "It was good talking to you. See you tonight at seven at the orientation meeting. It should go quickly. It's going to be a very small crew of only twenty-four people."

The meeting passed without a hitch. We introduced ourselves, shook hands with each other, and received an overview of the rehearsal and shootings schedule. I happened to get acquainted with Raul Armendiraz who would be playing the part of Carlos Sandoval, whom Ignatz befriends. Raul was a very affable, good-looking fellow, whose dark melancholic eyes, stub-nose and his shock of curly black hair faintly reminded me of Luis, a vaquero at the hacienda. We clicked right away. He spontaneously invited me for a glass of wine and, clinking our glasses, we toasted to our co-operation. Strange as it may seem, we almost fell into our film roles before we'd even begun rehearsing. He was Carlos and I, Ignatz, his friend.

Next day we delved into the rehearsals, which incidentally were also attended by Carolina. According to the script, the shooting would start off with actions more than with words — turmoil in choppy, shark-infested water. But unlike in *They Came From Afar*, this time I'd play the part of the rescuer who snatches Carlos and Cecilia (Elea Avila), his girlfriend, from the jaws of death by drowning or being torn to shreds by sharks. Senor Alarcon stressed that this rescue was of utmost importance because it would nail down the friendship between Ignatz and Carlos. Since Raul and Elea were anything but sporty types, he suggested that the most physical part of the scene should be rehearsed in the hotel's swimming pool. Still, even in this controlled environment both failed to meet Senor Alarcon's expectations.

"You kick and thrash around; you wave and flail your arms as if you'd just been released from a lunatic asylum and stuck into a water polo team," he shouted, shaking his head. "Have you never watched somebody drowning?"

The old fox got so livid, he stripped himself down to his underpants, jumped in and demonstrated hands-on how they should move their limbs, heads and bodies. He even urged them to gulp down water. Needless to say, it took them a while before they caught on.

The rest of the rehearsal proceeded without a wrinkle, including administering first aid, the mouth-to-mouth breathing and the extended treatment at the hospital, where Carlos and Cecilia were treated for oxygen deprivation. This didn't pass without a tragic note demanded by the script. For Cecilia help had come too late. Try as they might, the doctors weren't able to resuscitate her. But Carlos survived, miraculously so, without any serious injuries to his heart and lungs. Three days later he was declared fit again, or so the script demanded.

Let me add, during the coaching with Carolina I had come up with a Spanish, tinged with a slight Viennese accent. In my dialogue with the doctors I tried to nuance my vocal expressiveness by stressing words and phrases. I slowed down a line of speech only to speed it up again. Anyway, Senor Alarcon was full of praise. "Good job, Fred! You hit the right notes. You found the accent, the intonation, the gestures and the timing. You portrayed Ignatz exactly the way I envisioned him."

"Most of the credit should go to Carolina," I commented. "She was the one who coached me."

Antonio, however, didn't fare that well. The old zorro faulted him for not showing enough grief following the death of Cecilia. "You're far too theatrical," he explained. "As if you walked out of a comedy. You should restrain yourself a little. Remember, you just had a brush with death and saw your girlfriend die."

Carlos's release would be followed by a big party, an *accion de gracias,* in Mexico City, where Ignatz, as well as all of Cecilia's and Carlos's friends and relatives showed up. At first there would be a memorial service for Cecilia attended by a priest. It would be followed by a special ceremony where Carlos swears an oath to true friendship between Ignatz and him. However this party was scheduled to be staged and shot later, once we'd be back at the studio in el D.F.

To begin the action, all Senor Alarcon needed was a bout of stormy weather. It came two days later, as fierce winds sweeping in from the north whipped up the waves, even capping them. To protect myself, I insisted that the makeup artist put it on thick, changing my facial appearance to where I was hardly recognizable. Later, we all ventured out onto the waves with a fancy motorboat, a yacht, as well as a fishing boat. In some ways it was a daring undertaking, requiring a fair amount of nerve and grit. Having heard of recent shark attacks on humans, Raul and particularly Elea feared for their lives. Nor did I prove to be a model of self-confidence who'd want to spite their dread. Luckily, those razor-toothed rippers would choose to stay away.

Our stay in Veracruz was a short but a most enjoyable sojourn, despite the burden of the shooting schedule. Actually I was almost starry-eyed that I hit it off so well with Senor Alarcon. I figured that his praise would lend me wings for the more difficult, verbal parts of the script. But no less important was the rapport I achieved with Carolina. It had been some time since I saw her in such a cheerful and fulfilled mood. Gone were the grating sounds that had popped up during our exchanges in the past few months. I dare say our relationship almost approached the harmony that had been prevalent during the first few months of our infatuation.

On the way back we again stopped in el D.F. While I took up lodgings at the Hotel Monte Carlo, where Don Leonardo, but also the English writer

384

D.H. Lawrence famously stayed, Carolina wound her way on to San Miguel. Still we managed to get together almost every weekend. Either she came to visit me in the city, or I headed home to San Miguel. But from Monday to Friday I continued to be very busy rehearsing and shooting in el D.F., either at the CLASA studio or outdoors, often way into the night. Thanks to the rigorous coaching and my good start in Veracruz, I was able to hold my own, occasionally even earning more praise from Senor Alarcon. Yet I'd be fudging if I claimed everything moved along without a ripple. It didn't. I often faced more challenges than I thought I could handle. Among the most unsavory ones I encountered were, curiously enough, the various love scenes requiring me and my female opposite to appear in the nude. Although these shots, which simulated actions behind closed doors, presented some of the most intimate moments in the film, they necessarily had to be performed publicly, as a bevy of technicians watched us from the sidelines. I couldn't help it, something in me rebelled when making out with a woman while a camera and two dozen eyes were watching us. Who but a full-fledged exhibitionist would be comfortable presenting himself in public as a lover fired up by passion under such circumstances?

As Senor Alarcon had already informed us, impassioned love scenes of that kind required unique, sangfroid acting skills, simply because they were by nature anything but passionate. "If you feel your oats, wait until the shooting's done," he warned us. "Or else we may have to recast the scene." All I can say, it felt odd to be lying entwined on a crumpled bed, mouth-to-mouth, eyes shut, seemingly spellbound by our ardor, waiting for the cameraman to grumble, "I can barely see your cheeks and noses. Can't you turn a little to the left so I can catch your mouth?"

I dare say, it happened to me.

I grappled. Yet somehow, as if by a miracle, I managed to pass muster. Don't ask me how. It must have been the charged atmosphere, the tension when such a scene was about to be shot. As the clapperboard shut for the take and Senor Alarcon barked "Action!" I was no longer myself. It felt as if I'd been stripped of my identity and usurped the life of Ignatz. Not so Raul, my partner, fictional friend and study object. He also grappled with his love scenes, as if he didn't have other nuts to crack. Luckily with time and the generous support of Juan, an experienced actor and personal friend of Senor Alarcon, Raul, eventually managed to find his voice, pitch and gestures. That helped to make the shooting smoother, less tense, while reducing the fear of retakes.

I might add that aside from the love scenes, I had immense fun acting the part of Ignatz, speaking Spanish with a German-Viennese accent, intermittently injecting the words *Wahrheit* (truth), *Liebe* (love) and *Heimweh* (homesickness) in a cracked voice. Let's face it, what was acting but a flight from an irksome, often unpleasant reality into the high-flying fictitious mood of possibilities? Who wouldn't occasionally pine for converting the subjunctive 'what if' mood into the indicative, a real act or objective fact? For me it resembled daydreaming, of entering the golden haze of fairy tale. It felt a little bit like the blessed moments I experienced at the beach. Momentarily at least, I blissfully forgot the dread of being swept up by the judiciales, the fear of facing another Mexican jail, or the burden of guilt for having served a murderous regime. Several times, when I came off the set, I felt so enwrapped in my fictitious role play that I barely eluded a point-blank collision with reality.

In one instance things turned out to be particularly hazardous. Dusk was settling as I came off the set to head out of the studio. Trying to catch a bus, I wound my way across the much traveled boulevard and, a heady Ignatz that I was, right into the arms of a tamarindo, a traffic cop. Me of all people! What a rude awakening it was.

The cop, a burly fellow with wide shoulders, a broad Mayan head and small, riveting eyes, instantly nailed me, accusing me of violating the law. Hearing an accent, he asked for an identification. I pulled out my passport and handed it to him. He studied my face, opened the booklet and checked the photograph. My face was still made up, which must have thrown him off.

"This can't be you," he growled pointing at the picture.

"Yes it is," I said. "You see, I'm a movie actor working in the studio over there. I just came off the set. I'm still wearing my makeup."

He shook his head and cleared his throat. "Well, I think we may have to check you out at the precinct. Of course, you could also pay the *infraccion,* an official fine. It's 500 pesos." He held my passport in his right hand and, clenching his teeth, tapped it against the knuckles of his left hand. "However, in your case I'd turn a blind eye if you handed me 300 pesos. But you'll have to promise that from now on you'll obey the law."

I opened my wallet and handed him 300 pesos, with a mental sigh of relief. If that incident taught me anything it was the lesson that I should never take my eyes off reality.

Lest I forget, while I stayed in el D.F., I frequently rubbed elbows with Jorge as well. Usually we got together in cafes in Coyoacan or the Historic District, where we chewed the fat over a cup of coffee or antojitos. As a voracious reader, Jorge closely followed the events in Europe, particularly Germany and Austria. We threshed out the division of Germany into four zones, a Russian, an American, a British and, curiously enough, also a French one. True to his Jewish roots, Jorge was particularly eager to exchange views over the harrowing, tormenting stories emerging from the concentration camps, the sadistic henchmen who were in charge of them, the setting up of the Nuremberg war crime tribunals against twenty-four leading Nazi figures and the burden of the collective guilt the Germans would have to face.

"It is a stain on the Germans that may well stick for a thousand years," he said. "That'll be the only legacy the Thousand-Year Reich will leave behind."

What could I say? All I could do was choke down another slice of humble pie.

It was not until we touched on the question of atonement, particularly on the harsh life the German people had to endure, that I came back to a semblance of life. Yet, here again, while I felt grateful for enjoying such a life of comfort and relative wealth, I couldn't quite elude occasional pangs of guilt for escaping the hunger and cold in their icy, rubble-strewn cities.

MY FIRST COUCH DOCTOR

On the last day before my departure, Jorge and I met one more time at the Cafe El Popular. We had barely taken our seats in this offbeat, smoke-filled place, when Jorge handed me an article he'd cut out of the New York Times just three days ago. "I thought you might want to know what's happening in this odd relationship between Mexico and the United States," he said. "It always reminds me of a bad marriage, where the hardworking husband keeps finger-stabbing his wife for being sloppy and inept, and for failing to live up to the demands and duties of their marriage contract."

"But what has that got to do with me?"

"Well, you'll have to read it. We can talk about it later, as soon as I get back. You'll have to excuse me, I just have to say hello to a longtime acquaintance over there." He pointed to a table in the corner, where three gentlemen argued and gesticulated about some hot-button issue.

Meanwhile, I began reading it which wasn't all that easy because of the poor light. Let me summarize: It dealt with the exasperation of Uncle Sam with his southern neighbor. Washington accused the Camacho government of incompetence and failure to live up to its commitments. Besides holding back on the delivery of oil and other necessary raw materials, Mexico had miserably failed to secure its border, allowing too many Mexicans to enter the U.S. illegally, bringing along drugs, disease and, yes, crime. It was especially critical of its lack of commitment to the extradition treaty both countries signed. The most stinging attack was directed at the Mexican law enforcement agencies. Quoting J. Edgar Hoover, it stated that in the years between 1943 and 1945 a staggering number of violent criminals, altogether 16,453, had fled to Mexico to escape the American justice system. Yet hardly any of them had ever been caught, much less sent back. Wrapping up, the scoop stated that in the face of the Mexican foot-dragging the Truman administration was seriously considering quashing Mexico's status as a most favored nation, renegotiating the trade agreement, as well as to canceling the Bracero program (of letting Mexican agricultural laborers work on American farms). Uncle Sam would also get tough on illegal immigration, incarcerating trespassers and bussing them back.

"Damn, that's all I need!" I heard myself hissing, when Jorge came back. "I better hone my skills in dodging and ducking. I can see why the Americans are so upset."

"So can I."

"If anything, Camacho will be under tremendous pressure. He'll be forced to put the screws to the various departments, most of all on law enforcement, the Federal Chief Prosecutor and the judiciales, his lickspittles. I better be on my toes."

"I agree, it doesn't look good. At the same time, nothing's eaten as hot as it's been cooked up. Don't forget, there's always our Mexican bureaucracy. When orders from above come trickling down, they'll inevitably be diluted. Besides, many Mexicans, including me, are for sheer patriotic reasons either skeptical about the intentions of the gringos, or they despise them. They simply don't want the Americans meddling in our affairs. It's as simple as that."

"Well, I pray you're right. In the meantime, I'm going to be all eyes and ears."

Regrettably, the resolution of being all 'eyes and ears' wasn't all that easy to fulfill. More often than not, I was dead-tired owing less to my acting than to the lack of sleep. Though I tried, I was unable to shake off the possible threat Jorge's article roused within me, his soothing words notwithstanding. I couldn't help it, I was haunted by one nightmare after another. Usually it involved raids by the judiciales, but also scenes I experienced at the jail in Chihuahua, often intermingled with harrowing scenes of bloodstained Aztec warriors tearing pulsating hearts out of their victims' chests. The only way I could fend them off was by staying awake, but that was easier said than done. In one sequence a whole squad of well-armed judiciales appeared, tied me up and tortured me. They threatened to cut off my penis, fry it and then hand it to Carolina.

Dawn announced itself with a silvery pale sliver, a crack in the cloud cover along the eastern horizon. Somewhere in town muted church bells began to toll, summoning the faithful to mass. Drained from torturous dreams, I rolled out of bed, shuffled to the bathroom and threw some cold water on my face. That helped rouse me.

It was the first day after my return to San Miguel, and I hoped to slough off my troubles that had plagued me in el D.F. and gird myself for a new beginning. So I put on underpants, shorts and socks, pulled a knit shirt over my torso, slipped into sneakers and headed out for a morning jog. It was goose-pimply chilly. I had long worked out a loop that jogging east, up the slope, would take me up and around old town and then lead me back down on the southwestern side again. From the start, it was nothing but a test of tenacity, willpower, not least because of the rise in elevation. Although I had no taste for masochistic exercises, I was never averse to testing my will and endurance to the point where it actually began hurting. For me it was a question of mind over matter, an aspiration to a more lofty summons of the spirit.

Well, already pushing myself up the first rise made me huff and puff like an old geezer. And attempting the second, I would — sad to say — soon falter. I simply didn't have the oomph. That had never happened to me before, at least I couldn't remember any incident of that sort. It was disheartening. *Damn, was I getting old and frail?*

When at last I found my way back home, I felt like a beaten old rag. Sweating, I treated myself to a hot shower and, having put on some clothes, I joined Carolina, Enrique and Juanita for a hearty breakfast of huevos rancheros with scoops of pintos and stacks of tortillas. That made me feel a little better. Still, the dark cloud that hovered over me showed no sign of dissipating. And forget about any silver lining!

"Something must be bugging you," Carolina said after taking a sip of coffee. "You tossed, turned, and even shouted something last night. I could hardly catch some sleep. You've told me the filming had gone rather well and Senor Alarcon was very satisfied with your performance. So what's the problem?"

"Well it may be the article Jorge handed me."

I told her what it is about, highlighting the extradition treaty Mexico had signed with the United States. "It's crazy, during the daytime I can deal with it pretty well. But as soon as I lie down and try to catch some sleep, all hell breaks loose. I have one nightmare after another. And the worst thing is that I know of no way to stop it. Somehow I have no control over it; it's as if my head is running away with me. Occasionally I even have the feeling that it was a mistake of having taken on the part of Ignatz. I'm afraid the judiciales may recognize my face. It was far too risky. I may have to pay a heavy price for my vanity."

"Now you're going crazy. Your makeup was so deceiving that even people who knew you didn't recognize you."

"I wish you were right. But I'm afraid you are dreaming." I handed her the article. She read it and we discussed it.

"It sounds really threatening," she conceded. "At the same time, you have to look at it from the historical perspective of American-Mexican

390

relations going back hundreds of years. Because that's how long the gringos have been bugging us."

She essentially agreed with Jorge, betting on the Mexican bureaucracy to weaken the thrust of it. "Don't forget that Camacho had a hell of a time convincing the Mexican people to enter the war on the side of America," she claimed. "There was a lot of resistance. Some high officials openly opposed him, calling him Roosevelt's lapdog. It took nothing less than the sinking of a Mexican tanker by German subs to justify our entry on the side of America."

In any event, in her estimation, the judiciales, even if they were pressured from above, would probably be toothless. I was much less sure: Had I not been in their crosshairs ever since the raid at the hacienda? All I could do was hope they wouldn't ferret out our hideout here in San Miguel. In case they did, there was of course the tunnel which would give me a momentary edge. But after that I'd be condemned to be on the run. A bleak outlook indeed. And I had hoped that Hoover would slack off, now that the war had ended, with a victory no less.

"What frustrates me most is my inability to stop the nightmares," I told her. "They are killing me. The only antidote I know is waking up. But that's no solution. I can't stay awake twenty-four hours a day. What I need most of all is a sound sleep."

"I wouldn't know how to stop nightmares. But if you're looking for a sound sleep, sleeping pills might help. I hear there are good ones around. I'd check the drugstore. It probably has a pretty good selection. If not, you could see a doctor who could prescribe a more potent pill."

"I doubt they'll help but they can't hurt."

Half an hour later I found myself in the drugstore, rummaging the shelves. Eventually a saleslady who claimed to be knowledgeable about sleeping pills helped me, recommending some capsules that contained valerian and other natural substances that had a soothing effect on the nerves. She assured me they would help me sleep better. Well, I bought them. Come bedtime, I swallowed three mini bombs, and as far as I could tell they did indeed help me fall asleep. But then, around one o'clock, the nightmares surged back again. I found myself in a mess hall of a Mexican jail, where I was ambushed by vicious gangs with machetes who threatened to cut off my head if I didn't pay a sum of 100,000 pesos. I woke when their leader took a swipe at me with his butcher knife. In another scene I was hunted down by a group of six heavily armed judiciales. I was running for my life when all of a sudden I was facing a dense thicket of cacti. Desperate,

I headed straight into it. But as I stumbled over a huge barrel cactus I woke drenched in sweat.

It was twelve past four.

Cursed, I woke Carolina who grumbled, "You're impossible. I couldn't get any sleep. You shouted, moaned, and whimpered as if you were being tortured."

"I'm very sorry," I pleaded. "I've once again been rattled by these violent dreams. I don't know what to do any more, except... I think the only way to let you catch some sleep is for me to move out to my study."

"That's awful," she said, teary-eyed. "You know what people say of couples who no longer sleep together?"

"Well, if you know a better option, let me know."

Sighing, I grabbed my mattress, the bedding, and my clothes and withdrew to my study, where I continued to lay awake, even though I was dead tired. At six o'clock, I put on some clothes and shoes and ventured outside. Once again I was too drained to jog. So I just took a walk up to town, which was still asleep, save for the bell ringers at the various churches. It was so peaceful, yet I was too tired and tormented to enjoy it.

When I came back a little more than an hour later, Carolina glared at me as if I'd slinked out of the bughouse. "Where were you?"

"In town."

"Look, this can't go on. You have to do something. I've heard there is an American psychiatrist in town. His name is Dr. Earnest Frommer. A lot of people rave about him. Maybe he could help. I could go along with you if you like."

"You mean one of those couch doctors who treat maniacs? Well I'm not a maniac. Not yet anyway."

"I didn't say that. But you *do* need help."

"Let me sleep on it."

Well, after another harrowing night crammed with nightmares and anxiety attacks, I finally bowed. Carolina promptly made an appointment with Dr. Frommer, and three days later I sat in his office. Office? Actually it looked more like a living room, furnished as it was with a sofa, a coffee table and three comfortable armchairs, surrounding a fireplace. A little way off, next to the left wall, stood the hallowed couch. The walls were covered by soothing oil paintings of pastel landscapes and older, dignified women, as well as various degrees, honors and awards Dr. Frommer had received over his long professional career.

He was fifteen minutes late, but apologized as he introduced himself, giving me a soft, feminine handshake. He was an amiable, soft-spoken man in his sixties, with a shiny bald head, puffy cheeks, a fleshy nose and small watery-blue eyes hiding beneath almost hairless brows. These were countered by flamboyant tufts of reddish hair-whorls jostling out of his ears as if to prove, I suppose, that he was very much part of our simian heritage. "How can I help you, Senor de Keyser?" he wanted to know.

Well, I began poking around in my maladies, describing my nightmares, my anxiety attacks and sleepless nights but stopped short of revealing anything about my past. I was well aware that merely describing the symptoms begged the question, and Dr. Frommer quickly pointed that out, repeatedly stressing that anything I said would remain strictly confidential and nobody would have access to any disclosures I made, not even Carolina. That was not only sensible but also reassuring. If I still held myself back, it should be attributed to my inborn reluctance to surrender vital tidbits about my private life, fearing I'd be judged by them. But that didn't seem to discourage him. Quite the contrary, armed with an arsenal of charm and wiles, he gradually, step by step, wheedled me into disclosing the emotional roots of my suffering, including my past encounter with the judiciales and my fears of what might happen in the future. While I talked, he busied himself taking notes and posing supplementary questions. Unfortunately, we soon ran out of time.

Even though I promised to be back next week, I walked out with an ambivalent feeling. I liked Dr. Frommer, his sunny personality, his smooth approach and engaging manner, although that didn't detract from my doubts about his ability of helping me. At the same time, I did feel a little better, possibly because of the belief that I had taken the first step toward healing myself. That's what I also told Carolina who was most eager to hear my impressions of my first session. As to my reservations, she thought it was far too early to judge the effectiveness of the therapy. That might take months to bear fruit. I should be patient.

The night I spent in the study seemed to be a little more tamed as well. Or was it merely the fact that Carolina was not disturbed by my turning, tossing and moaning? I had no way of knowing.

Next week I was back at the therapy session. After greeting me, Dr. Frommer suggested I place myself on his couch. It would relax me, he claimed, and help me uncover the roots of my emotional distress and reverse my repressed defense mechanisms. What he hoped to accomplish was to shift the *angst* from the nooks and crannies of the unconscious into the realm of conscious thought. In any event, I felt much more comfortable and poured out my personal experiences, going back all the way to my escape from the POW camp to the violent crossing of the border. As before, he diligently took notes but also posed questions whenever he felt in doubt. Yet he was very careful to judge or second-guess my or anybody else's actions. According to him they were neither good nor bad. They just 'were'.

It was as if time had doubled its velocity, and when I shook hands and walked out the office I felt visibly relieved, as if the burden weighing on my shoulders had greatly diminished. That was encouraging news. I hadn't felt that hopeful for some time, indeed, not since I'd left the studio thirteen days ago.

Back home, as I stepped into our *entrada*, Carolina didn't fail to notice that something had changed. "You must've had a good session," she said, smiling. "It's the first time I have seen you smiling since you came back from el D.F."

"Oh really?" I told her what had taken place. "I can't explain it, but just talking to somebody you respect and trust really uplifted me. Let me add, Dr. Frommer is a very intuitive man; he has a unique, almost magical capacity for projecting himself into somebody else's mind, making you feel understood and cared for. His goal was to hand me a rope in the breakwater of angst. And he did. I could have gone on and on, to the point of feeling let down when he reminded me that the session was over."

"I've heard this is what happens when you see a good psychiatrist."

"Yeah, it felt as if he'd massaged my mind. But I wonder if my upbeat feeling isn't just a fluke. Somehow the fear that it may not last has never left me."

"Time will tell. In the meantime, you might as well enjoy it while you have it."

After taking a short walk with Enrique, who was already able to do it unaided, and puttering in the garden, I sauntered up the worn cobbled streets to the Jardin, the center of town. On the way I stopped at facades of old buildings where the paint had flaked off, showing five different colors, most still vibrant. I thought about my own face and all the makeup it had to endure the past few years. Having reached the center, I headed to a cafe where I treated myself to a cup of Mayan brew and some dulces. Pen and writing pad in hand, I kept watching people, listening to their conversations and keeping an eye on their gestures. Since my sojourn into acting, I had become much more sensitized and curious about the way people looked and carried on in public. And the cafe was like a stage to me, where short, often comical scenes were being performed. Needless to say, they provided me with an inexhaustible amusement, not to mention inspiration. I couldn't resist taking notes of phrases I heard or sketching an unusual face or head that struck me. I might add, some of the guests were Americans who, as a rule, were smart and well educated, even though they often tended toward the comical. Off the cuff, they were blissfully unaware that they presented such an easy target for the pen of a satirist, standing out by the way they dressed and handled themselves. In fact, at the table next to me sat an elderly American couple — she crinkly-mouthed with a blue-rinsed coif, Rococo-framed glasses and baby-pink slacks, while her husband, whose nose and eyes reminded me of F.D.R., attracted attention by donning a checkered, varicolored jacket, a pair of raspberry-hued pants and huge two-toned dress shoes. Whenever he stopped talking, he nervously poked at his teeth with a toothpick, shading his right, active hand with his left. Every once in a while a waft of perfume mixed with deodorant and aftershave came my way, surging up my nostrils. I hope to be forgiven but this pair looked and smelled as though they'd spent half of their lives in a highly sanitized bathroom whose walls had never heard of a hale and hardy fart, much less reeked of any doo-doo. Indeed, if the adage cleanliness is nearest to godliness were in search of an image, it would have to be this couple. Unsurprisingly, they chatted in a diphthong-laden southern drawl about how hopelessly backward we Mexicans were, how dirty our streets, how unsanitary our bathrooms, wondering how we could live that way.

When I got back home, I noticed there was something or other that had ruffled Carolina. "Everything all right?" I inquired.

"Definitely not! Half an hour ago Senor Alarcon called, telling me that three judiciales barged into his office this morning asking for Senor Lars Stenson. They wanted to talk to him."

I held my breath. "Stenson? You must be kidding!"

"I wish I were."

"Oh Lord!" I sighed. "Here we go again! Shit, mierda. They must have recognized me on the silver screen playing the professor in *Dulce*."

"I doubt it. With all that makeup and the wig, you looked so different, like a stranger."

"Well, I specifically asked Sancho, the makeup artist, to do what he could to change my face. But apparently it wasn't enough. Why else would they show up at Senor Alarcon's office?"

"Well, some people may have seen you there."

"Possibly, but not likely. Did Alarcon tell you what he told them?"

"He claimed to have told them that he had no idea where you were, that he had no contact with you. He also told them you'd mentioned of going back to America again because the pay was so lousy here."

"Not bad, drawing a red herring across the trail. It can't hurt. Whether it'll help me is another question. You know, I wouldn't be surprised if one

395

day they'll be standing in front of our gate insisting on speaking with Senor Stenson. The pressure is on. I better see to it that the tunnel is free of cobwebs and black widows. Who knows when I'll have to make use of it. In the meantime, I better drag the mattress back into the study or even into the basement."

As all this kept tumbling in my mind, other unpleasant concerns popped up. "I wonder how Senor Alarcon will react toward me? I know I've been in good standing with him. But he might change his mind if the judicales keep bothering him. What if the head honcho accuses him of harboring an American fugitive? The deferential treatment I received may well end. He may no longer feel free to offer me parts in his productions. Say, how was the tone of his voice?"

"Quite good, I had the feeling that he was very much on your side, otherwise he wouldn't have mentioned that you wanted to go to America."

"Yes, that was his own rather clever invention. It was a sly hint that I may no longer be in Mexico and their hunt for me is useless, that it would have to be the FBI's job to nab me, not the judicales."

"I agree, he may have tried to protect you."

"That's possible. But he can't, really."

The news of yet another raid sent me to the doldrums. What disheartened me most was watching my options of living a normal life shrinking to near zero. I felt stuck between two giant boulders, which were slowly but relentlessly closing in on me. Hapless and helpless, I braced for fate knocking on my door. It was not a question of 'if' but 'when' the judicales would show up at our doorstep. This state of uncertainty relentlessly gnawed at me, robbing me of my sleep, tiring me, turning me back into a sorry bundle of dread and angst.

Thank God I still had Dr. Frommer, Carolina and — lest I forget — also Enrique, or I might well have been ripe for a psychiatric asylum. I clung to all three like a leech to an old man's leg. They picked me up and helped me get on my feet. At least twice a week I enjoyed the privilege of discussing my phobias with Carolina, often suggesting practical measures I could take to keep them in check. Yet, even more beneficial were my sessions with Dr. Frommer. They continued to be highlights for me I didn't want to miss.

He was such a gentleman, humble, smart, unpretentious and refreshingly flexible. Having in the meantime found out that I'd had some experience in acting, he encouraged me to integrate it into my therapy. So under his guidance I began acting out in a sort of soliloquy hidden feelings, thoughts, phobias, anxieties and traumas, using not only words but also a rich pallet of gestures. Expressing my hidden mental baggage and exposing it to bright daylight worked wonders, begetting a veritable cleansing action or, in Dr. Frommer's psychiatric jargon, "a catharsis."

REGAINING MY FOOTING

Dr. Frommer's therapy, coupled with the talks I had with Carolina, helped me regain some of my footing. It was far from perfect but, thanks to my low expectations, I was able to make the best of it. A most welcome diversion was spending time with Enrique. Actually I felt a little guilty for not taking a greater part in raising him. Aside from occasionally taking him on short walks, there were long stretches of time when I didn't see him at all. And Carolina justly chided me for paying too little attention to him. Perhaps my negligence was partially attributable to my growing up as an ophan. I lacked a father figure, as Dr. Frommer had reminded me of.

Since Enrique was already able to move quite confidently, even climb steps, I made more time than usual to take him to the backyard to play ball, fully cognizant that such an exercise required several other skills he still had to learn. Though he might have been able to reach for the ball, he was unable to catch it. But once he had it in his possession, he'd pick it up and then throw it back underhand. What fascinated him most was finding an object, a rock, or a toy, I'd hidden someplace. Nervous with energy, he'd search every nook and cranny, leaving no stone unturned. And having finally found it, he'd hold it up like a trophy, beaming from ear to ear, while his eyes sparkled with joy.

I also took him on little strolls, first around the yard and gradually out onto quiet streets. If the walk was a bit long, he might occasionally stumble and fall. Yet he'd quickly shake off his slip-up, get up with a smile and keep on going. Sometimes when he happened to be full of vim and vigor I might even walk with him all the way to the Jardin. He seemed to be drawn to this place, particularly its sand box, presumably because it offered excitement, particularly other children, boys and girls, with whom he could interact, not always peacefully, I regret to say. For instance, one day I watched him swipe another boy's wooden truck only to be confronted by him. It took some time, sometimes even pushing and shoving, before he realized he was in the wrong. Thankfully I was also privileged to have watched him show a more gracious side. Two days after his first confrontation I saw him picking up a small boy who had been pushed down by an older one. He even offered the victim a hug while taking a threatening stance toward the perpetrator.

Mentally, he was wide awake, frequently pointing at things that caught his eyes, preferably animals, food and toys, as if he expected me to name them. He'd usually try to repeat what I said but oftentimes his words came rushing out garbled, unintelligible. Yet he was also able to utter meaningful spurts, containing three to four words. "Me go to Jardin?" he'd say in Spanish, looking at me as if seeking approval. He was especially versed in expressing certain needs. "Me hungry now," he'd say when his stomach growled. And at that point I'd better listen, or he might well work himself up into a temper tantrum. Yes, he could be very stubborn, asserting his will to the point of refusing to cooperate in getting dressed or putting on his shoes.

He liked to listen to Carolina or me read simple stories to him, most notably those which were interspersed with pictures. He was also fond of rhymes and songs, and when I presented them he would try to join in. Most often his attempts were far beyond his grasp, let alone skills, resulting in funny twists bringing me close to laughter. Much of what he'd do was unwittingly comical anyway.

Yet there were also times when I couldn't help but shake my head. Once at the Jardin I caught him and another boy playing with dog doo-doo. Using their hands, they tried to knead the turds into little bricks, which they stacked up to make it look like an adobe building, as though they were working with common dirt. Both were very upset when I and the other boy's mother dragged them away and buried their project with dirt. At another time, it was shortly after a good rain, I found him out in the backyard, kneeling near a flower bed with a fat earthworm in his mouth. The worm was still struggling, twisting and writhing. I instantly made him spit it out, squeezing his cheek and mouth, while lecturing him that earthworms belong to the earth but never in the mouth. He answered with an extended temper tantrum, gathering all his strength to push my hands away. What can I say, watching him may have covered the whole spectrum from funny to yucky and beastly. Yet it was never dull. More often than not it was very enjoyable. It made me focus on the present moment, making me forget, momentarily at least, the dark clouds that still continued to hover over my head.

If I wasn't busy with looking after Enrique, working in the garden or fixing something around the house, I'd saunter up to the cafe, where, over a dark-roast cup of coffee and some dulces, I'd spend a couple of hours watching people. Since I usually came at a set time in late afternoon, after the siesta, I invariably encountered familiar faces among the mixed crowd, made up of well-to-do Mexicans as well as *norteamericanos* and other expats. This being Mexico, we would, after first flashing smiles at each other, exchange greetings that could occasionally be accompanied by some small talk about the weather — being in the middle of the monsoon season offered a dramatic sideshow — or the local political scene.

One day in late June, a middle-aged Mexican man I'd chit-chatted with before, happened to approach me at the table. Introducing himself as Rudolfo Herrera, he asked me if by any chance I was Senor Stenson, the actor, who played the role of the German sailor in *They Came From Afar*.

Startled, I wavered for a few seconds but then nodded, "Yes, that's me."

"Congratulations! Your performance was absolutely stupendous. I was so taken by it that tears came to my eyes. My wife thought you were one of the best movie actors she had ever seen, and good-looking, too."

Rudolfo was a small but sturdy, well-nourished fellow with a broad, round-cheeked face, a low forehead, a pair of black button eyes, and a vibrant thatch of black hair that tended to divert my glances from his flaring, bat-like ear conches.

I invited him to take a seat, and we began to chat about the movie, the suffering of those refugees and the flattering ending. One thing led to another and pretty soon we were deep into our own lives, our families, our jobs and life in San Miguel. He told me he was married, had three children and worked for the tourist and visitors section in the town hall. He'd held this job for eighteen years and knew San Miguel better than his own pocket. Being an affable busybody with a nose for news, he was aware of who was coming and going, the number of foreigners living here and where they came from, most of them anyway. He liked it here; his only complaint: The pay was lousy. "It's hand to mouth," he claimed. "We can hardly scrape by with the money I bring home." In passing, he also touched on the shadowy world of crime, claiming that it was far more vibrant than meets the eye. That was at least the assessment of a prominent police officer he was chummy with.

'Police officer?' Was there anything more piquant that could've pricked up my ears? But I held back from prying for fear he'd think of me harboring a closet full of skeletons.

In any event, during the next few months I often got together with Rudolfo and we eventually befriended each other. Mindful of his lack of means, I often invited him for antojitos and drinks. And he knew how to appreciate getting a treat. In the course of our conversations, I once insinuated that, being a foreigner, I may accidentally have overstayed my time here in Mexico and that I was worried that one day the Federales might be looking for me.

Rudolfo found that funny and laughed. "Come on, Fred, you are in Mexico, not in los Estados Unidos. I wouldn't worry about that."

"Well, you don't know because you're not sitting in the same boat. But I feel vulnerable. I just wonder… What if they came looking for me? I heard they are a nasty bunch."

"Well, as a rule they are 'cause there's nobody who is checking on them. And that is always dangerous in Mexico. But in your case you could clear your name by paying a mordida of 100 pesos. That's all."

"How about if I'd disappear for a day or two, so they couldn't find me?"

"Well, that would be the best. You'd save the mordida."

"If only I knew when they were coming."

"Oh, I may be able to help you with that. I could ask my friend Arturo at the police precinct to inform me about such visits. He usually knows. And then I…"

We shook hands.

In early July, Carolina and I headed to el D.F. for the red-carpet premiere of 'Sweets and Red Chili'. Actually, I had already seen the final version at the private showing presented at the Studio Theater three weeks before. But Carolina hadn't, and she was eager to get a taste of 'Sweets'. She also wanted to visit with Jorge, the Aznars and do some shopping. Jorge, generous as always, offered us his apartment for the stay. And Carolina had already promised to take his offer. Yet I was leery, insisting that I'd rather be safe than sorry. As usual, Carolina promptly accused me of being paranoid again.

I shot back, pointing the finger at her lack of intuition. "Somehow you can't project yourself into my mind. I've a *reason* to be scared. How many times were the judiciales looking for me? May I remind you that even Dr. Frommer took cognizance of that."

Well, she eventually bowed, and we finally settled on staying at the Hotel Monte Carlo again. As an additional bonus, we were assigned the very room the English writer D.H. Lawrence had once occupied, or so the manager tried to inveigle us into believing.

The premiere itself was just as flamboyant as the previous one. We actors and actresses, but also the producer Senor Alarcon, were at the center of attention. The reporters and movie critics descended on us as if we were the makers of heaven and earth. Flashing the lights on us and shoving the microphones into our faces, they bombarded us with such questions as the future of sensuality and love, if we believed in another Mexican revolution and whether communism was a possible answer to corruption and the sorry state of the indigenas, the Indian population.

The movie itself received ravishing applause, not least because of the many lurid, tantalizing love scenes and the contemporary Marxist revolutionary fervor. After the show we gathered behind the stage for a lively reception, where pretty, high-bosomed girls in short skirts served wine, champagne and appetizers. We mingled with the artists, critics and movie buffs. The most sought after man happened to be Senor Alarcon again. He was surrounded by a dense halo of movie critics from various papers who shot pointed questions at him. As usual, he was in a blithe and cheerful mood, giving succinct and witty answers that sparked roars of laughter.

During a lull way at the end I also had a chance to get into a chit-chat with him. Actually as we walked past, he turned his head and hollered, "Hola! Carolina and Fritz... I mean... Fred. Good to see you both."

I was dumbfounded. "How do you know my real name?"

"Oh, your name? Why would you want know? At any rate, I'm working on a new movie script with an intriguing plot, whose leading roles were a German SS officer who falls in love with a Jewish woman. Apparently, it really happened a little more than two years ago in Russia."

"Yes, I have heard about it," I added. "It happened in the Bukovina."

"Oh, really? So you know about it?"

"Yes."

He glanced at me as if I'd fallen from a batch of clouds. And catching himself, he went on, "All the better. To write a credible movie script about the lieutenant, I desperately need somebody who knows the German Army from the inside, the ins and outs, how it ticks. I've been told that you served in it."

"Who in the hell told you that?" I remember pressing him.

"Well, let's not get into it. In any event, I would like to ask you if you can help me with the script. And if you like the part of the officer also play it, or at least help during shooting."

"You flatter me. I'd be delighted to help you with the script and also play the part of the officer, even though I have great reservations representing a member of Himmler's SS."

"You should. If it's all right, we can work on the script together. As soon as I write a few scenes, I'll send them to you for a thorough critique. I want you to be the devil's advocate, to make suggestions, changes, always keeping in mind that the scenes should be authentic, the way they could have happened in real life."

"That goes without saying. When, do you think, could I get the first scenes?"

He told me in about four weeks or so. He would keep me informed.

I also tried to broach the recent visit of the judiciales but he'd put me off politely saying he couldn't stand these asses with ears and goggles. He still added that he'd be flying to Hollywood early in the morning. He wouldn't be back until the middle of next week.

"Hollywood?" I burst out.

"Yes there is a good chance that I'll find a distributor for 'Sweets' in the United States. The Americans very much relish its anti-communist stance. They're crazy about it."

"That would be great. Good luck!"

"I may need it."

BECOMING MORE MEXICAN?

Boy, was it soothing to be back in San Miguel. I was surprised how much this town had taken root in me. When I was criss-crossing this fetid, quake-riven crock called el D.F., I hankered for the steep, cobblestoned streets and old houses gathered around churches and squares, the clanging of church bells swashing over the roofs and up the hill; I longed for the clean air and starry sky, the sounds of tranquility, the roosters cock-a-doodle-dooing, the burros braying, the mariachis' whining laments of heartbreak and loss under the portals near the Jardin; I yearned for Enrique with his laughter and all his foibles, for our comfortable home with its cozy corners and its inviting patio, the profusion of greenery, the riot of flowers and, last though not least, the unabashed mop of a purple bougainvillea.

I originally came here to escape from the claws of the judiciales and, unbeknownst to me, found a home, a place that warmed the cockles of my heart. Yet why do I catch myself again and again rubbing my horseshoe and knocking on wood? Because deep in a cranny of my cabeza a somber voice keeps whispering that my hearth couldn't last, the day of reckoning would inevitably come, when the judiciales would be barricading our gate and demanding my scalp. Not to worry, some may say. True, I am prepared; after all, I have a tunnel I can use to escape. But where would I go? And for how long? I couldn't be on the run forever.

I discussed my worries with Carolina, in the wake of our first supper after our return. Her position: To quell these bothersome voices, I should drop being so German and infuse my mind with a more relaxed attitude and become more Mexican. I could, for instance, keep a slacker rein on myself and devote myself to living more in the present, in the tangible moment, similar to what I'd promised myself in the dialogue with Rodrigo, my skull. What she had in mind was for me to take a different, more passive attitude toward time. To underpin her thrust, she referred to a Mayan poem she had recently read a translation of. It deals with our attitude toward the notion of time, depicting the course of the day in Mayan culture. As the poet made us believe, the day would show up in the east and then start walking. It would be on a journey, and we humans were bound to be woven into its fabric, although we were unable to shape it.

"In other words, the day is inherently mightier than the human will," Carolina claimed. "Think about it. Wisdom hints at us to better pull along and fall in step with it."

I took a gulp of coffee. "Quite original," I offered with a smile. "But I'm sniffing your old 'ojala' again, now wrapped in a new garb, the 'Mayan day'. We humans can't do anything 'cause that's the way the ball bounces or the cookie crumbles. I concede, to think and live like that may be more soothing but it leads to irresponsible behavior with potentially fatal consequences. Daily many people die because of it. Rudolfo recently told me that one of his relatives, a young, well-known soccer player, died in an accident. Apparently, somewhere in southern Chiapas a bridge collapsed and a bus full of soccer players and fans tumbled into a roaring river a hundred meters below. More than thirty people perished, including his relative. Only four survived. And you know what Rudolfo said? *'Ni modo'*. (Nothing can be done. It can't be helped.)That's what he said. 'But Rudolfo, you can't be serious,' I flashed back, shaking my head. 'More than thirty people died! Somebody must be held responsible. The bridge should have been inspected and, if found wanting, repaired or torn down. Somebody screwed up. In other words, the accident could've been prevented.'

"Maybe in Germany or in the United States but not in Mexico," Rudolfo claimed, shrugging his shoulders. "Have you ever heard of hen's teeth? No, they don't exist. Well, it's the same with responsibility."

"So it'll happen again, tomorrow, somewhere in Chihuahua."

"*Sí.*"

"That's what Rudolfo said," I explained to Carolina. "In other words, responsibility is as scarce as hen's teeth. That's why you'll never find a desk where the buck stops. Remember the papazote? He struck the same note. In Mexico, you can literally get away with murder."

"If that's true, how come you're so scared of the judiciales?"

"The judiciales are not the problem. They'd have long dropped me. It's the Americans who keep pushing them."

"I know what you're driving at," Carolina added. "But you must also admit that falling in step with an all-powerful day does indeed lighten the burden and soothes your mind. It makes you feel freer. The irony is, your obsession with the judiciales, your paranoia, actually fences you in. It's like another, self-made prison that is robbing you of the freedom you're trying to hang onto. I think you could enjoy life much more if you wouldn't worry so much about all these sinister things that could happen to you."

"I believe you, that may all be true but at what price? It would be so high it wouldn't be worth paying for it. I know what it's like. I got badly burned once. When I was seventeen, I literally fell in step with our German fate. We called it Adolf Hitler. I had put all my faith in his leadership, to the point of dying for him. I was greener and dumber than a young pea pod. Had it not been for sheer luck, my bones would've been rotting away in Russia. Most of my comrades experienced precisely such a fate. Luckily I was able to wake up, at the last moment, when one of my friends was hanged by those Nazi zealots. And the first action I took was jackknifing the line. Looking back, that was the first sensible move I made and it still fills me with pride.

"I know you have the best of intentions, Carolina, but if I had followed your advice, I'd have been food for worms in a forsaken area of Texas. I owe my life to my wits, my will, some gambling and oodles of luck. And, by the way, if somewhere in Mexico a bridge collapses or a cookie crumbles, I'd want to know who was in charge. I'd ask why they were so fragile and if the engineer or baker had done their job. Were they attentive and competent, or did they come to work drowsy with eyelids down and a pint of tequila rushing through their blood vessels? That's why I have a tough time falling in step with the Mayan day."

VALE OF TEARS

At the end of August, on the evening of the 25th, Carolina received a phone call from her mother. Imelda was so swamped with emotion that Carolina could barely grasp what she was saying. She stumbled and muddled that Don Leonardo had been struck down by a severe stroke and had been committed to a hospital in Chihuahua. The doctors who treated him informed her that he could well pass away. She just wanted to let Carolina know. Jorge's been informed as well.

Carolina promptly called Jorge and they agreed to zoom up there and pay their father a visit, possibly their last. Actually they urged me to come along as well. But I declined, arguing that Don Leonardo had shown nothing but disdain for me. Besides, Chihuahua would only awaken old demons I wouldn't want to stir up.

"Shame on you," Carolina countered. "You're very ungrateful. You keep forgetting, my dear, it was my dad who loaned you the money for the ransom to get you out of jail, without so much as a nod or a gesture of thanks from you. Think about it. Had it not been for him, you'd have been nothing but food for *zopilotes,* turkey vultures. And as to your remarks about Chihuahua, you tend to forget that it was the Gutierrezes, Francisco and Erlinda that unlocked Mexico for you. They took you in and also recommended you to Guillermo. Had it not been for their help, you wouldn't have had a job and we'd never have met."

No doubt, she had a point, indeed, more than one. And, I hasten to say, also a companion to accompany her on the journey — me. In any event, Jorge came by in the early afternoon to pick us up and together we barreled north to Chihuahua. We rented a room at a hotel and, having dropped off our luggage, rushed over to the hospital.

Although Don Leonardo was still alive when we stepped into the sickroom, he was so frail and tired we weren't even sure he'd recognize us. Deep, dark gouges underscored his eyes sitting in a pitifully ashen face. Having emitted an anguished howl, he was overcome by a paroxysm of coughing, eventually chucking up some mucus he spat into a spittoon.

All in all, we stayed on for eight days and, together with Imelda, went on our daily pilgrimage to the hospital to spend time with the prodigious, but very frail hacendado. Unfortunately, things looked grim. His health declined rapidly. The whole left side of his face and part of his body became paralyzed. We all braced for the inevitable. But then, quite unexpectedly, he managed to perk up again. Clinging to a straw, everybody, the nurses, doctors, as well as Imelda, Carolina, Jorge and I rejoiced. Jorge brought several bottles of champagne, and circling his bed, we all toasted to his health. *"Long live Don Leonardo!"* was the huzzah we belted out.

Yet, just as the celebration was about to reach its climax, Don Leonardo rose from his bed and, staring at us and flailing like a madman, began shouting a garbled volley of words we could barely decipher. "Stop it, you fools! Life? What life? Having my bottom wiped and pushed around in the wheelchair! I'd much rather be dead than keep on living in such misery." At that point, he collapsed, covered his face and started sobbing and mewling like a baby.

A hush settled over the room, filling every corner, nook and cranny. Taken aback, embarrassed, we, Imelda, Carolina, Jorge and I, as well as the doctors and nurses, sheepishly looked at one another. Nobody uttered a word. Eventually the doctors and nurses slinked out of the room, leaving us relatives behind, all deeply shaken. Watching that proud man, whose life had been lived according to a strict aristocratic demeanor, breaking down in the face of such a tragic fate was so gripping, I couldn't help but commiserate with him. I was moved to tears, pursing my lips and clenching my teeth. Nor was I alone. Imelda, Carolina, and Jorge were seized by even starker emotions.

At last, having regained his composure, Don Leonardo gave me a stare, then stretched out his hand, thumb up. After wobbling a second or two, I bent over and, without saying a word, locked hands with him. It was one of those gestures which would never be rinsed out of my memory till the end of my days.

Lest I forget, while we stayed in Chihuahua I paid the Gutierrezes, Francisco and Erlinda, an unannounced visit. Stunned, both received me with open arms, thanking me profusely for the bouquet of flowers and the bottle of champagne I'd brought along, not to mention the Christmas cards I'd sent them over the years. Sadly, both had aged, particularly Francisco, who looked very frail. He was racked with pain and had a hell of a time walking, owing to his bad back and arthritic knees. We popped the bottle of champagne and raised the glasses to our health. Erlinda fixed some tasty antojitos and we sat around the table and chewed the fat, catching up on the events that had touched us the past two years.

Francisco informed me that Pablo was still working on the farm in Colorado and sending money home, and greetings to me. They had bought a lot for him nearby, where he would build a house upon his return. But that would take another two to three years. Guillermo, the foreman at the hacienda who had hired me, had recently announced the birth of another son. He was still busy as a *capataz*. The Gutierrezes obviously hadn't heard the latest news, and when I told them that Don Leonardo had been struck down by a stroke and that he was trying to recuperate at the hospital here in Chihuahua, they were bowled down. Erlinda instantly offered to send a fervent prayer to the Virgen de Guadalupe, begging her to intervene on Don Leonardo's behalf.

They also wanted to know about Carolina, where we lived, if we had any children and what I was doing. They were amazed when I revealed that I made my living by acting in movies, which to them was a *terra incognita* they might want to visit one day.

At the end of our journey to the north, Carolina, Jorge and I also seized the opportunity to wind our way up to the hacienda, where we stayed for a couple of days. Actually I, just to be safe, spent the nights in the very shack where Carolina and I used to meet for our amorous rendezvous. As to the state of the hacienda, it struck me from the beginning that it had seen better days. Starting with the shape of the road, the mansion and the bunkhouse, many things were in disrepair or simply falling apart. It showed that Don Leonardo, having been ailing for some time, had long lost his ability to keep a tight rein on the running of the estate and we all wondered what would happen, once he returned, if, indeed, he would. Jorge, for one, did not mince words, suggesting it ought to be sold. But his dad had always resisted and would probably continue to do so. In that case nothing could be done, at least until he'd pass away.

Three weeks later, Carolina received a call from her mother who broke the news that Don Leonardo had passed away shortly after he'd been released from the hospital. On his first Sunday, he'd called on Demesia, to help him put on his Sunday suit, his hat and strap on his fanciest riding boots. Clueless, she made him climb into his wheelchair, as was his wish, then pushed him up to the horse stable, close to his favorite horse. There she was told to go back to the mansion. Well, a few minutes later they heard a shot blasting off. Startled, they all stared at each other, until Demesia broke down in tears, stuttering out Don Leonardo's last request. Her suspicion proved true. Minutes later they found their hacendado slumped in his wheelchair, splattered with blood. Part of his skull had been blown off, with a bullet of a Colt that was now lying at his feet.

The funeral was scheduled to take place three days later. A Catholic priest and a Rabbi led the ceremony. He'd requested to be buried at the hacienda, close to the horse stable, where he'd chosen to end his life. Jorge, Carolina, I and Enrique attended, as well as close to two hundred people from all walks of life. It was a most solemn occasion with funeral rites conducted in Spanish, but also in Hebrew, including a long eulogy. And when the coffin was lowered into the grave six cowboys, armed with rifles, lined up and gave their hacendado a festive farewell.

Shocked to the core by her husband's death, Imelda fell into a deep trough of grief from which she never fully recovered. Jorge and Carolina still managed to move her to el D.F. for treatment. But, having lost her will to live, she soon succumbed to a bout of pneumonia. She died a month later, shortly after the celebration of her seventy-third birthday.

Since neither Jorge nor Carolina showed interest in taking over the hacienda, it was eventually sold, albeit in parcels. Most of the land, including the mansion, was swallowed up by the Mennonites. Thus ended four hundred years of family ownership. Carolina broke down in tears, when the last piece with the mansion came up for bids. And I was on the verge of it. Deprived of its corporeal existence, the hacienda would continue to live on in both of our memories as a Shangri-la, where we'd spent the happiest days of our lives.

Shortly after my return from Chihuahua, I received the first badge of scenes from Senor Alarcon. I right away plunged into them. A novice that I was, I'd never done such a task of critically reading a screenplay before. Moreover, I was very unsure of myself, not least because it was written in Spanish. Again and again I had to engage Carolina who helped me understand the script, the characters, the plots, including its countless nuances. Having no academic background, I also wrestled with my role as critic. Standing in awe of Senor Alarcon, it took extraordinary courage and a concerted effort to pass judgment on his characterizations. Was he not my mentor? A screenwriter, a celebrated director and producer of motion pictures?

What helped me getting over the hump was my familiarity of the German military. I flattered myself of having a definite edge over the old zorro, as far as the story of the SS-lieutenant was concerned. Besides discussing it on end with my comrades during the Russian campaign, I was also well acquainted with the ethos of the German Army, the conduct and demeanor of its soldiers. It provided me with some backbone, steadying my hand to add comments, suggest changes and inject nuances, thus improving the script by making it more authentic.

Once I had finished the job, I wondered if my comments had been a tad too harsh, the more so since the pages resembled a collection of battle scenes. *Could I have pricked my mentor's pride?* And having sent them off, I braced for Senor Alarcon's response.

Well, four days later I received a call from him. And what a relief it was to hear an accolade of praise. "Good job!" I heard the old fox saying. "What you did easily surpassed my expectations. How in the hell did you do all that in such a short time? If you continue on that path I won't be able to deny you the co-authorship of the screenplay."

I was enraptured, carried away. I couldn't think of anything that could have raised the level of my self-confidence more than Senor Alarcon's words.

PANIC ATTACK

"Senor de Keyser, there is a phone call for you," Juanita, our housemaid, hollered at me. "It's a gentleman by the name of Rudolfo."

I was outside, carrying sacks of oats from the car over to the horse stable. "Rudolfo?" My adrenaline rising, I rushed to the phone.

"Sorry to disturb you, Fred," Rudolfo hustled in his high-pitched voice. "But I just talked to Arturo, my friend at the police department, and he informed me the judiciales have been in town since last night. Sorry I'm so late. I just found all of that out a minute ago."

My pulse started galloping; I choked to the point of suffocating. "Did Arturo tell you why they're here?"

"He doesn't know. Generally, the judiciales don't tell them. I just wanted to let you know. Anyway, good luck."

"Thanks for telling me."

Flustered, I informed Carolina about the news. She tried to calm me down, claiming there could be many reasons why they'd pay the town a visit. "Of course, it doesn't hurt to clear the tunnel of spiderwebs," she admitted. "Just in case."

Bracing for the cops to show up any time, I told Juanita to position herself at the gate and watch for anybody *desconfiado,* suspicious. If that were to happen, she should immediately ring the bell.

In the meantime I scrambled down to the basement to check out the tunnel. Save for some spiders, among them black widows, and a couple of small puddles way toward the exit — a remnant from the torrential rain two days ago — everything appeared to be in fair shape.

Well, on the way up the stairs, I stumbled and fell. Down on my knees, I suddenly panicked, shivering, uncontrollably, as if in a mortal dread. Cold sweat ran down my spine. I was so detached from myself, I can't even recall what exactly happened. I faintly remember that Carolina tried to calm me down, accusing me of being crazy. What I can tell with a fair degree of certainty, I found myself heading west along the agricultural plain toward Guanajuato. As I plodded along I eventually changed direction, turning north toward Dolores Hidalgo, possibly San Luis Potosi. I hoped to eventually reach the thinly settled, wide, open spaces of the border states, Tamaulipas, Chihuahua, and even Sonora. I figured that they'd boost my chances of remaining incognito. Naturally, my thoughts hinged on the hope that Carolina and Enrique could join me later, once I'd settled down. But all that was nothing more than a hot gust of brainstorming.

I must have walked about eleven kilometers and intermittently hitchhiked another thirty-two, passing small farming communities and groups of people, usually Indians, working in fields, until at last I reached Dolores Hidalgo. A tired sun had barely settled way in the west as I stepped out of a rattling old Ford jalopy. Ambling around the Plaza Principal the heart of the town, I found a room at a friendly *casa de huespedes* called Posada Dolores. Later I treated myself to a meal of tacos al carbon and two bottles of Bohemia. Gradually, very gradually, as the meal began to settle, I regained a semblance of peace. And once back at the reception, I placed a call to Carolina, more than eager to find out how the visit of these sinister guests had proceeded.

"Where are you?" Carolina wanted to know. "Are you all…"

"In Dolores Hidalgo. Tell me, what happened? Are they gone?"

"What do you mean? They weren't even…"

"Stop playing the secret-monger. How did they treat you? Were they as wicked as before, at the Aznar's?"

"Fred, sober up, please! There were no judiciales anywhere, *nadie*."

"Come on…"

"The whole scare existed only in your imagination that bubbled out of your warped and paranoid mind. Just as I told you before you were storming out."

"I wouldn't be so quick to judge. How can you be so sure? They may still show up. What if they're at the gate tomorrow morning?"

"Yes, like the great white shark popping up in a sprawl of cacti."

I had a torturous night, filled with bizarre dreams, topped by a frightful nightmare. I was at home when seven banditos, armed with machetes, came crashing through the door. When they surrounded Enrique, Carolina and me, I tried to fight them off, throwing candle holders, flower pots and chairs at them. But they kept on coming, shouting repeatedly at me, "We remember you from the Chihuahua prison. We will get you, bastard. This time, we'll cut your throat."

I rolled out of bed with the rising sun. Dead tired and sweaty, I dragged myself to the bathroom, where I showered cold. That sobered me up, helping me regain my footing. Last night's exchange with Carolina wouldn't let go of me. It was beyond embarrassing.

Having dressed, I headed to a nearby cafe, where I swilled down three shots of tequila. That helped me easing up a little. For breakfast, I scoffed down a heap of *huevos motulenos*. Yesterday's loss of face gnawed at me relentlessly. Still I felt drawn to heading back home. So I wound my way to the bus station, where I found out that the buses to San Miguel left about every two hours. In fact, I saw a Flecha Amarilla standing there revving up its engine. But I was not quite ready to hop aboard. I wanted to make damned sure I wouldn't bump into a bunch of judiciales who might still be practicing their duplicitous searches. So instead I picked up a couple of newspapers, found a cafe close to the Plaza Principal, where I, hunched over a cup of coffee and shot of tequila, perused the papers for the latest news.

The afternoon dragged on like a frazzled piece of cloth loosely woven with used and stolen moments. Shortly before five, I trudged back to the bus station, boarded the bus and less than an hour later stepped off in San Miguel. Mercifully, I didn't detect any sign of the judiciales. Nor had they paid a visit to Carolina in the morning, as I soon found out. It was all reassuring, indeed, worthy of raising glasses of champagne. Yet Carolina was not in the mood to celebrate. Quite the contrary, seldom had I seen her so filled with raw anger. She pounced on me, starting a violent quarrel, to the point where we almost came to blows. According to her, I was hopelessly paranoid, mentally ill, ready to be committed to the loony bin. She even threatened to file for divorce, if this would ever happen again.

Actually, my ill-timed anxiety attack which caused such a stir should have been placed squarely in Dr. Frommer's bailiwick. The session I had with the gentleman less than two weeks later begged for it. Yet I felt so embarrassed about it, I didn't dare mention it to him. Instead, I let myself be guided into the dusty, spider-webbed dungeons of my childhood at the orphanage. Don't get me wrong, it was well-meant but I doubted that it pulled up anything worth my while.

After we had shaken hands, I strolled up to the cafe where I sipped several cups of coffee, read the paper and watched people. A street musician, squatting on the steps nearby, passed on a rich offering of breakneck guitar licks, minutely crafted string runs and subtle vibratos, all topped by boisterous chords and bent notes. As usual, shortly past five Rudolfo came in to join me. He'd recently received a raise, which had visibly lifted his mood. Curious, I pried him about the visit of the judiciales and why they'd appeared in here the first place. He suggested that their goal was to go after some drug dealers who were staying at the Hostal

Internacional and the Casa de Huespuedes. According to Arturo at the local police station they were able to question four suspects, two Mexicans and an American couple whom they later arrested and put behind bars at the federal penitentiary in el D.F.

Rudolfo also enlightened me about the use and trafficking of drugs here in San Miguel, claiming there was a very lucrative market, owing to the large colony of foreigners, people with means no less than needs. That served as the primary reason why the town had moved in the crosshairs of the judiciales and why they might raid it more often in the future.

"I'd really appreciate if you could inform me *before* their arrival," I told him, handing him 100 peso bill.

"I'll try my best." He smiled as he snatched it and shoved it into his pocket.

Incidentally, I never told Carolina about the reason for the judiciales' visit. It would only have given her even more firepower against me.

Time ran through my fingers like fine sand. I didn't so much feel it, as I was able to witness it while watching Enrique grow and develop. It was simply amazing. As his baby fat gradually receded, his chest and neck grew in volume. Never immune from a certain swagger, he was very fond of walking around on tiptoes, or even jumping. But his favorite occupation was to play ball, getting a kick out of kicking or throwing a big soccer ball toward or at me. I had long staked out a small soccer field and put up a cage. I'd try to keep goal, and whenever he'd be able to outwit and get the ball past me, he'd glow with pride. And when I applauded him, he'd curl his right hand into a fist, jerk it up and roar with laughter.

When we walked up to town, we often got stuck at the most unusual of places, simply because something he didn't know caught his attention. Forever curious, he'd point at the object or pick it up and ask me to name it. He always tried to repeat the word, although sometimes he garbled it and out came his own creation. When I hastened to correct him, he'd turn very stubborn, mulish. Sometimes he'd yell angrily at me, as if I were at fault of his mispronunciation. His curiosity also carried over to the stories Carolina would read to him almost every evening before he was sent to bed. Not only would he listen very attentively, he might also inject comments about the characters. "He is a bad man," he'd say. Or, "I like her!" He was particularly fond of tales containing riddles and suspense, where he was challenged to guess the outcome.

Owning a coloring book, pencils and crayons, he'd also try to paint and draw, especially forts and castles. But often his imagination ran ahead of his ability to put something meaningful on paper. That frustrated him and he could easily lose his composure, throwing his pencil or crayon against the wall. But let him get his hands on rocks or, better yet, on mud, and he'd unfold the patience of Job. As soon as the rain showed signs of letting up, he ventured out into the backyard to the pile of dirt, which he'd shape into small adobe bricks to build castles or forts with.

I often wondered how *I* carried on when I was his age, but unfortunately I couldn't remember all that much, at least before the age of six. That blank slate had already come up at a session with Dr. Frommer, and I often wondered why it took me so long to become conscious about myself and my surroundings. I guess I was simply a late-bloomer, as the wise old gentleman had dubbed me.

THE SORROWS OF THE KOMMANDANT.

Quite frankly, the co-operation between Senor Alarcon and me couldn't have been smoother or more fruitful. Over the next few months I must have received more than five batches of scenes I was asked to critique, and each time my mentor was full of praise for my work. Trusting my judgment, he'd gradually drift more and more in my direction. He relied on me not only in the development of the characters, the lieutenant and the Jewish women, but also willingly took my advice on the plot.

"It's going to be a most gripping story," he once said over the phone, "and you're doing a terrific job. I don't think I could write it without your input. You have a keen ability to go through the script to find the underlying emotional truth." Now that was a compliment from a man who can sniff out a pivotal scene like a seasoned pig in search of truffles.

On the first Friday in January, during a severe cold spell, which nipped many of our tropical plants, I received another call from the old fox. Thanking me for my last critique, he let me know that the script was pretty much done. The provisional title should be 'The Sorrows of Lieutenant X', adding that he'd still like to introduce me to Alicia Stoltenberg who is interested in playing the part of Esther Silbermann. He invited me and Carolina to dinner at the Bar La Opera, where we'd met before, and asked what day would be convenient for us.

"Tuesday would be fine for me," I said, after checking the calendar.

"Good, see you Tuesday night." He gave me a tentative time when we could meet. In case he couldn't get a reservation, he or a secretary would call me back and suggest another place.

When I informed Carolina about the invitation, she expressed a willingness, even eagerness, to join me. She was always drawn to Senor Alarcon because he was not only a man who wore his smarts lightly, but a gentleman to boot. What's more, while she was in el D.F. she also thought of getting together with Jorge whom she hadn't seen since September.

On Tuesday morning we barreled down to el D.F. The lush green the monsoon season had so generously allotted us had vanished. Nature had put on its tan coat and its burlap dress for the dry season. As bad luck would have it, the city's air was as bad as ever, perhaps even worse. Popocatepetl, the proud sentinel, was hidden behind a thick layer of brownish-grey haze, jamming the whole valley.

Yet the Bar La Opera on Cinco de Mayo appeared to be even more opulent than before, a supreme visual as well as culinary treat. Senor Alarcon was already waiting for us, seated as he was far back in the corner. His nose buried in a script, he occasionally nipped on a drink and puffed his cubano. As usual, he greeted Carolina with a hand kiss and me with a warm embrazo. "By the way, Alicia Stoltenberg had a small accident," he said. "She's going to join us a little later."

He first ordered a Spanish cava and we toasted to our exemplary collaboration. For a starter the old fox had ordered *anguilas,* baby eels, with maize crackers. For the main dish I favored their *pollo verde almendrado,* chicken with green tomatillo-almond sauce, and a full-bodied Argentinian Malbec, while Carolina went for *pescado a la veracruzana*, tossed off by a Chilean Sauvignon Blanc.

Senor Alarcon right away delved into 'Dulce', informing us that it was doing rather well, in part because of the strident controversy it aroused. Some critics with left leanings called it a debauched, self-indulgent testimony of a belated capitalist ideology, while other pundits on the right praised it as a deep and very enlightening exploration of life in the twentieth century, showing the utter bankruptcy of the communist ideology and its followers. Smiling, he was quick to add that various communist organizations had even staged demonstrations in front of those movie theaters that were showing the flick. To no one's surprise, Diego Rivera, Frida Kahlo and Alfaro Siqueiros, as well as other left-leaning artists had also participated.

"Let them demonstrate," he sputtered, raising his eyebrows and casting an impish twinkle at us. "Every protest and boycott are free ads for our film. They are too dumb to notice that." He took a bite of his *puntas de filete,* quartered beef filet ends, chasing it with a gulp of Malbec.

"There she is," he suddenly paused, rising from his chair.

Approaching our table with self-assured steps was a young, captivating blonde with perfectly symmetrical facial features, a cute little nose, a broad forehead and a pair of wide-set eyes of a gossamer blue that doll manufacturers tend to pick for their choicest dolls. She was dressed in a purple spencer with a broad black collar and a ruffled light-blue skirt.

"I'm glad you could make it," Senor Alarcon said, mimicking a hand kiss. And turning toward us, he went on, "May I introduce you to Alicia Stoltenberg. As I told you, Miss Stoltenberg has expressed interest in playing the part of Esther Silbermann."

After we had shaken hands, she took a seat next to Senor Alarcon.

"So it worked out," Senor Alarcon told her, rubbing his chops with a napkin.

"Yes, it wasn't easy. What can you do? You can't choose your parents."

I might add, I was deeply impressed by Miss Stoltenberg, not only on account of her looks but also on the way she moved and smelled. Did I not detect a waft of lavender drifting across the table?

After she had ordered a dish of *pescado a la veracruzana* and a glass of white wine, she leaned toward Senor Alarcon and gazed at him in expectation. The old wizard cleared his throat. "As promised, let me add a little meat to the skeleton I've given you last week. By the way, it will all be in the screenplay you'll get at the end. The title I've settled on is 'The Sorrows of the Kommandant'. It's a human drama that takes place in the western Ukraine during the war, or so Fred tells me, and he should know. Fred, maybe you can give Miss Silbermann an overall picture of what happened when the German Army pushed its way into the area."

"Sure," I snickered, overjoyed to take up the slack. "The regular German Army entered many villages and towns that were populated by Jews but also by Germans. Although most Germans had already left the area for Germany, some, especially left-leaning idealists, stayed on. With the subsequent arrival of Himmler's rabid SS troops, horrible things happened, especially to the Jewish population. Some were either shot on the spot or herded together and sent to the concentration camps. But a few of them also tried to go into hiding," I went on, riveting my eyes on Miss Stoltenberg. "Among them were the Silbermanns, a well-to-do, highly educated Jewish family. Well, one of their two children happened to be a strikingly beautiful, nineteen-year-old girl who was endowed with a shock of reddish-blond curls, captivating facial features, long legs and a curvaceous, buxom body."

"Needless to say, that would be your part, Miss Stoltenberg," Senor Alarcon butted in. "Unfortunately, the Silbermanns, being Jews, were also caught in their dragnet. As she watches her family being taken away, Esther happens to be struck by an indomitable will to live. And when a lieutenant wants to know what her name is, she claims it is Helga Krause and that she is of pure German blood, going back to the earliest German immigrants that poured into Russia under Catherine the Great. Luckily, she has the looks to prove it. In addition, she chooses not only to speak a highly refined German, but she's also familiar with most of the pillars of German *Kultur*. Thanks to her looks, her demeanor and her command of the German language and culture, she immediately catches the eye and ear of Wolfgang Wagner, the SS Kommandant.

"That's where Fred enters," Senor Alarcon went on, turning toward me. "The Kommandant is captivated, smitten. He calls for a tank, orders his troops to fall into a perfect circle around it, then scales it and raises Helga upon it. 'Comrades, soldiers and fighting men', he bellows, 'I want you to take a good look at Helga Krause. Here we have a perfect example of a pure-blooded German girl, in Russia of all places, the new *Lebensraum* that we'll soon have conquered all the way to the Urals and beyond. Our Fuehrer, the whole German *Volk,* would be proud of her. *Heil Hitler! Sieg Heil'!*"

"Wow!" I heard Miss Stoltenberg remarking. "What a scene."

"But as the affair between Helga Krause and the Kommandant unfolds, two Ukrainians who cooperated with the Germans, bristle that he the Kommandant, fell victim to a lie; that the presumed Helga Krause is none other than Esther Silbermann, a full-fledged Jewess. Other witnesses also come to the fore, and in the end she confesses to the Kommandant who by then is head over heels in love with her."

Here Senor Alarcon paused, hollering to a passing waiter to refill our glasses. Once the waiter had left, he resumed. "As expected, the Kommandant is crestfallen, mortified. He lets her know that he must immediately cut off all contacts; that he has sworn absolute loyalty to his Fuehrer, to the racial purity of the German *Volk*; that in sleeping with a Jewess he has betrayed and soiled the very idea of the Third Reich. He suffers, he squirms and twists as if under a curse. Yet, tied up in bondage to her, he falls into a slough of despond from which he'd never rise. And six days after her confession, he sticks a P-38 in his mouth.

"His death, not to mention the events preceding it, kicks up a hell of a row and outrage, particularly in Berlin. But they are quickly hushed up. The government's obituary notice to his wife simply states that Wolfgang Wagner has died an heroic death fighting for the Fuehrer and the German *Vaterland.*"

Senor Alarcon took a swig of wine and brushed his mouth with his sleeve. "Where was I… Ah, yes… While the Kommandant ends his life, he saves Esther Silbermann's. He keeps on worshipping her until the bitter end. He sees to it that she's put up in an nice apartment, that she's fed and receives identity papers under the name of Helga Krause. And two weeks later she pops up in Berlin, where she is destined to spend the rest of the war years, working as a German-Russian translator and interpreter for the government. During one of the air raids she is wounded. That's how she meets a German physician whom she marries and gives birth to two children. In secret, she keeps working on her memoirs. Shortly after the war she emerges from her shadow, drops her German identity and becomes Esther Silbermann again. She divorces her husband, takes her two children and is on her way to Israel. Still working as a translator, she finishes her memoirs, which is destined to become an international bestseller."

"Once again, it's a most gripping and captivating story," Miss Stoltenberg blurt out. "It's even up a few notches from the original version two months ago. Congratulations! I feel greatly honored that you offered me to play a part in it." She shook Senor Alarcon's hand.

"Hold it! Fred is just as deserving as I am, perhaps even more so. Let me just say, I could not have done the job without him."

"Oh?" Miss Stoltenberg said. "Well, thanks to you, too, Fred. You both did a superb job. I'm really looking forward to the challenge."

"Wonderful!" Senor Alarcon shouted. "What a happy occasion! Let's drink to it."

We clinked our glasses.

"Incidentally, here is the synopsis and a preliminary screenplay," my mentor said, handing Miss Stoltenberg and me a sheaf of papers. "Keep in mind, there are a few scenes we may still change. If you have any suggestions of your own, please let us know. We may start shooting sometime in May, if things go as planned. I thank you for a most marvelous evening."

TUCKS AND PULLS

Carolina had always been against it. She'd liked my looks from the beginning, since she first caught sight of me. "You've lived almost a dozen lives," she spouted off one evening at supper, when I once again mentioned plastic surgery as a possible option for my dilemma.

We were sitting outside on our porch. The air was mellow. A light breeze kept stroking the leaves of the jacaranda and the blossoms of the bougainvillea.

"You've been a poor orphan, a committed Nazi soldier, a German POW," she'd bicker, stabbing into a piece of chicken. "Then you turned into a repentant anti-Nazi, a happy-go-lucky cowboy, a hunted criminal, a jail bird, a family man, a Don Juan and an actor who has played two different roles already, with more to come. And now you're talking about changing your face once again to become yet somebody else you aren't. Think about it, all these changes are bound to have an effect on you. Aren't you scared of losing your identity? One day you'll look in the mirror and conclude that your only true identity is the mask you constantly change."

I took a swig of Malbec and savored it on my tongue. "Wow! Are you sure you haven't missed some roles?" I came back, chuckling. "But the crux of your comments is your Jesuit logic, and there you're way off. If I look back on my life, I can only see that every change in my appearance led to growth and enrichment, while I tried to adapt to new circumstances. Adapt or die! It's Darwin, sheer survival. As a spinoff, it has also turned into a colorful booty of memories I wouldn't want to miss for anything. Nor is there any evidence that this has led to a loss of my identity or character, as you claim. At least I haven't noticed it. At the core I'm still the same: Fritz, the rootless and restless orphan. Aside from that, aren't we, you, me, all of us, stuck in the amber of early lessons learned?"

To reiterate, the question of adaptation and survival was uppermost in my mind. After all, I was still mortally threatened, and would probably continue to be. And the public image of my identity was my face, unfurled in my mugshots. Figuring that the judiciales had at least two of me — one they received from the FBI and the other from the Chihuahua jail — I'd always put a great effort into hiding my original face, to give myself a different look.

Way back, while I tried to get my present passport, I recall having discussed my quandary with Moritz. He had also brought up the option of *physically* changing my features by way of surgical procedures. He made it sound so easy, assuring me that a few tucks and pulls around the forehead, eyes, nose and mouth would make me much less recognizable, thus improving my safety. He'd even given me the name and address of Dr. Joaquin Lopez, a surgeon who was allegedly *the* expert in the field.

Since I had been busy with my acting career at the time, I hadn't followed up. But the last scare would once again remind me of this option. I was afraid, the judiciales might well recognize my face on the silver screen had already, for all I knew. Looking back, my appearance in the role of Ignatz in 'Sweets and Red Chili' already cost me countless hours of sleep. And playing the 'Kommandant' with my present facial features would ratchet up the risk to unknown heights, giving me untold of jitters, or worse.

I continued to wrangle with her, painfully aware that I needed her support. But try as I might I simply couldn't make her to slip into my skin. "Things being as they are," I remember saying, while the evening was dawdling into the night and our eyelids waxed heavy. "I'm convinced that my career, indeed, my life, depended on facial changes. And, frankly, it should be in your interest as well. Would you want to become a widow?"

From all I could tell, the last sentence seemed to mellow Carolina a little.

To make things short, the morning after our long discussion, I threw up my hands and called Dr. Lopez, the plastic surgeon Moritz had recommended. I might add, I found his staff to be very forthcoming, encouraging me to make an appointment. But before I did, I had a talk with Jorge, just to hear what he had to say. Not only was he on my side, but he was also familiar with the clinic, claiming that Dr. Lopez was reputed to be one of the best facial surgeons in Mexico. In fact, one of his women friends, Marta, who had been treated by him for the removal of wrinkles around her eyes and a bony hump on her nose, raved about him.

Having hung up, I dialed the clinic and made an appointment for a consultation. When I informed Carolina about it, she just shook her head, saying, "There is no end in sight."

But two days later, she seemed to be a little more accommodating. "I still think your fear of being recognized is overblown," she said. "Yet if it absolutely has to be, I wouldn't mind accompanying you."

"Thank you so much, that's very nice of you. You're not thinking of having something done on *your* face as well? Smoothing out some wrinkles?"

"Oh, no, just to help *you* make good choices. After all, it's me who has to look at you every day."

Dr. Lopez was a tall, haggard Catalan from Barcelona who'd fled Franco's Spain in 1938. Bald-headed, he was just skin and bones, with a fallen-in face that emphasized his prominent cheekbones, a bony wedge of a nose and simian eyebrows that shaded two shifty, deep-seated, dark-brown eyes.

He was a bit tense and helpless, and when he looked at my face he acted as though there was nothing which needed to be changed. But when I insisted on doing it anyway, he came around and took a closer look, finally saying he'd do whatever I requested. I should make suggestions, and he would try to follow through on them.

Callow, I started with the forehead, insisting he smooth out two deep forehead wrinkles, as well as the two vertical frown lines jutting down my lower forehead to the eyebrows and, yes, lift the outer ends of the eyebrows. Farther down, I asked him if there was a way to get rid of the fine wrinkles around my eyes, to reduce the flare of my nostrils, to make my cheekbones more visible, to lift the corners of my mouth, and to pull in the ears a tiny bit. To give him a clue to my wishes, I showed him a photograph of a young, good-looking Swedish actor Sten Lindgren I'd lifted out of a magazine. Although his head had a similar overall shape as mine, he looked different, possessing most of the features that met my wishes.

Dr. Lopez took a good look at the photograph and added that he could try to model my appearance to the Swede's. At the same time, he didn't have any divine powers to simply make me look like him. He claimed he could do all these procedures in one session, if I wouldn't mind being under the knife for up to three-and-a-half hours.

He set a date. We shook hands.

On the 21st of February I appeared at his clinic. I was anesthetized and went under Dr. Lopez's knife. The operation proceeded smoothly, without a glitch, and three hours later I was released, looking like a veritable victim of a head-on collision. My whole head was swaddled in gauze with four drainage tubes sticking out. Next I was turned over to Carolina who chauffeured me back to the hotel where I spent some very uncomfortable, occasionally painful, days and nights, mercifully without complications. It helped immensely that my novia was with me. Like a nurse, she saw to it that the drainage tubes remained clean, that I got something to eat and that I swallowed my pain pills. Two days later Carolina hauled me back to my *brujo* for a checkup. Thankfully, there was no bother; everything proceeded according to plan, indeed even better. In any event, Dr. Lopez did encourage me to start moving around to get my blood flowing.

Thanks to my good physical health the healing made good strides. The swelling and puffiness receded and within five days Dr. Lopez was able to remove the drainage tubes and lift the gauze. Needless to say, my face looked awful, badly bruised, dominated as it was by a palette of blue, brown and yellow smudges. Yet I could already recognize the Swede in me. It was especially soothing that Carolina liked my new face, saying it was just as attractive as my old one, possibly even more so.

After twelve days, the discoloration of the skin gradually began to disappear, but I had to wait yet another two weeks before I was back to normal. The first person I paid a visit to happened to be Moritz. Although he instantly recognized me, I looked odd to him. "Gee, what happened to you?" he wanted to know, his eyes riveted on my face as though he were a dermatologist.

"Well, guess. You're the one who first told me about Dr. Lopez. I finally saw him and I don't regret it, although it was a pain in the you-know-where."

He chuckled. "So it's time for a new passport?"

"How did you guess?"

He insisted, we first have a drink, Moritz's top choice of Tequila reposado, which loosened not only our tongues. He couldn't wait to tell me, Elsie wasn't doing well at all, that she might be suffering from ovarian cancer, in which case she'd have to have an operation. He expressed the wish to take a boat to New York to accompany her during her difficult time. He asked me how Carolina and Enrique were doing and how life in San Miguel kept unfolding. Curious, he looked upon it as a big 'shtetl' and he wanted to know if I regretted having moved out of the big city.

Finally getting down to business, he shuffled to his photo nook, waved me over, told me to take a seat, pulled out his Leica and snapped a series of pictures.

"How about the various entries?" he wanted to know. "Are they going to be the same as in your last passport?"

"I'm glad you asked."

I pulled out my old passport and checked them. "Yes, except for the name. My new name is going to be Frederik Erikson."

"A bit boring and frosty, maybe, but it'll fit your new face like an old shoe," he said with a grin.

"I sure hope so. So, how much do I owe you, Moritz?"

"Oh, let's say about 4,000 pesos."

"Here are 5,000, four grand for the passport and one for the ticket to New York. I hope you make it to New York and pray that Elsie will snap back. Please give her a warm hug from me. When, do you think, will you take the trip?"

"I don't know yet. There's a liner leaving Veracruz in three weeks. I might as well take it."

"*Gute Reise! Buen viaje!* I wish you a happy trip!"

I hugged him and placed a smack on his forehead.

A week and a half later I received the passport by registered mail. Once again, I was amazed by the meticulous work of the forgery. It looked so real, so official. I compared it to Carolina's specimen, yet I couldn't make out any difference. If anything, it looked even more authentic than the passports the Mexican government issues.

Incidentally, attached to the document was a short letter in which Moritz thanked me for the 1,000 pesos, saying it helped him pay for the ticket. He'd leave on the 11th of April, expressing great relief that there are no German U-boats trawling the Gulf of Mexico any more.

THE FILMING OF THE KOMMANDANT

I couldn't wait to delve into the final version of the screenplay, which Senor Alarcon had sent me by mail. It continued to leave a deep impression on me, most notably my part, the role of the title hero. The act appeared to be so demanding that I got the shivers. What strengthened my backbone was the experience I had before I took on the part of Ignatz in *Dulce*. It had scared the living daylight out of me, and yet... So I buckled down, working at it every day, often deep into the night, and eventually with the help of Carolina, I scrambled on top of it. I particularly relished looking at the words with the underlying emotional truth in mind. I was fully aware that I had to tame my present aversion to Nazism, if I aimed for a credible performance of the "Kommandant'. What helped me most was my digging down into my former mental state, when I still stuck in the boots of a faithful Nazi zealot, a dedicated fighter for the Fuehrer and the German fatherland.

On the third of June I slipped into the cocoon of a Flecha Amarilla on my way to el D.F. for the shooting. Like most of the actors and actresses who lived outside of the Moloch, I chose to be quartered at the Pelican, a small, nondescript hotel in the suburb of Churubusco, close to the famous Azteca Studios. Early next day all the acting staff, as well as the technical crew gathered at the studio for an orientation meeting. There were nearly two hundred people present. Waiters and waitresses served wine, beer and appetizers. We shook hands and got to know one another.

I was particularly eager to engage with Miss Stoltenberg. In the meantime, I'd heard from Senor Alarcon and others that she was actually a well-known actress who'd played prominent parts in several successful productions, two even in Hollywood.

"Elvira Mendez is a midget compared to her," I remember the old zorro telling me, as if I'd had some doubts.

The rehearsals that were scheduled to follow the next eight days unwound unusually well. I was pleased to notice a real team spirit unfolding, a feeling we were all in this together. Unlike in past productions, everyone of us had our lines down pat, promising a smooth shooting. In any event, Senor Alarcon was delighted and, after tweaking the performance of two lieutenants a little and helping Alicia act out a few additional scenes, he actually put on a pair of rose-colored glasses.

Owing to our exemplary cooperation, the preparations for the filming began already on the 13th of June, even earlier than the schedule called for. Our set construction crew had in the meantime been busy erecting a perfect replica of a Ukrainian shtetl, including a market square surrounded by public buildings and representational homes of the merchant class. And when we got there, we encountered a whole company of spiffy SS-troops in black uniforms. Actually they were soldiers from the Mexican Army whom Senor Alarcon had hired and wrapped into the infamous diabolical SS-garb, decorated with those infamous double runes. They were waiting for us, but it took us, the actors, the makeup artists, as well as the camera team and sound mixers, almost two hours before we got ready. Finally, we, the lieutenants, the non-commissioned officers and I appeared in our black SS-uniforms prepared to shoot the first scene. Things fell into place, and once our clapper slapped the board shut and hollered "Action", the shooting began to move with the smoothness of a ballet performance.

Once the arrival of the SS-troops and the heinous scenes of hunting down Jews, herding them into cattle cars, or shooting them point-blank, were behind us, Senor Alarcon turned his attention to Esther Silbermann's high-wire act of deception, although most of these latter scenes had to wait until next day and the day thereafter.

It deserves mention that Alicia played her part with absolute perfection. Mentally focused, she served her ruse cold, mouth pursed. Her claim of being Helga Krause, followed by her recitation of German poetry, including a few of Gretchen's lines from Goethe's *Faust,* couldn't have been more persuasive. She was so captivating, so bewitching that everybody, including me — especially me! — fell head over heels in love with her. She demonstrated beyond even a dot of doubt that intelligence and beauty, combined with a pinch of cunning, could overwhelm any racist zealotry. The most pivotal scene, when I lifted her onto the tank to show how the ideal of a racially pure German girl looks like, murmurs of awe and adoration rushed through the ranks of our SS-troops, some of whom appeared to be close to swooning. The whole scene resembled a religious ceremony, where a Germanic goddess, flanked by muscular, naked torch bearers, is heaved onto a pedestal. Only the incense was missing.

That same evening, after supper, I invited Alicia for a glass of wine at the hotel's cafe, proposing we chat about the next scenes. She agreed but not without casting a knowing smile at me. The cafe turned out to be filled to the brim and so smoky we could barely breathe. But we stuck it out. Over a glass of wine, we chatted about the love scene we were scheduled to shoot next day. She looked at it as a purely professional sequence our acting skills would simulate to be real, whereas I caught myself arguing for a more emotional involvement. I let her know that I had a crush on her, as if she hadn't known already. I recall, she simply laughed it off, insinuating that I may have had too much wine.

Shortly before eleven, she was ready to leave. "Tomorrow, we've got a big day ahead of us," she said. "I do need my eight hours of sleep."

So I accompanied her to the door of her room, not without an anticipation of delight. My heart was beating in my throat. I looked forward to an adventure, to the thrill and the tension of its hidden strings. Embracing her, I pressed her against the doorframe and let my hand explore the configurations of her back. Wary, she repeatedly turned away. Worse, she pushed me off, pleading, "Fred, please! You are married. Behave yourself!" The harder I tried, the more she resisted, to the point of getting increasingly more upset. At that point, I finally bowed and, wishing her a good night, tuck tail.

I had a fitful, disquieting night. I was flung out of the saddle of my self-assurance in a high arc, becoming painfully aware of my fecklessness. At the same time, the intensity of my feelings for her rose to unknown heights. I was fixed on her, her alluring face, framed as it was by vigorous, reddish-blond curls, her shapely lips, her soulful eyes, her cute flanges of her nose, not to mention her small and tight bosom and supple body. I would raise her onto a pedestal like a goddess, as if taking lines out of the screenplay and making them my own. Before I realized, I had turned into Wolfgang Wagner, the character I was playing in the movie. It was a complete, seamless, as well as scary Stanislavskian fusion, one of a pair. *Was Carolina right after all?* I began asking myself. *Was I losing my identity?* I recalled, even Dr. Frommer had mentioned much the same once, although he'd used a convoluted psychiatric jargon I couldn't quite understand.

Be that as it may, next morning during the shooting of the first love scenes involving Alicia I faced some unusual challenges. Smitten that I was, I rushed into it full throttle, making her feel very uncomfortable. And not only her, but also Senor Alarcon. Especially him. It didn't take him long to notice what was going on and he lost no time to call a spade a spade.

"Fred, you should know better," he growled, visibly upset. "You're far too explicit. Remember what I've told you. I want you to be more suggestive. I want touch, tenderness, mystery, imagination, not rushing to coitus. I want professionalism, control. We've got to do a retake."

Needless to say, my mentor's voice burned into me like a stroke with a rawhide whip. Egg on my face, I shrunk back. It was a wake-up call, a sobering reminder to drop the animal in me for the mature actor, master of his emotions. Let me add, the public shaming worked: My performance in the retake was flawless, earning me praise. As did the acting of the most demanding part, the Kommandant's realization of having become a victim of Helga Krause's ruse.

Incidentally, not unlike the Kommandant's spellbound fixation on Esther Silbermann, I was not able to shake off my infatuation for Alicia. For all I know, it may even have increased a few notches. And since she insisted on showing me the cold shoulder, I clenched my teeth and resigned myself. Still, like a true companion, she continued to be in my mind's eye long after the filming had ended, as the one who gave me an icy shoulder.

FLICKS OF MY SUBCONSCIOUS

I was torn out of my sleep by rumbles and crashes. Seconds later they came smashing into our bedroom, five of them, Aztec warriors in full regalia, with colorful, feathered headdresses and bright-red loincloths, equipped with daggers and obsidian-edged clubs. Smelling of pulque, they carried large torches pointed at me and Carolina. "Finally, we caught up with you," one of them, their leader, shouted. "Get the hell out of bed, both of you, with hands up."

I remember raising my arms and getting out of bed, but then, at a split of a second, I tried to jump on the leader. Unfortunately, they all came to his rescue, piling up on me. And once they had clubbed me to the ground, the leader, whose face reminded me of J. Edgar Hoover, shouted at me, "You thought you could get away from us. Nobody will escape the judiciales who will see to it that you're brought to justice." As they dragged me away, I woke up, drenched in sweat. But instead of being relieved, I was downcast, traumatized. It was still dark and quiet as a tomb. It was shortly past three a.m. Everybody was still fast asleep. I tried to get up but was unable to, feeling as if my limbs were paralyzed. Yet neither could I get back to sleep, ending up tossing, turning and regurgitating my dream. Since I lay on the cot in my study I didn't disturb Carolina.

Eventually, more than an hour later, I pulled myself together and managed to rise. My watch showed 4:35. After a quick cat's lick, I put on some clothes and shoes and staggered up to the Jardin. It was hauntingly hushed, ghostlike. I didn't see or hear a soul. Feeling like a walking corpse, I meandered through the whole old part of the town, including a cemetery, until dawn showed up on the eastern horizon.

When I got back, Carolina had just risen. "You look terrible, like an el D.F. homeless who slept under a bridge," she said, when she caught me heading into the bathroom. "Are you all right?"

"Well, I feel a little better, after my long walk through the town." I told her about my terrifying dream and the sleepless aftermath, including my crippling paralysis. "These nightmares have been bothering me for the third day in a row. They are very similar, with only slight variations here and there. But all of them show the involvement of the Aztecs and the judiciales in some way or other."

"Fred, I greatly worry about your mental health," Carolina said, shaking her head. "You've got to get a grip on these problems. I would try to get an emergency appointment with Dr. Frommer. He'd be able to help. But in the event he can't, he might be able to refer you to somebody who can. It's worth a try."

It seemed to be a reasonable suggestion, and after breakfast I rushed to call the office of Dr. Frommer. Luckily Clara Jimenez answered. She still remembered me. But when I asked for an emergency appointment with Dr. Frommer, she reminded me that he'd passed away four months ago and that the practice had been taken over by Dr. Snyder.

"I'm sorry to hear that," I said. "Dr. Frommer was such a gentleman. I desperately need some help. I just wonder if I could see Dr. Snyder."

"Well, let me check. It looks like he's pretty much filled up. But I think I could squeeze you in for an emergency appointment at four o'clock in the afternoon."

"That would be very helpful. Thank you."

Weary, I spent the day doing errands, taking short naps and going on a long walk with Enrique. Shortly before four, I wound my way to Dr. Snyder's office. As I stepped in, I noticed right away that things had changed radically. What were once premises that looked like an old-fashioned, stuffy apartment with antiquated furniture, heavy drapes and pictures of Dr. Sigmund Freud and Vienna at the turn of the century, was now a modern, bright, businesslike office.

After chit-chatting with the secretary for a minute, I took a seat and waited for my turn. Shortly past four I shook hands with Dr. Snyder who may have been in his seventies already. Though small, he was a flinty fellow with a shiny, balding head and a bony, wedge of a nose dominating his face. His dark, piercing eyes which hid under his hooded brows gave him a rigid, almost sinister appearance.

Greeting me with a plucky handshake, Dr. Snyder informed me that he had my records from Dr. Frommer in his possessions, although he hadn't had a chance to take a look at them. At any rate, he wanted to hear from me, what was troubling me. Well, I told him, things had actually been fairly peaceful lately. There were only a few flare-ups. "It wasn't until three nights ago that nightmares began haunting me again, robbing me of my sleep, making my blood run cold and wearing me to a frazzle. They went from bad to worse, with the most frightening happening last night."

"Tell me about it, the last one, I mean."

Well, I began spilling my dream. He proved to be an attentive listener and feverishly scribbled down notes. And when I had ended, he took on a very professorial mien and said with a self-satisfied smile, "As you might know, dreams or nightmares are flicks of your subconscious, or even your id. They can tell you what's stirring deep inside the netherworld of, what we used to call, the soul. They mirror your wishes, desires, fantasies and yearnings, as well as your fears, apprehensions, dreads and anxieties. Oftentimes you need something to activate them. Do you recall any event that might have triggered them?"

I told him about the occasional bouts of paranoia and anxiety attacks I've been suffering from. I made specific mention of the last embarrassing incident some months ago, when I got so scared that I hightailed out of town.

"You just mentioned the Federal Police, the judiciales. But why would they want to arrest you? You're not dealing with drugs, are you?"

"No, of course not. I'm quite sure it's because I originally crossed the border into Mexico illegally, without papers. And somehow they must have gotten wind of it. Because since then they've been after me. They've got me in their crosshairs."

He shook his head. "Are you sure?"

"Yes, very sure. They've tried to arrest me at least four times. Luckily I was able to duck out or get away. That's been going on for more than ten years or so."

"More than ten years? Forgive me, but it sounds like you suffer from anxieties based on a paranoid obsession. You think you're being persecuted, that you are a victim, that there is a conspiracy in the government threatening your life?"

"No, I know so." To back it up, I rehashed the various efforts by the judiciales to arrest me.

He looked at me as if I had made it all up. "Are you sure they all happened?"

"Dead sure! I have witnesses. Besides my wife, there are at least four or five other people who could verify what I told you."

"Hm, initially you said that lately it has been rather peaceful."

"Yes, but that didn't mean I was free of the fear of being arrested. It's like a dark cloud that hovers over me."

"I understand. Your mind seems to be caught in an internal maelstrom fed by your anxieties. That's where chaos reigns. What I'd like to do is put up some guardrails and strengthen them. I'm afraid it'll take many sessions before we can accomplish that, plus countless more to root out the poisonous weed of your *angst*. As for now, all I can do is prescribe some anti-anxiety medication. I should warn you, it's no panacea but it should provide you with some handrails you can hold on to. I also want you to do some homework consisting of learning a number of relaxation techniques and other strategies that could help you facing your angst." He gave me some sheets detailing what I ought to do.

Feeling a little more at ease, I walked out of the office and made my way to a pharmacy, where I bought the anti-anxiety pills and started swallowing them. Granted, they did calm me, helping me momentarily to shake off my anxieties. At the same time, they were also accompanied by some very unpleasant side effects: They made me very drowsy, worse, dizzy, causing me to lose my coordination. I was sluggish and listless, walking around with an unsteady gait as if drunk. All I did was fill my day with sleeping, sauntering up to the cafe and puttering around in the backyard. At best I could be drawn into guarding the goal in the soccer games with Enrique, Pablo and Manuelito, his friends from school, or get my fishing gear and take Enrique down to the lake to catch some fish.

Any spark I may have had was gone, drained out of me. According to Carolina I was an idler, a drifter and wastrel, with a slurred speech to boot. On my desk lay a screenplay, 'A Gringo In Puerto Vallarta', a comedy, that Senor Alarcon had handed me three weeks ago. Yet I was incapable of devoting myself to it, as was my wont. Only on rare occasions was I able to pull myself together to peruse it. Even then, after ten or fifteen minutes, I caught myself dropping it. The same was also true of the homework Dr. Snyder had given me. I couldn't even make sense of it.

No question, it was gnawing at my substance, and after three weeks of idling, I couldn't take it any more. So I made my way back to Dr. Snyder to inform him of my misgivings about the remedy. He was unusually gruff, lecturing me that all medications worth their money have side effects. He compared them to arranged marriages: hopefully good outcomes outweigh bad ones, such as mine. Besides, each patient reacted differently to the very same medication.

Getting back to my case, he still held on to his optimism. With his help, I could face up to these attacks, even conquer them, at least momentarily. He claimed that he had in the meantime researched my case and come to the conclusion that I suffer from an underlying frightful narrative or nightmare that had settled in my memory. It had nestled in the limbic system of my brain, and he was confident that he, with my help, could somehow sweep it out.

"Having decoupled itself from the processing of your daily experiences," he claimed, nervously twiddling his thumbs, "it leads his own autonomous life down there. Unfortunately, it's very hard, almost impossible to dislodge it outright. But it's feasible to change the narrative of it in such a way that the outcome is not as dreadful. In your case, you could say that you've always welcomed to get these problems settled peacefully. So now you finally have the means to hire a team of sharp lawyers who'd defend you and see to it that justice prevails."

"Barnackle-backs like the papazote, who got me out of the jail in Chihuahua," I threw in.

"There we go. When you do that, you change the nightmare by attaching your own, more hopeful ending. In that case, you cut the vicious circle of the narrative. Now here is what I'd want you to do. I want you to sit down and write out the nightmare with your own ending. Then you place it besides your bedstead and read it twice before you go to sleep. And when your nightmare arouses you again, you'd grab your own version and recite it several times, aloud, almost like a poem."

Frankly, I wondered. What he offered seemed too smooth, sleight of hand. But seeing no alternative on the horizon, I tried what that whizz of the mind proposed. I sat down at my desk, gave Rodrigo — my skull — a twinkle and wrote out the narrative of my dreams with my own ending. Before dropping off at night, I read it again. And in the early morning, when the nightmare would awake me, I'd recite, with the zeal of a monk pitching in a fervent prayer to heaven.

That's what I did for more than a week. At first nothing changed, nil. I literally had to wait nine days before this exercise finally gained some traction. From then on, the nightmare would gradually languish and eventually give up its ghost.

Incidentally, I saw Dr. Snyder one more time. I thanked him for his help, also praising his wizardry. That put him in a back-patting mood and, smiling from ear to ear, he congratulated me for sticking it out.

At the same time he could not resist also adding a warning. "Nightmares have a way of coming back," he said in a somber tone of voice, "depending on the stimulant they receive from a person's daily experiences. But they may be different."

He did not go into details, but I strongly suspected that he was referring to my bouts of paranoia, or rather what his pigeonholing mind diagnosed as such. His previous outburst, "You give me the impression that everyone is out to get you," was still fresh in my mind.

Having my limbic system momentarily in shackles, I was able to go back to my passion of acting, of reading scripts, learning dialogue, of working with actors or actresses in studios and remote locations. And these had taken off unusually well. I had several streaks of luck, especially since the release of 'El Commandante', which was a huge box-office success, not only in Mexico, but also in Latin America, the United States and Europe. My hope was that I'd get to be known; that in the eyes of the public the name Frederik Erikson would stand for uniqueness, a distinct appearance, a peerless style of acting, but also for good entertainment.

In the meantime, Carolina had become more and more actively involved in my acting career. Her support became invaluable to me. Not only did she assist me with my Spanish, but also — I'd say even foremost — with the business aspect of my career. She had nominally become my agent who had taken charge of my public relations.

I had long noticed that, aside from being well-paid, there was yet another bonus for my full engagement in the acting profession: My daily apprehensions were shoved onto the back burner. The more I focused on learning a part, the more I held my nose tightly to the grindstone, the less I ruminated on a possible raid by the judiciales. Such worries came mainly to the fore during a lull in activities, when I had finished one film project but hadn't taken on a new part.

ENRIQUE, OUR FLEDGLING

Enrique sprouted fast, turning into a gangly teenager with a goofy defiance and a hormonal rush that sparked pimples, as well as a pronounced weakness for — surprise! surprise! — girls. Although his grades in school were good, but that may've been more attributable to low standards than genuine achievement. He certainly didn't take learning seriously. Being smart, he approached school as a necessary evil we parents had foisted on him. Never did I see him exerting himself, studying into the night for an exam or writing a long term paper. Carolina and I admonished him frequently, stressing that learning was paramount, laying the foundation for a good vocation or profession later in life. But it was all for naught. We just wasted our breath.

To stir him up, we agreed to place him at a private college, following graduation from high school. Carolina argued, we send him to a Jesuit prep school here in Mexico, the one she had attended. While I thought very highly of the schools run by a religious order, I feared they were a bit too parochial. I hoped to expose him to a more open, competitive environment, to a world where the future would be shaped. In short, I wanted him to receive a solid liberal education in the United States. I had no beef with Spanish. At the same time, I thought it helpful if he'd learn English well because I sensed that this jumble of a tongue would sooner rather than later be the *lingua franca* of the world. Rueing the cuts in my own eyeteeth, I wanted to give him a good start in life.

One evening we discussed our differences with the Perkins, Richard and Nancy, American expatriates from Los Angeles, whom we met at a party. Richard was a retired professor who had taught English literature at Occidental College, a liberal arts college nestled in the Eagle Rock area of Los Angeles. He praised it just short of heaven, claiming it was one of the best private colleges in the United States. Having shown us some appealing pictures of the campus, he also offered his help in gaining admission, a process he characterized as being very tough.

After some arguments pro and con, Carolina and I agreed that Occidental was worth a try. When we informed Enrique of our decision, he first recoiled, taking offense at not having been consulted. He insisted on enrolling at UNAM, the National University in el D.F., even without our support. "Because that's where the action was," he let us know, with an emotional fervor no less. He referred to his infatuation with certain leftist student organizations that clamored for a revolution and the installment of a communist government. Mercifully, two weeks later, once he had settled down, he wasn't so sure any more. And as soon as the admission forms from Occidental arrived, he couldn't wait to fill them out, with the help of Professor Perkins. And, lo and behold, two months later he received a letter of admission.

At first he was overjoyed but later doubts began to creep into his mind, or so he confessed to me one day. *Would my English be good enough to keep up with the curriculum and lectures?* He was also worried that the students and professors might think of him as a lazy, *manana*-infused Mexican who, crouched on the shoulder of the highway, is begging for a free ride. For us, this was a good sign, hoping that a pinch of pride would make him stir his stumps a little.

On the 3rd of August, Carolina with Enrique in tow flew to Los Angeles. An employee of the college picked them up at the airport and chauffeured them cross-town to the campus. As they wound their way through this park-like academic enclave, they were bedazzled. "It's breathtakingly beautiful," I heard Carolina gush into the mouthpiece next day. "It's very Mediterranean, with covered walkways and shady trees. All the buildings have tiled roofs. You'd never guess that this is America. I thought this is what Italy or Spain must be like. Enrique is excited as well; he's all fired up. What a learning environment! I'm so glad we followed Professor Perkins' advice."

On Christmas, 1967, Enrique paid us a visit, and we all celebrated the holidays together. Jorge also joined us. I had scrounged up a shapely, two-meter high fir from a local vendor, which we decorated together with bulbs, Mexican straw-angels and *santos*, tinsel and live candles. That in itself lifted our spirits, dealing an additional boost by wetting them with champagne. For our Christmas day dinner I roasted a young goose I'd stuffed with prunes, chestnuts and *foie gras,* to be served with braised leeks and red cabbage and tossed off with a full-bodied red Burgundy and a German Traminer I'd picked up in a special el D.F. liquor store. Later we also stirred up our vocal cords for some Christmas carols, followed by an exchange of gifts.

The next day, we grabbed our bathing suits and plenty of towels and headed out to the hot springs where we spent all day, bathing, eating, drinking and chewing the fat. Enrique came alive as well, relating his experiences in America, specifically at Occidental, which he characterized as very challenging, given that his knowledge of English was — ouch! — even worse than he'd assumed.

"I know many Mexicans don't like America," he let us know. "But it has been very good to me. Sure it has some problems, like the rise in violent crime and the lack of safety in certain cities. But that's also true of Mexico. Here it's just not being reported or punished. No doubt, there's a lot to find fault with in America but it's not for us Mexicans to point the finger. What I particularly like about America is the openness, the emphasis on personal freedom and the sheer unlimited opportunities it offers. I almost forgot to add that Americans are not nearly as indulgent toward corrupt practices as we are."

"You sound like you don't even want to return to Mexico any more," I replied, with Cole Porter's 'freedom' song stirring in my mind.

"Certainly not to San Miguel. Don't get me wrong, it's nice for retirees but not for young people. I'd certainly want to stay in America beyond graduation."

"That's in May, isn't it?" Carolina asked.

"Yes, in May, at the end of the spring semester," he said with a pinch of self-importance. "My friends and I would be flattered if you'd attend the ceremony. Will you?" He looked at both of us.

"I'd love to," Carolina prattled.

"How about you, Dad?"

That put me on the spot, and in a bind as well. I couldn't tell him why I didn't want to join Carolina. It would have taken a whole day, no, weeks. Besides, he wouldn't have understood my predicament anyway.

"Don't get me wrong, I'd like to," I said, trying to display a sober mien. "But I'm afraid I can't. I've already committed myself to playing a part in one of Senor Alarcon's comedies."

It was nothing but a pretext, and Enrique quickly picked up on that. "Come on, Dad," he said with the look of a disdainful beggar. "You still have five months. You can plan it if you really want to."

"Sorry, Enrique, but I can't. I already promised, and Senor Alarcon expects me to be on the set."

It was painfully embarrassing.

Being on the verge of tears, he still felt an urge to say something, but then choked. From then on he avoided me whenever he could. And when, two days later at the airport, we bid each other farewell, he wouldn't even let me embrace him. That hurt.

Incidentally, he'd barely left when Carolina took me to task, calling me a cruel father, worse, a heartless and callous ass. Her verdict: "Enrique will never ever forgive you."

NO END TO SCARES

I received my miracle the way the Virgen de Guadalupe did her *nino*. First of all, I'd barely evaded the devastating earthquake on Thursday, the 19th of September, 1985. Only the day before, I was at the studio rehearsing for a small part in a comedy called 'Trust Me Pablo'. Shortly past one, Senor Alarcon received a call from his in-laws, informing him that his brother had been badly injured in a serious traffic accident near Guadalajara. Obliged to assist him, he suspended the rehearsal until Monday the next week. So on Wednesday afternoon, I headed back to the hotel, gathered my clothes and placed them into my luggage. Ironically, part of my outfit, a pair of shoes, pants, as well as a shirt, were still sitting near the door in preparation for a temblor, as if bracing for one. Well, I slid into the car, revved up the engine and took off, pulling into our driveway shortly after darkness settled over San Miguel.

It wasn't until late next morning, while listening to the radio, that I heard about that horrific quake which shook Mexico to its core. According to unconfirmed reports, the damage to the city was nothing short of catastrophic, as if all those vengeful Aztec gods had risen from their muddy depths of the ancient lake Tenochtitlan and, swaggering, had torn open the torso of this vain and pompous city to rip out its pulsating heart. A staggering ten thousand people were known to have perished, but the real number may have been closer to thirty thousand. Hit hardest was the Historic District where the Templo Mayor, the Aztec ceremonial center, was supposed to have stood. Countless buildings, including the Monte Carlo, where I'd stayed, had totally collapsed or burned to the ground due to exploding gas lines, leaving behind nothing but rubble and misery.

Moreover, I was also able to steer clear of the judiciales. It so happened that when, descending into San Miguel, I turned onto our street I saw them standing right before our gate, two of them, in the company of a local cop and an old Chevy that carried the insignia of the San Miguel police department. Except for the cop, they were dressed in civilian clothes. One of them held on to a slip of paper and wildly gesticulated about something or other. *Holy shit! What to do?* Stopping the car would only have attracted unnecessary attention. I recalled what Wolfgang Riem, the theater director at the camp said to one actor who was scared to forget his lines. If you abandon yourself to fear, you're dropping the very lever that will eradicate it. The lever? My acting ability. So I pulled myself together and trundled on. And when I'd pulled even with the cops, I eased to a halt, rolled down the window, smiled, and *sangfroid* cracked, "Good afternoon, gentlemen. Can I be of any help?"

They looked at me dumbfoundedly, until one of them, who wore a strapping Pancho Villa mustache, opened his muzzle and said, "No, that's nice of you. Thank you, sir."

I smiled, rolled up the window, stepped on the pedal and off I was, heading toward Guanajuato, where I spent the rest of the day. Relieved that things worked out so well, I leisurely strolled around, stopped at a bubbly cafe, where I ate some antojitos, slurped several cups of coffee, leafed through several newspapers and indulged in my favorite pastime — people-watching. I didn't return until darkness had settled.

"Where have you been?" Carolina wanted to know, when I entered. "You told me over the phone that you'd be back early afternoon."

"Never mind. But tell me first, what did you tell the judiciales?"

"The judiciales? What judiciales? I was at Sybil's place. I didn't get back until six o'clock."

I told her what had happened. She just shook her head, questioning repeatedly my assertion that they, the judiciales, were standing in front of our gate, as though she didn't believe me.

Two days later I found out that they had indeed visited San Miguel, even our area. But it must have been a mixup. The suspect whom they finally arrested lived farther up. He was an American drug dealer, or so Rudolfo, whom I bumped into at the cafe a day later, informed me. He apologized profusely for having failed to warn me ahead of their visit.

"Didn't you tell me you'd be staying in el D.F.?" he asked. "I truly worried that the temblor might have killed you."

WHO COULD REFUSE?

"I just received an offer from Bob Daly, the chairman of the Warner Brothers studio this morning," Senor Alarcon told me after the shooting of the comedy 'Trust Me, Pablo'."

"I might add that the Warner Brothers are one of the giants in the American movie business, and they invited me to produce 'Paris Needs Help', another war movie at their studio. It deals with the last days of Paris under the German occupation and the battle of liberation."

"Congratulations!"

"Thank you, I really appreciate that. It's in recognition of my work as script writer and producer. Incidentally, Daly raved about the 'Kommandant'. I really feel flattered. And so should you. — Anyway, I've been working on the script, and once again, I need your input, your expertise on the German military. You see, one of the protagonists is a seasoned German captain who is on the staff of General Dietrich von Choltitz, the German commandant of Paris. In the script he's partially responsible for saving Paris from destruction by the German Army. 'Cause that's what his croaking Fuehrer insisted on, in case of surrender."

"I might mention that the captain's chivalry didn't exactly fall from heaven. Or, come to think of it, maybe it did after all. You see, he had hopelessly fallen in love with Giselle, a very attractive French woman. And as is the habit of lovers, they frequently engage in pillow talks."

"Shrewd!"

"You mean realistic, down to earth. We're all biological creatures, at least those of us who are young and healthy enough, like the captain."

"Like the Kommandant."

"Precisely! But as tragic irony would have it, neither his good deed, nor his love relationship are being rewarded. When the Germans finally surrendered on August 25th, 1944, he was hanged by the Parisian mob on one of those fancy rod-iron streetlights. And Giselle was publicly shamed as a collaborating whore. Her head shaved and her beautiful locks burned, she was banished from society until the end of her life."

"It's the second time the main character dies at the end," I recall saying. "I hope…"

"Yes, I haven't even thought about it. In any event, that's the way I envision the plot. So are you ready to help me with putting it all on paper? I need your expertise."

"I'd be delighted. The story sounds very gripping."

"Of course, the script would have to be translated into English. Although that would be no problem. My second question is: Would you be ready to take on the part of the captain and run with it? Knowing you, I think you'd do a superb job. And you might like it, too. Of course, we'd have to make you look quite a bit younger, but that could easily be done. I've already talked to Reynaldo, our makeup artist, and he assured me that this wouldn't be a problem. As to the stay, it should take about four months, give or take a few weeks. So are you ready to go to Hollywood with me?"

I was so fired up, I could barely recover my composure. "Well, thank you. It's nice that you thought of me. The part sounds exciting, thrilling. But Hollywood? I'll have to think about it."

"Come on, Fred, what's the hangup? There are no judiciales in Hollywood, if that's what you're afraid of. Hell, it would be even safer than here. You'd be a complete stranger up there, the tip of a needle in a haystack. And let me just add, Warner Brothers pays very well, I mean tops. They'd also take care of the plane tickets, the accommodations and the visas. Everything would be paid for. They'd pick us up at the airport and drive us to our hotel, one of the most luxurious in town. We'd be treated like kings and queens. Carolina could come along as well. Didn't you tell me not too long ago that Enrique, your son, lives and works in California?"

"Yes, at Berkeley, close to San Francisco. Anyway, thanks for the offer. It sounds very tantalizing. I'll talk it over with Carolina as soon as I get back to San Miguel."

"Let me know as soon as you can. By the way, I'll give you the pages I've written so far. As for the other scenes, we'll do it the same way as with the 'Kommandant': per mail. How does that sound?"

I was almost speechless. A new screenplay! A peach of a part! Hollywood! America! What else could I ask for? It sounded like a dream come true. And yet…

After I got home two days later I couldn't wait to discuss the offer with Carolina. Sitting on our patio, the fragrance of fresh-brewed coffee in the air, watching the hummingbirds feasting on the nectar of our tropical plants, I delved head over heels into Senor Alarcon's proposal, keeping mute about my own opinion.

Not unexpectedly, Carolina was very enthusiastic, urging me to grab it. "It's the chance of a lifetime," my agent and promoter gushed. "It offers you a catchy set of promises that would be a booster rocket for your career. I'm not even talking about the money."

I took a big gulp of coffee. "Granted, that might all be very exciting, if it weren't for the pivotal question of — well, you know what — safety. What if the bloodhounds of the FBI track me down and arrest me. Remember for them I'm still the Nazi fugitive of justice."

"But Fred, sober up." She had a load of huevos a la Mexicana on her fork, but then suddenly dropped it. "It's almost forty-two years after the war. And more than fourteen years after death of J. Edgar Hoover, your pet peeve. Chances are they've long forgotten about you. I'd bet that your file's buried under a thick layer of dust. At worst, you'd be on their back-burner. But even if that weren't the case, the FBI would most surely suspect that you were still hiding somewhere in Mexico. You've said it yourself, the danger comes from the judiciales."

"Well, yes. But they are a danger only because they are under intense pressure by the FBI and the American government as a whole."

"That may well be the case. At the same time, nobody, neither the judiciales nor the FBI, would expect you to be working in the United States, especially in a Hollywood film studio. That means nobody would be looking for you there. Frankly, I couldn't think of a better hiding place than among the international film crowd that has gathered in that sprawling hotchpotch of Los Angeles. Hell, they couldn't find you even if they were looking for you. You'd be the proverbial needle in the haystack you always wanted to be. Besides, the FBI has more than its hands full chasing important American criminals. It won't have time for an outdated case like yours. I don't want to rub it in, but you're not as important as you might think."

"Hell, you almost sound like the old zorro."

She turned away and devoted herself to her breakfast. I, on the other hand, continued to ponder her words, wondering if she spoke more for herself, her own appetite for breathing in the glamor of Hollywood, than for me and my safety.

"It just occurred to me," she suddenly perked up again, after taking a swig of coffee. "There is another facet that might help protect you. The fact is, your face looks radically different than it did forty years ago. Not only have you aged, but you've also had some plastic surgery. Now, as far as we know, the only pictures the FBI has of you is from the year 1943, when you were a very young German POW. Most likely that's also the one they've got on their arrest warrant. I doubt that they have your mugshot from the time you were in the Chihuahua penitentiary. But that would also be ancient."

"Your argument makes perfect sense. But I still can't quite shake off the angst of being nabbed, put on trial and then face the gallows. It's deep-rooted, buried in my subconscious."

"Sure, but you have that feeling regardless of where you are, in Mexico or in America. I can't see much of a difference. You know, sometimes you have to pull yourself together and take a little risk, sort of the way you did when you escaped from the POW camp. Sorry for rubbing it in, but you repeatedly told me that your most favorite song was *Don't Fence Me In*. You used to be so obsessed with freedom, so full of vim and vigor. And then, once we'd left the hacienda, you turned into a fraidycat. Don't you see, you're stuck in a viscous circle. What you mostly fear is fear itself. You'll have to find a new narrative, a way of breaking out. Where has your youthful spirit gone?"

That hurt, the more so since Carolina may have been right.

HOLLYWOOD OPENS ITS ARMS

Having not seen him for several years, I was shocked how old and frail, how dowdy he was. Unshaved like a bum, he let wisps of grey hair hang down from the sides of his skull. Only his eyes sparkled, as always.

I asked about Elsie, but instantly regretted it. It didn't take much to notice that I'd touched a very sensitive nerve.

"She passed away," he whispered, tears welling up from his eyes, "five months ago. Of ovarian cancer."

I hugged him, yet failed to pursue in more detail what exactly happened or where. I had the impression that it was too painful for him to bring that up.

"What gives me the pleasure of your visit?" he said, setting off his Adam's apple and waving me over to his musty sofa.

To digress, I told him that I had been invited to work in Hollywood and I intended to travel to America, to Los Angeles, admitting I was scared facing the passport control and asking him if he had any suggestions. He gave me the usual hints: I should act as normal as possible, put my tongue on a short leash, let the officials do the talking and do what they say. But he also wanted to take another look at the passport he'd forged seven years ago. Opening it, he pulled out a magnifying glass and studied it, especially the photograph, then compared it to my real face.

"What do you think?" I was curious to know. "Would I be safer if I had a new passport with a more recent picture?"

"Oh no, you'd want to avoid a precise match between the photograph and your real face. Think about it, this passport was issued seven years ago. People's faces change, they age. What you could do is grow a three-day-old stubble beard. You could even use a conventional razor and shave yourself. I'd do it a little sloppily, nicking yourself here and there, as if done with a shaky hand. Older gentlemen tend to do this. I'd also make your face look pale, tired and waxy, even a little sickly, you know, blue of jowl. It's always smart to elicit a pinch of pity."

"I'm curious, how the officials conduct themselves when they check somebody's identity. What would their attitude toward me, an older Mexican gentleman, be?"

"Pretty much like with any other traveler. They tend to look at your face first, trying to keep your features in their mind's eye. Then they'd ask for your papers, the purpose of your visit and also look at the photograph. For a smooth passage, it doesn't have to be a complete match with your real face. They seldom are anyway. All they're looking for are similarities. It's also helpful to wear a tie, a turtleneck, or a scarf. You don't want to look like a *paisano*. A small, eye-catching distraction usually helps."

"Good point."

"Since you're a Mexican, they may ask you if you're carrying any drugs and if you've traveled to Colombia or other Latin American countries. I'd stress that you were invited by a Hollywood studio to act in a movie, possibly a comedy. It's always good to show them papers, if you have any. That impresses them. As does a nice smile. It always goes very far in America. Remember, you want them to roll out their welcome mat."

"I just wonder, could it help if I had one or two official stamps from a U.S. customs office on the visa pages showing that this was not my first visit to the United States?"

"Not a bad idea. I can easily put them in, if you want me to. I can do it in a week."

On the morning of January 24th, 1989, Carolina and I made our way to the Benito Juarez Airport, where we joined Senor Alarcon and two handfuls of actors, actresses and technicians, all of whom boarded a sleek and glistening cocoon of the Boeing 747 for a five-hour flight to Los Angeles. I had prepared myself, having slipped into a dark-brown tweed jacket, grey pants and a white turtleneck. Using some makeup, I'd given my face a pale, almost sickly hue. In addition to toning my hair with a grayer tint, I'd also grown a three-day-old beard. And, not to forget, I purposely nicked myself twice, on the chin and the cheek. My appearance, needless to say, didn't go unnoticed.

"You look like a feeble old man," Carolina sneered, when I emerged from the bathroom of the hotel we stayed for the night.

The flight was quiet, uneventful, up the blue Sea of Cortez, which stood in stark contrast to shades of brown and sallow. Once the cloud cover lifted I enjoyed a bird's eye view of the thin sliver of the Baja California peninsula to the west and the ragged Sierra Madre to the east, on whose eastern slopes lay the spread of the hacienda. The latter conjured up nostalgic feelings, memories of cheerful, carefree times in an enchanting hideout, of falling in love, illicit rendezvous, challenging hikes in raw nature, riding horses and playing a carefree, happy-go-lucky vaquero. This was Mexico at its best, a state of grace. When I shared them with Carolina who occupied the window seat, we both reveled in delightful memories.

"I can even see the cottonwood," I teased my novia, pointing toward a large canyon.

"The murmur of the cottonwood," she said dreamily. "These were times."

We couldn't let go reminiscing about the past until we crossed the border into California. What a change it was! Everything looked so clean, orderly, so vibrant. Most astonishing was the brimming green of the landscape. *Almost like Germany.* Still on a northwestern trajectory, the aircraft barely ventured into the wide open Pacific. As we began to turn toward the north-east a cluster of islands, resembling a pod of humpbacks, inched into our view. Meanwhile toward the east a humungous horseshoe of a basin struck our eyes. It was filled to the rim-like foothills with a grey-brown haze reminiscent of el D.F. Our vision was so blurred, we could barely recognize any objects on the ground.

"Where in the hell is the city?" I wondered.

"Enrique told me, there's none," Carolina jested, "that L.A., as he called it, is nothing more than a million homes and five hundred shopping center in desperate search of a city."

But then as we descended I spotted a small concentration of high-rise buildings.

"Nestled way back in the foothills is the campus of Occidental College," she pointed out

We finally touched down. It was a smooth landing. *Now I am in America again,* I whispered to myself. *But no barbed wire for a change. I can't believe it.* I felt a wild fluttering of butterflies in my stomach. It was to grab hold of my horseshoe and squeeze it.

Once we had disembarked, we rushed through the air bridge tunnel and entered the passenger terminal, where Senor Alarcon gathered our Mexican party. As he led us to the Baggage Claim, three gentlemen, one carrying a large sign 'Warner Brothers Studios', came shuffling toward us. Senor Alarcon immediately engaged with them. They bid us a warm welcome, announcing that they'd help us pick up our luggage and pass customs. And once we had gathered our luggage, we all marched to the passport control. I was tense, jittery, as I, with Carolina in tow, walked up to the booth. It was manned by an officer, a swarthy, hollow-eyed gentleman with a crooked nose and large gaps between his lower incisors.

"From Mexico?" he barked, as he opened the passport, checked the photograph and scrutinized my face. "What's the purpose of your visit?"

"He is an actor," a voice from the background shouted. "He's working for us, Warner Brothers. And the lady is his wife."

"Get you!" the official snapped.

As he flipped through Carolina's passport he let a smile creep over his lips. "Is it gonna be a comedy?" he wanted to know as he handed our passports back.

"Kind of."

Having been waved through, I allowed myself a couple of deep sighs. Fully aware that this was only the first hurdle, we took our luggage and marched to the customs gates.

We braced.

"Where you from?" the burly official mumbled.

"Mexico."

"Any weapons? Drugs? Have you been to Colombia lately?"

"No."

"Open them suitcases."

We unzipped the lids and flipped them open. He stuck his beefy hands into our belongings, probing them from various sides and angles. *Like a butcher in the entrails of a pig.*

"Okeydoke," he finally snapped and waved us on.

"Boy, am I relieved!" I whispered to Carolina, as we made our way to the waiting representatives of Warner Brothers. We all piled into a van and within forty minutes we arrived at the Beverly Hills Hotel on Sunset Boulevard, also known as the 'Pink Palace'. Here the creme de la creme of the movie world, the staple of actresses, actors, movers, shakers and moguls traditionally assembled, or so we were told. And, indeed, it couldn't have been a fancier, more frivolous setting. Surrounded by lush tropical gardens and dotted with exotic flowers, honey-slurping humming birds, this luxury accommodation would be our prospective home for the next three months or more.

We were assigned a spacious, deluxe room with more comforts than I dared imagine, plus a view of the city, if the smog would allow it. As soon as we had tipped the bellboy we headed down to the restaurant, where our Mexican flock was scheduled to meet. Seated in a small side-room we were first served French champagne and some appetizers, followed by a dinner that was accompanied by choice French wines and a lavish dessert.

Once we had taken care of our bodily needs, we were turned over to a business manager from Warner Brothers. His intent? Initiating us into the "California Way of Life," as he called it. Slightly condescending and offering us a heavy dose of self-congratulation, he began by introducing us to the traditions, the customs, manners and taboos, the dos and don'ts of Hollywood. Curious for this freedom-loving land, there were far more 'don'ts' than 'dos'. As if we were savages, we were reminded that a woman's 'No' means 'No' (even if her body language says otherwise), girls under eighteen are innocent and very vulnerable little creatures, the service personnel, waitresses and chamber maids, are not *servants,* but *employees,* and that it is strictly *verboten* to pinch their 'nether regions'. And, yes, that free speech is celebrated, except when it involves any praise of socialism or, God forbid, communism, and less favorable comments about Blacks and Hispanics, yes, even Mexicans.

What astonished us most about the 'Land of the Free', was the warning not to take a stroll after dark along residential streets, lest we might get arrested by the police or — worse — robbed. In the end, we all received keys to Cadillac DeVille Luxury Coupes. Insurance, service, potential repairs and parking in the hotel's garage were part of the package. All we had to pay was the gasoline.

When we got back to our room, we were dog-tired, worn to a frazzle. We showered and turned in, counting sheep or other woolly critters. At least we hoped we could. In vain! We both had a restless, agitated night. Being used to quiet surroundings, we couldn't stomach the noise. First it was the roar of engines and the sound of sirens. Later, we were kept awake by the chopping and clattering of helicopters. We simply couldn't figure out why they would want to fly at night. It wasn't until two hours before sunrise when we were able to catch up on some sleep.

Cursed that I was, even the doze turned out to be a mixed blessing. I was haunted by a strange dream, in which I was followed and eventually apprehended by people in white coats and hauled to an insane asylum.

After a sumptuous breakfast, we were picked up by a van and chauffeured to the Warner Brothers Studios in Burbank, where we were taken on a guided tour. It was amazing just standing there and letting our eyes wander. We were awed at the sheer size of the place and the buildings, the gigantic back lots, the sets and sound stages, the various specialized departments, the offices, cafes, restaurants. "A city unto itself," as the guide boasted. "And crowded with throngs of people, like Times Square." Granted, many were tourists. Yet there were also plenty of employees who, like ants, were busily flitting back and forth, or single-mindedly going about their work, sawing and hammering sets, cutting out and sewing costumes, touching and brushing on makeup and shifting and focusing cameras. Others were steering cars, trucks and forklifts, hauling oddments from one place to another, all reeking of industriousness. At one point, while visiting a backlot, we watched a flock of long-legged, taut-assed, bosomy girls in tiny swimsuits leaving the shooting of a beach scene, full of chatter and chirpiness as they scattered. Everybody hustled and bustled, scurried and hurried, all in the service of a huge dream factory, scrambling to achieve the peculiar goal — of making fake look real and raking in the dollars.

We spent about six hours there, including a lunch and two coffee breaks. And later, as I squinted at this ant hill from afar, I wondered how we'd fit in, find our niche, if indeed we could, and where. I braced myself, knowing we Mexicans would have to start hustling as well. After all, we were in America now!

On the third day Enrique came down from Berkeley for a visit. It was a joyous reunion and we spent the whole afternoon and evening with him, chatting, dining, drinking champagne, wine and tequila, as well as strolling down the memory lane. He proudly announced that he had recently been promoted from instructor to assistant professor, which no doubt helped lift him into a good mood. What put me on edge was his attitude toward me. I could tell that he continued to bear me a grudge. Perhaps he was still miffed at me for not attending the graduation ceremonies at Occidental and at Stanford, where he finally earned a Ph.D. in comparative literature. While I continued to praise him for having achieved such a lofty level of education from some of the best schools in the United States, he never posed a single question about *my* life, my well-being or my acting career. Only once, conscious of the quid pro quo, did he make a halfhearted attempt to return the compliment, applauding my career as an actor.

As the night progressed and alcohol loosened our tongues, we began digging into the dim recesses of our minds, dredging up many witty anecdotes from the past. He told us tidbits about ourselves we'd either long forgotten or had never been aware of. Way toward the end — it must have been past one — he gingerly asked me about my past, my youth in Germany and how and why I came to Mexico. It was the first time he was curious about my past. Feeling awkward, I mentioned only that it was too painful to recapitulate; I wanted to let sleeping dogs lie for fear they might bark, snarl or, God forbid, even bite. Besides, he wouldn't understand since he's from a different generation and culture.

Gradually we managed to orient ourselves in this megalopolis, and on the fourth day of our arrival we hurled ourselves into the rehearsals of 'Paris Needs Help'. 'We' meant the five Mexican actors and actresses, as well as more than a dozen Americans. It dragged a bit, not least because three of us

Mexicans had some difficulty with the English pronunciation, particularly the American diphthongs, the 'Rs' and the intonation. Although they were supposed to play French men and women, Senor Alarcon still insisted they speak almost flawless English, preferably with a slight French accent. To achieve this, he ordered them to take lessons in English and French pronunciation and articulation.

That helped, although at the cost of valuable time. And make no mistake, time was 'money', as Bob Daly never forgot to remind 'our Mexican friends'. From day one our lackadaisical attitude toward time was a cause of considerable friction. Exacerbating was the fact that Senor Alarcon bent over backward to avoid being seen as a Mexican who was oblivious to time. It was no secret that the word *manana* and the image of a squatting Mexican lazing away the day under a big sombrero was nothing short of a disgrace to him. That's why he demanded of everyone who worked under him to be punctual, mercilessly chewing out all latecomers with a vehemence bordering on zealotry. My Mexican colleagues never stopped rolling their eyes, mumbling openly that he outdid the gringos just to demonstrate that he was not a stereotypical Mexican.

Maybe I should mention that at one time I, *too*, experienced the misfortune of becoming a victim of his wrath. It so happened that during our second week I was held up in a traffic jam on La Cienega Boulevard grounding me for almost an hour. (Actually I'd called Senor Alarcon's secretary but somehow the message got lost.) And when I finally arrived at the set, half an hour late, Senor Alarcon could barely contain himself. Perching high on his director's chair, he stared me down, chopping a white towel like an hyena would a tough chunk of meat. Then, taking said towel out and throwing it at me, he began to unleash a frightful row, as if I'd somehow planned to stage an uprising against him and the head honcho Bob Daly. I viewed it as a gust of overcompensation leaving everybody, including me, standing there in an embarrassed silence, sheepishly staring at the ground for an answer. Somehow, we couldn't quite swallow that this was the same man we had always known to be a forgiving, tolerant *hidalgo*.

There was yet another of our boss's sensitivities that struck a similar note, goading the ire of my Mexican colleagues just as much, if not more. Once again it touched on an acting style that was widespread in Mexico, namely the expression of feelings with a flamboyant animation in the form of pronounced gestures and volatile facial expressions. Time and again he'd halt a rehearsal reminding my Mexican colleagues that such a style was not only infantile but that it actually cheapened the emotions.

"We're not in a comedy or a farce and you are not buffoons or madcaps," he'd remind us. "Always remember, you're performing for a critical audience that expects serious acting — a presentation with a reserved demeanor, restraint and credibility. So stop the honied ham acting."

FRIENDLY COPS

It wasn't that I hadn't been warned. I recalled that Enrique had alerted us to the rising crime rate here in America. "There are some areas of Los Angeles where the threat of being robbed or shot dead are so high that even the toughest police force hesitated to enter," I remember him telling us. Indeed, almost on a daily basis the newspapers were crammed with scoops about gang warfare, muggings, robberies and killings. But somehow I shoved all that murder and mayhem away from me, as though assuming that they invariably happened only to others, never to us.

Well, I was in for a rude awakening. I happened to be fond of visiting East L.A., an area settled mainly by Hispanics and Mexicans, where I enjoyed the restaurants, the stores, the sound of Spanish, the whole ambiance. I loaded up on Mexican groceries there, dined on savory tamales, enchiladas and carne adovada. I purchased my mescal and my tequila there. I could go on and on. Oftentimes, while experiencing these pastimes, I felt as if I were in Mexico. It was a rich, satisfying feeling that conjured up countless pleasures and joys. Call it mexistalgia if you will, showing, I suppose, that I'd become more Mexican than I was willing to admit, or so Carolina joyfully liked to rub it in.

Just two days after I'd received the gush of bile from Senor Alarcon, I happened to drop into East Los Angeles again. It was a hot day owing to the Santana, an unpleasant desert wind that was blowing into the basin from the east. It was known to dry throats, make skins feel itchy and shorten tempers. After bagging a number of groceries and some gifts, I headed to La Azteca, a highly acclaimed restaurant I had visited before. It had the best antojitos outside of Mexico, or so the owner, with whom I occasionally had a chat, continued to boast. Well, it turned out to be another sensory experience and, once I'd downed a shot of tasty tequila, I took my hat, stepped outside and headed to the far end of the parking lot, where I'd parked my Cadillac. Wary, I noticed already from afar that something was stirring inside the cab. And wouldn't you know it, that 'something' turned out to be a juvenile who was crouched behind the steering wheel, fiddling around with something or other, I suspected the ignition. Seconds later, as I drew closer, I got more than an eyeful: a smashed window and a youngster of about eighteen, who was joined by another character, sitting in the passenger seat. Two other scoundrels were hanging around close-by, doped by the thump and giddy bounce of a boombox. An unsavory lot, they were dressed in baggy, low-riding jeans with the crotches almost strangling their knees. Their arms, even the foreheads of some, were covered with such lurid tattoos that would make any woman instantly shrink into a fetal curl.

When I was about to confront these pigheaded monsters, they skipped, ready to bolt. But, closing in from the left flank, I caught the presumed leader by the arm and whirled him around. "What in the hell were you doing in my car?" I shouted, fuming.

"Le'me go," he spat at me. "I ain't done nothin'."

Meanwhile the other rascals rallied around him, making threatening gestures.

"What do you mean?" I said. "You wanted to steal my car."

"That's not true," he said cockily, hoping to shake me off. Worse, he even tried to punch me. Luckily, I caught his arm.

I was beside myself. "You fucking punk!" I shouted, taking him by the scruff of the neck and landing a solid hook on his chin. I was so angry, I may have given myself to gasps of perverse delight watching his head snap back.

Not unexpectedly, the other three punks tried to pile up on me, but I managed to keep them at a distance. I lashed out like a howling dervish, until two of them pulled out knives and came at me. Flashbacks of scenes at the prison in Chihuahua gripped me and, scared shitless, I was about to turn and bolt. At that point a car pulled into a parking lot about a hundred feet away and a couple stepped out. I shouted, "Please help! I need your help!" But they acted as if they didn't hear me and quickly scurried away. Still, it made the punks slow down. Just in time two tall and beefy security guards came charging toward us, shouting, "Stop it, stop it right now."

Luckily the punks bowed to them, especially after the latter fondled their pistols. They pulled back their knives, and a little lull settled in. The presumed leader just stood there, holding his jaw, while the other three acted as if they didn't know what to do.

"What's the problem?" one of the guards pressed.

"He started the fight," one of the punks barked. "He kept attacking us."

"They wanted to steal my car," I shot back, pointing to the broken windshield. "I had to defend myself. I had no choice."

Accusations flew back and forth, until an LAPD patrol car, lights flashing and siren howling, showed up. Two burly cops jumped out and, palpating their belts and pistols, came striding toward us. Seconds later a backup came. Now there were four. Although I welcomed them, I also felt apprehensive. They were cops, after all. And I was Fritz Graf!

While two took on the foulmouthed villains, the others turned toward me, frisking me for weapons. They also inspected the car and took shots of the broken window. And after they had radioed the routine information to the dispatcher, they wanted to see my ID, my driver's license and proof of my insurance. A deep-seated fear gripped me, keeping me on tenterhooks. *Did not the leading cop with his stocky built and his square jaws look like a doppelgänger of J. Edgar Hoover?* I braced as he leafed through Finkelstein's fake, checking the entries, my picture and my face. It felt like a slow-motion scene. Finally, he handed the booklet back to me, breaking into a smile. I held it in my hand and heaved a long sigh of relief. The only stumbling block left turned out to be my Mexican driver's license. One cop claimed it was invalid in the United States, while the other seemed to be more forgiving. Luckily the latter gained the upper hand. In the end, with all three of us making ourselves comfortable in my car, they began probing me to tell what precisely had happened.

Having calmed down, I was as factual as possible, stressing time and again that I was a victim of the youngsters' aggression. Mercifully, the outcome of both investigations clearly shifted the question of guilt or innocence into my favor, helped by the fact that most of the reprobates had run-ins with the police before. Two carried knives and one allegedly even had a concealed gun stashed away in his pocket — news that made me shudder. According to the leading cop, they'd all be arrested and charged with stealing my car, as well as aggravated assault. I, meanwhile, would get off with the best of all wishes regarding my acting career.

A BRUSH OF WINGS — A SEQUEL
by Prof. Enrique Gomez-Stenson

Fate dragged its feet and ran one day late, picking the 14th of February. Yet it struck with full force, away from Hollywood's tinsel, whirls and claptrap, leaving my father struggling for his life. I was at an utter loss when I heard of this heartrending calamity.

Let me just dash off a short summary of the course of events, appending a muted warning, if I may. Since neither my mother nor I had witnessed this terrifying incident, we were forced to rely on secondary information, on television coverage, newspaper reports and most of all on conversations with Senor Alarcon, colleagues and members of the crew who were present at the site.

According to the information I was able to gather, it took place during the filming of a scene of *Paris Needs Help* on location in Ventura County. The producer, Senor Alarcon, opted for a bird's eye shot of the German captain (my father) and his sergeant, riding in his German bucket jeep to the front line a little outside of Paris. According to the script, they were supposed to be under fierce fire by American sharpshooters. The unpaved road was rocky and uneven at best. As usual, the camera technicians had mobilized a movie truck, equipped with a tall crane, topped by a basket. It was supposed to follow the jeep. Everything seemed to proceed according to plan. Unfortunately, as the jeep came around a hairpin curve, the truck reportedly hit a trough, forcing the crane to whip forward so haplessly that it smashed headlong into the windshield of the jeep, killing the cameraman and critically injuring the American actor Robert Wycliff, as well as my father, Frederik Erikson.

Within minutes medical personnel had rushed to the site, pulling the cameraman out of the basket and my dad and Robert Wycliff of the bucket jeep. As if jinxed, the basket had not only crushed their rib cages but also struck their heads, badly mauling them. Both were unconscious and bleeding heavily. A medical helicopter was radioed to the scene and both men were whisked to the emergency room at the Ventura County Medical Center, where physicians attempted to stabilize them. Chased by bad luck, Robert Wycliff soon succumbed to his injuries while my father managed to hang on to life, though barely. At one point his cardiogram was as flat as a pancake. Surgical specialists kept him under the knife for more than six hours.

My mother, who was informed of the accident before nightfall, was told that, Dad being under the knife, she wasn't allowed to visit him until early next morning, when he'd been released from the trauma center. She called me shortly past eight, her voice so agitated, shaky and trembling that I could hardly understand her. I thought she was close to facing a nervous breakdown. I tried to soothe and comfort her, promising that I'd be in Ventura late in the morning.

When Mom showed up at the medical facility very early in the morning, Dad had just been released from the trauma center. The ether still clung to him. As I entered the room two hours later, she was sitting at his bedside, her eyes badly smudged by tears. She was busy dabbing Dad's cheeks, nostrils and lips with cool mineral water and whispering soothing words into his ears. And, frankly, there was no one around who needed it more. Never had I seen him in such a feeble, wailful state. Eyes shut, his face had a pale, waxen shine to it. Still more worrisome: He breathed with a frightful rattle, like an old coal miner with a black lung. A tangle of tubes trailed his nose and mouth, while part of his face, neck and arms were covered with red, purple and brown smudges, as well as yellow stains of surgical cleanser, faintly reminding me, if I may say so, of Kandinsky's experimental paintings. He was punctured by needles, dialyzed and irrigated. His right hand lay on a sheet, lightly curled, each finger a short chain of polished bones wrapped in translucent skin. It was hard to imagine that barely two days ago blood pulsated in them, promising a ruddy hue and an iron grip, a trademark of his.

"*Hola mama!*" I said, giving her a long, warm hug. "How are you doing?"

"*Muy mal.*" Drooping, she buried her head in her hands and began to sob, sucked out from a deep well of despair.

I hugged her again and we both moaned. It took a while before we were able to regain our composure.

Meanwhile two gurneys with new patients rattled past in the hallway.

Mom rose and bent over Dad. "Fred, Enrique has just arrived," she whispered, touching his hand. "He wants to find out how you're doing."

Dad opened his eyes and, giving me a hint of a smile, was about to say something. But all that came across his lips was an extended gurgle. He pulled back his hand and, clenching his teeth, tried to grope for something under his sheet.

459

"I bet he's looking for his horseshoe," Mom offered. "His good luck charm. He usually carries it in his pockets. Why don't you rush down to the reception and ask for his clothes. It must be in his German uniform."

I left and twenty minutes later came back with the horseshoe and a bundle of Dad's blood-spattered uniform of a German captain.

Mom right away placed the horseshoe in Dad's hand. He grabbed it and squeezed it. A hint of a smile hushed across his face. Unfortunately, he instantly fell back into his mental haze again. We heard some intestinal rumblings and gaseous pops, reminiscent of the distant bleat of a goat. Seconds later he screwed up his eyes and dropped his jaw, as if to shriek.

"I'm afraid he's in pain," Mom said in a shaky voice.

"Let's call Dr. Chubb," I told Thelma, the nurse. "He may need some morphine."

His breath rattled, caught on a gob of phlegm. We heard some cracklings, gutteral sounds and fragments of German.

Less than five minutes later, Dr. Lawrence Chubb whisked into the room and, having shaken hands, got busy. He was a lanky fellow with a shiny, bald head, penetrating eyes and a big fleshy nose that seemed at odds with his sparse cheeks and a narrow jaw.

He quickly called on Dad. At first, there was no response. But when he tapped his shoulders, Dad opened his eyes. "Who are you?" he mumbled in his light German accent, glaring at him. "You must be one of the judiciales?"

Hushed dumb, we all glanced at each other, puckering our brows.

"Judiciales? What are you talking about? No, I'm Dr. Chubb, your doctor. Mr. Erikson, are you with me? How's your pain? Let me give you a morphine shot."

Though Dad perked up for a few seconds, he fell back into an extended pneumonic rattle again, followed by a gurgle and a sudden release.

"Oh my God!" Mom burst out biting her fist.

I braced for the worst, gazing at the monitor, but couldn't make sense of it.

Pricked by our reaction, Dr. Chubb rushed to check Dad's pulse and other vital signs. "Actually, he may not sound or look like it," he said visibly relieved, "but from all I can tell, he appears to be pretty stable for now. Call me, whenever he hits some rough spots again."

Once Dr. Chubb had left, Dad continued to gasp, wheeze, cough and rattle, but eventually settled down, as if falling into a slumber. All we heard was a light snore and the gurgling and burbling of the infusion device.

Shortly past three, Senor Alarcon and Bob Daly, the head of Warner Brothers, came visiting us, loaded with flowers, sweets and encouraging words. As soon as Dad heard Senor Alarcon's voice, he brightened up. Yet he failed to respond, when they tried to talk to him.

Both started off by apologizing to Mom and me for the horrible accident, blaming it on the maintenance of the equipment. They promised, they'd leave no stone unturned to help him.

"Although he has received very good care so far," Bob Daly assured us, "we suggest that we transfer him to the Cedars-Sinai Medical Center in Los Angeles. That's a very renowned medical facility with some of the best doctors in the world. It's also much closer to the Beverly Hills Hotel as well and would help make visits easier for you. The transfer could be done as early as tomorrow morning."

We both nodded vigorously.

They also praised Dad's extraordinary physical and mental toughness and resilience, expressing hope that he'd recuperate quickly.

The visit must have given Dad another boost. After all, it was none other than the head of one of the most important cinematographic enterprises who took his time to pay him a visit.

The following day, a Friday, Dad was buzzed by helicopter to the Cedars-Sinai Hospital, where he was quartered in a fancy medical suite with a view of Los Angeles and the surrounding foothills.

Mom and I came visiting shortly past eleven, carrying a ghetto blaster, a CD and a bottle of Tequila reposado. We were impressed by the facility and the treatment. The slew of doctors whom we talked to were cautiously optimistic that Dad would pull through it, but also warned of serious setbacks that could pop up anytime.

Dad happened to be asleep, but he must have heard us because shortly later he emerged from his slumber. "Did you see the judiciales?" he mumbled, as he emerged from his mental haze.

"Fred, I want you to stop worrying," Mom told him. "You are in America now. There are no judiciales here. There are only friendly American cops. Don't you remember how they helped you at the Azteca restaurant in East Los Angeles?"

"Yeah, Azteca," he murmured, grinning.

"I wondered if you'd like to hear a little music?" Mom asked.

He nodded.

Once we'd set up the ghetto blaster on Dad's night stand, Mom slid the CD into the slot and started pushing a few buttons. Within seconds, the old tune of Cole Porter's cowboy hit *Don't Fence Me In* began to fill the suite.

And, *que milagro!* Dad instantly opened his eyes and let a smile hush across his face. He also grabbed his horseshoe and squeezed it.

"That's curious," I said, uplifted. "Tell me, what's the significance of that cowboy hit?"

"I know it sounds funny, but it's the song of his life, at least his life in America and in some sense also Mexico. It's mainly about his quest for freedom and leaving his Nazi past behind. He first heard it and learned by heart at the POW camp in Colorado."

"Oh, are you saying he had a Nazi past?"

"Yes, he got brainwashed as a youngster."

"The song really had a grip on him. I could see it in the reaction on his face, the way he pursed his lips and nodded. Come to think of it, I've got something else that may help cheer him up as well." I pulled a small bottle of Tequila reposado out of my pocket, opened it and poured half a shot onto a washcloth.

"Let's play the song again," I said, countering her puzzled look.

She did and as the song hit the air, I began dabbing the washcloth under his nose. And once again Dad opened his eyes and started smiling. He even mumbled something we couldn't grasp and groped for our hands.

In the afternoon, eleven actors, actresses, as well as members of the technical crew showed up, showering him with flowers, sweets, liquors, smiles, laughter and good wishes. At one time there were more than thirty people in the room. The commotion seemed to overwhelm him, making him turn away.

Meanwhile, we continued to visit Dad every day, often separately, staying several hours. We were delighted by the steady progress he made, although there were also some setbacks that made us shiver and break out in cold sweat. One of them, a stubborn arrhythmia, accompanied by a rattling breath, lasted almost two days. But thanks to the exemplary treatment and care, Dad managed to pull out of it. He also developed a hearty appetite and within two weeks, the doctors encouraged him to get up and walk around the ward. Actually it was *he* who badgered them. Comparing his bed to 'a feathered tomb', he couldn't wait to get out of it and start walking. Fittingly, it was Mom and me who took him on one of his first walks, propping him up and guiding his steps. It was a wobbly affair, not least because Dad insisted on pushing himself to the limits. At a price, I might add. Coming around a sharp curve, his knees buckled, making him stumble and fall badly. Thank heavens he didn't break anything. Actually, he surprised everyone in the way he shook off his spill and hustled to bounce back. Hours later, while zestfully tucking away his Mexican lunch, he'd even rise above himself by begging me to fetch him his movie script. And after lip-reading a certain scene for an hour or more, he'd be up again to go on his walk, sometimes with me, at the times with Mom. That pretty much became a habit with us, and every day we were seen crisscrossing or circling the floor.

His head wrapped in a white towel and acting as if he was a dignified Sikh, he'd greet everybody who seemed to be approachable, often falling into a chit-chat with them. He'd frequently mention something absurd, like straining a gnat or swallowing a camel, or an off-the-wall joke. While closely watching the stunned faces, he'd immerse himself in peals of laughter, sounding as though he were about to enter the Bower of Bliss.

CPSIA information can be obtained
at www.ICGtesting.com
Printed in the USA
LVHW092324021221
705157LV00005B/297